SPACE DANDY

CONTENTS

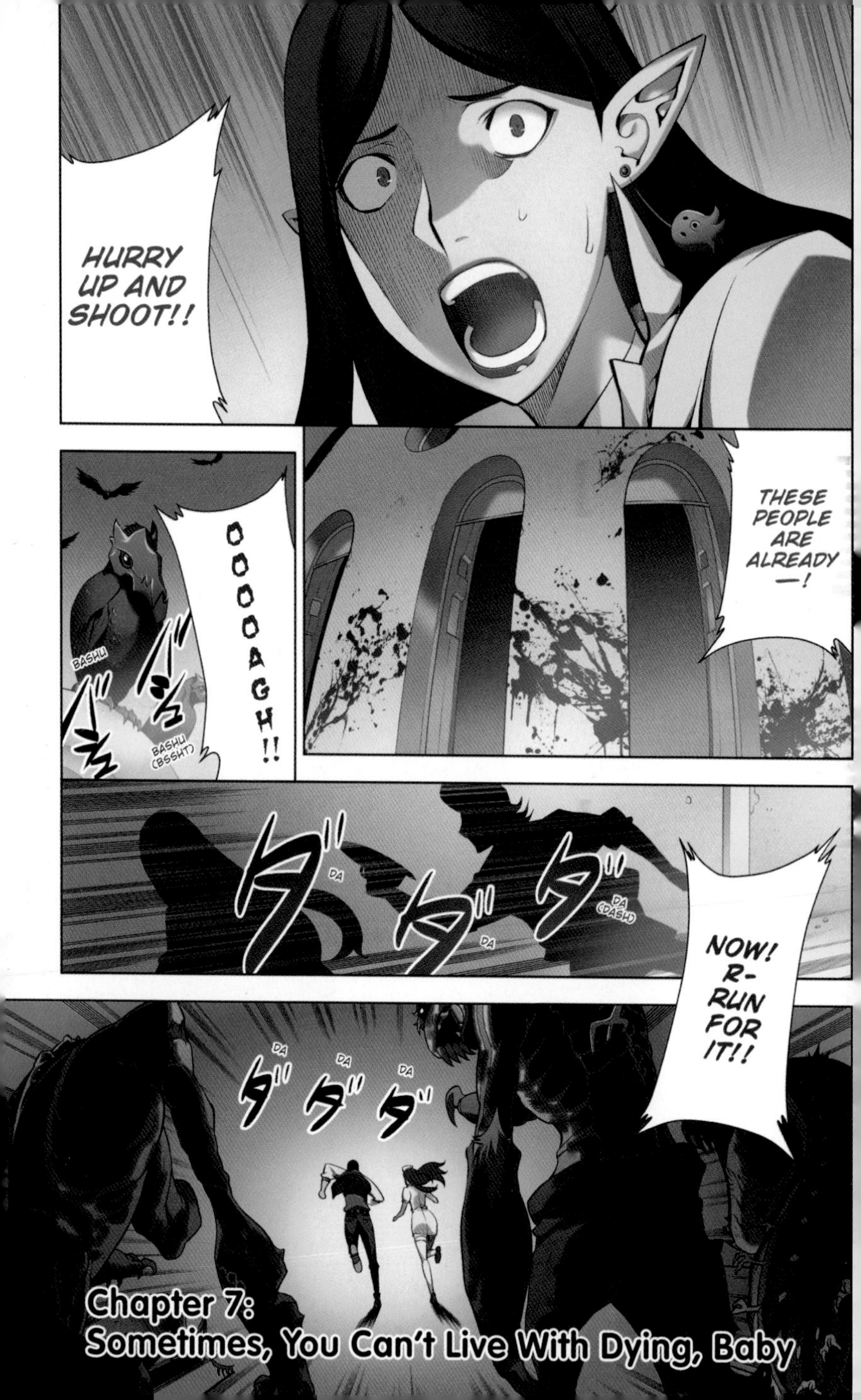
HURRY UP AND SHOOT!!
THESE PEOPLE ARE ALREADY—!
OOOOOAGH!!
BASHU
BASHU (BSSHT)
DA
DA
DA (DASH)
NOW! R-RUN FOR IT!!
DA DA DA

Chapter 7: Sometimes, You Can't Live With Dying, Baby

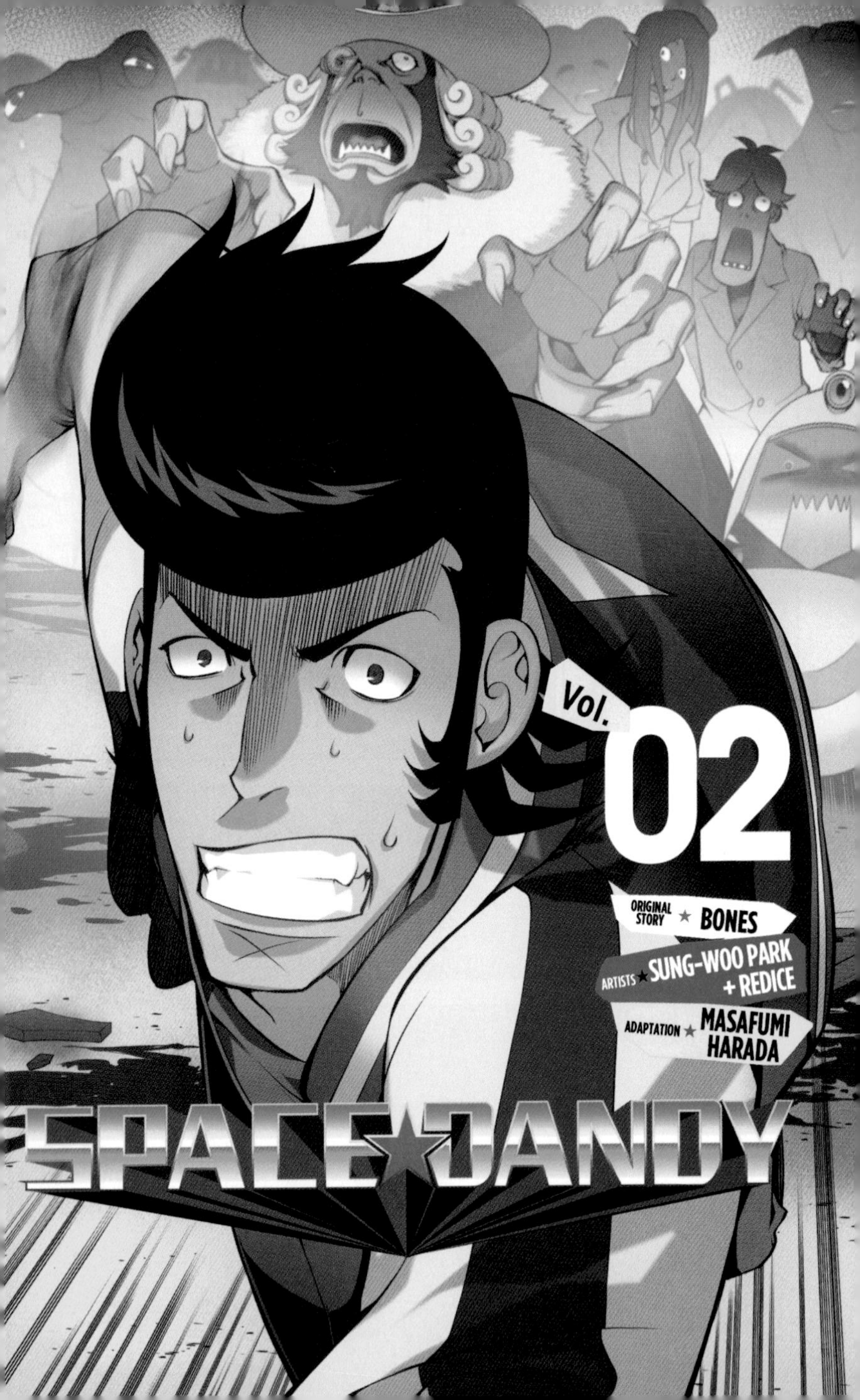
Vol.
02
ORIGINAL STORY ★ BONES
ARTISTS ★ SUNG-WOO PARK + REDICE
ADAPTATION ★ MASAFUMI HARADA
SPACE★DANDY

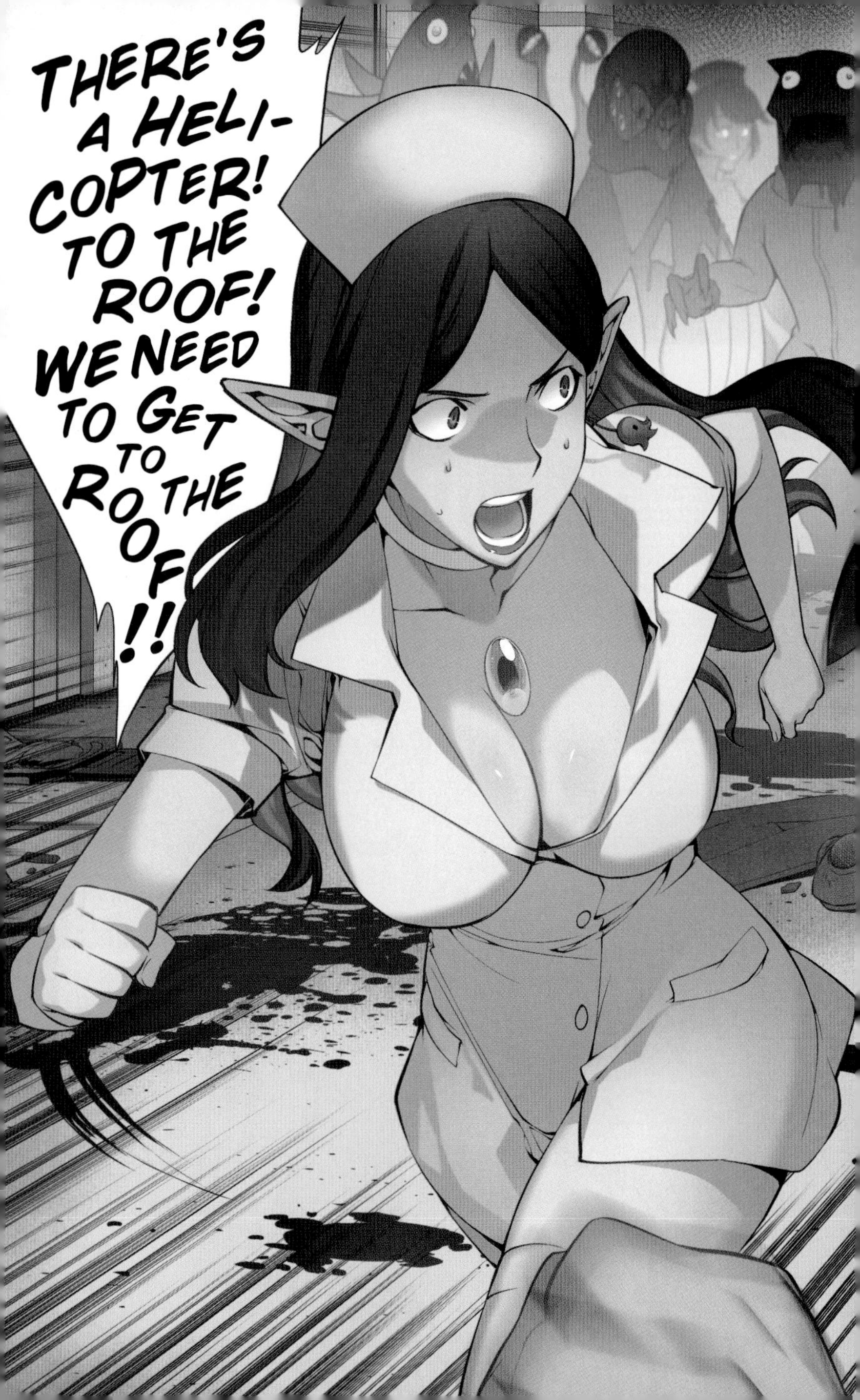
THERE'S A HELI-COPTER! TO THE ROOF! WE NEED TO GET TO THE ROOF!!

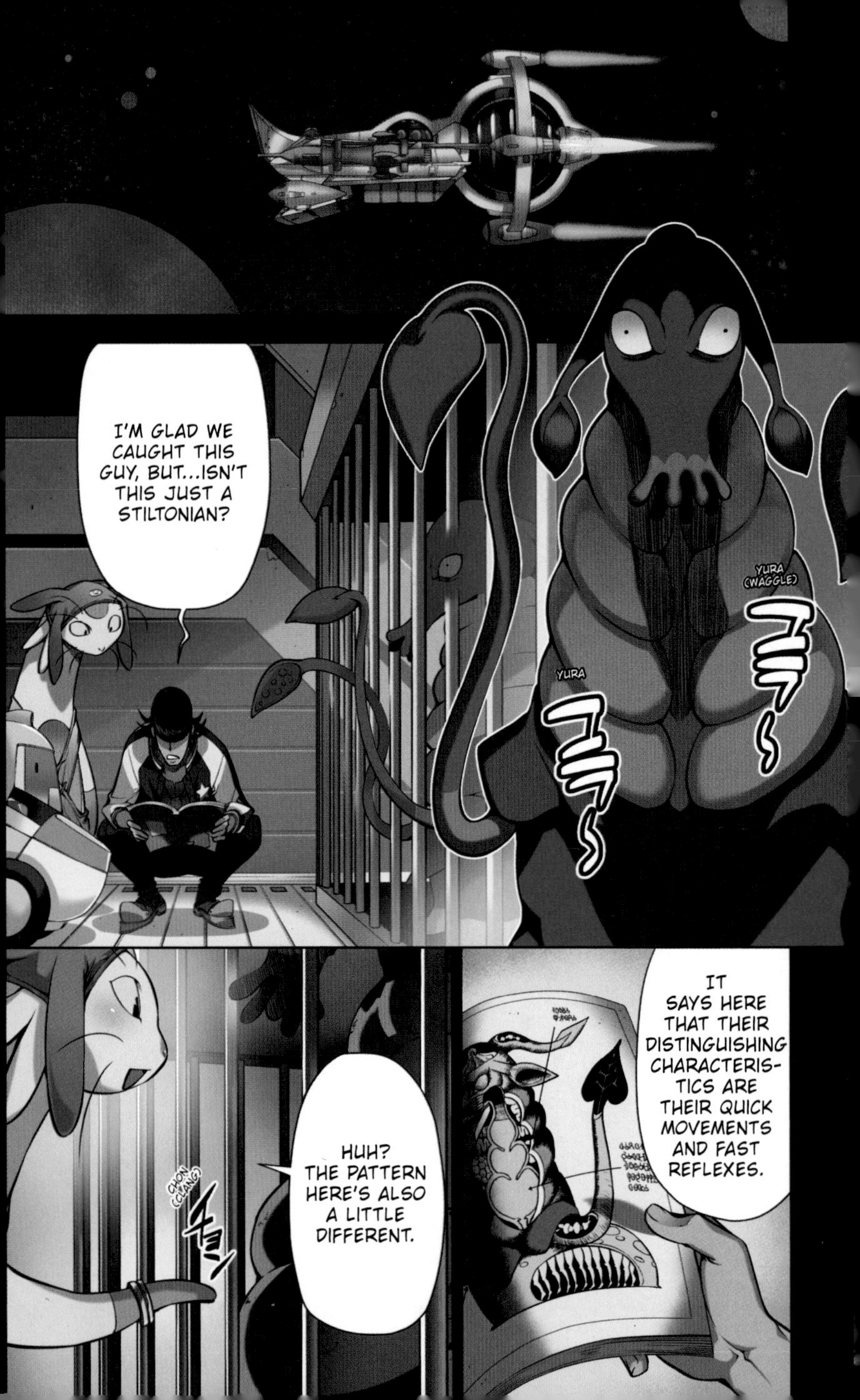
YURA (WAGGLE)
YURA
I'M GLAD WE CAUGHT THIS GUY, BUT...ISN'T THIS JUST A STILTONIAN?
IT SAYS HERE THAT THEIR DISTINGUISHING CHARACTERIS-TICS ARE THEIR QUICK MOVEMENTS AND FAST REFLEXES.
HUH? THE PATTERN HERE'S ALSO A LITTLE DIFFERENT.
CHON (CLANG)

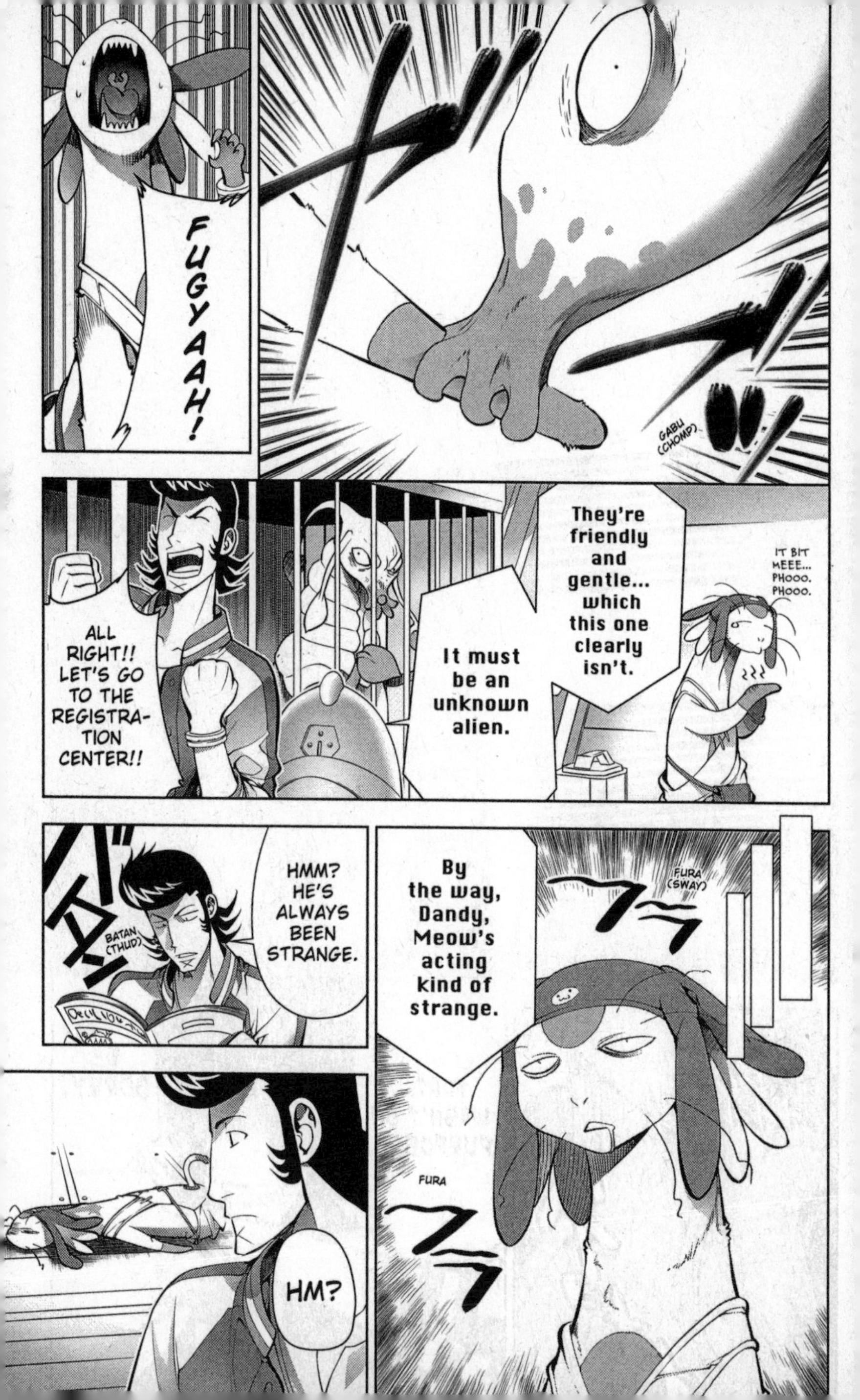
GABU (CHOMP)
FUGYAAAH!
IT BIT MEEE... PHOOO. PHOOO.
They're friendly and gentle... which this one clearly isn't.
It must be an unknown alien.
ALL RIGHT!! LET'S GO TO THE REGISTRATION CENTER!!
FURA (SWAY)
By the way, Dandy, Meow's acting kind of strange.
FURA
HMM? HE'S ALWAYS BEEN STRANGE.
BATAN (THUD)
HM?

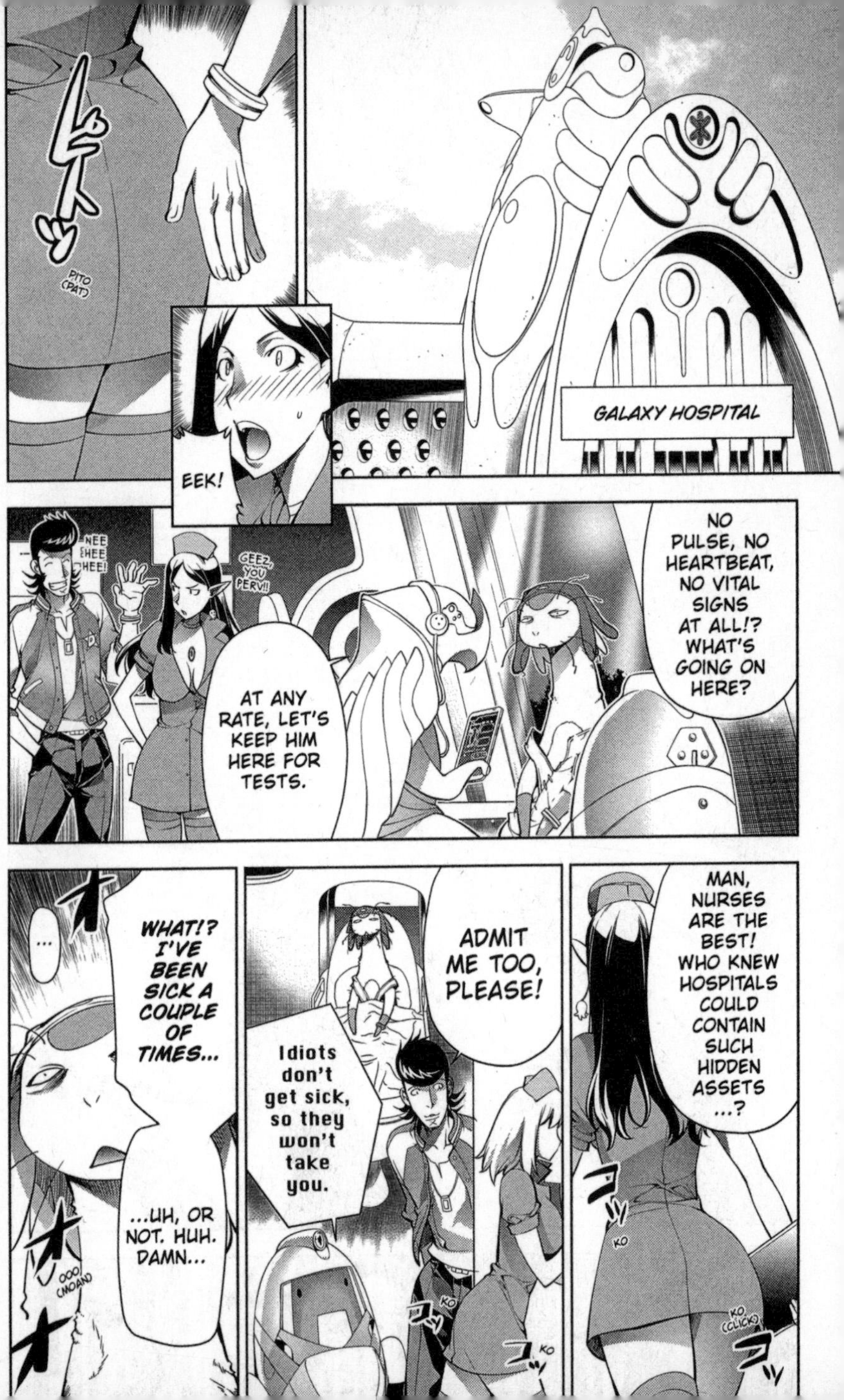
GALAXY HOSPITAL
PITO (PAT)
EEK!
NO PULSE, NO HEARTBEAT, NO VITAL SIGNS AT ALL!? WHAT'S GOING ON HERE?
AT ANY RATE, LET'S KEEP HIM HERE FOR TESTS.
GEEZ, YOU PERV!!
NEE HEE HEE!
MAN, NURSES ARE THE BEST! WHO KNEW HOSPITALS COULD CONTAIN SUCH HIDDEN ASSETS ...?
KO
KO (CLICK)
ADMIT ME TOO, PLEASE!
Idiots don't get sick, so they won't take you.
KO
KO
...
WHAT!? I'VE BEEN SICK A COUPLE OF TIMES...
...UH, OR NOT. HUH. DAMN...
OOO (MOAN)

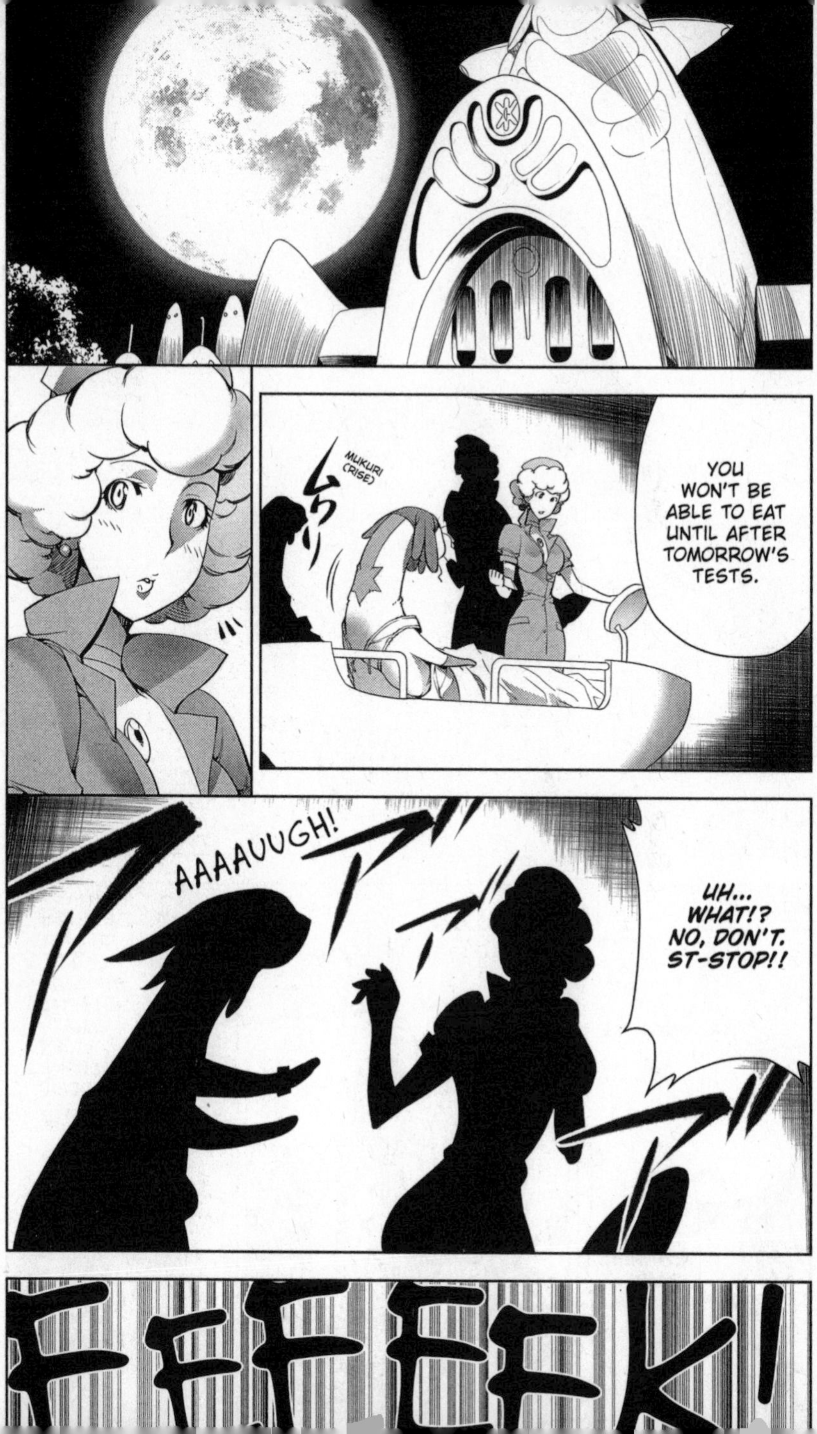
YOU WON'T BE ABLE TO EAT UNTIL AFTER TOMORROW'S TESTS.
MUKURI (RISE)
UH... WHAT!? NO, DON'T. ST-STOP!!
AAAAUUGH!
EEEEEK!

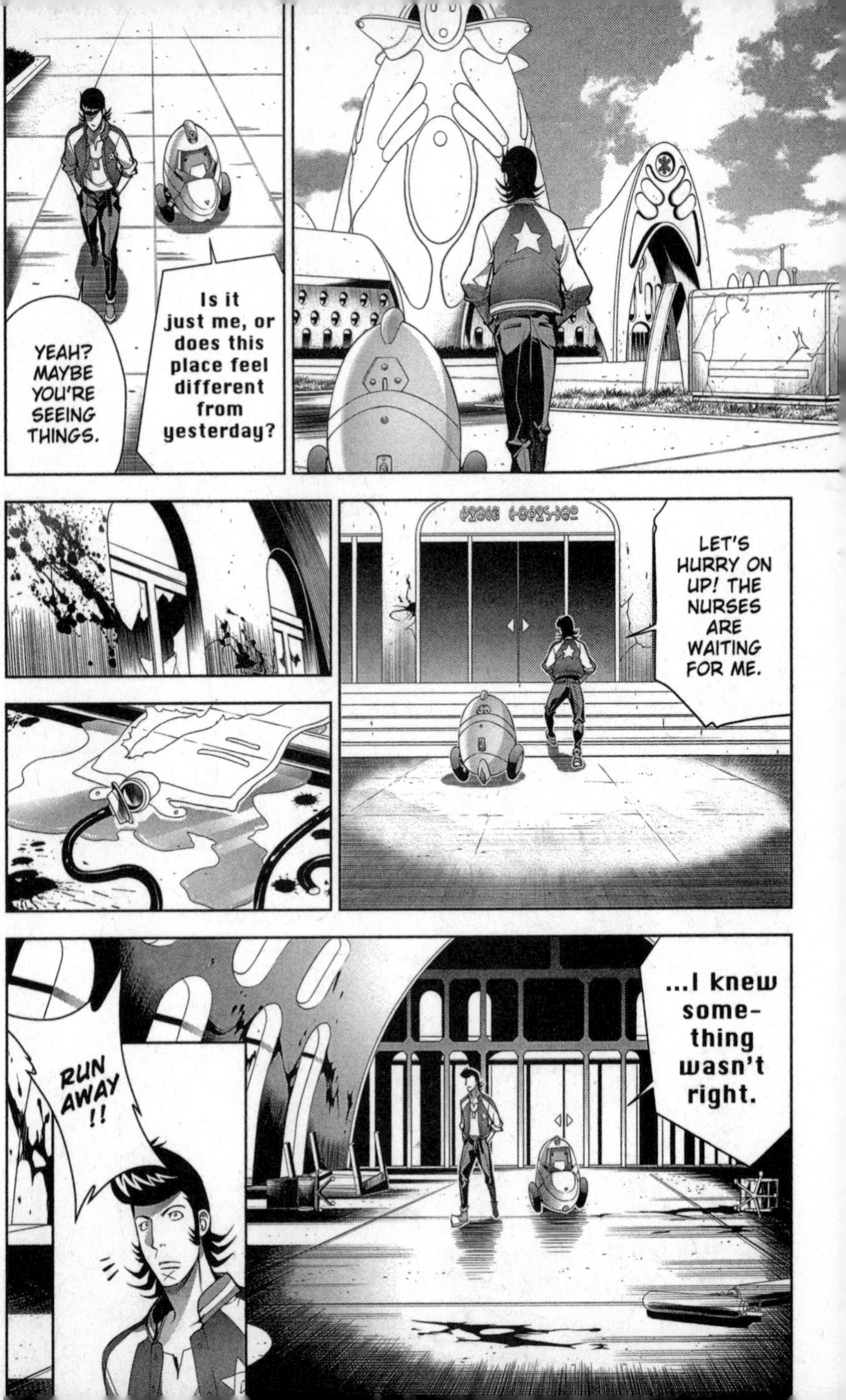
Is it just me, or does this place feel different from yesterday?
YEAH? MAYBE YOU'RE SEEING THINGS.
LET'S HURRY ON UP! THE NURSES ARE WAITING FOR ME.
...I knew something wasn't right.
RUN AWAY!!

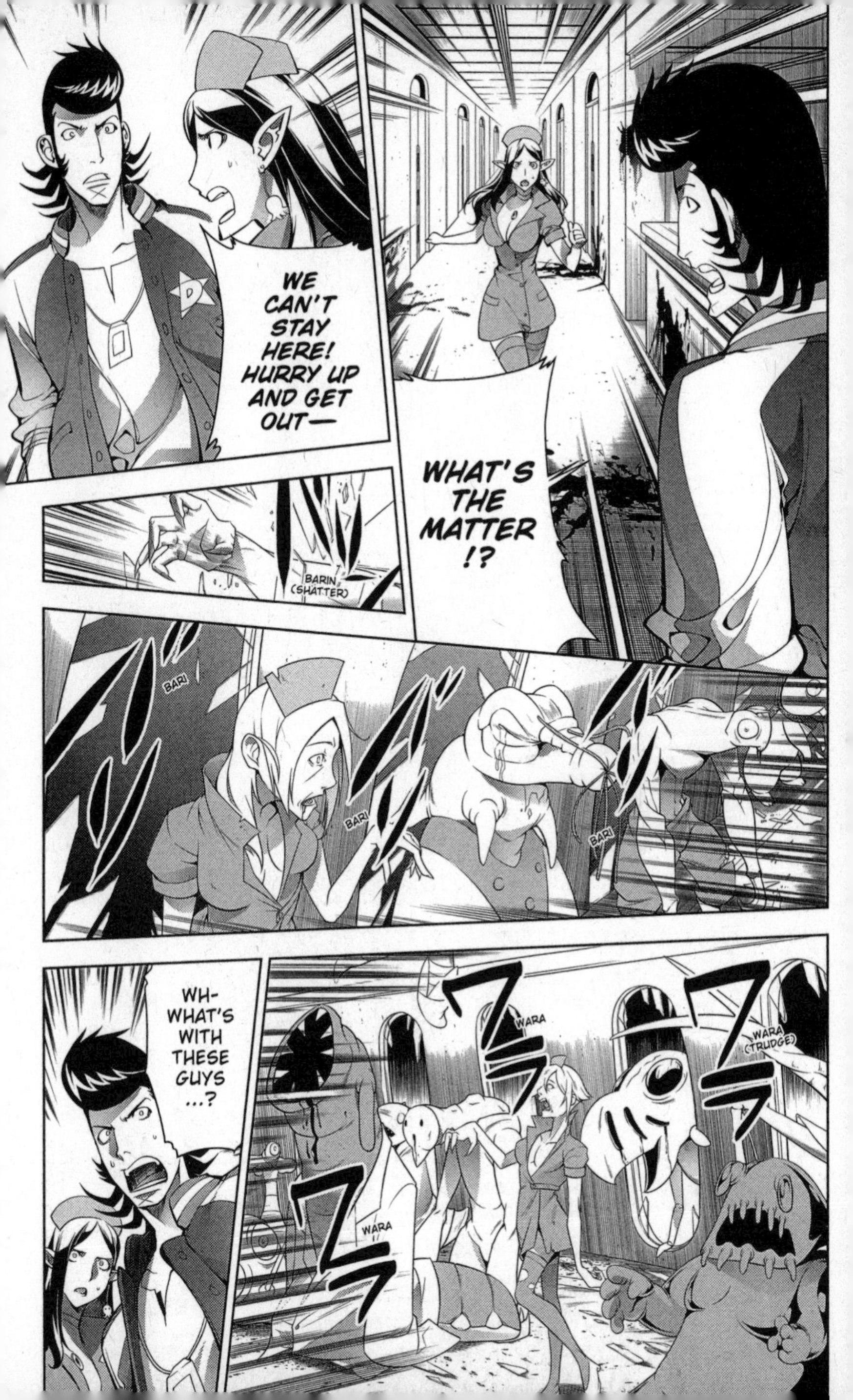
WHAT'S THE MATTER !?
WE CAN'T STAY HERE! HURRY UP AND GET OUT—
BARIN (SHATTER)
BARI
BARI
BARI
WARA (TRUDGE)
WARA
WARA
WH-WHAT'S WITH THESE GUYS ...?

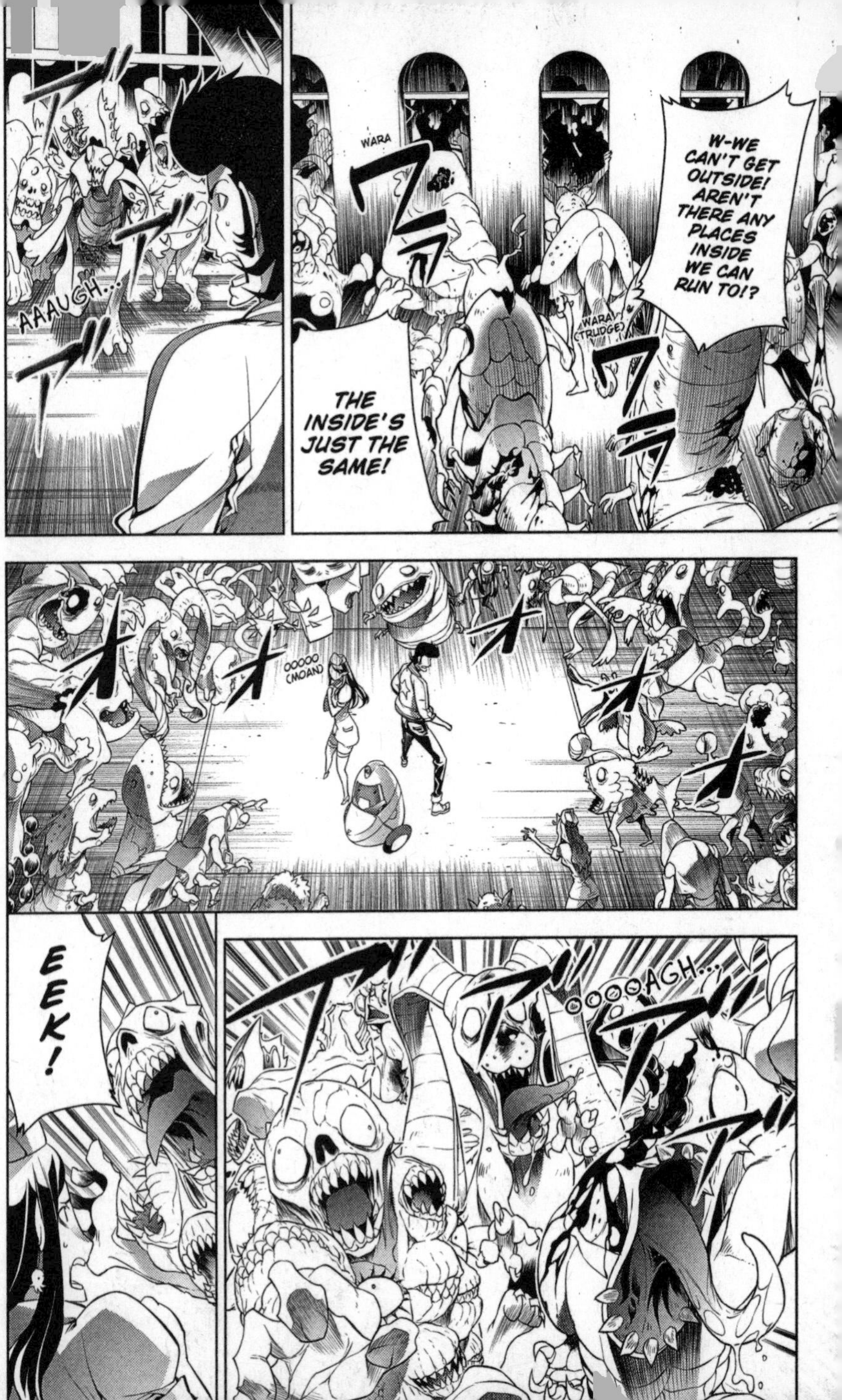
W-WE CAN'T GET OUTSIDE! AREN'T THERE ANY PLACES INSIDE WE CAN RUN TO!?
WARA (TRUDGE)
WARA
THE INSIDE'S JUST THE SAME!
AAAUGH...
OOOOO (MOAN)
OOOOAGH...
EEK!

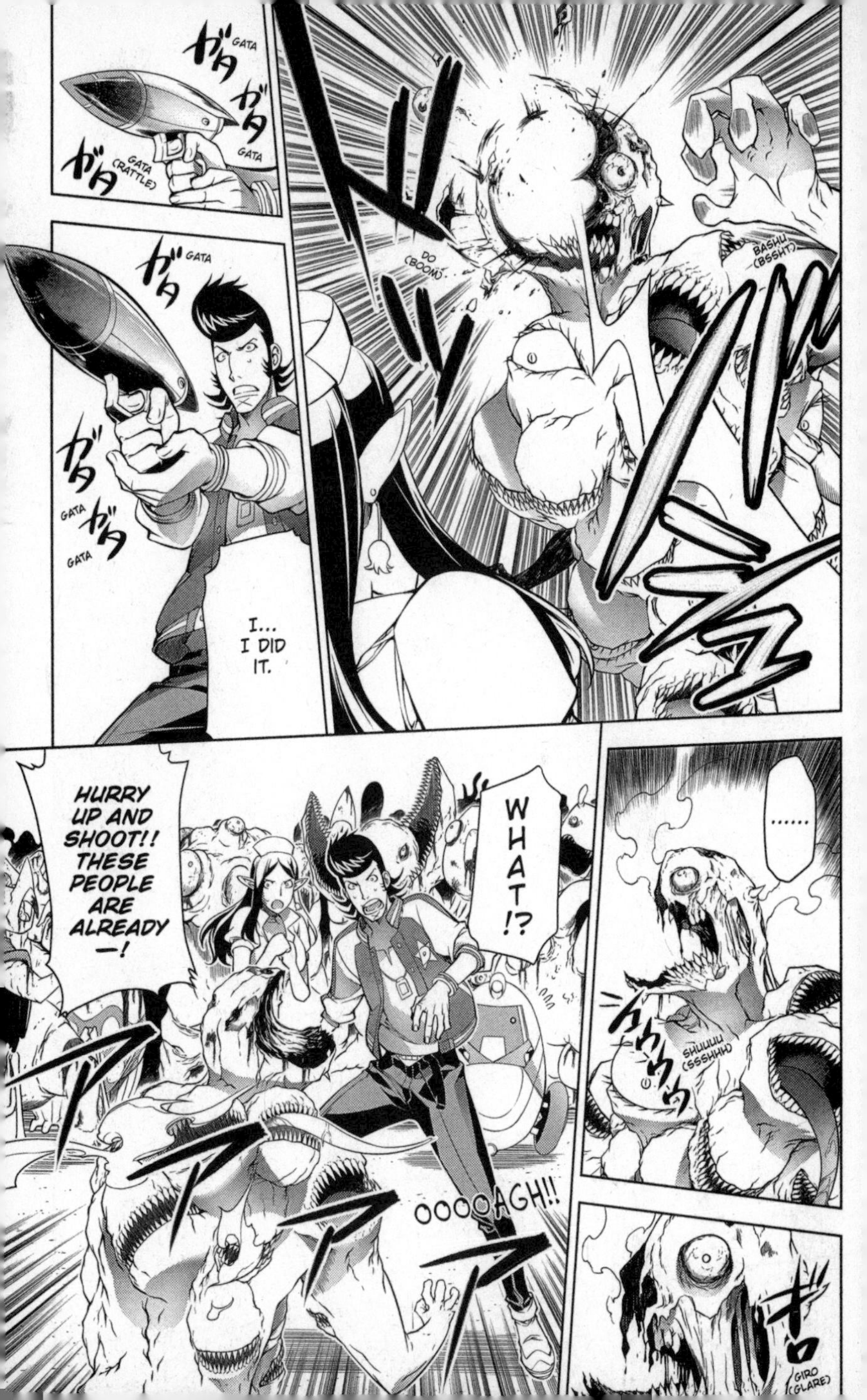
BASHU (BSSHT)
DO (BOOM)
GATA
GATA
GATA (RATTLE)
GATA
GATA
GATA
I... I DID IT.
......
SHUUUU (SSSHHH)
GIRO (GLARE)
WHAT!?
HURRY UP AND SHOOT!! THESE PEOPLE ARE ALREADY—!
OOOOAGH!!

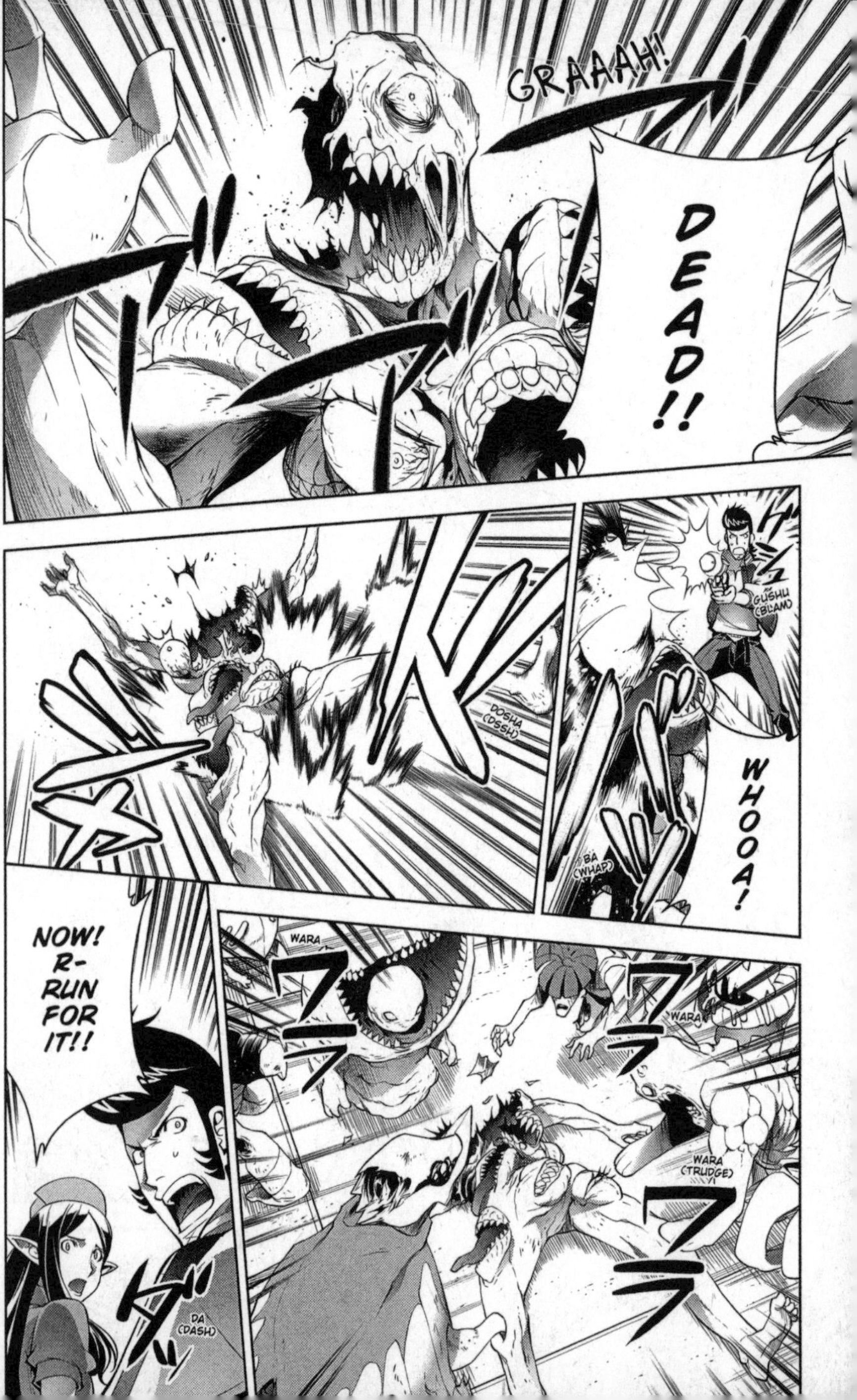
GRAAAH!
DEAD!!
GUSHU (BLAM)
WHOOOA!
BA (WHAP)
DOSHA (DSSH)
WARA
WARA
WARA (TRUDGE)
NOW! R-RUN FOR IT!!
DA (DASH)

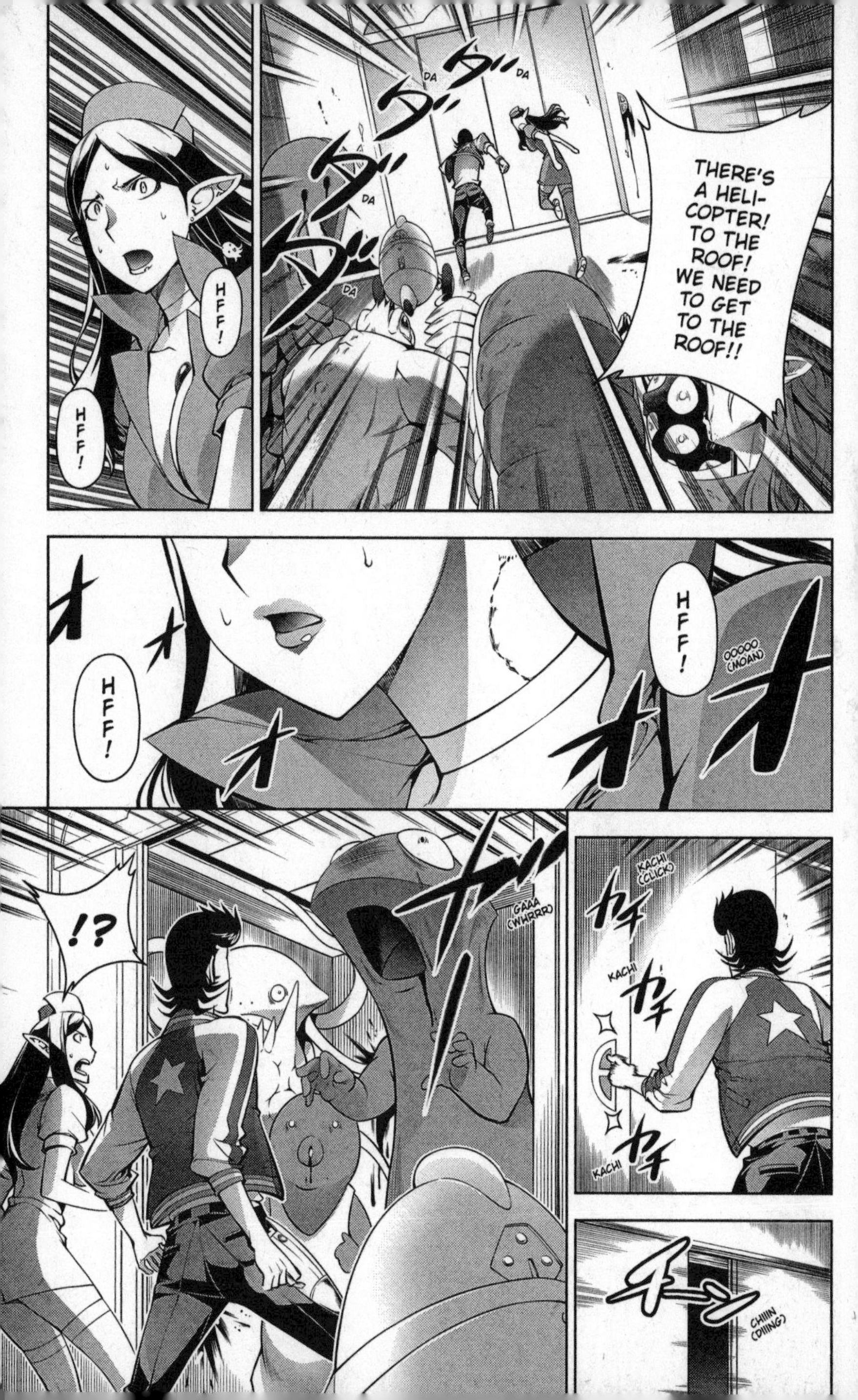
DA
DA
DA
DA
DA
THERE'S A HELI-COPTER! TO THE ROOF! WE NEED TO GET TO THE ROOF!!
HFF!
HFF!
HFF!
OOOOO (MOAN)
HFF!
KACHI (CLICK)
KACHI
KACHI
CHIIIN (DIIING)
GAAA (WHRRR)
!?

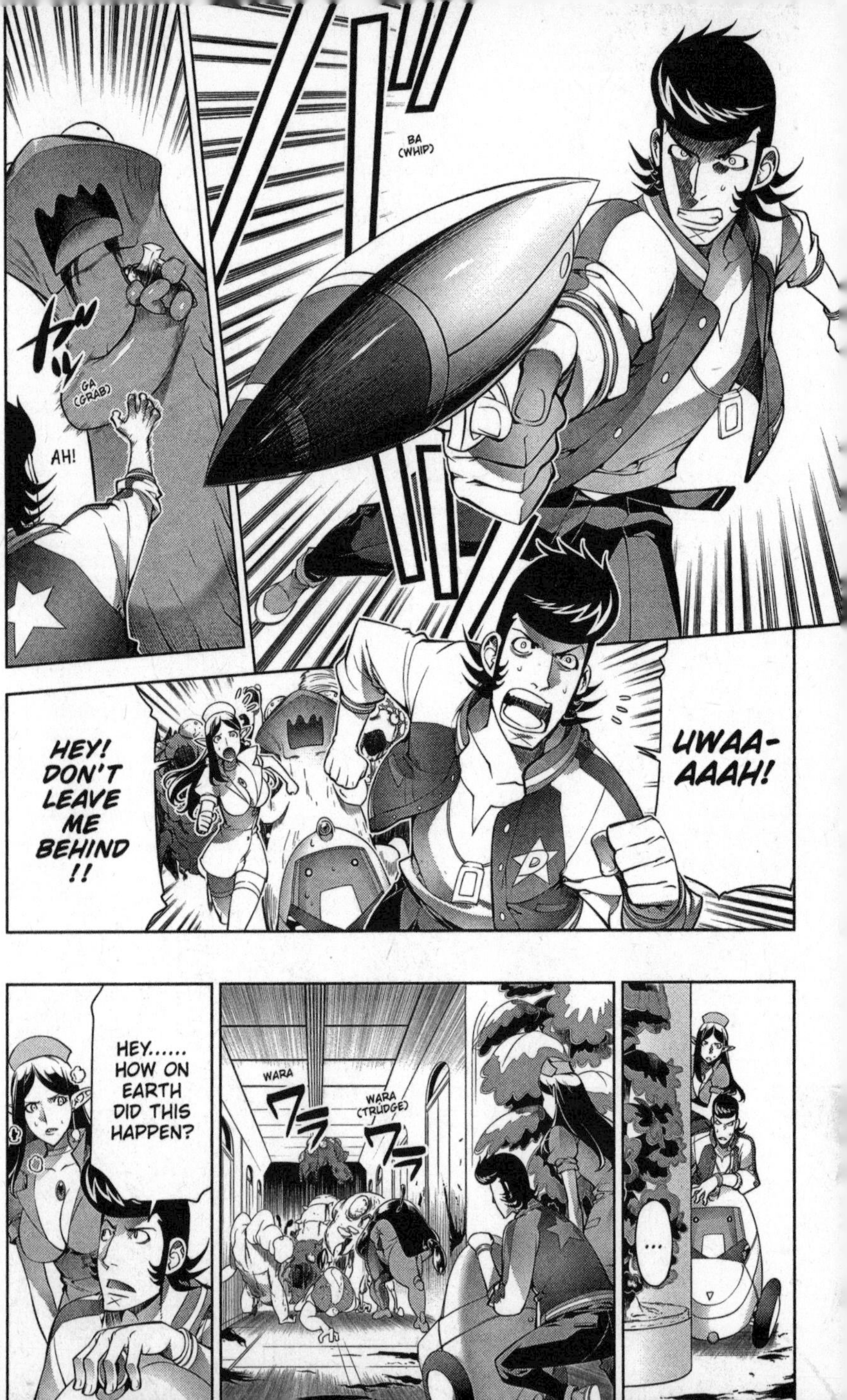
BA
(WHIP)
GA
(GRAB)
AH!
UWAA-
AAAH!
HEY!
DON'T
LEAVE
ME
BEHIND
!!
....
WARA
WARA
(TRUDGE)
HEY......
HOW ON
EARTH
DID THIS
HAPPEN?

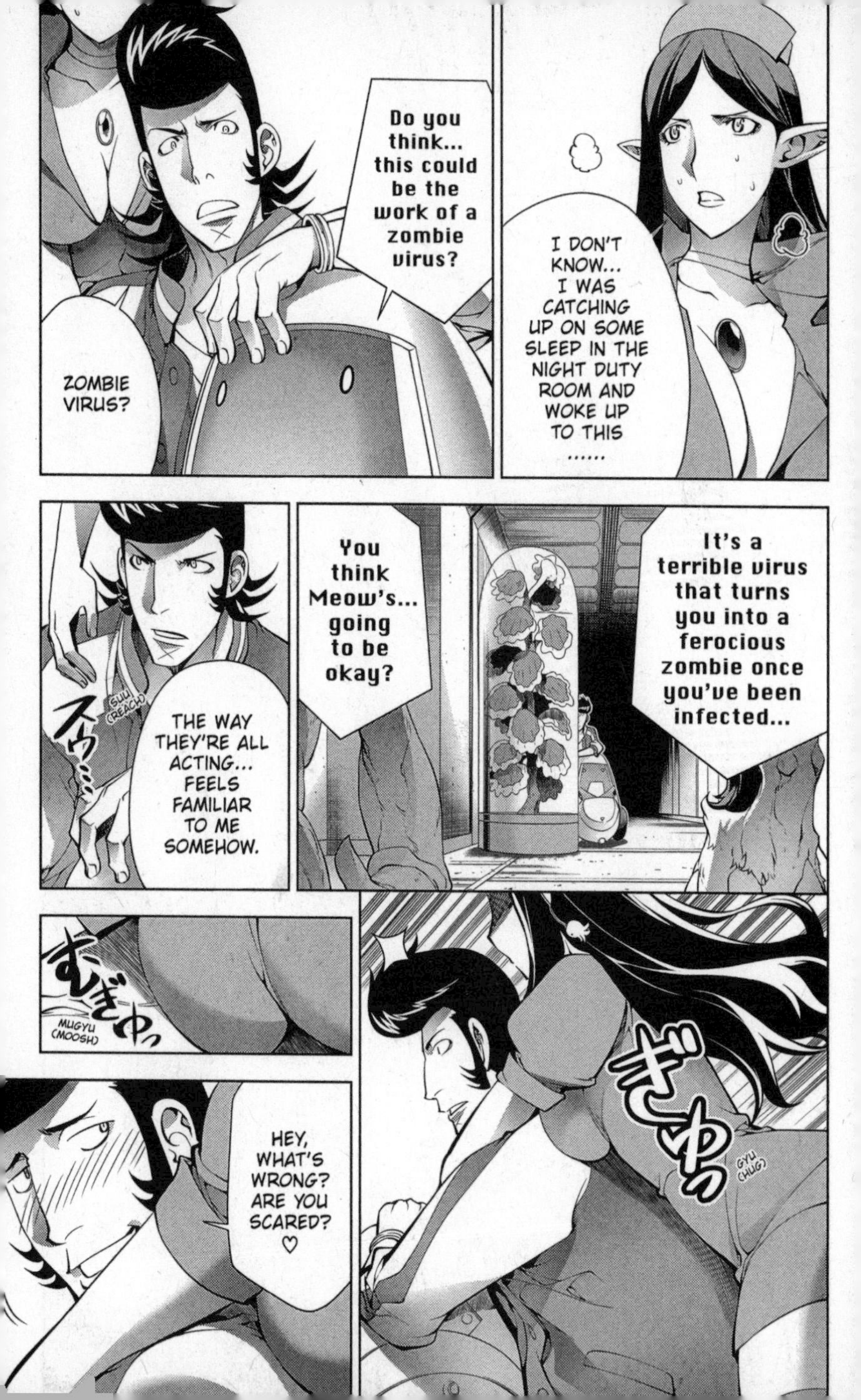
I DON'T KNOW... I WAS CATCHING UP ON SOME SLEEP IN THE NIGHT DUTY ROOM AND WOKE UP TO THIS ......
Do you think... this could be the work of a zombie virus?
ZOMBIE VIRUS?
It's a terrible virus that turns you into a ferocious zombie once you've been infected...
You think Meow's... going to be okay?
THE WAY THEY'RE ALL ACTING... FEELS FAMILIAR TO ME SOMEHOW.
SUU (REACH)
GYU (HUG)
MUGYU (MOOSH)
HEY, WHAT'S WRONG? ARE YOU SCARED? ♡

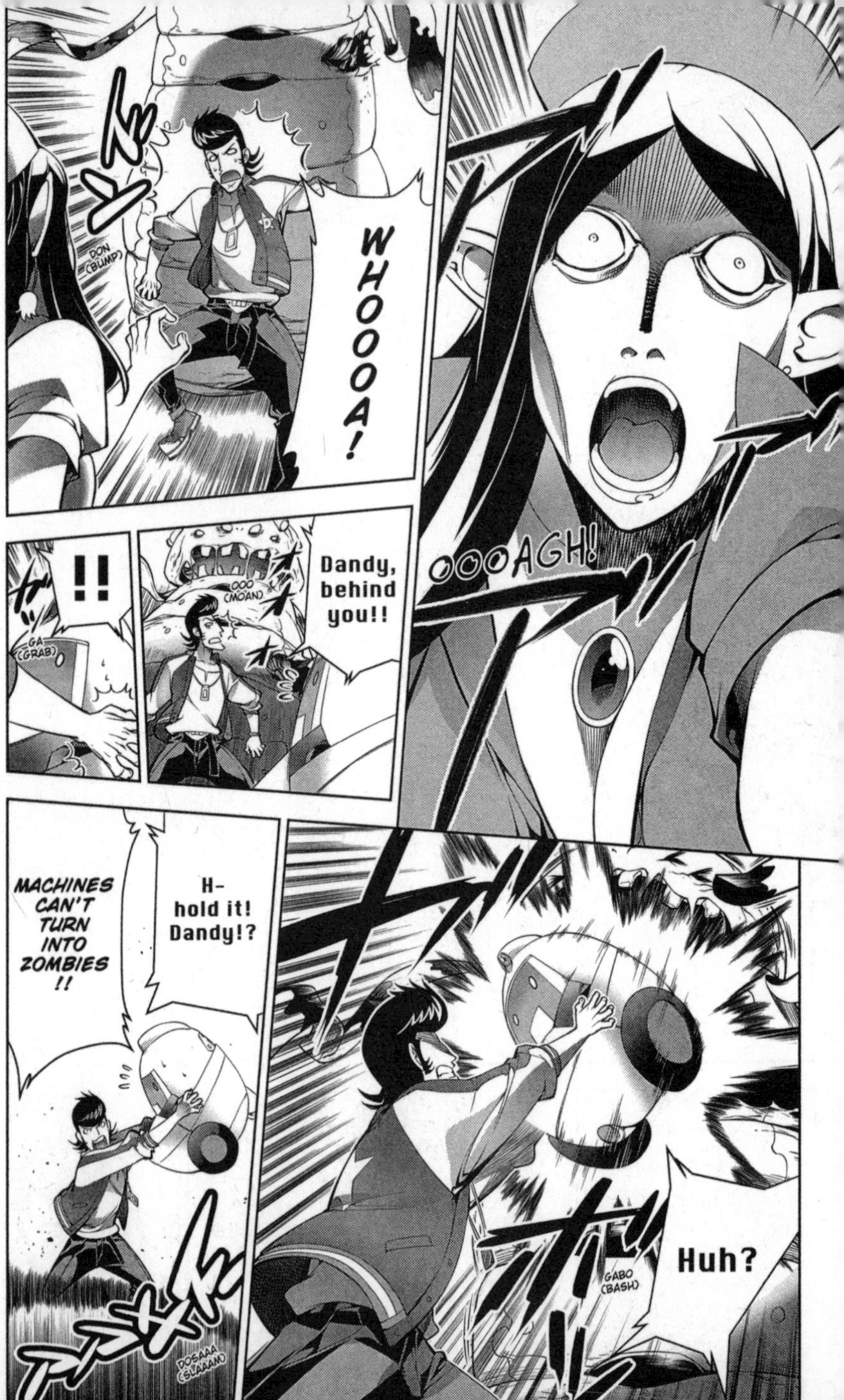

OOOAGH!
WHOOOOA!
DON (BUMP)
Dandy, behind you!!
OOO (MOAN)
!!
GA (GRAB)
Huh?
GABO (BASH)
H- hold it! Dandy!?
MACHINES CAN'T TURN INTO ZOMBIES!!
DOSAAA (SLAAAM)

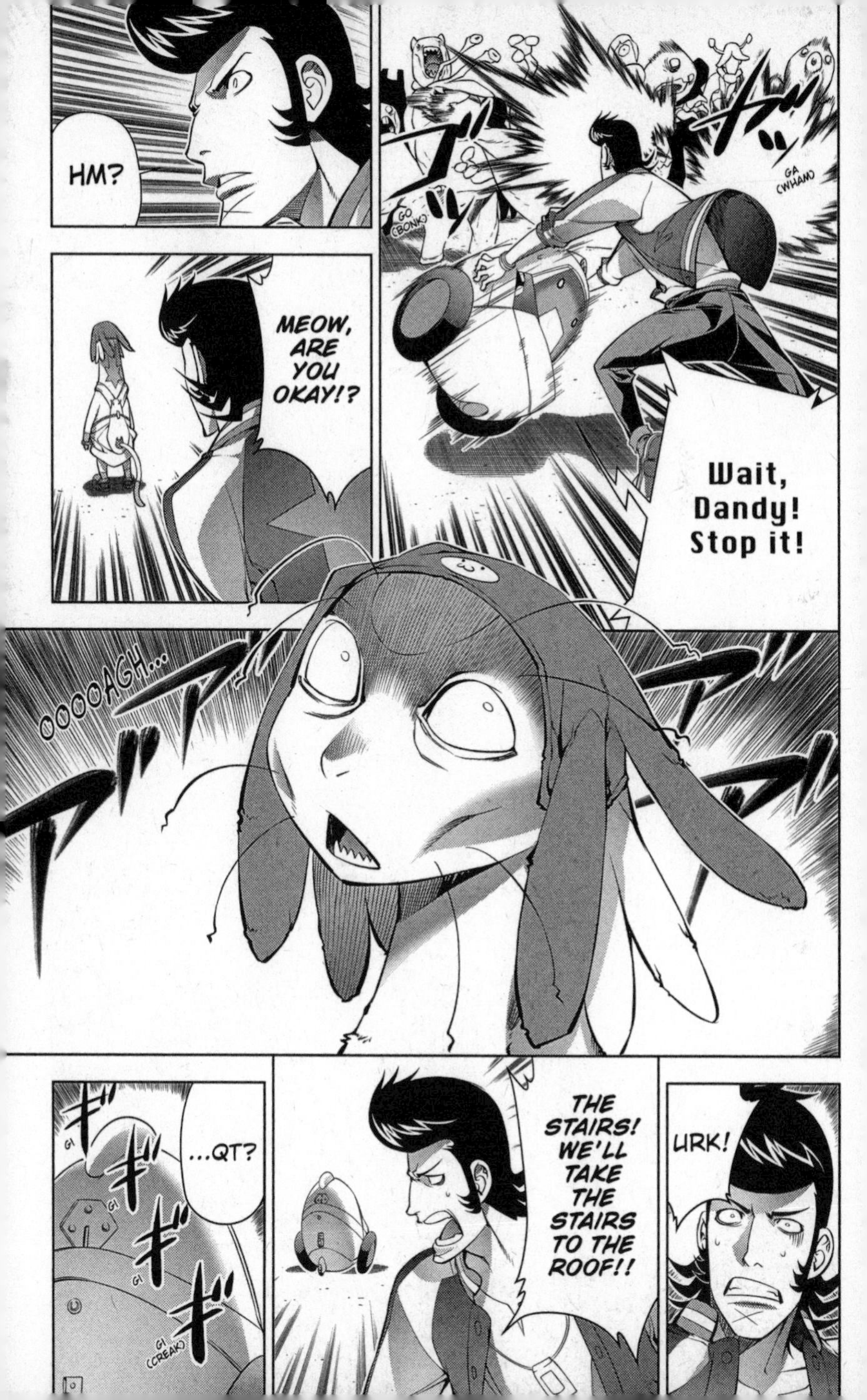
GA (WHAM)
GO (BONK)
Wait, Dandy! Stop it!
HM?
MEOW, ARE YOU OKAY!?
OOOOAGH...
URK!
THE STAIRS! WE'LL TAKE THE STAIRS TO THE ROOF!!
...QT?
GI
GI
GI
GI (CREAK)

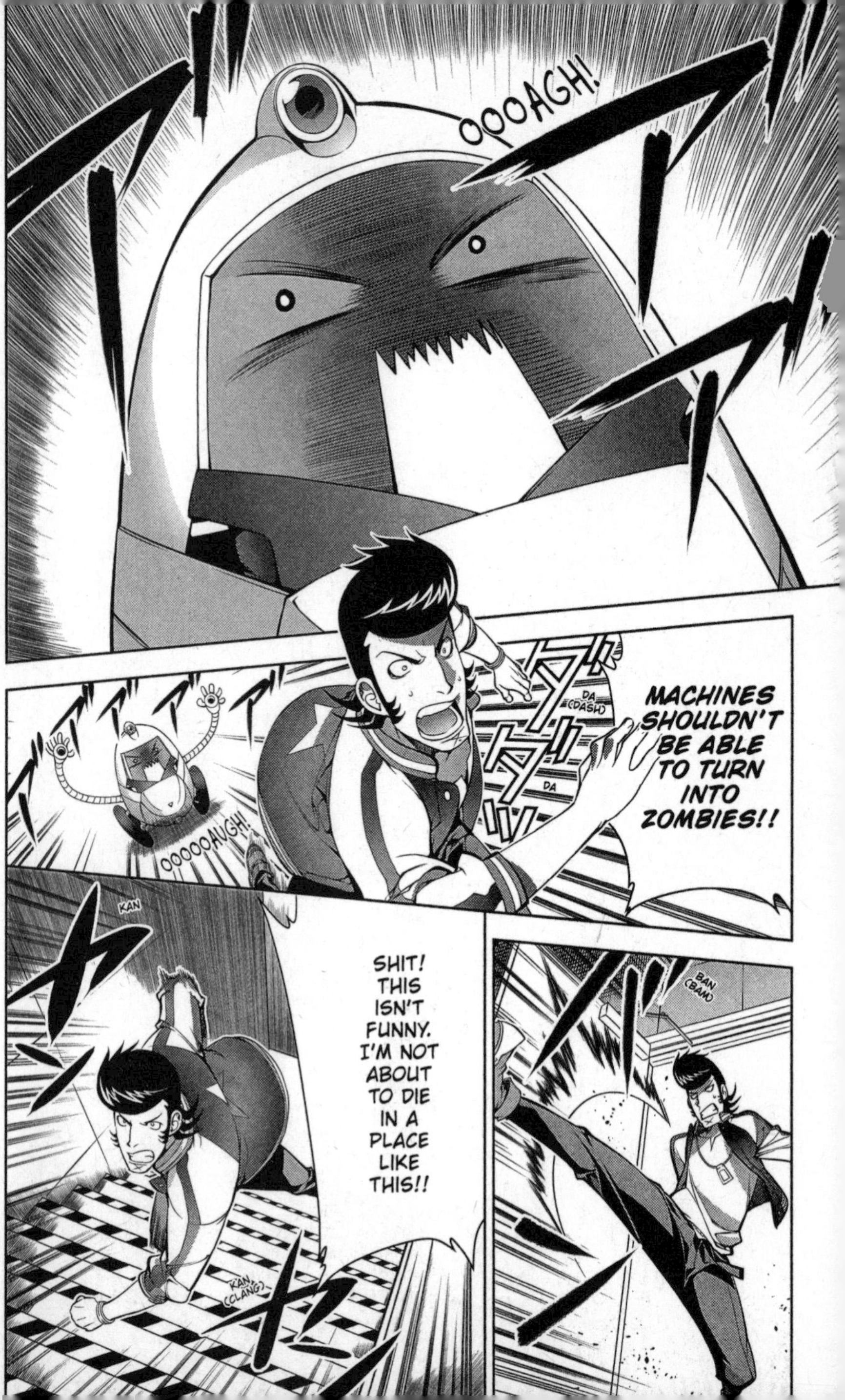
OOOAGH!
MACHINES SHOULDN'T BE ABLE TO TURN INTO ZOMBIES!!
DA (DASH)
DA
OOOOOAUGH!
BAN (BAM)
KAN
SHIT! THIS ISN'T FUNNY. I'M NOT ABOUT TO DIE IN A PLACE LIKE THIS!!
KAN (CLANG)

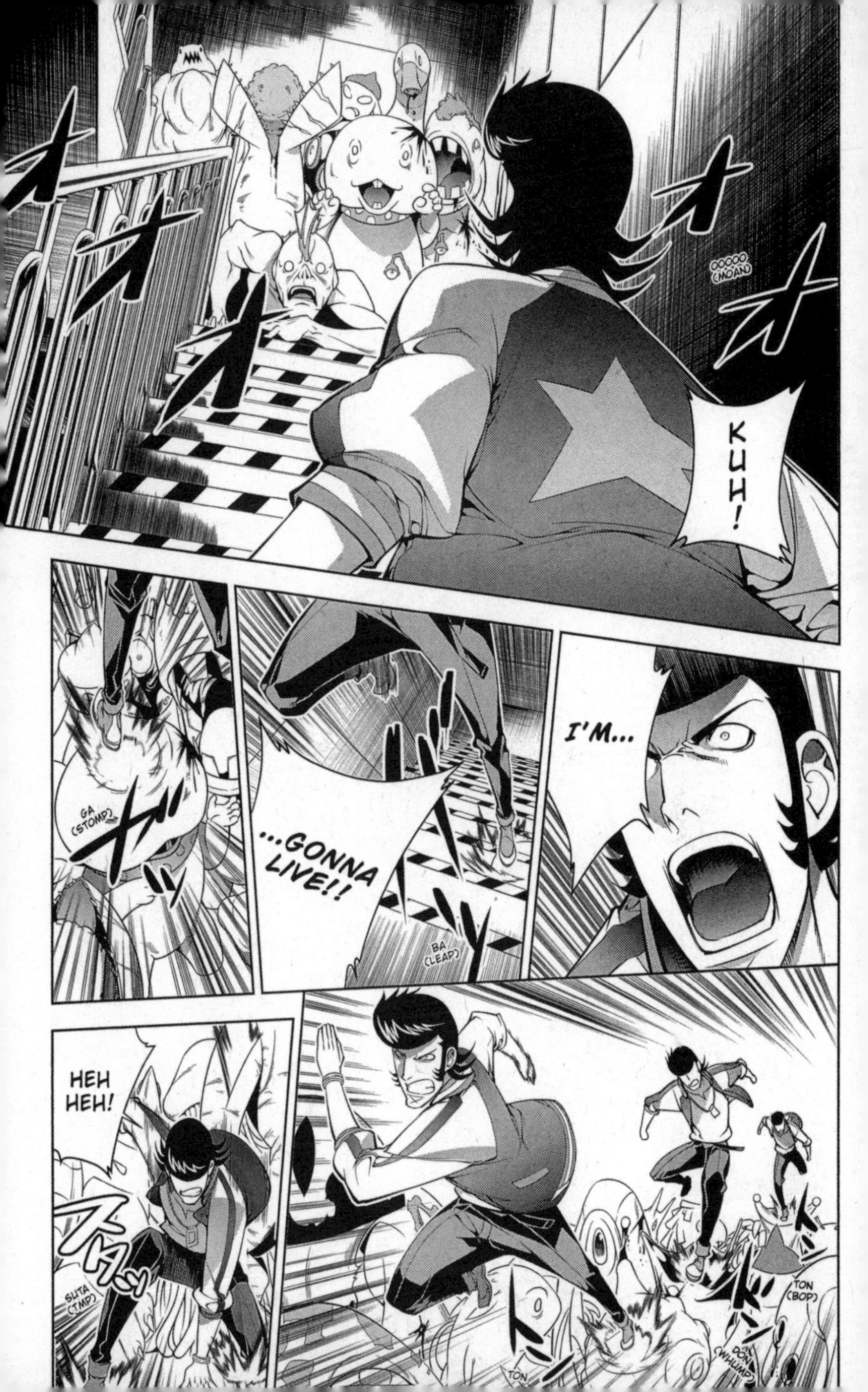

OOOOO (MOAN)
KUH!
I'M...
...GONNA LIVE!!
BA (LEAP)
GA (STOMP)
TON (BOP)
DON (WHUMP)
TON
HEH HEH!
SUTA (TMP)

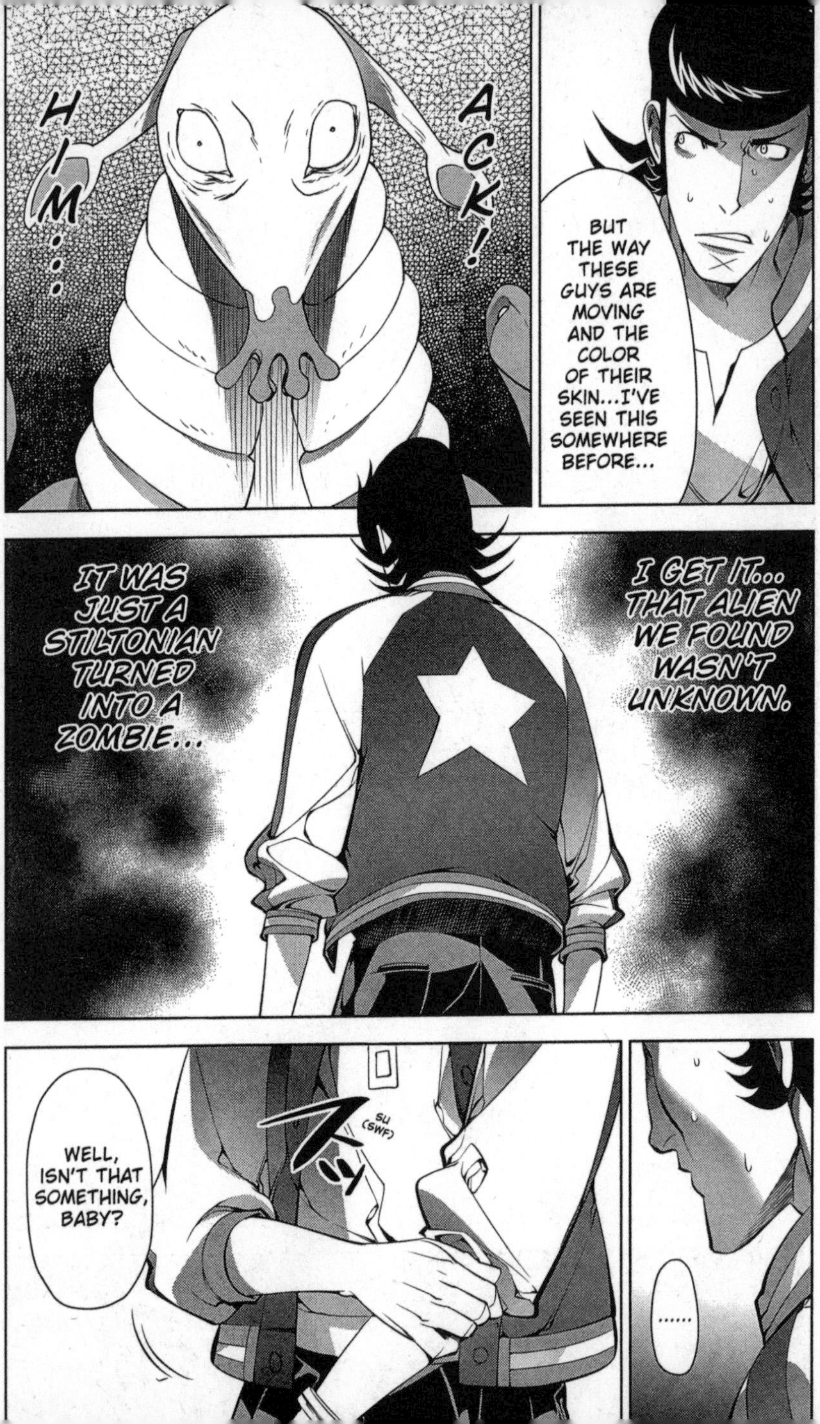
BUT THE WAY THESE GUYS ARE MOVING AND THE COLOR OF THEIR SKIN...I'VE SEEN THIS SOMEWHERE BEFORE...
ACK!
HIM...
I GET IT... THAT ALIEN WE FOUND WASN'T UNKNOWN.
IT WAS JUST A STILTONIAN TURNED INTO A ZOMBIE...
......
SU (SWF)
WELL, ISN'T THAT SOMETHING, BABY?

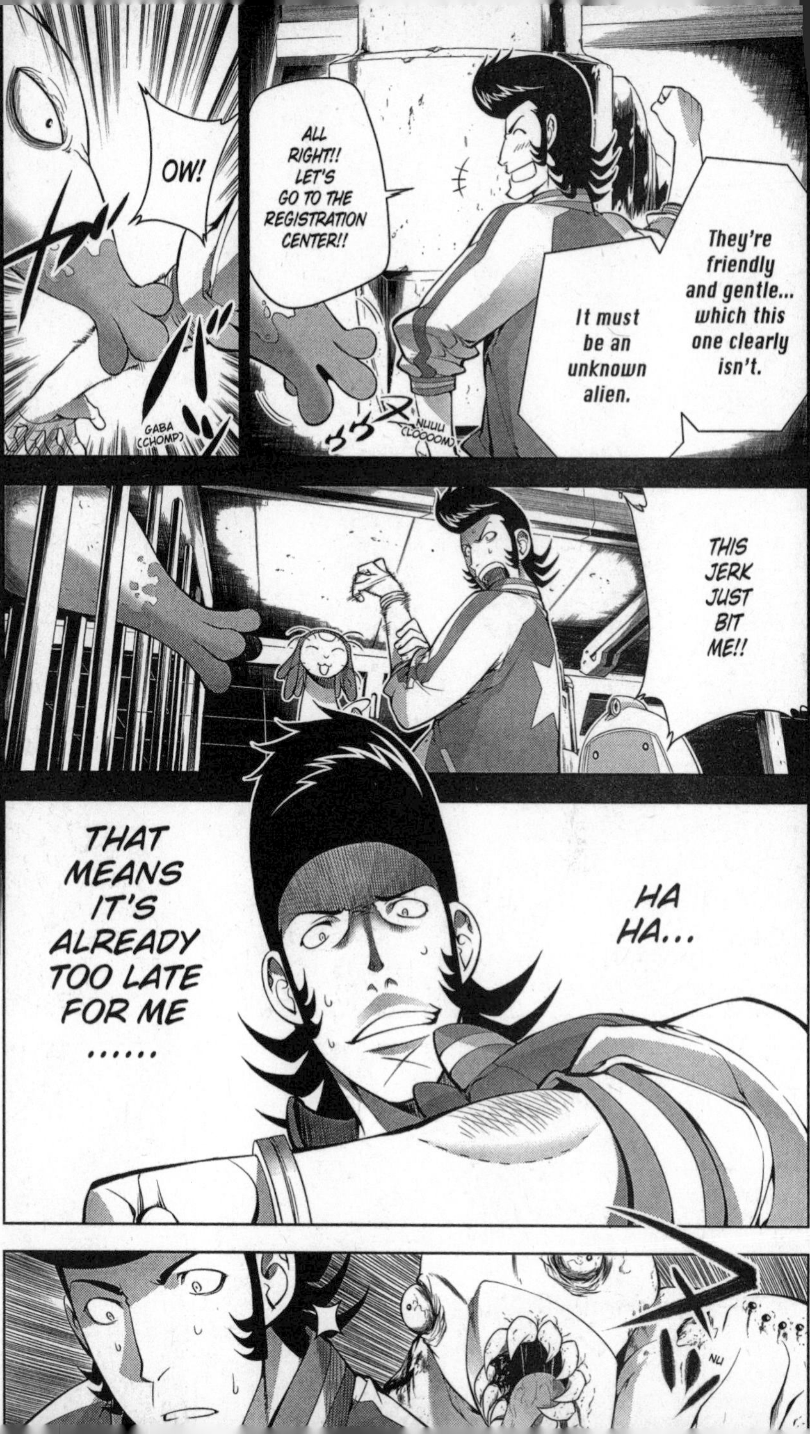
ALL RIGHT!! LET'S GO TO THE REGISTRATION CENTER!!
They're friendly and gentle... which this one clearly isn't.
It must be an unknown alien.
NUUU (LOOOOM)
OW!
GABA (CHOMP)
THIS JERK JUST BIT ME!!
HA HA...
THAT MEANS IT'S ALREADY TOO LATE FOR ME ......
NU

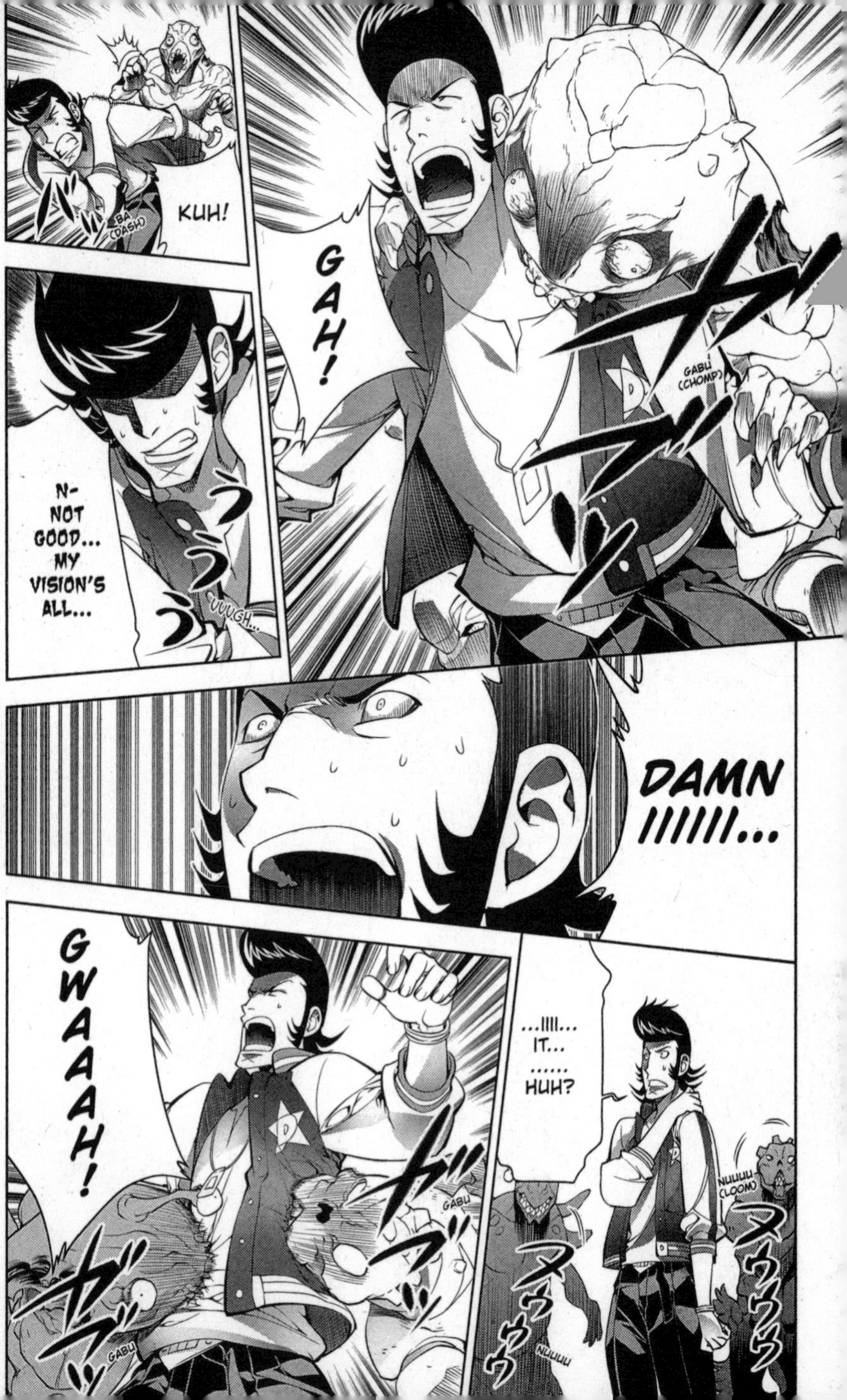
GAH!
GABU (CHOMP)
BA (DASH)
KUH!
N-NOT GOOD... MY VISION'S ALL...
UUUGH...
DAMN IIIIII...
...IIII... IT... ...... HUH?
NUUUU (LOOM)
NUUUU
GWAAAAH!
GABU
GABU

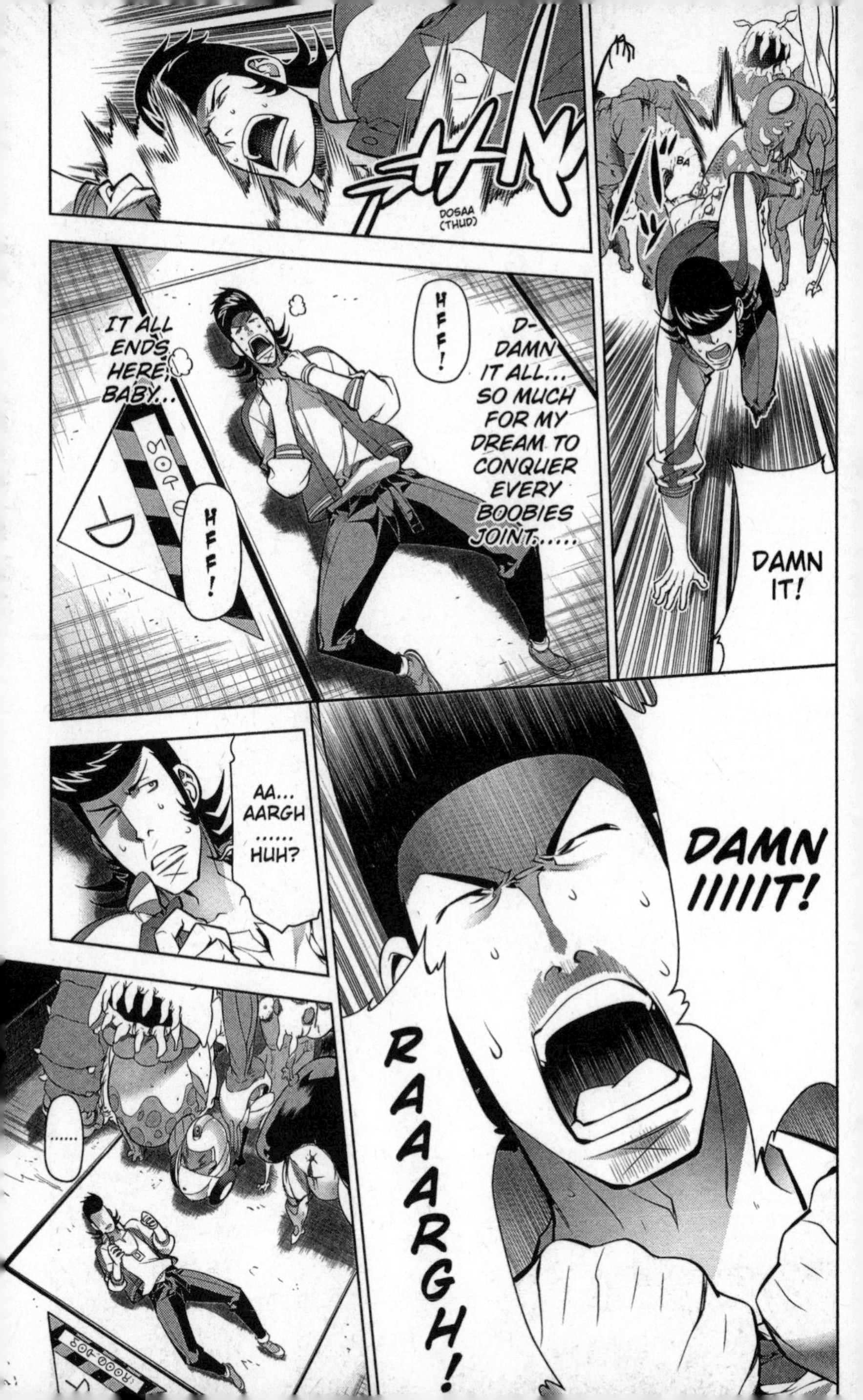
BA
DAMN IT!
DOSAA (THUD)
HFF!
D- DAMN IT ALL... SO MUCH FOR MY DREAM TO CONQUER EVERY BOOBIES JOINT.....
IT ALL ENDS HERE, BABY...
HFF!
DAMN IIIIIT!
RAAARGH!
AA... AARGH ...... HUH?
......

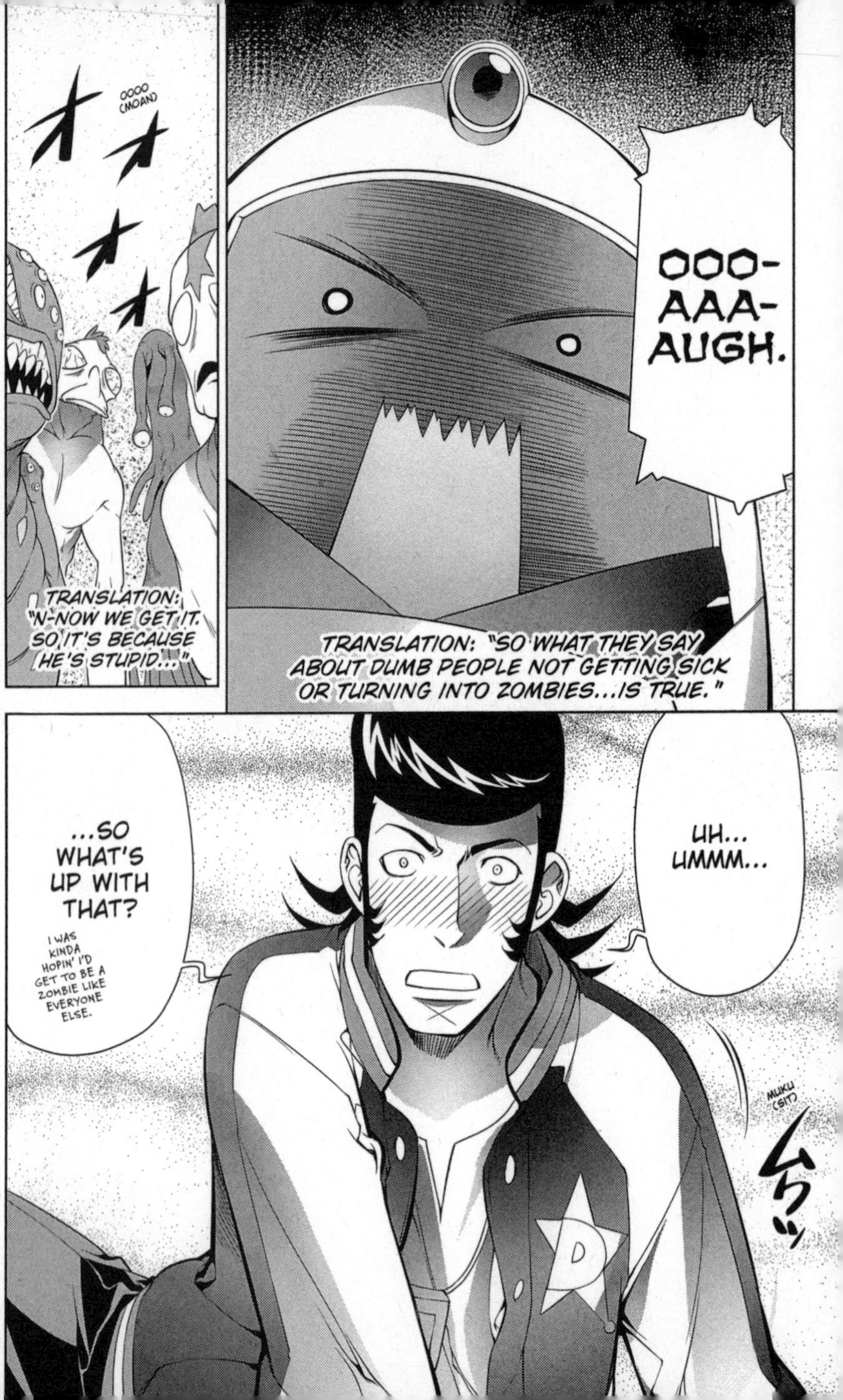
OOO-AAA-AUGH.
TRANSLATION: "SO WHAT THEY SAY ABOUT DUMB PEOPLE NOT GETTING SICK OR TURNING INTO ZOMBIES...IS TRUE."
OOOO (MOAN)
TRANSLATION: "N-NOW WE GET IT. SO IT'S BECAUSE HE'S STUPID..."
UH... UMMM...
MUKU (SIT)
...SO WHAT'S UP WITH THAT?
I WAS KINDA HOPIN' I'D GET TO BE A ZOMBIE LIKE EVERYONE ELSE.

SPACE DANDY

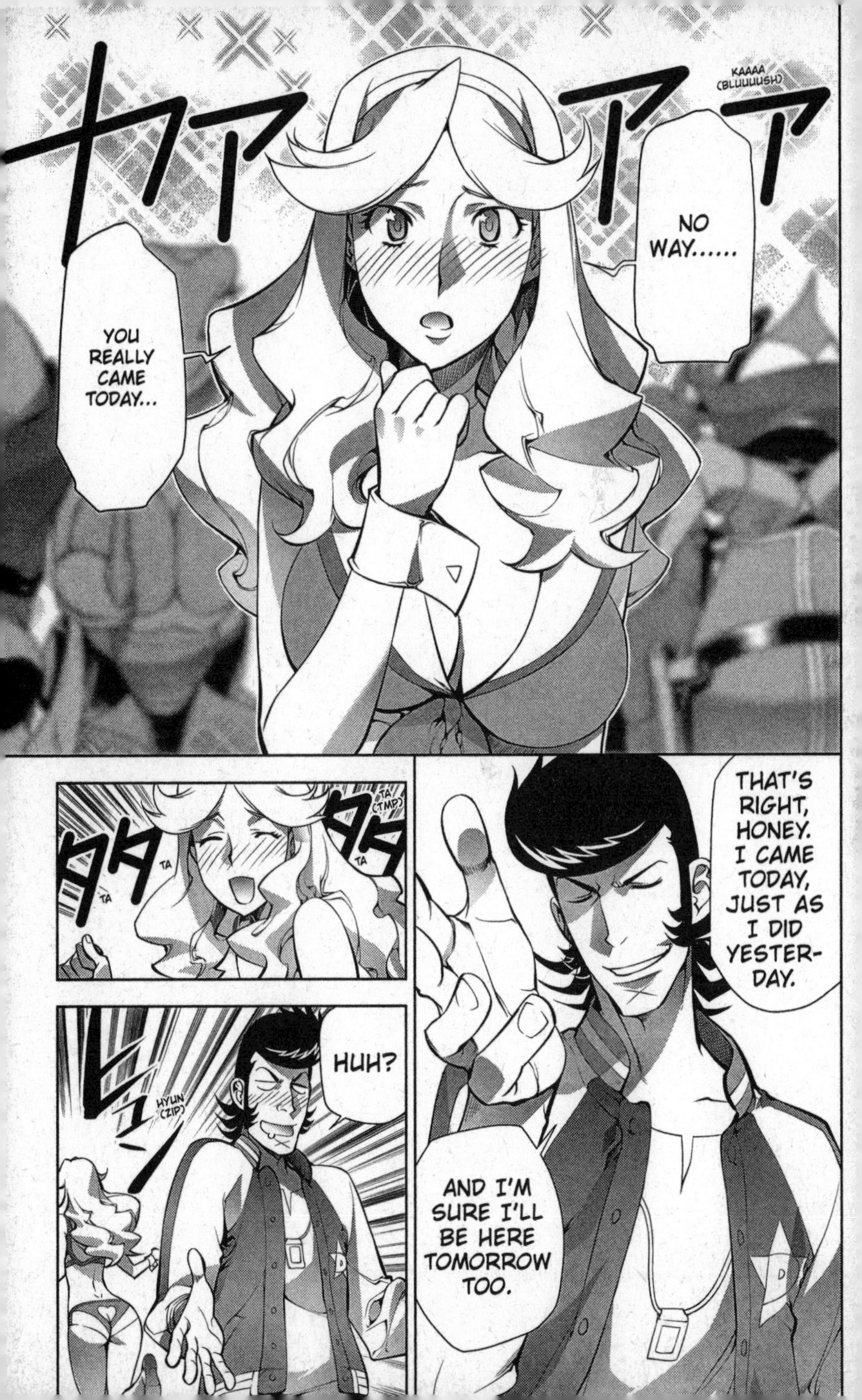
KAAAA (BLUUUUSH)
NO WAY......
YOU REALLY CAME TODAY...
THAT'S RIGHT, HONEY. I CAME TODAY, JUST AS I DID YESTER-DAY.
AND I'M SURE I'LL BE HERE TOMORROW TOO.
TA (TMP)
TA
TA
TA
HUH?
HYUN (ZIP)

Chapter 8: A Race in Space Is Dangerous, Baby (Part I)

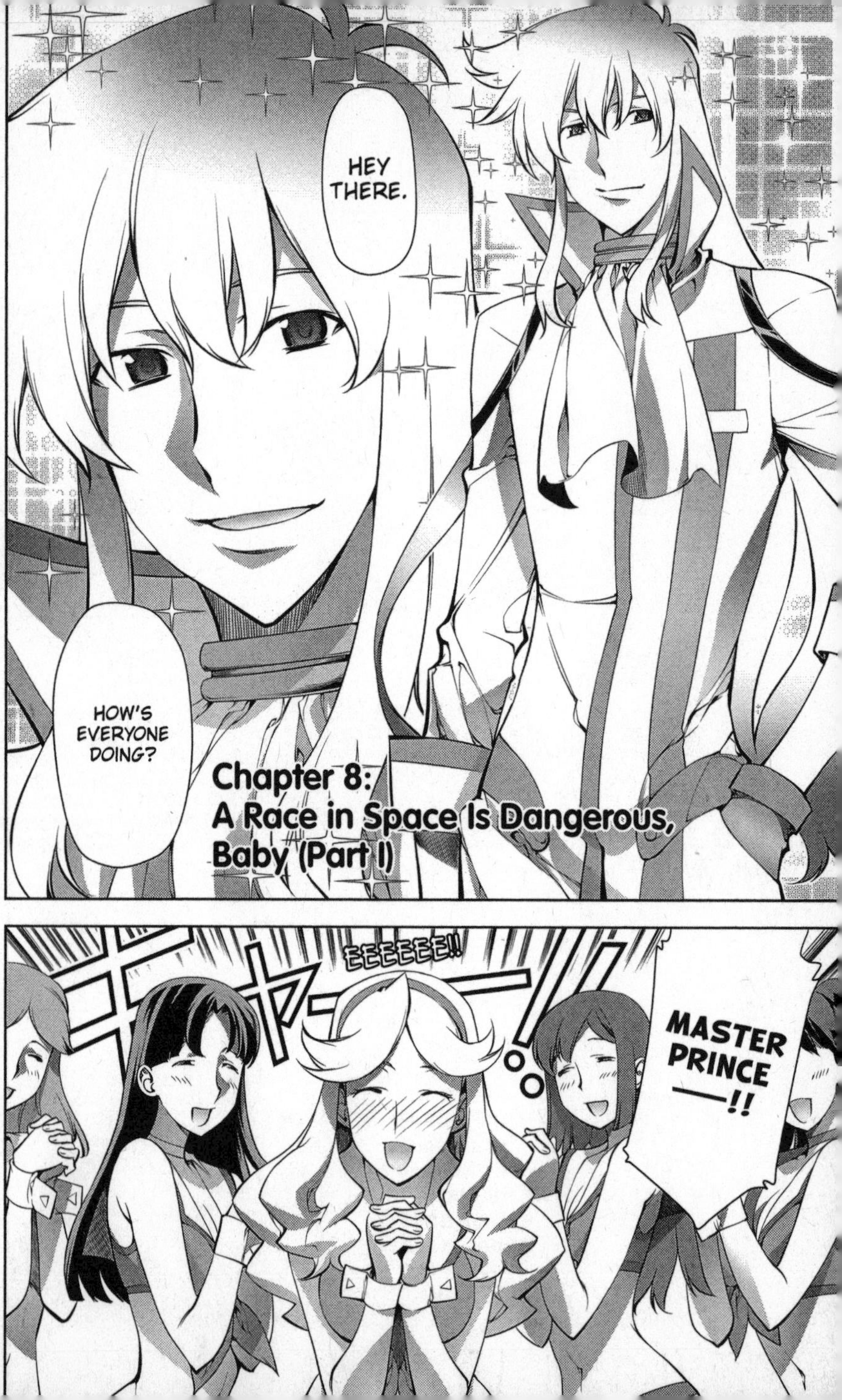
HEY THERE.
HOW'S EVERYONE DOING?
EEEEEE!!
MASTER PRINCE—!!

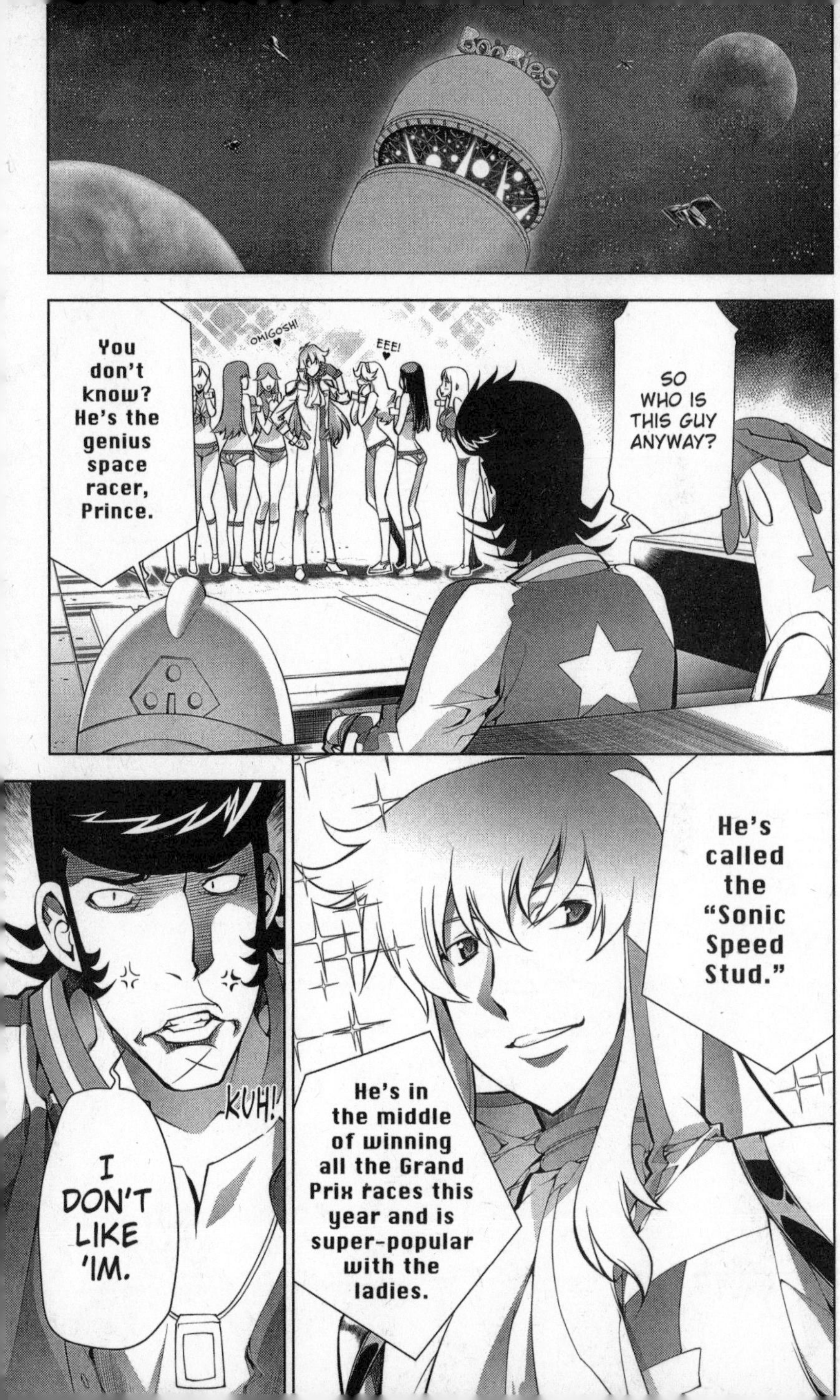
SO WHO IS THIS GUY ANYWAY?
EEE! ♥
OMIGOSH! ♥
You don't know? He's the genius space racer, Prince.
He's called the "Sonic Speed Stud."
He's in the middle of winning all the Grand Prix races this year and is super-popular with the ladies.
KUH!
I DON'T LIKE 'IM.

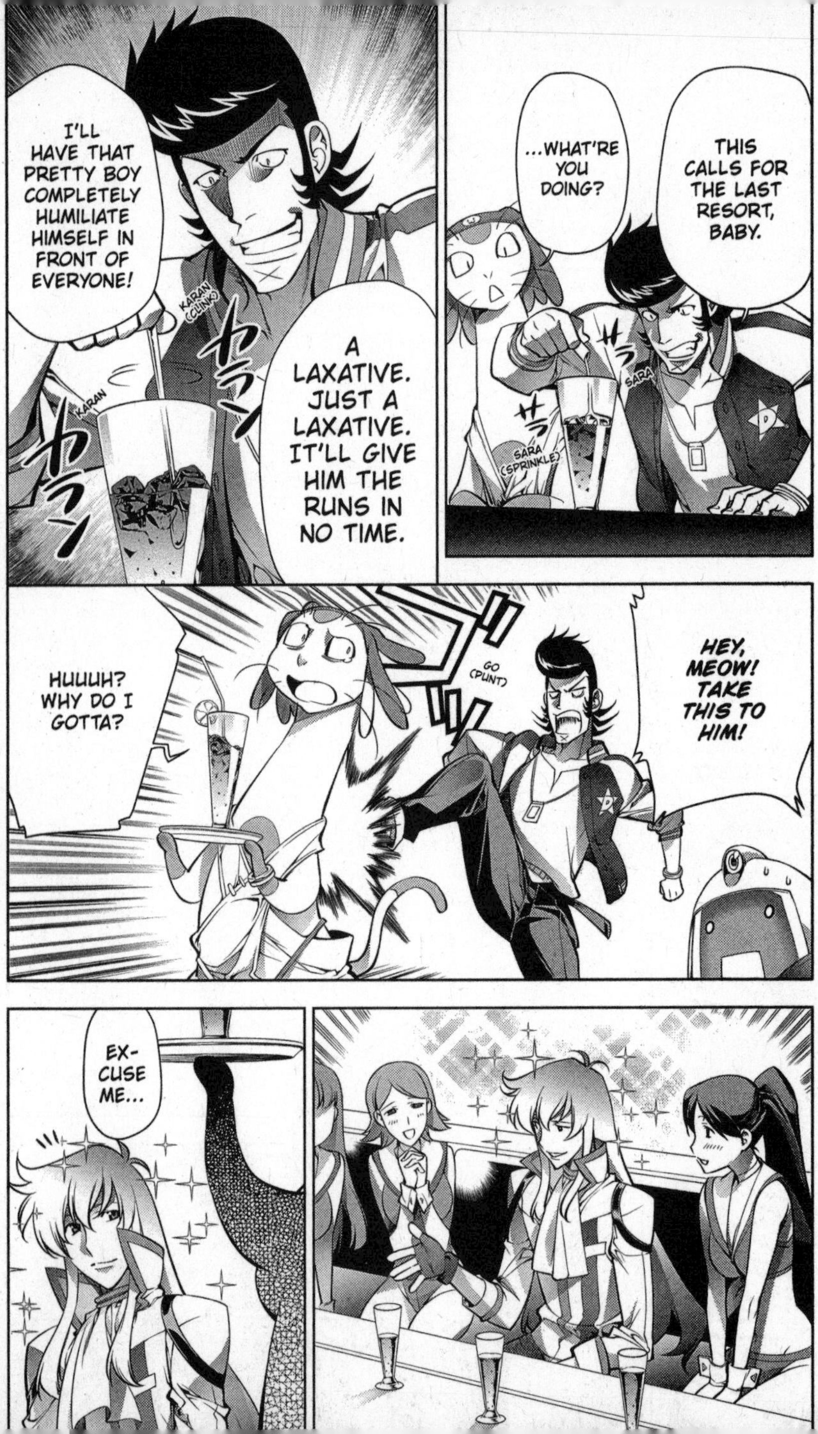

THIS CALLS FOR THE LAST RESORT, BABY.
...WHAT'RE YOU DOING?
SARA
SARA (SPRINKLE)
KARAN (CLINK)
A LAXATIVE. JUST A LAXATIVE. IT'LL GIVE HIM THE RUNS IN NO TIME.
I'LL HAVE THAT PRETTY BOY COMPLETELY HUMILIATE HIMSELF IN FRONT OF EVERYONE!
KARAN
HEY, MEOW! TAKE THIS TO HIM!
GO (PUNT)
HUUUH? WHY DO I GOTTA?
EX-CUSE ME...

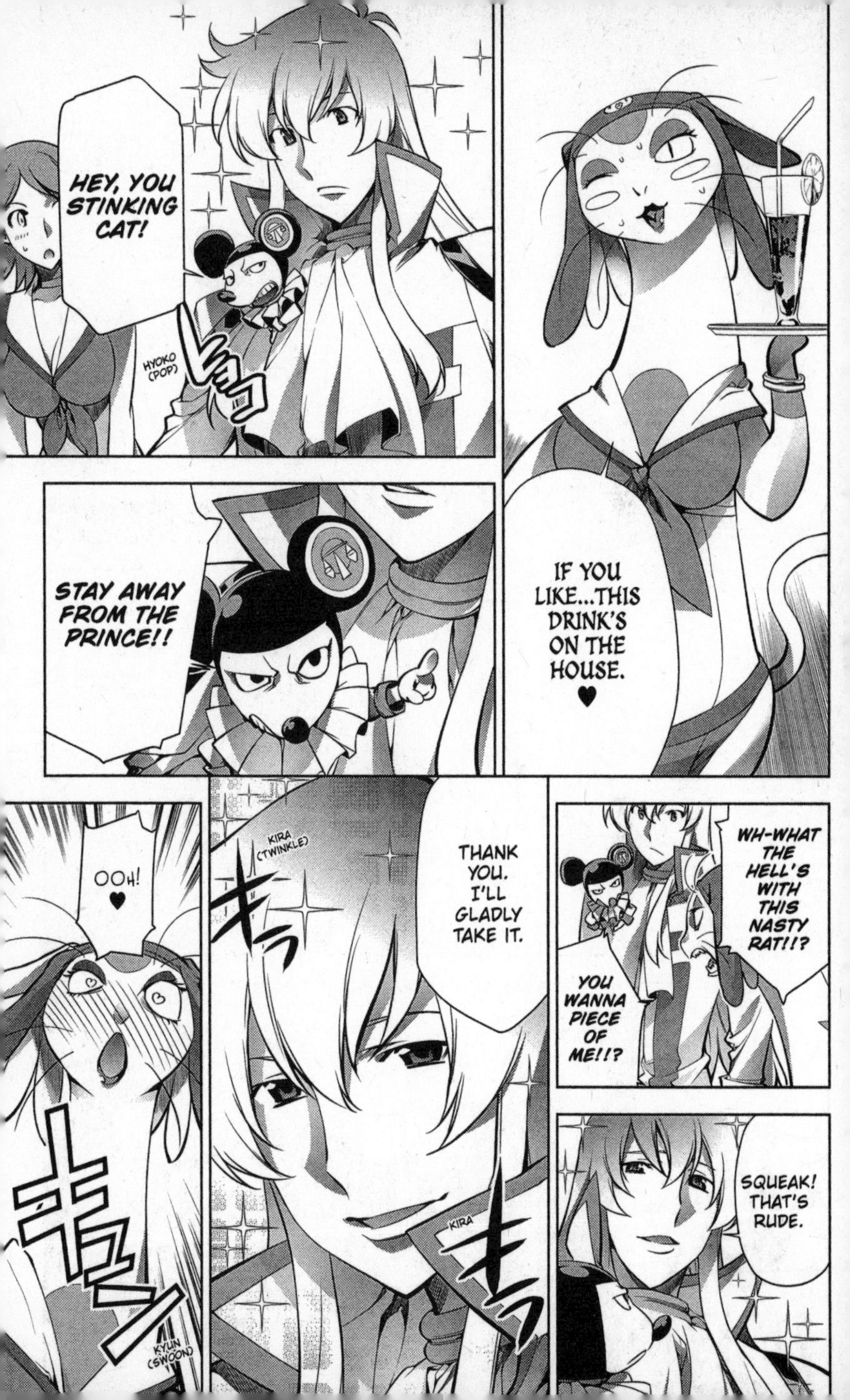
IF YOU LIKE...THIS DRINK'S ON THE HOUSE. ♥
HEY, YOU STINKING CAT!
HYOKO (POP)
STAY AWAY FROM THE PRINCE!!
WH-WHAT THE HELL'S WITH THIS NASTY RAT!!?
YOU WANNA PIECE OF ME!!?
SQUEAK! THAT'S RUDE.
KIRA (TWINKLE)
THANK YOU. I'LL GLADLY TAKE IT.
KIRA
OOH! ♥
KYUN (SWOON)

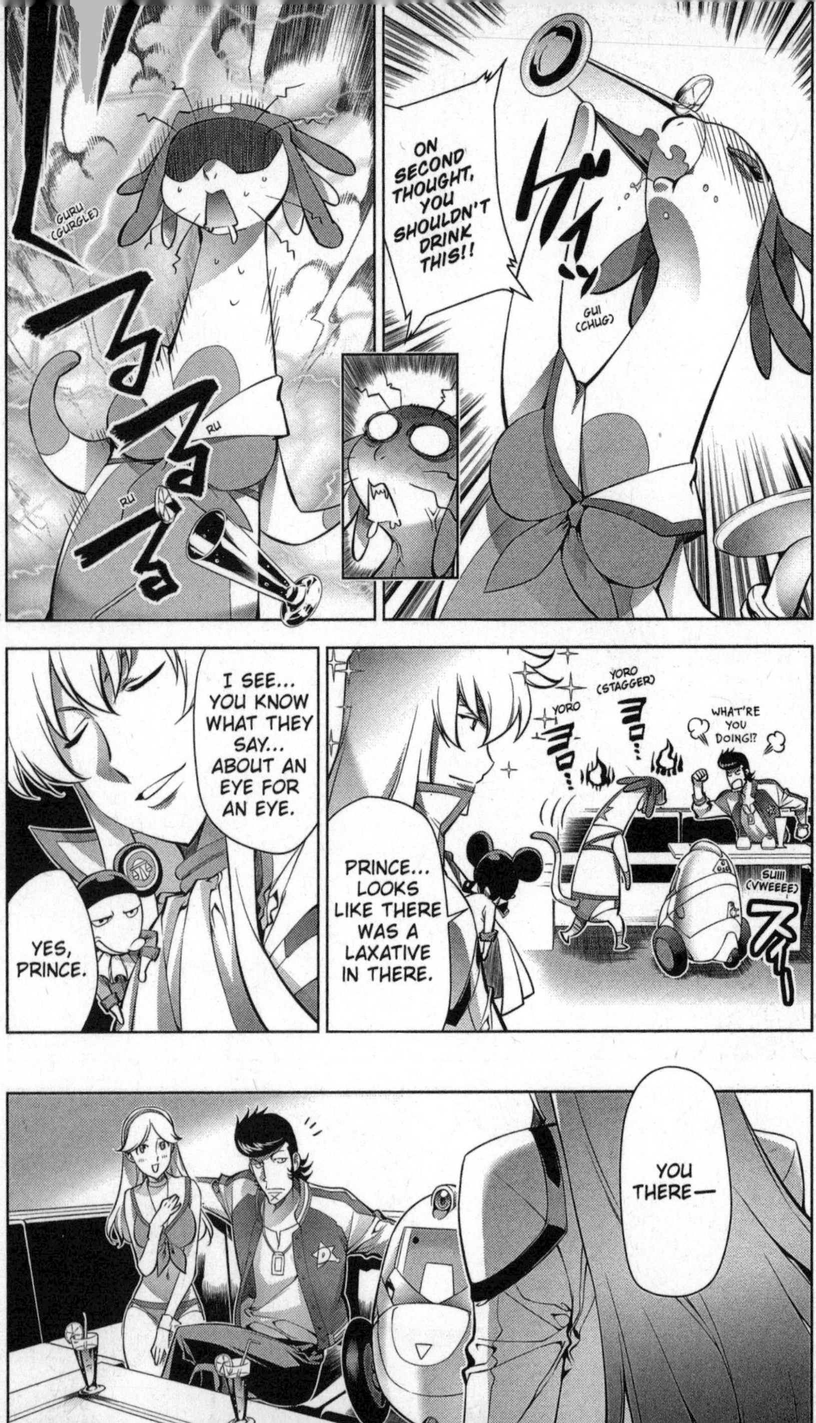
ON SECOND THOUGHT, YOU SHOULDN'T DRINK THIS!!
GUI (CHUG)
GURU (GURGLE)
RU
RU
WHAT'RE YOU DOING!?
YORO (STAGGER)
YORO
SUIII (VWEEEE)
PRINCE... LOOKS LIKE THERE WAS A LAXATIVE IN THERE.
I SEE... YOU KNOW WHAT THEY SAY... ABOUT AN EYE FOR AN EYE.
YES, PRINCE.
YOU THERE—

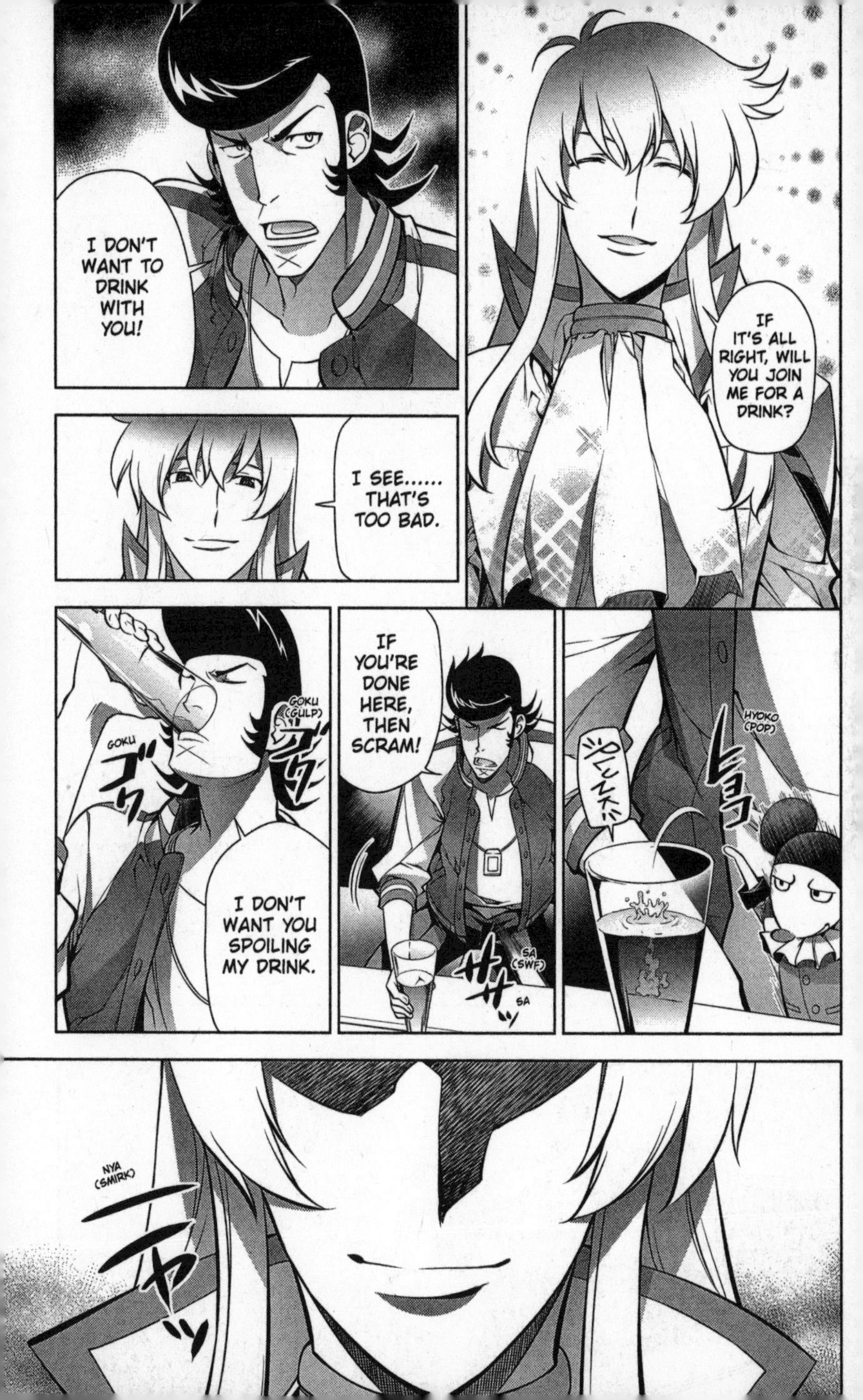
IF IT'S ALL RIGHT, WILL YOU JOIN ME FOR A DRINK?
I DON'T WANT TO DRINK WITH YOU!
I SEE...... THAT'S TOO BAD.
HYOKO (POP)
PLUNK!
IF YOU'RE DONE HERE, THEN SCRAM!
SA (SWF)
SA
GOKU (GULP)
GOKU
I DON'T WANT YOU SPOILING MY DRINK.
NYA (SMIRK)

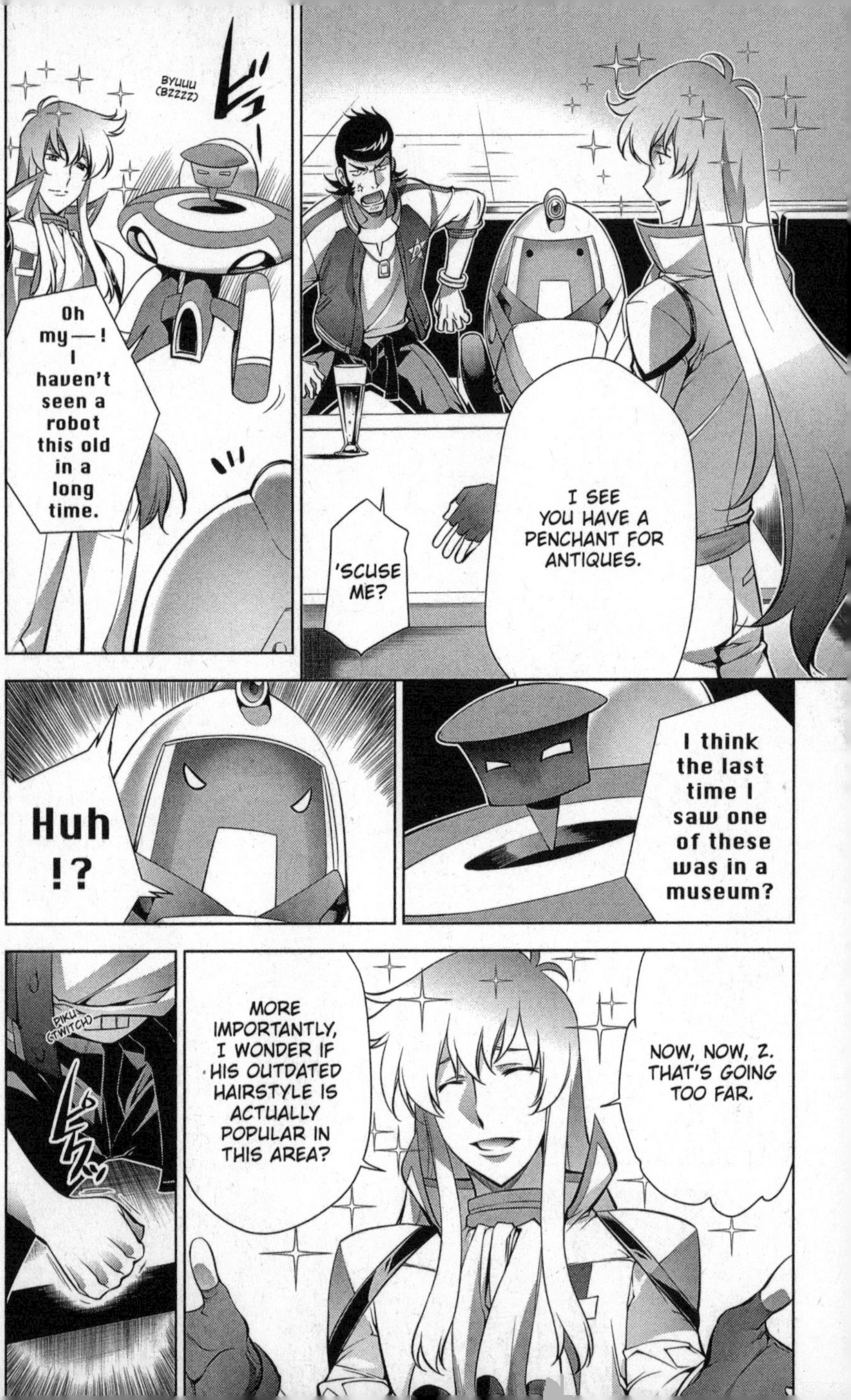
I SEE YOU HAVE A PENCHANT FOR ANTIQUES.
'SCUSE ME?
BYUUU (BZZZZ)
Oh my—! I haven't seen a robot this old in a long time.
I think the last time I saw one of these was in a museum?
Huh!?
MORE IMPORTANTLY, I WONDER IF HIS OUTDATED HAIRSTYLE IS ACTUALLY POPULAR IN THIS AREA?
NOW, NOW, Z. THAT'S GOING TOO FAR.
PIKU (TWITCH)

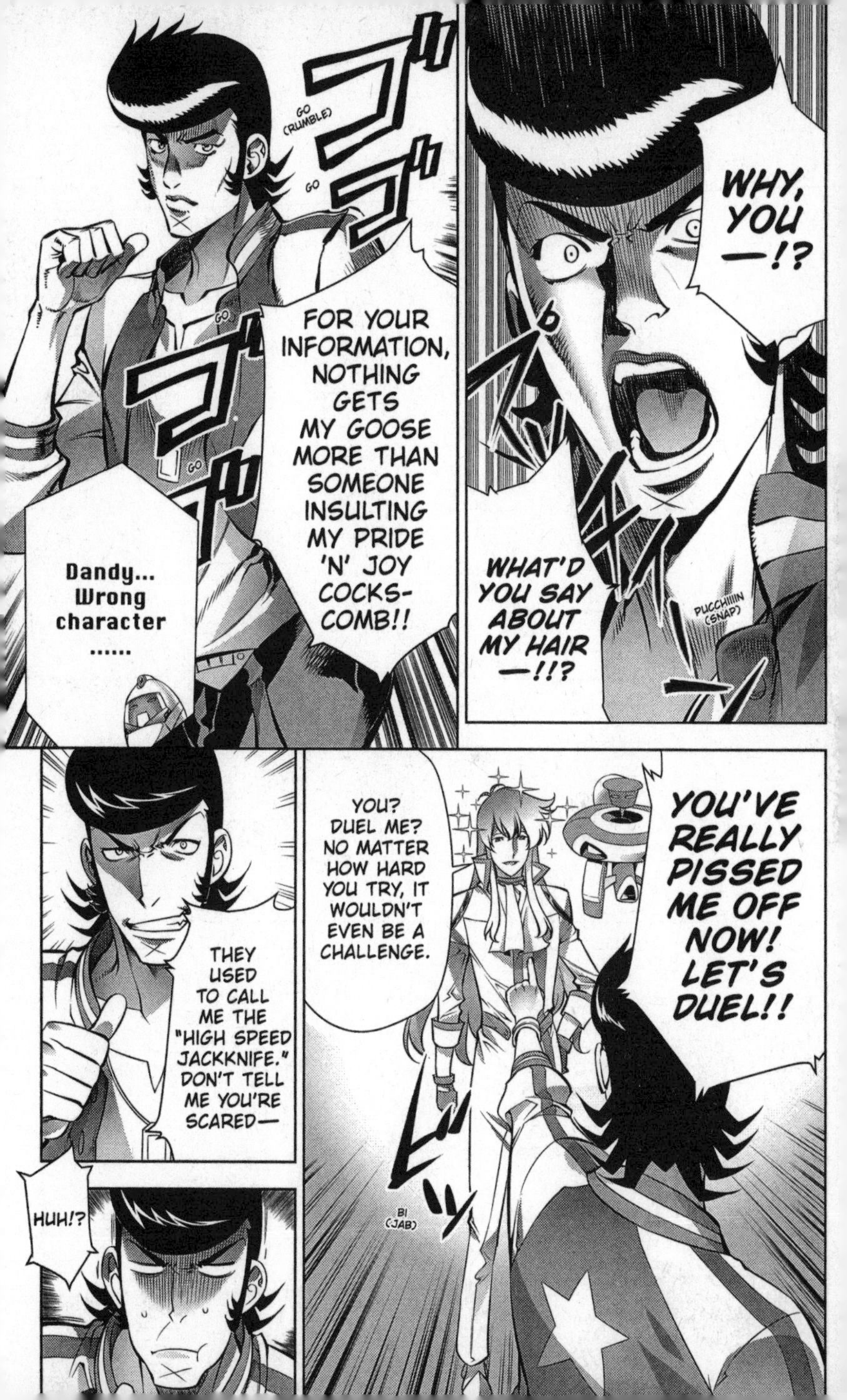
WHY, YOU—!?
WHAT'D YOU SAY ABOUT MY HAIR—!!?
PUCCHIIIN (SNAP)
GO (RUMBLE)
GO
GO
GO
FOR YOUR INFORMATION, NOTHING GETS MY GOOSE MORE THAN SOMEONE INSULTING MY PRIDE 'N' JOY COCKSCOMB!!
Dandy... Wrong character ......
YOU'VE REALLY PISSED ME OFF NOW! LET'S DUEL!!
YOU? DUEL ME? NO MATTER HOW HARD YOU TRY, IT WOULDN'T EVEN BE A CHALLENGE.
BI (JAB)
THEY USED TO CALL ME THE "HIGH SPEED JACKKNIFE." DON'T TELL ME YOU'RE SCARED—
HUH!?

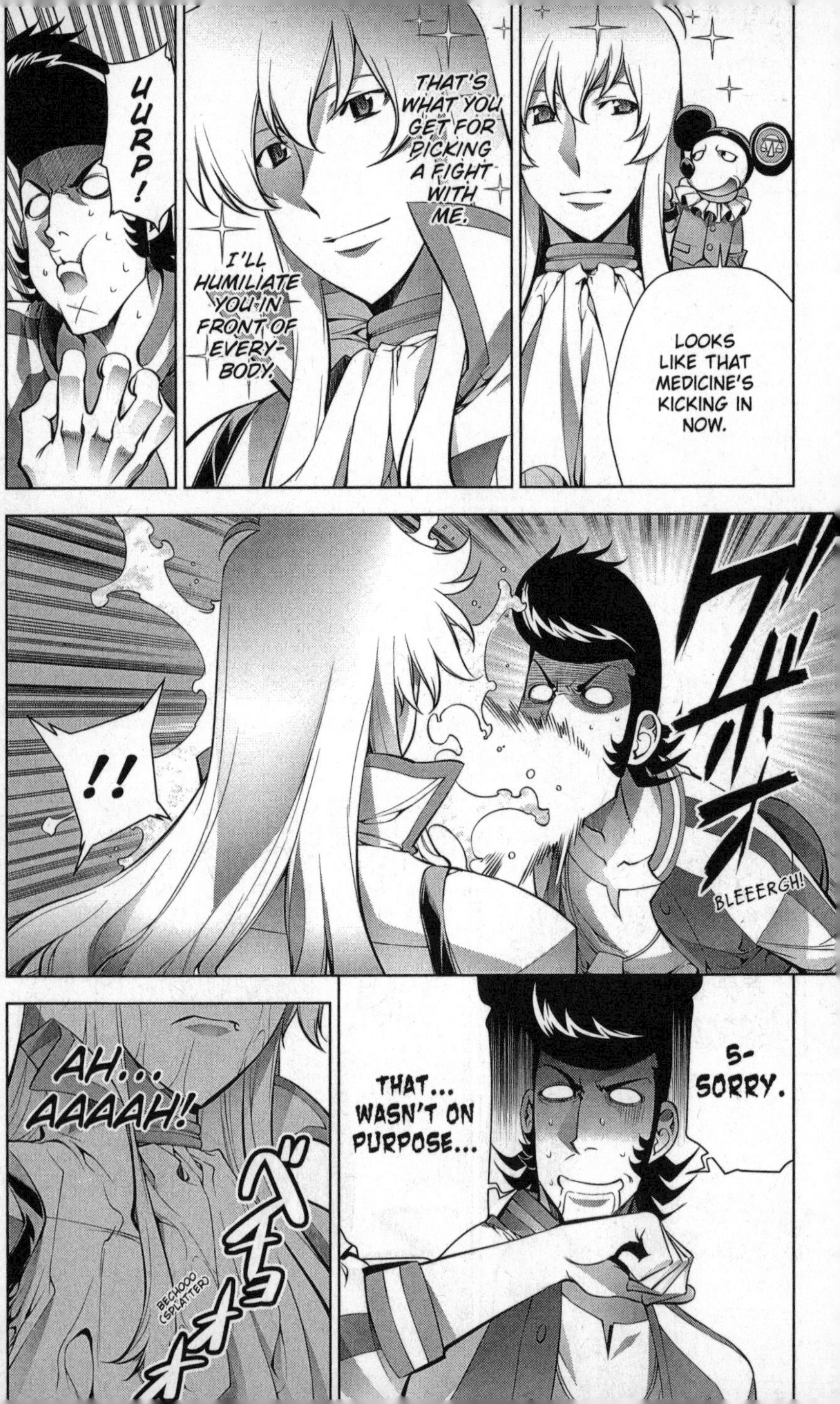
LOOKS LIKE THAT MEDICINE'S KICKING IN NOW.
THAT'S WHAT YOU GET FOR PICKING A FIGHT WITH ME.
I'LL HUMILIATE YOU IN FRONT OF EVERY-BODY.
UURP!
BLEEERGH!
!!
S- SORRY.
THAT... WASN'T ON PURPOSE...
AH... AAAAH!
BECHOOO (SPLATTER)

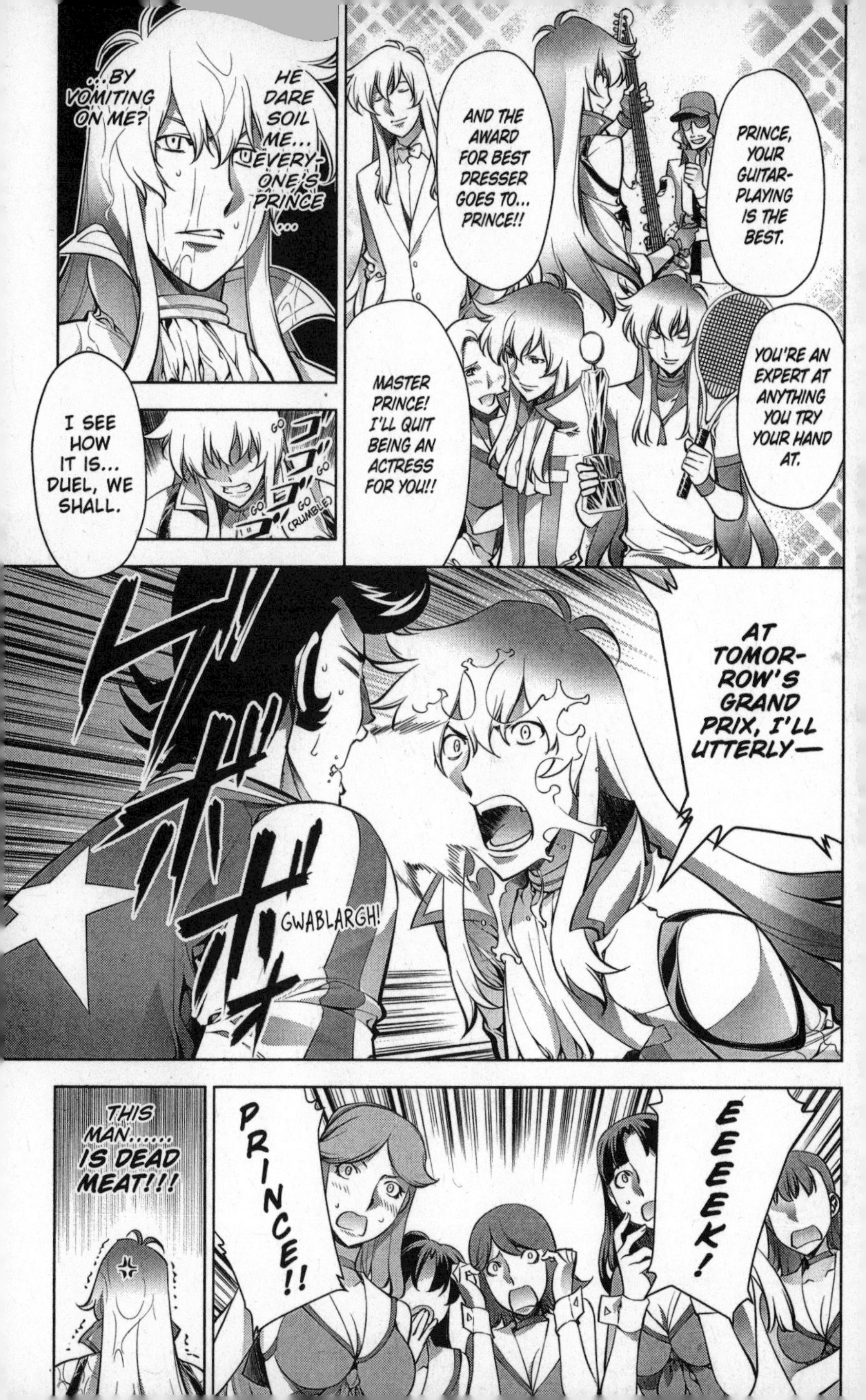
PRINCE, YOUR GUITAR-PLAYING IS THE BEST.
AND THE AWARD FOR BEST DRESSER GOES TO... PRINCE!!
YOU'RE AN EXPERT AT ANYTHING YOU TRY YOUR HAND AT.
MASTER PRINCE! I'LL QUIT BEING AN ACTRESS FOR YOU!!
HE DARE SOIL ME... EVERYONE'S PRINCE...
...BY VOMITING ON ME?
GO GO GO GO (RUMBLE)
I SEE HOW IT IS... DUEL, WE SHALL.
AT TOMORROW'S GRAND PRIX, I'LL UTTERLY—
GWABLARGH!
EEEEEK!
PRINCE!!
THIS MAN...... IS DEAD MEAT!!!

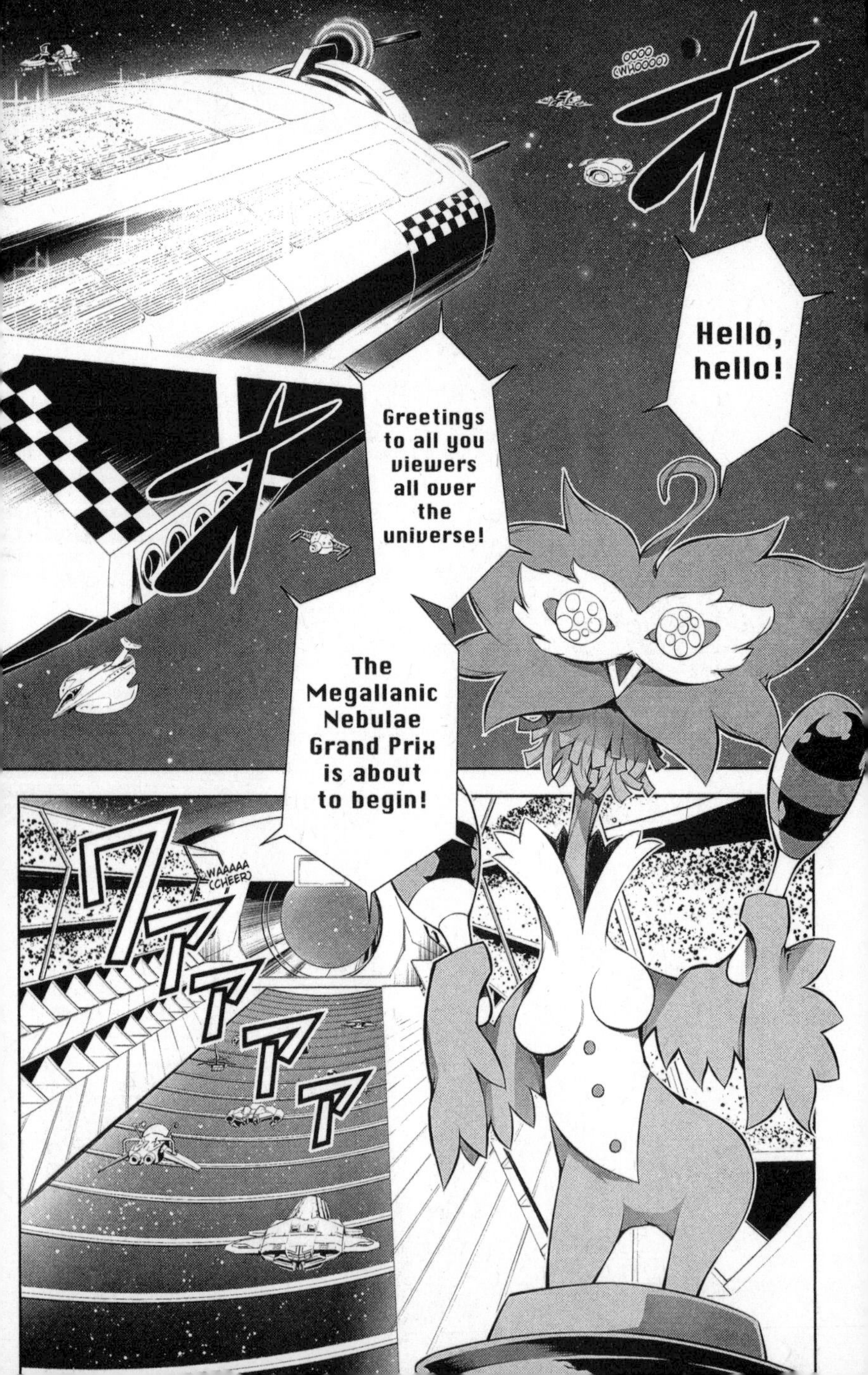
OOOO (WHOOOO)
Hello, hello!
Greetings to all you viewers all over the universe!
The Megallanic Nebulae Grand Prix is about to begin!
WAAAAA (CHEER)

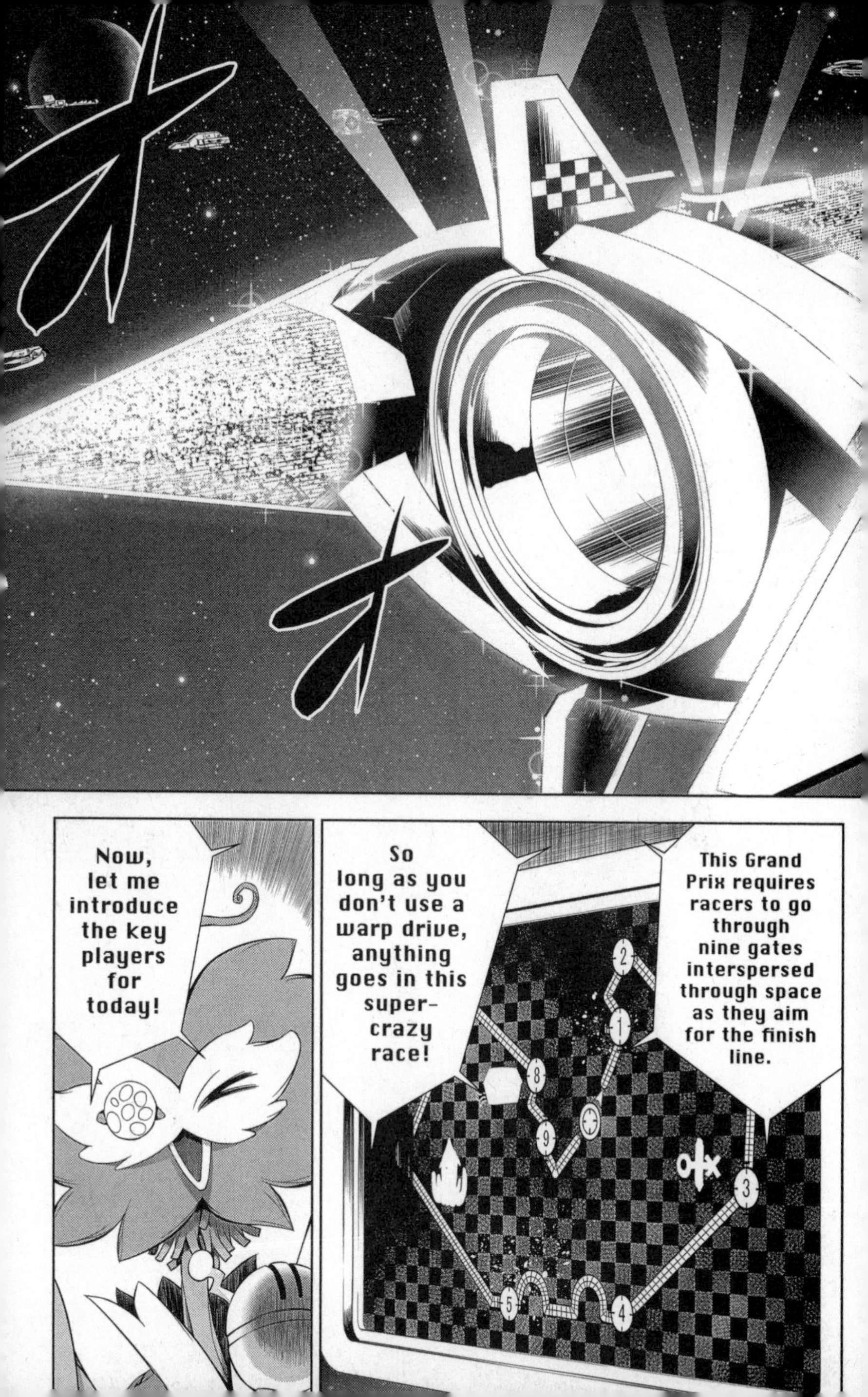

This Grand Prix requires racers to go through nine gates interspersed through space as they aim for the finish line.
So long as you don't use a warp drive, anything goes in this super-crazy race!
Now, let me introduce the key players for today!

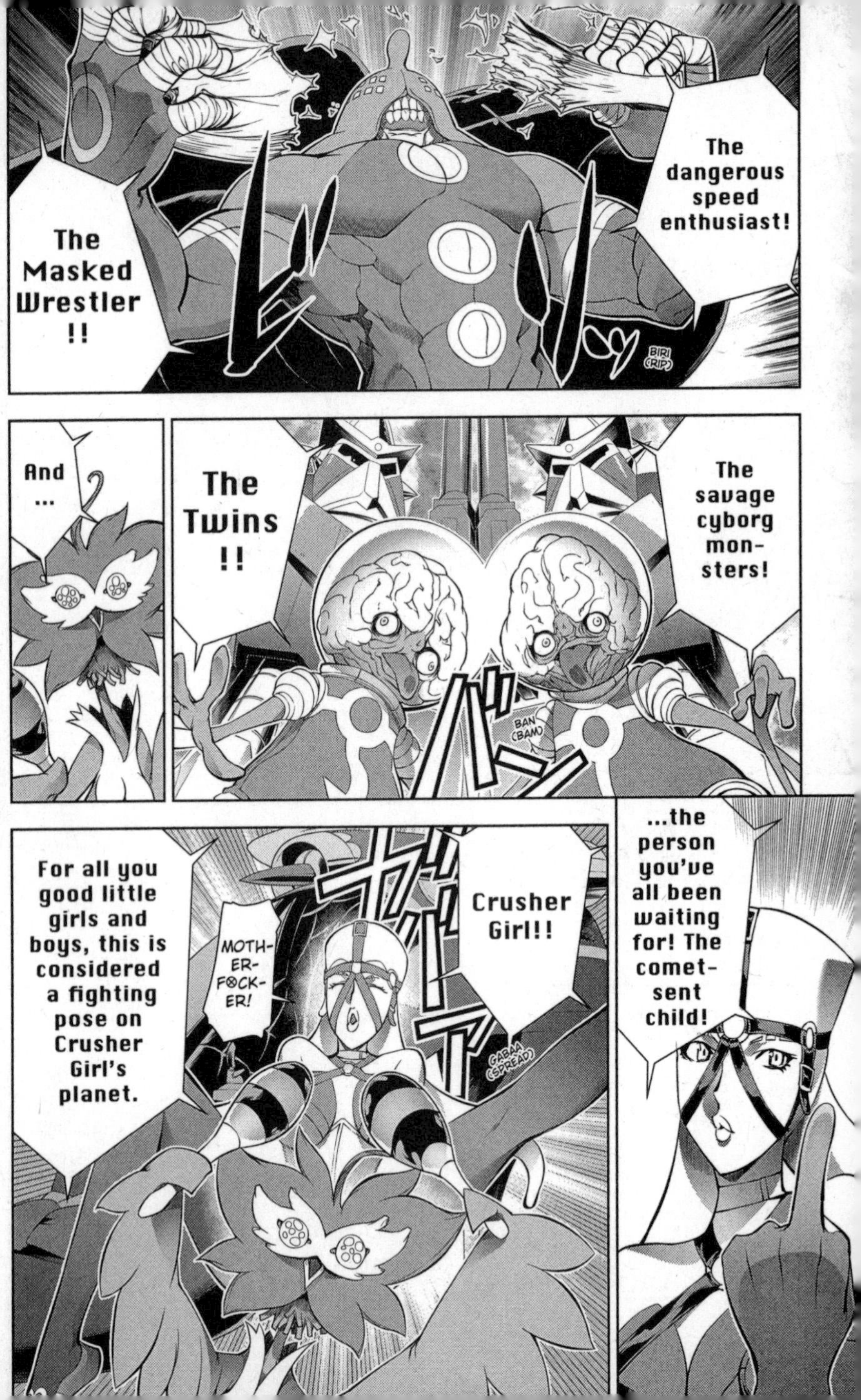
The dangerous speed enthusiast!
The Masked Wrestler!!
BIRI (RIP)
The savage cyborg monsters!
The Twins!!
BAN (BAM)
And ...
...the person you've all been waiting for! The comet-sent child!
Crusher Girl!!
MOTHER-F⊗CKER!
GABAA (SPREAD)
For all you good little girls and boys, this is considered a fighting pose on Crusher Girl's planet.

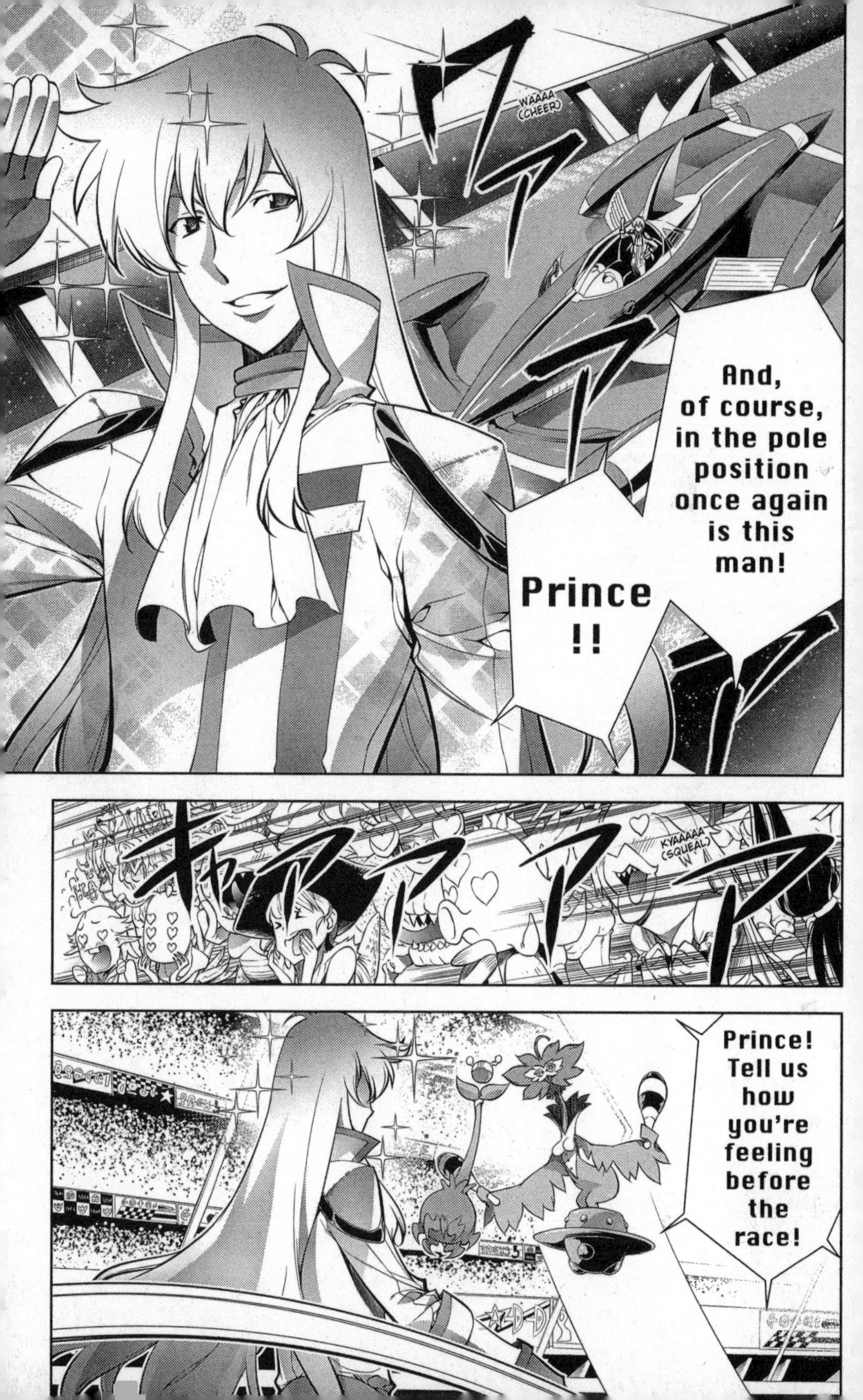
WAAAA (CHEER)
And, of course, in the pole position once again is this man!
Prince !!
KYAAAAA (SQUEAL)
Prince! Tell us how you're feeling before the race!

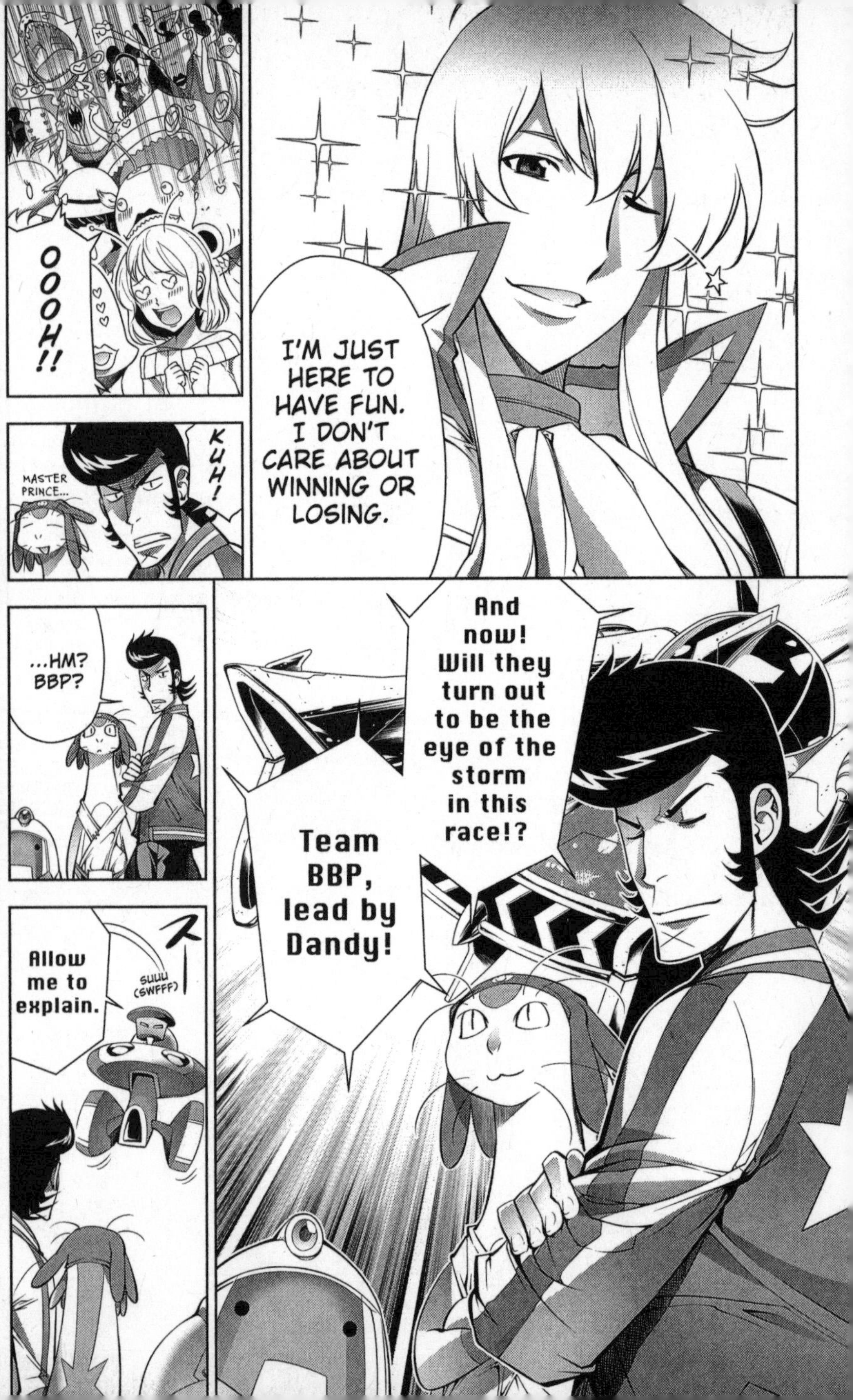
I'M JUST HERE TO HAVE FUN. I DON'T CARE ABOUT WINNING OR LOSING.
OOOOH!!
KUH!
MASTER PRINCE...
And now! Will they turn out to be the eye of the storm in this race!?
Team BBP, lead by Dandy!
...HM? BBP?
SUUU (SWFFF)
Allow me to explain.

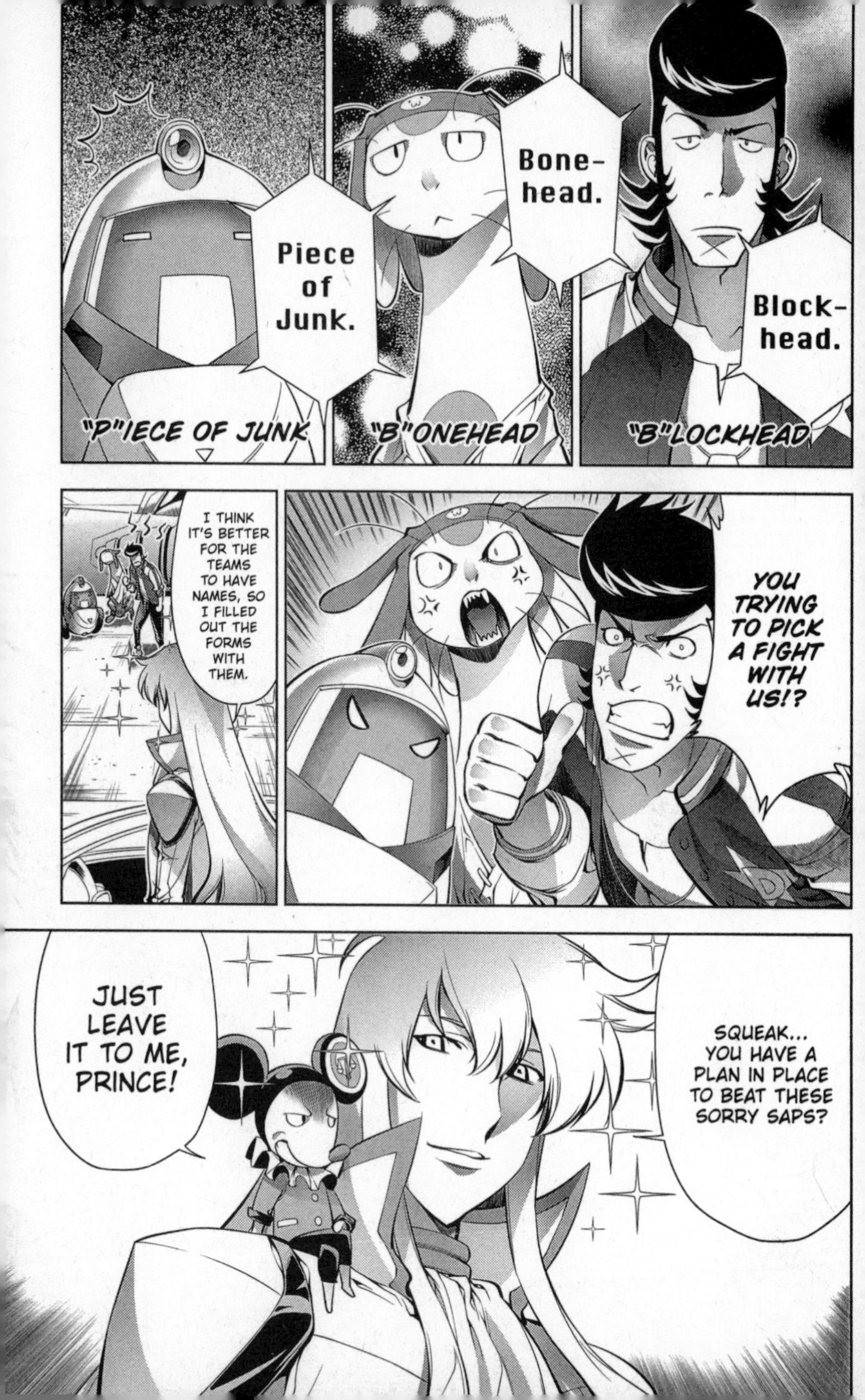
Block-head.
"B"LOCKHEAD
Bone-head.
"B"ONEHEAD
Piece of Junk.
"P"IECE OF JUNK
YOU TRYING TO PICK A FIGHT WITH US!?
I THINK IT'S BETTER FOR THE TEAMS TO HAVE NAMES, SO I FILLED OUT THE FORMS WITH THEM.
SQUEAK... YOU HAVE A PLAN IN PLACE TO BEAT THESE SORRY SAPS?
JUST LEAVE IT TO ME, PRINCE!

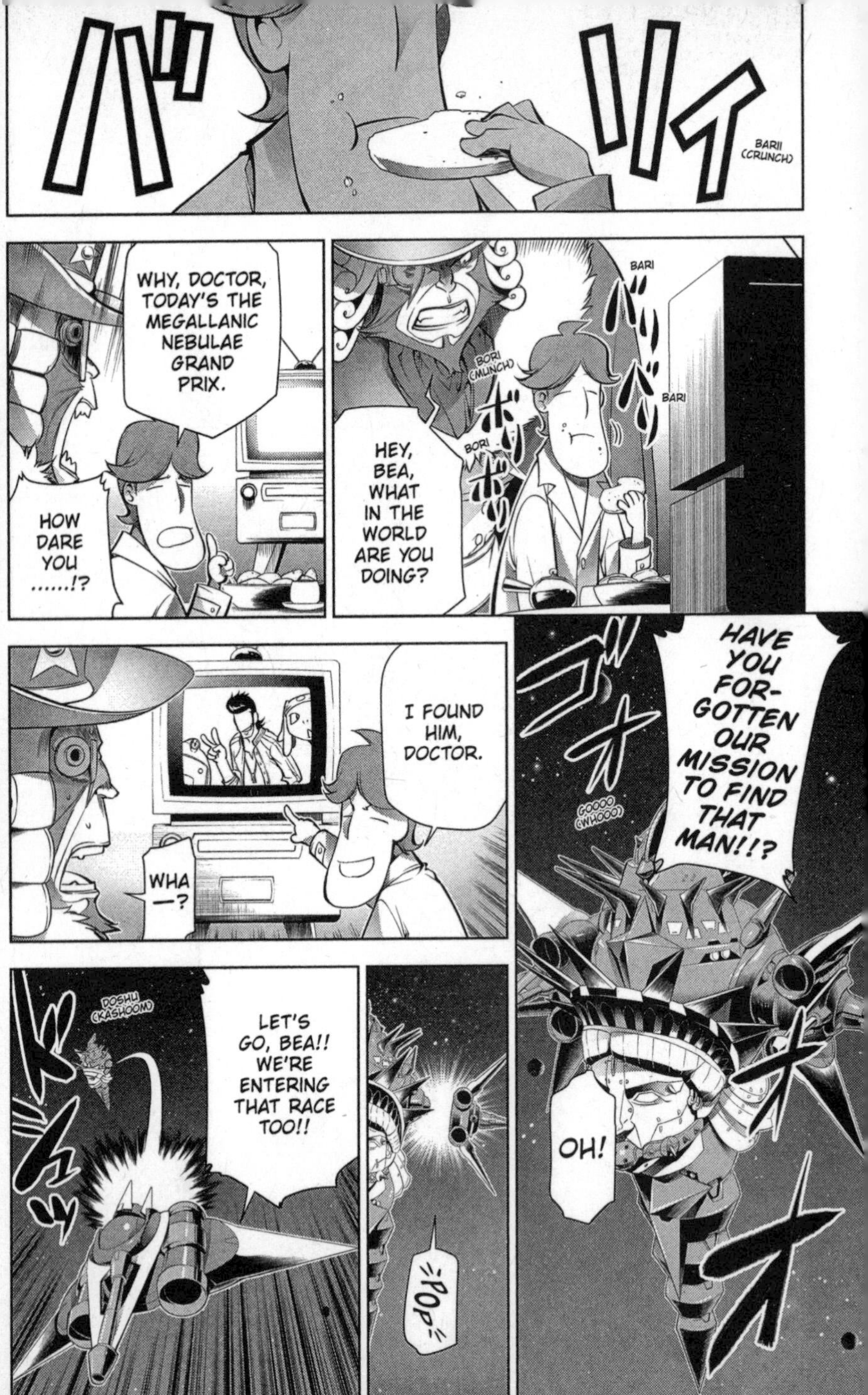
BARII (CRUNCH)
BARI
BARI
BORI (MUNCH)
BORI
HEY, BEA, WHAT IN THE WORLD ARE YOU DOING?
WHY, DOCTOR, TODAY'S THE MEGALLANIC NEBULAE GRAND PRIX.
HOW DARE YOU ......!?
HAVE YOU FOR-GOTTEN OUR MISSION TO FIND THAT MAN!!?
GOOOO (WHOOO)
OH!
I FOUND HIM, DOCTOR.
WHA—?
POP
LET'S GO, BEA!! WE'RE ENTERING THAT RACE TOO!!
DOSHU (KASHOOM)

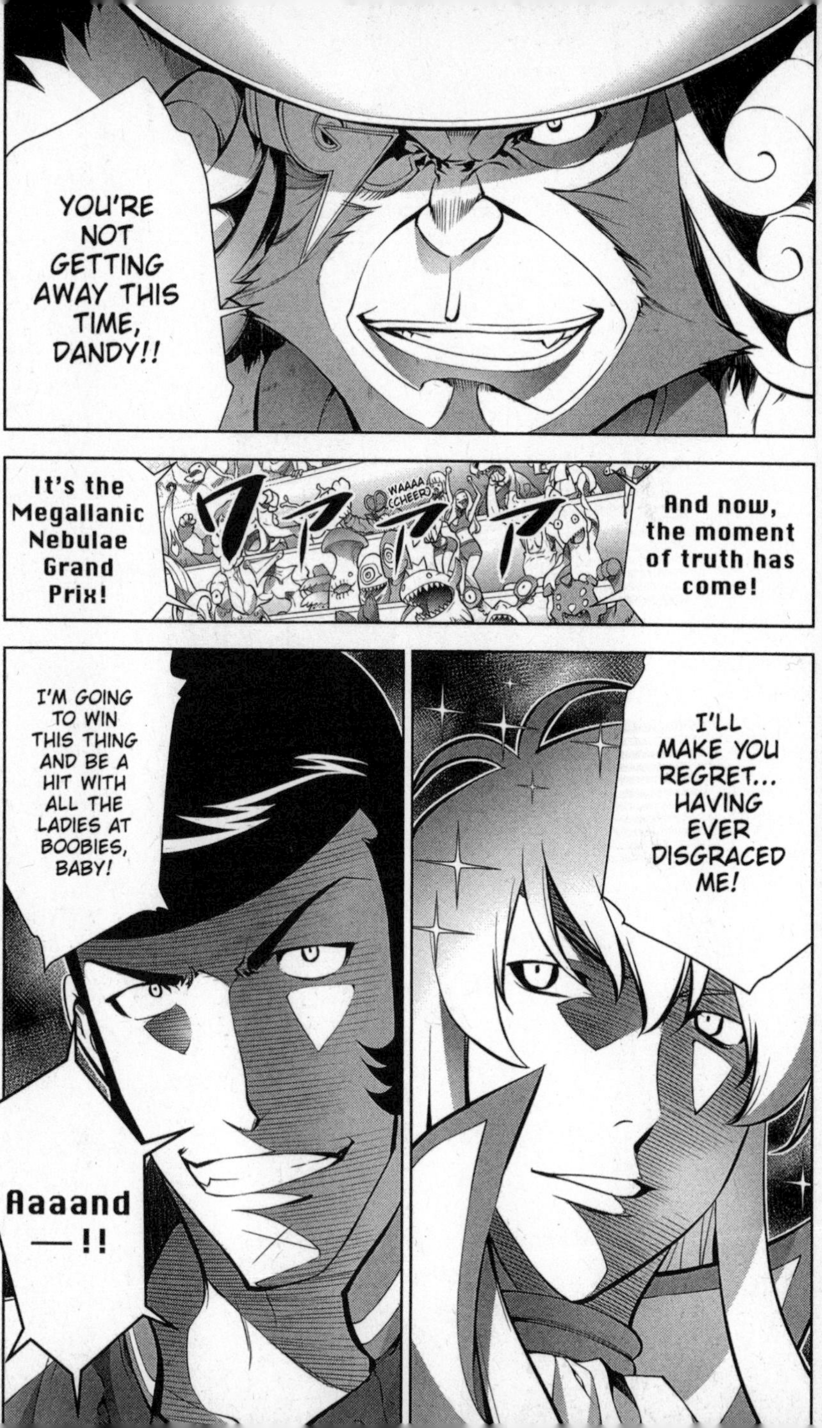
YOU'RE NOT GETTING AWAY THIS TIME, DANDY!!
And now, the moment of truth has come!
WAAAA (CHEER)
It's the Megallanic Nebulae Grand Prix!
I'LL MAKE YOU REGRET... HAVING EVER DISGRACED ME!
I'M GOING TO WIN THIS THING AND BE A HIT WITH ALL THE LADIES AT BOOBIES, BABY!
Aaaand —!!

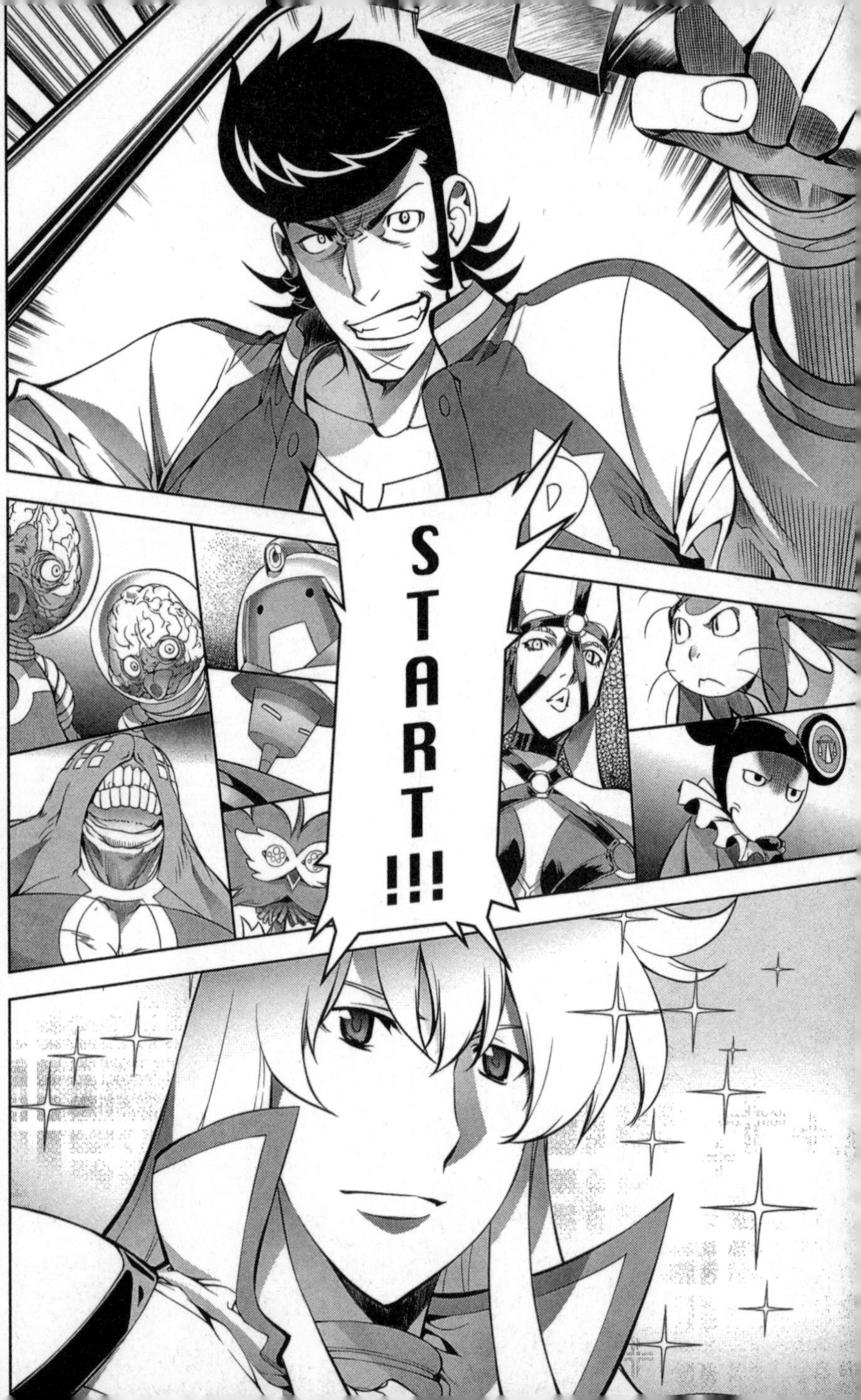
START!!!

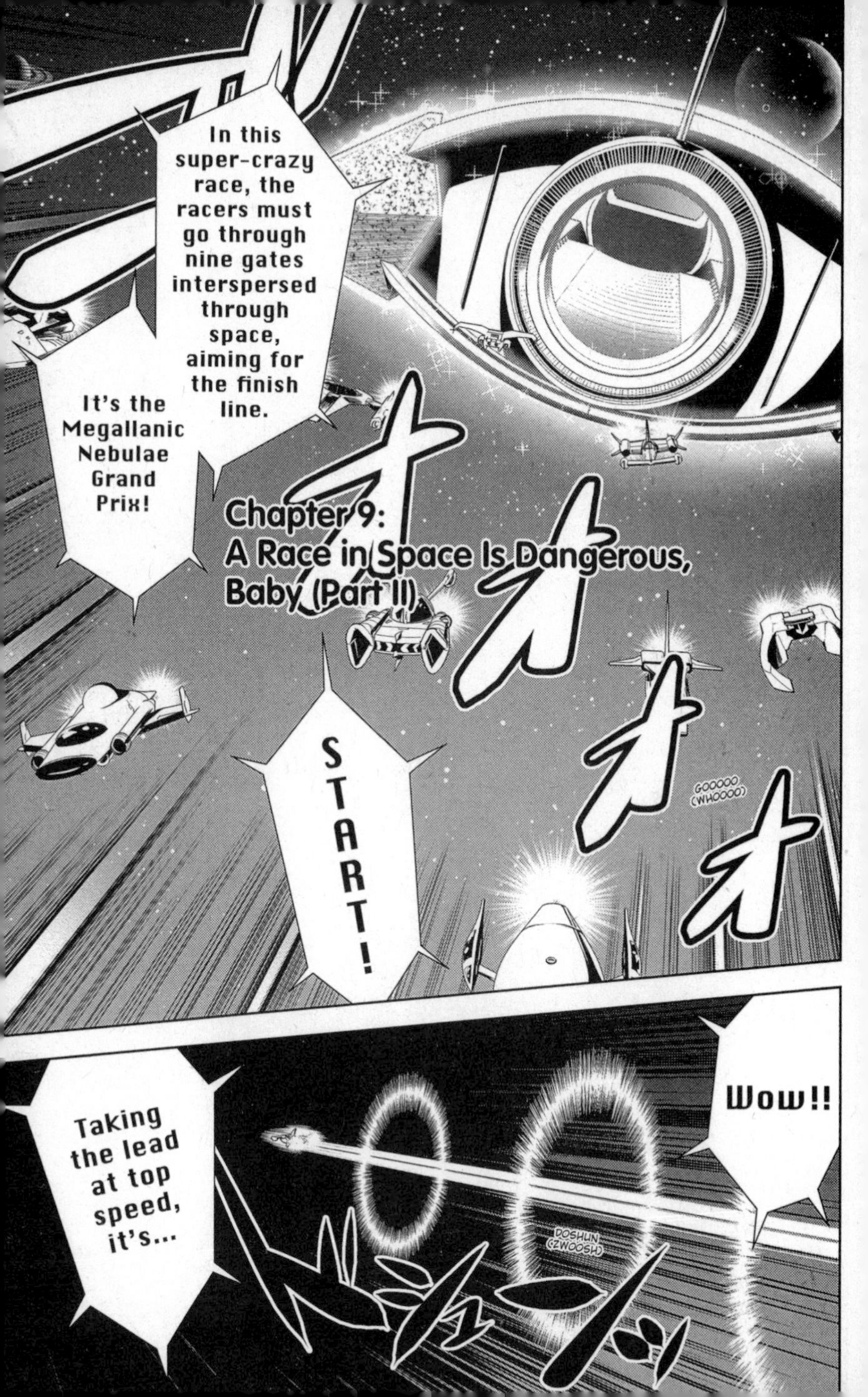
In this super-crazy race, the racers must go through nine gates interspersed through space, aiming for the finish line.
It's the Megallanic Nebulae Grand Prix!
Chapter 9: A Race in Space Is Dangerous, Baby (Part II)
GOOOOO (WHOOOO)
START!
Wow!!
Taking the lead at top speed, it's...
DOSHUN (ZWOOSH)

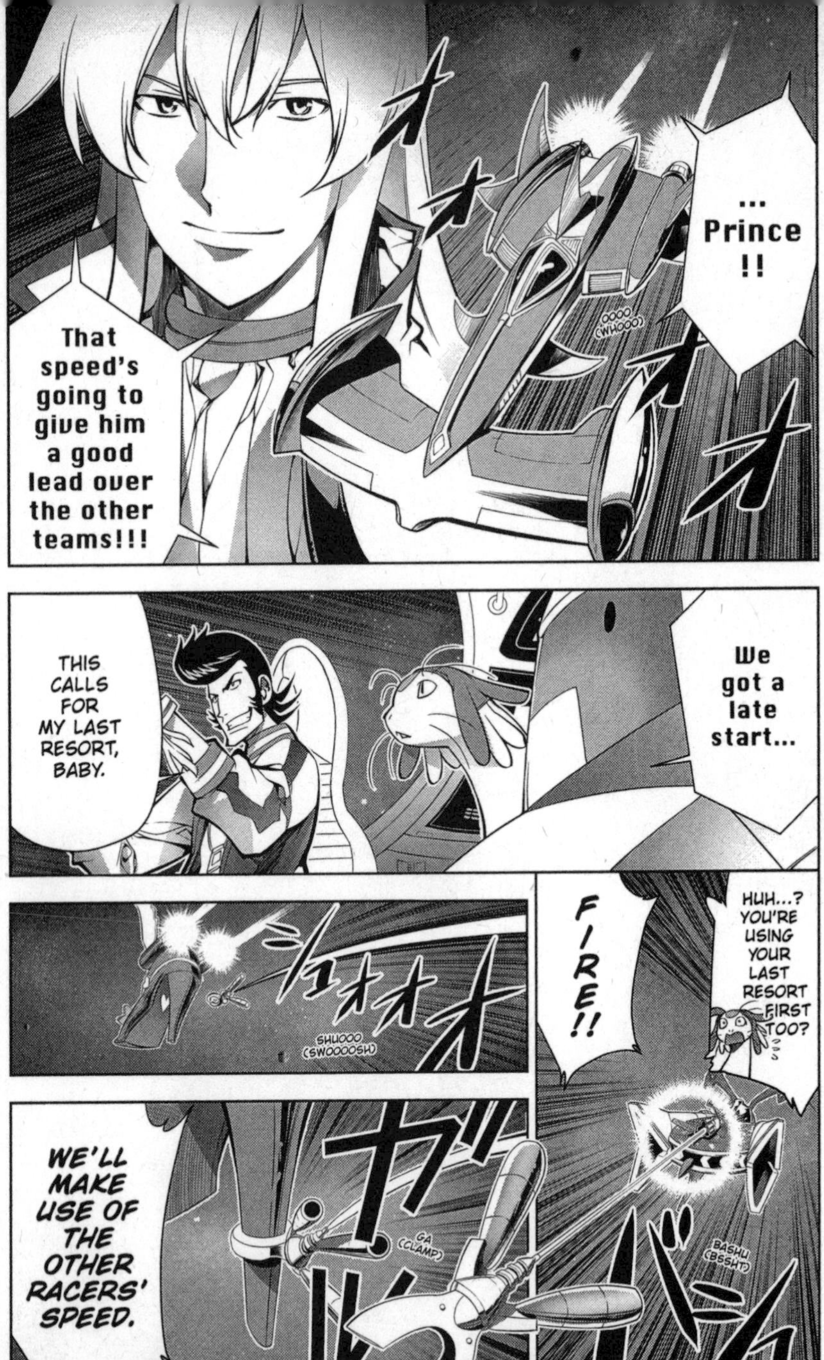
...Prince!!
OOOO (WHOOO)
That speed's going to give him a good lead over the other teams!!!
We got a late start...
THIS CALLS FOR MY LAST RESORT, BABY.
HUH...? YOU'RE USING YOUR LAST RESORT FIRST TOO?
FIRE!!
BASHU (BSSHT)
SHUOOO (SWOOOOSH)
WE'LL MAKE USE OF THE OTHER RACERS' SPEED.
GA (CLAMP)

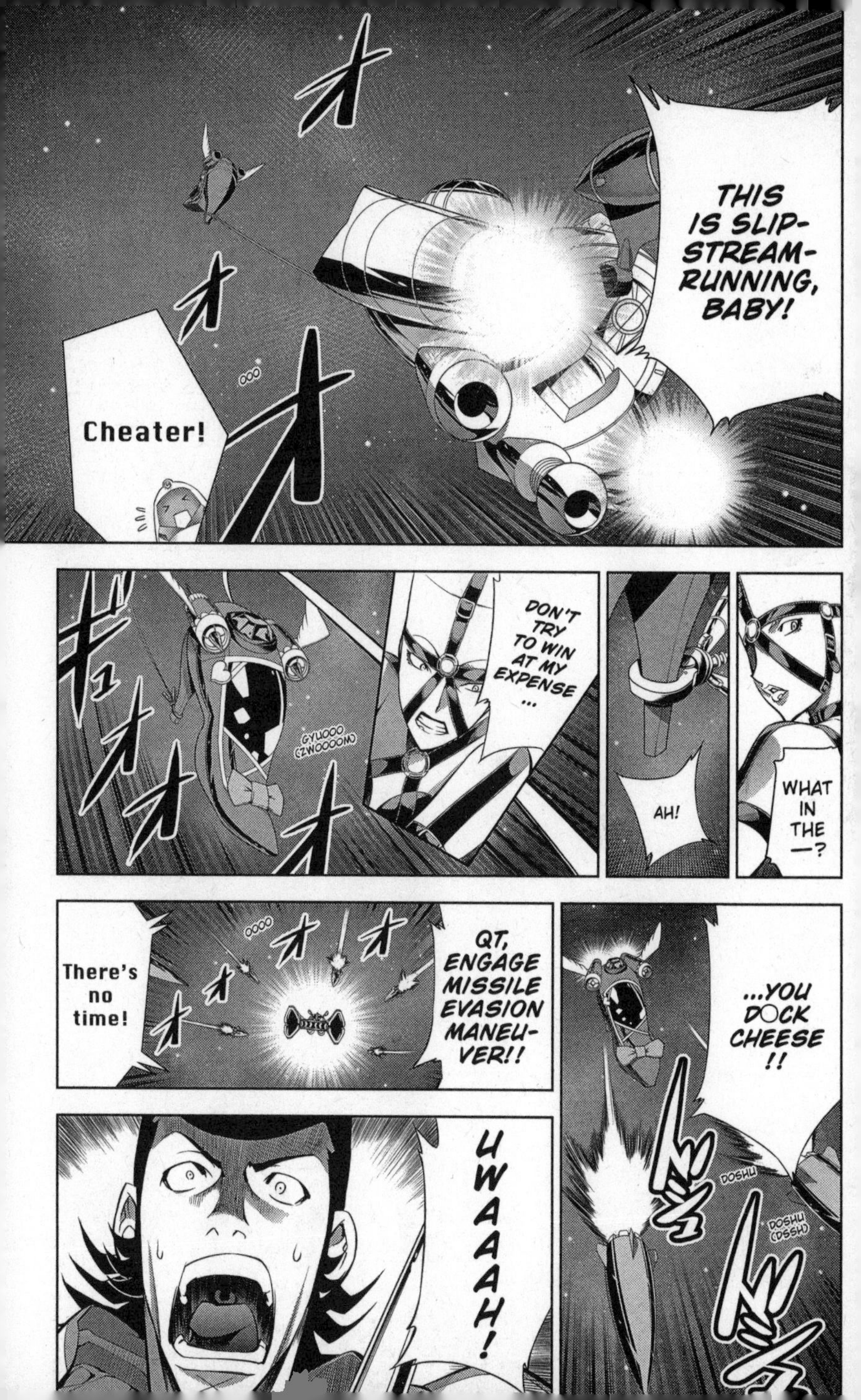
THIS IS SLIP-STREAM-RUNNING, BABY!
ooo
Cheater!
WHAT IN THE—?
AH!
DON'T TRY TO WIN AT MY EXPENSE...
GYUOOO (ZWOOOOM)
...YOU D○CK CHEESE!!
DOSHU
DOSHU (DSSH)
QT, ENGAGE MISSILE EVASION MANEUVER!!
oooo
There's no time!
UWAAAAH!

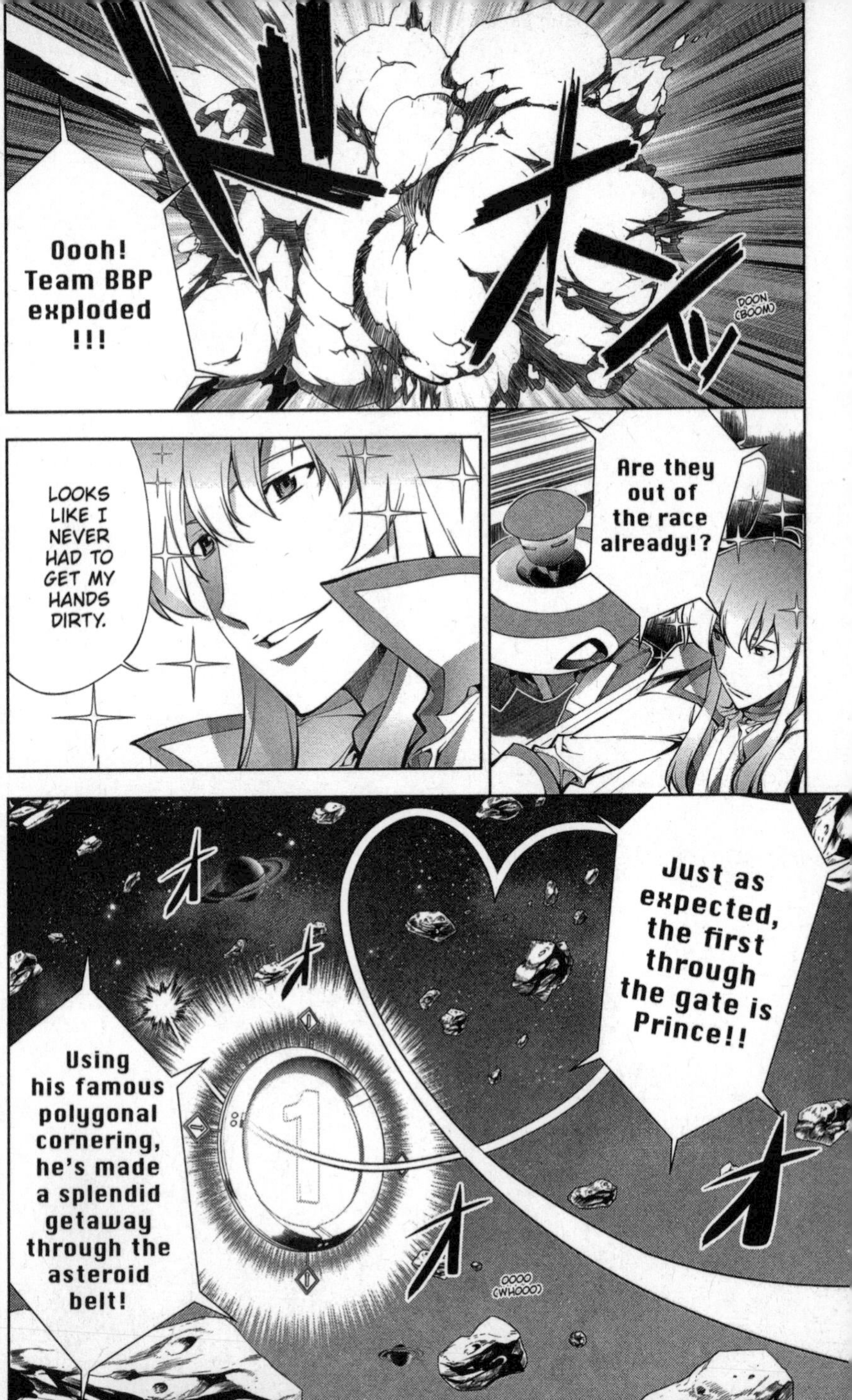
Oooh! Team BBP exploded!!!
DOON (BOOM)
Are they out of the race already!?
LOOKS LIKE I NEVER HAD TO GET MY HANDS DIRTY.
Just as expected, the first through the gate is Prince!!
Using his famous polygonal cornering, he's made a splendid getaway through the asteroid belt!
OOOO (WHOOO)

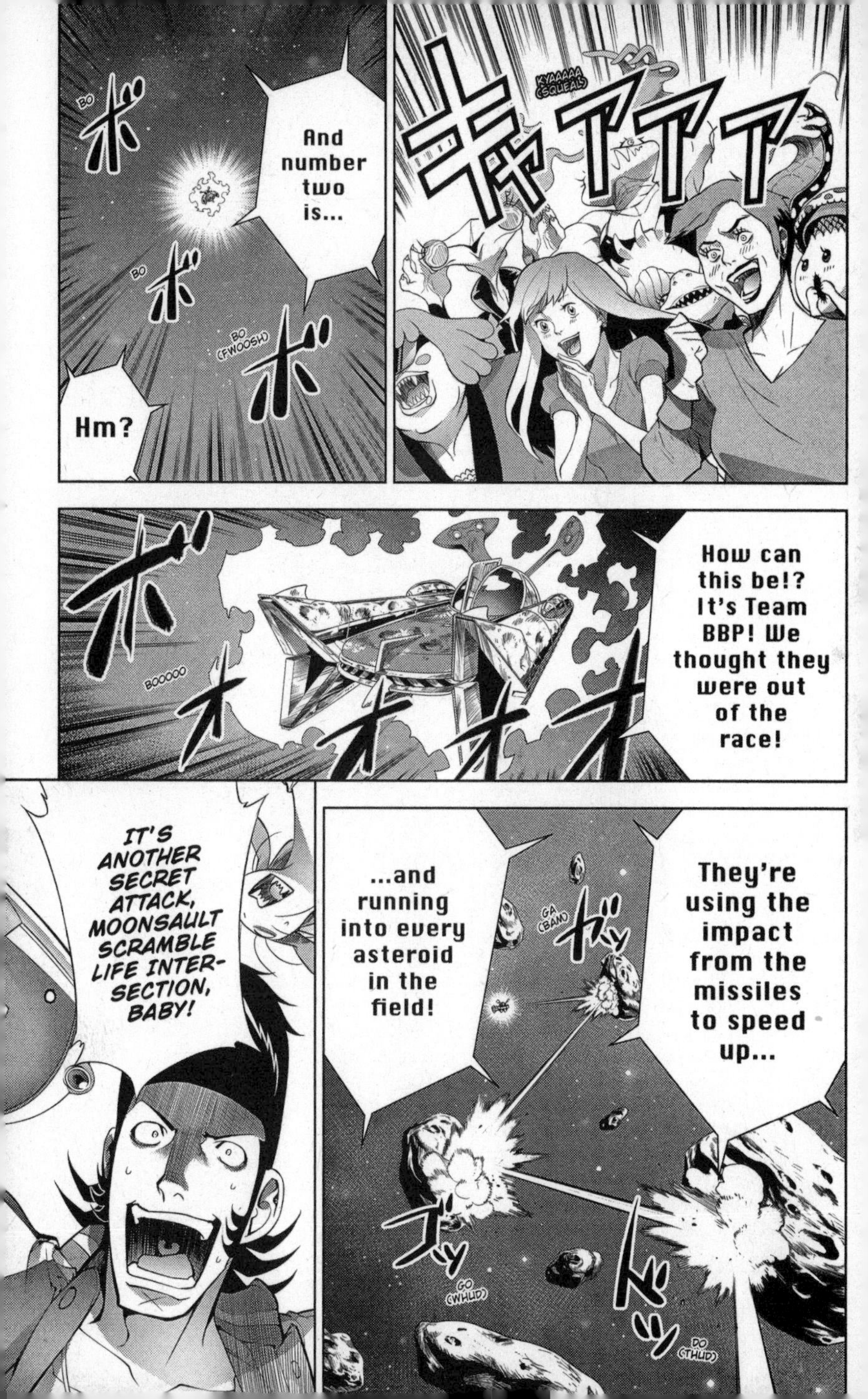
キャアア
KYAAAAA (SQUEAL)
And number two is...
ボ
BO
ボ
BO
ボ
BO (FWOOSH)
Hm?
How can this be!? It's Team BBP! We thought they were out of the race!
ボオオオ
BOOOOO
They're using the impact from the missiles to speed up...
...and running into every asteroid in the field!
ガッ
GA (BAM)
ドッ
DO (THUD)
ゴッ
GO (WHUD)
IT'S ANOTHER SECRET ATTACK, MOONSAULT SCRAMBLE LIFE INTER-SECTION, BABY!

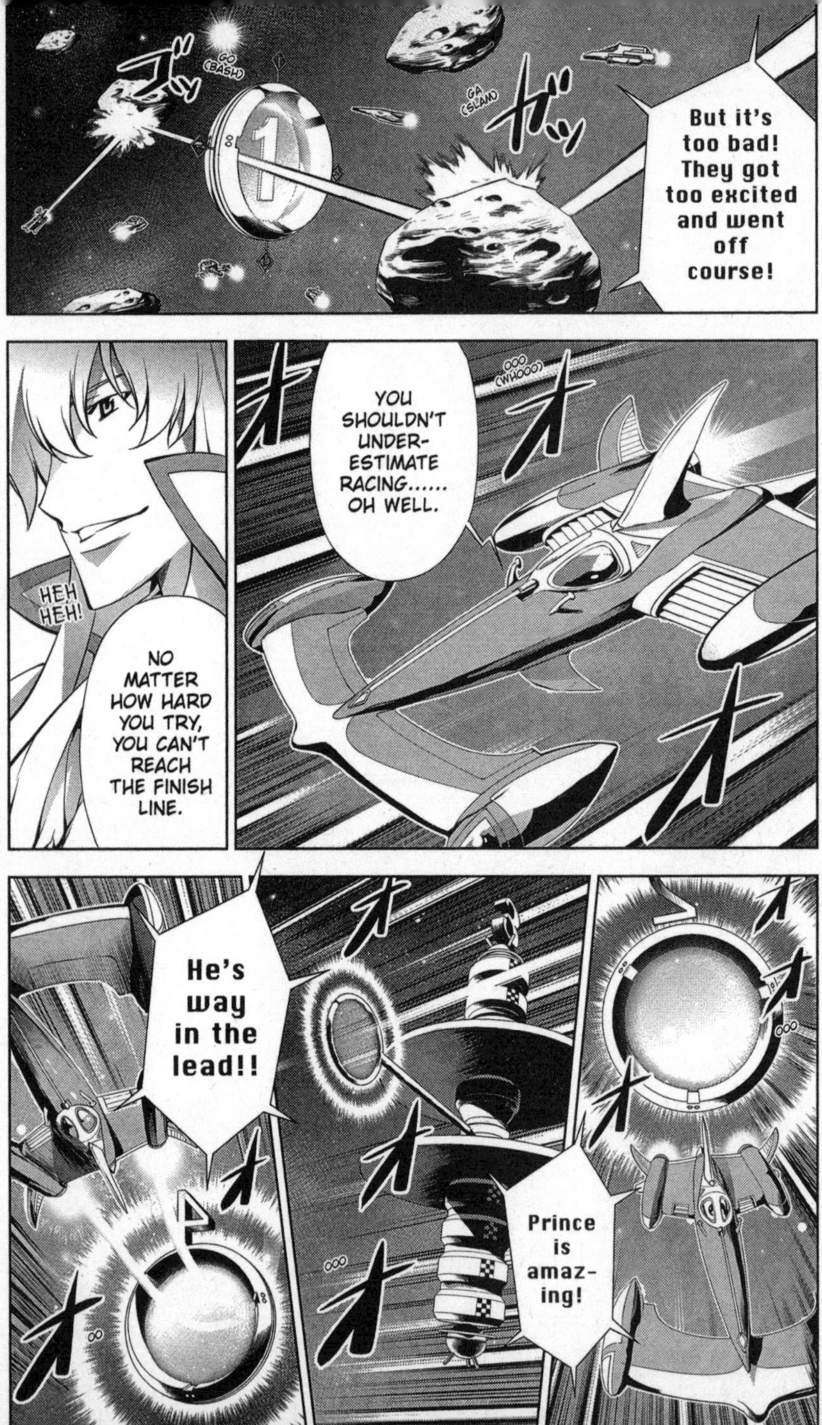
But it's too bad! They got too excited and went off course!
GA (SLAM)
GO (BASH)
OOO (WHOOO)
YOU SHOULDN'T UNDER-ESTIMATE RACING...... OH WELL.
HEH HEH!
NO MATTER HOW HARD YOU TRY, YOU CAN'T REACH THE FINISH LINE.
OOO
Prince is amaz-ing!
OOO
He's way in the lead!!

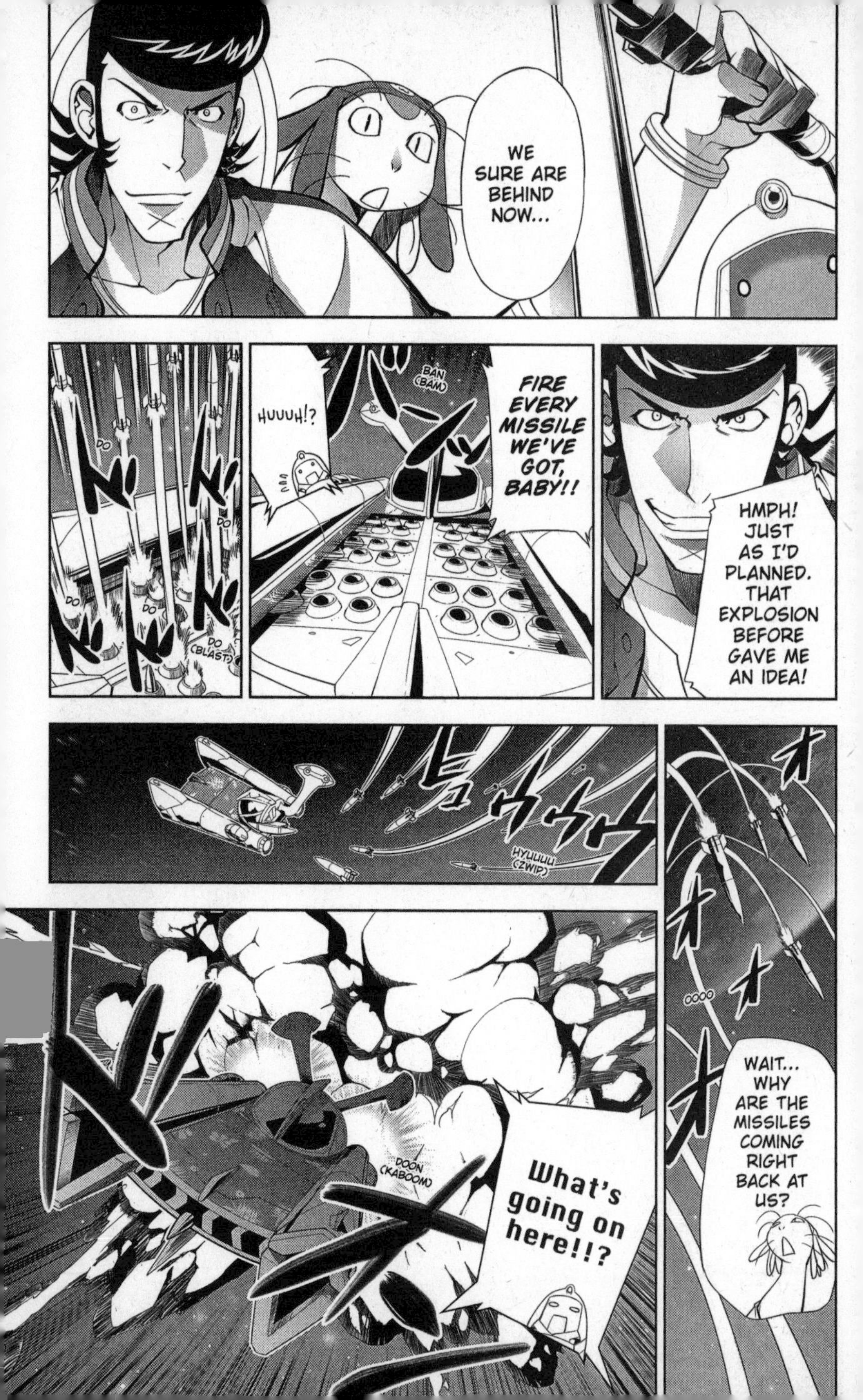
WE SURE ARE BEHIND NOW...
HMPH! JUST AS I'D PLANNED. THAT EXPLOSION BEFORE GAVE ME AN IDEA!
BAN (BAM)
FIRE EVERY MISSILE WE'VE GOT, BABY!!
HUUUH!?
DO
DO
DO
DO
DO (BLAST)
OOOO
WAIT... WHY ARE THE MISSILES COMING RIGHT BACK AT US?
HYUUUU (ZWIP)
DOON (KABOOM)
What's going on here!!?

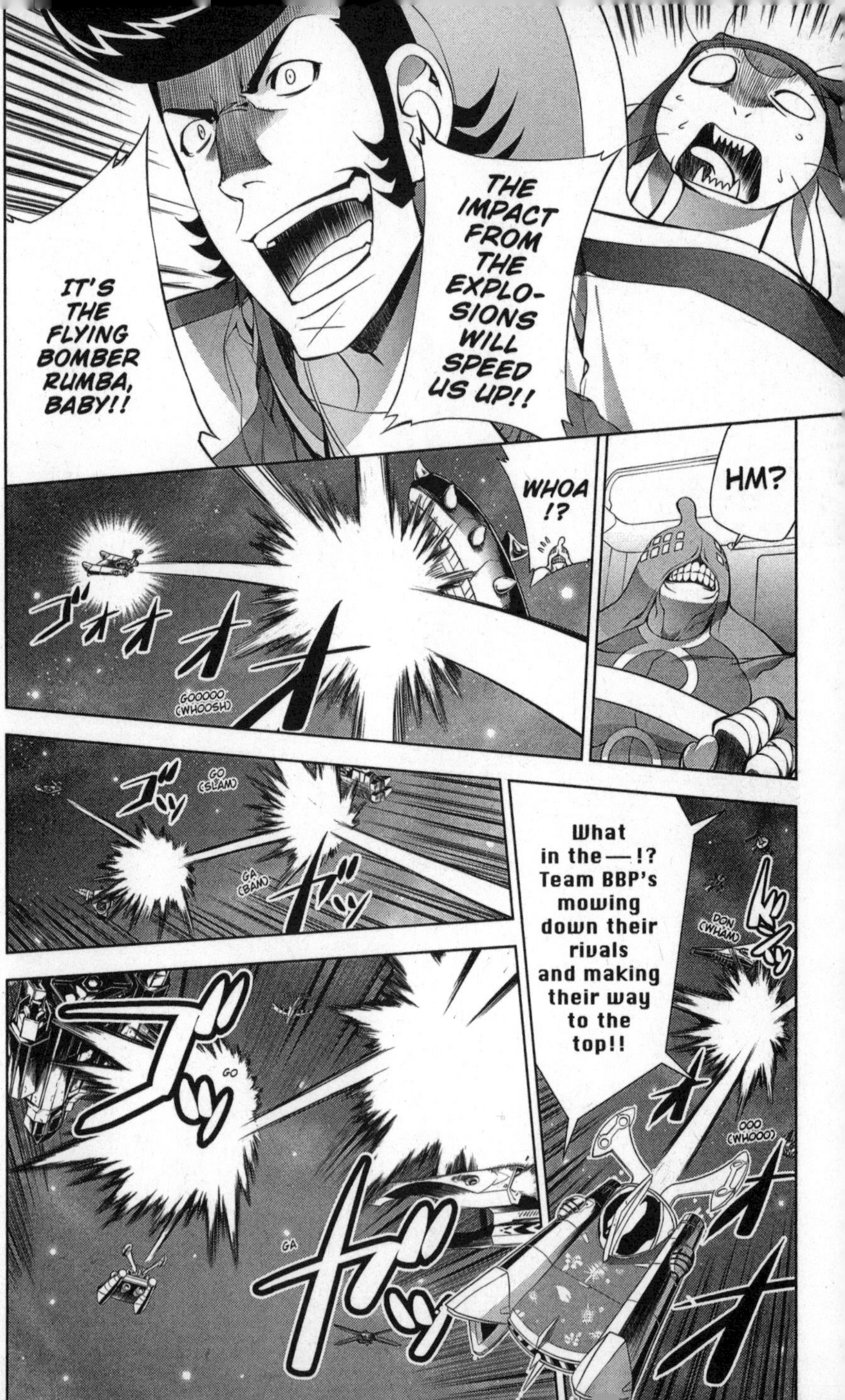

THE IMPACT FROM THE EXPLOSIONS WILL SPEED US UP!!
IT'S THE FLYING BOMBER RUMBA, BABY!!
HM?
WHOA !?
GOOOOO (WHOOSH)
What in the—!? Team BBP's mowing down their rivals and making their way to the top!!
DON (WHAM)
OOO (WHOOO)
GO (SLAM)
GA (BAN)
GO
GA

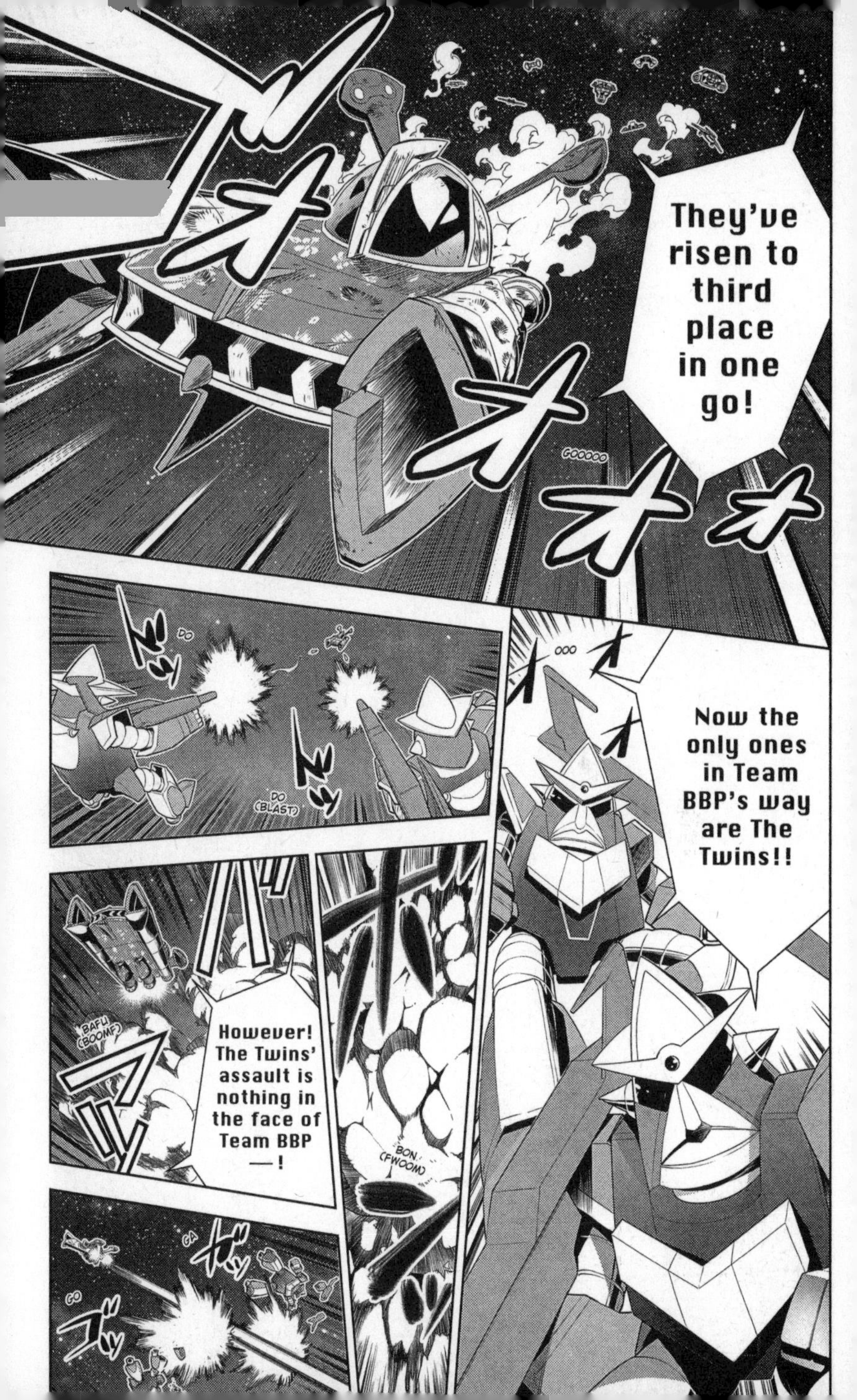
They've risen to third place in one go!
GOOOOO
OOO
Now the only ones in Team BBP's way are The Twins!!
DO
DO (BLAST)
BON (FWOOM)
BAFU (BOOMF)
However! The Twins' assault is nothing in the face of Team BBP —!
GA
GO

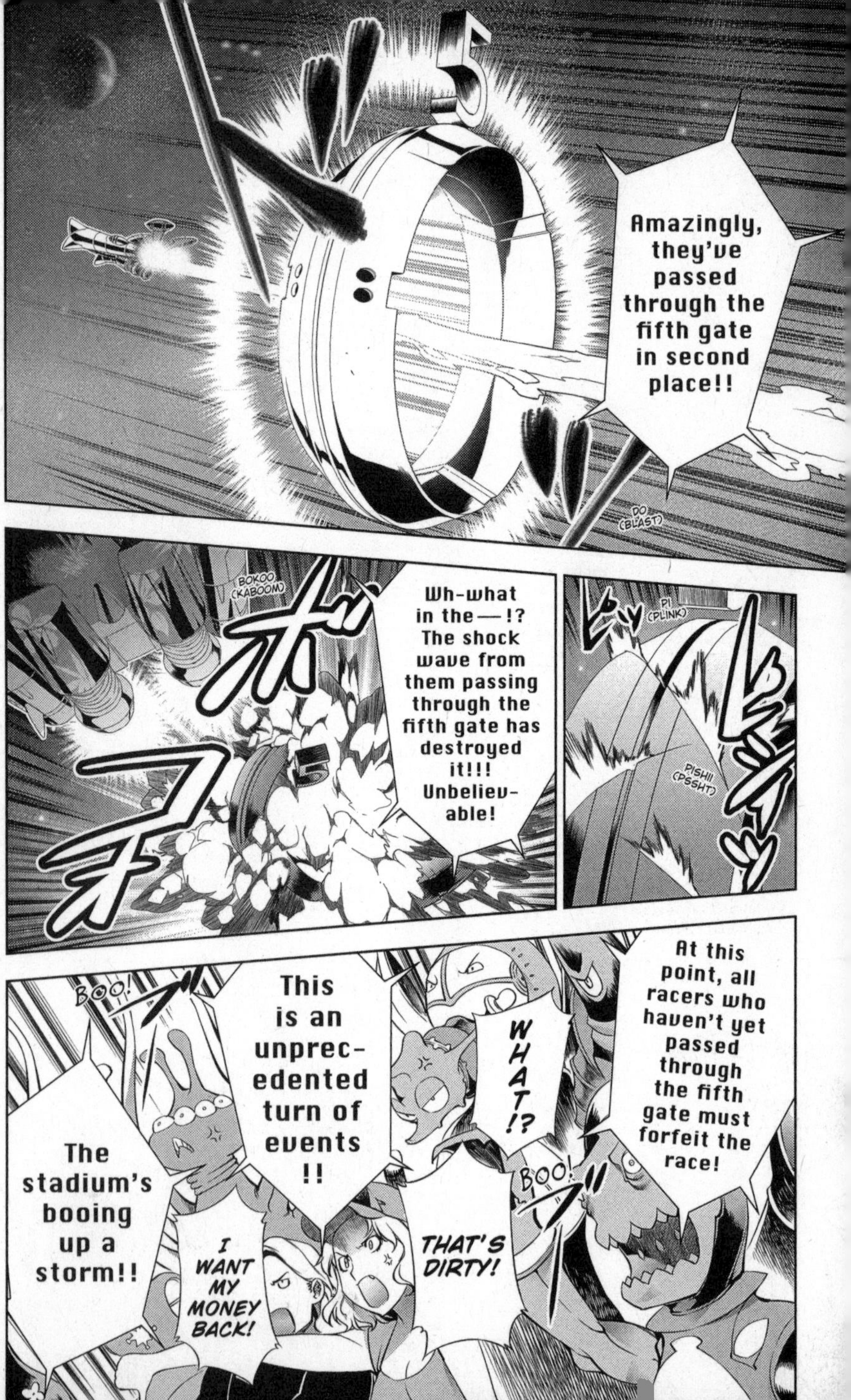
Amazingly, they've passed through the fifth gate in second place!!
DO (BLAST)
PI (PLINK)
PISHII (PSSHT)
BOKOO (KABOOM)
Wh-what in the—!? The shock wave from them passing through the fifth gate has destroyed it!!! Unbeliev-able!
At this point, all racers who haven't yet passed through the fifth gate must forfeit the race!
WHAT!?
BOO!
This is an unprec-edented turn of events!!
BOO!
THAT'S DIRTY!
I WANT MY MONEY BACK!
The stadium's booing up a storm!!

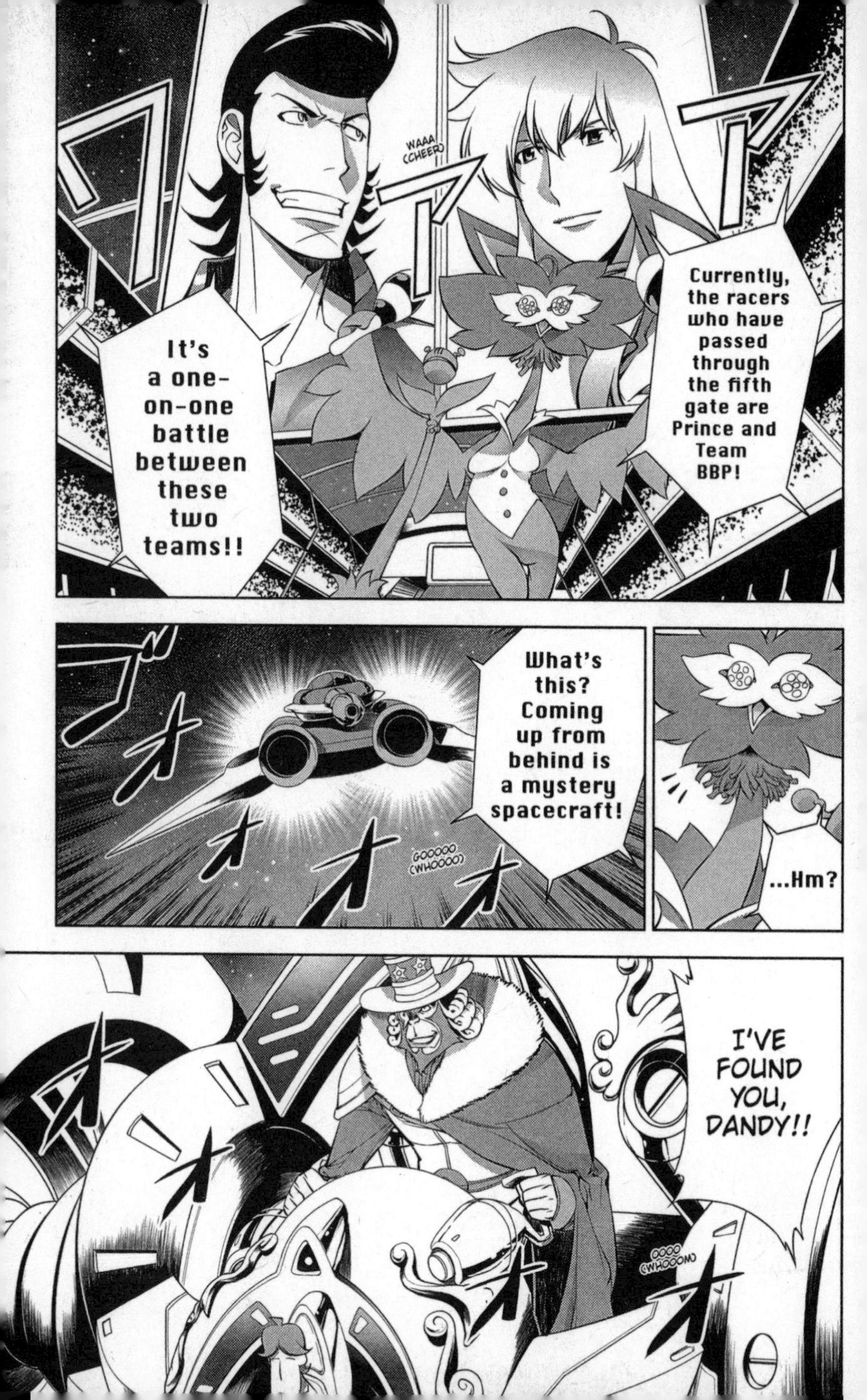
Currently, the racers who have passed through the fifth gate are Prince and Team BBP!
WAAA (CHEER)
It's a one-on-one battle between these two teams!!
...Hm?
What's this? Coming up from behind is a mystery spacecraft!
GOOOOO (WHOOOO)
I'VE FOUND YOU, DANDY!!
OOOO (WHOOOM)

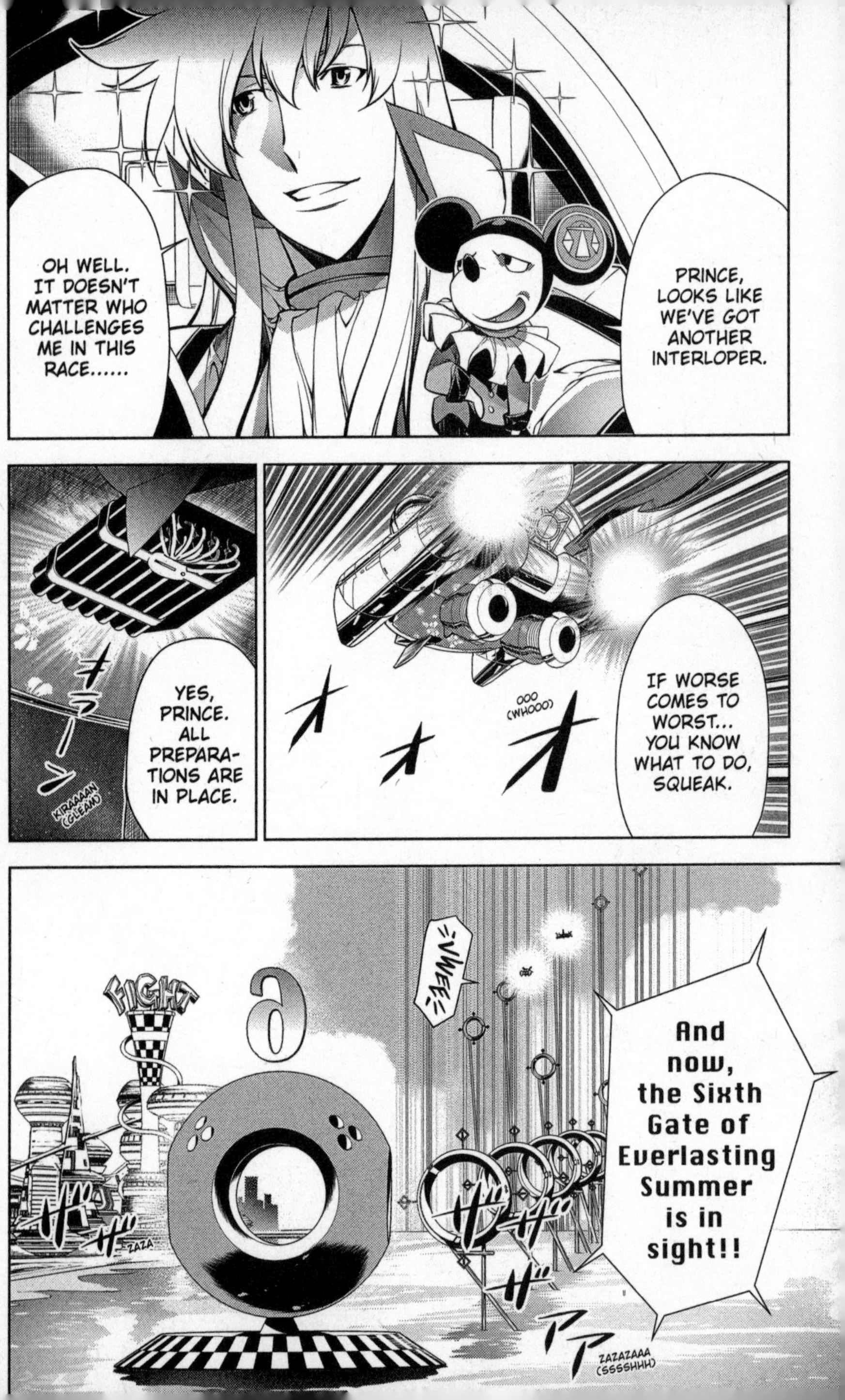
PRINCE, LOOKS LIKE WE'VE GOT ANOTHER INTERLOPER.
OH WELL. IT DOESN'T MATTER WHO CHALLENGES ME IN THIS RACE......
IF WORSE COMES TO WORST... YOU KNOW WHAT TO DO, SQUEAK.
OOO (WHOOO)
YES, PRINCE. ALL PREPARA-TIONS ARE IN PLACE.
KIRAAAAN (GLEAM)
And now, the Sixth Gate of Everlasting Summer is in sight!!
VWEE
FIGHT
6
ZAZA
ZAZAZAAA (SSSSHHH)

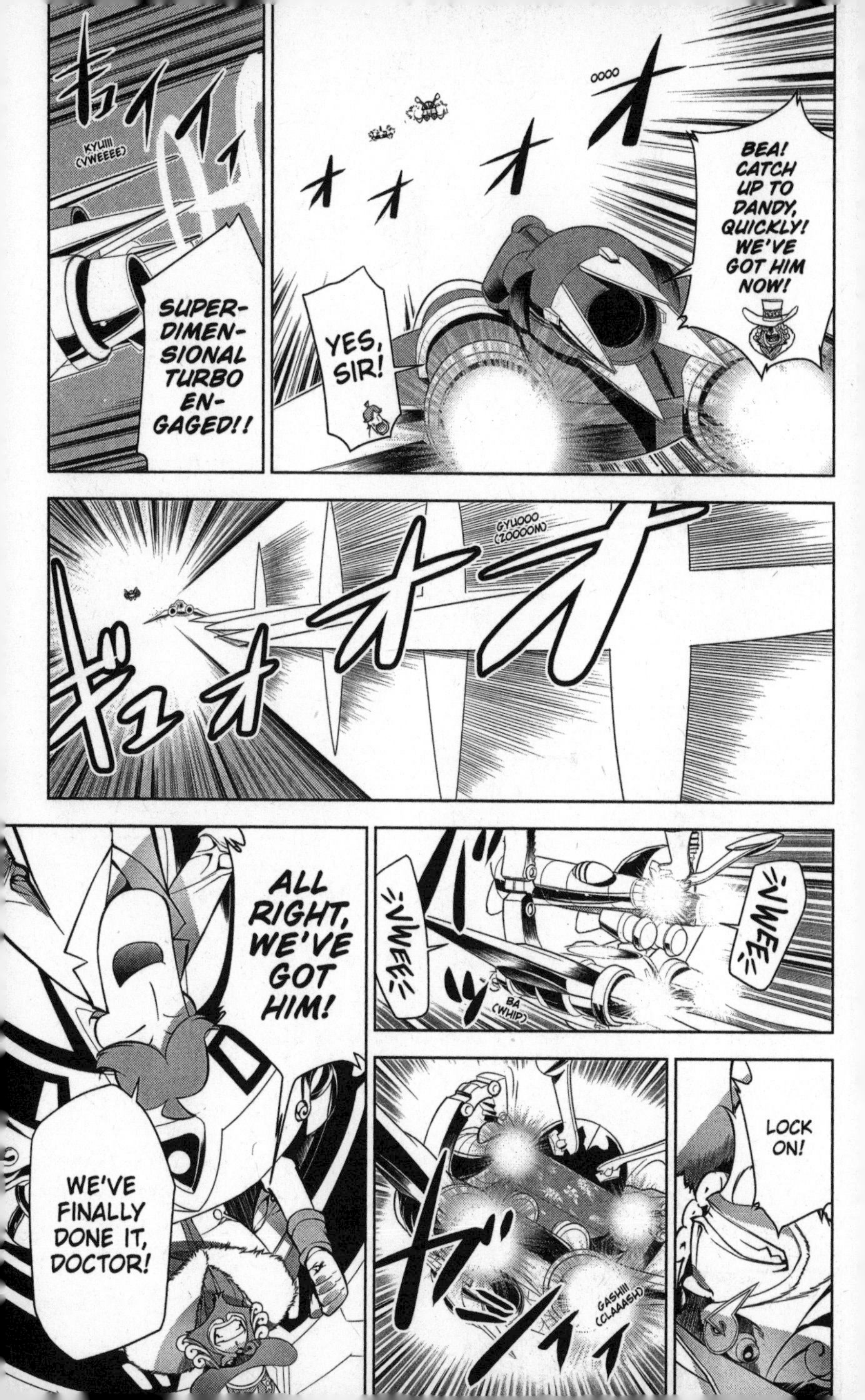
oooo
BEA! CATCH UP TO DANDY, QUICKLY! WE'VE GOT HIM NOW!
YES, SIR!
KYUIII (VWEEEE)
SUPER-DIMENSIONAL TURBO ENGAGED!!
GYUOOO (ZOOOOM)
VWEE
VWEE
BA (WHIP)
LOCK ON!
GASHIII (CLAAASH)
ALL RIGHT, WE'VE GOT HIM!
WE'VE FINALLY DONE IT, DOCTOR!

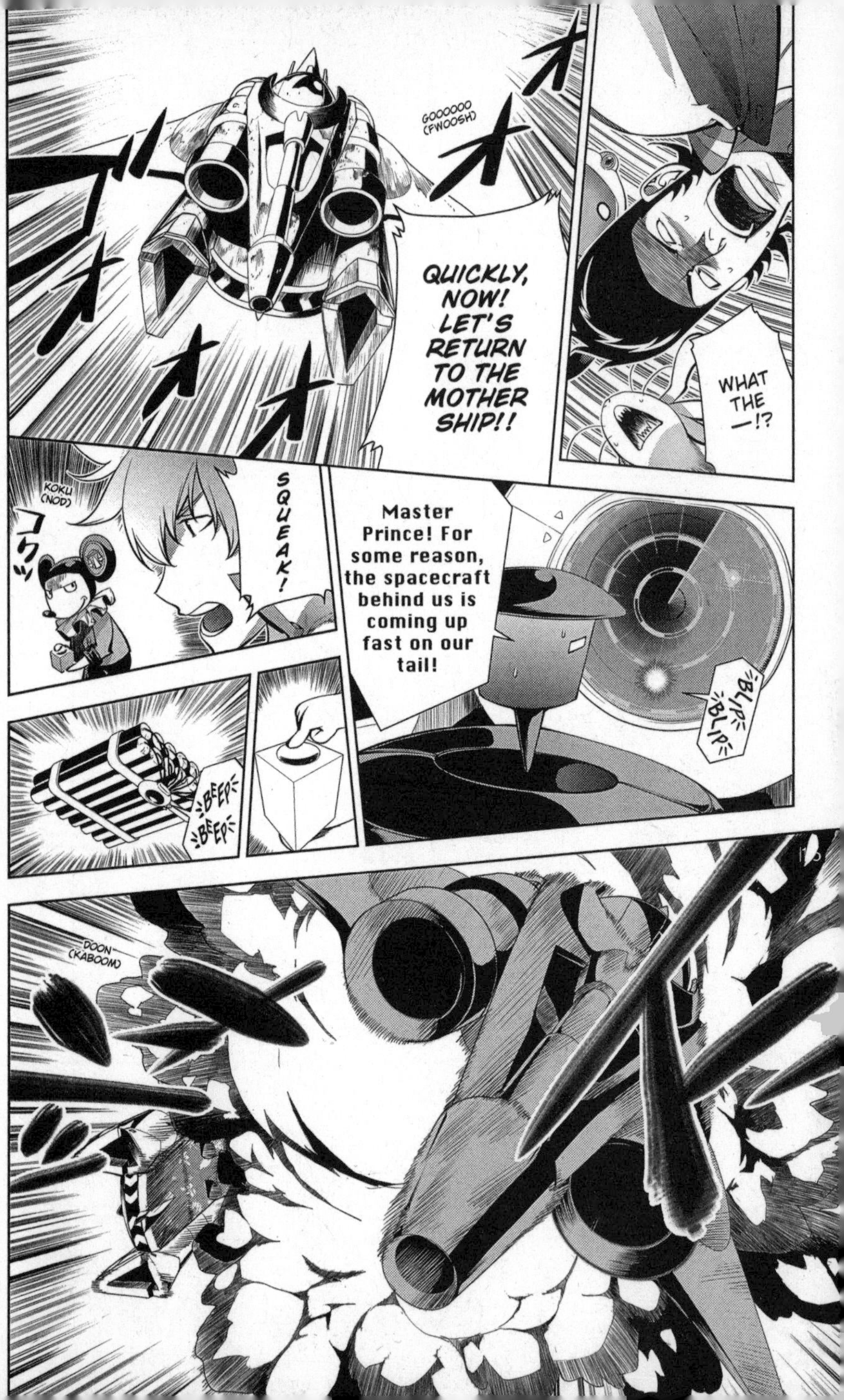
WHAT THE—!?
GOOOOOO (FWOOSH)
QUICKLY, NOW! LET'S RETURN TO THE MOTHER SHIP!!
Master Prince! For some reason, the spacecraft behind us is coming up fast on our tail!
BLIP BLIP
SQUEAK!
KOKU (NOD)
コクッ
BEEP BEEP
DOON (KABOOM)

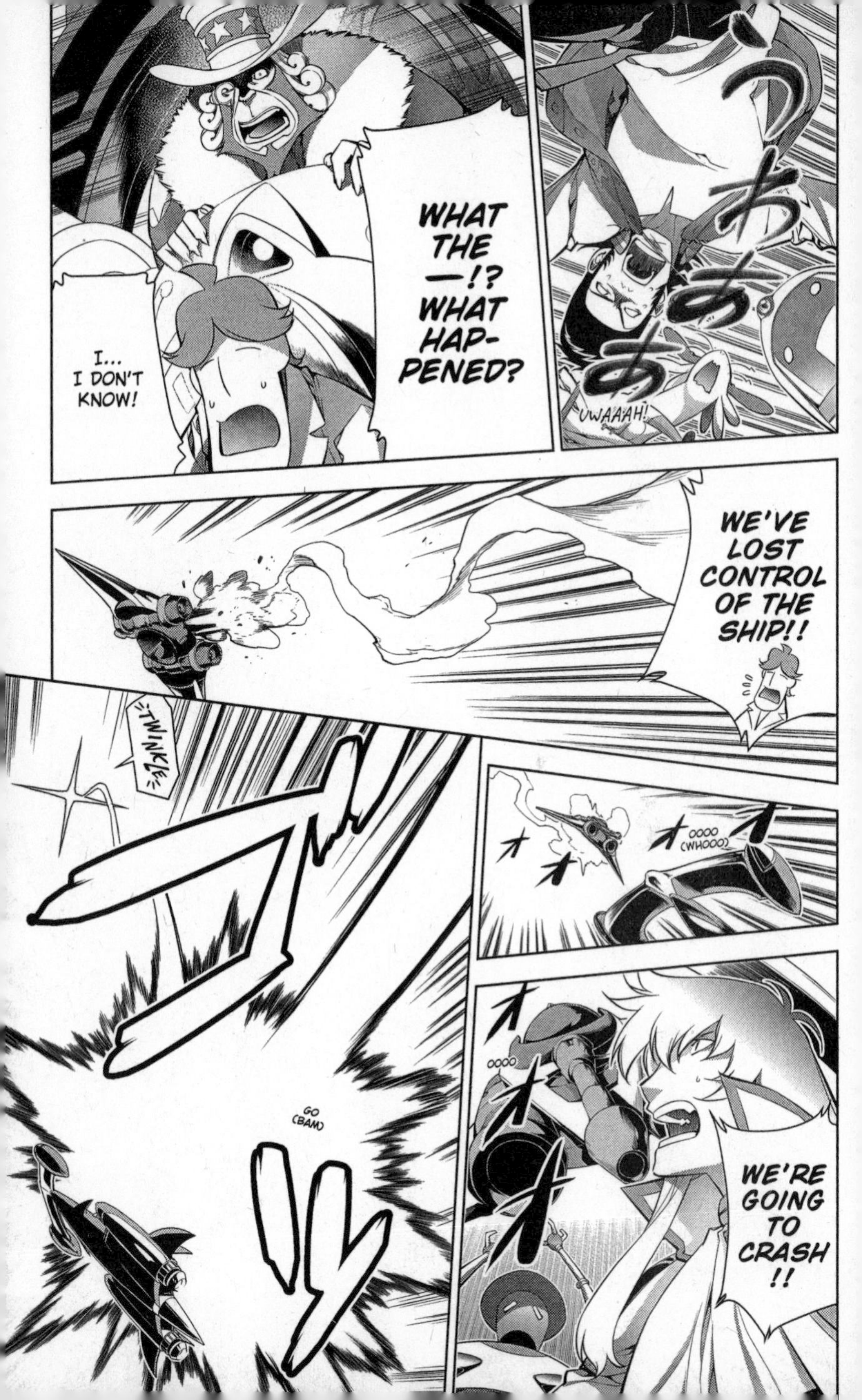
UWAAAH!
WHAT THE—!? WHAT HAP-PENED?
I... I DON'T KNOW!
WE'VE LOST CONTROL OF THE SHIP!!
OOOO (WHOOO)
OOOO
WE'RE GOING TO CRASH!!
TWINKLE
GO (BAM)

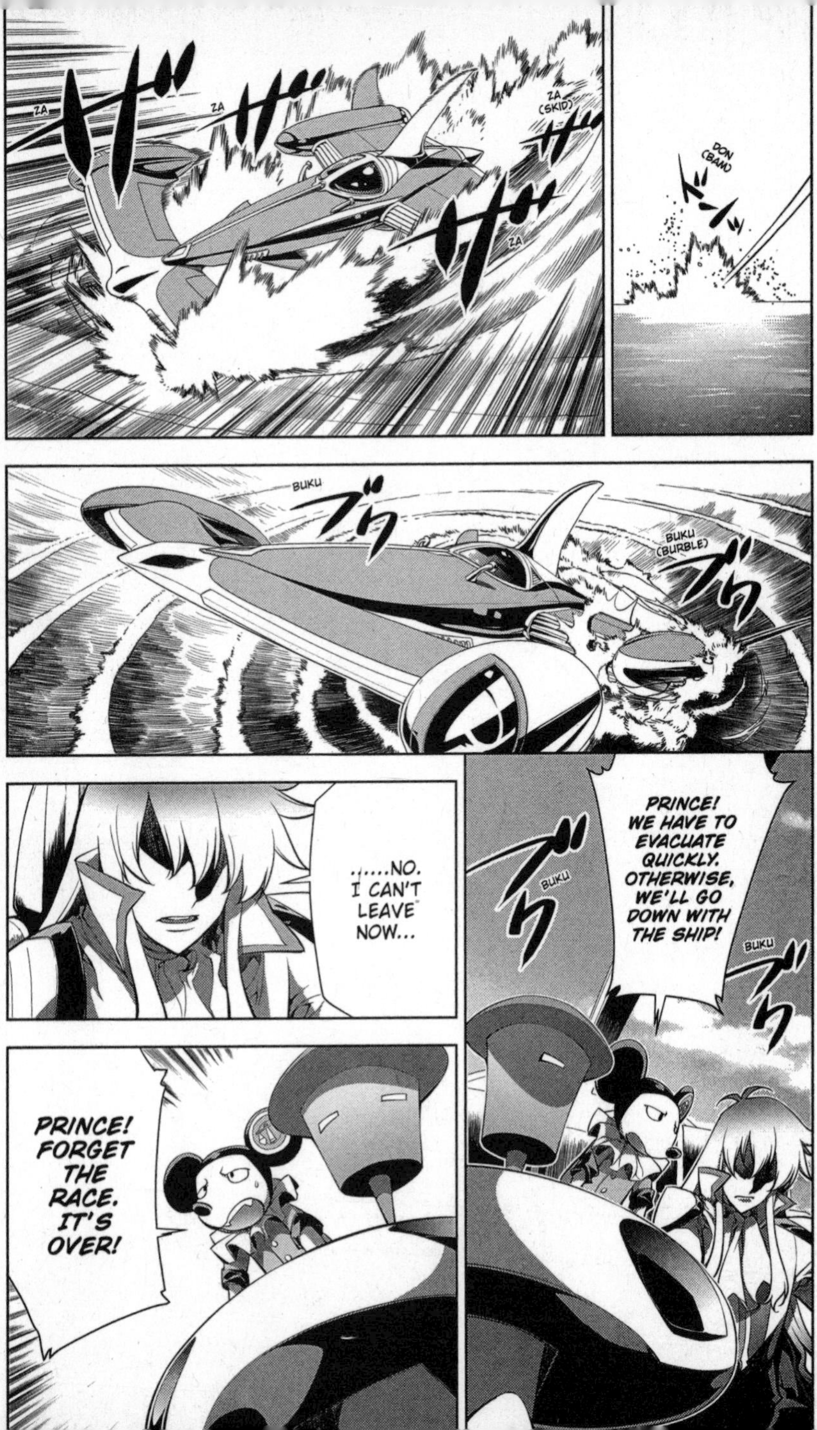
DON (BAM)
ZA (SKID)
ZA
ZA
ZA
BUKU (BURBLE)
BUKU
PRINCE! WE HAVE TO EVACUATE QUICKLY. OTHERWISE, WE'LL GO DOWN WITH THE SHIP!
BUKU
BUKU
......NO. I CAN'T LEAVE NOW...
PRINCE! FORGET THE RACE. IT'S OVER!

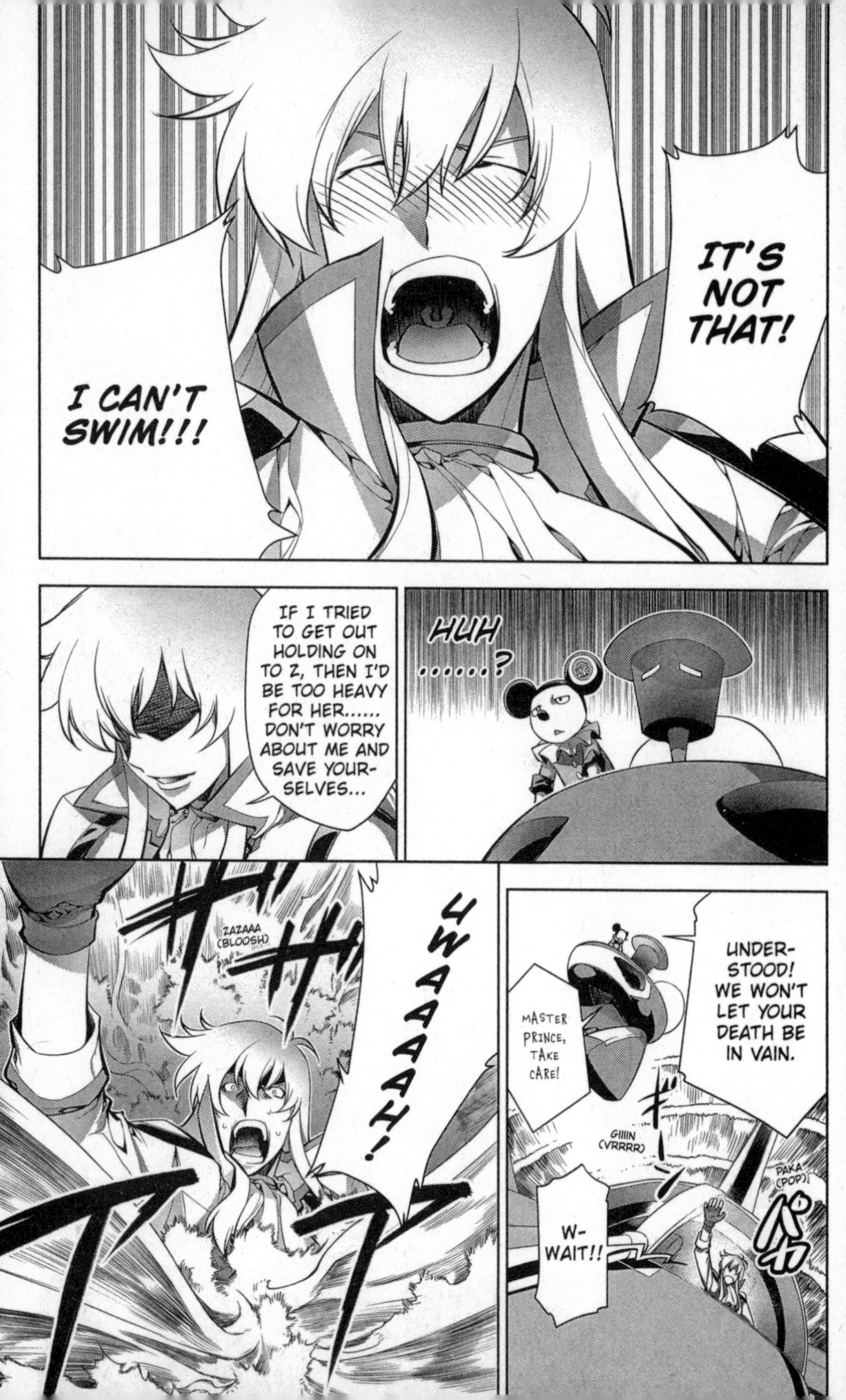
IT'S NOT THAT!
I CAN'T SWIM!!!
HUH ......?
IF I TRIED TO GET OUT HOLDING ON TO Z, THEN I'D BE TOO HEAVY FOR HER...... DON'T WORRY ABOUT ME AND SAVE YOURSELVES...
UNDERSTOOD! WE WON'T LET YOUR DEATH BE IN VAIN.
MASTER PRINCE, TAKE CARE!
GIIIN (VRRRR)
PAKA (POP)
W-WAIT!!
ZAZAAA (BLOOSH)
UWAAAAAAH!

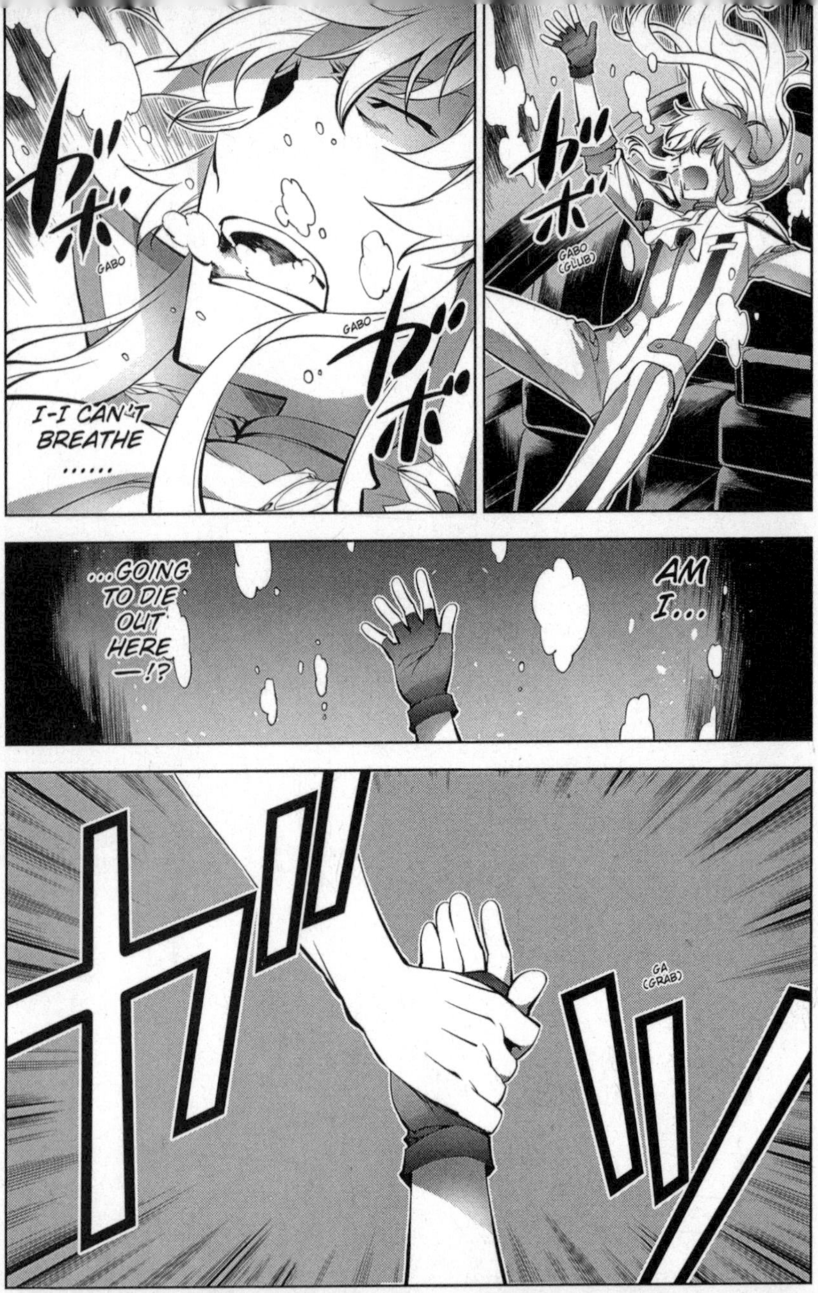
ガボ
GABO (GLUB)
ガボ
GABO
ガボ
GABO
I-I CAN'T BREATHE ......
AM I...
...GOING TO DIE OUT HERE—!?
ガッ
GA (GRAB)

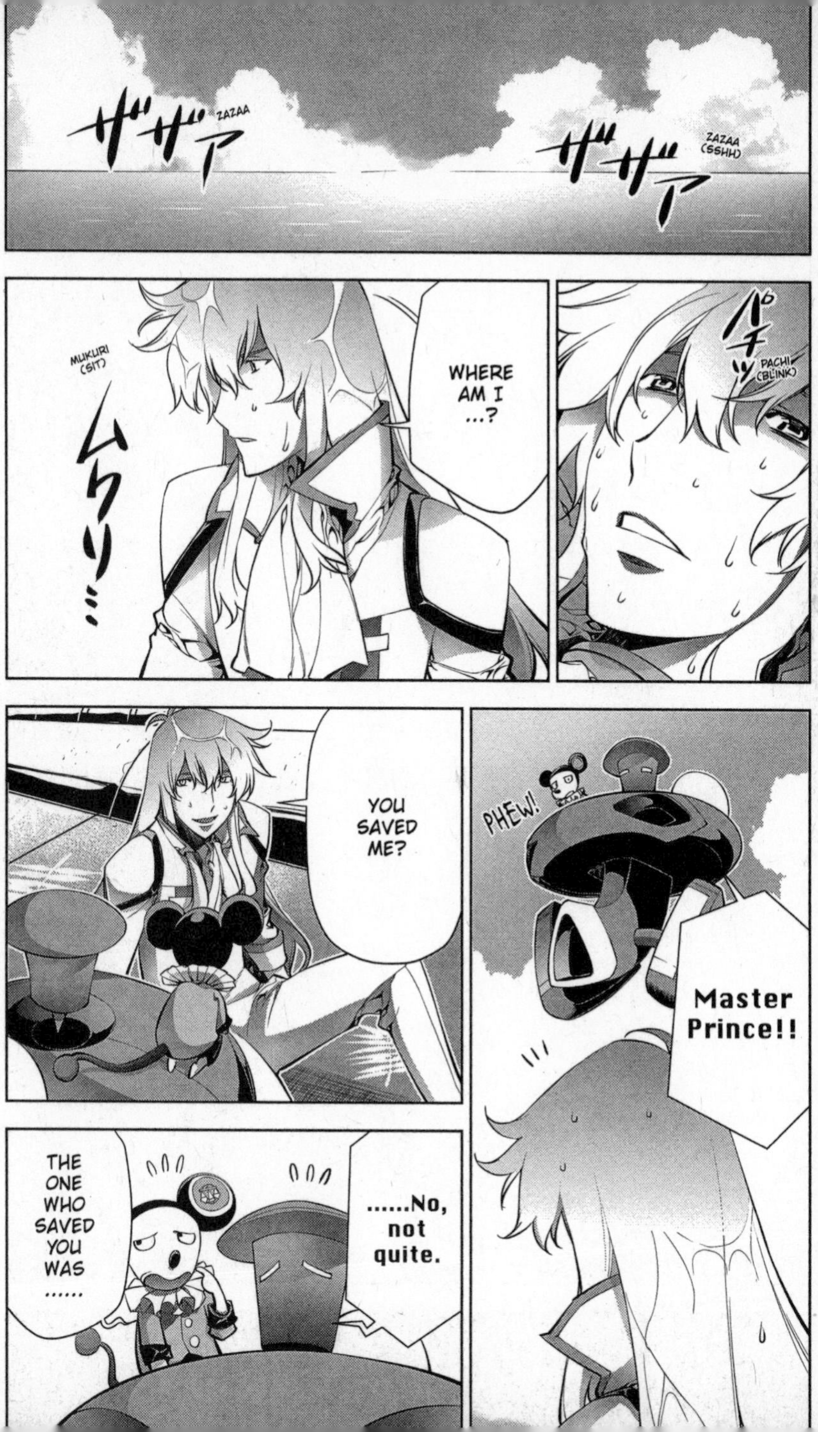

ザザア
ZAZAA (SSHH)
ザザア
ZAZAA
パチッ
PACHI (BLINK)
WHERE AM I ...?
MUKURI (SIT)
ムクリ…
PHEW!
Master Prince!!
YOU SAVED ME?
......No, not quite.
THE ONE WHO SAVED YOU WAS ......

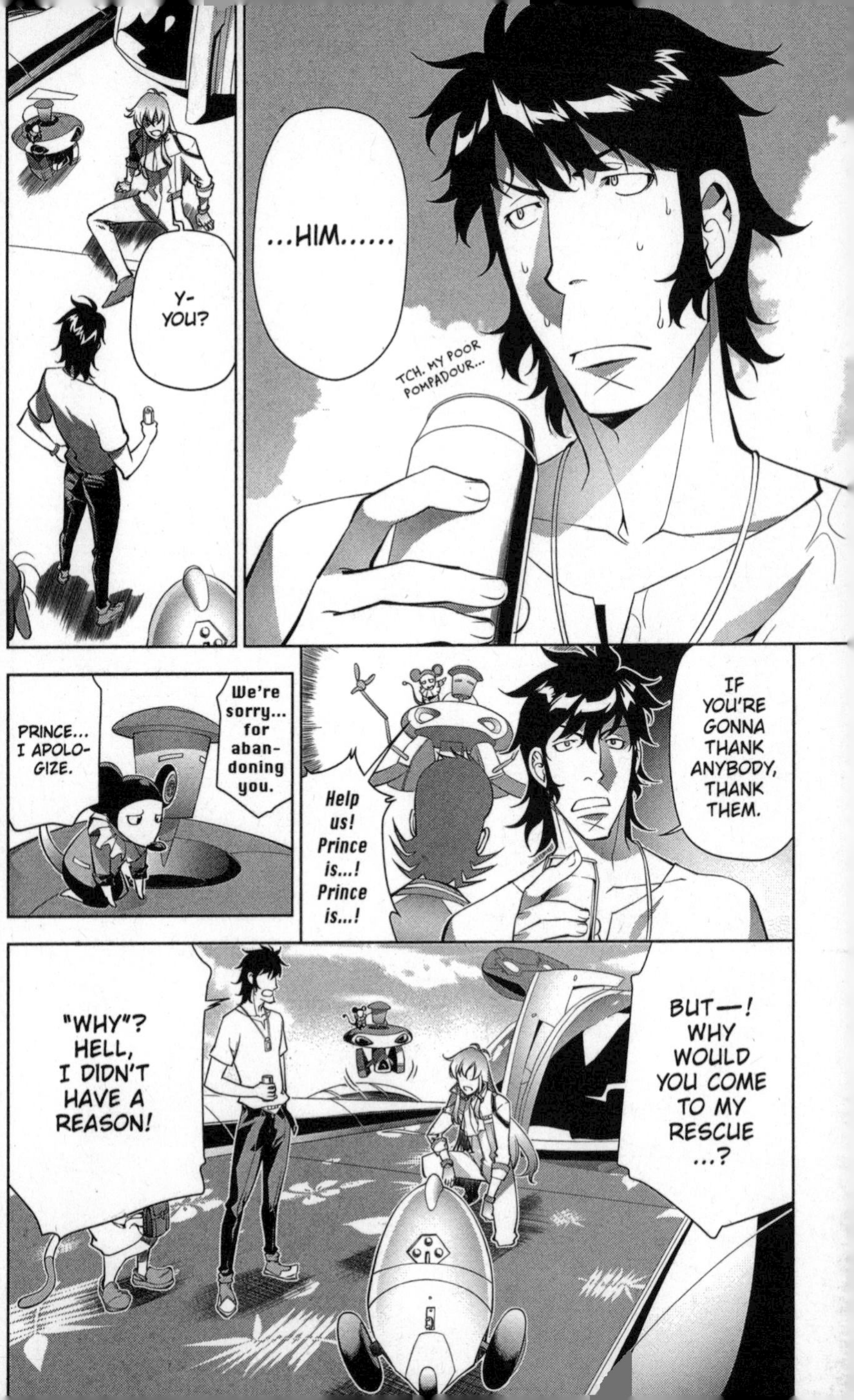
...HIM......
TCH. MY POOR POMPADOUR...
Y-YOU?
IF YOU'RE GONNA THANK ANYBODY, THANK THEM.
Help us! Prince is...! Prince is...!
We're sorry... for abandoning you.
PRINCE... I APOLOGIZE.
BUT—! WHY WOULD YOU COME TO MY RESCUE ...?
"WHY"? HELL, I DIDN'T HAVE A REASON!

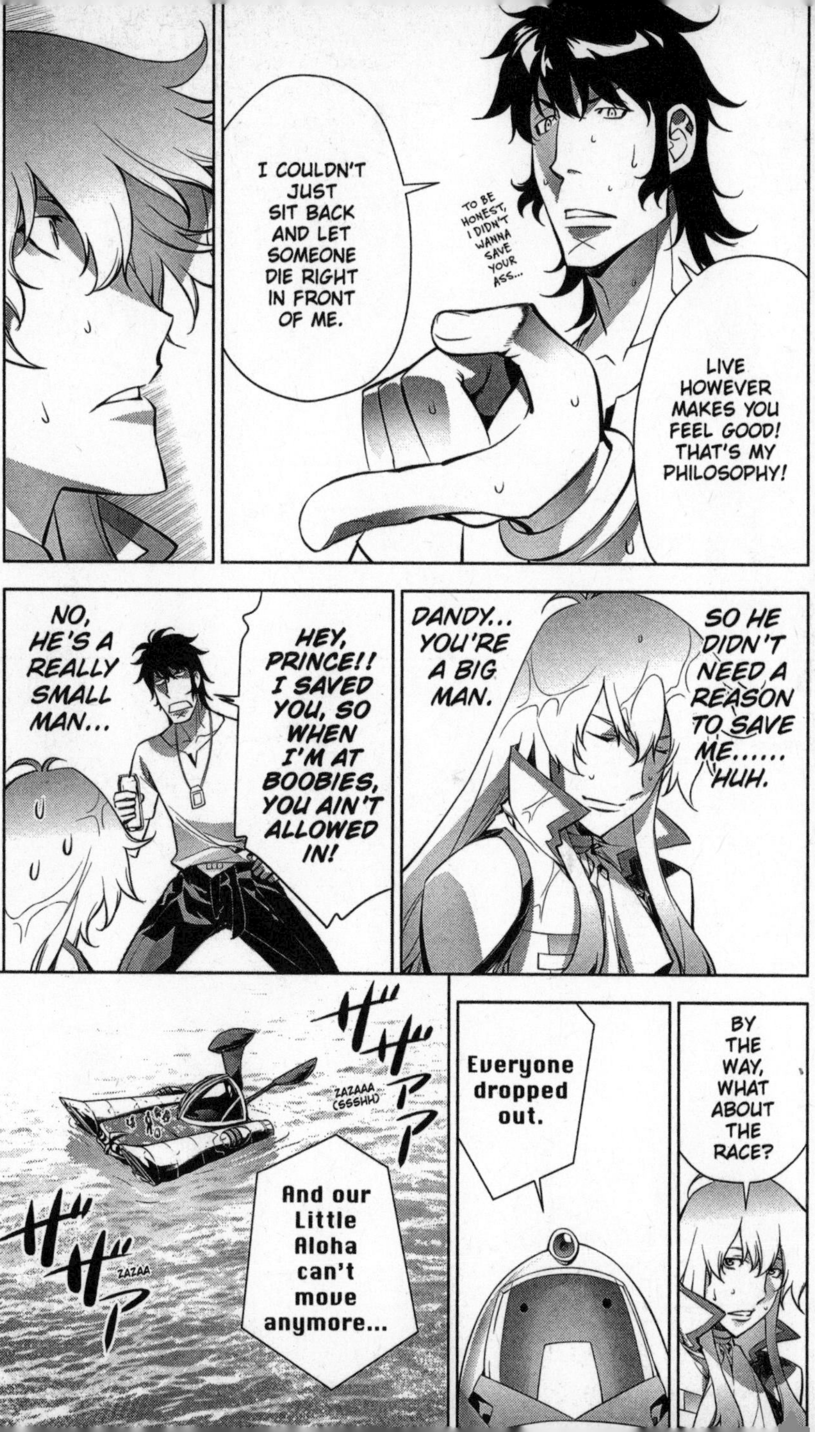
TO BE HONEST, I DIDN'T WANNA SAVE YOUR ASS...
I COULDN'T JUST SIT BACK AND LET SOMEONE DIE RIGHT IN FRONT OF ME.
LIVE HOWEVER MAKES YOU FEEL GOOD! THAT'S MY PHILOSOPHY!
SO HE DIDN'T NEED A REASON TO SAVE ME...... HUH.
DANDY... YOU'RE A BIG MAN.
HEY, PRINCE!! I SAVED YOU, SO WHEN I'M AT BOOBIES, YOU AIN'T ALLOWED IN!
NO, HE'S A REALLY SMALL MAN...
BY THE WAY, WHAT ABOUT THE RACE?
Everyone dropped out.
ザザァ
ZAZAAA (SSSHH)
And our Little Aloha can't move anymore...
ザザァ
ZAZAA

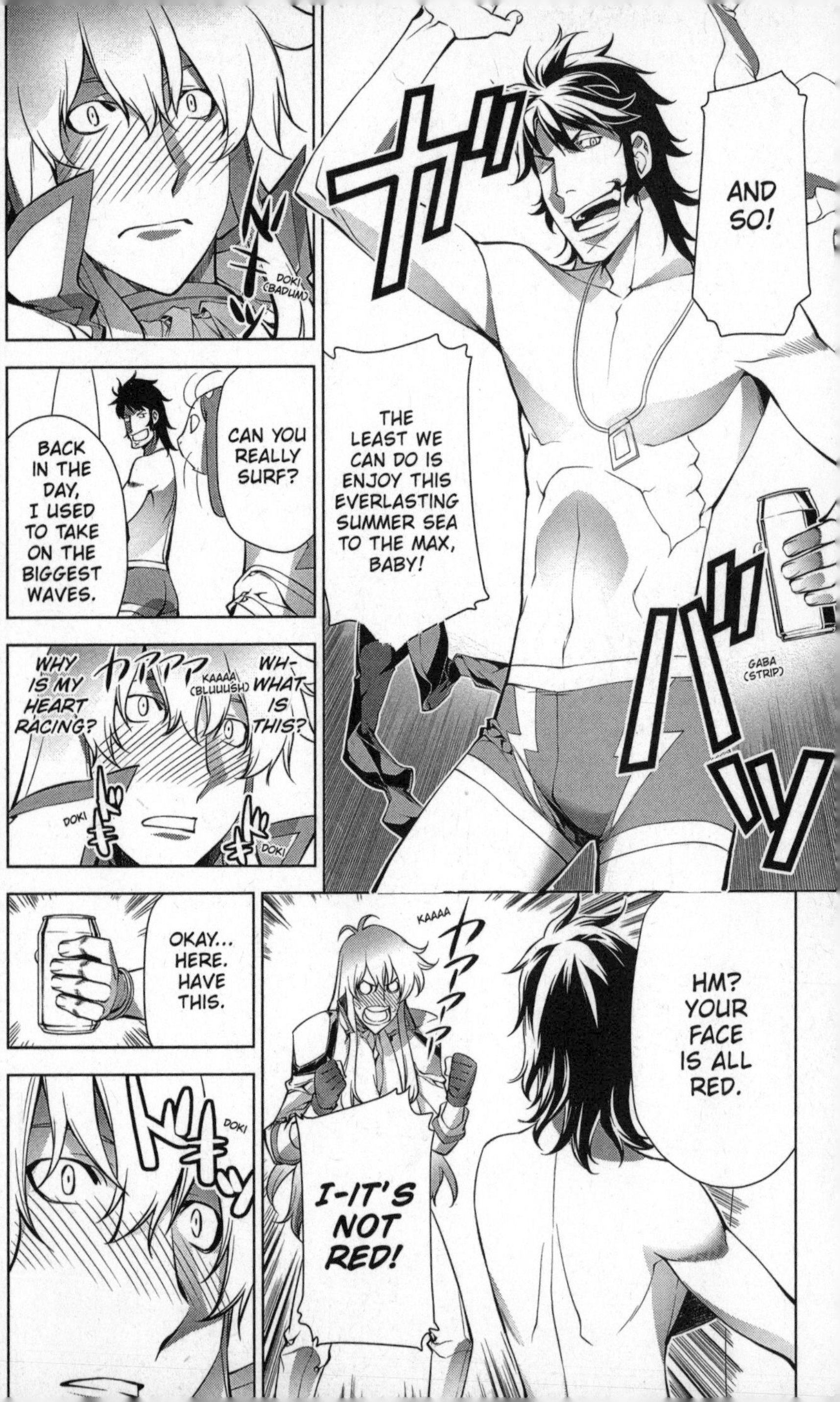
AND SO!
THE LEAST WE CAN DO IS ENJOY THIS EVERLASTING SUMMER SEA TO THE MAX, BABY!
GABA (STRIP)
DOKI (BADUM)
CAN YOU REALLY SURF?
BACK IN THE DAY, I USED TO TAKE ON THE BIGGEST WAVES.
WH-WHAT IS THIS?
KAAAA (BLUUUSH)
WHY IS MY HEART RACING?
DOKI
DOKI
HM? YOUR FACE IS ALL RED.
KAAAA
I-IT'S NOT RED!
OKAY... HERE. HAVE THIS.
DOKI

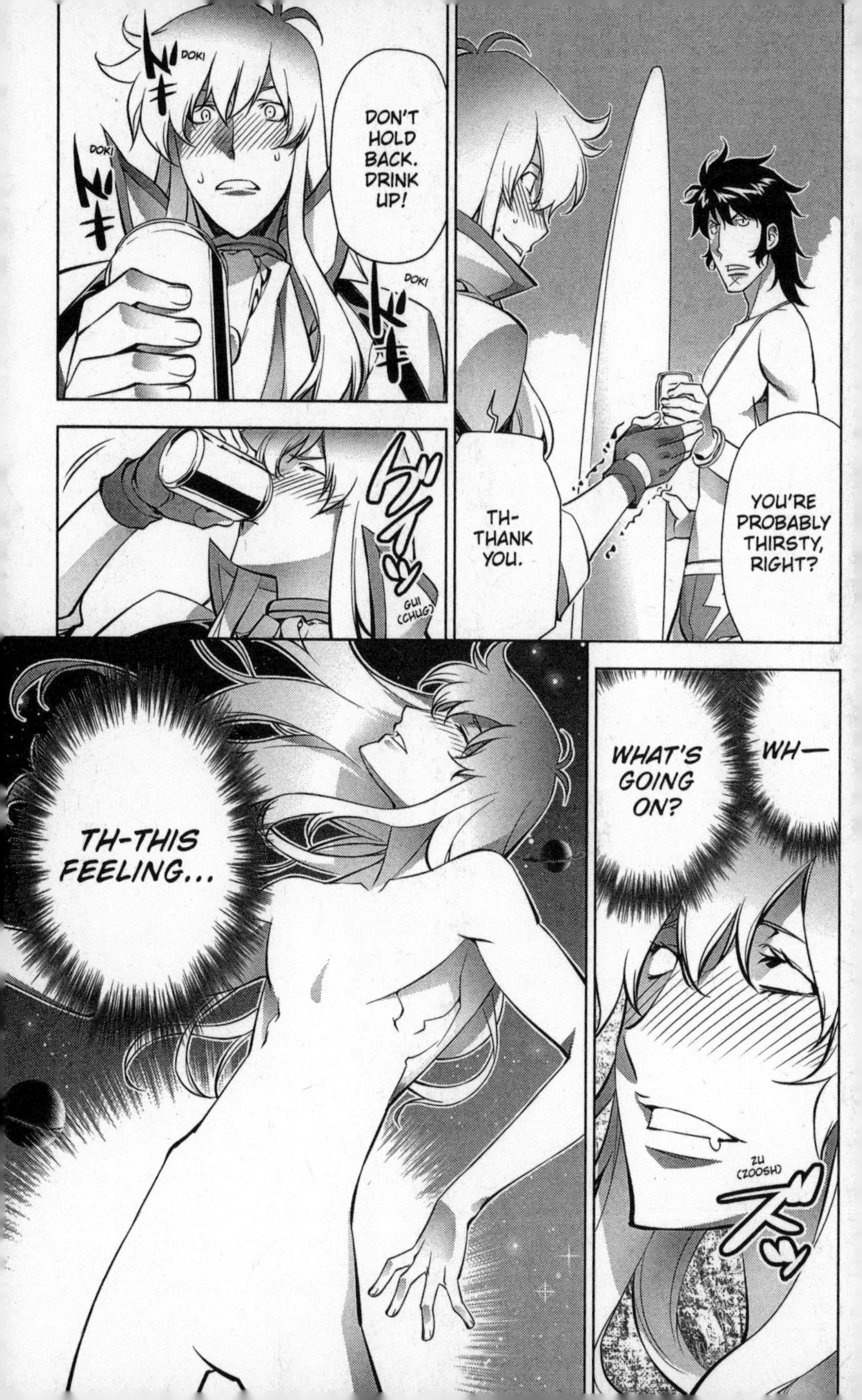
YOU'RE PROBABLY THIRSTY, RIGHT?
TH- THANK YOU.
DOKI
DOKI
DON'T HOLD BACK. DRINK UP!
DOKI
GUI (CHUG)
WH—
WHAT'S GOING ON?
ZU (ZOOSH)
TH-THIS FEELING...

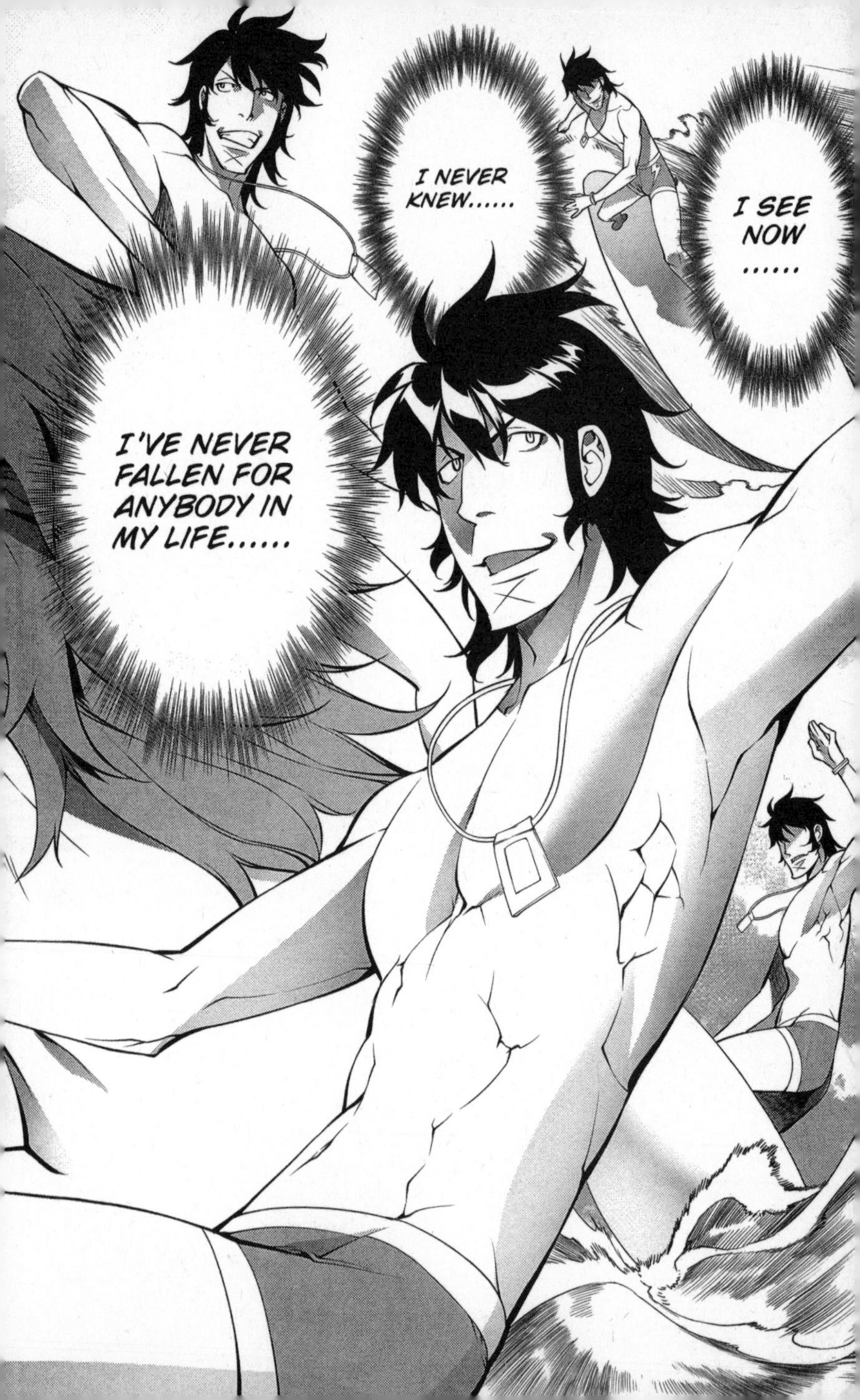
I SEE NOW ......
I NEVER KNEW......
I'VE NEVER FALLEN FOR ANYBODY IN MY LIFE......

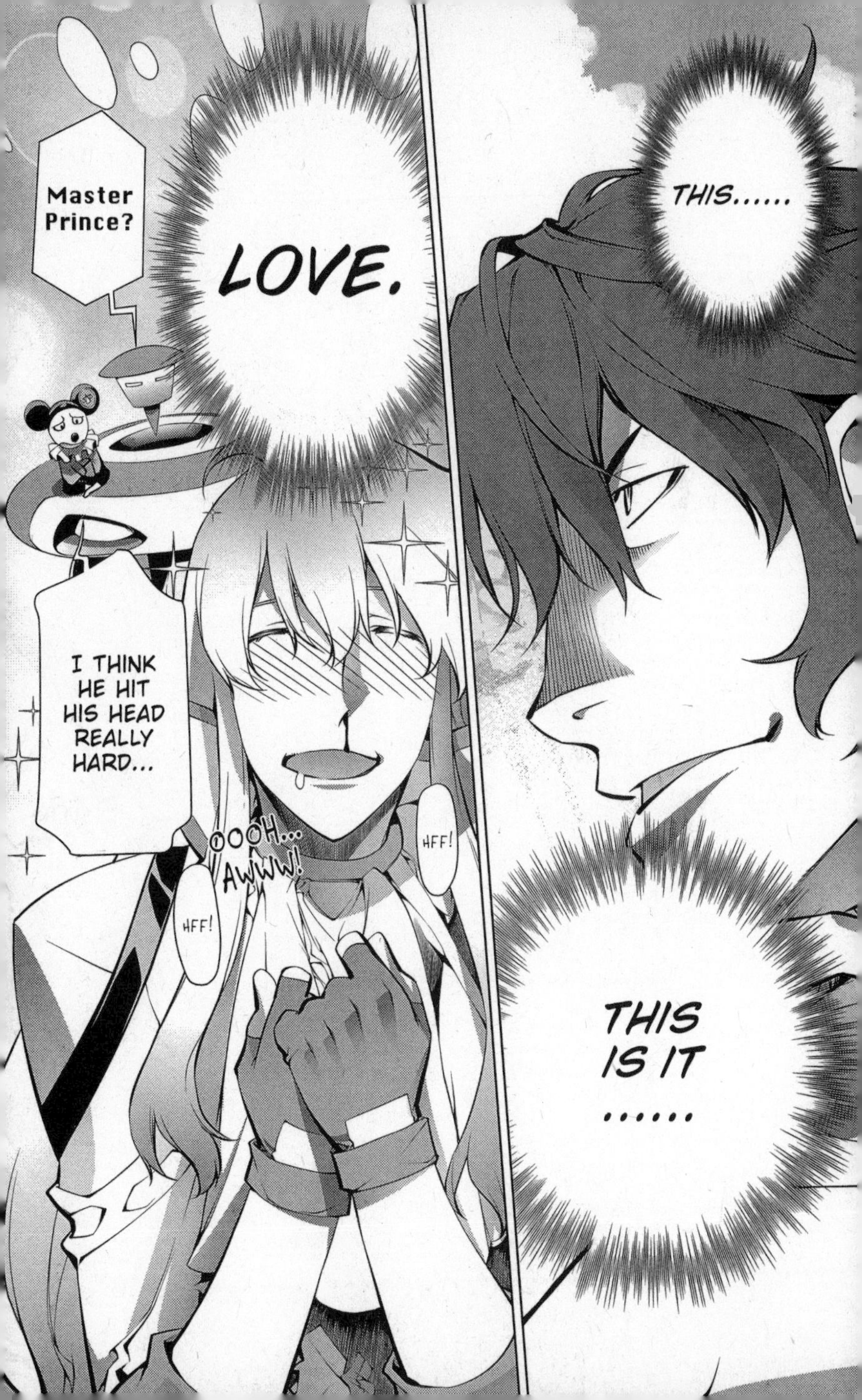
THIS......
THIS IS IT ......
LOVE.
Master Prince?
I THINK HE HIT HIS HEAD REALLY HARD...
HFF!
OOOH... AWWW!
HFF!

Chapter 10: This Gal's Got a Violent Streak, Baby

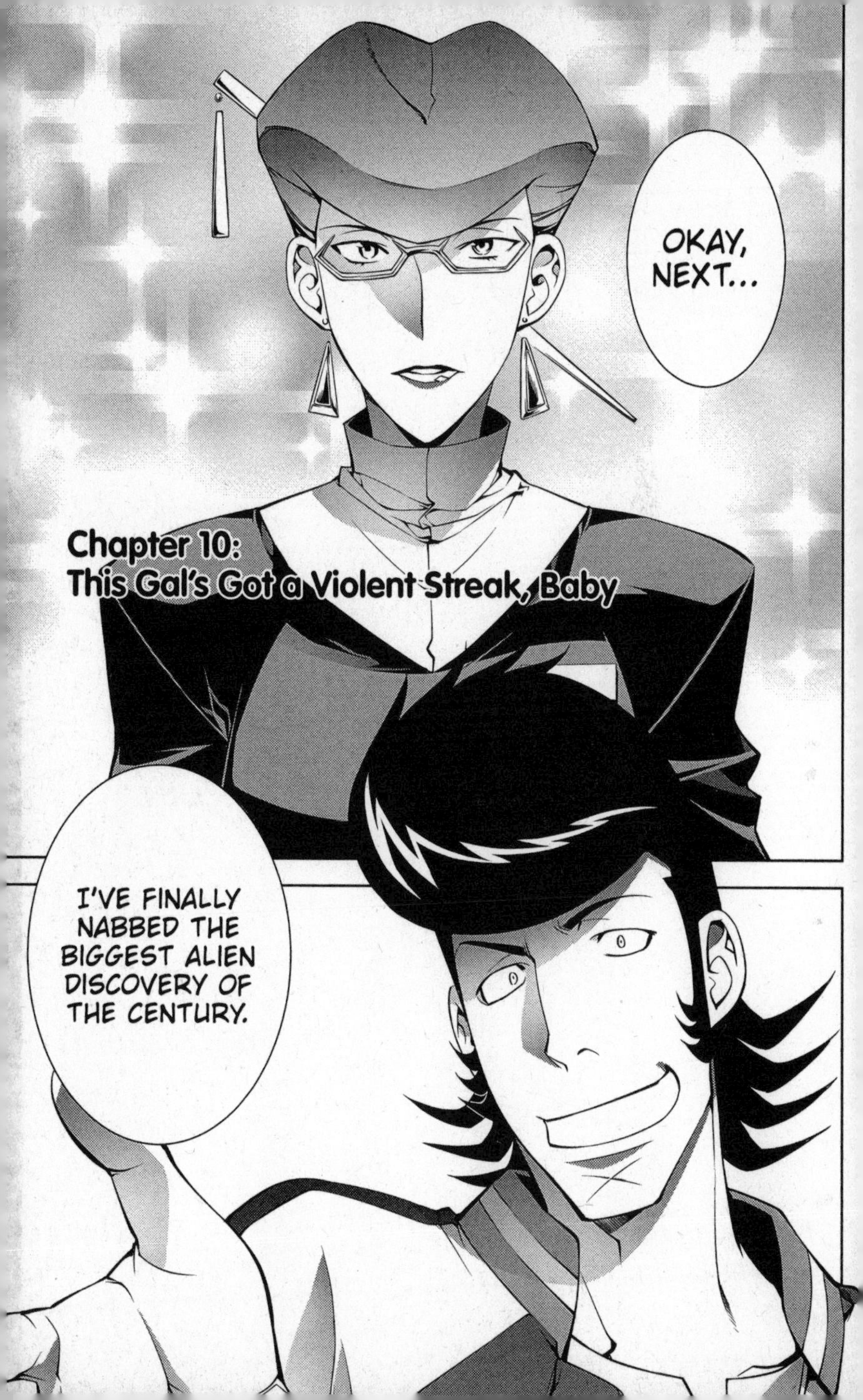
OKAY, NEXT...
I'VE FINALLY NABBED THE BIGGEST ALIEN DISCOVERY OF THE CENTURY.

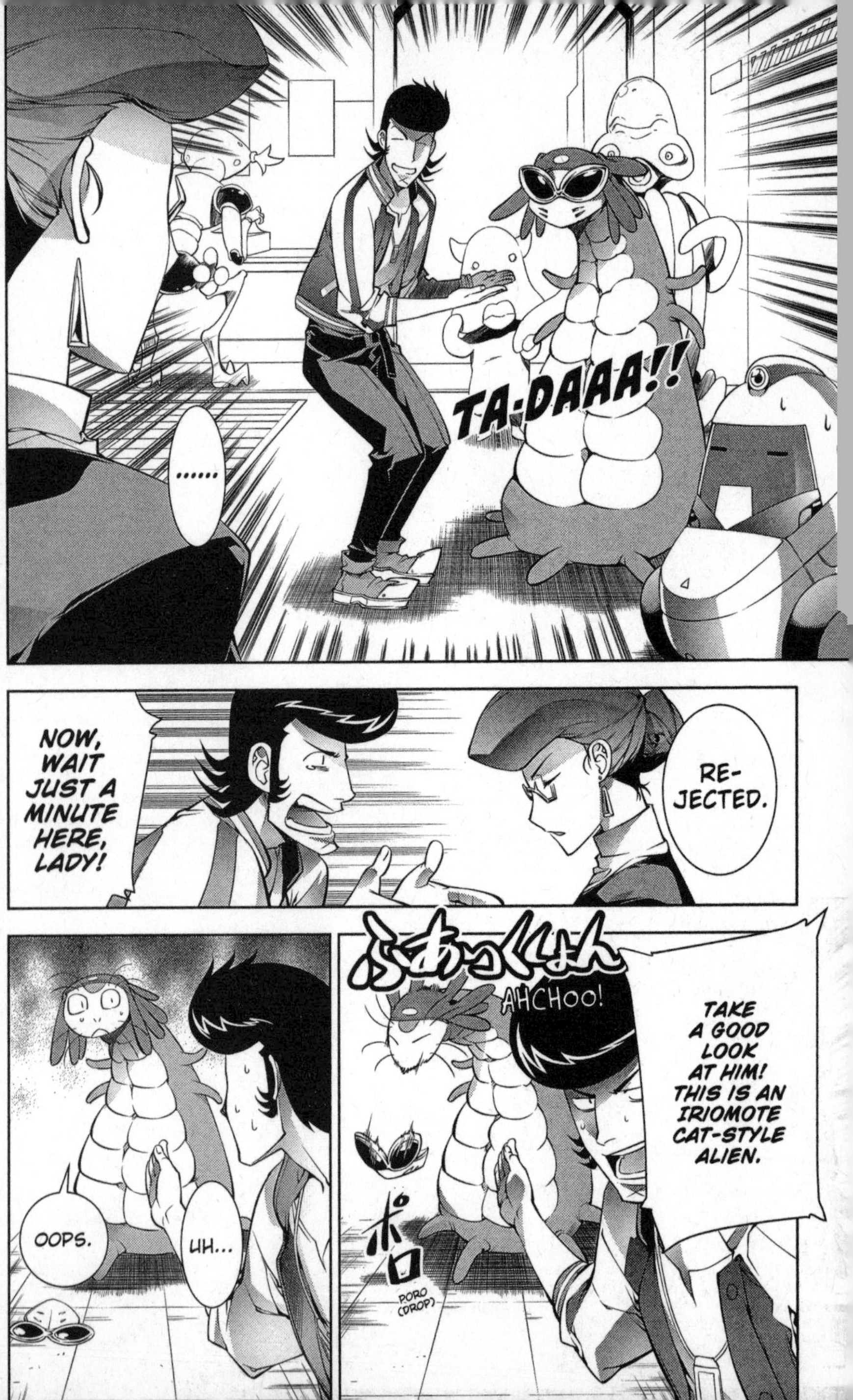
TA-DAAA!!
......
RE-JECTED.
NOW, WAIT JUST A MINUTE HERE, LADY!
ふぁっくしょん
AHCHOO!
TAKE A GOOD LOOK AT HIM! THIS IS AN IRIOMOTE CAT-STYLE ALIEN.
ポロ
PORO (DROP)
UH...
OOPS.

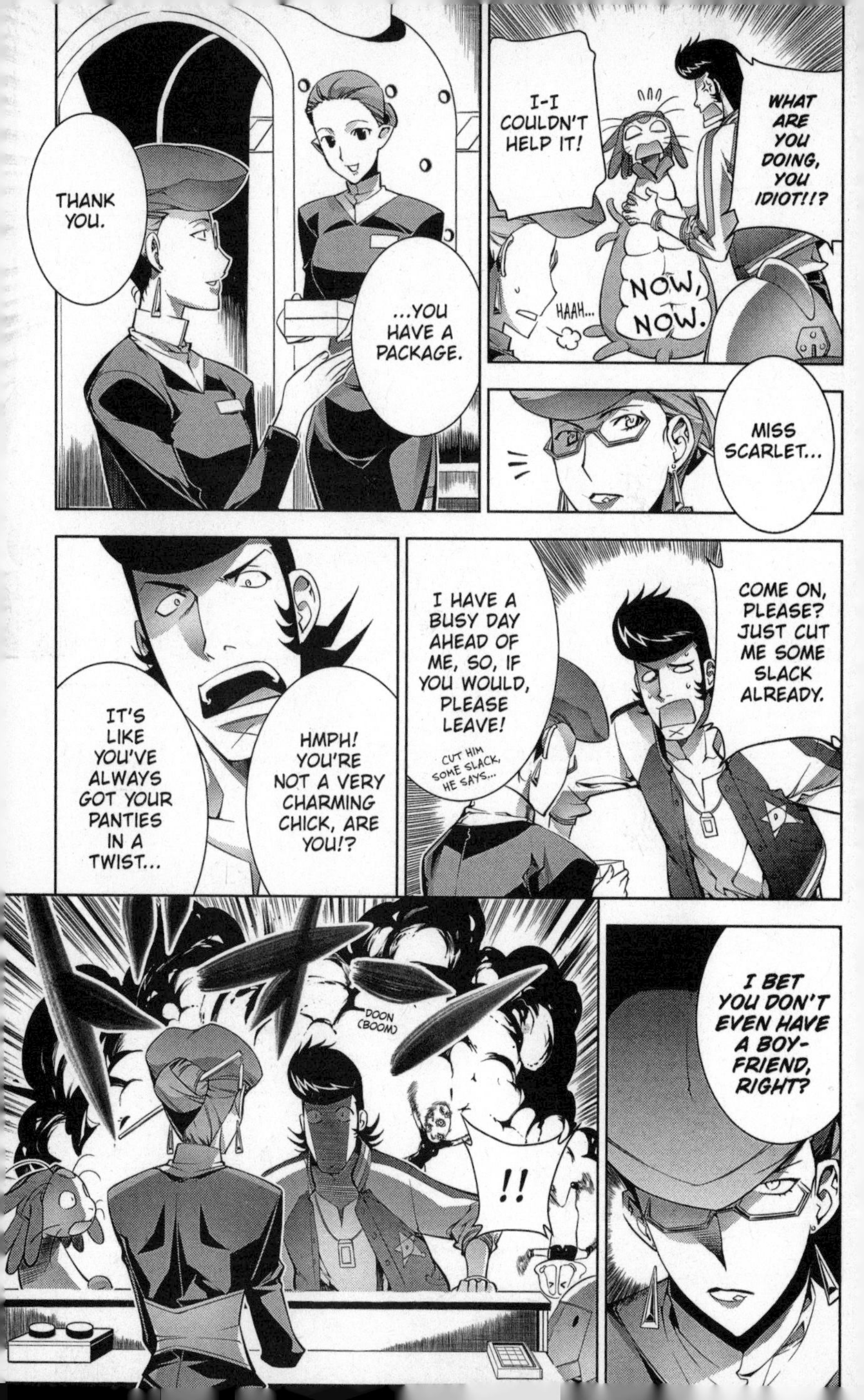
WHAT ARE YOU DOING, YOU IDIOT!!?
I-I COULDN'T HELP IT!
NOW, NOW.
HAAH...
MISS SCARLET...
...YOU HAVE A PACKAGE.
THANK YOU.
COME ON, PLEASE? JUST CUT ME SOME SLACK ALREADY.
I HAVE A BUSY DAY AHEAD OF ME, SO, IF YOU WOULD, PLEASE LEAVE!
CUT HIM SOME SLACK, HE SAYS...
HMPH! YOU'RE NOT A VERY CHARMING CHICK, ARE YOU!?
IT'S LIKE YOU'VE ALWAYS GOT YOUR PANTIES IN A TWIST...
I BET YOU DON'T EVEN HAVE A BOY-FRIEND, RIGHT?
DOON (BOOM)
!!

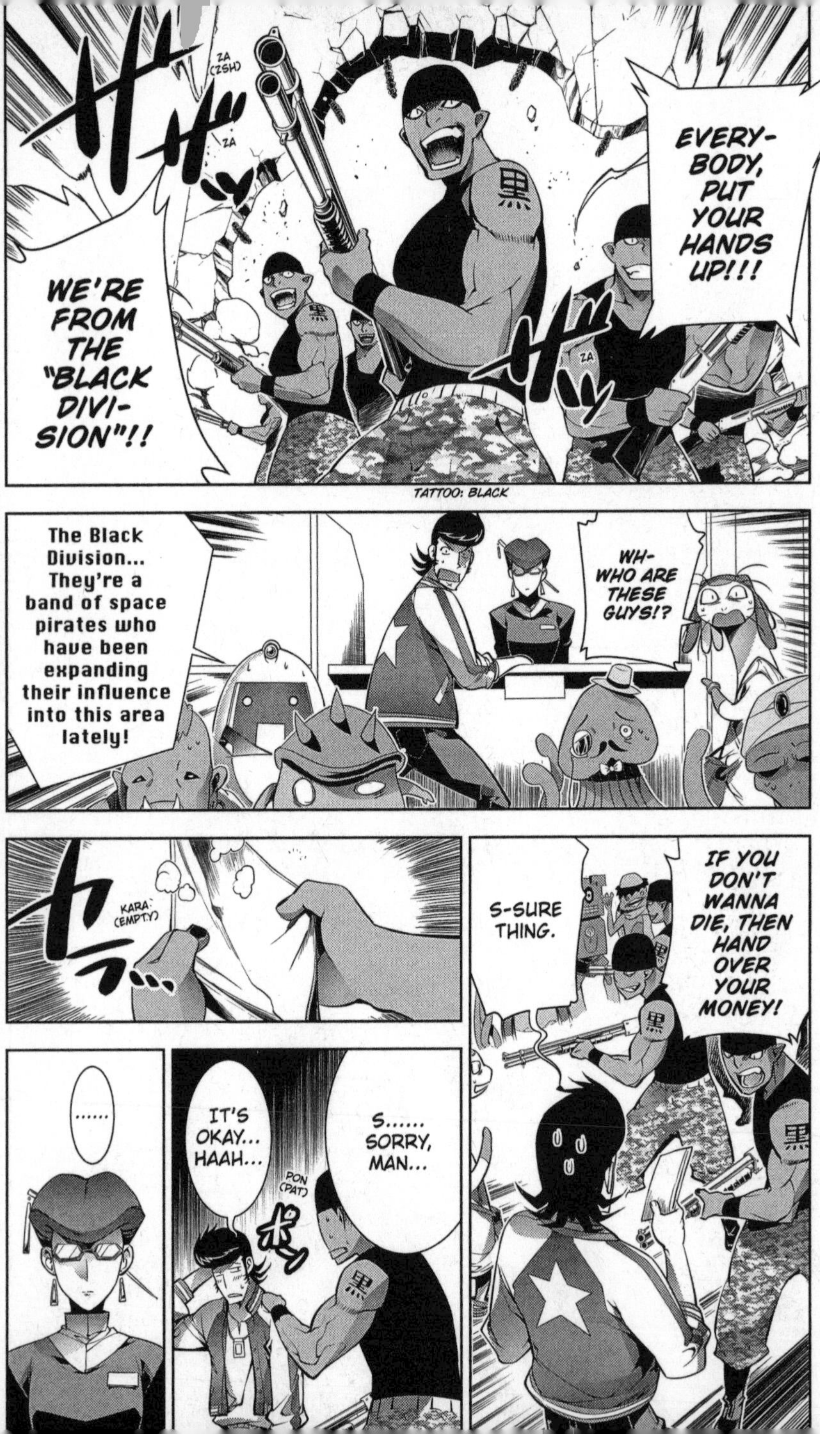
EVERY-BODY, PUT YOUR HANDS UP!!!
ZA (ZSH)
ZA
ZA
WE'RE FROM THE "BLACK DIVISION"!!
TATTOO: BLACK
WH- WHO ARE THESE GUYS!?
The Black Division... They're a band of space pirates who have been expanding their influence into this area lately!
IF YOU DON'T WANNA DIE, THEN HAND OVER YOUR MONEY!
S-SURE THING.
KARA (EMPTY)
S...... SORRY, MAN...
IT'S OKAY... HAAH...
PON (PAT)
......

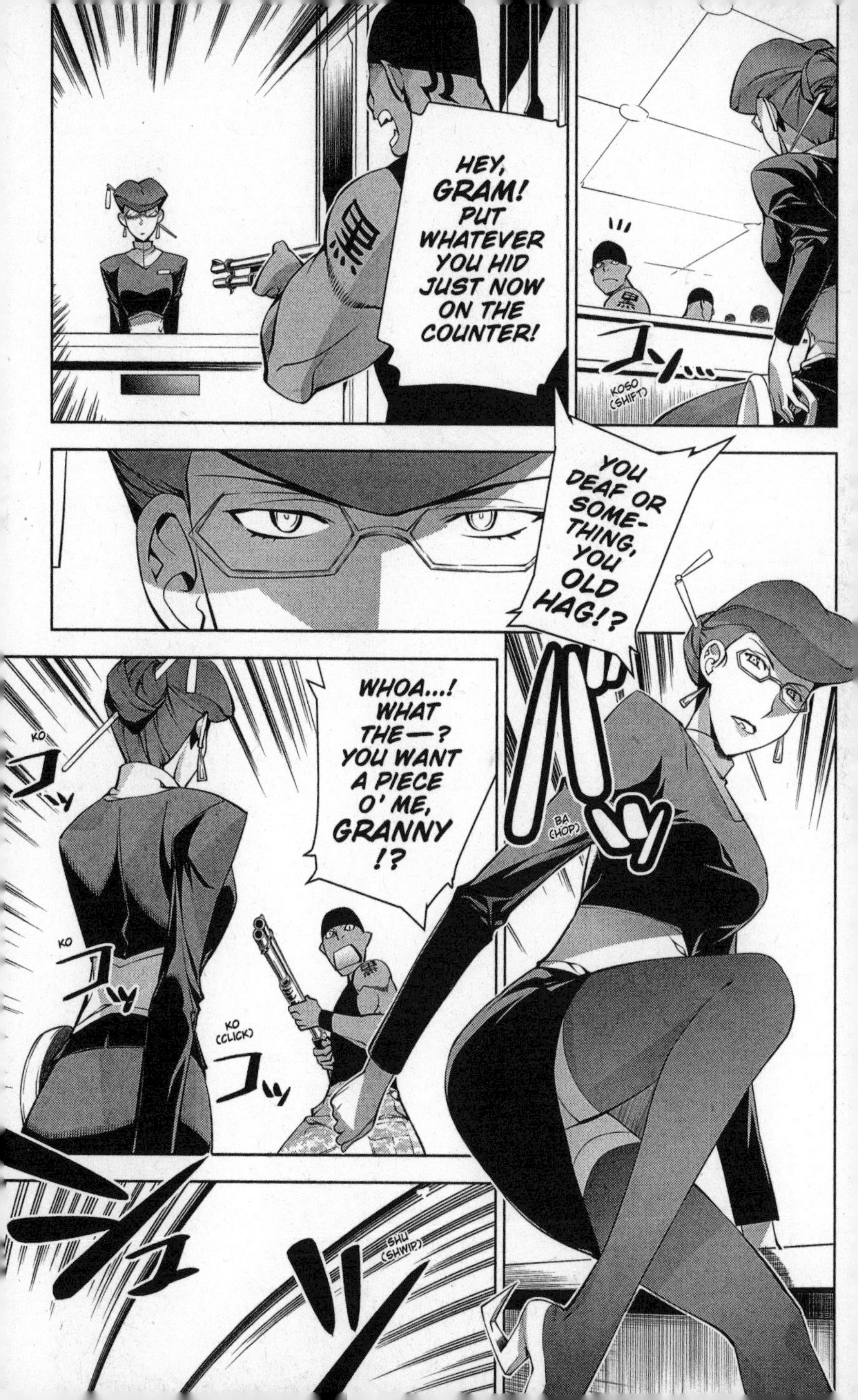
KOSO (SHIFT)
HEY, GRAM! PUT WHATEVER YOU HID JUST NOW ON THE COUNTER!
YOU DEAF OR SOME-THING, YOU OLD HAG!?
BA (HOP)
WHOA...! WHAT THE—? YOU WANT A PIECE O' ME, GRANNY!?
KO
KO
KO (CLICK)
SHU (SHWIP)

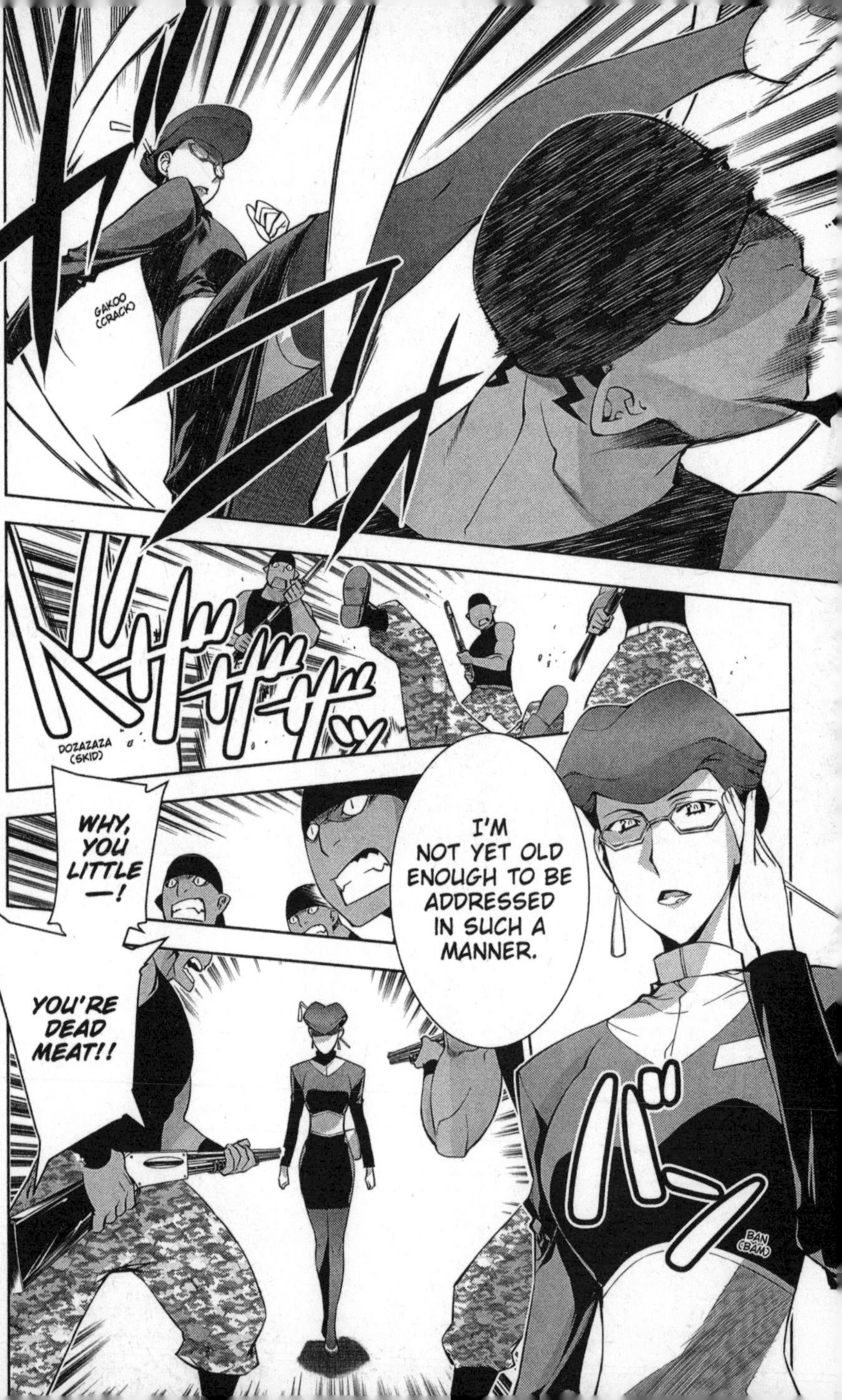

GAKOO (CRACK)
DOZAZAZA (SKID)
I'M NOT YET OLD ENOUGH TO BE ADDRESSED IN SUCH A MANNER.
WHY, YOU LITTLE—!
YOU'RE DEAD MEAT!!
BAN (BAM)

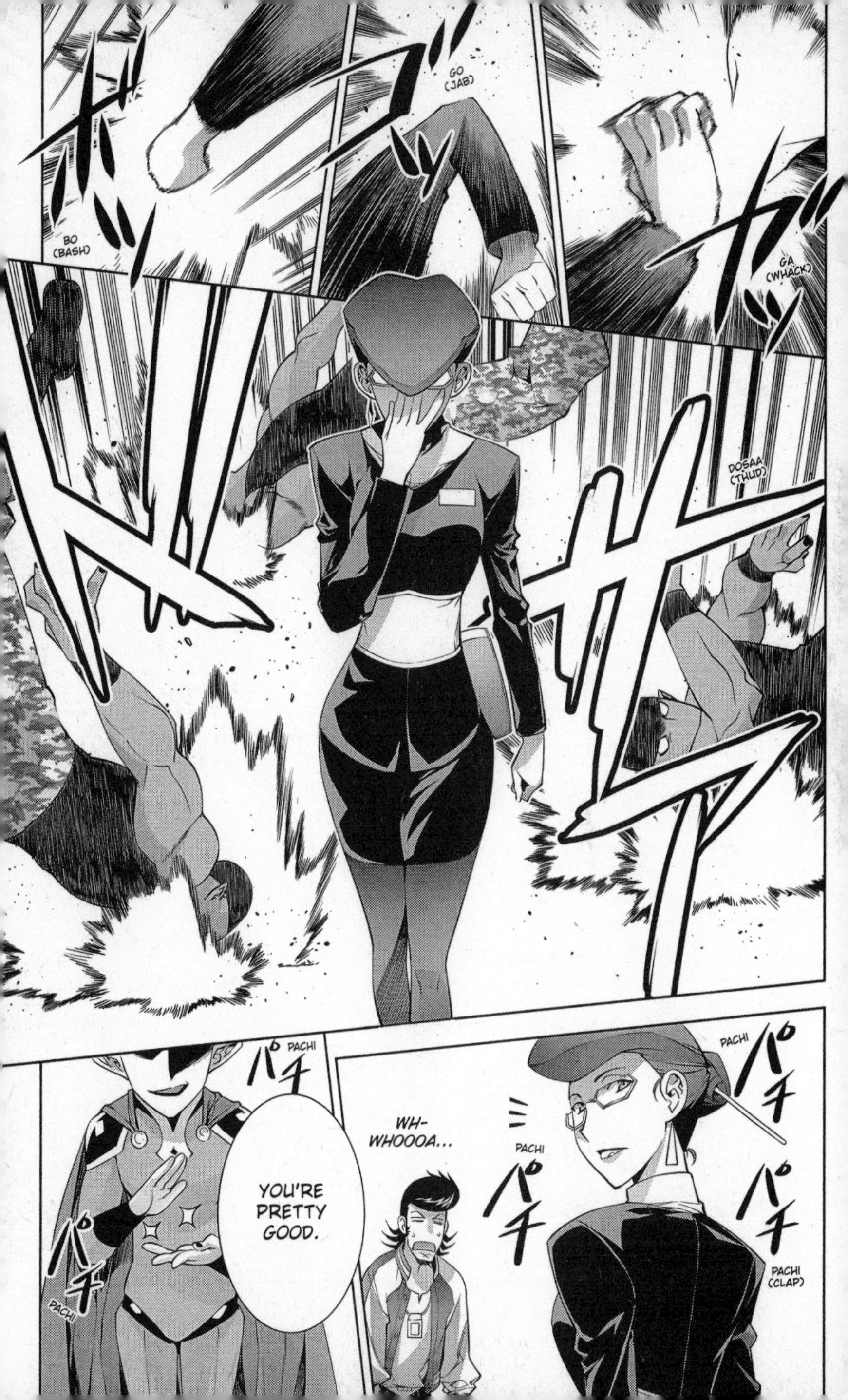
GA (WHACK)
GO (JAB)
BO (BASH)
DOSAA (THUD)
PACHI
WH- WHOOOA...
PACHI
PACHI (CLAP)
PACHI
YOU'RE PRETTY GOOD.
PACHI

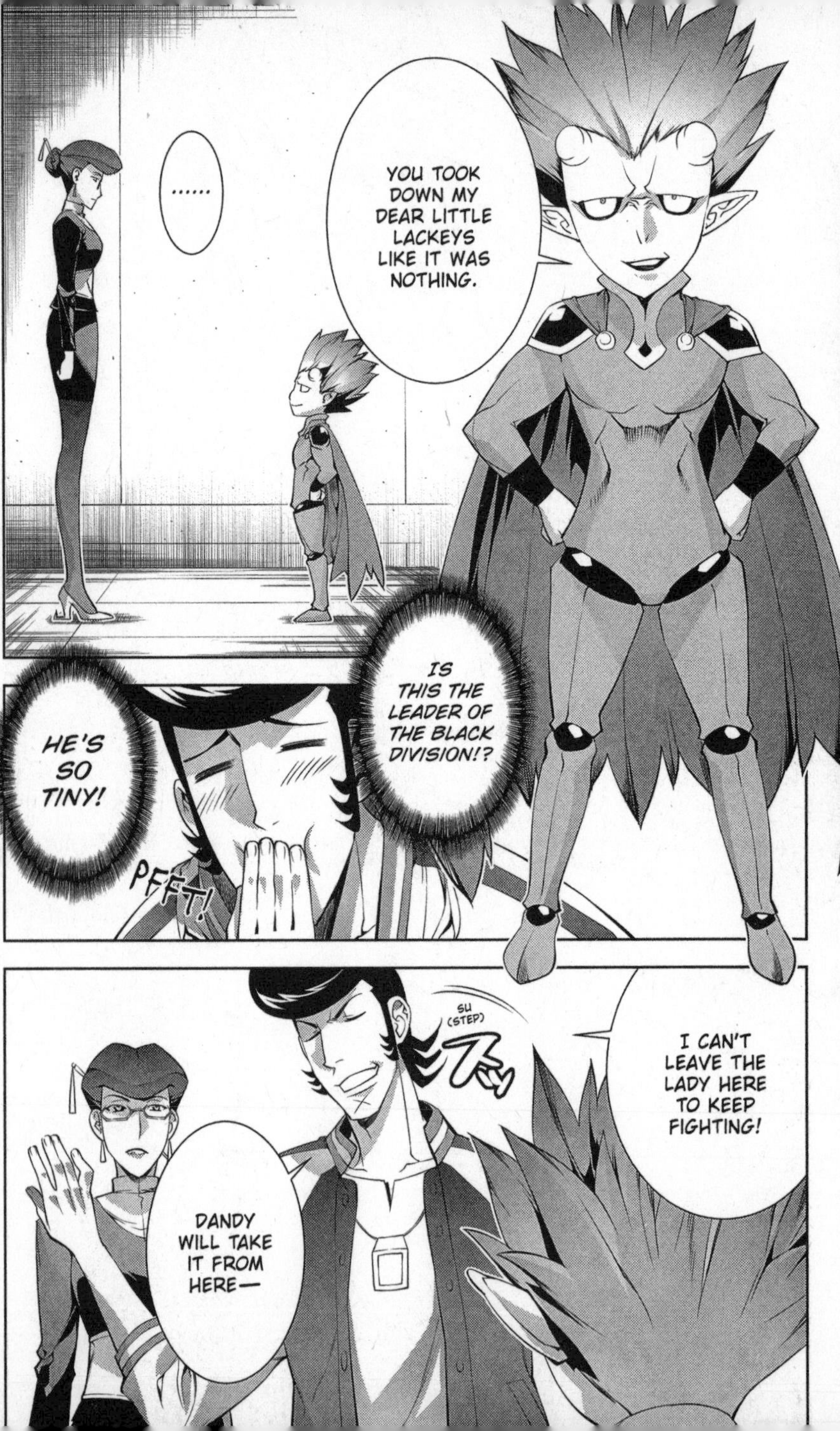
YOU TOOK DOWN MY DEAR LITTLE LACKEYS LIKE IT WAS NOTHING.
......
IS THIS THE LEADER OF THE BLACK DIVISION!?
HE'S SO TINY!
PFFT!
I CAN'T LEAVE THE LADY HERE TO KEEP FIGHTING!
SU (STEP)
DANDY WILL TAKE IT FROM HERE—

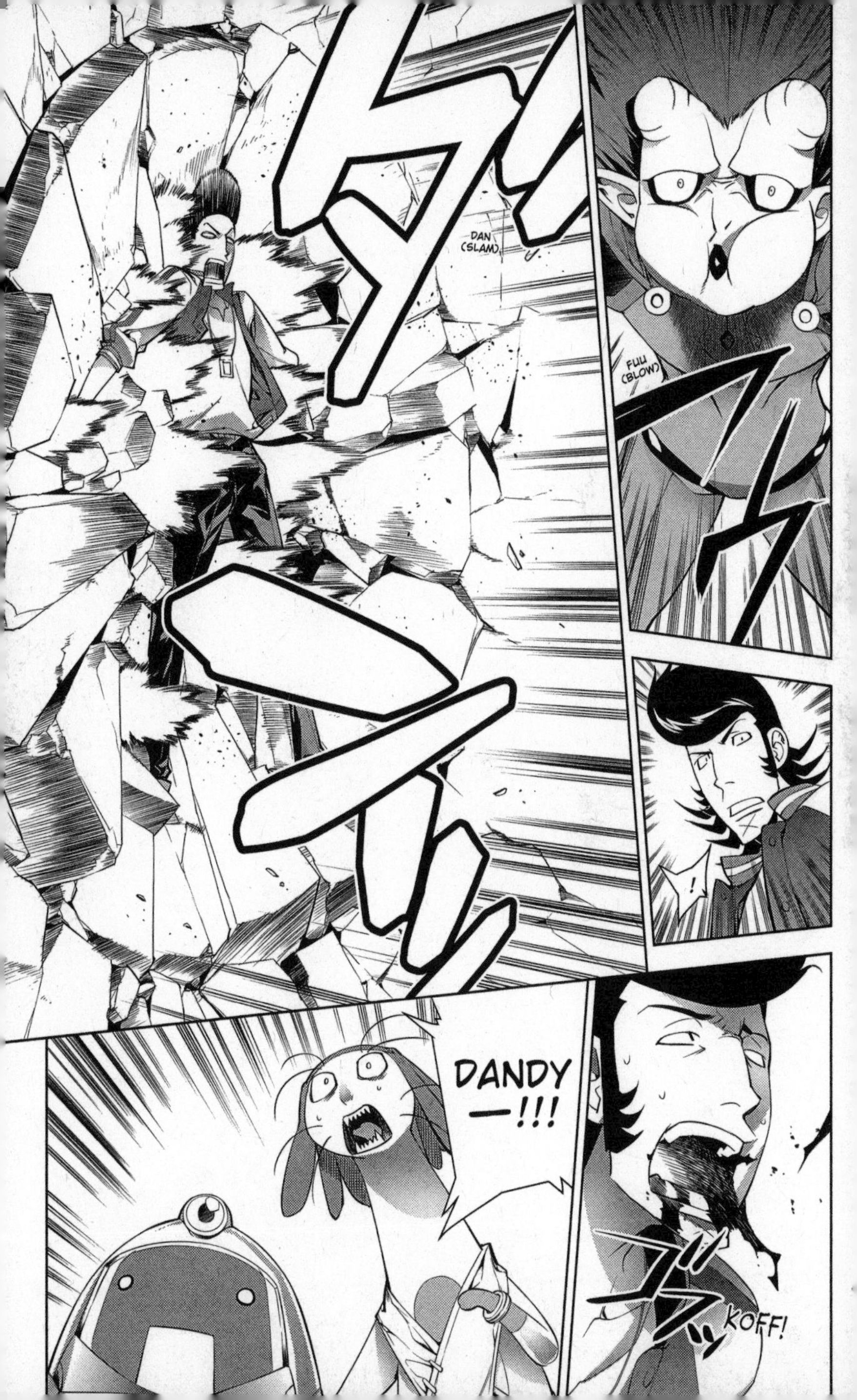
FUU (BLOW)
!
DAN (SLAM)
KOFF!
DANDY —!!!

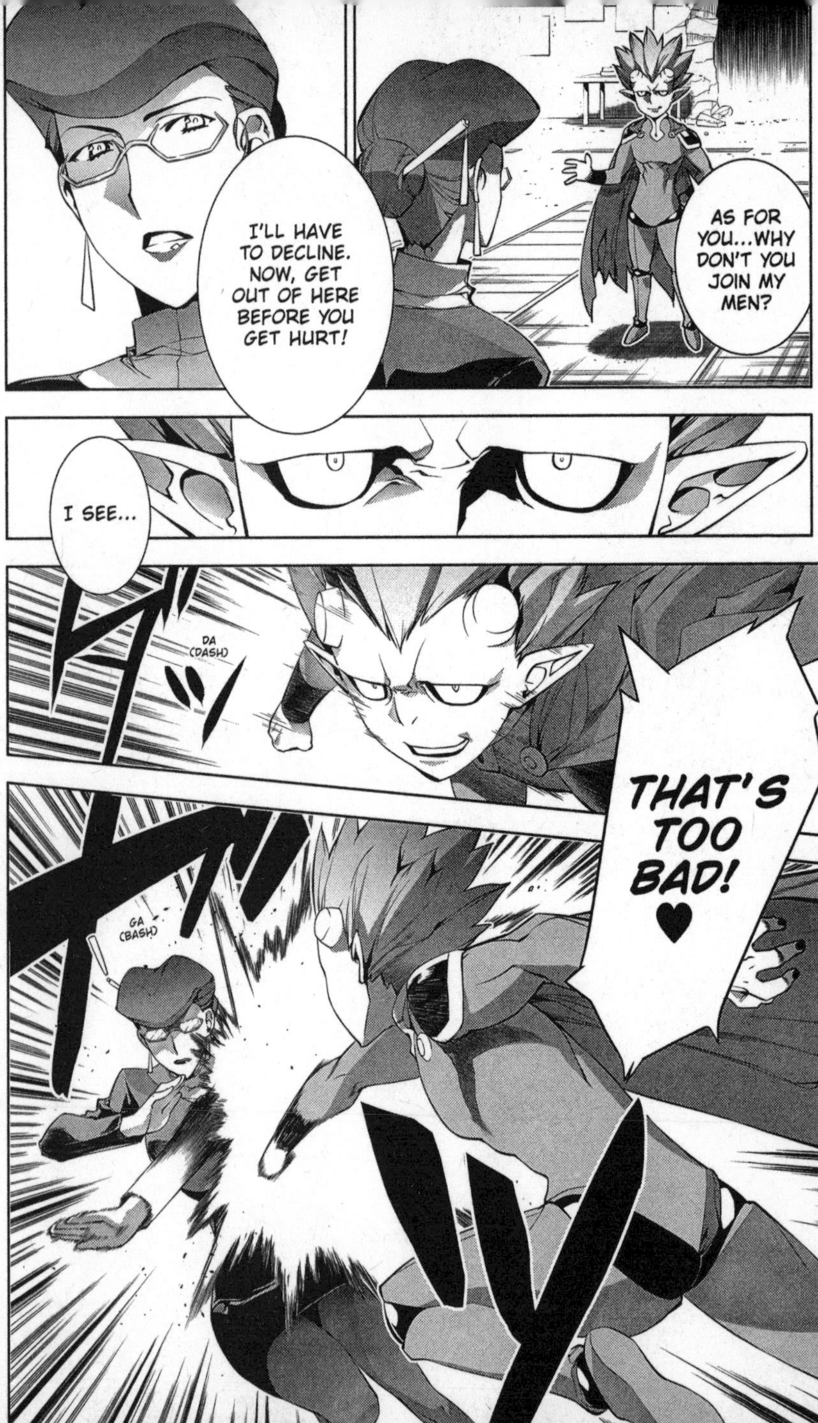
AS FOR YOU...WHY DON'T YOU JOIN MY MEN?
I'LL HAVE TO DECLINE. NOW, GET OUT OF HERE BEFORE YOU GET HURT!
I SEE...
DA (DASH)
THAT'S TOO BAD! ♥
GA (BASH)

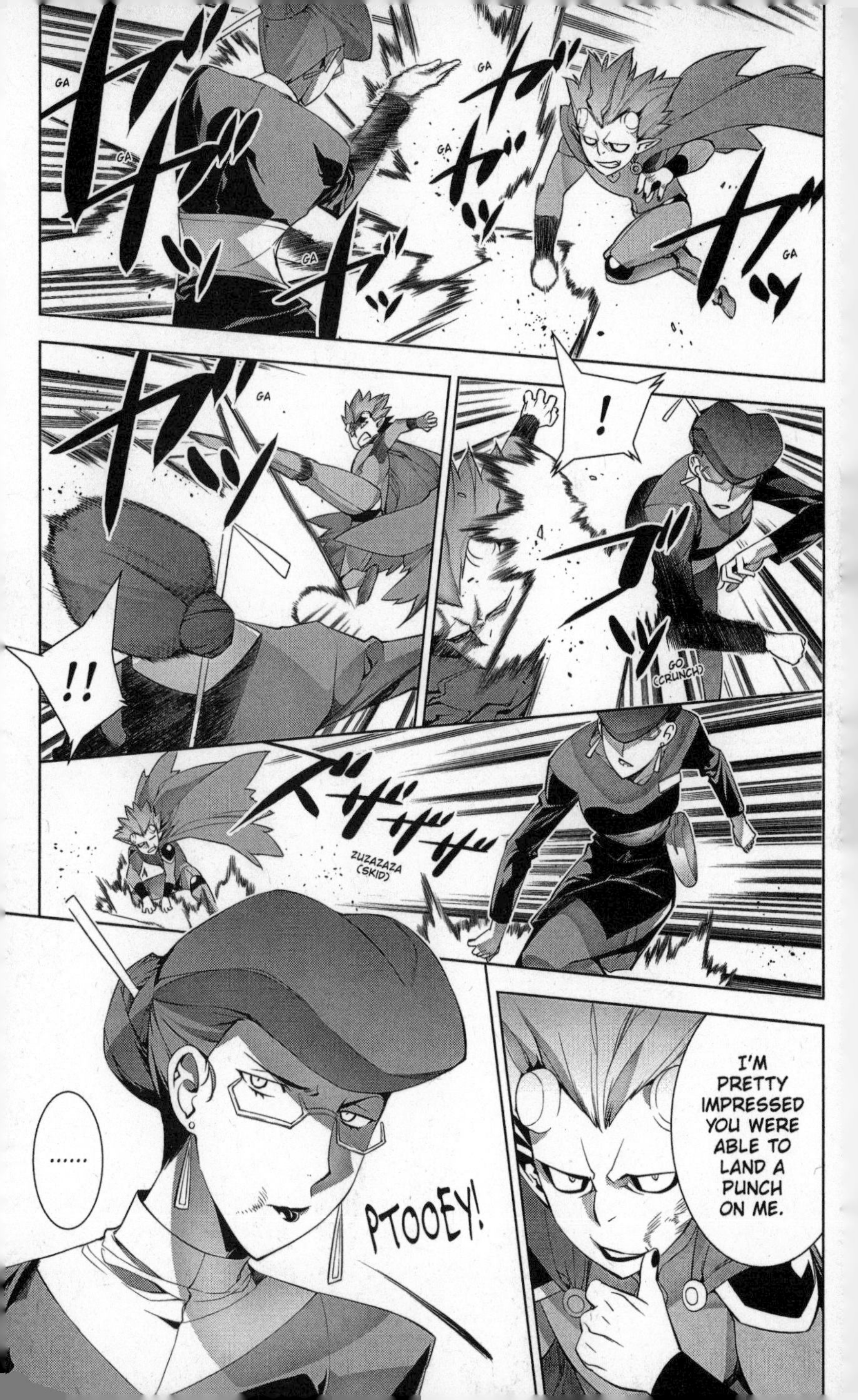
GA
GA
GA
GA
GA
GA
!
GO (CRUNCH)
GA
!!
ZUZAZAZA (SKID)
I'M PRETTY IMPRESSED YOU WERE ABLE TO LAND A PUNCH ON ME.
PTOOEY!
......

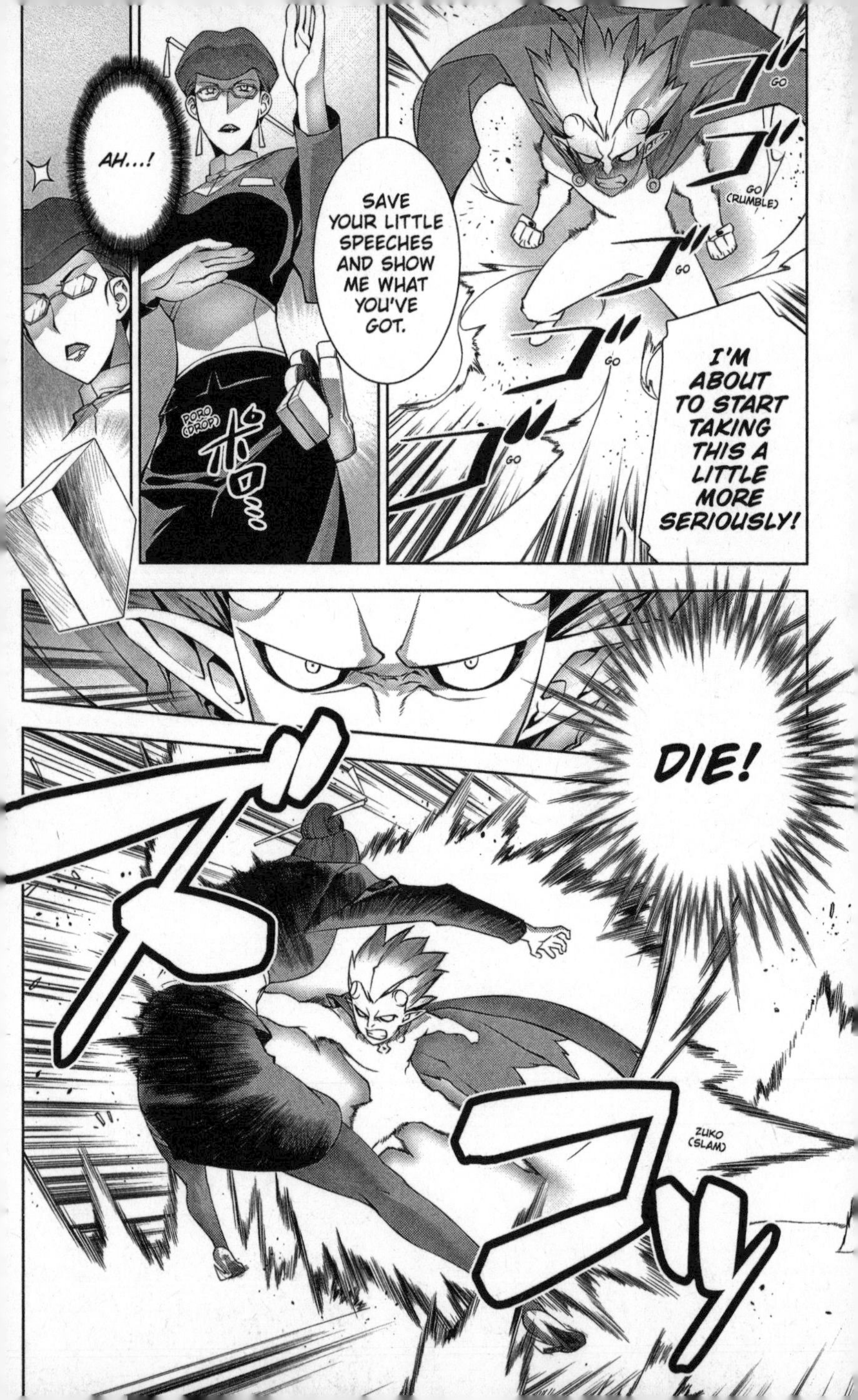
GO
GO (RUMBLE)
GO
GO
GO
I'M ABOUT TO START TAKING THIS A LITTLE MORE SERIOUSLY!
SAVE YOUR LITTLE SPEECHES AND SHOW ME WHAT YOU'VE GOT.
PORO (DROP)
AH...!
DIE!
ZUKO (SLAM)

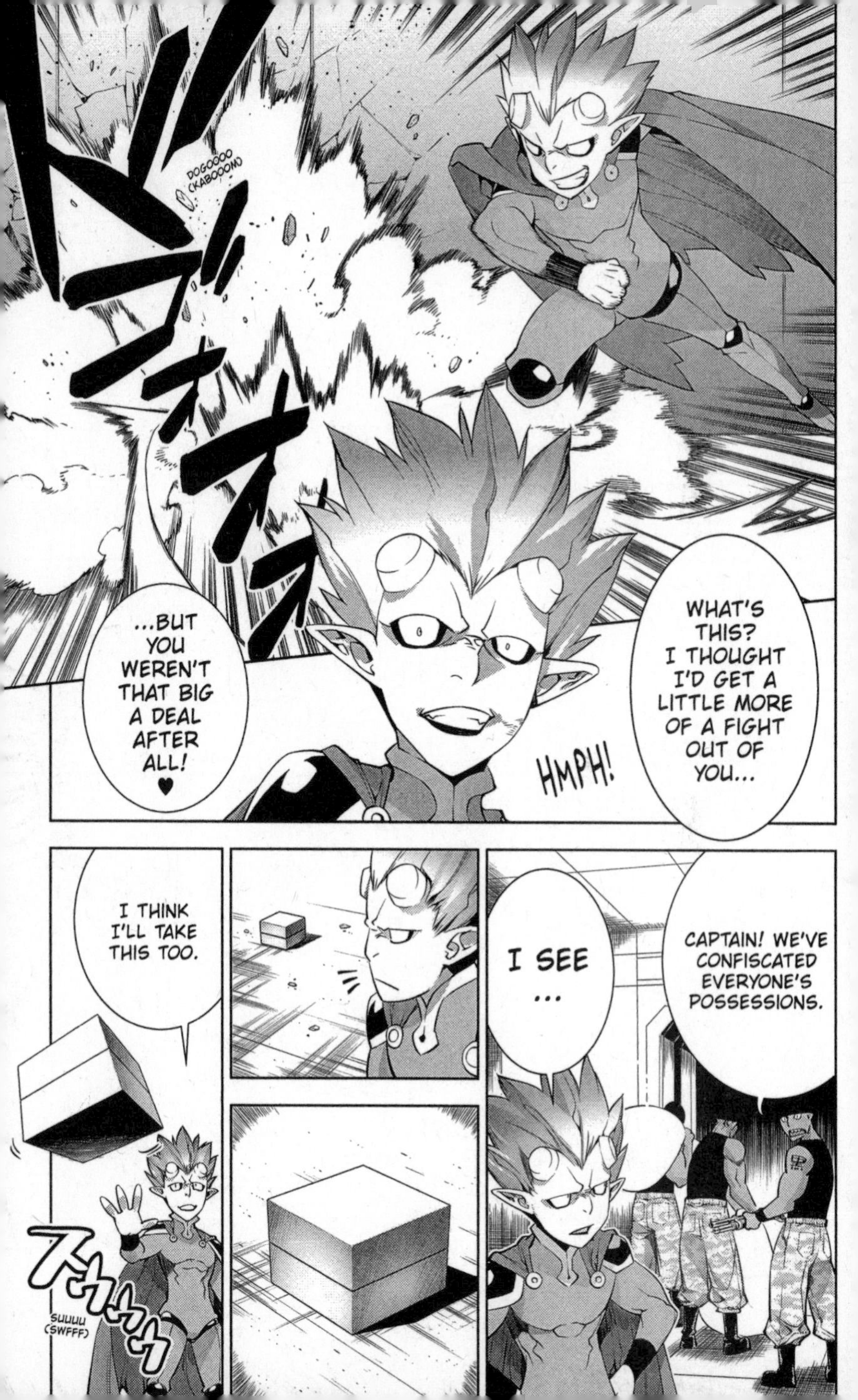
DOGOOOO (KABOOOM)
WHAT'S THIS? I THOUGHT I'D GET A LITTLE MORE OF A FIGHT OUT OF YOU...
HMPH!
...BUT YOU WEREN'T THAT BIG A DEAL AFTER ALL! ♥
CAPTAIN! WE'VE CONFISCATED EVERYONE'S POSSESSIONS.
I SEE ...
I THINK I'LL TAKE THIS TOO.
SUUUU (SWFFF)

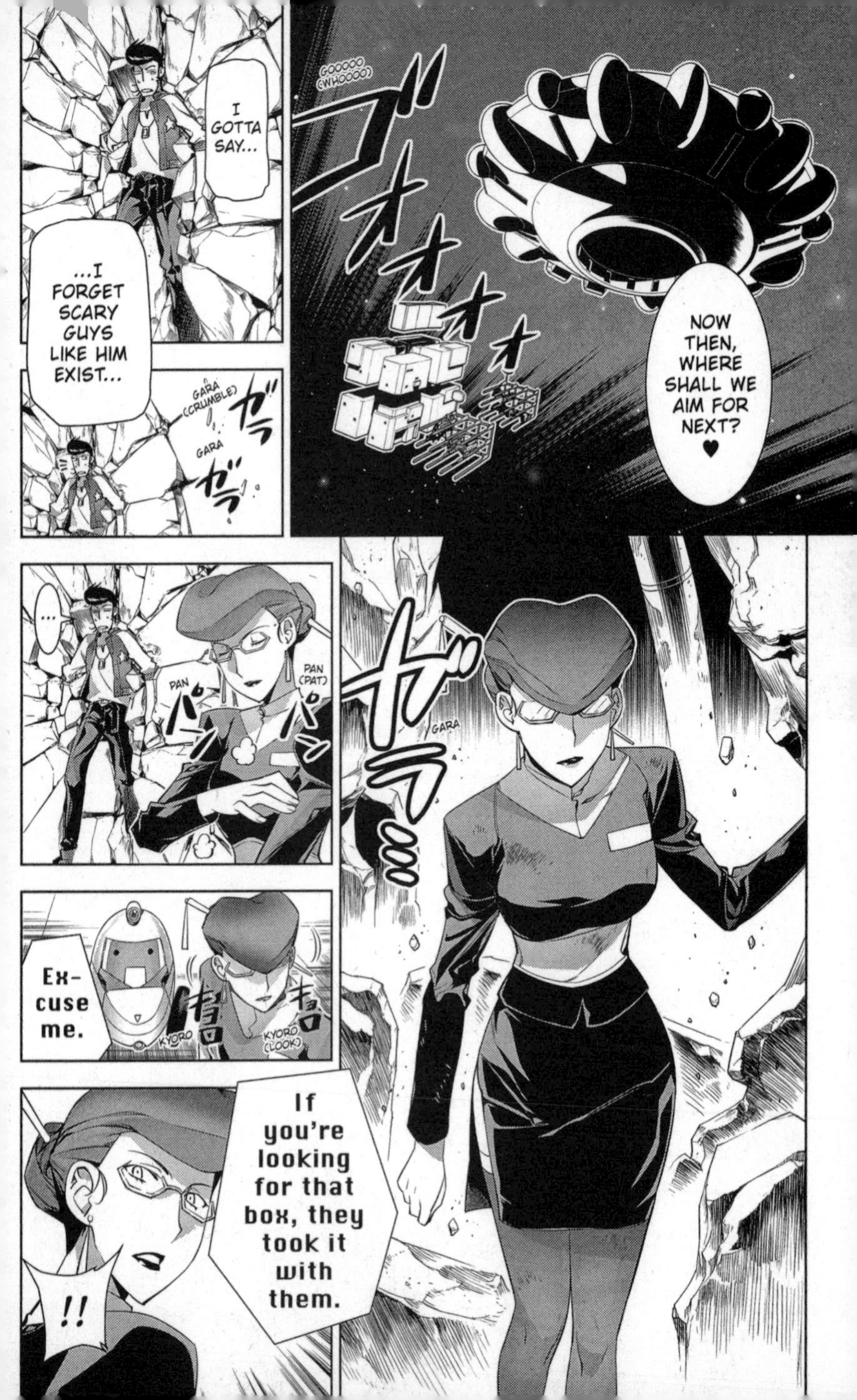
GOOOOO (WHOOOO)
NOW THEN, WHERE SHALL WE AIM FOR NEXT? ♥
I GOTTA SAY...
...I FORGET SCARY GUYS LIKE HIM EXIST...
GARA (CRUMBLE)
GARA
GARA
...
PAN (PAT)
PAN
Ex-cuse me.
KYORO (LOOK)
KYORO
If you're looking for that box, they took it with them.
!!

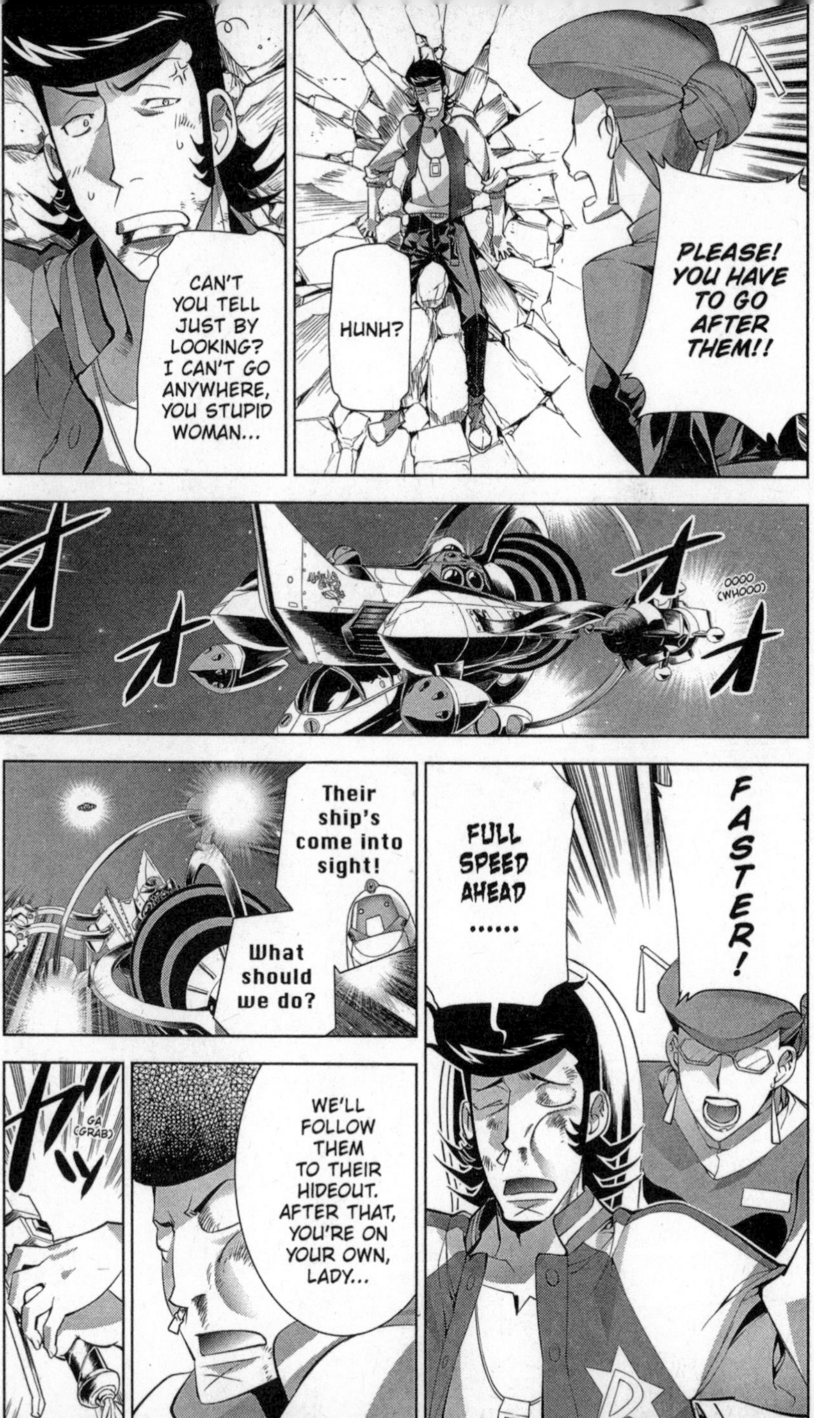
PLEASE! YOU HAVE TO GO AFTER THEM!!
HUNH?
CAN'T YOU TELL JUST BY LOOKING? I CAN'T GO ANYWHERE, YOU STUPID WOMAN...
OOOO (WHOOO)
FASTER!
FULL SPEED AHEAD ......
Their ship's come into sight!
What should we do?
WE'LL FOLLOW THEM TO THEIR HIDEOUT. AFTER THAT, YOU'RE ON YOUR OWN, LADY...
GA (GRAB)

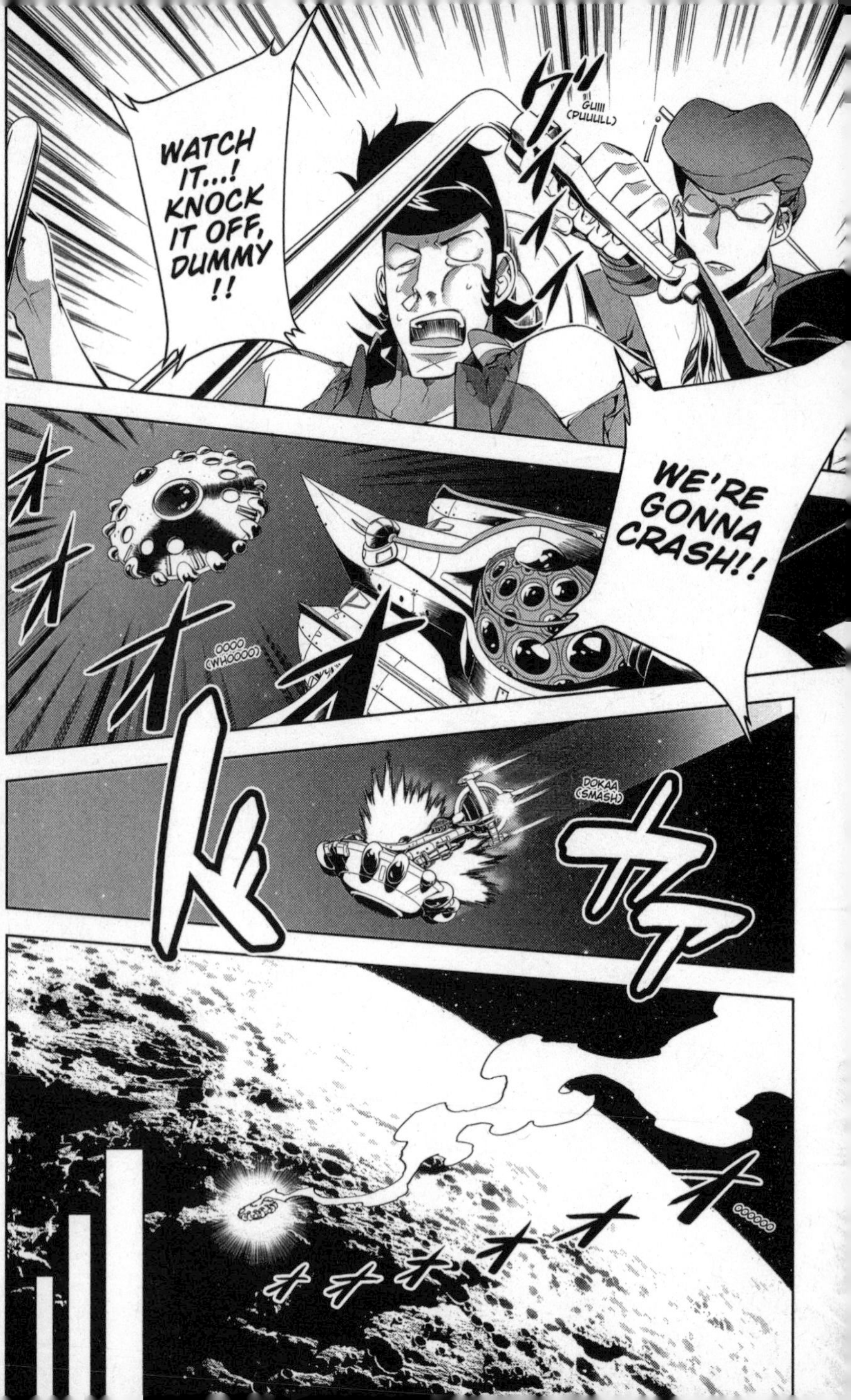
GUIII (PUUUULL)
WATCH IT...! KNOCK IT OFF, DUMMY!!
WE'RE GONNA CRASH!!
OOOO (WHOOOO)
DOKAA (SMASH)
OOOOOO

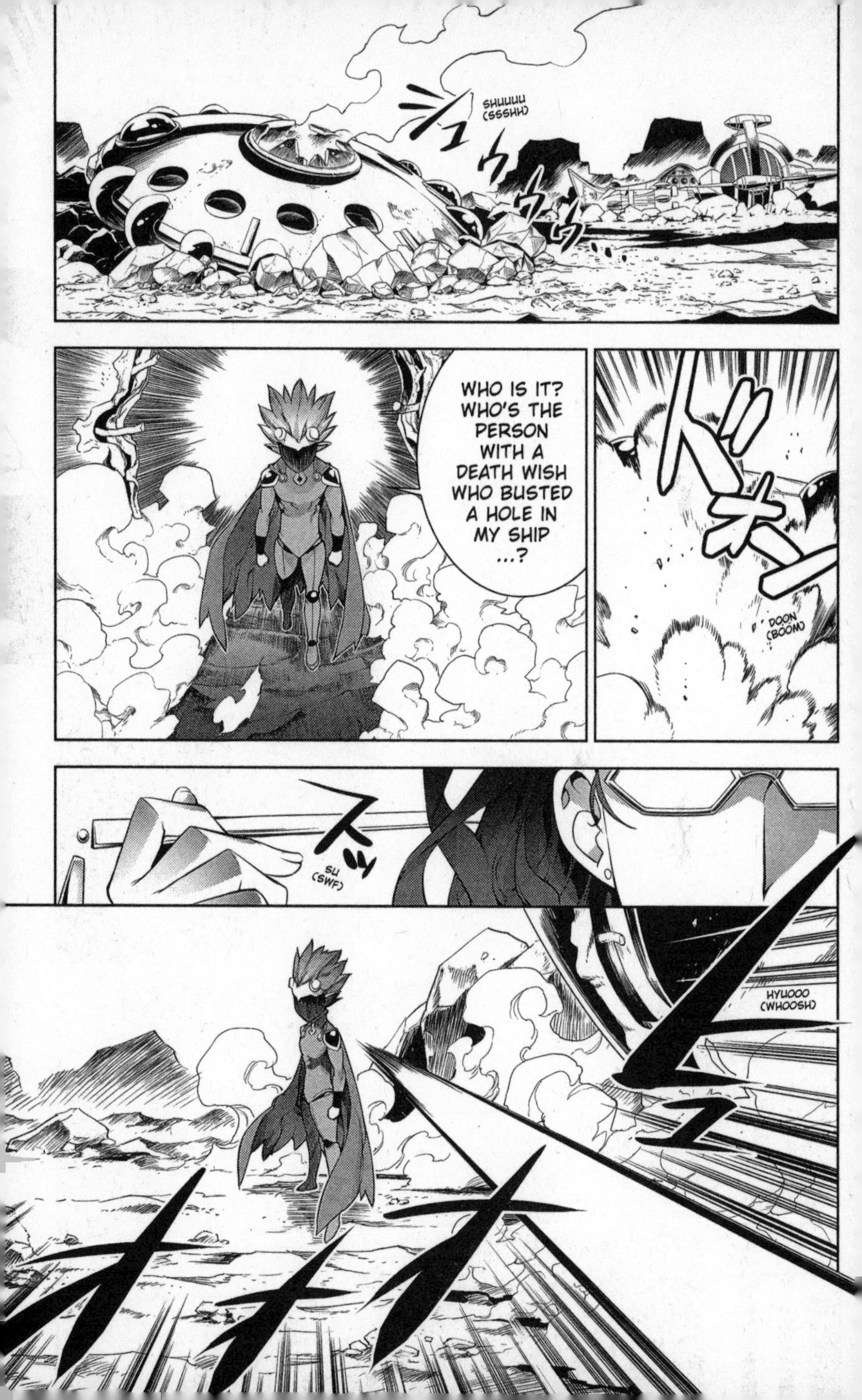
SHUUUU
(SSSHH)
DOON
(BOOM)
WHO IS IT? WHO'S THE PERSON WITH A DEATH WISH WHO BUSTED A HOLE IN MY SHIP ...?
SU
(SWF)
HYUOOO
(WHOOSH)

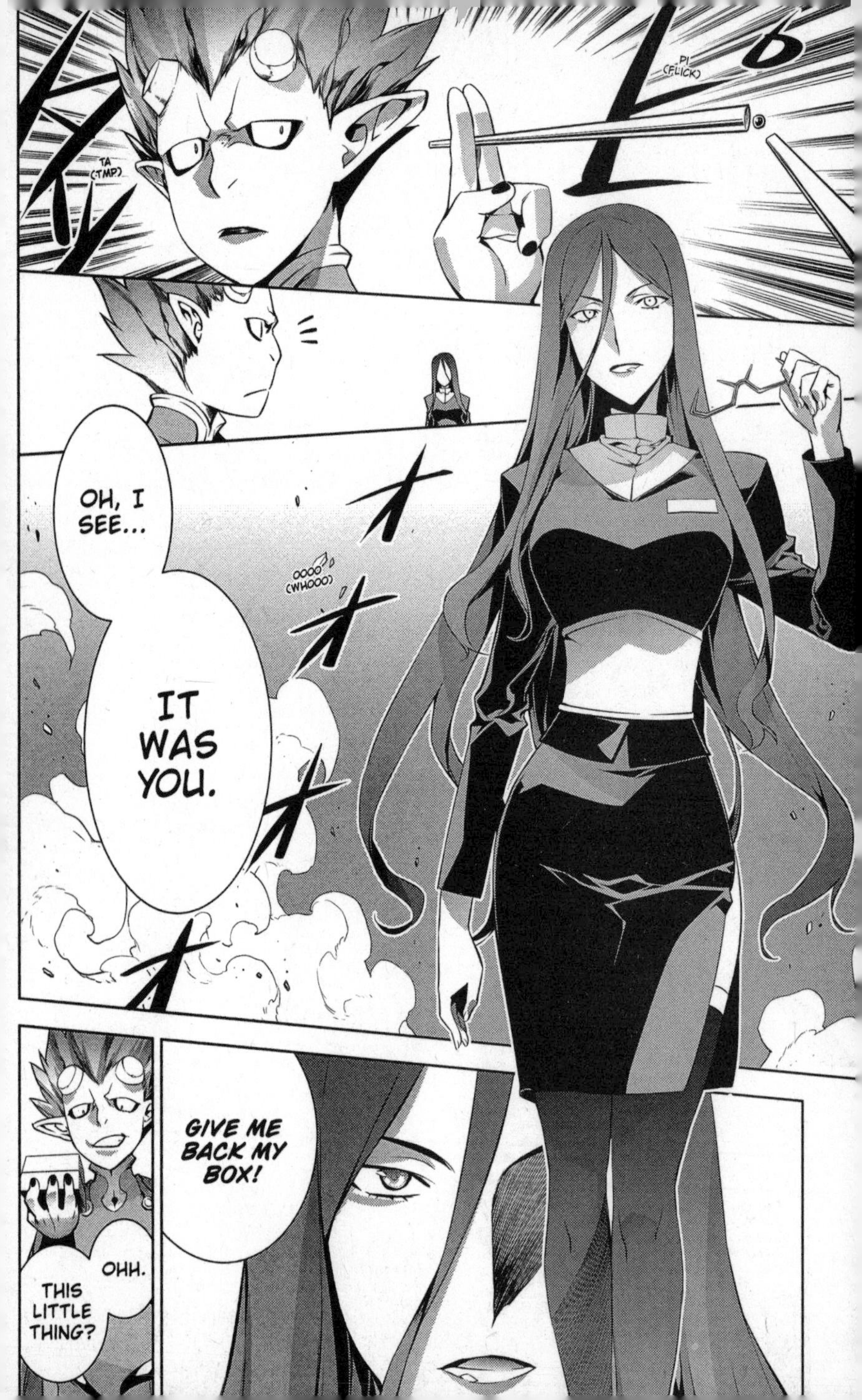
PI (FLICK)
TA (TMP)
OH, I SEE...
IT WAS YOU.
OOOO (WHOOO)
GIVE ME BACK MY BOX!
OHH.
THIS LITTLE THING?

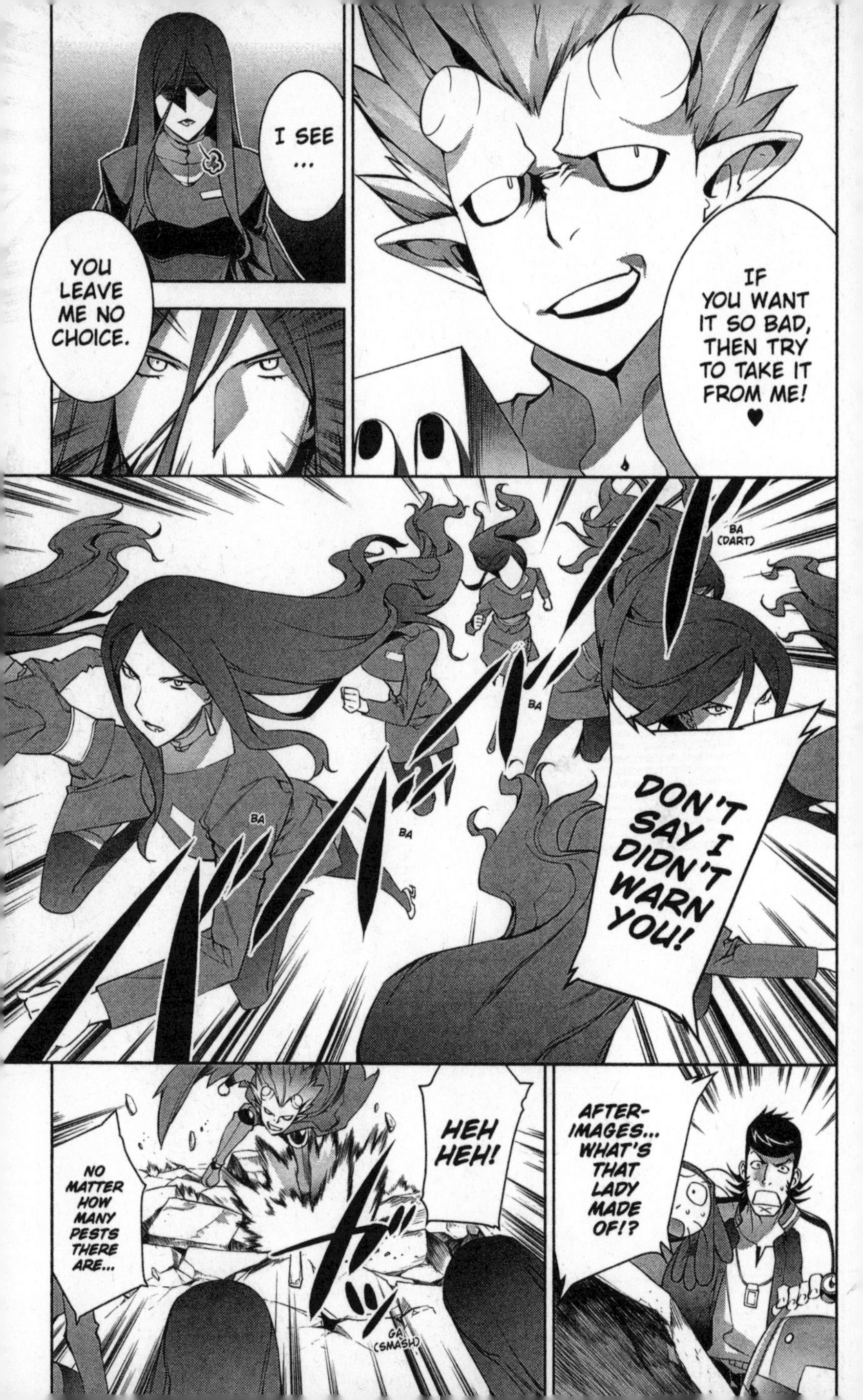
IF YOU WANT IT SO BAD, THEN TRY TO TAKE IT FROM ME! ♥
I SEE ...
YOU LEAVE ME NO CHOICE.
BA (DART)
DON'T SAY I DIDN'T WARN YOU!
BA
BA
BA
AFTER-IMAGES... WHAT'S THAT LADY MADE OF!?
HEH HEH!
NO MATTER HOW MANY PESTS THERE ARE...
GA (SMASH)

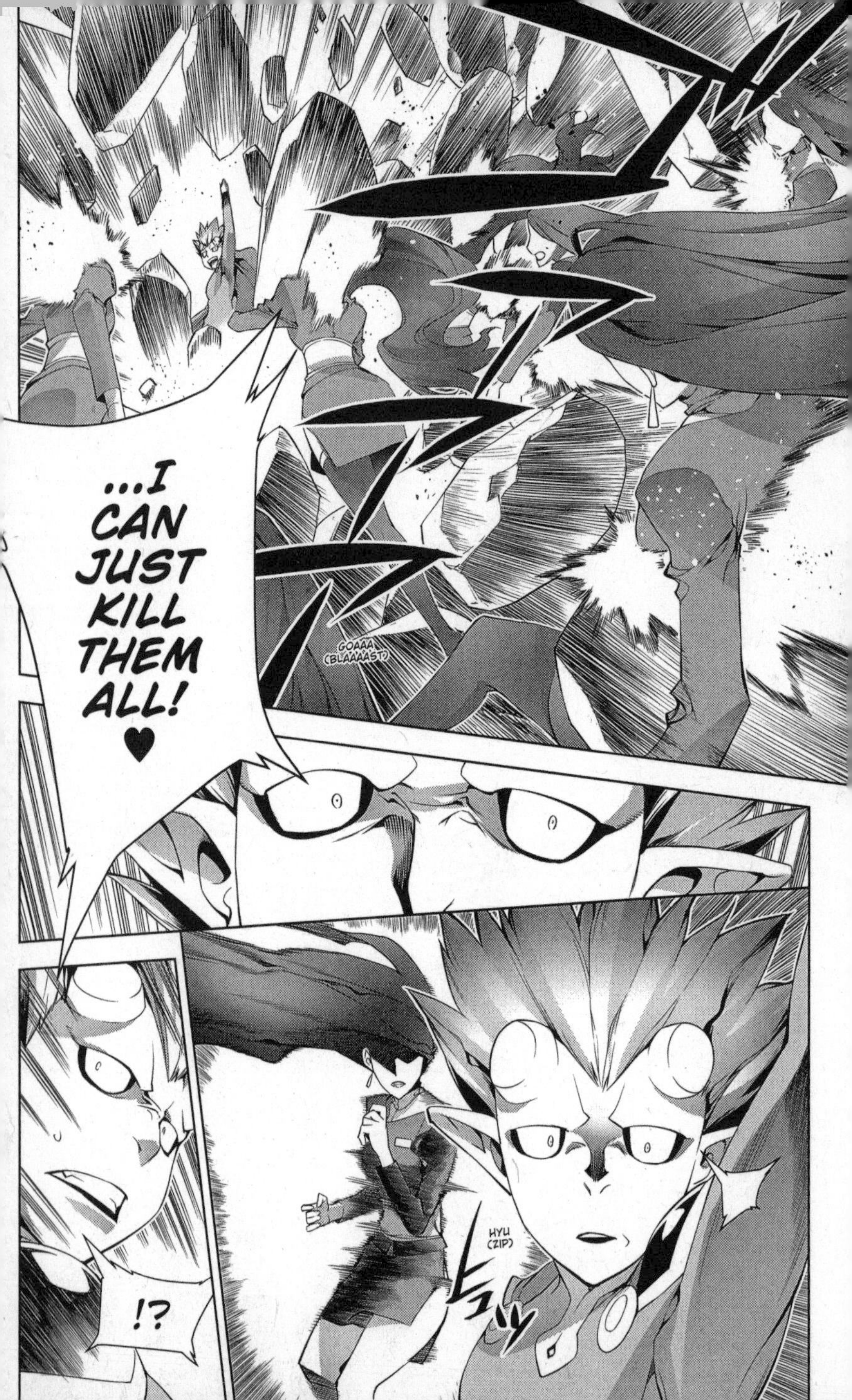
GOAAA (BLAAAAST)
...I CAN JUST KILL THEM ALL! ♥
HYU (ZIP)
!?

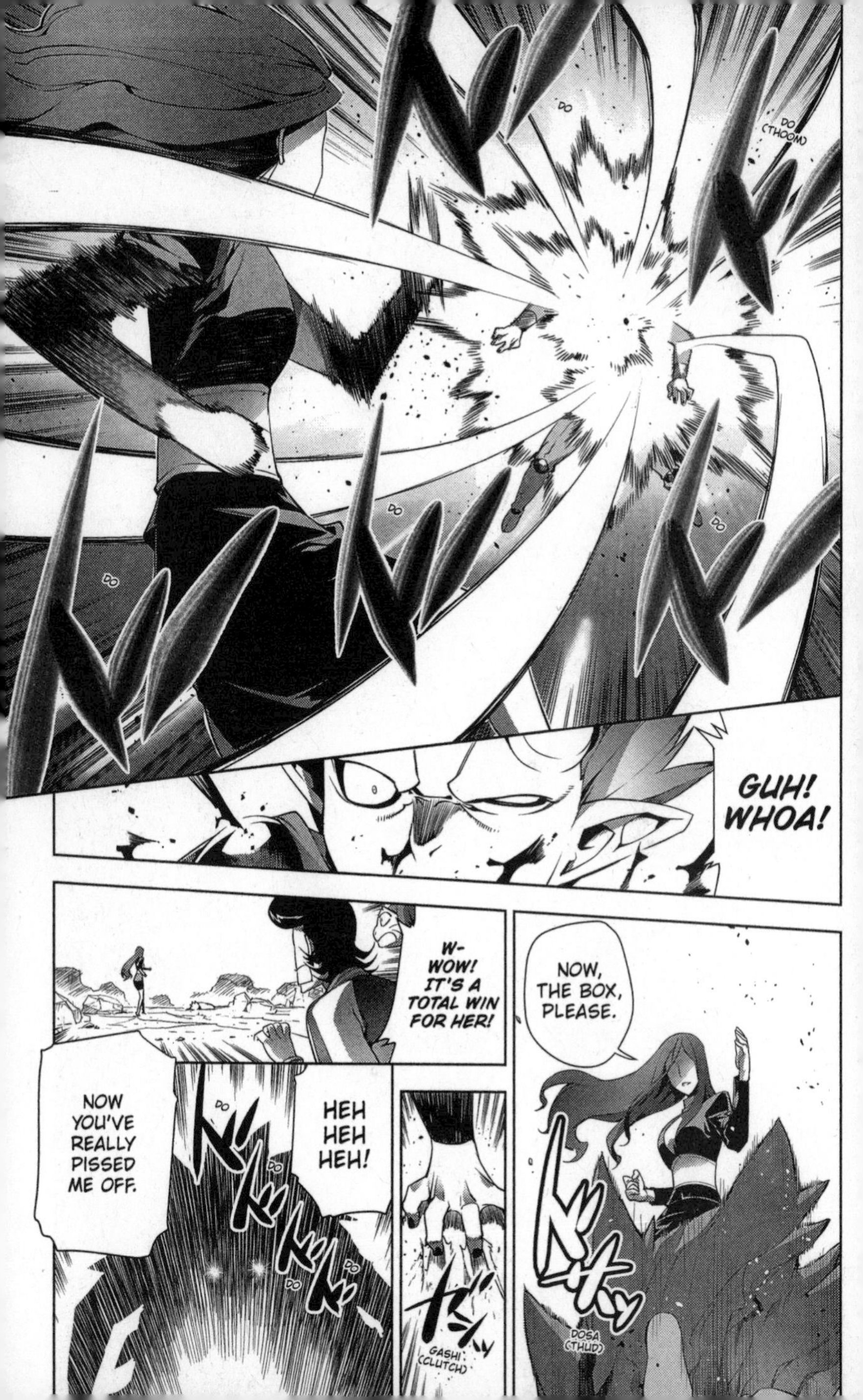
DO
DO (THOOM)
DO
DO
DO
GUH! WHOA!
NOW, THE BOX, PLEASE.
DOSA (THUD)
W-WOW! IT'S A TOTAL WIN FOR HER!
HEH HEH HEH!
GASHI (CLUTCH)
NOW YOU'VE REALLY PISSED ME OFF.
DO
DO
DO
DO

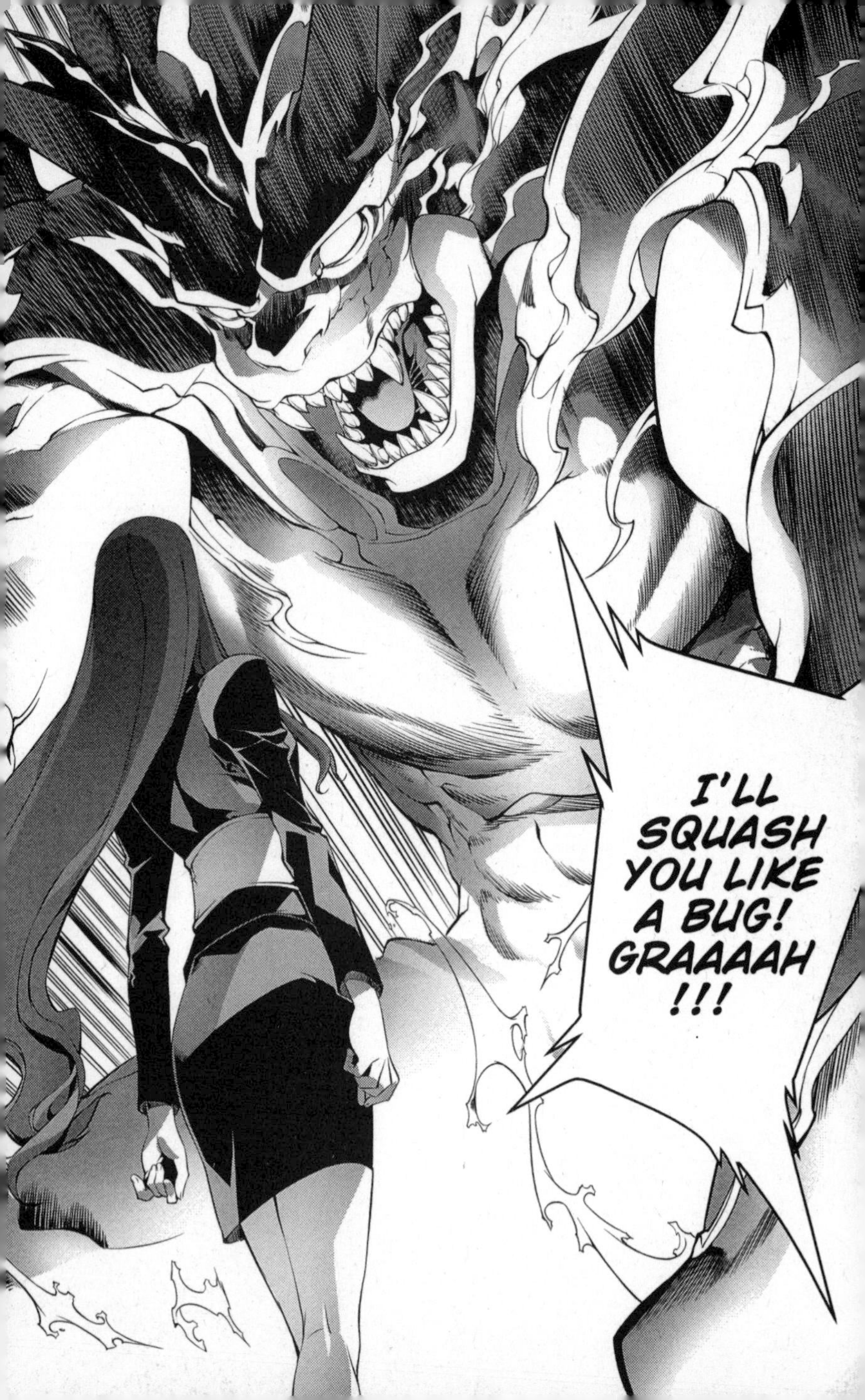
I'LL SQUASH YOU LIKE A BUG! GRAAAAH !!!

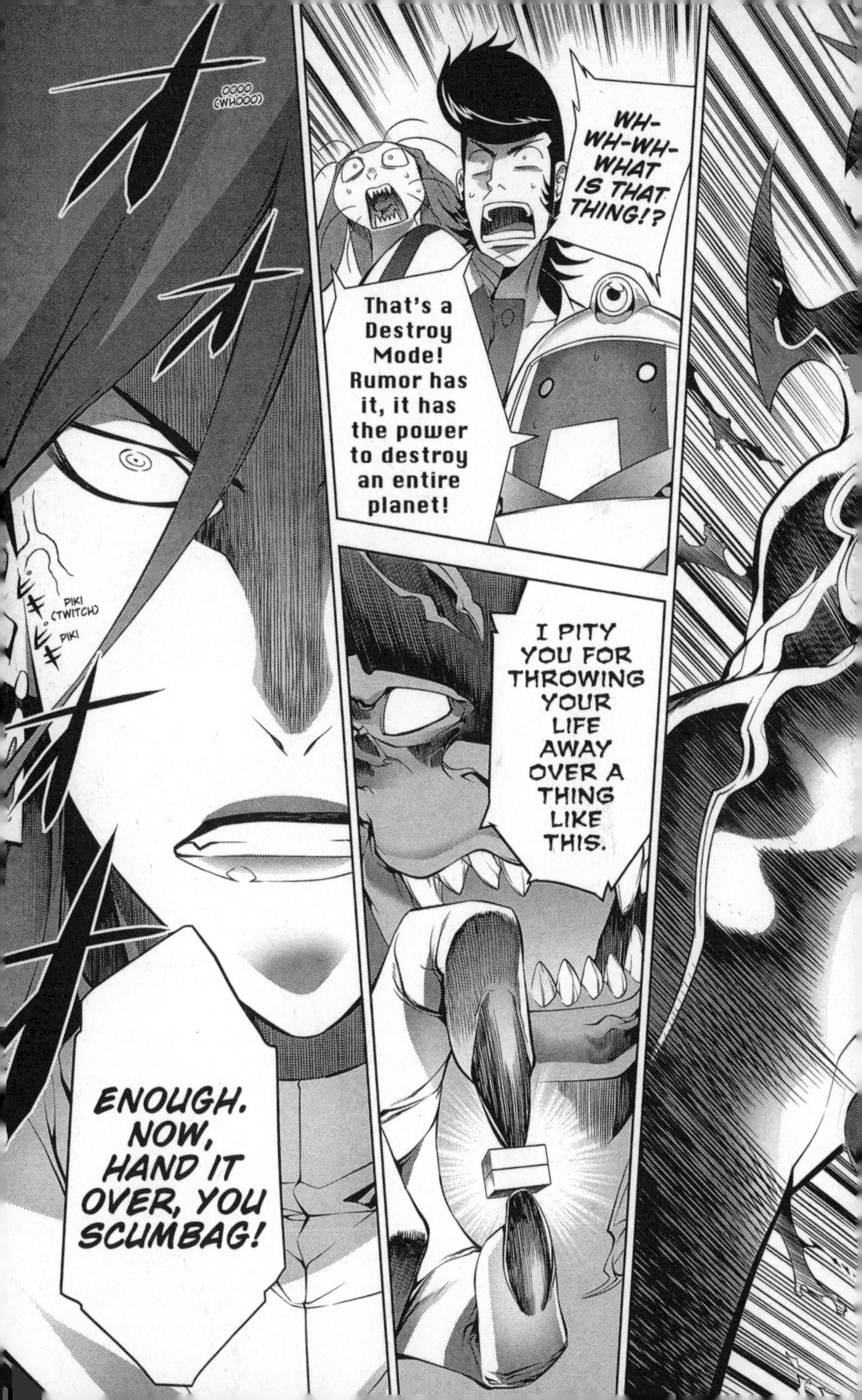
WH-WH-WH-WHAT IS THAT THING!?
That's a Destroy Mode! Rumor has it, it has the power to destroy an entire planet!
I PITY YOU FOR THROWING YOUR LIFE AWAY OVER A THING LIKE THIS.
OOOO (WHOOO)
PIKI (TWITCH) PIKI
ENOUGH. NOW, HAND IT OVER, YOU SCUMBAG!

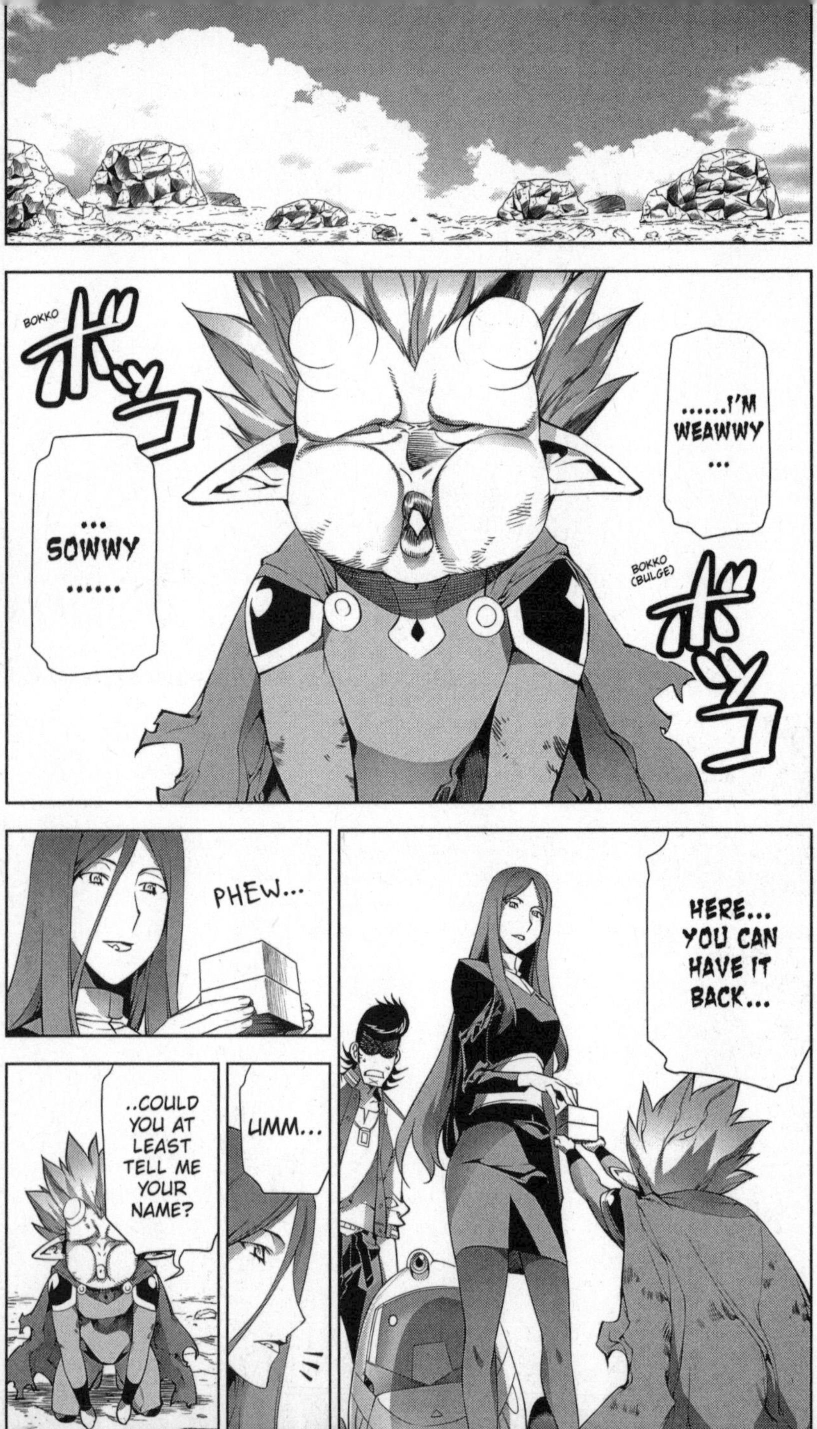
BOKKO (BULGE)
ボッコ
......I'M WEAWWY ...
BOKKO
ボッコ
... SOWWY ......
HERE... YOU CAN HAVE IT BACK...
PHEW...
UMM...
..COULD YOU AT LEAST TELL ME YOUR NAME?

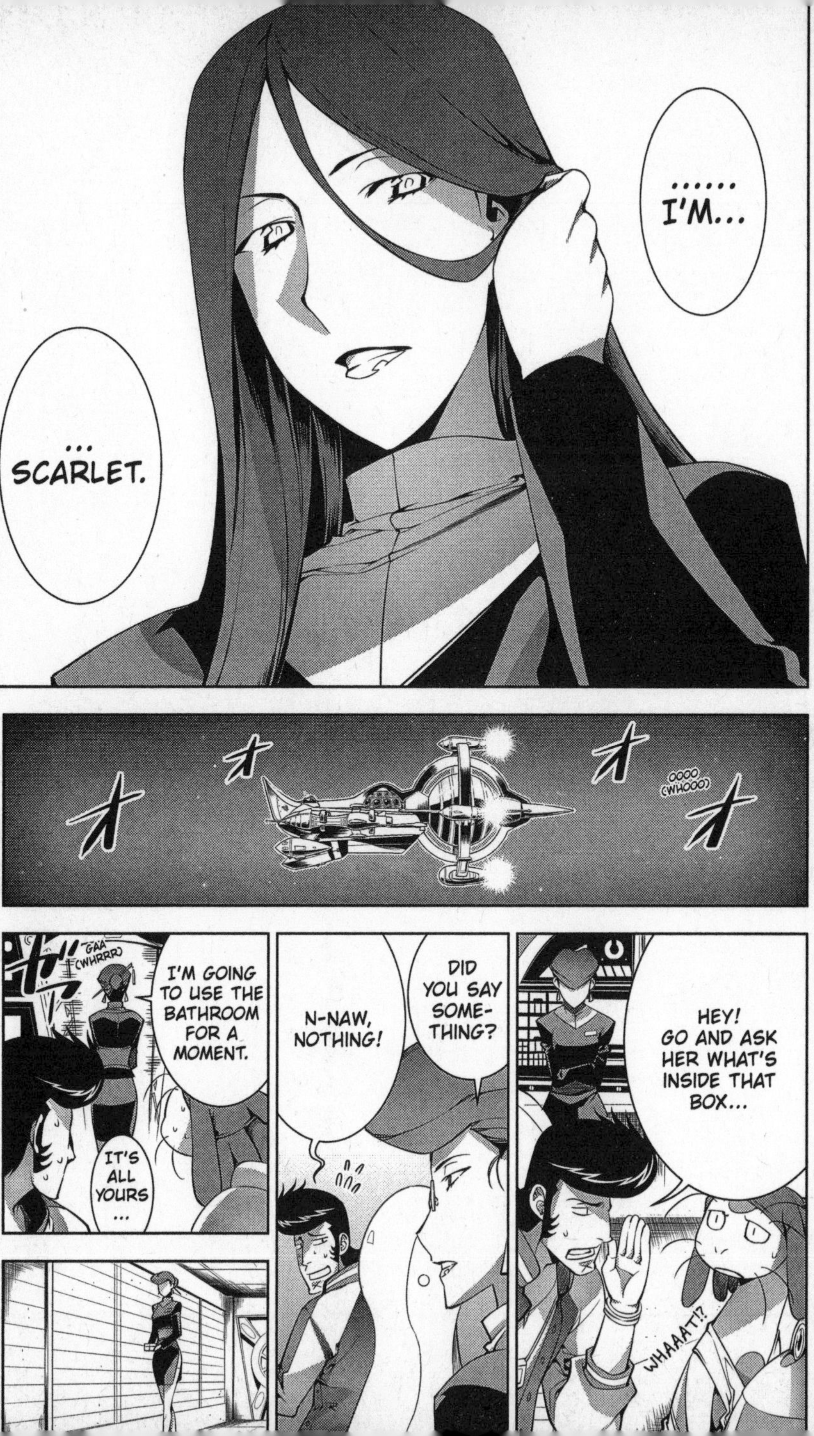
......
I'M...
...
SCARLET.
OOOO
(WHOOO)
HEY! GO AND ASK HER WHAT'S INSIDE THAT BOX...
WHAAAT!?
DID YOU SAY SOME-THING?
N-NAW, NOTHING!
GAA
(WHRRR)
I'M GOING TO USE THE BATHROOM FOR A MOMENT.
IT'S ALL YOURS ...

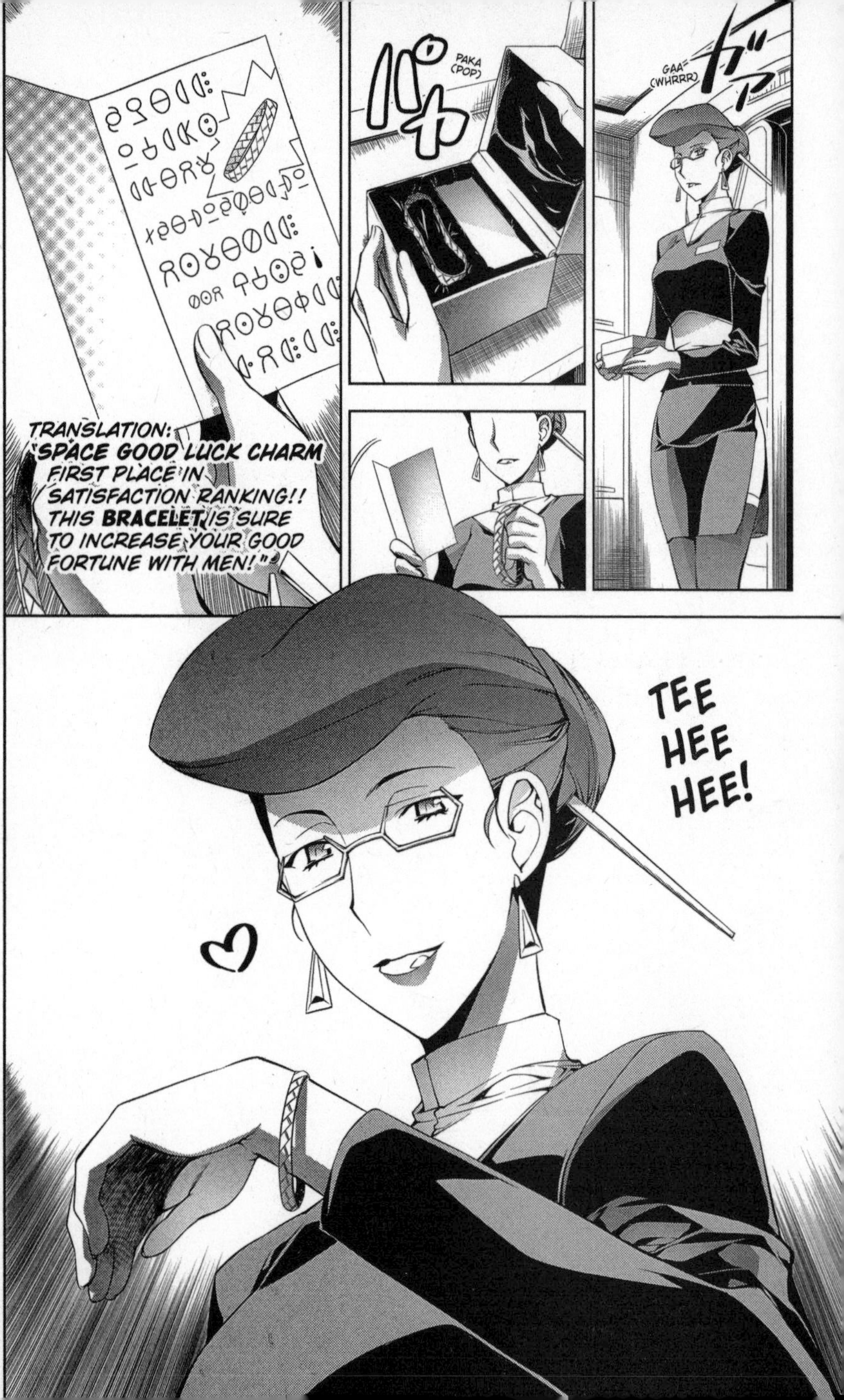
GAA (WHRRR)
PAKA (POP)
TRANSLATION: "SPACE GOOD LUCK CHARM FIRST PLACE IN SATISFACTION RANKING!! THIS BRACELET IS SURE TO INCREASE YOUR GOOD FORTUNE WITH MEN!"
TEE HEE HEE!

SPACE★DANDY

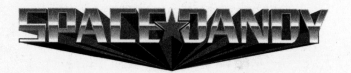

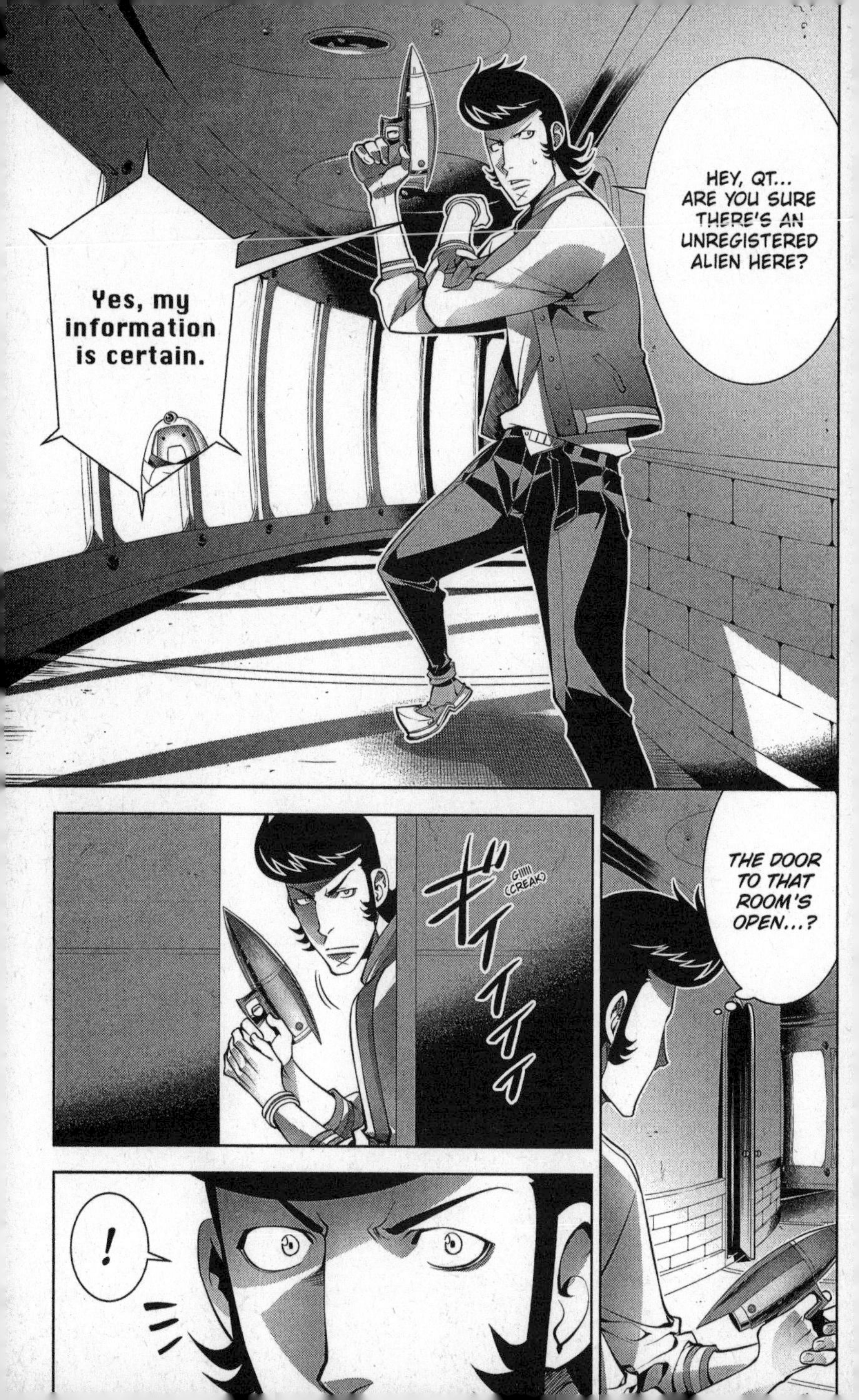
HEY, QT... ARE YOU SURE THERE'S AN UNREGISTERED ALIEN HERE?
Yes, my information is certain.
THE DOOR TO THAT ROOM'S OPEN...?
GIIIII (CREAK)
!

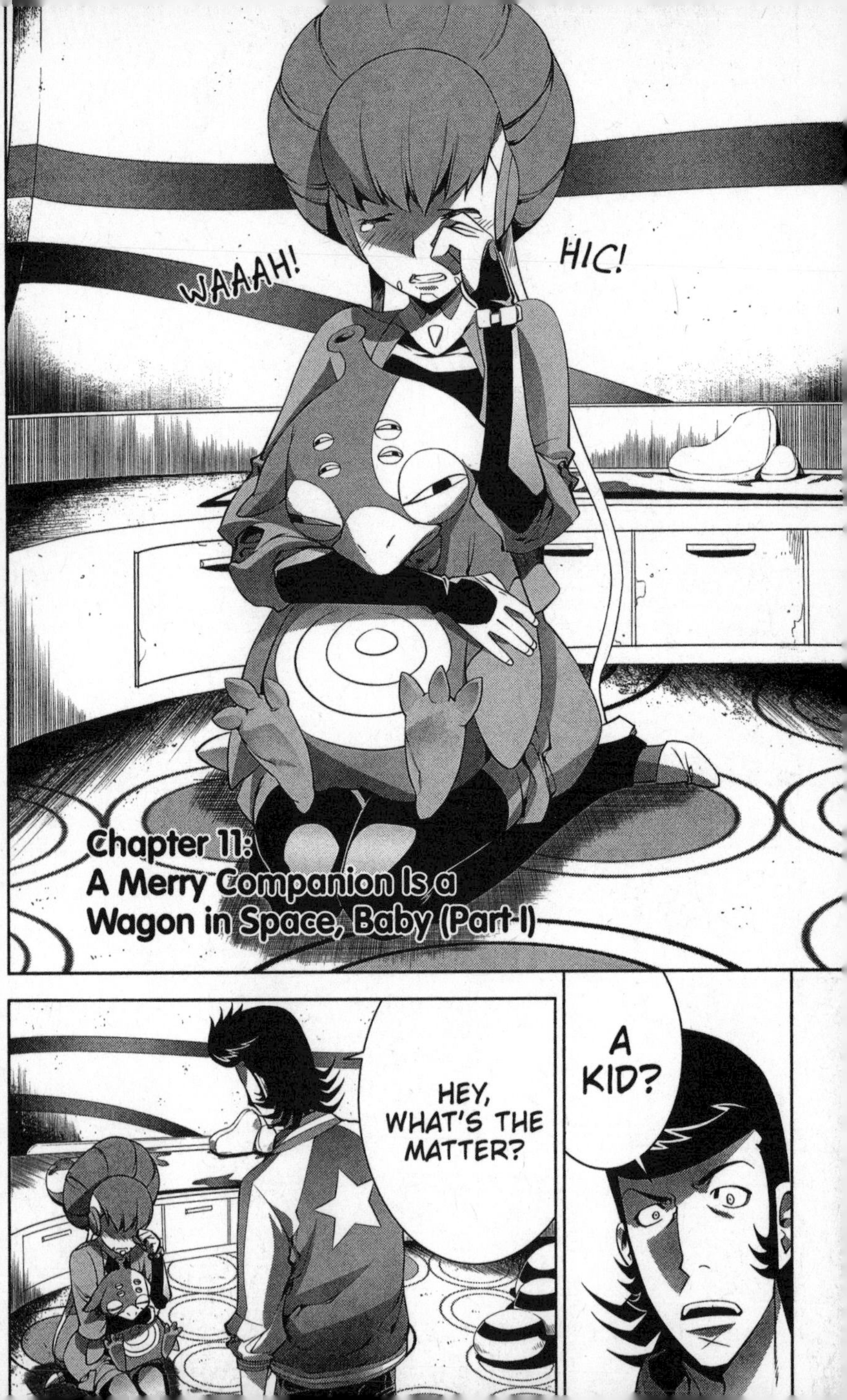
HIC!
WAAAH!
Chapter 11:
A Merry Companion Is a Wagon in Space, Baby (Part I)
A KID?
HEY, WHAT'S THE MATTER?

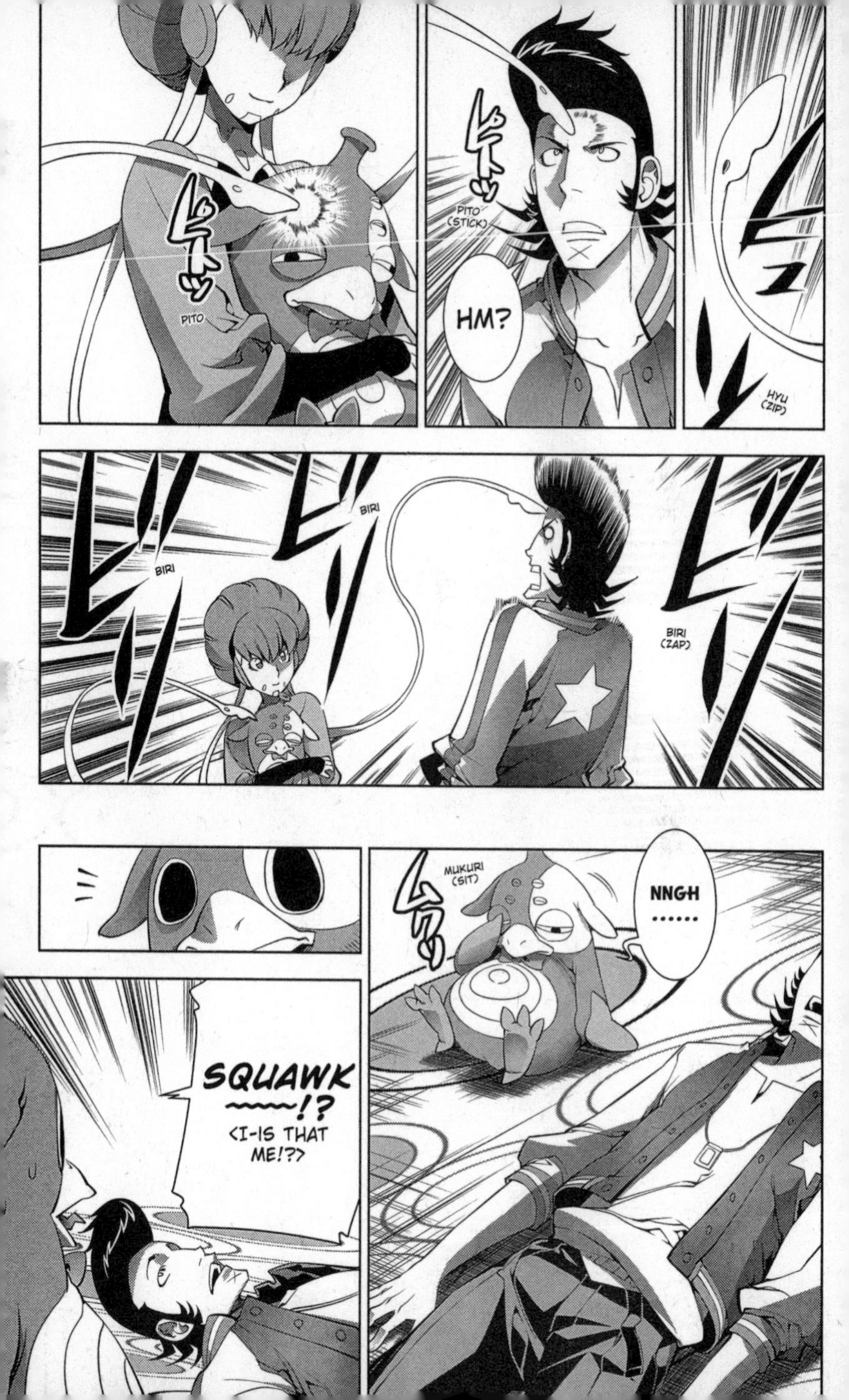
HYU (ZIP)
PITO (STICK)
HM?
PITO
BIRI (ZAP)
BIRI
BIRI
MUKURI (SIT)
NNGH ......
SQUAWK ~~~!?
<I-IS THAT ME!?>

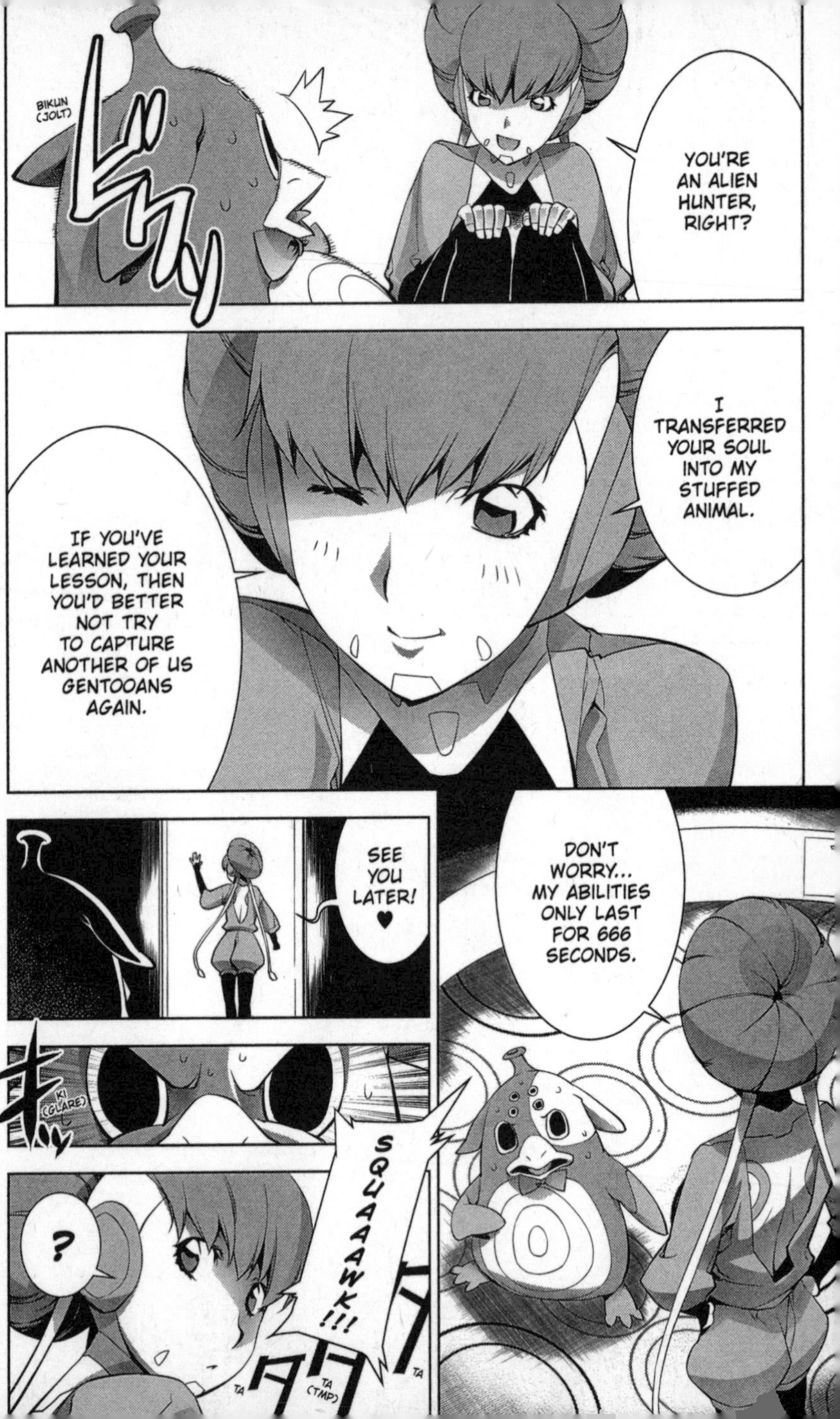
YOU'RE AN ALIEN HUNTER, RIGHT?
BIKUN (JOLT)
I TRANSFERRED YOUR SOUL INTO MY STUFFED ANIMAL.
IF YOU'VE LEARNED YOUR LESSON, THEN YOU'D BETTER NOT TRY TO CAPTURE ANOTHER OF US GENTOOANS AGAIN.
DON'T WORRY... MY ABILITIES ONLY LAST FOR 666 SECONDS.
SQUAAAAWK!!!
TA
TA (TMP)
TA
SEE YOU LATER! ♥
KI (GLARE)
?

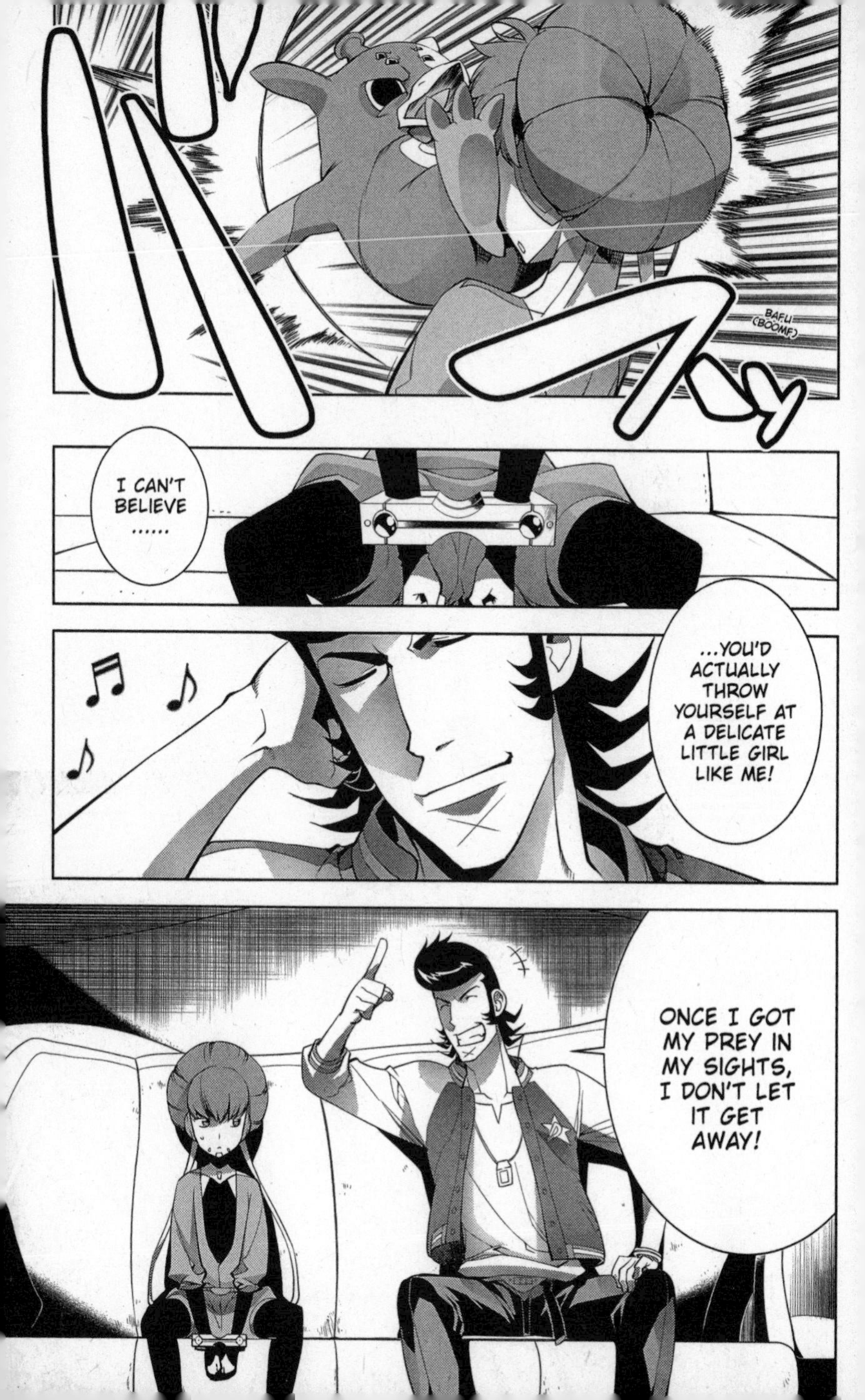
BAFU (BOOMF)
I CAN'T BELIEVE ......
...YOU'D ACTUALLY THROW YOURSELF AT A DELICATE LITTLE GIRL LIKE ME!
ONCE I GOT MY PREY IN MY SIGHTS, I DON'T LET IT GET AWAY!

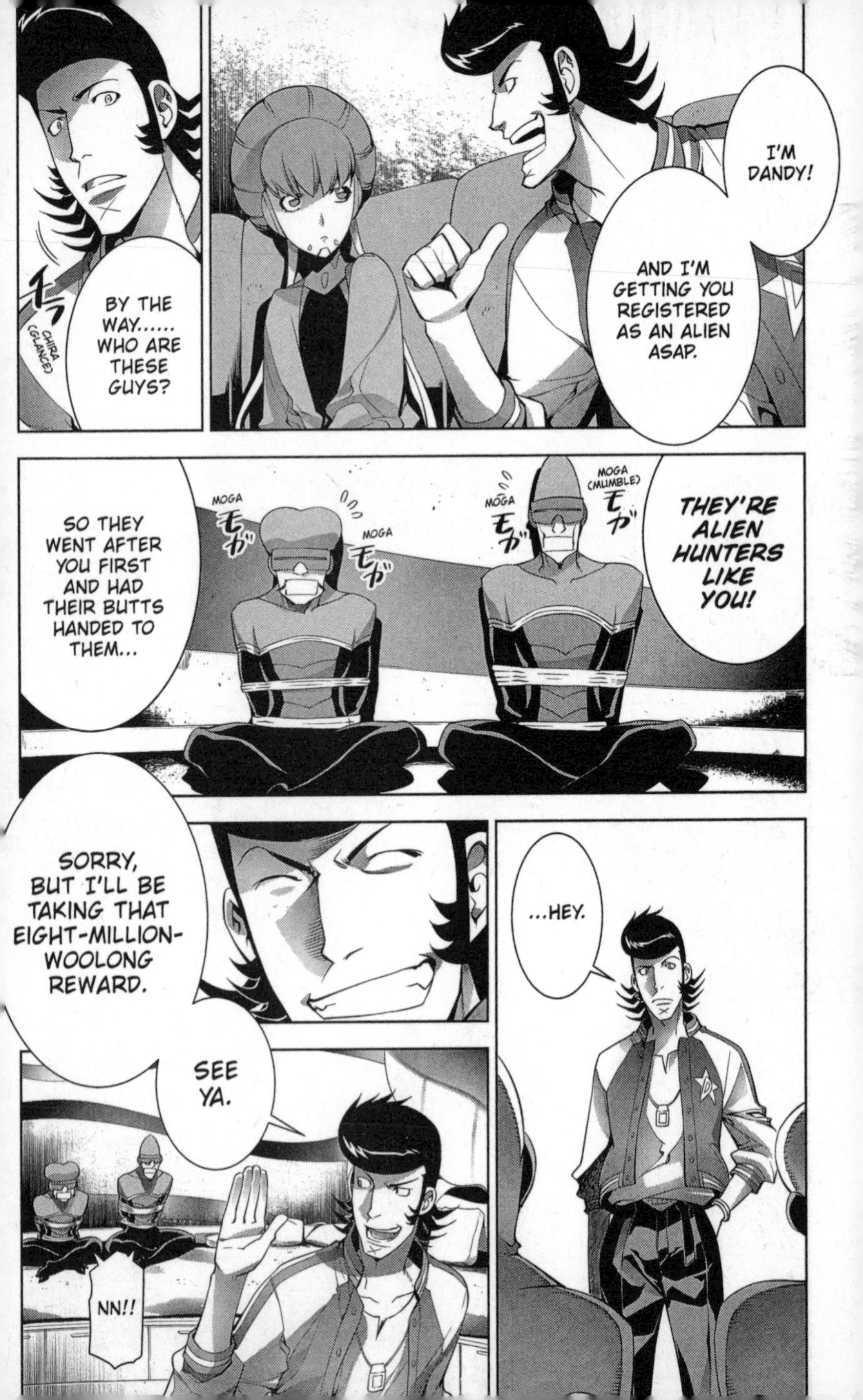
I'M DANDY!
AND I'M GETTING YOU REGISTERED AS AN ALIEN ASAP.
CHIRA (GLANCE)
BY THE WAY...... WHO ARE THESE GUYS?
THEY'RE ALIEN HUNTERS LIKE YOU!
MOGA (MUMBLE)
MOGA
MOGA
MOGA
SO THEY WENT AFTER YOU FIRST AND HAD THEIR BUTTS HANDED TO THEM...
...HEY.
SORRY, BUT I'LL BE TAKING THAT EIGHT-MILLION-WOOLONG REWARD.
SEE YA.
NN!!

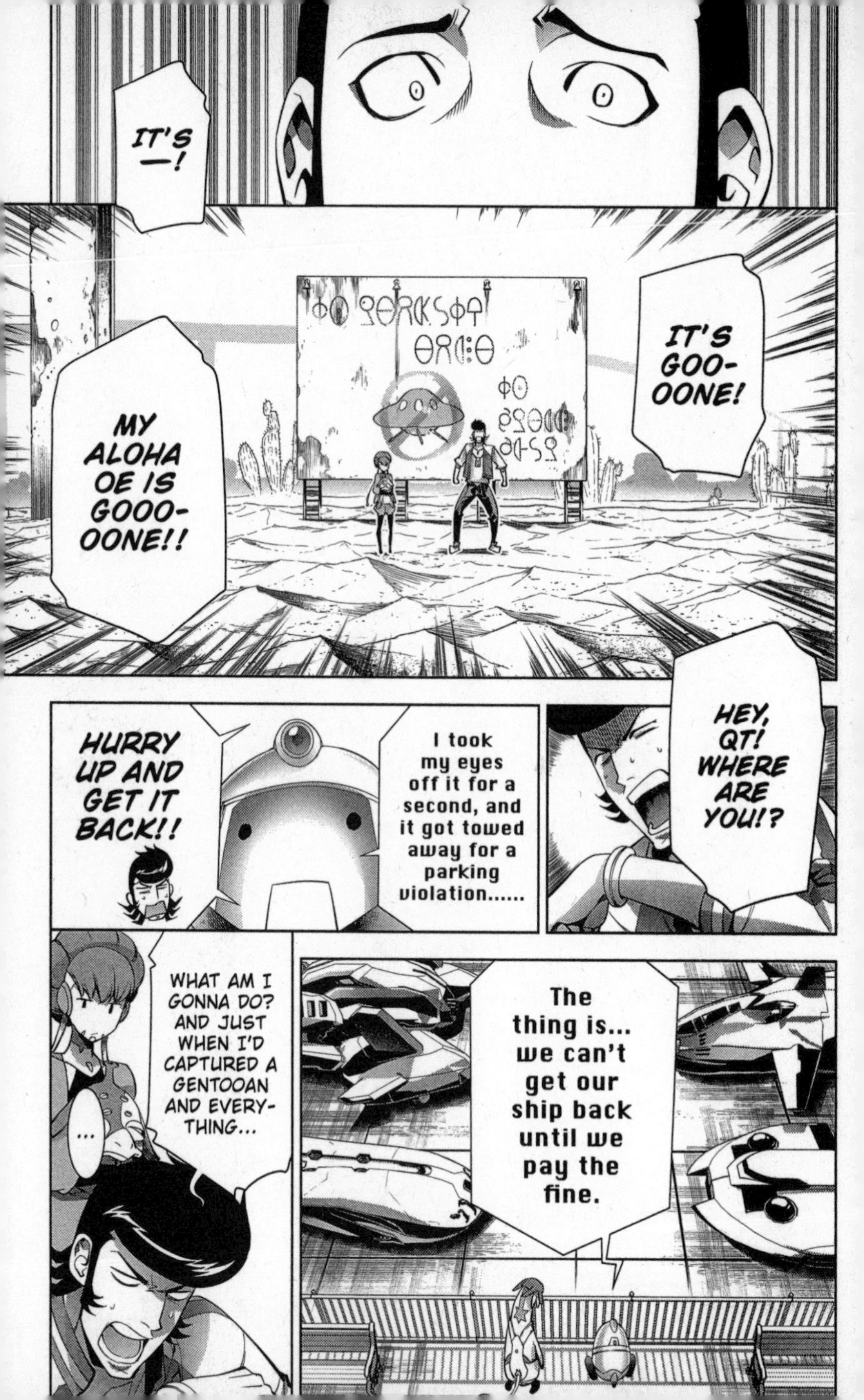
IT'S —!
IT'S GOOO-OONE!
MY ALOHA OE IS GOOOO-OONE!!
HEY, QT! WHERE ARE YOU!?
I took my eyes off it for a second, and it got towed away for a parking violation......
HURRY UP AND GET IT BACK!!
The thing is... we can't get our ship back until we pay the fine.
WHAT AM I GONNA DO? AND JUST WHEN I'D CAPTURED A GENTOOAN AND EVERYTHING...
...

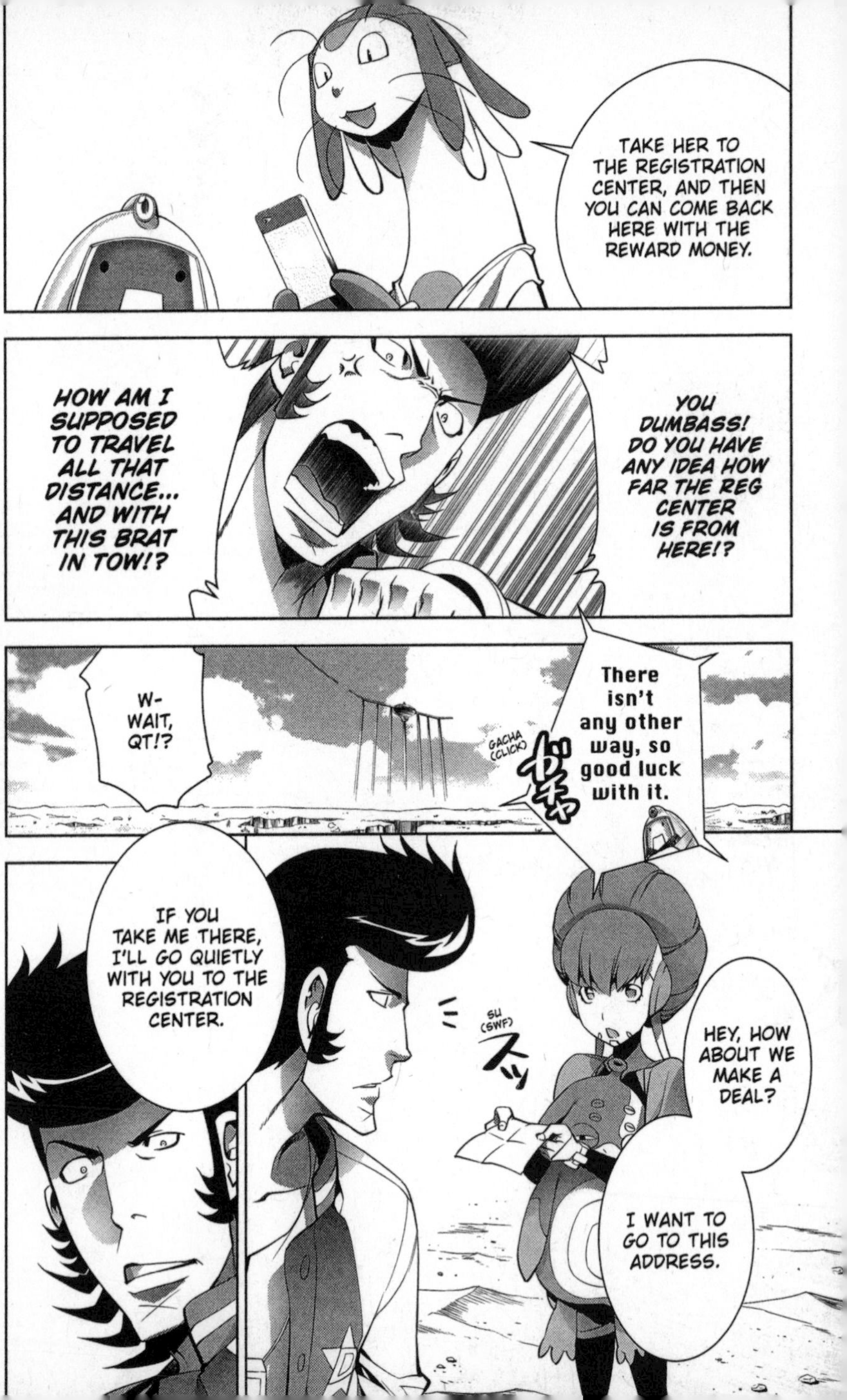
TAKE HER TO THE REGISTRATION CENTER, AND THEN YOU CAN COME BACK HERE WITH THE REWARD MONEY.
YOU DUMBASS! DO YOU HAVE ANY IDEA HOW FAR THE REG CENTER IS FROM HERE!?
HOW AM I SUPPOSED TO TRAVEL ALL THAT DISTANCE... AND WITH THIS BRAT IN TOW!?
There isn't any other way, so good luck with it.
ガチャ
GACHA (CLICK)
W-WAIT, QT!?
HEY, HOW ABOUT WE MAKE A DEAL?
I WANT TO GO TO THIS ADDRESS.
スッ
SU (SWF)
IF YOU TAKE ME THERE, I'LL GO QUIETLY WITH YOU TO THE REGISTRATION CENTER.

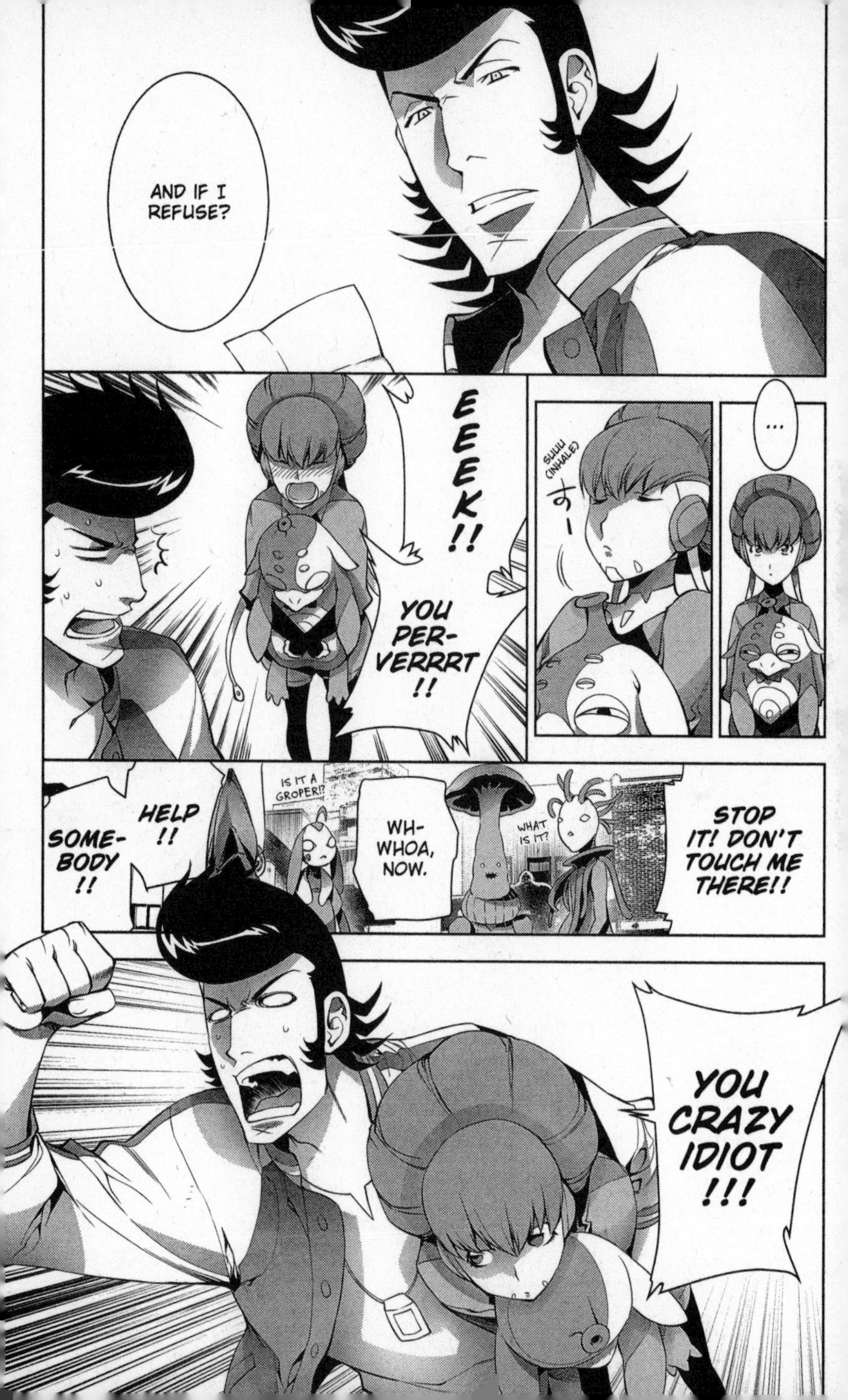
AND IF I REFUSE?
...
SUUU (INHALE)
すー
EEEK!!
YOU PER-VERRRT!!
STOP IT! DON'T TOUCH ME THERE!!
WHAT IS IT?
WH- WHOA, NOW.
IS IT A GROPER!?
HELP!!
SOME-BODY!!
YOU CRAZY IDIOT!!!

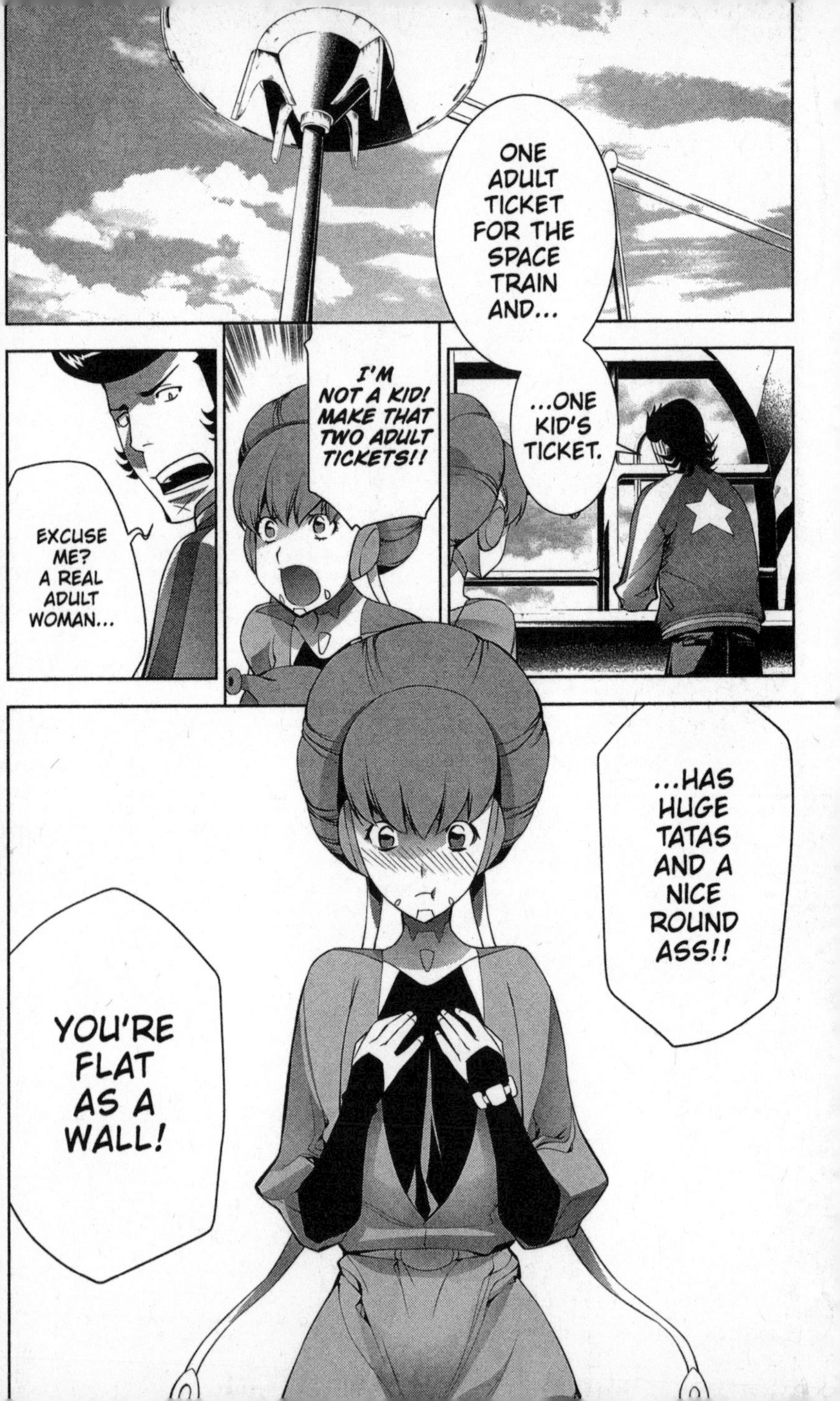
ONE ADULT TICKET FOR THE SPACE TRAIN AND...
...ONE KID'S TICKET.
I'M NOT A KID! MAKE THAT TWO ADULT TICKETS!!
EXCUSE ME? A REAL ADULT WOMAN...
...HAS HUGE TATAS AND A NICE ROUND ASS!!
YOU'RE FLAT AS A WALL!

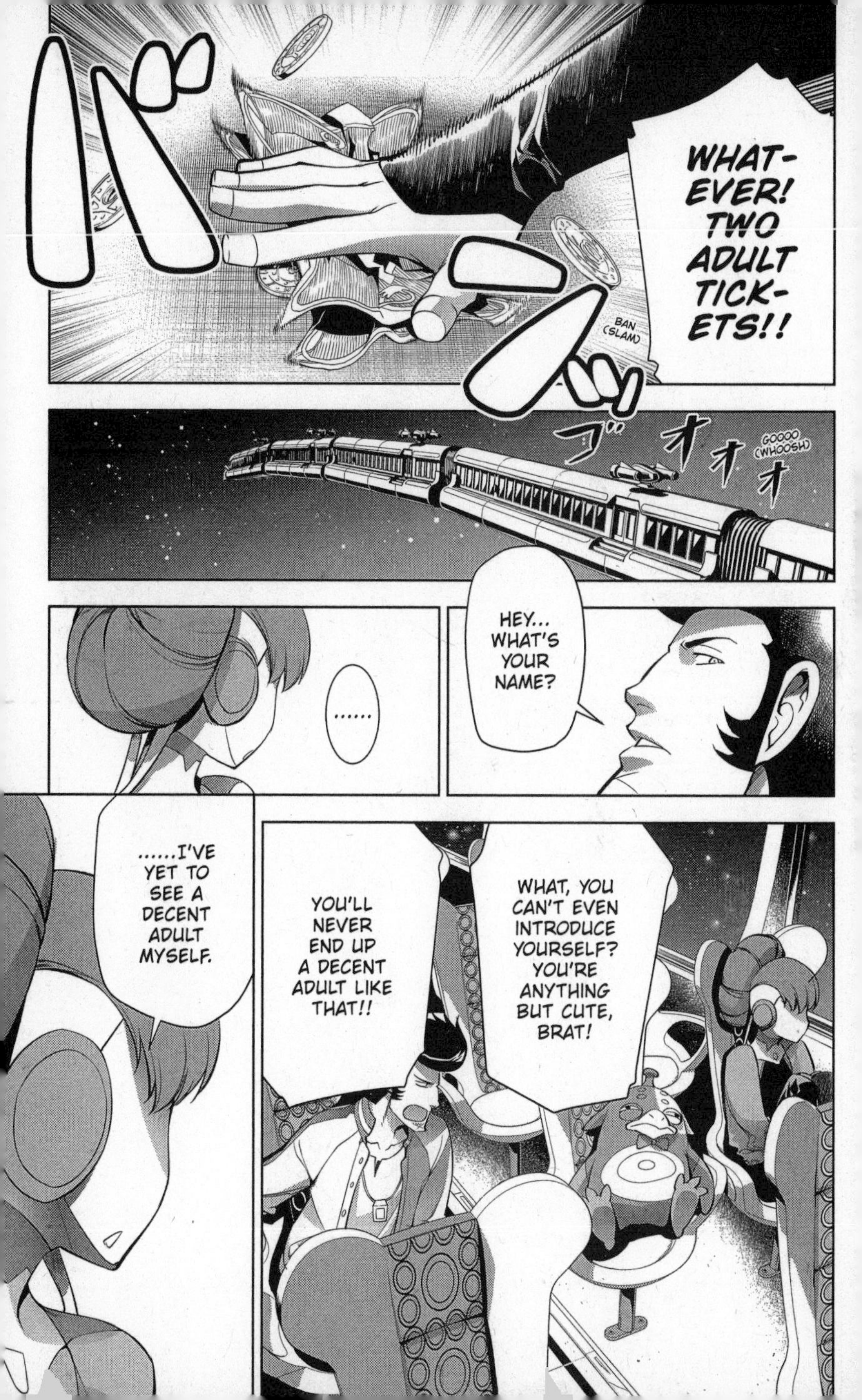
WHAT-EVER! TWO ADULT TICK-ETS!!
BAN (SLAM)
GOOOO (WHOOSH)
HEY... WHAT'S YOUR NAME?
......
WHAT, YOU CAN'T EVEN INTRODUCE YOURSELF? YOU'RE ANYTHING BUT CUTE, BRAT!
YOU'LL NEVER END UP A DECENT ADULT LIKE THAT!!
......I'VE YET TO SEE A DECENT ADULT MYSELF.

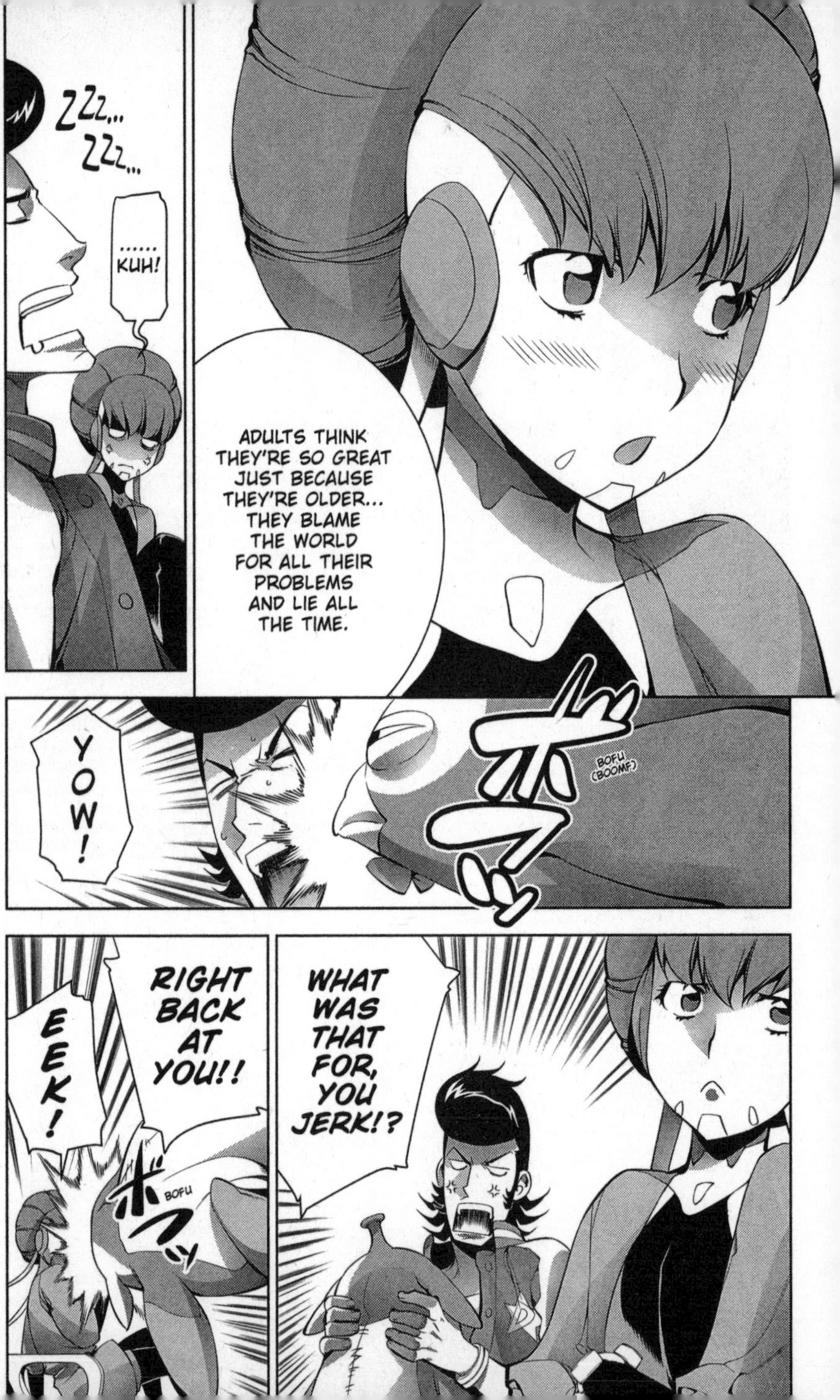
ADULTS THINK THEY'RE SO GREAT JUST BECAUSE THEY'RE OLDER... THEY BLAME THE WORLD FOR ALL THEIR PROBLEMS AND LIE ALL THE TIME.
ZZZ... ZZZ...
...... KUH!
BOFU (BOOMF)
YOW!
WHAT WAS THAT FOR, YOU JERK!?
RIGHT BACK AT YOU!!
EEK!
BOFU

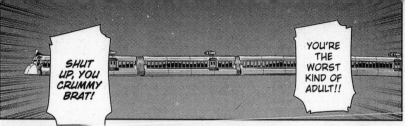

YOU'RE THE WORST KIND OF ADULT!!
SHUT UP, YOU CRUMMY BRAT!
BUSUUU (SULK)
...ADÉLIE.
THAT'S MY NAME.
DID YOU... LIVE IN THAT ROOM ALL BY YOURSELF?

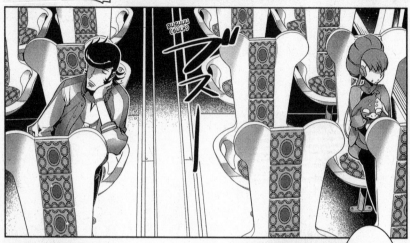

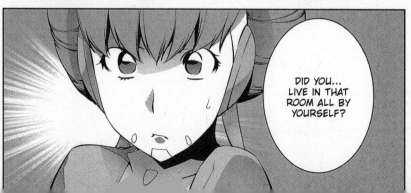

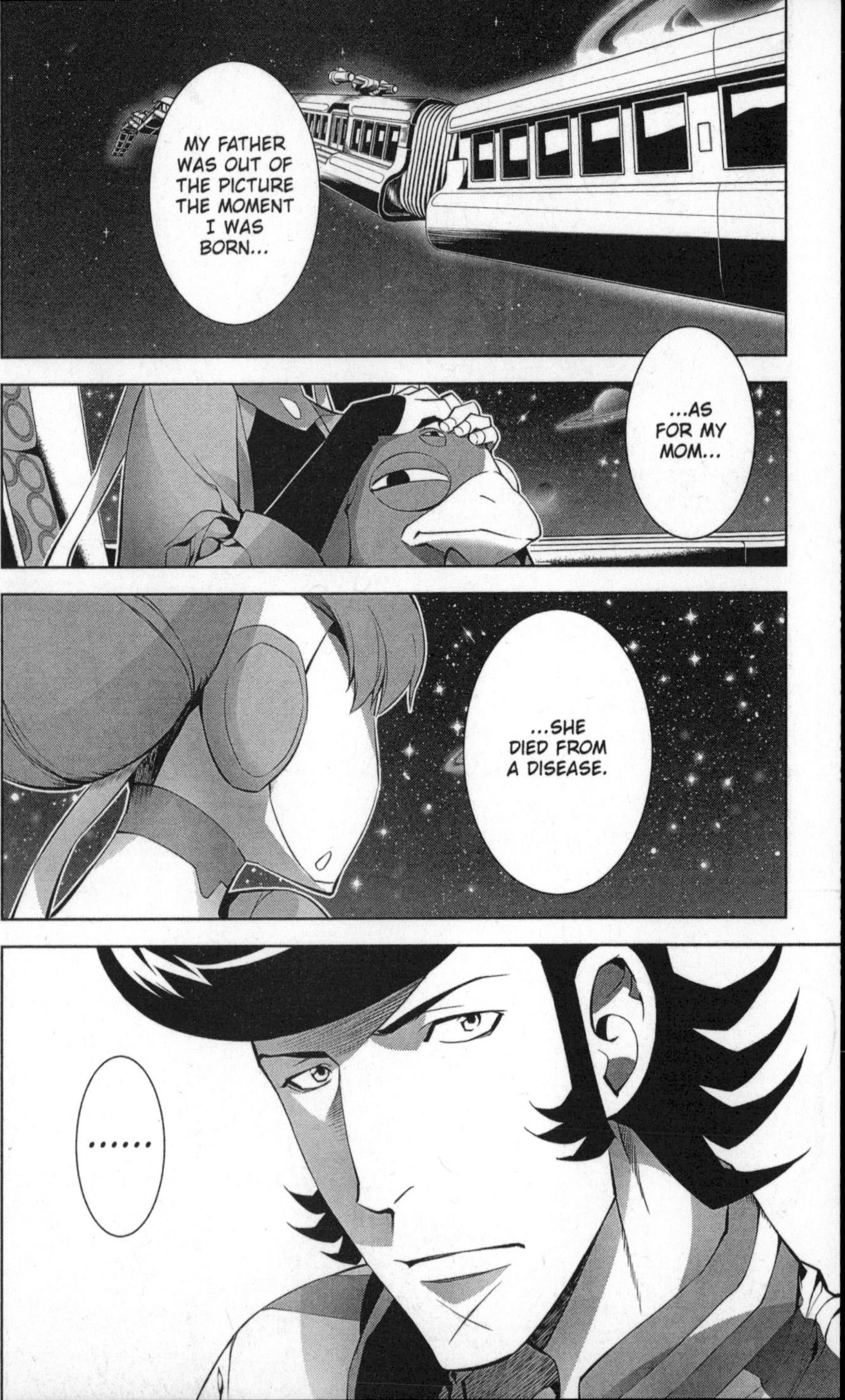
MY FATHER WAS OUT OF THE PICTURE THE MOMENT I WAS BORN...
...AS FOR MY MOM...
...SHE DIED FROM A DISEASE.
......

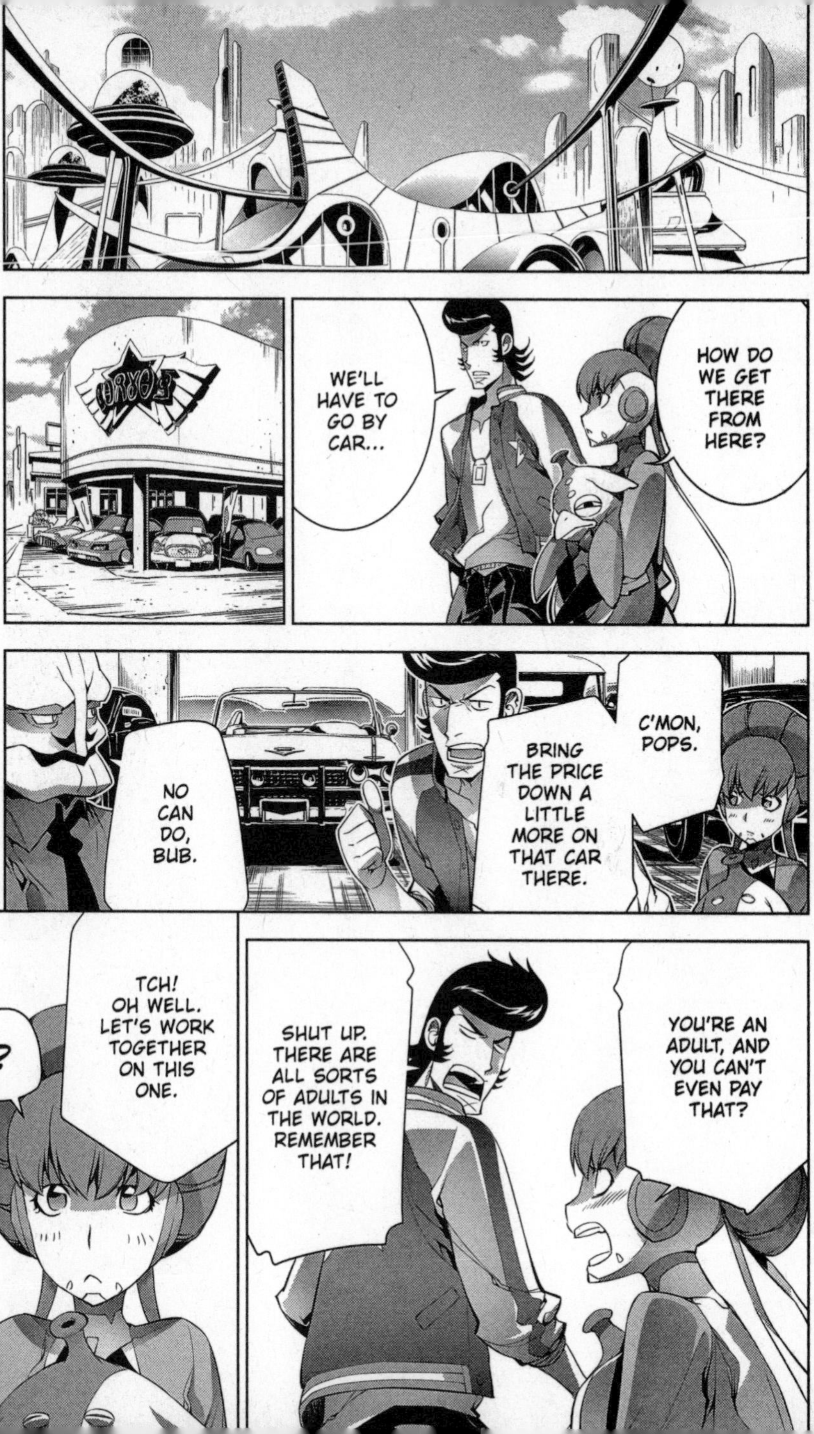
HOW DO WE GET THERE FROM HERE?
WE'LL HAVE TO GO BY CAR...
C'MON, POPS.
BRING THE PRICE DOWN A LITTLE MORE ON THAT CAR THERE.
NO CAN DO, BUB.
YOU'RE AN ADULT, AND YOU CAN'T EVEN PAY THAT?
SHUT UP. THERE ARE ALL SORTS OF ADULTS IN THE WORLD. REMEMBER THAT!
TCH! OH WELL. LET'S WORK TOGETHER ON THIS ONE.
?

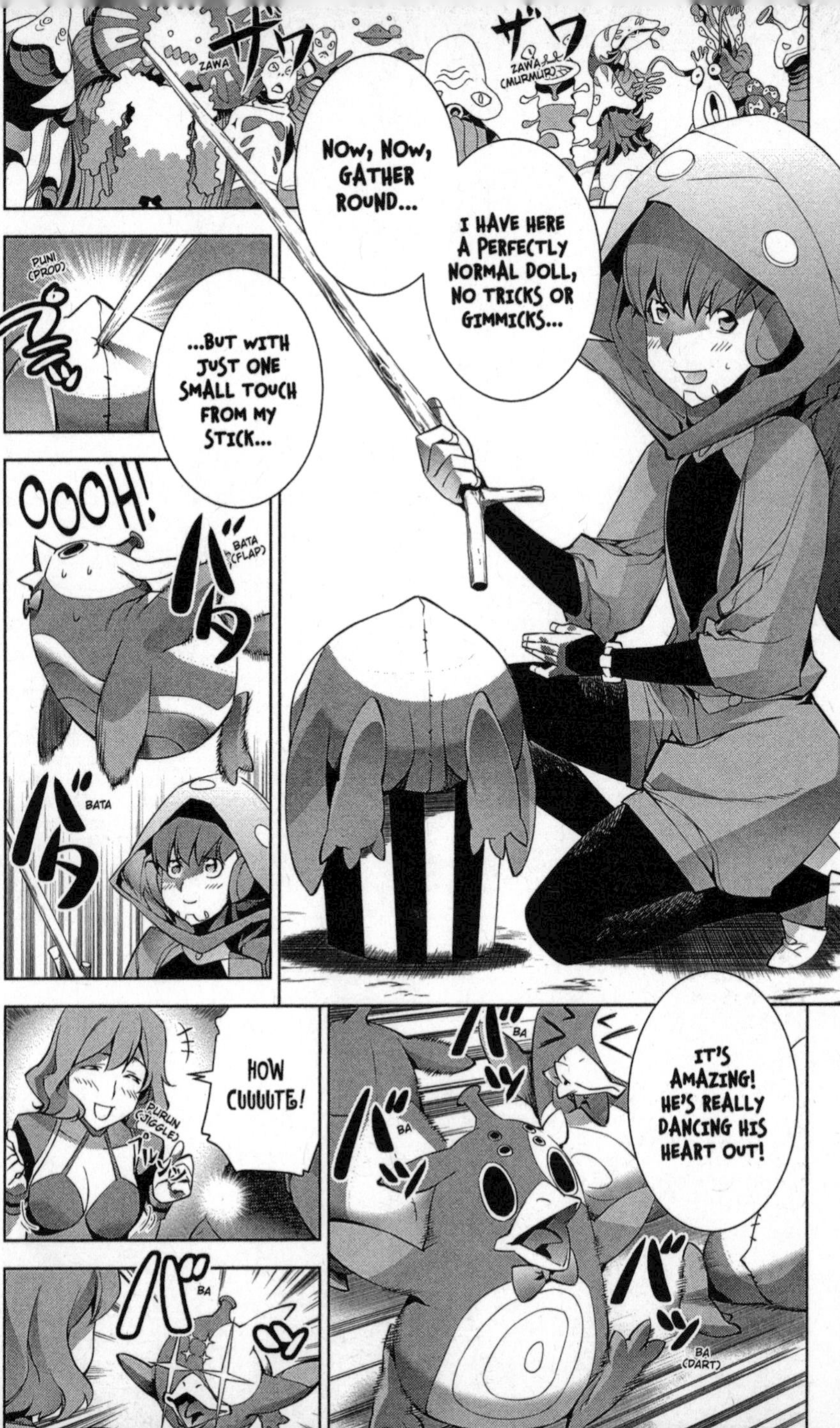
ZAWA (MURMUR)
ZAWA
NOW, NOW, GATHER ROUND...
I HAVE HERE A PERFECTLY NORMAL DOLL, NO TRICKS OR GIMMICKS...
...BUT WITH JUST ONE SMALL TOUCH FROM MY STICK...
PUNI (PROD)
OOOH!
BATA (FLAP)
BATA
IT'S AMAZING! HE'S REALLY DANCING HIS HEART OUT!
BA
BA
BA (DART)
HOW CUUUUTE!
PURUN (JIGGLE)
BA

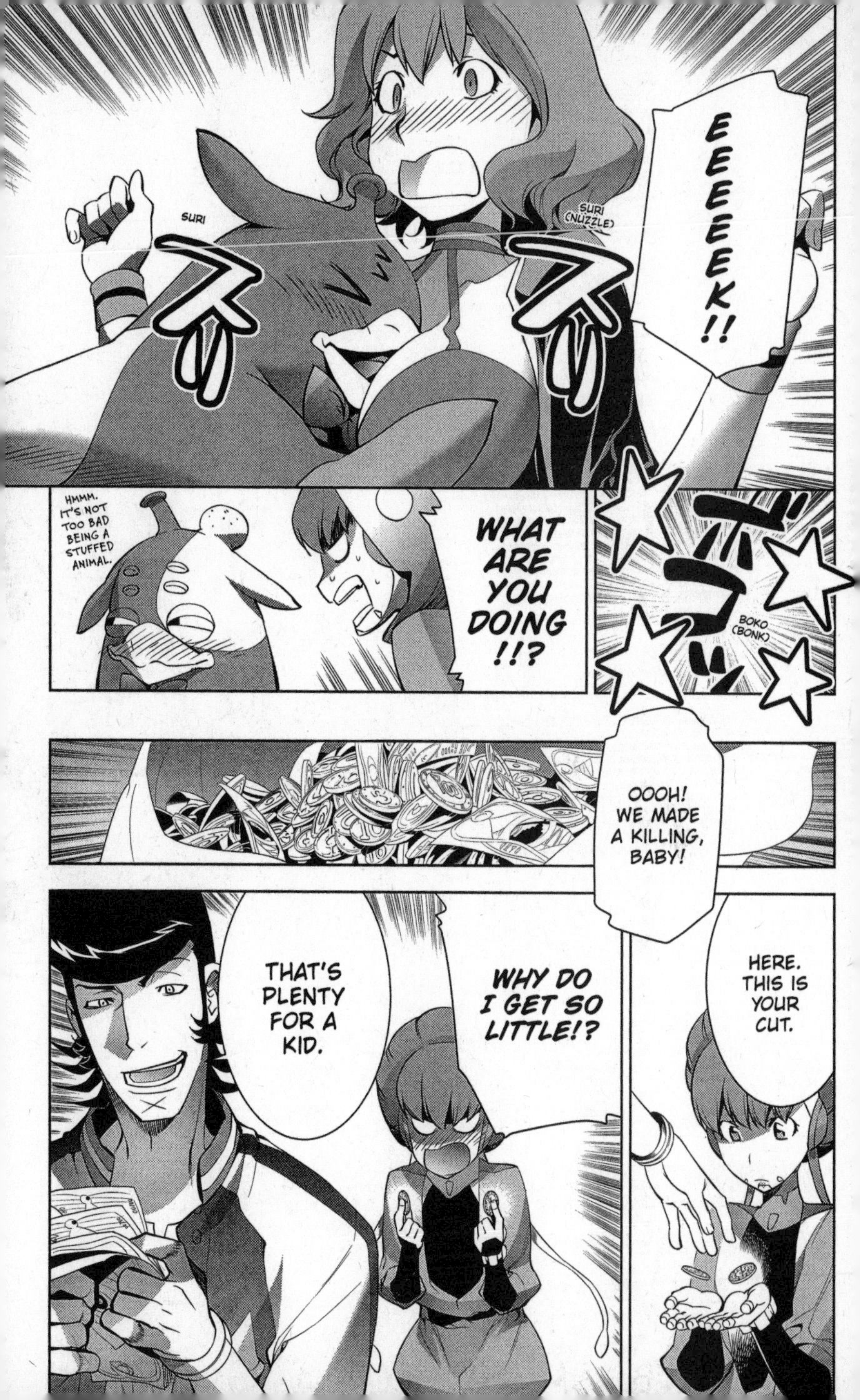
EEEEEEK!!
SURI (NUZZLE)
SURI
BOKO (BONK)
WHAT ARE YOU DOING!!?
HMMM. IT'S NOT TOO BAD BEING A STUFFED ANIMAL.
OOOH! WE MADE A KILLING, BABY!
HERE. THIS IS YOUR CUT.
WHY DO I GET SO LITTLE!?
THAT'S PLENTY FOR A KID.

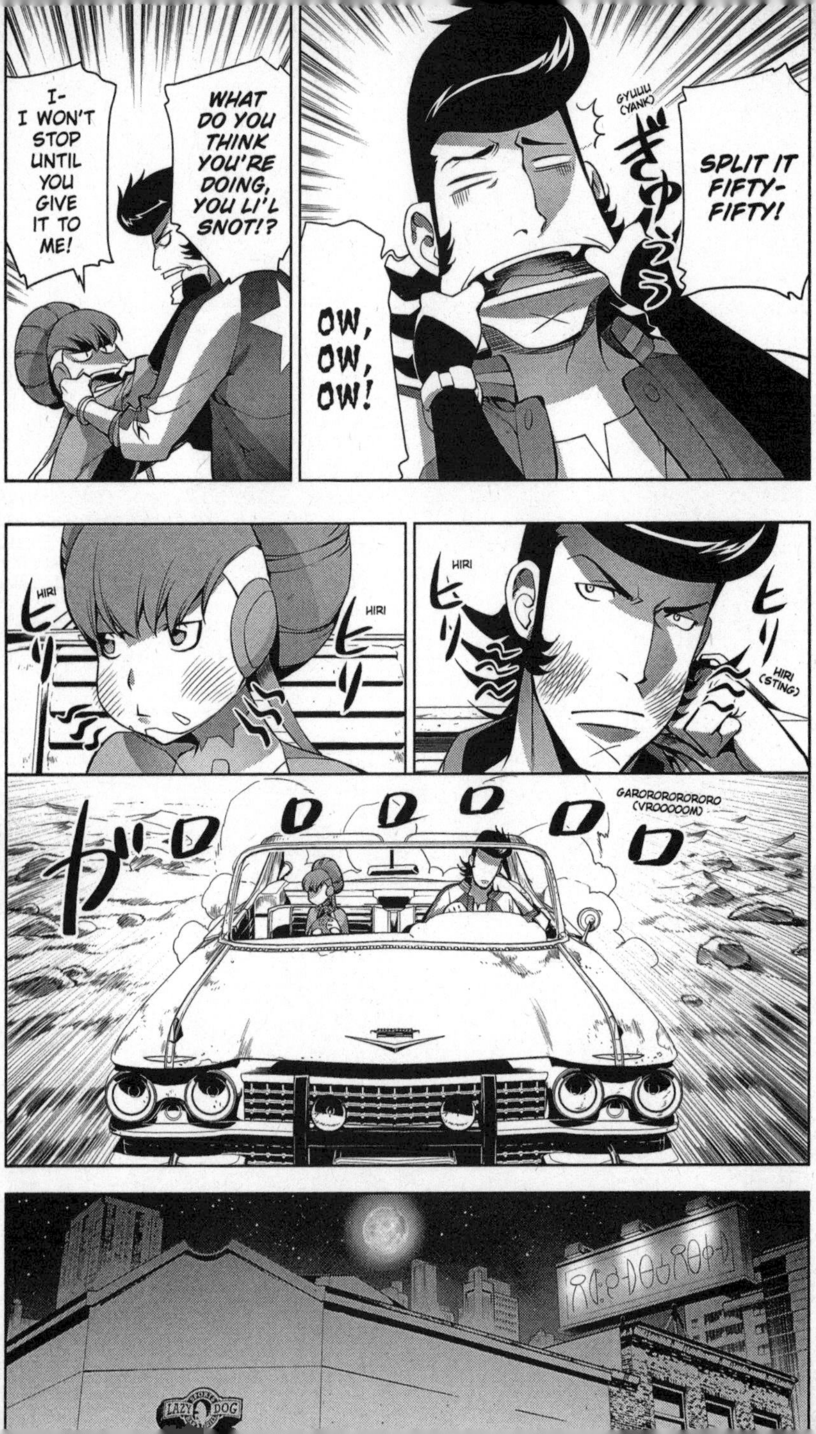
SPLIT IT FIFTY-FIFTY!
ぎゅううう
GYUUU (YANK)
OW, OW, OW!
WHAT DO YOU THINK YOU'RE DOING, YOU LI'L SNOT!?
I- I WON'T STOP UNTIL YOU GIVE IT TO ME!
ヒリ
HIRI (STING)
ヒリ
HIRI
ヒリ
HIRI
ヒリ
HIRI
ガロロロロロロロ
GARORORORORORO (VROOOOOM)
LAZY DOG

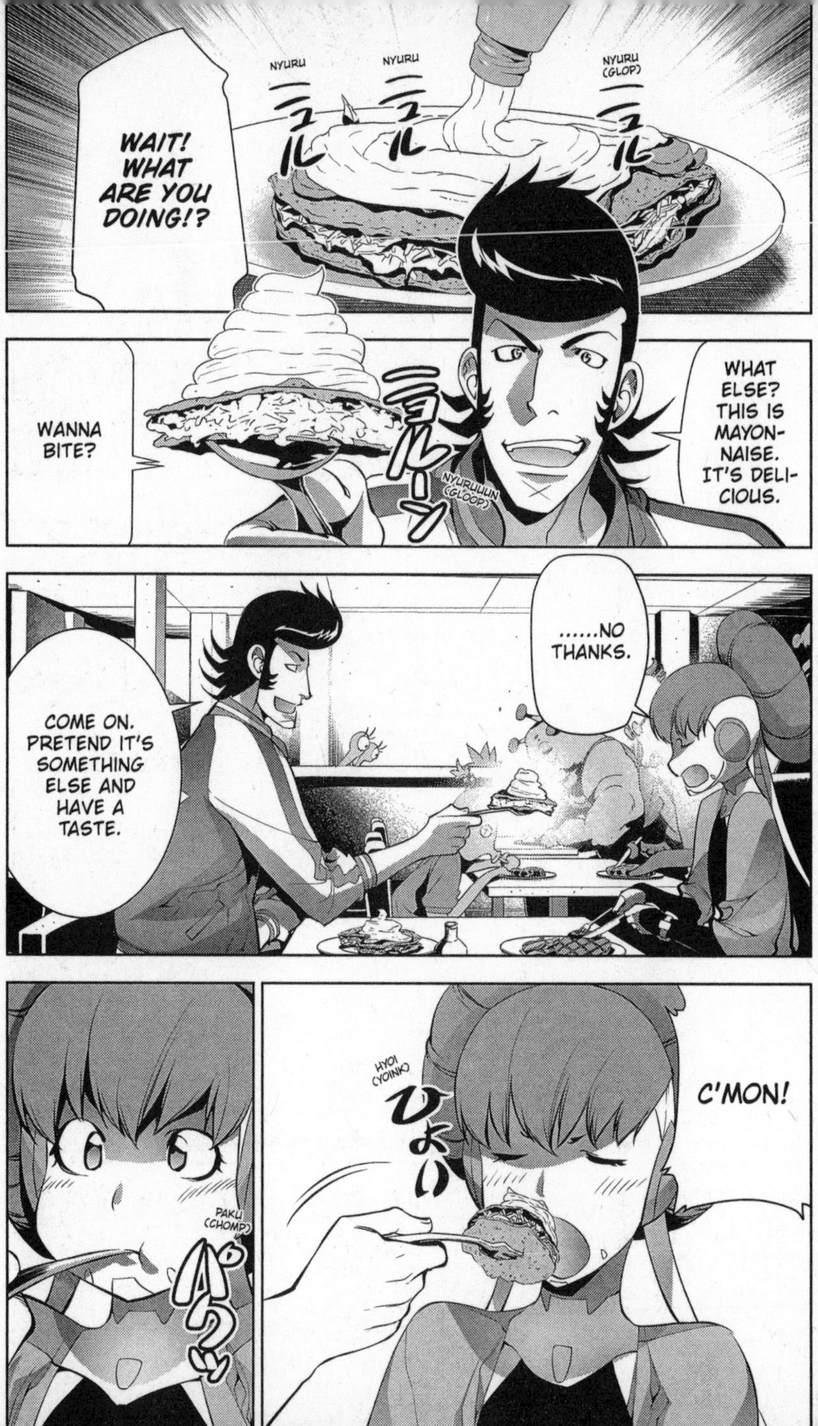
NYURU (GLOP)
ニュル
NYURU
ニュル
NYURU
ニュル
WAIT! WHAT ARE YOU DOING!?
WHAT ELSE? THIS IS MAYON-NAISE. IT'S DELI-CIOUS.
NYURUUUUN (GLOOP)
ニュルーン
WANNA BITE?
......NO THANKS.
COME ON. PRETEND IT'S SOMETHING ELSE AND HAVE A TASTE.
C'MON!
HYOI (YOINK)
ひょい
PAKU (CHOMP)
ぱくっ

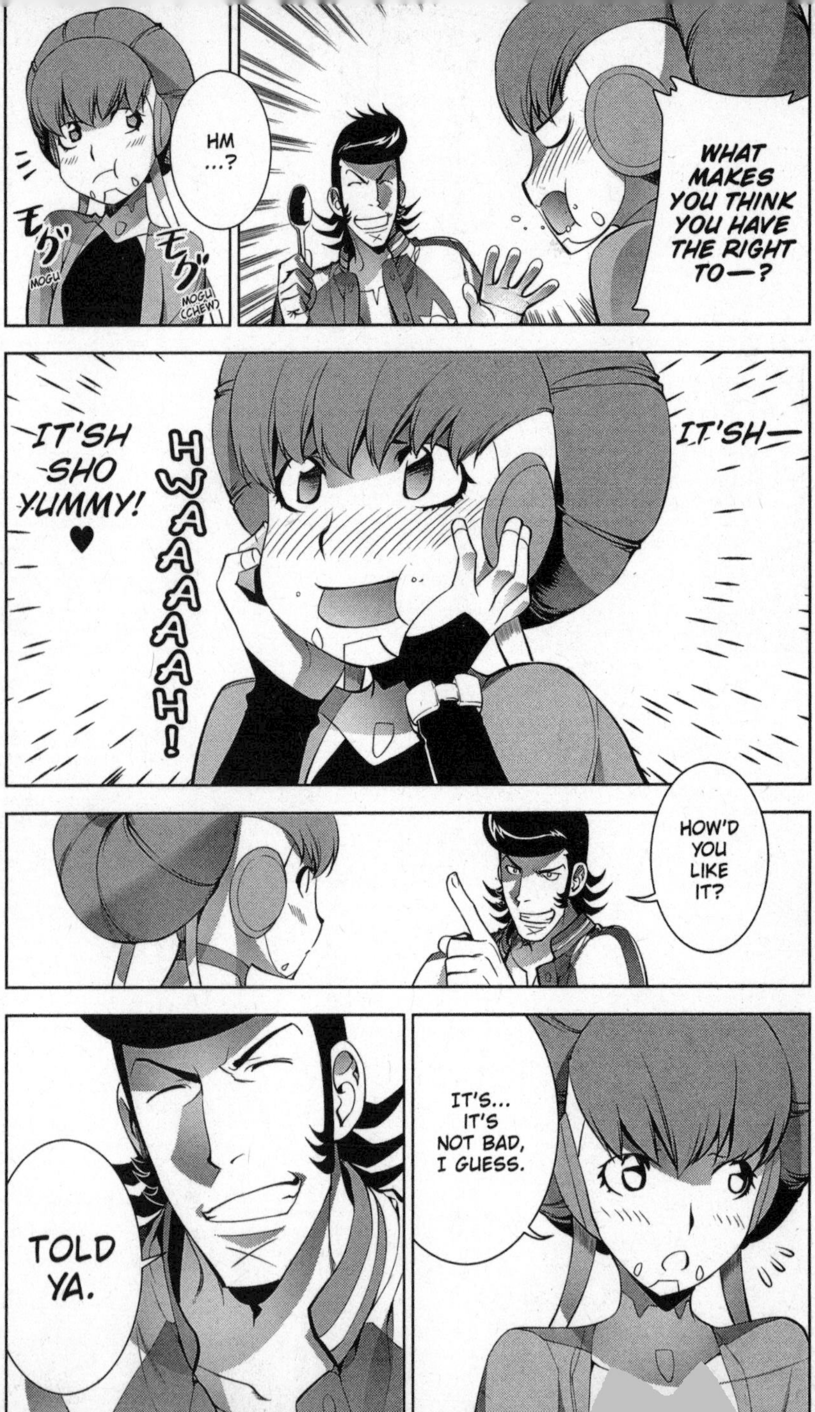
WHAT MAKES YOU THINK YOU HAVE THE RIGHT TO—?
HM ...?
モグ MOGU
モグ MOGU (CHEW)
IT'SH—
HWAAAAAAAH!
IT'SH SHO YUMMY! ♥
HOW'D YOU LIKE IT?
IT'S... IT'S NOT BAD, I GUESS.
TOLD YA.

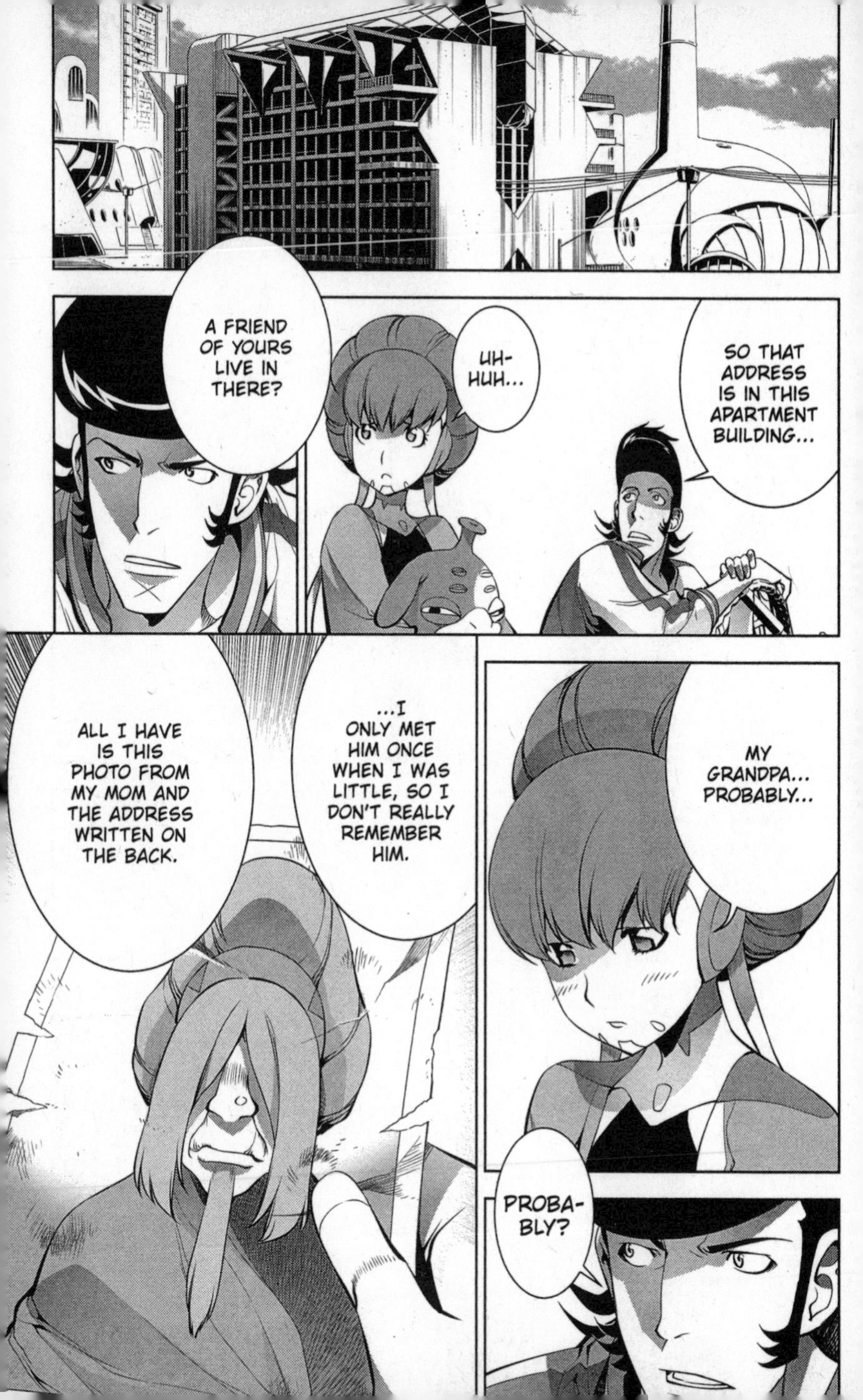
SO THAT ADDRESS IS IN THIS APARTMENT BUILDING...
UH-HUH...
A FRIEND OF YOURS LIVE IN THERE?
MY GRANDPA... PROBABLY...
PROBABLY?
...I ONLY MET HIM ONCE WHEN I WAS LITTLE, SO I DON'T REALLY REMEMBER HIM.
ALL I HAVE IS THIS PHOTO FROM MY MOM AND THE ADDRESS WRITTEN ON THE BACK.

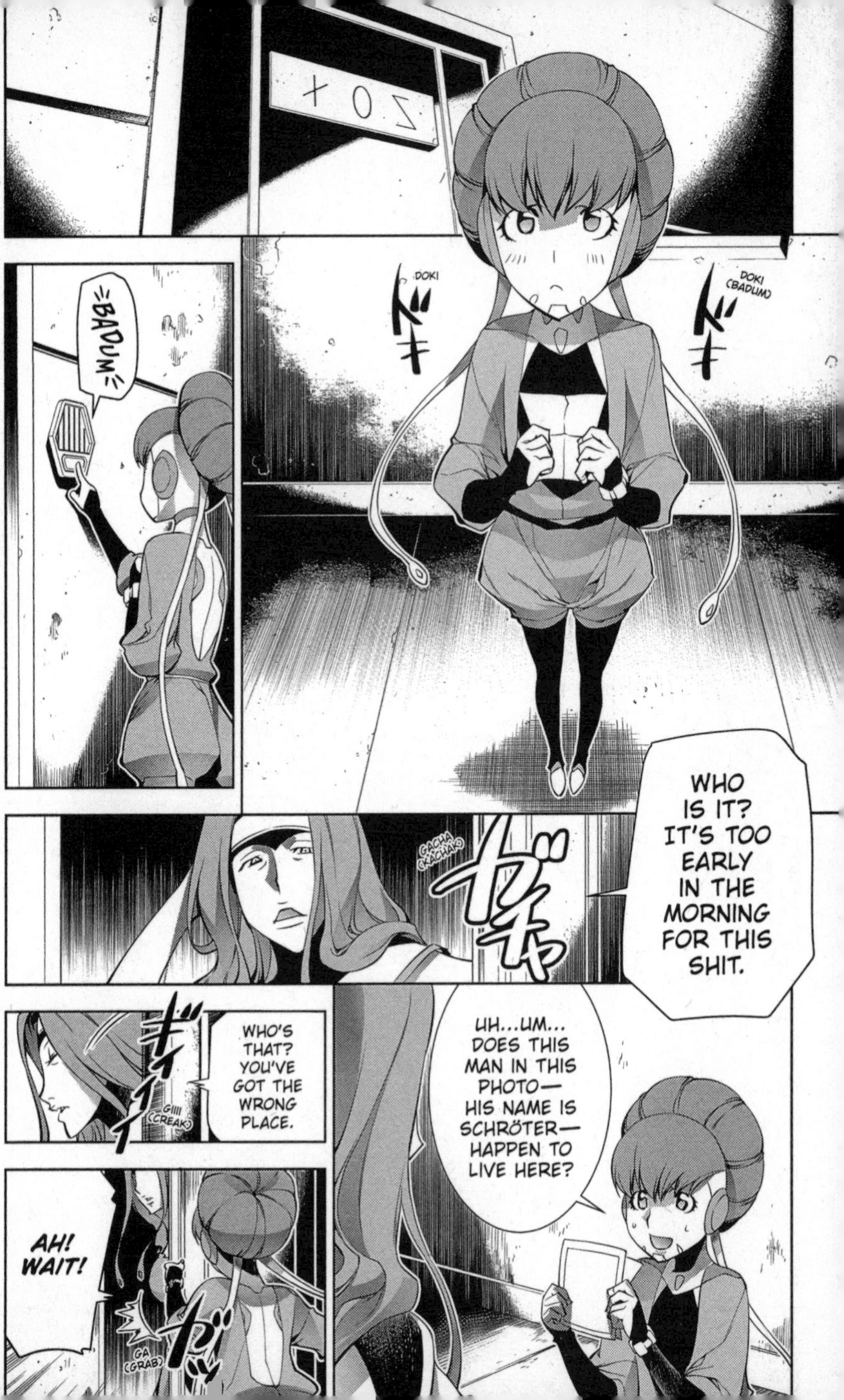
DOKI (BADUM)
DOKI
BADUM
WHO IS IT? IT'S TOO EARLY IN THE MORNING FOR THIS SHIT.
GACHA (KACHAK)
UH...UM... DOES THIS MAN IN THIS PHOTO— HIS NAME IS SCHRÖTER— HAPPEN TO LIVE HERE?
WHO'S THAT? YOU'VE GOT THE WRONG PLACE.
GIIII (CREAK)
AH! WAIT!
GA (GRAB)

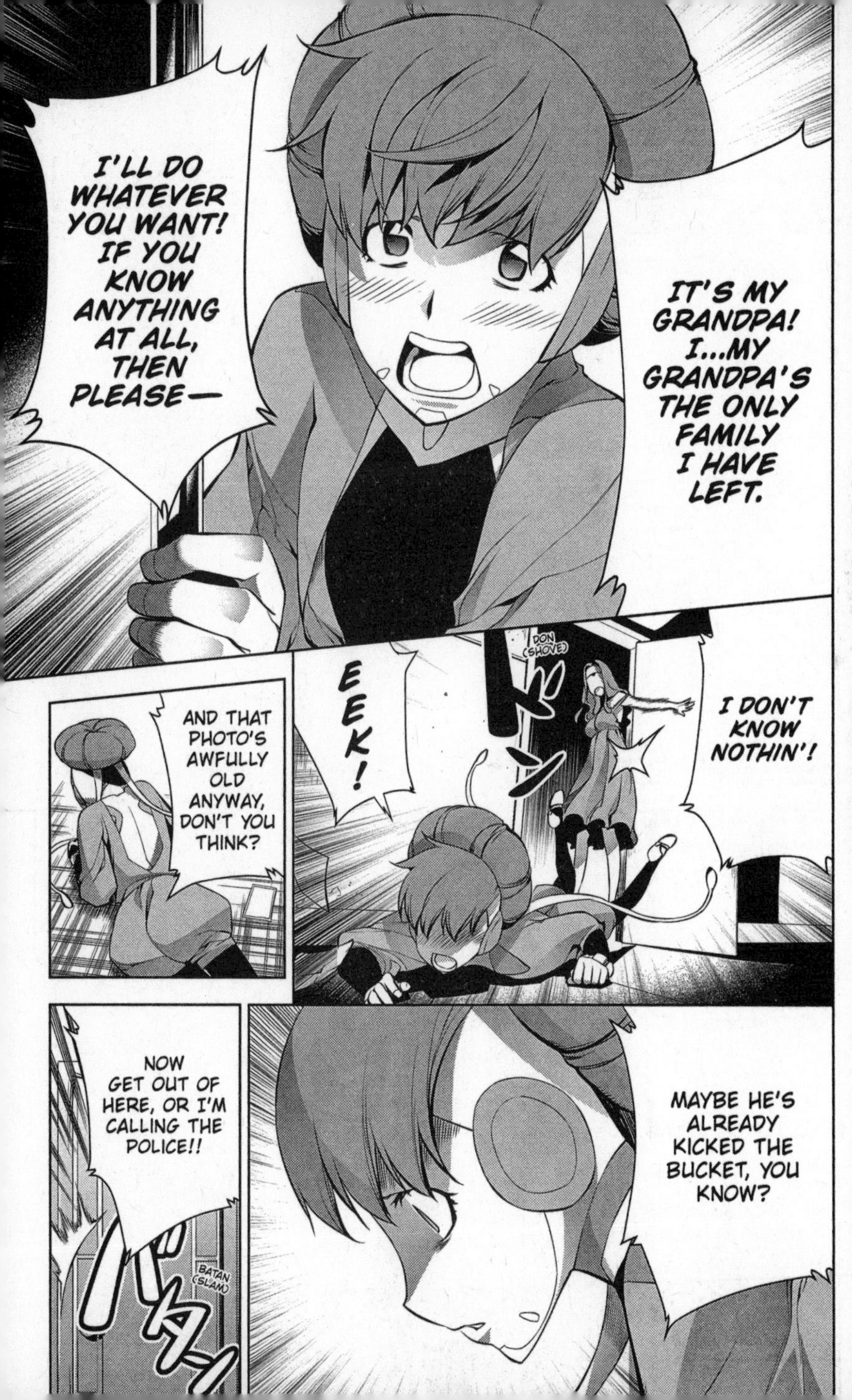
IT'S MY GRANDPA! I...MY GRANDPA'S THE ONLY FAMILY I HAVE LEFT.
I'LL DO WHATEVER YOU WANT! IF YOU KNOW ANYTHING AT ALL, THEN PLEASE—
I DON'T KNOW NOTHIN'!
DON (SHOVE)
EEK!
AND THAT PHOTO'S AWFULLY OLD ANYWAY, DON'T YOU THINK?
MAYBE HE'S ALREADY KICKED THE BUCKET, YOU KNOW?
NOW GET OUT OF HERE, OR I'M CALLING THE POLICE!!
BATAN (SLAM)

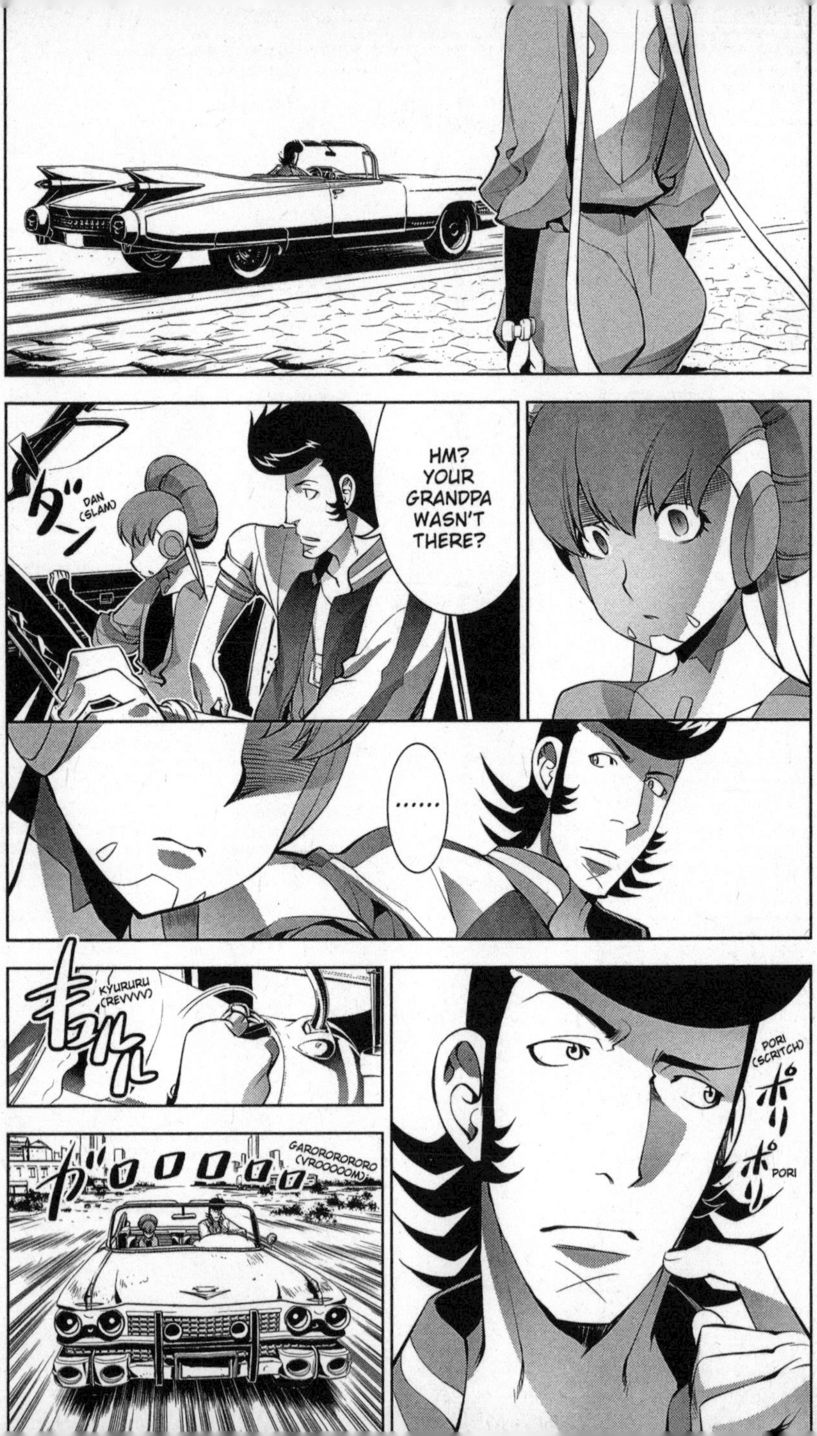
HM? YOUR GRANDPA WASN'T THERE?
DAN (SLAM)
......
PORI (SCRITCH)
PORI
KYURURU (REVVVV)
GARORORORO (VROOOOOM)

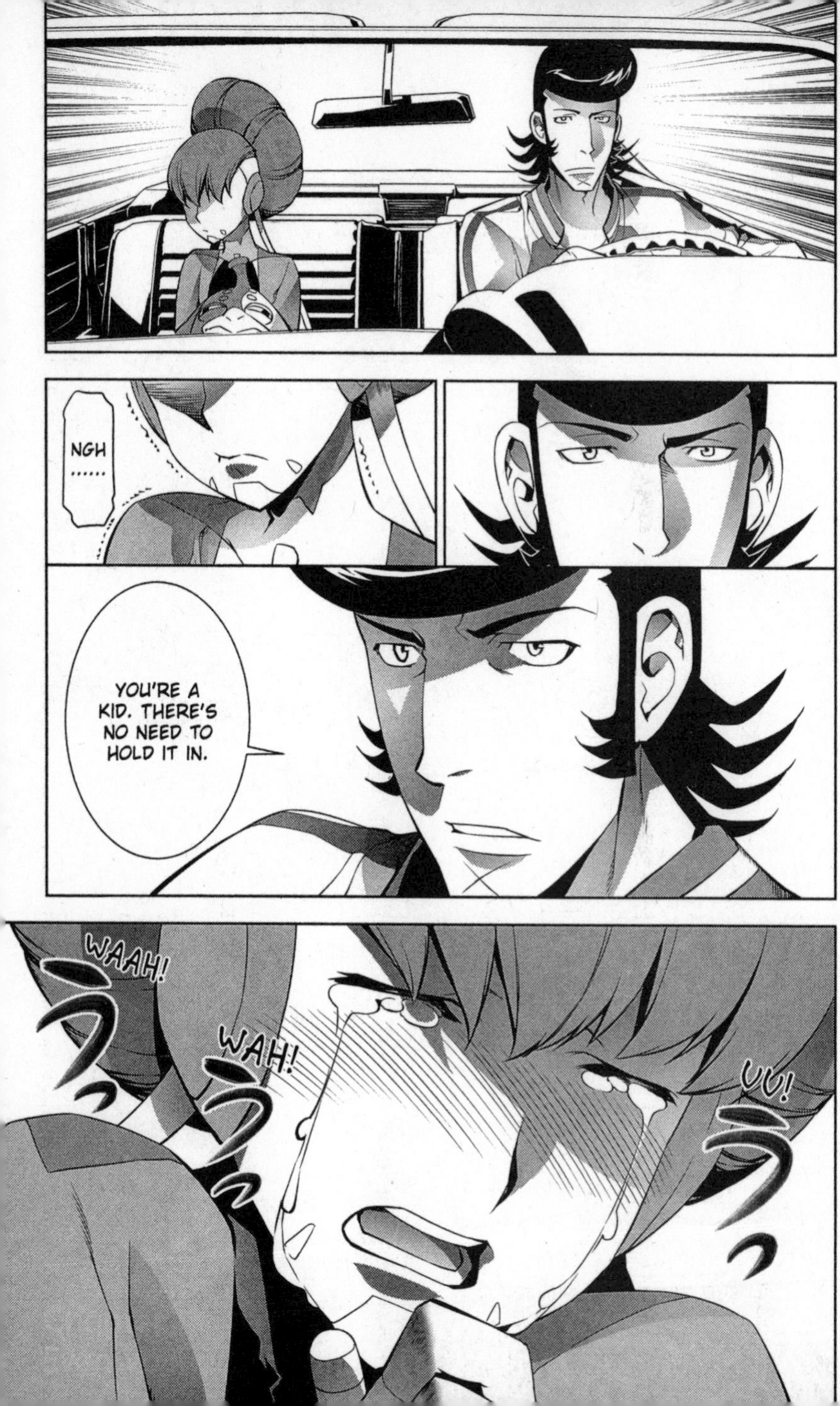
NGH ......
YOU'RE A KID. THERE'S NO NEED TO HOLD IT IN.
UU!
WAH!
WAAH!

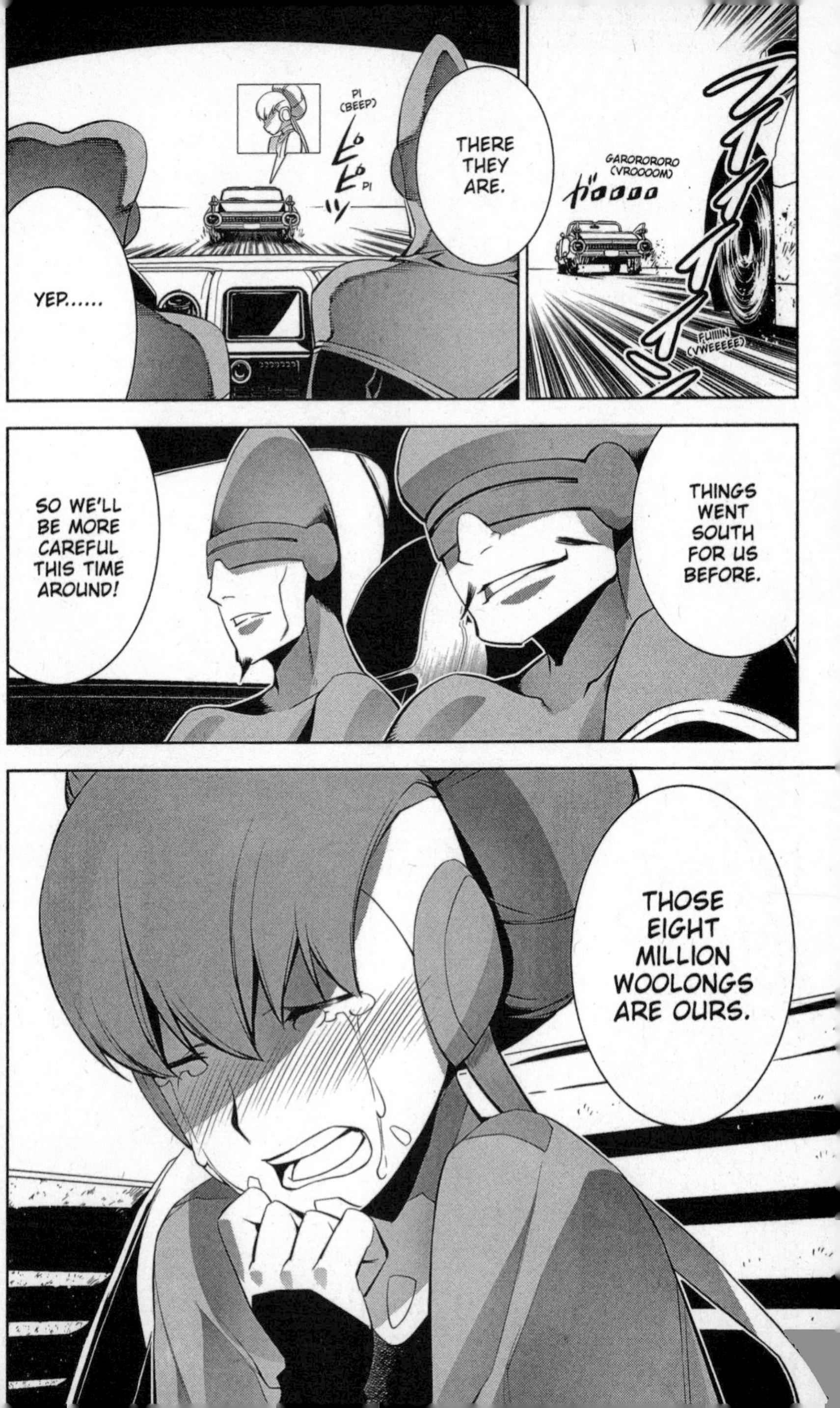
GARORORORO (VROOOOM)
FUIIIIN (VWEEEEE)
THERE THEY ARE.
PI (BEEP)
PI
YEP......
THINGS WENT SOUTH FOR US BEFORE.
SO WE'LL BE MORE CAREFUL THIS TIME AROUND!
THOSE EIGHT MILLION WOOLONGS ARE OURS.

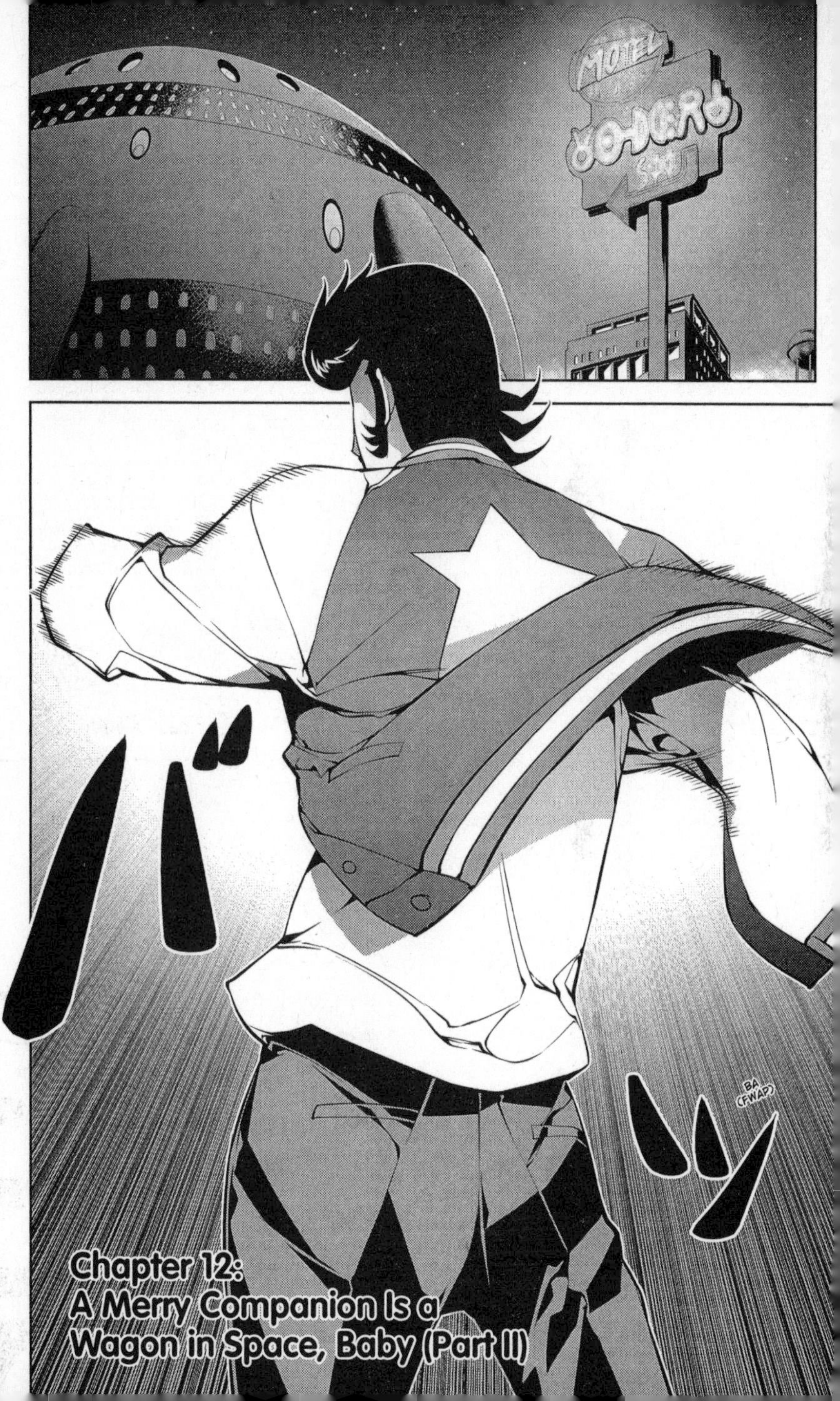
MOTEL
BA (FWAP)

Chapter 12: A Merry Companion Is a Wagon in Space, Baby (Part II)

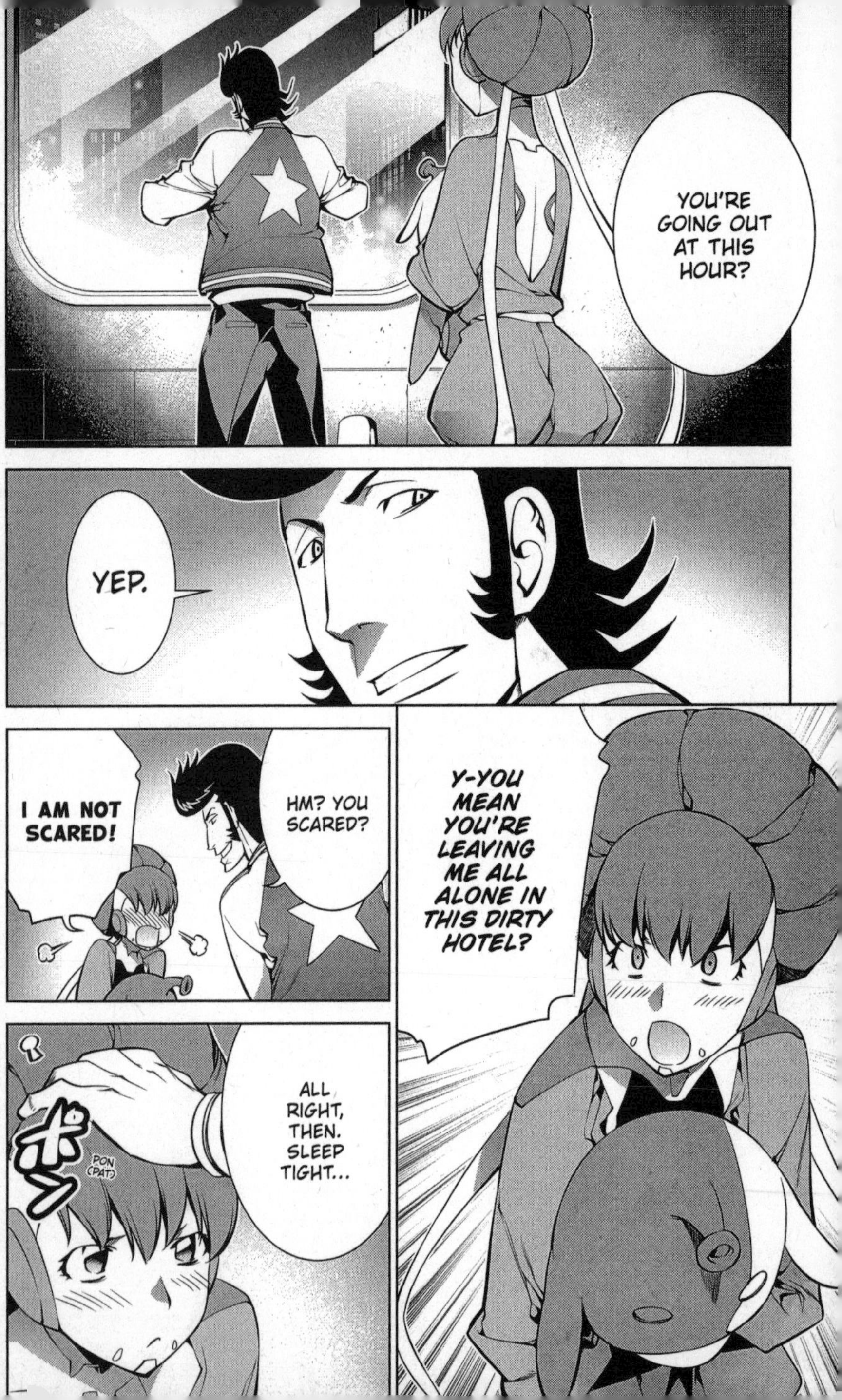
YOU'RE GOING OUT AT THIS HOUR?
YEP.
Y-YOU MEAN YOU'RE LEAVING ME ALL ALONE IN THIS DIRTY HOTEL?
HM? YOU SCARED?
I AM NOT SCARED!
ALL RIGHT, THEN. SLEEP TIGHT...
ポン
PON (PAT)

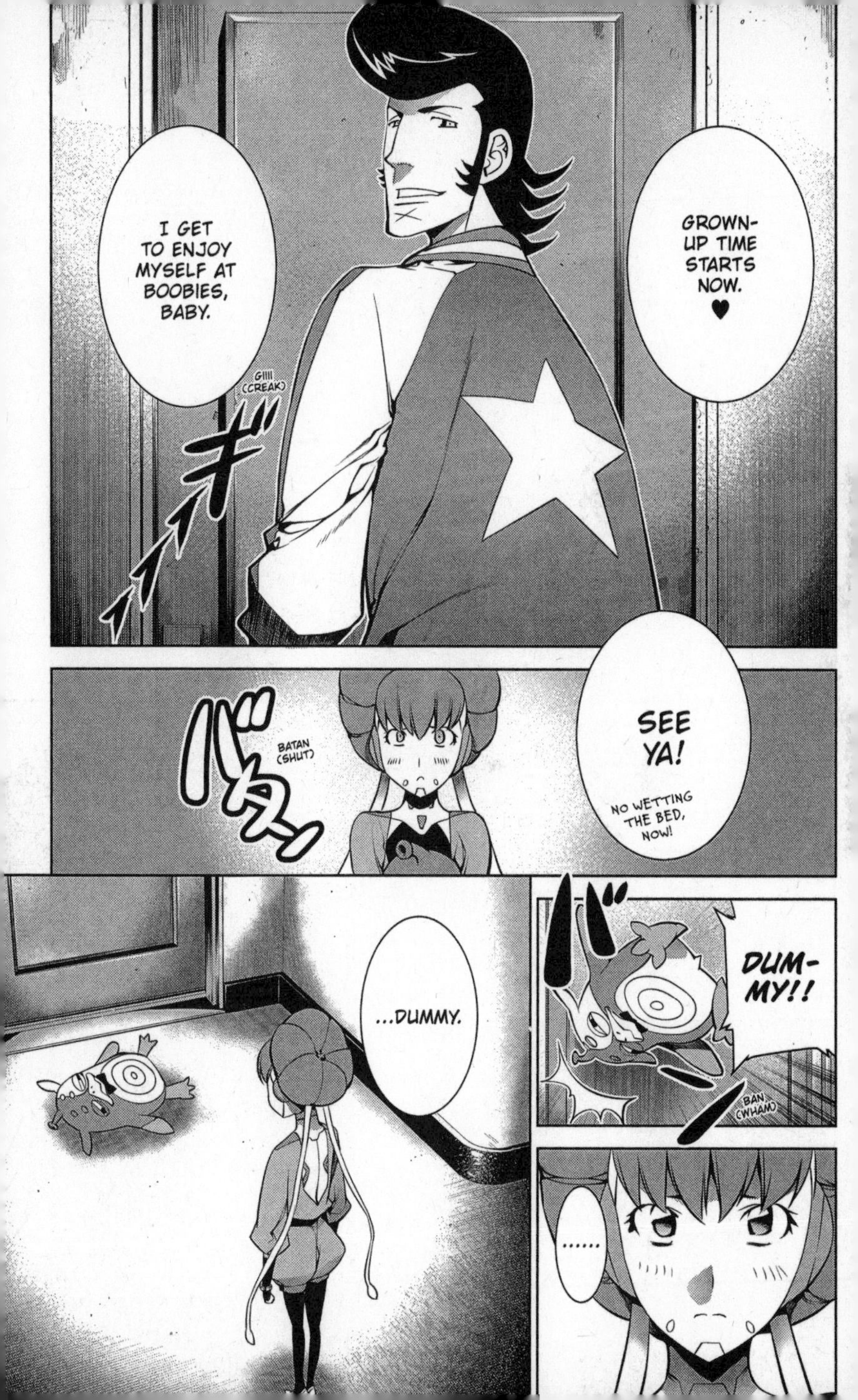

GROWN-UP TIME STARTS NOW. ♥
I GET TO ENJOY MYSELF AT BOOBIES, BABY.
GIIII (CREAK)
SEE YA!
NO WETTING THE BED, NOW!
BATAN (SHUT)
DUMMY!!
BAN (WHAM)
......
...DUMMY.

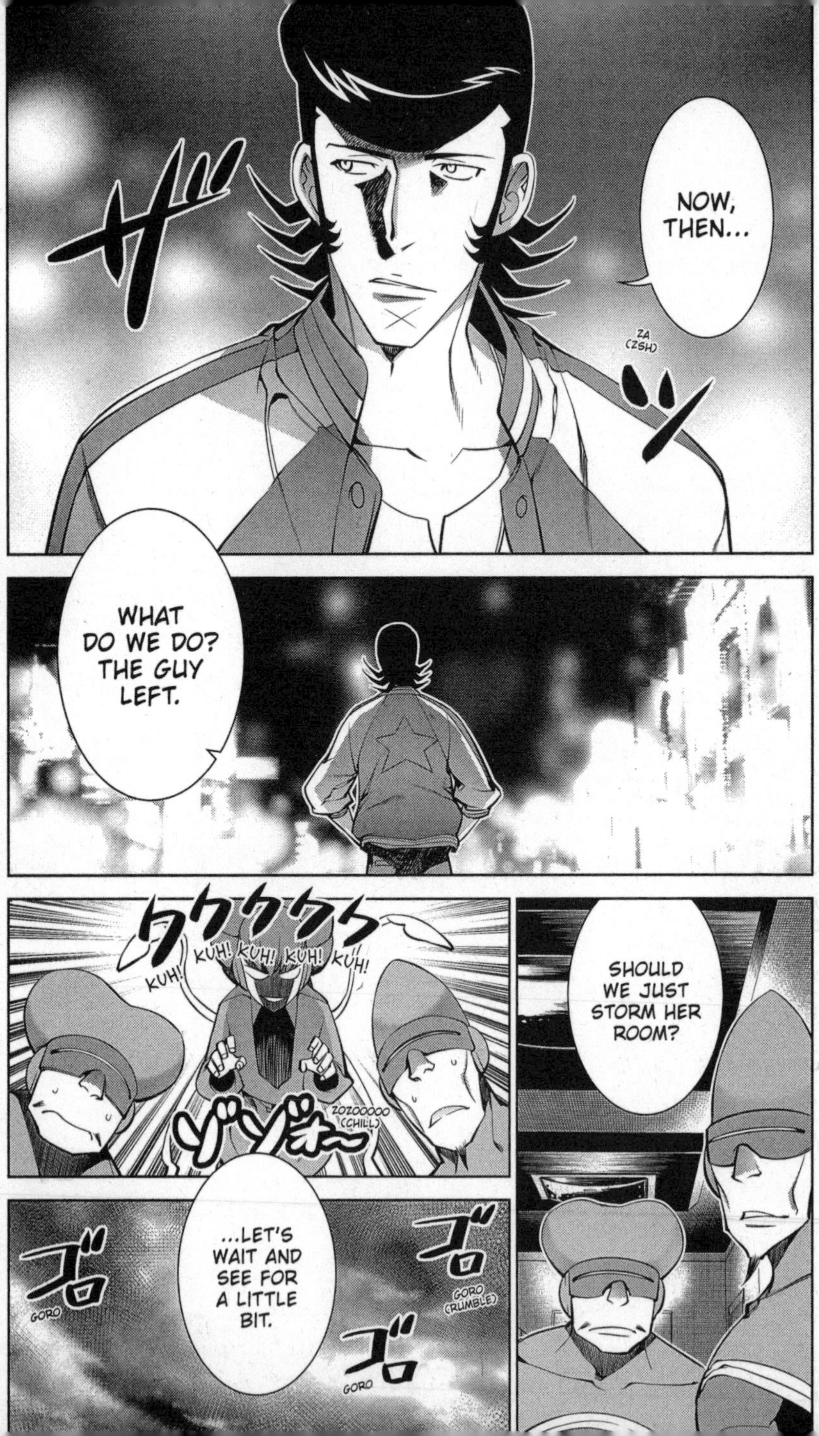
NOW, THEN...
ZA
(ZSH)
WHAT DO WE DO? THE GUY LEFT.
SHOULD WE JUST STORM HER ROOM?
KUH! KUH! KUH! KUH! KUH!
ZOZOOOOO
(CHILL)
...LET'S WAIT AND SEE FOR A LITTLE BIT.
GORO
(RUMBLE)
GORO
GORO

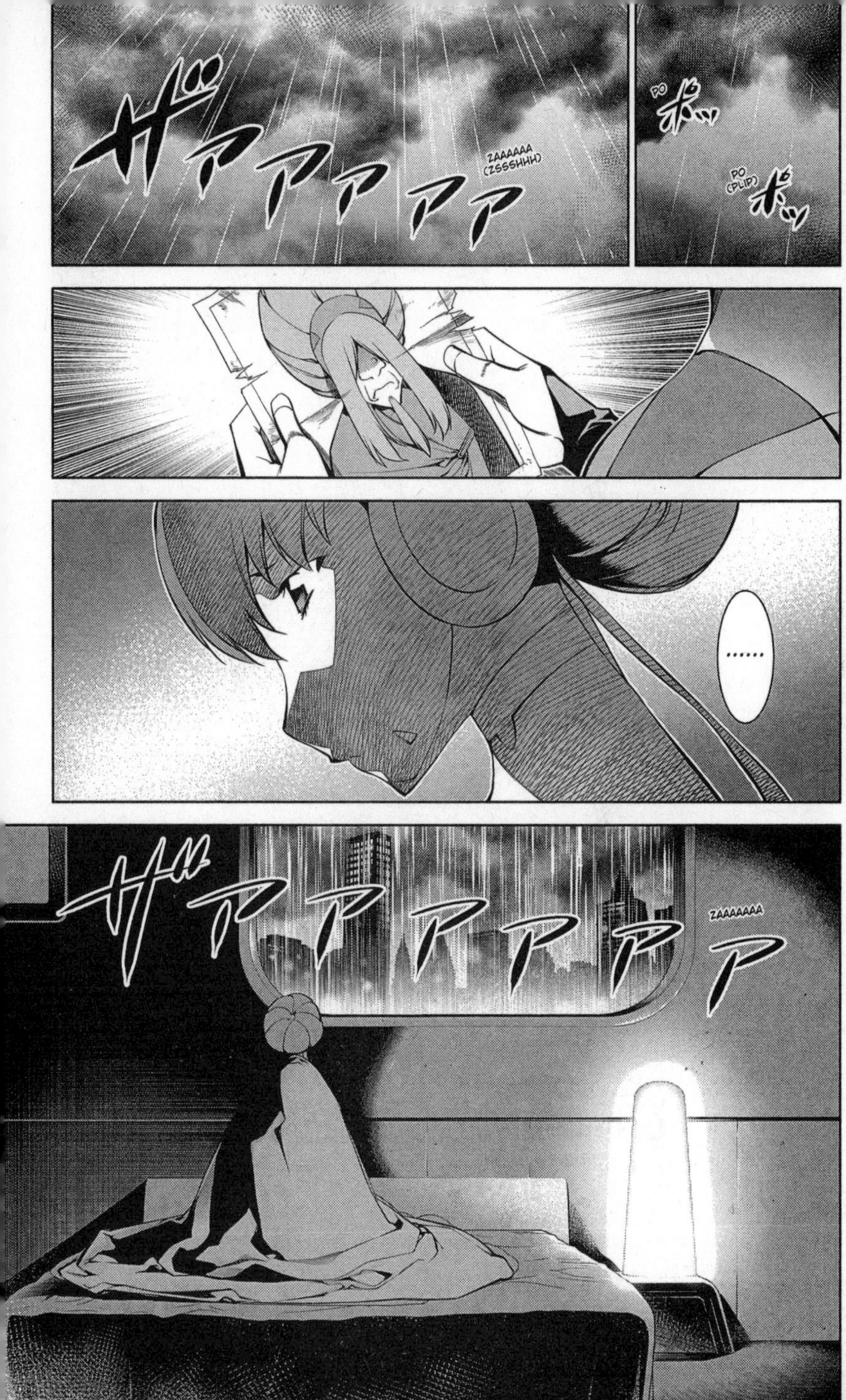
PO
PO (PLIP)
ZAAAAAA (ZSSSHHH)
......
ZAAAAAA

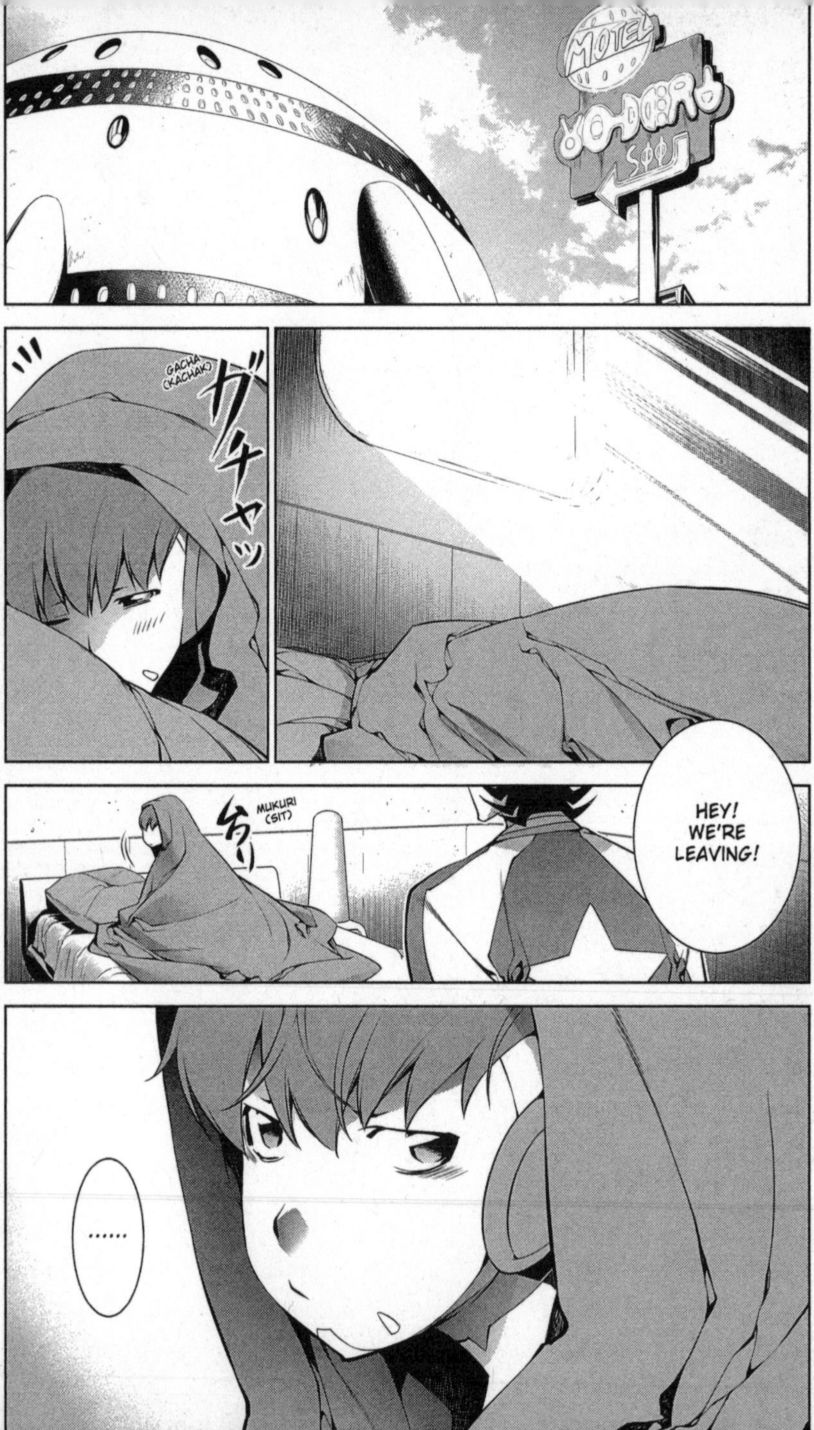
MOTEL
GACHA (KACHAK)
ガチャッ
HEY! WE'RE LEAVING!
MUKURI (SIT)
むくり
......

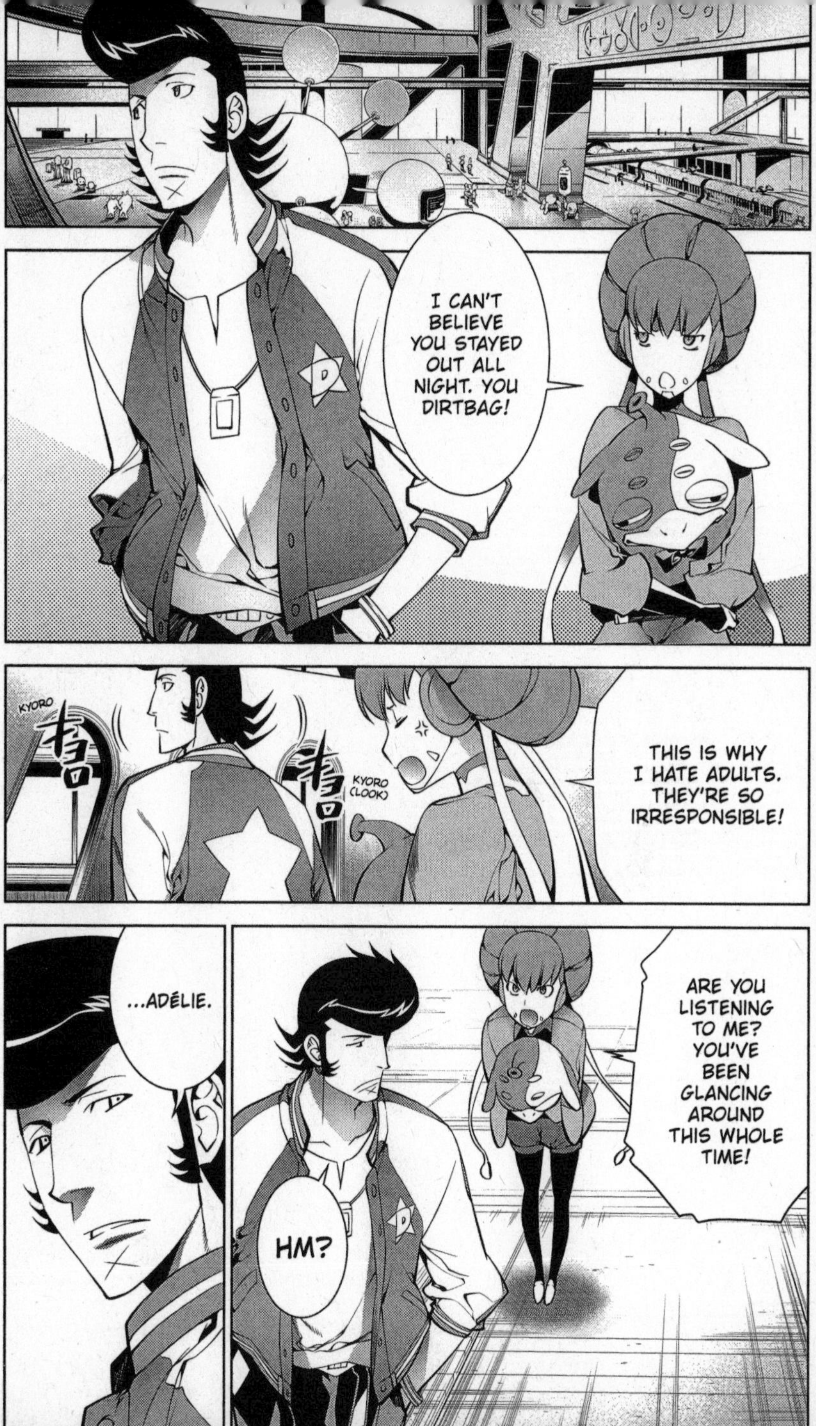
I CAN'T BELIEVE YOU STAYED OUT ALL NIGHT. YOU DIRTBAG!
THIS IS WHY I HATE ADULTS. THEY'RE SO IRRESPONSIBLE!
KYORO (LOOK)
KYORO
ARE YOU LISTENING TO ME? YOU'VE BEEN GLANCING AROUND THIS WHOLE TIME!
HM?
...ADÉLIE.

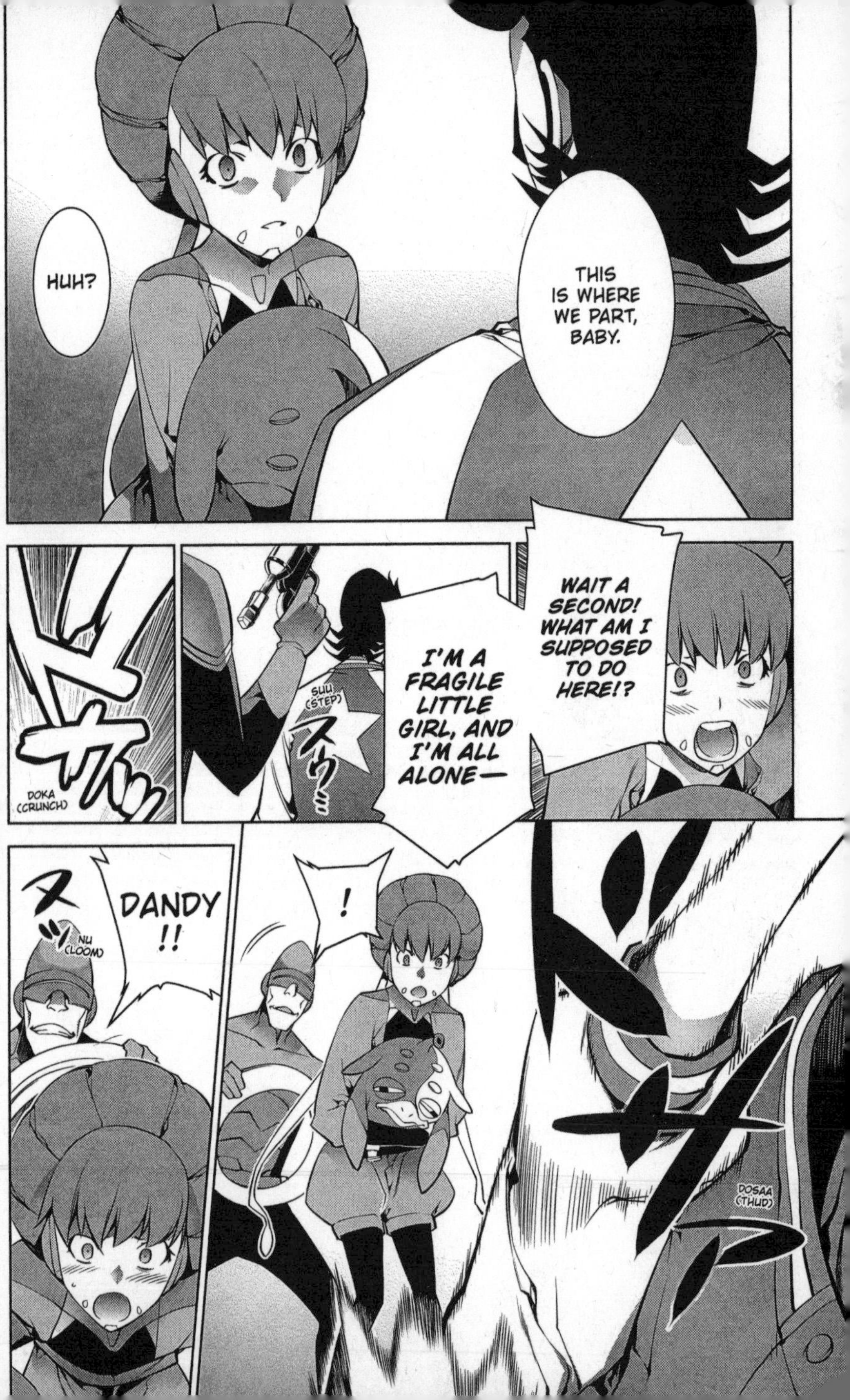
THIS IS WHERE WE PART, BABY.
HUH?
WAIT A SECOND! WHAT AM I SUPPOSED TO DO HERE!?
I'M A FRAGILE LITTLE GIRL, AND I'M ALL ALONE—
SUU (STEP)
DOKA (CRUNCH)
DOSAA (THUD)
!
DANDY!!
NU (LOOM)

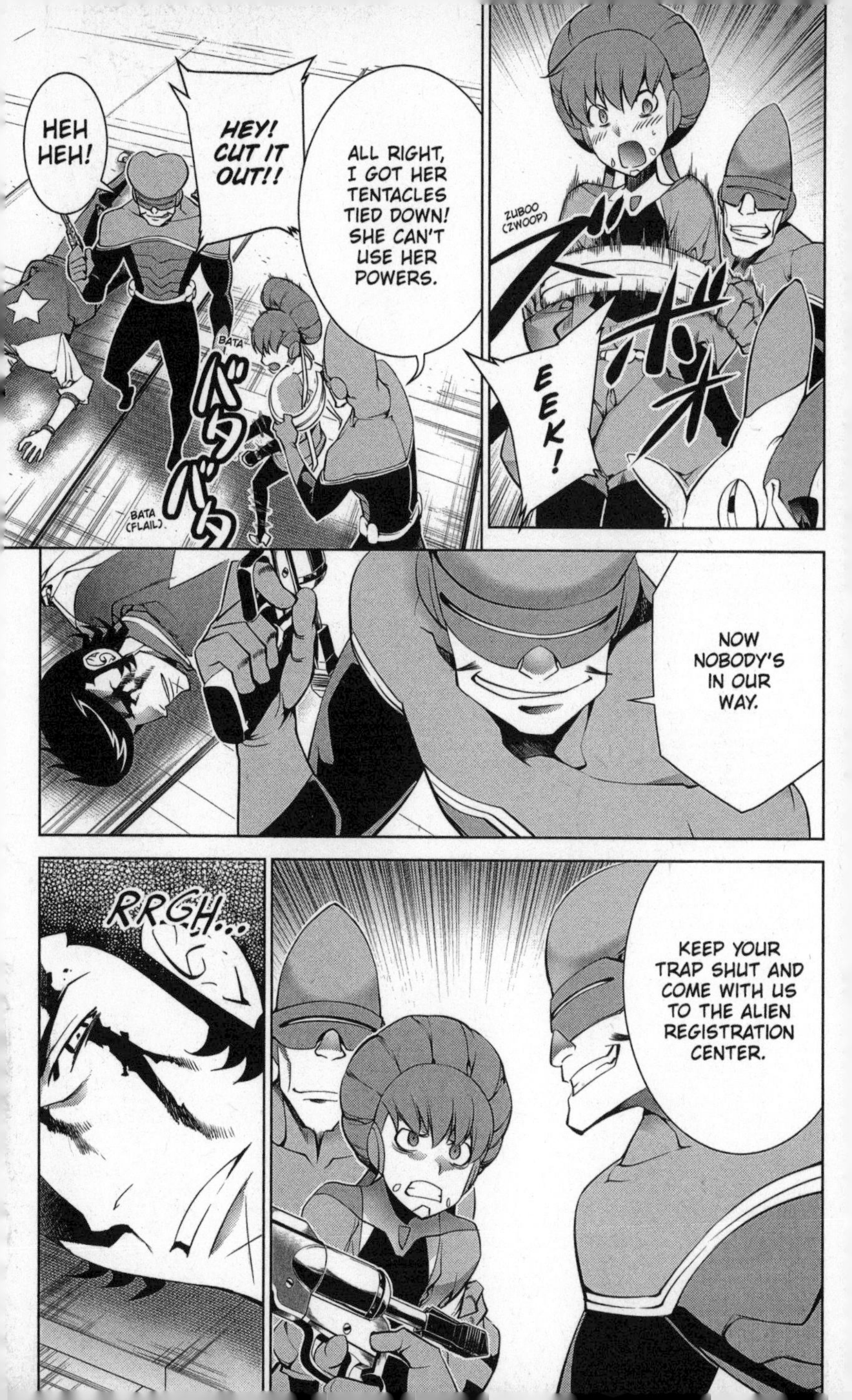
ZUBOO (ZWOOP)
EEK!
ALL RIGHT, I GOT HER TENTACLES TIED DOWN! SHE CAN'T USE HER POWERS.
HEY! CUT IT OUT!!
HEH HEH!
BATA
BATA (FLAIL)
NOW NOBODY'S IN OUR WAY.
KEEP YOUR TRAP SHUT AND COME WITH US TO THE ALIEN REGISTRATION CENTER.
RRGH...

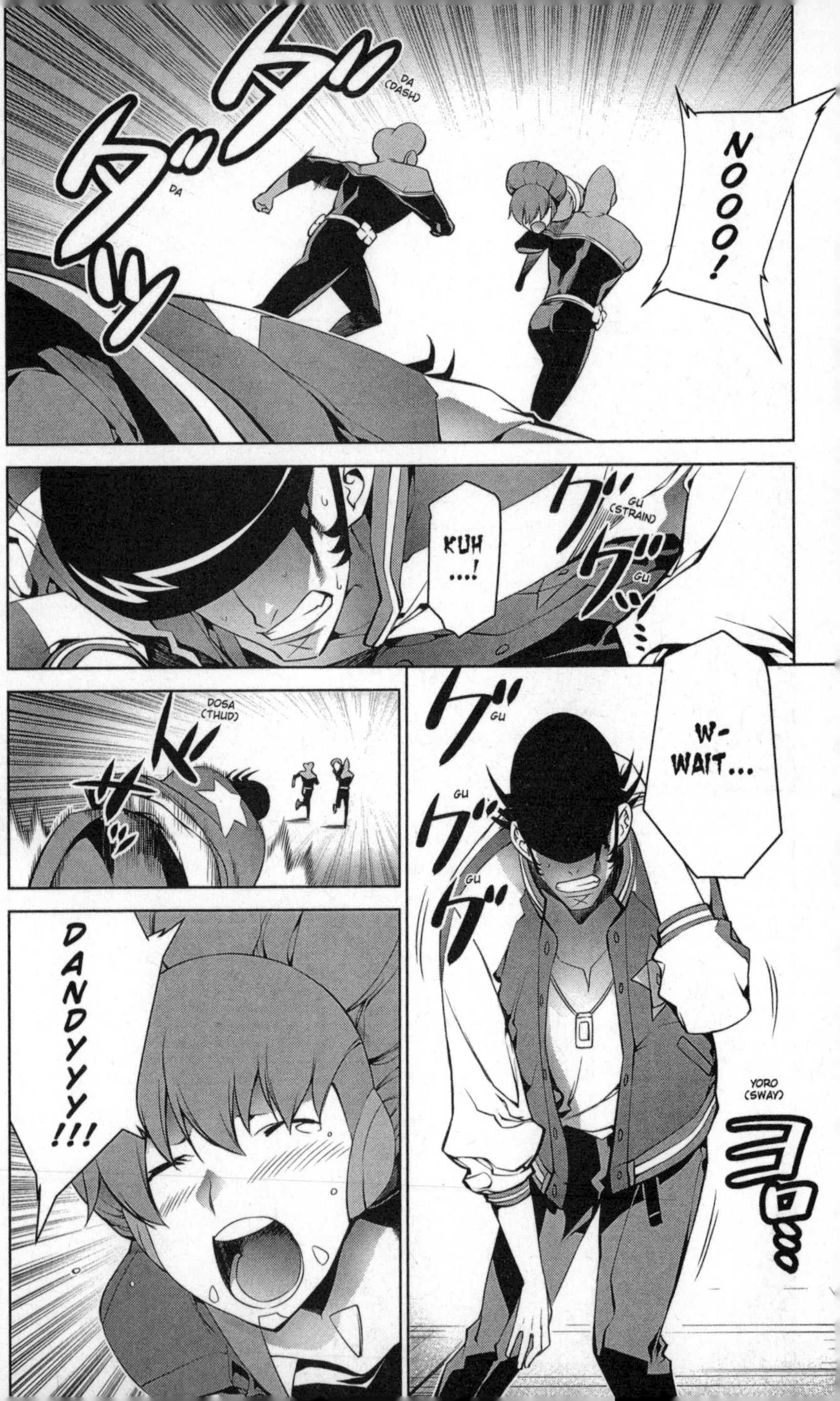
NOOOO!
DA (DASH)
DA
GU (STRAIN)
GU
KUH...!
W-WAIT...
GU
GU
GU
YORO (SWAY)
DOSA (THUD)
DANDYYYY!!!

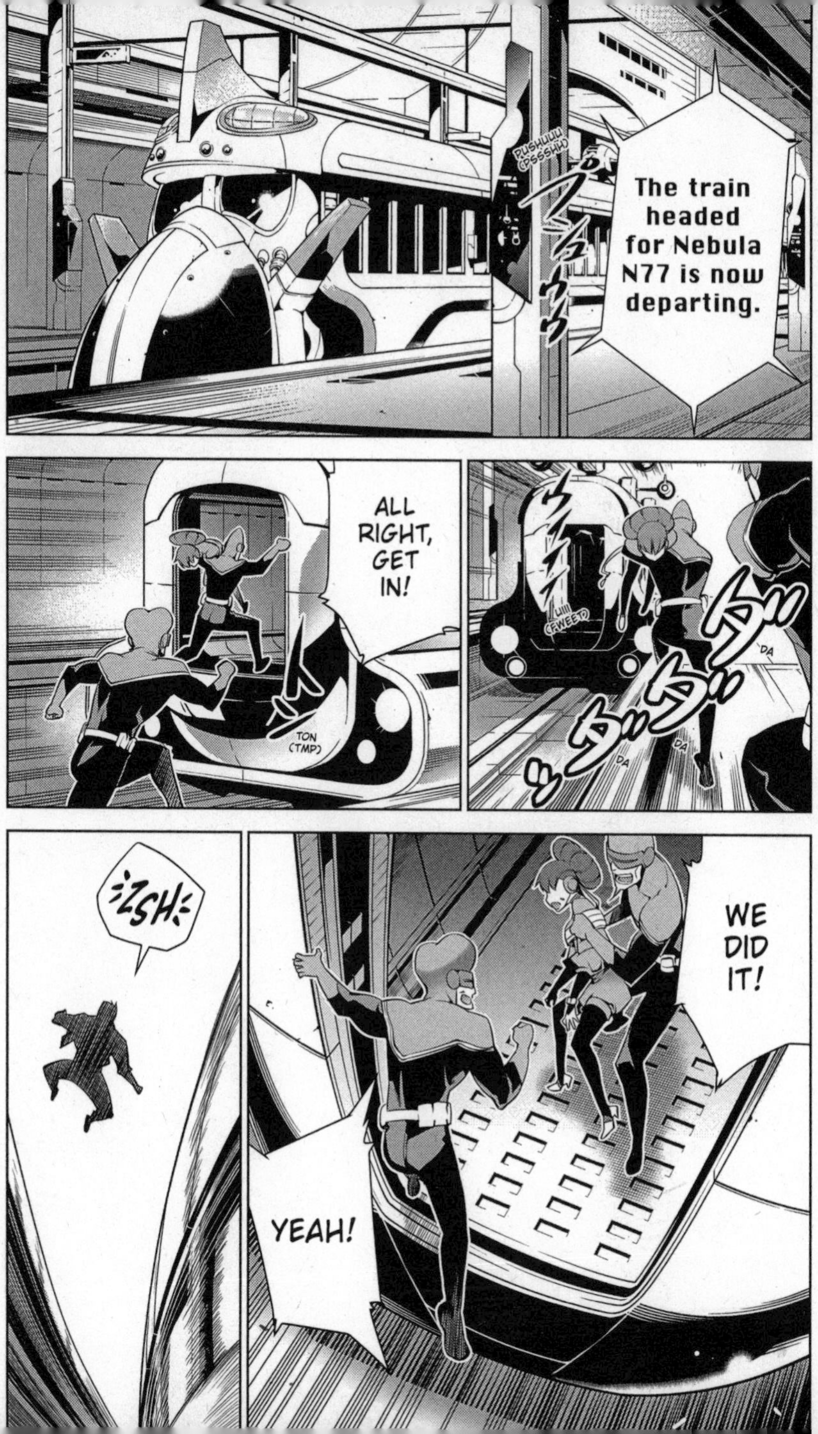
PUSHUUU (PSSSHH)
The train headed for Nebula N77 is now departing.
UIII (FWEET)
DA
DA
DA
ALL RIGHT, GET IN!
TON (TMP)
WE DID IT!
YEAH!
ZSH

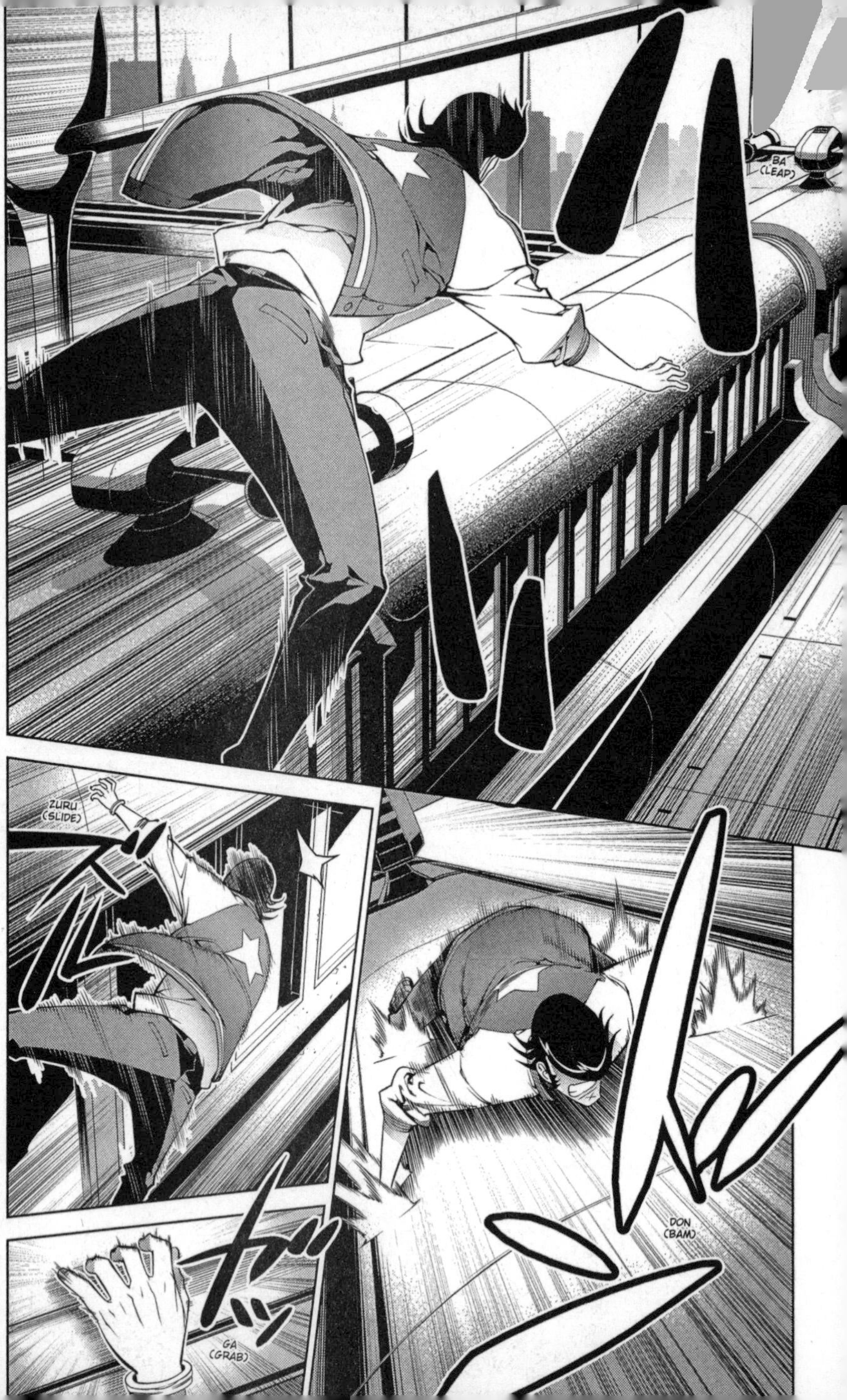
BA
(LEAP)
DON
(BAM)
ZURU
(SLIDE)
GA
(GRAB)

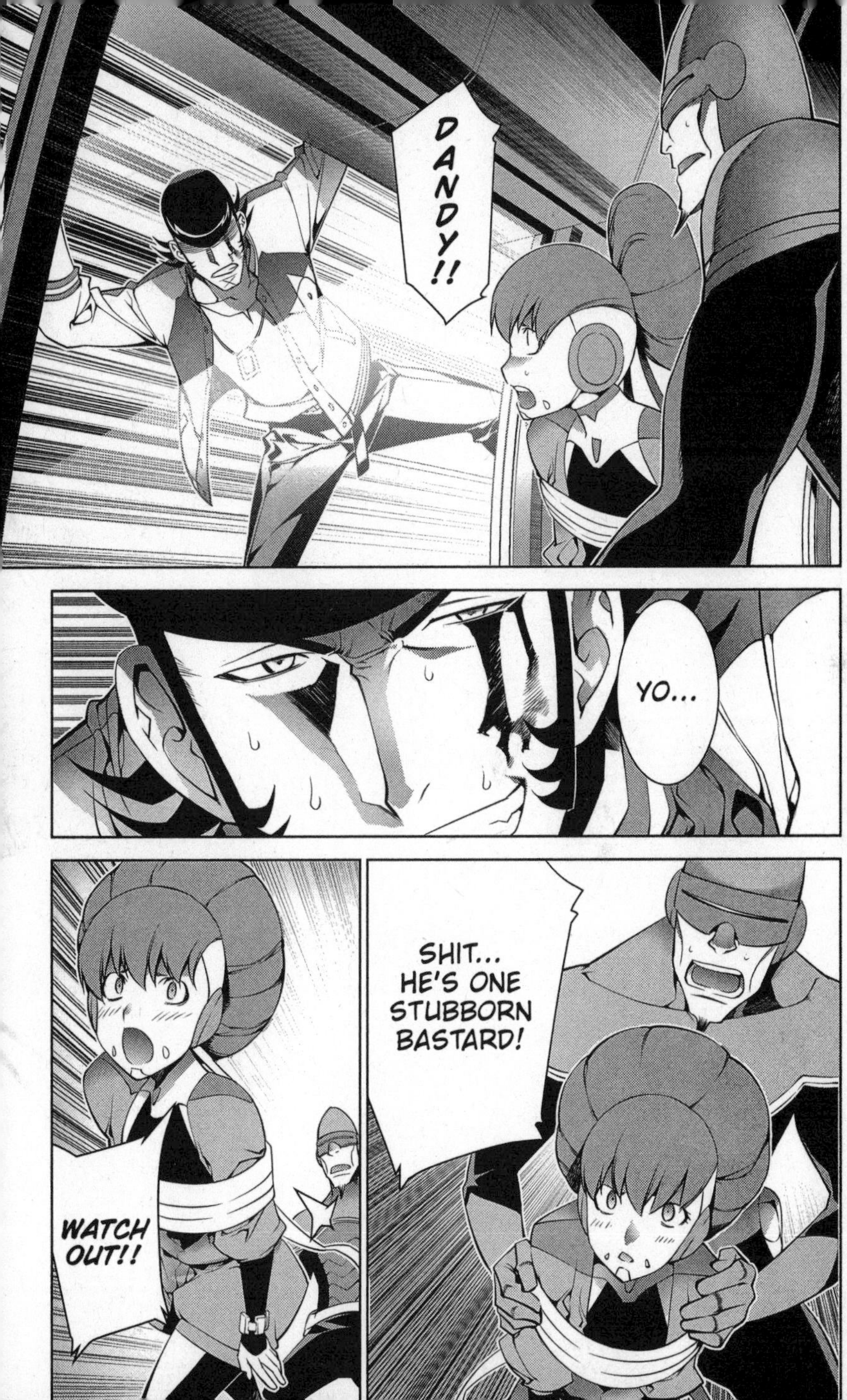
DANDY!!
YO...
SHIT... HE'S ONE STUBBORN BASTARD!
WATCH OUT!!

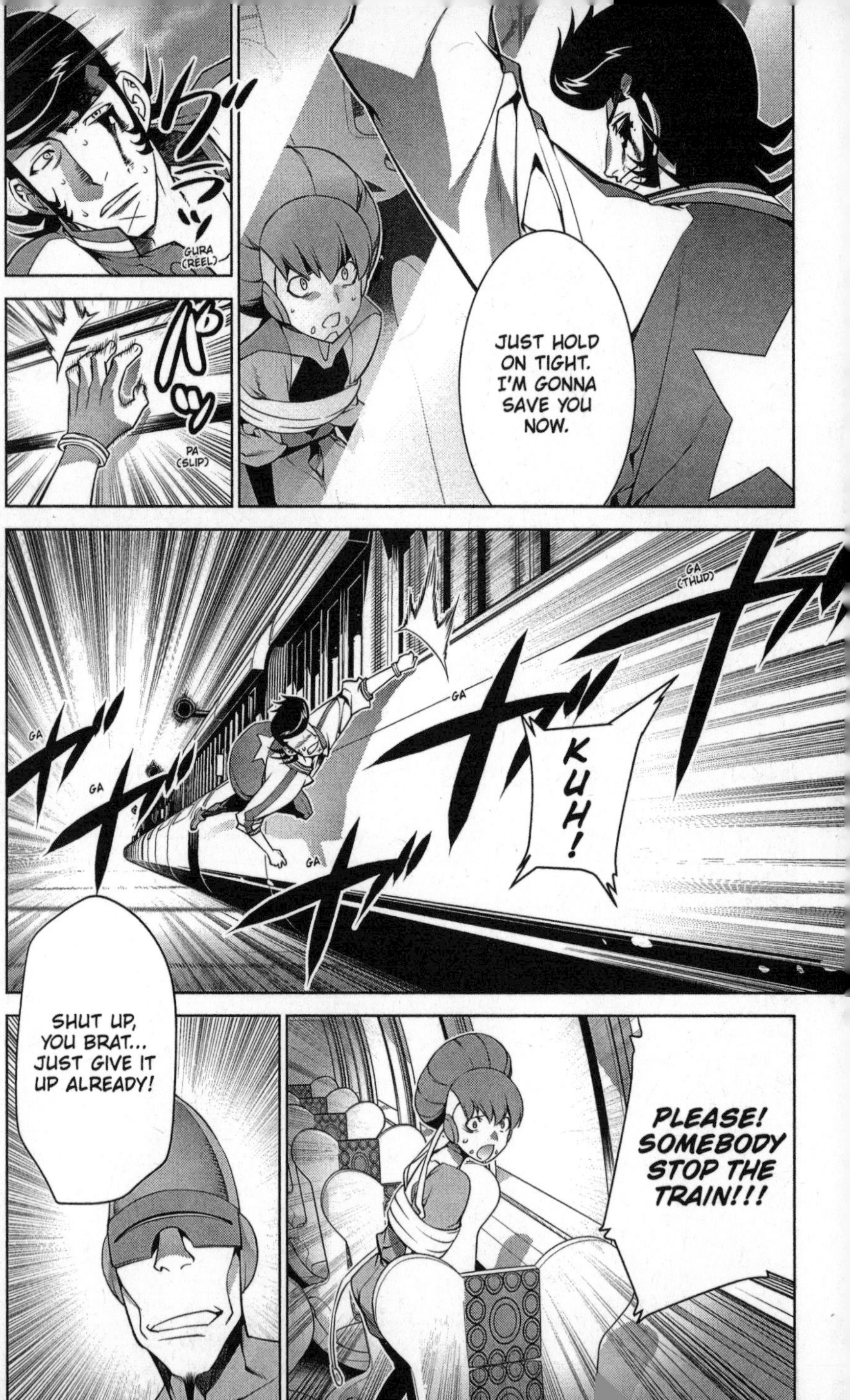
JUST HOLD ON TIGHT. I'M GONNA SAVE YOU NOW.
GURA (REEL)
PA (SLIP)
GA (THUD)
KUH!
GA
GA
GA
GA
PLEASE! SOMEBODY STOP THE TRAIN!!!
SHUT UP, YOU BRAT... JUST GIVE IT UP ALREADY!

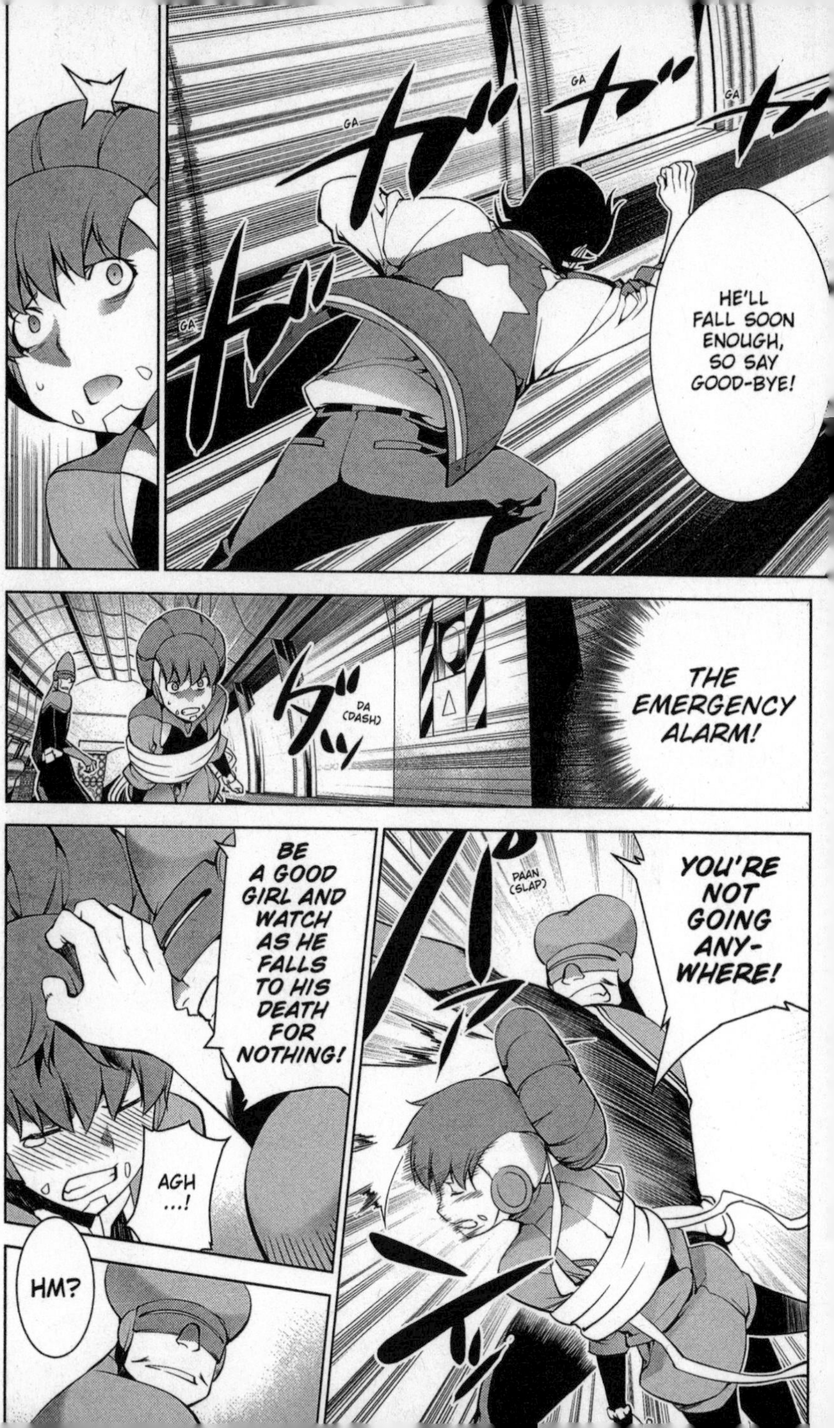
GA
GA
GA
GA
HE'LL FALL SOON ENOUGH, SO SAY GOOD-BYE!
THE EMERGENCY ALARM!
DA (DASH)
YOU'RE NOT GOING ANY-WHERE!
PAAN (SLAP)
BE A GOOD GIRL AND WATCH AS HE FALLS TO HIS DEATH FOR NOTHING!
AGH ...!
HM?

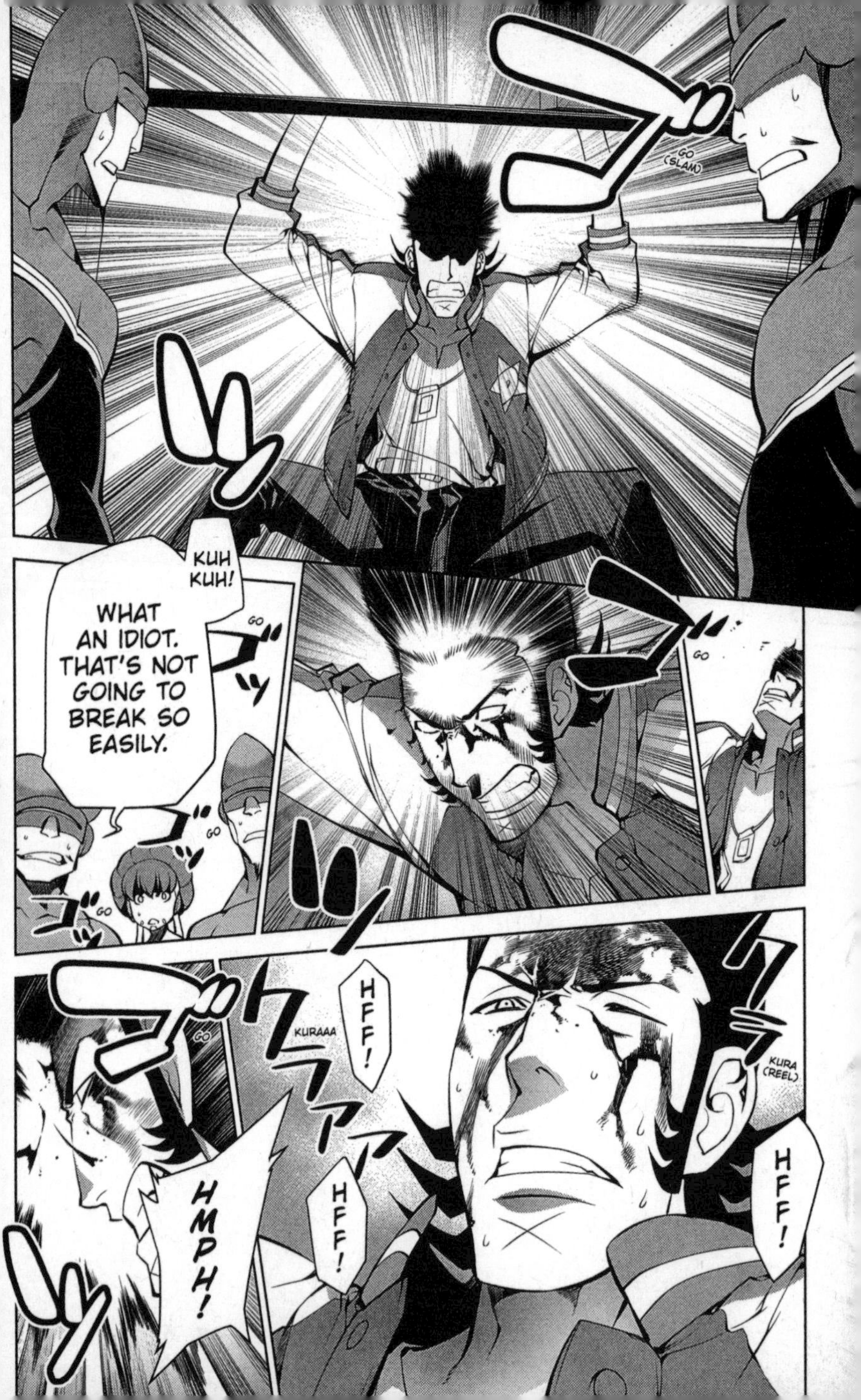
GO (SLAM)
KUH KUH!
WHAT AN IDIOT. THAT'S NOT GOING TO BREAK SO EASILY.
GO
GO
GO
GO
KURA (REEL)
HFF!
KURAAA
HFF!
GO
HFF!
HMPH!

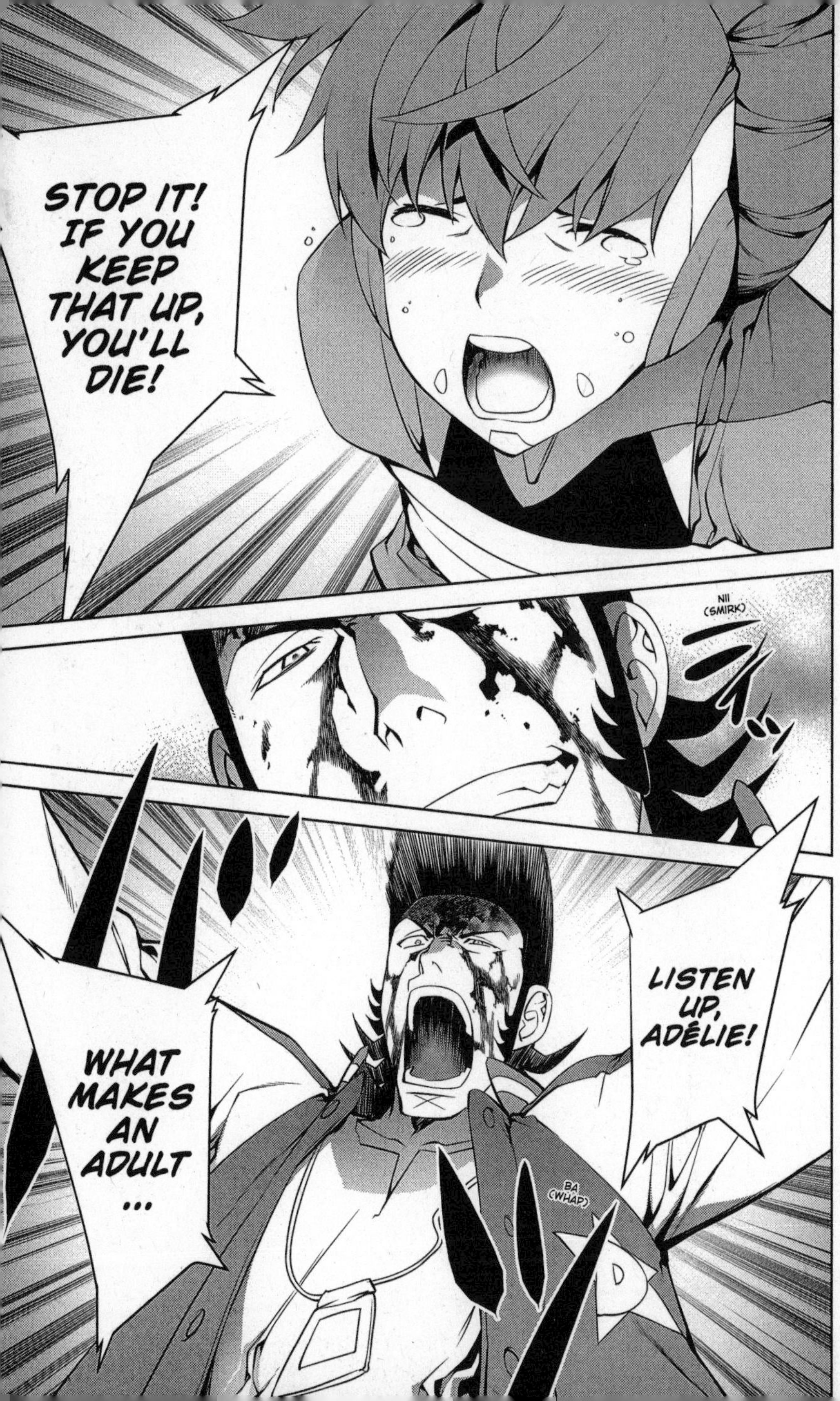
STOP IT! IF YOU KEEP THAT UP, YOU'LL DIE!
NII (SMIRK)
LISTEN UP, ADÉLIE!
WHAT MAKES AN ADULT ...
BA (WHAP)

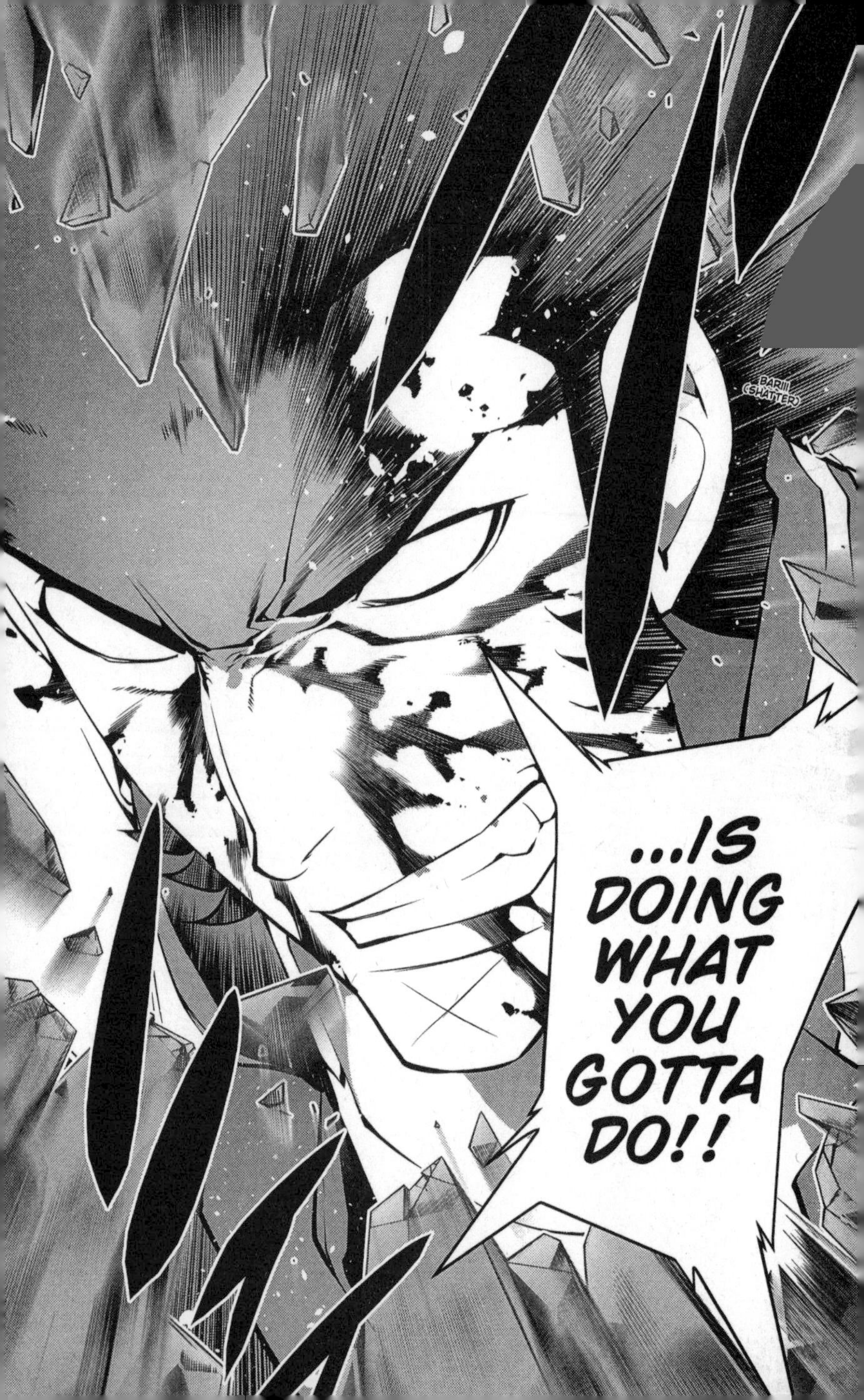
BARIII (SHATTER)
...IS DOING WHAT YOU GOTTA DO!!

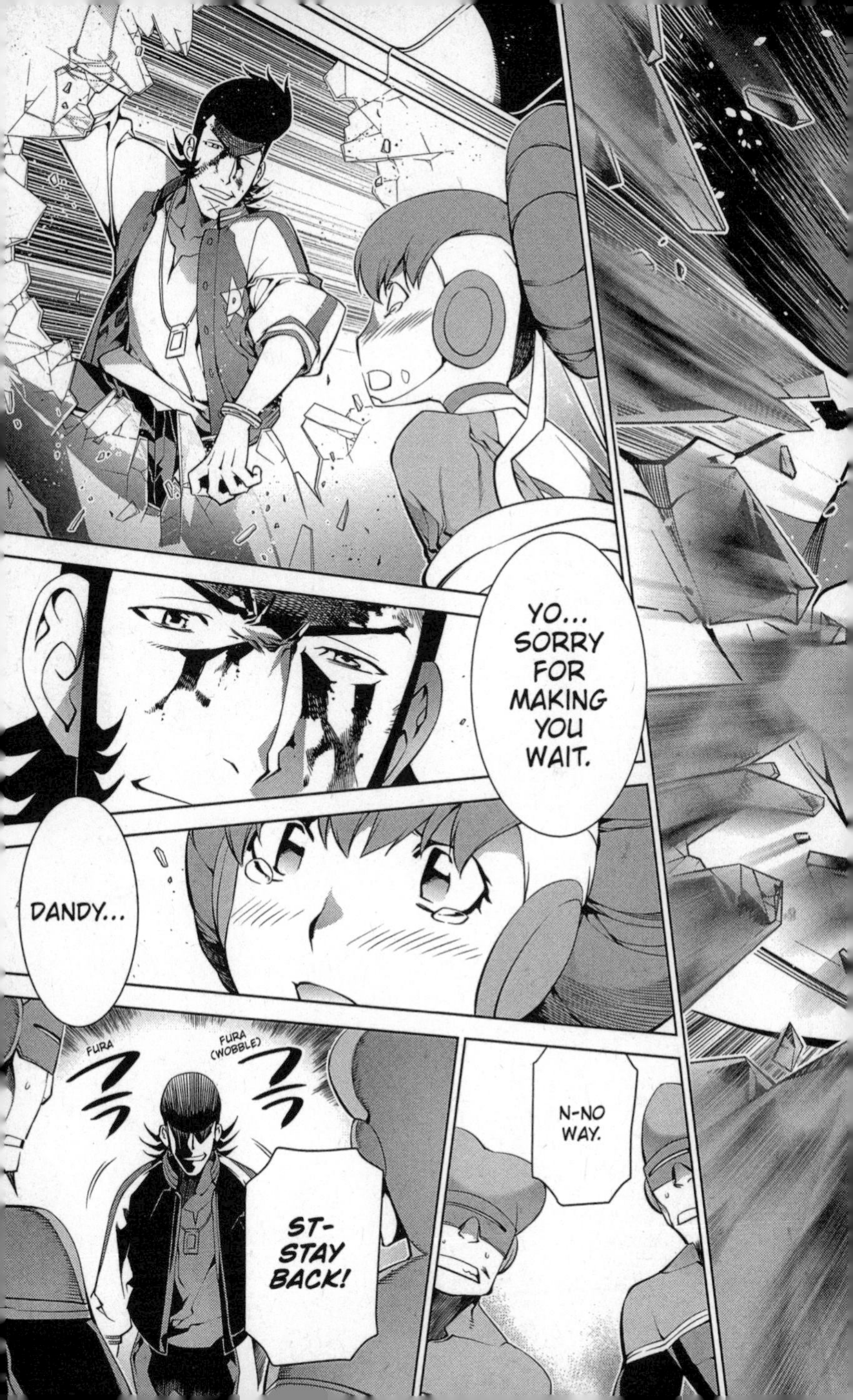
YO... SORRY FOR MAKING YOU WAIT.
DANDY...
N-NO WAY.
FURA (WOBBLE)
FURA
ST- STAY BACK!

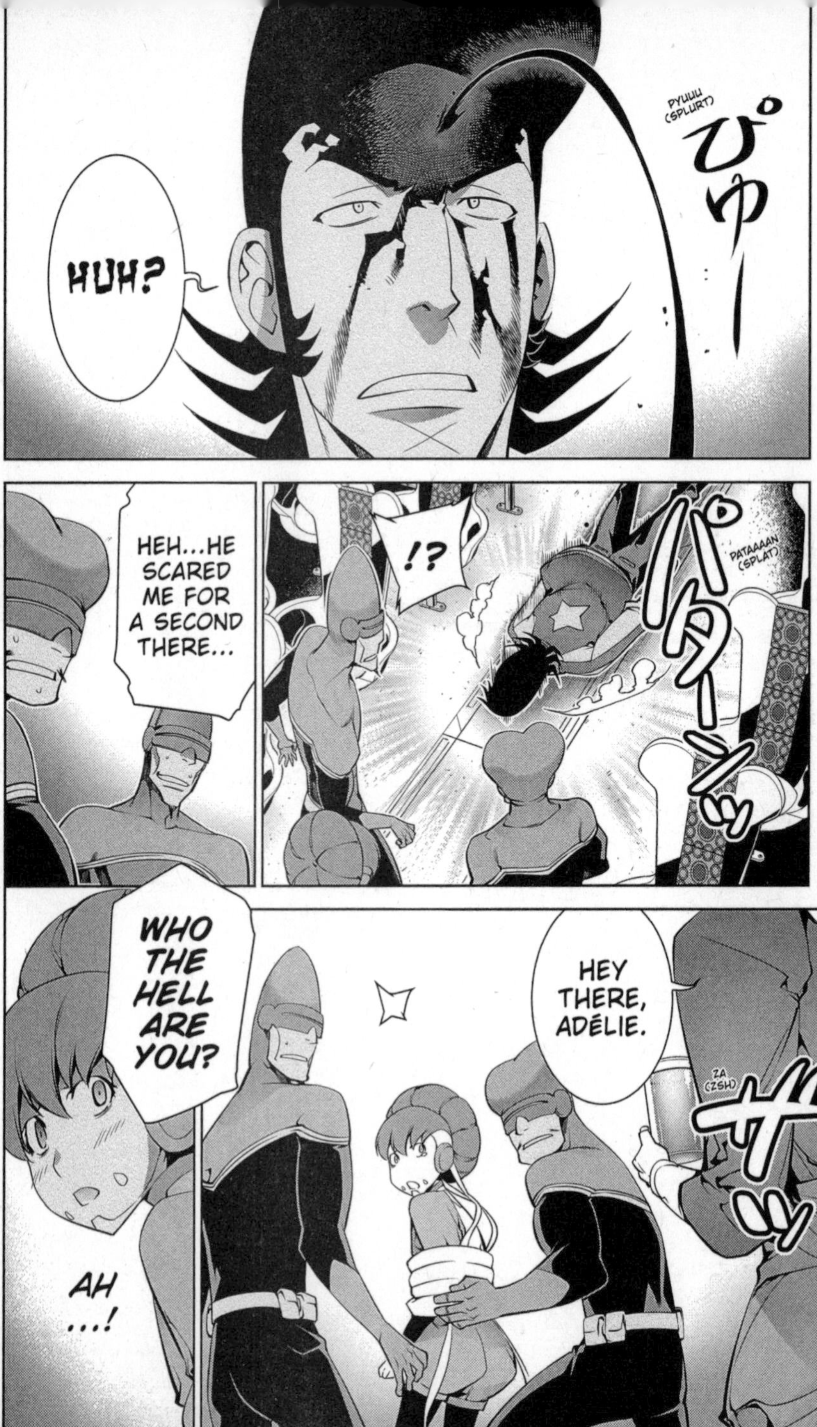
PYUUU (SPLURT)
ぴゅー
HUH?
PATAAAAN (SPLAT)
パターンッ
!?
HEH...HE SCARED ME FOR A SECOND THERE...
ZA (ZSH)
ザッ
HEY THERE, ADÉLIE.
WHO THE HELL ARE YOU?
AH ...!

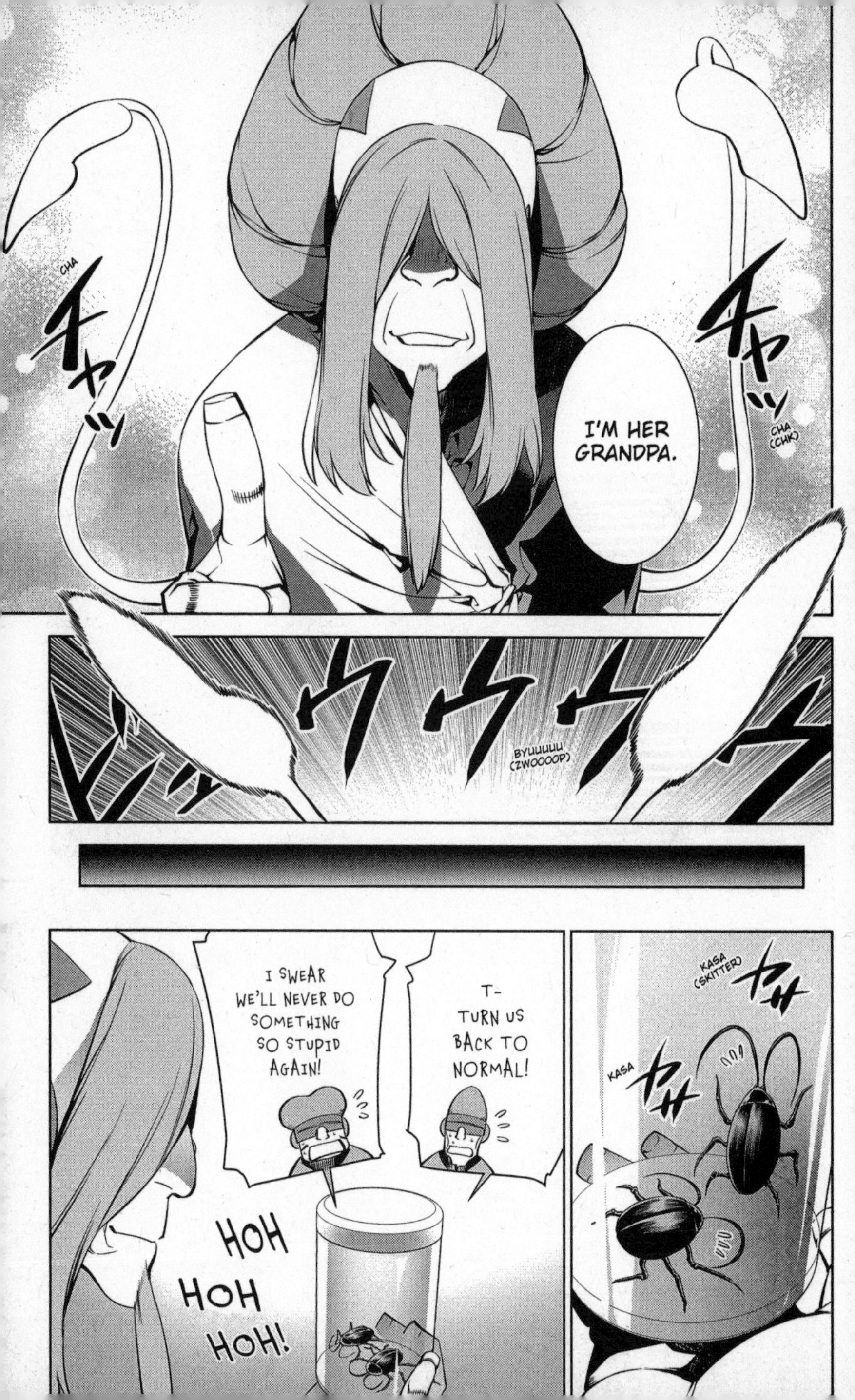
CHA (CHK)
I'M HER GRANDPA.
CHA
BYUUUUU (ZWOOOOP)
KASA (SKITTER)
KASA
T- TURN US BACK TO NORMAL!
I SWEAR WE'LL NEVER DO SOMETHING SO STUPID AGAIN!
HOH HOH HOH!

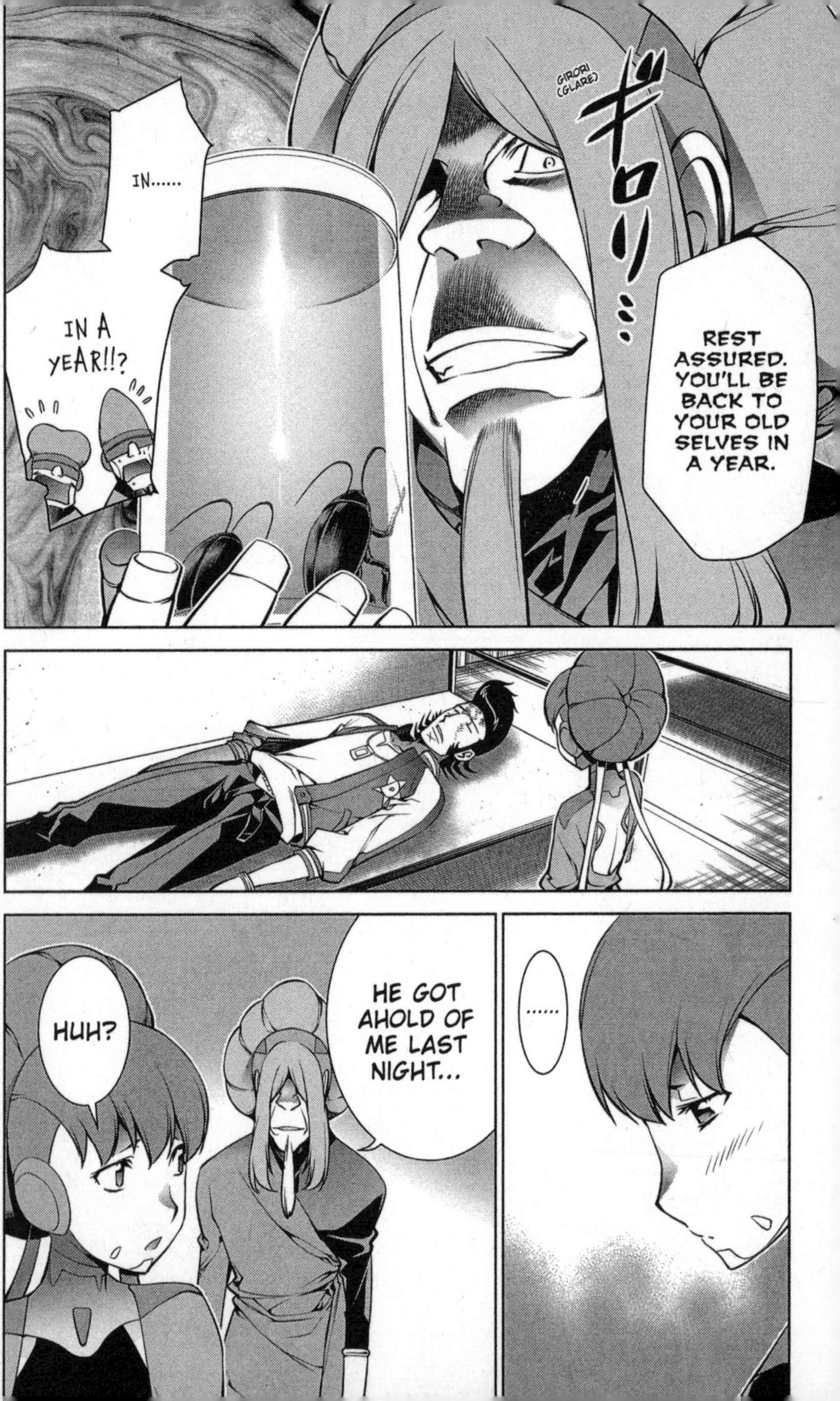
ギロリ
GIRORI (GLARE)
REST ASSURED. YOU'LL BE BACK TO YOUR OLD SELVES IN A YEAR.
IN......
IN A YEAR!!?
......
HE GOT AHOLD OF ME LAST NIGHT...
HUH?

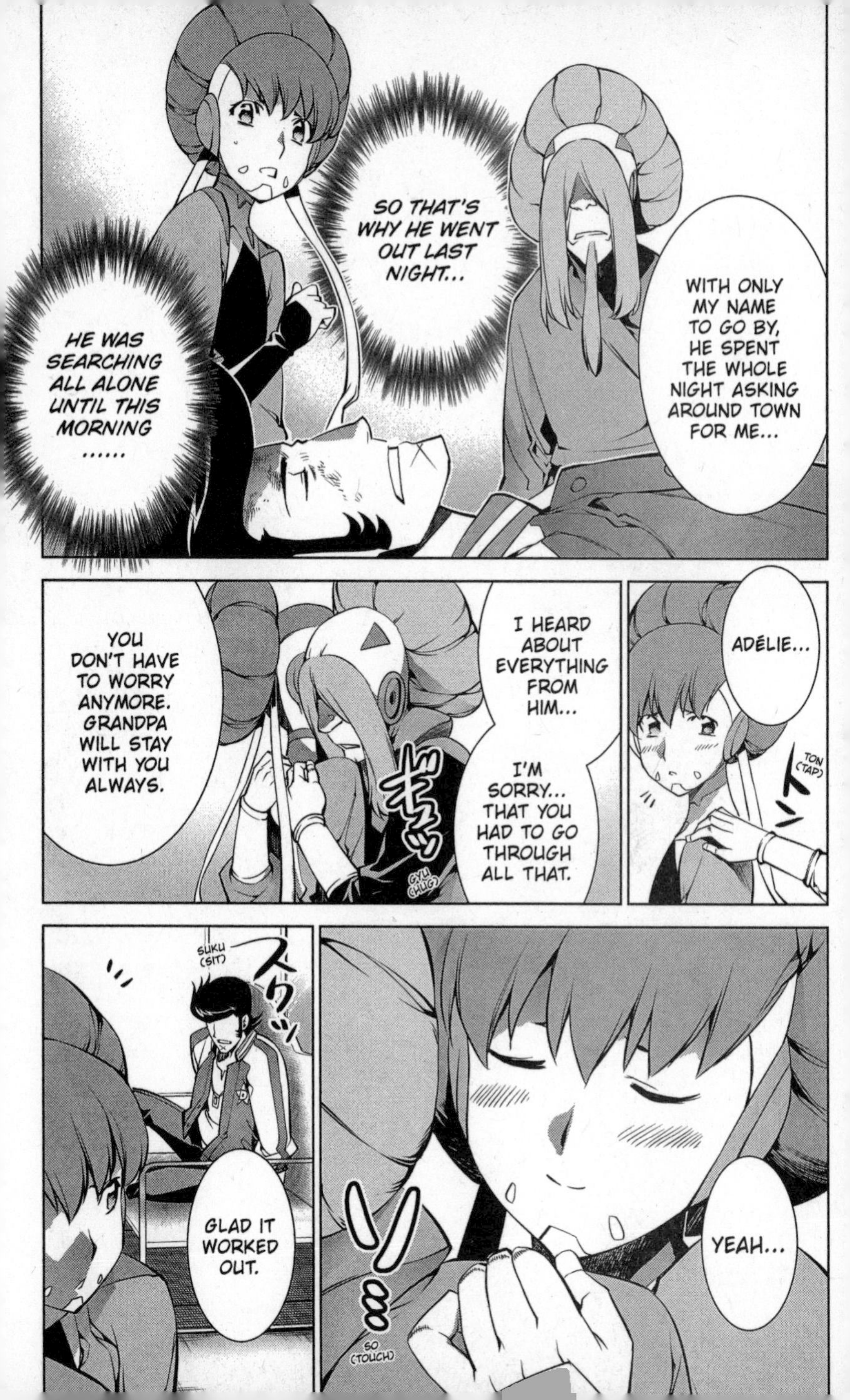
WITH ONLY MY NAME TO GO BY, HE SPENT THE WHOLE NIGHT ASKING AROUND TOWN FOR ME...
SO THAT'S WHY HE WENT OUT LAST NIGHT...
HE WAS SEARCHING ALL ALONE UNTIL THIS MORNING ......
ADÉLIE...
TON (TAP)
I HEARD ABOUT EVERYTHING FROM HIM...
I'M SORRY... THAT YOU HAD TO GO THROUGH ALL THAT.
GYU (HUG)
YOU DON'T HAVE TO WORRY ANYMORE. GRANDPA WILL STAY WITH YOU ALWAYS.
YEAH...
SO (TOUCH)
SUKU (SIT)
GLAD IT WORKED OUT.

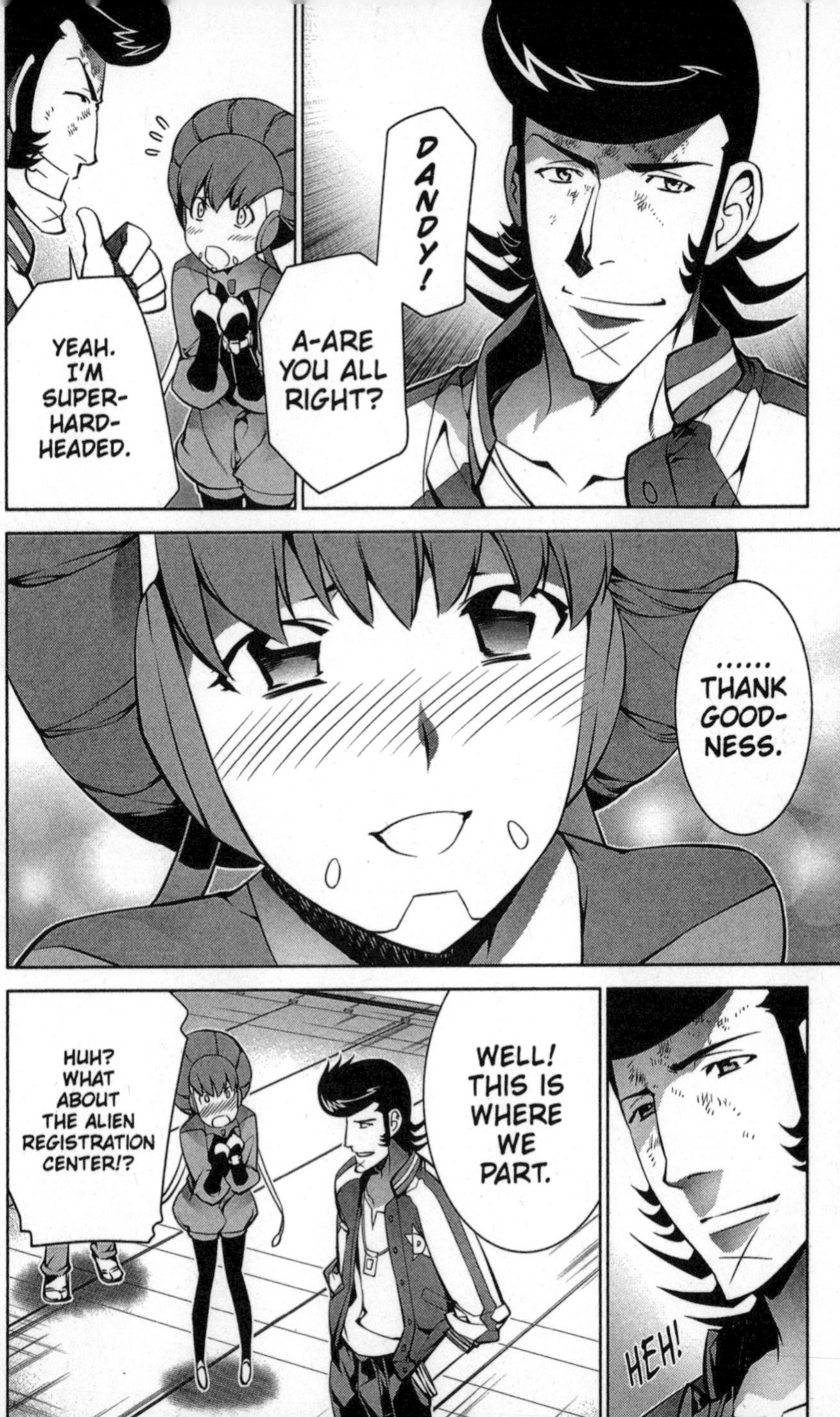
DANDY!
A-ARE YOU ALL RIGHT?
YEAH. I'M SUPER-HARD-HEADED.
...... THANK GOODNESS.
HEH!
WELL! THIS IS WHERE WE PART.
HUH? WHAT ABOUT THE ALIEN REGISTRATION CENTER!?

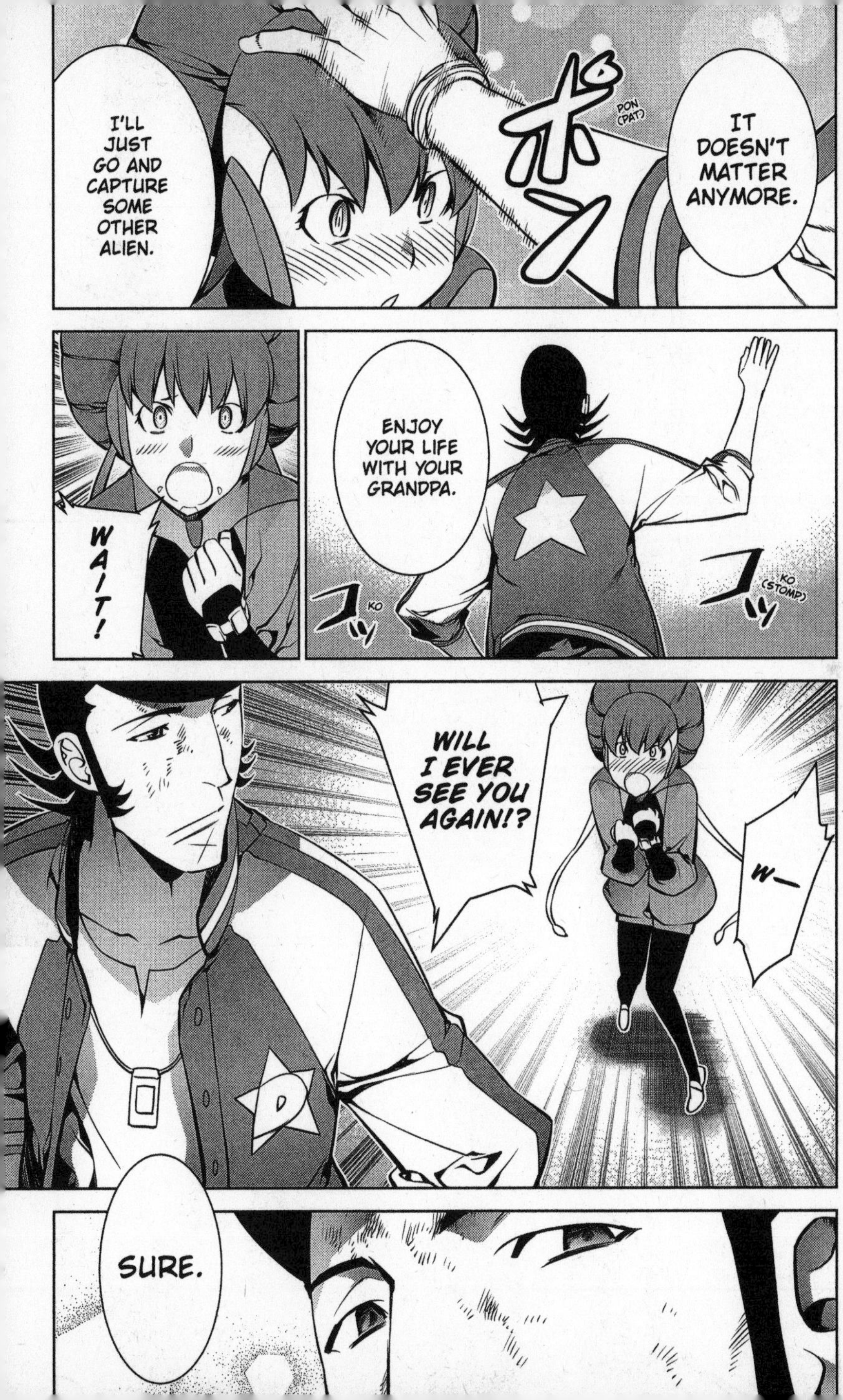
IT DOESN'T MATTER ANYMORE.
PON (PAT)
I'LL JUST GO AND CAPTURE SOME OTHER ALIEN.
KO (STOMP)
ENJOY YOUR LIFE WITH YOUR GRANDPA.
KO
WAIT!
W—
WILL I EVER SEE YOU AGAIN!?
SURE.

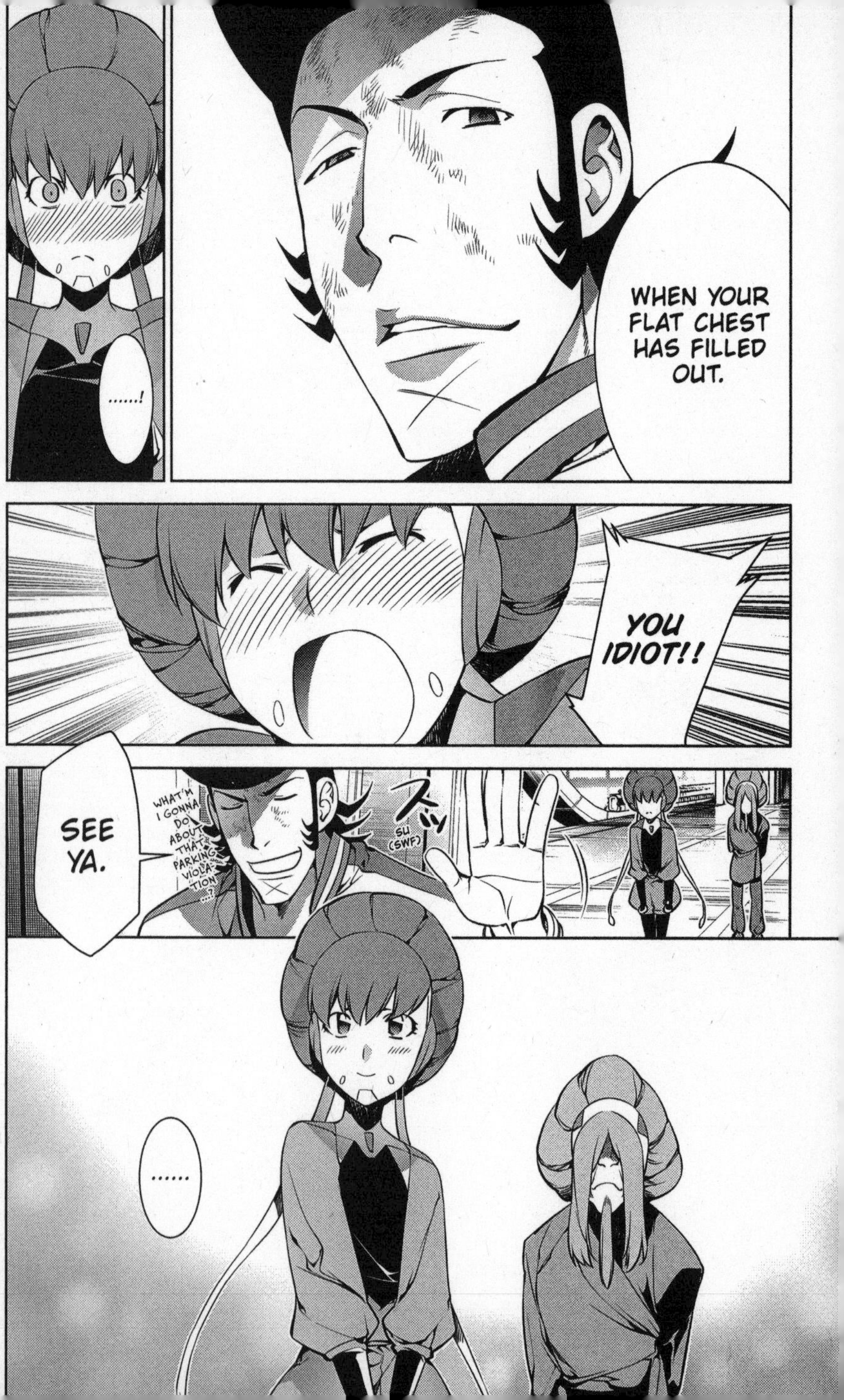
WHEN YOUR FLAT CHEST HAS FILLED OUT.
......!
YOU IDIOT!!
スッ
SU (SWF)
WHAT'M I GONNA DO ABOUT THAT PARKING VIOLATION ...?
SEE YA.
......

SPACE DANDY

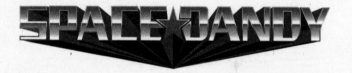

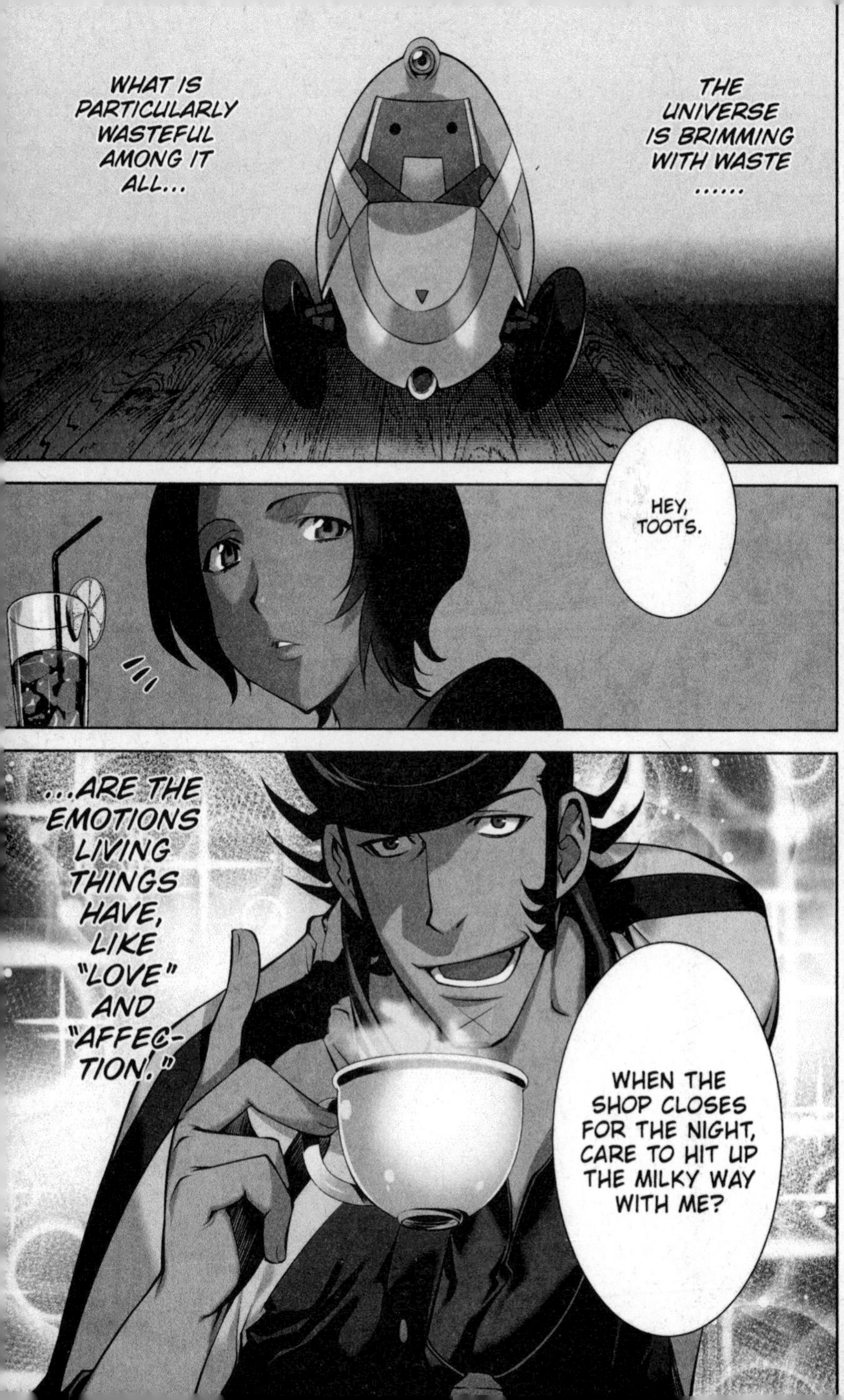
THE UNIVERSE IS BRIMMING WITH WASTE ......
WHAT IS PARTICULARLY WASTEFUL AMONG IT ALL...
HEY, TOOTS.
...ARE THE EMOTIONS LIVING THINGS HAVE, LIKE "LOVE" AND "AFFECTION."
WHEN THE SHOP CLOSES FOR THE NIGHT, CARE TO HIT UP THE MILKY WAY WITH ME?

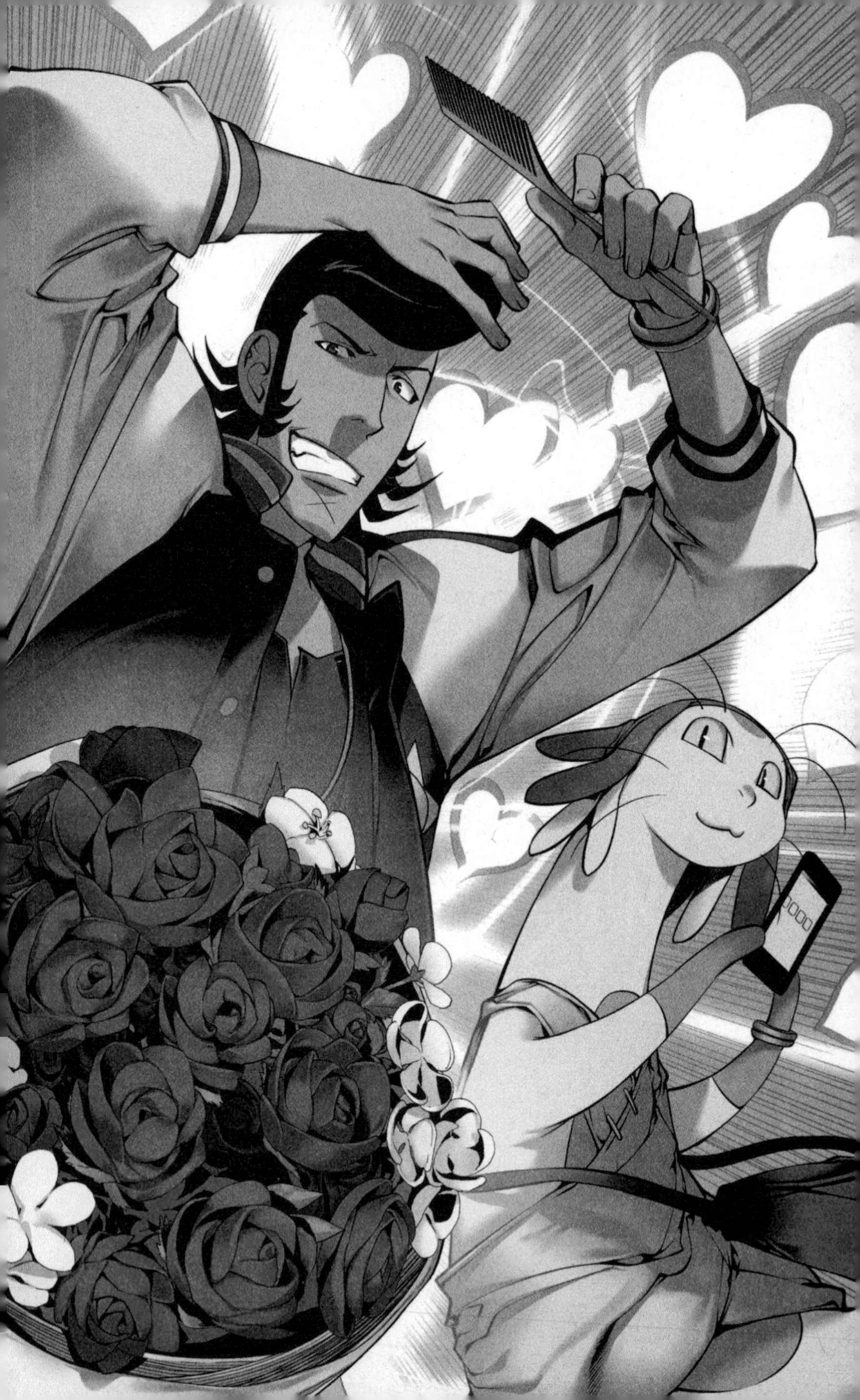

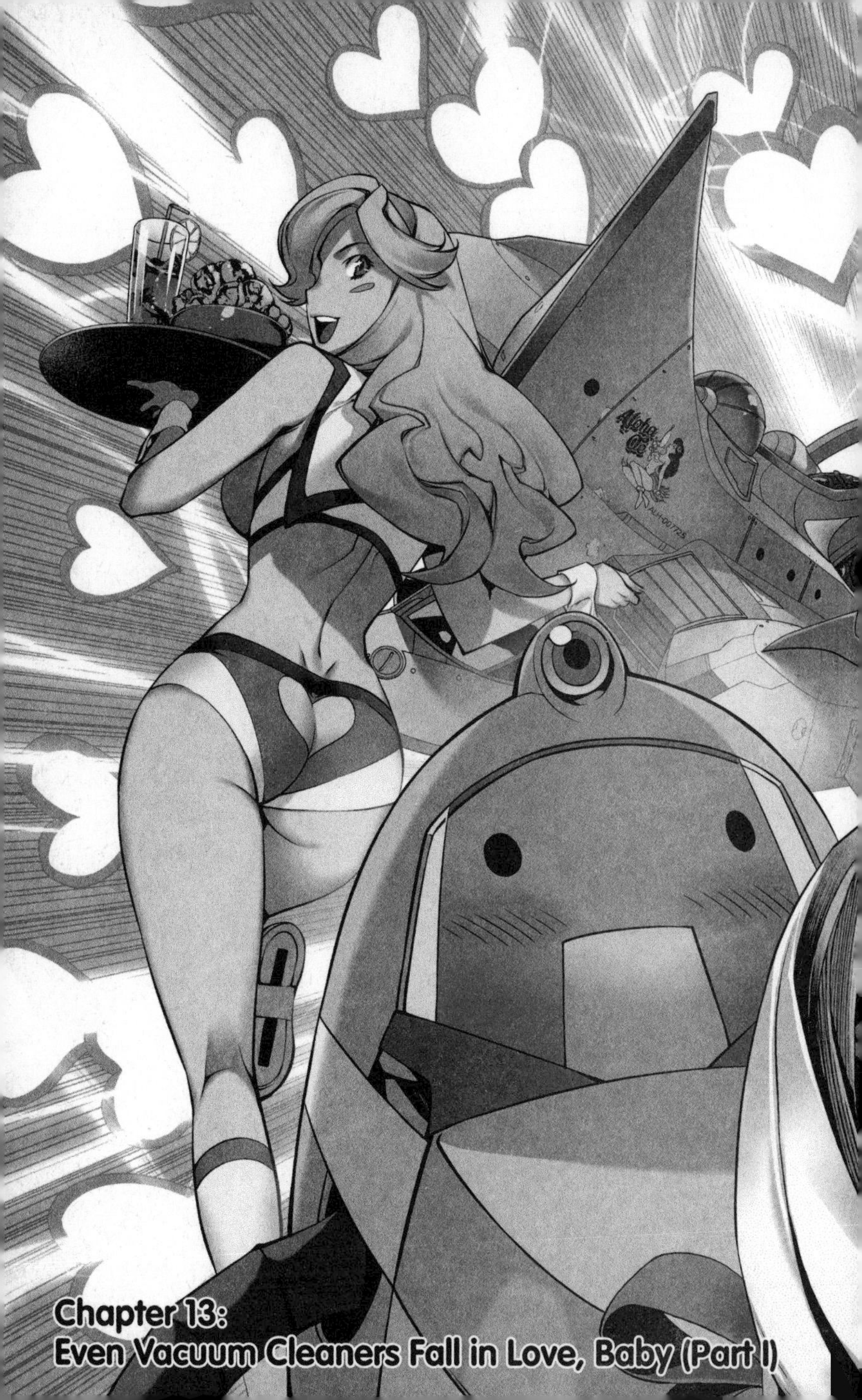

Chapter 13:
Even Vacuum Cleaners Fall in Love, Baby (Part I)

SPACE DANDY

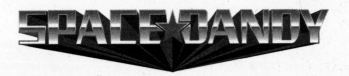

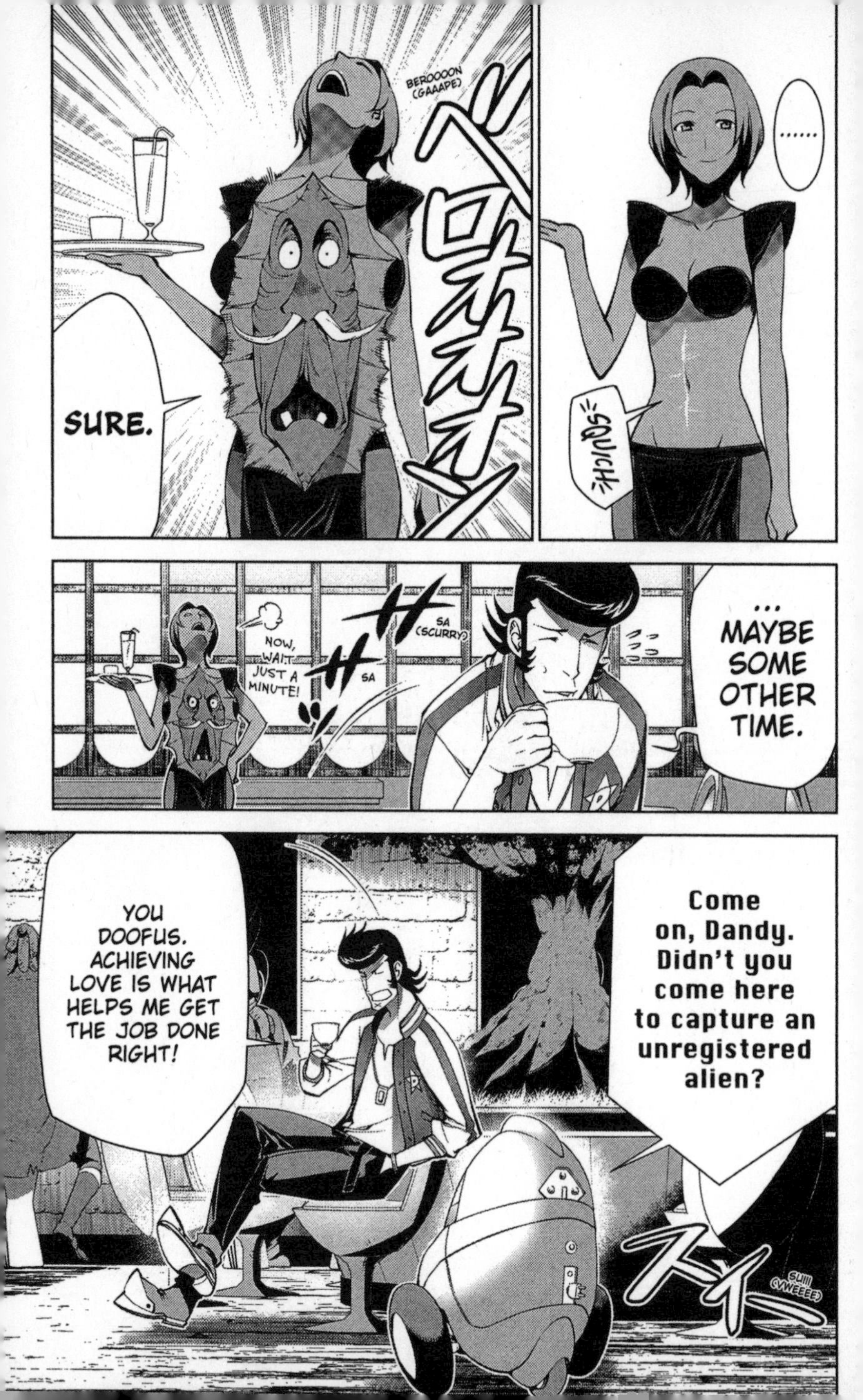
......
SQUICH
BEROOOON (GAAAPE)
SURE.
... MAYBE SOME OTHER TIME.
SA (SCURRY)
SA
NOW, WAIT JUST A MINUTE!
Come on, Dandy. Didn't you come here to capture an unregistered alien?
YOU DOOFUS. ACHIEVING LOVE IS WHAT HELPS ME GET THE JOB DONE RIGHT!
SUIII (VWEEEE)

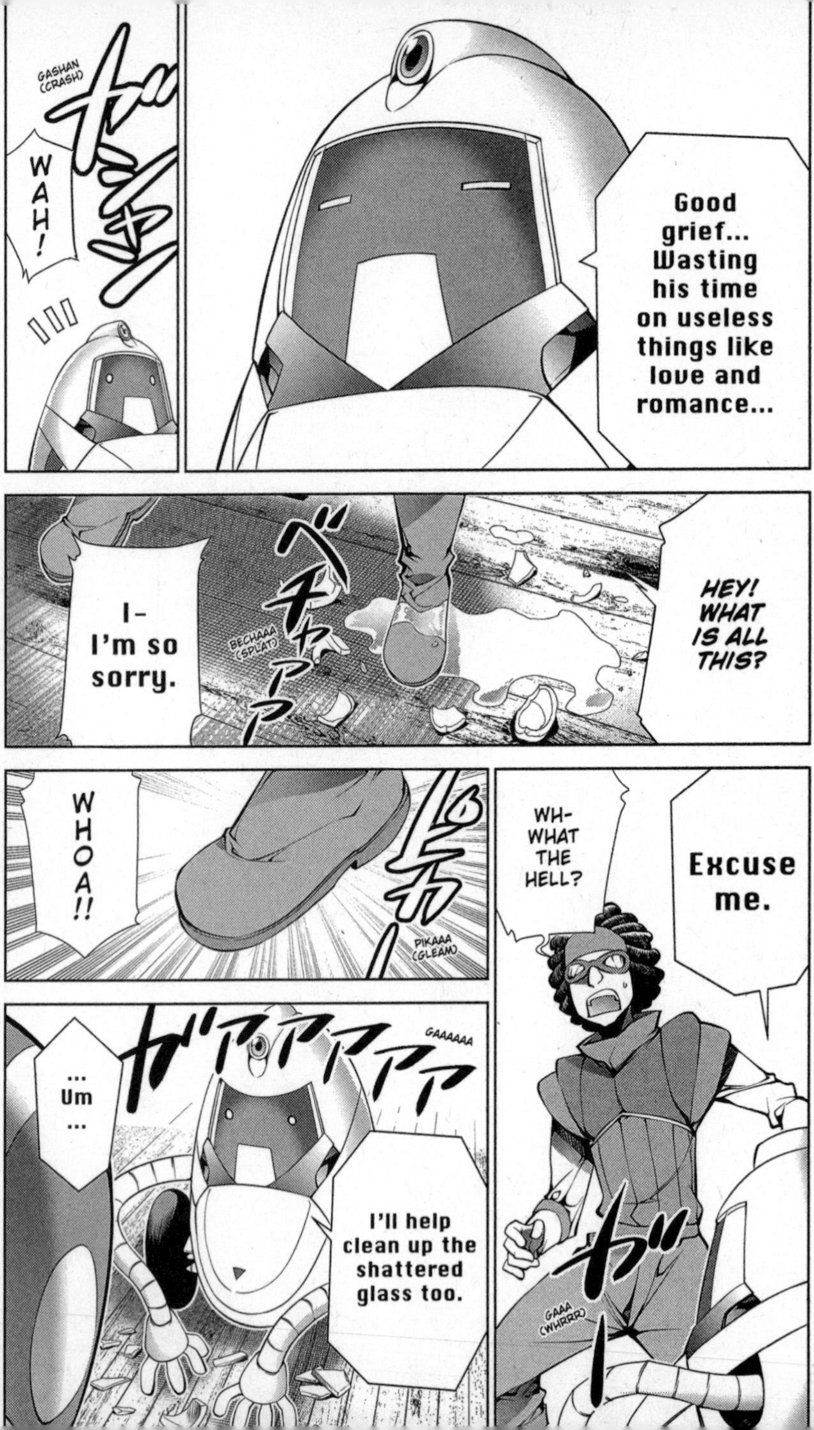
Good grief... Wasting his time on useless things like love and romance...
GASHAN (CRASH)
WAH!
HEY! WHAT IS ALL THIS?
BECHAAA (SPLAT)
I- I'm so sorry.
Excuse me.
WH- WHAT THE HELL?
GAAA (WHRRR)
PIKAAA (GLEAM)
WHOA!!
GAAAAAA
I'll help clean up the shattered glass too.
... Um ...

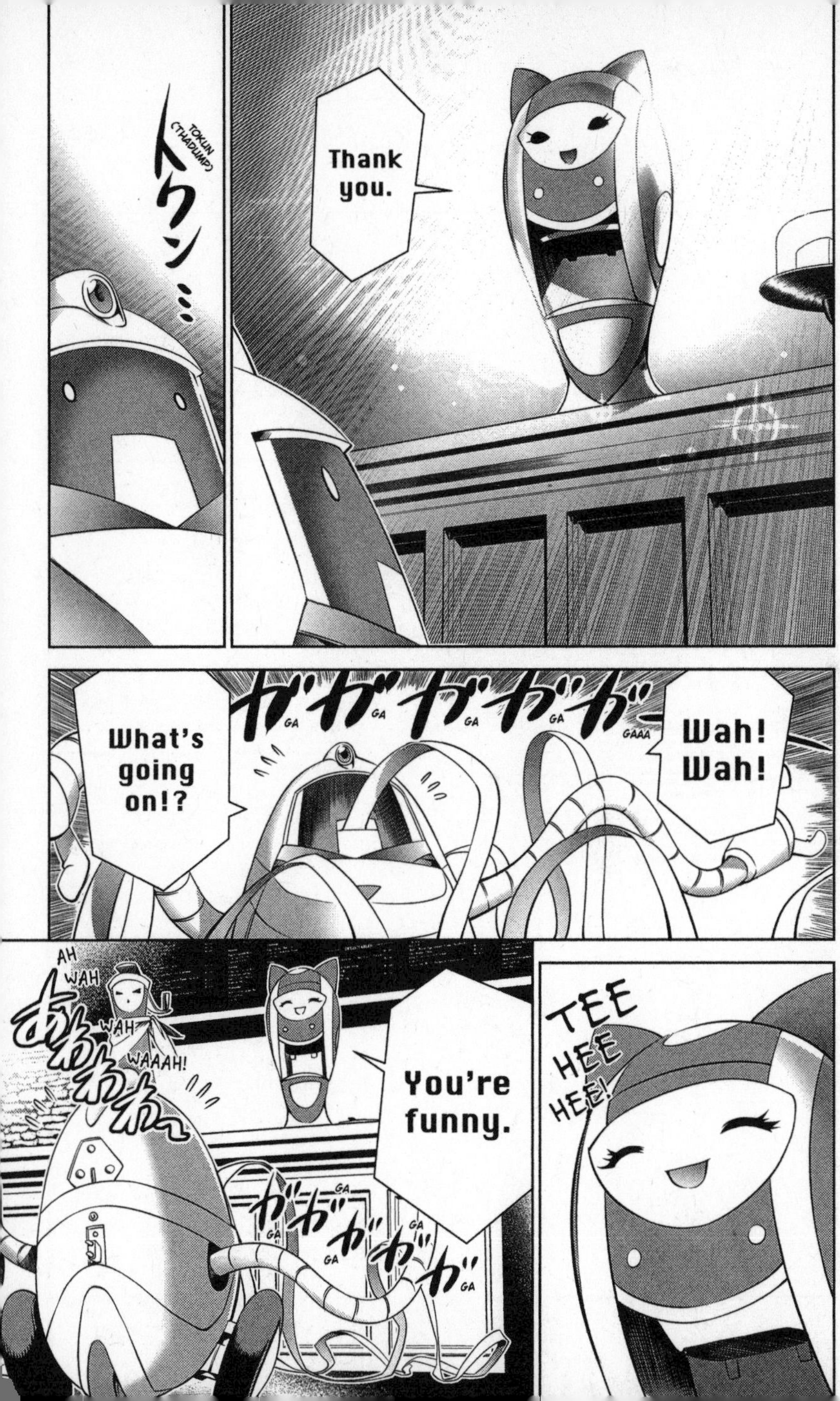
Thank you.
トクン…
TOKUN (THADUMP)
Wah! Wah!
ガガガガガー
GA GA GA GA GAAA
What's going on!?
TEE HEE HEE!
You're funny.
あわわわ〜
AH WAH WAH WAAAH!
ガガガガガ
GA GA GA GA GA

When it comes to making coffee, nobody can beat me.

I'm Coffee Maker.

Wh- when it comes to cleaning, nobody can beat me!

...I'm QT.

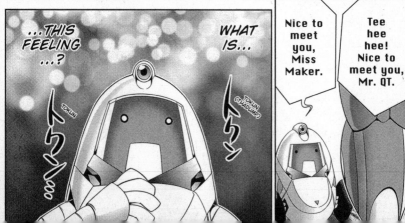

...THIS FEELING...?

WHAT IS...

Nice to meet you, Miss Maker.

Tee hee hee! Nice to meet you, Mr. QT.

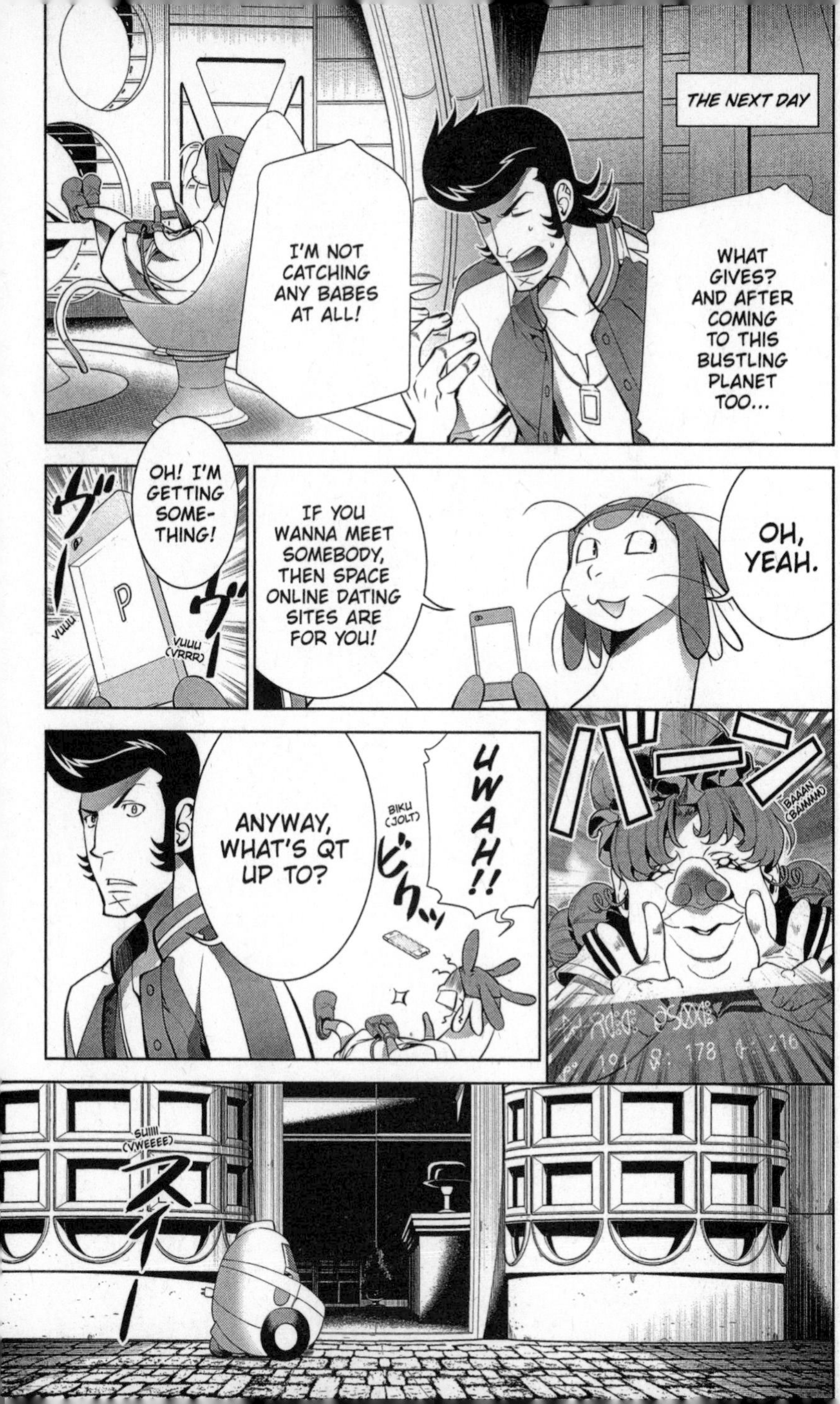
THE NEXT DAY
WHAT GIVES? AND AFTER COMING TO THIS BUSTLING PLANET TOO...
I'M NOT CATCHING ANY BABES AT ALL!
OH, YEAH.
IF YOU WANNA MEET SOMEBODY, THEN SPACE ONLINE DATING SITES ARE FOR YOU!
OH! I'M GETTING SOME-THING!
VUUU (VRRR)
VUUU
BAAAN (BAMMM)
UWAH!!
BIKU (JOLT)
ANYWAY, WHAT'S QT UP TO?
SUIIII (VWEEEE)

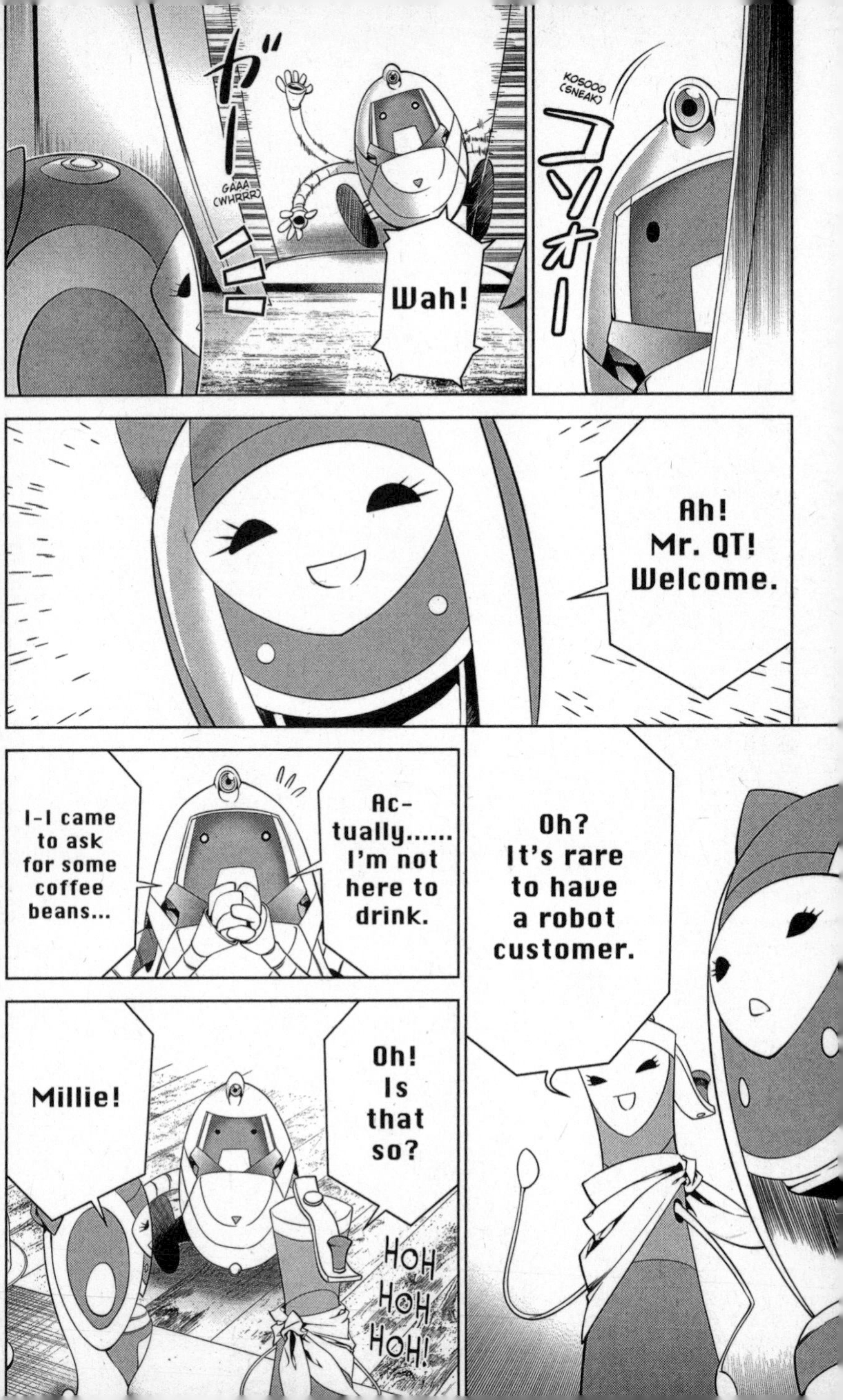
KOSOOO (SNEAK)
GAAA (WHRRR)
Wah!
Ah! Mr. QT! Welcome.
Oh? It's rare to have a robot customer.
Ac-tually...... I'm not here to drink.
I-I came to ask for some coffee beans...
Oh! Is that so?
Millie!
HOH HOH HOH!

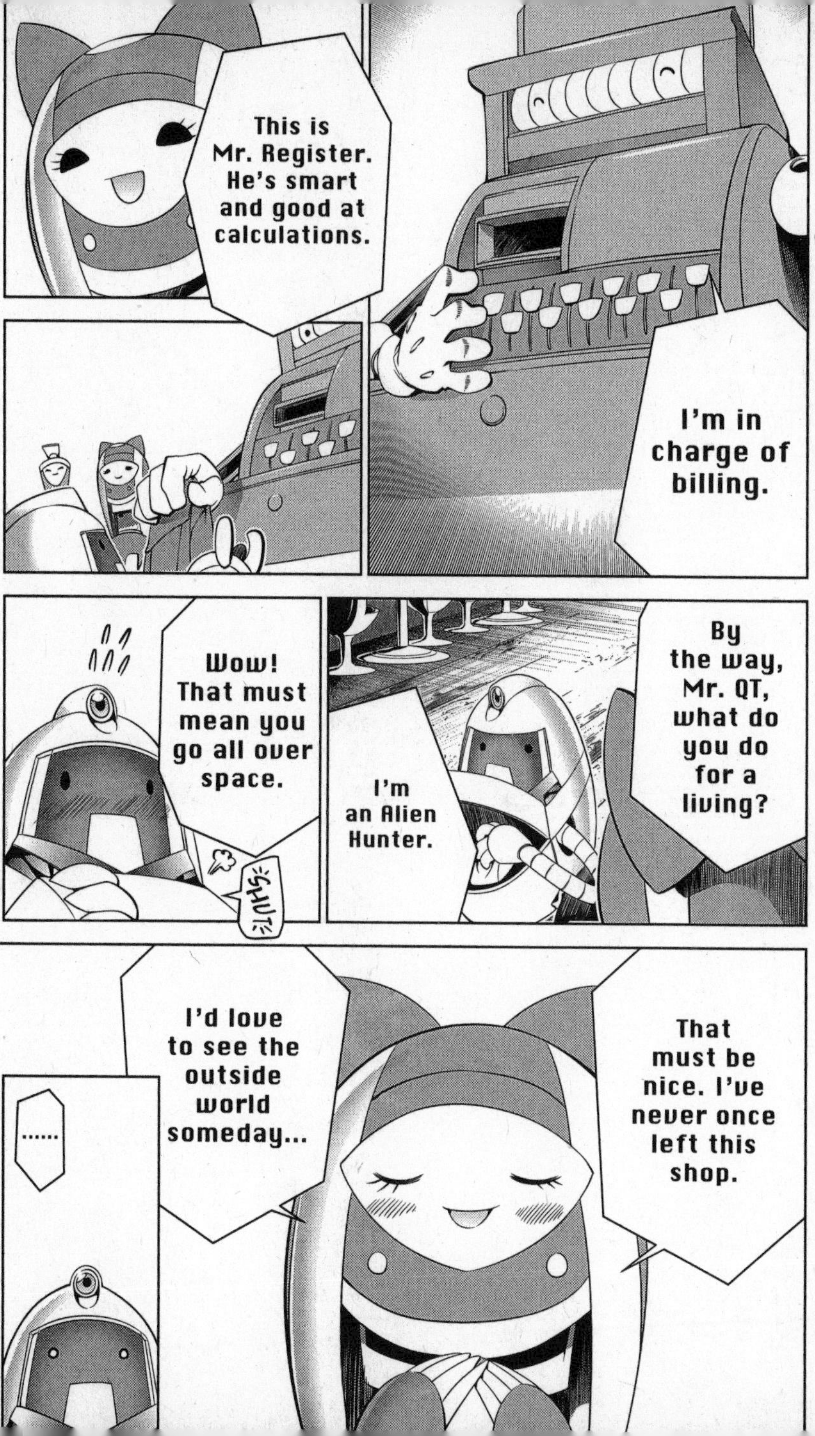
I'm in charge of billing.
This is Mr. Register. He's smart and good at calculations.
By the way, Mr. QT, what do you do for a living?
I'm an Alien Hunter.
Wow! That must mean you go all over space.
SHUT
That must be nice. I've never once left this shop.
I'd love to see the outside world someday...
......

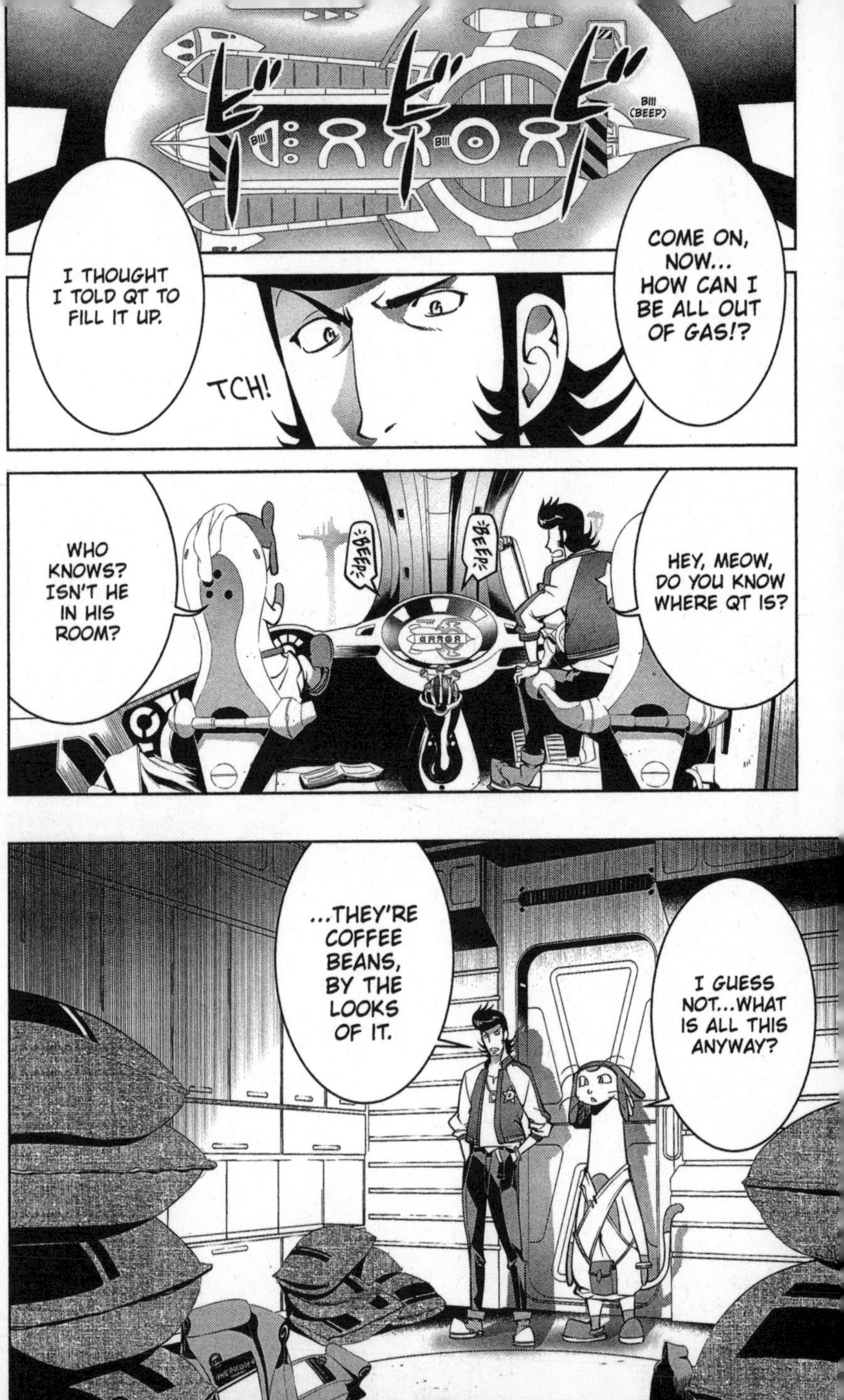
BIII (BEEP)
BIII
BIII
COME ON, NOW... HOW CAN I BE ALL OUT OF GAS!?
TCH!
I THOUGHT I TOLD QT TO FILL IT UP.
HEY, MEOW, DO YOU KNOW WHERE QT IS?
BEEP
BEEP
WHO KNOWS? ISN'T HE IN HIS ROOM?
I GUESS NOT...WHAT IS ALL THIS ANYWAY?
...THEY'RE COFFEE BEANS, BY THE LOOKS OF IT.

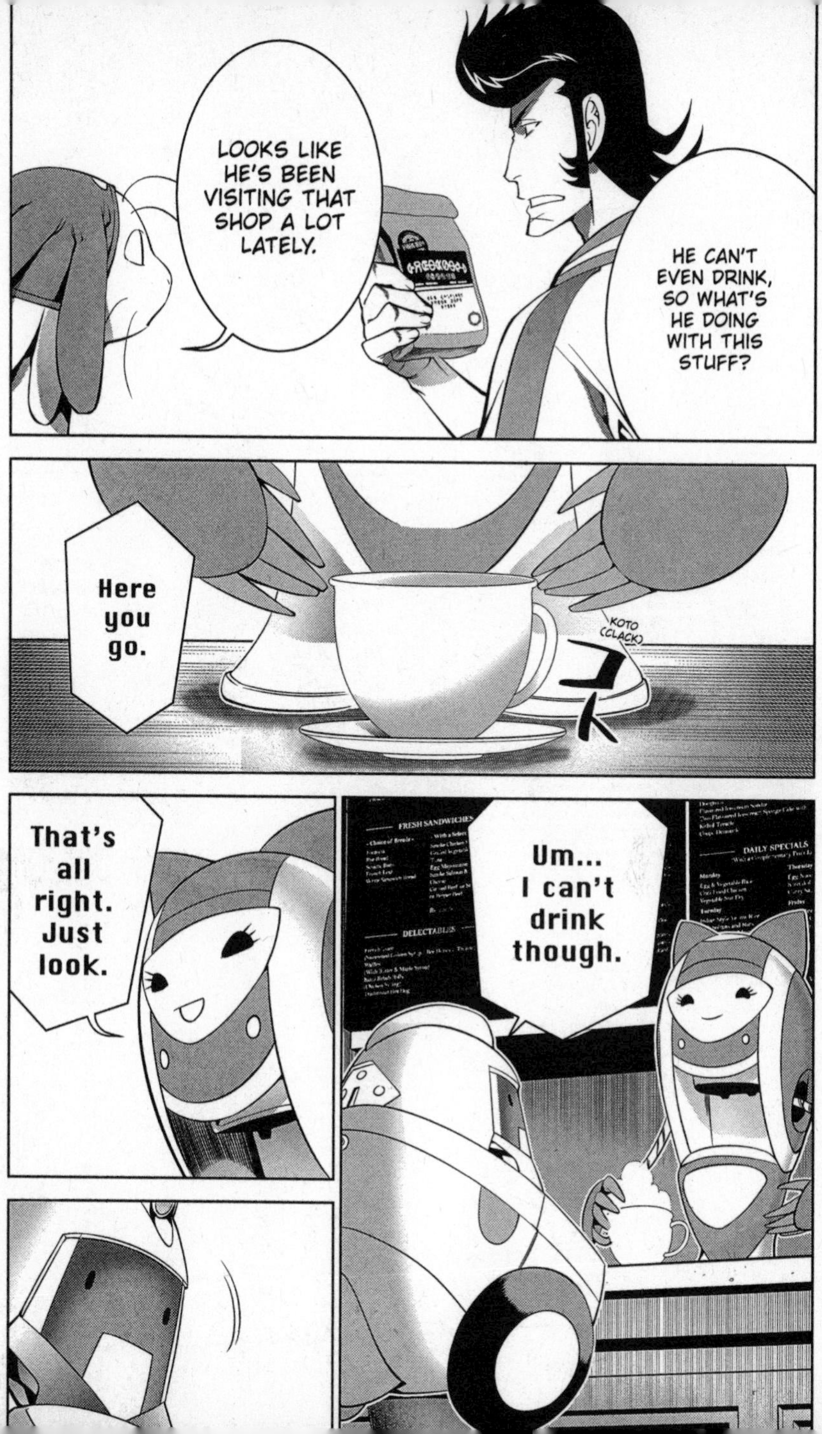
LOOKS LIKE HE'S BEEN VISITING THAT SHOP A LOT LATELY.
HE CAN'T EVEN DRINK, SO WHAT'S HE DOING WITH THIS STUFF?
Here you go.
KOTO (CLACK)
FRESH SANDWICHES
DELECTABLES
DAILY SPECIALS
Um... I can't drink though.
That's all right. Just look.

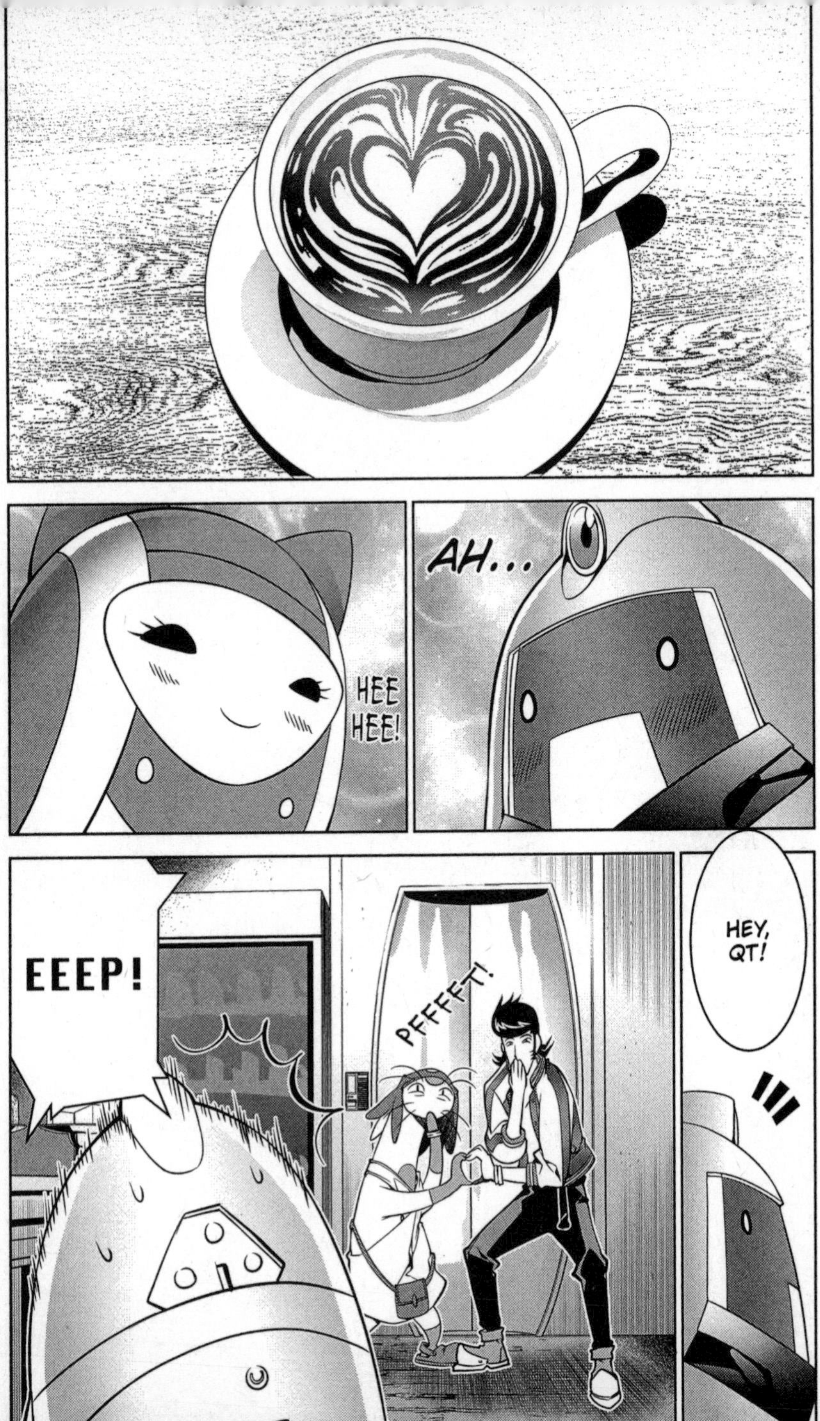
AH...
HEE HEE!
HEY, QT!
EEEP!
PFFFFT!

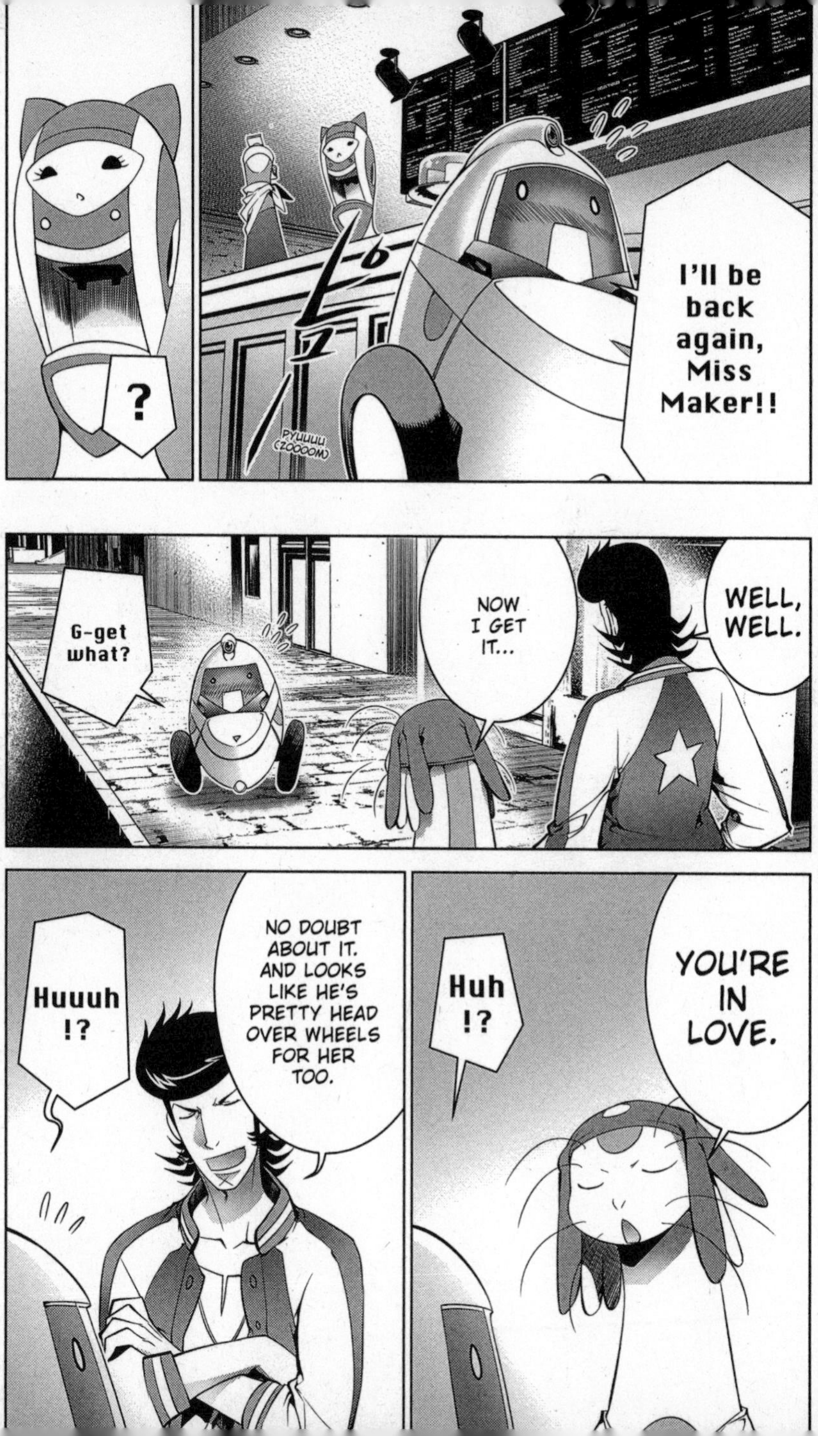
I'll be back again, Miss Maker!!
PYUUUU (ZOOOOM)
?
WELL, WELL.
NOW I GET IT...
G-get what?
YOU'RE IN LOVE.
Huh !?
NO DOUBT ABOUT IT. AND LOOKS LIKE HE'S PRETTY HEAD OVER WHEELS FOR HER TOO.
Huuuh !?

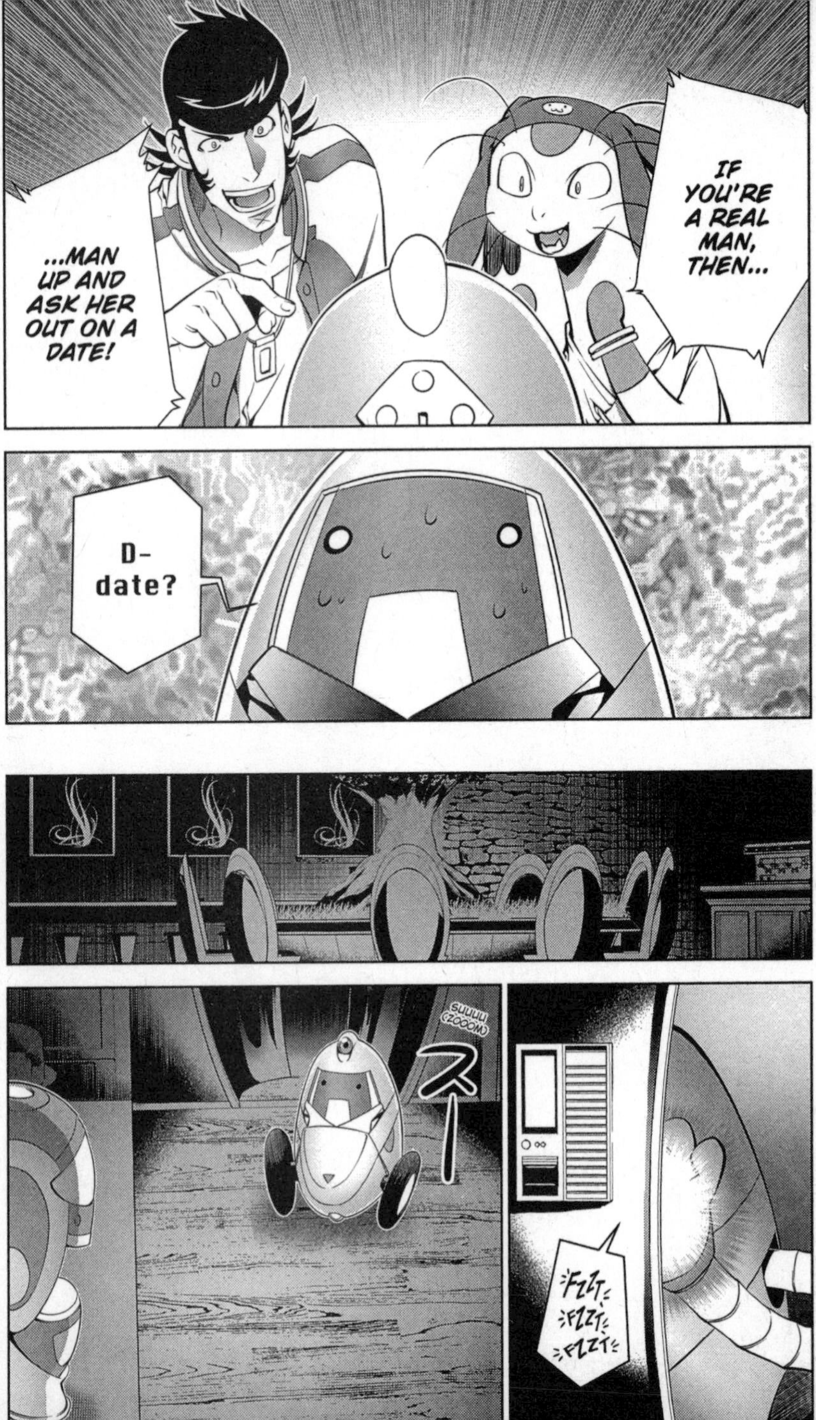
IF YOU'RE A REAL MAN, THEN...
...MAN UP AND ASK HER OUT ON A DATE!
D-date?
FZZT FZZT FZZT
SUUUU (ZOOOM)
スー

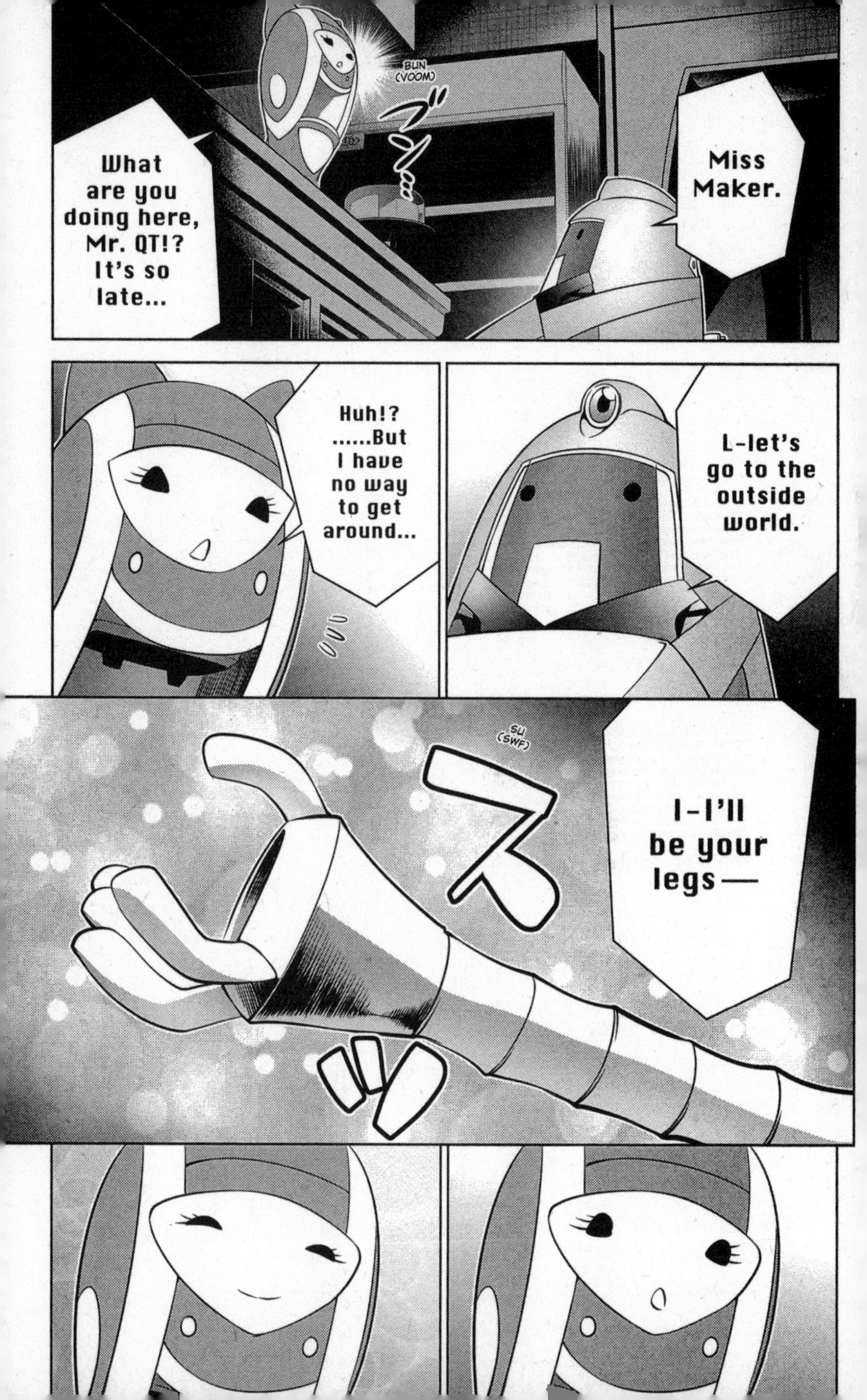
Miss Maker.
BUN (VOOM)
What are you doing here, Mr. QT!? It's so late...
L-let's go to the outside world.
Huh!? ......But I have no way to get around...
I-I'll be your legs—
SU (SWF)

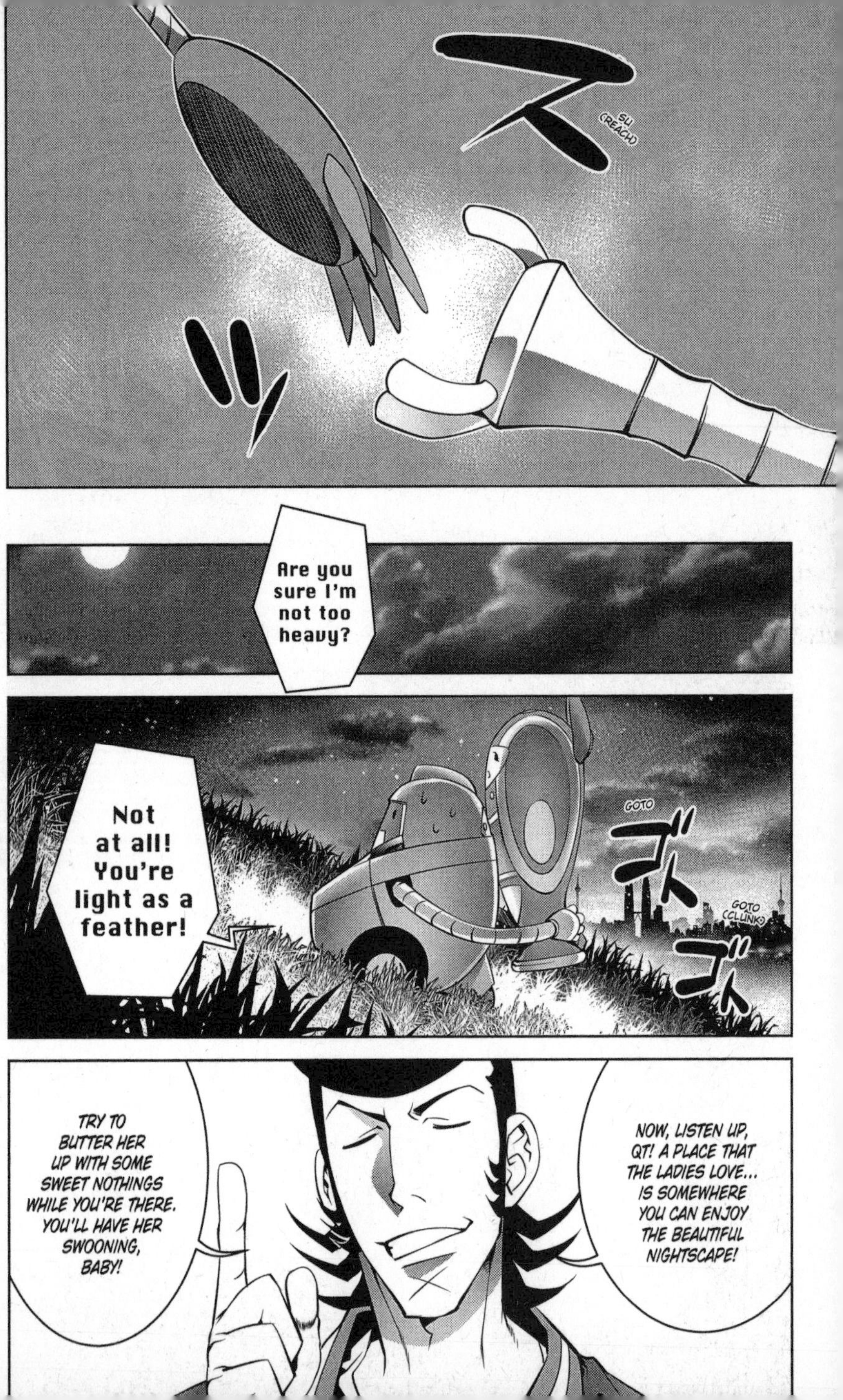
SU
(REACH)
Are you sure I'm not too heavy?
Not at all! You're light as a feather!
GOTO
GOTO (CLUNK)
NOW, LISTEN UP, QT! A PLACE THAT THE LADIES LOVE... IS SOMEWHERE YOU CAN ENJOY THE BEAUTIFUL NIGHTSCAPE!
TRY TO BUTTER HER UP WITH SOME SWEET NOTHINGS WHILE YOU'RE THERE. YOU'LL HAVE HER SWOONING, BABY!

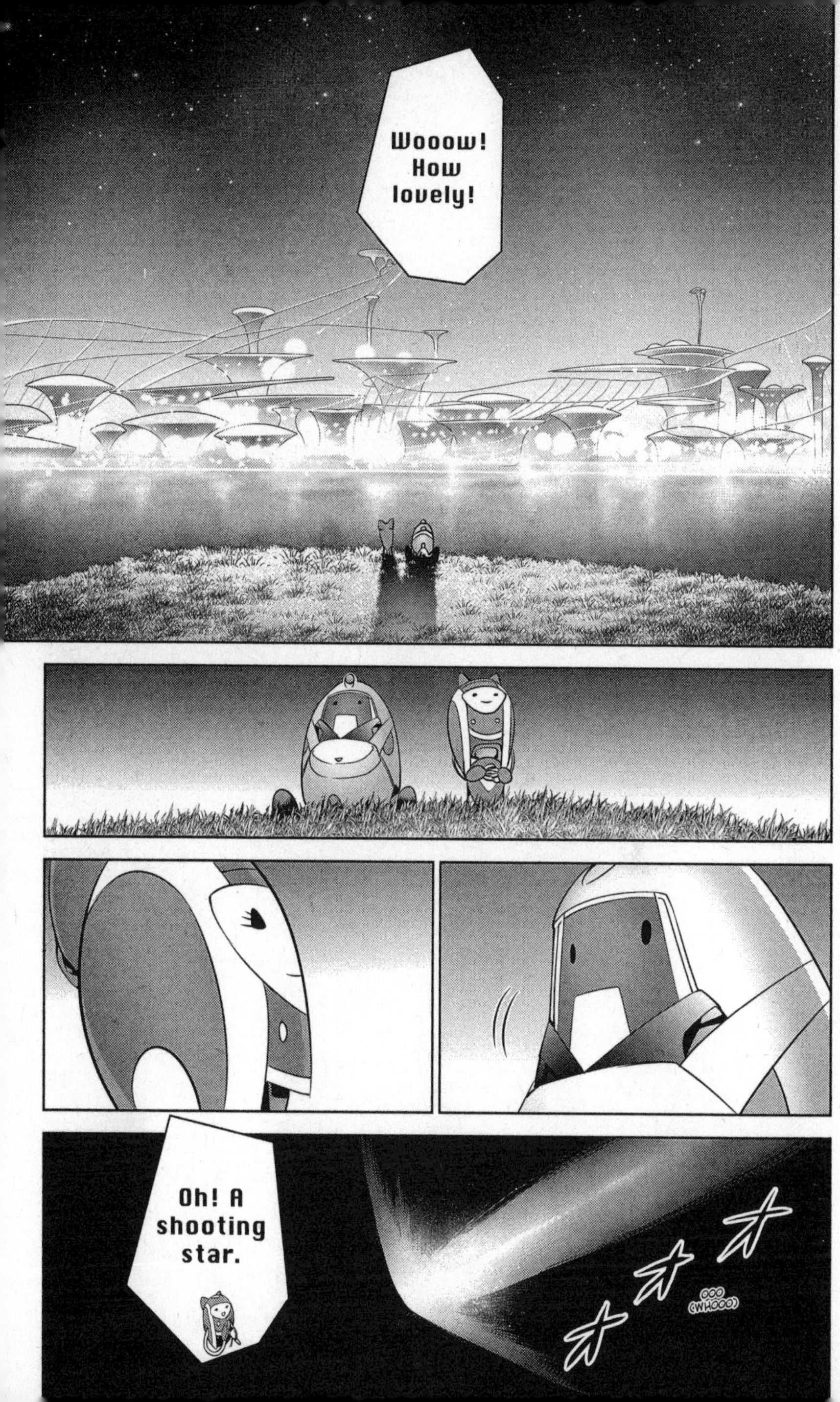
Wooow! How lovely!
Oh! A shooting star.
OOO (WHOOO)

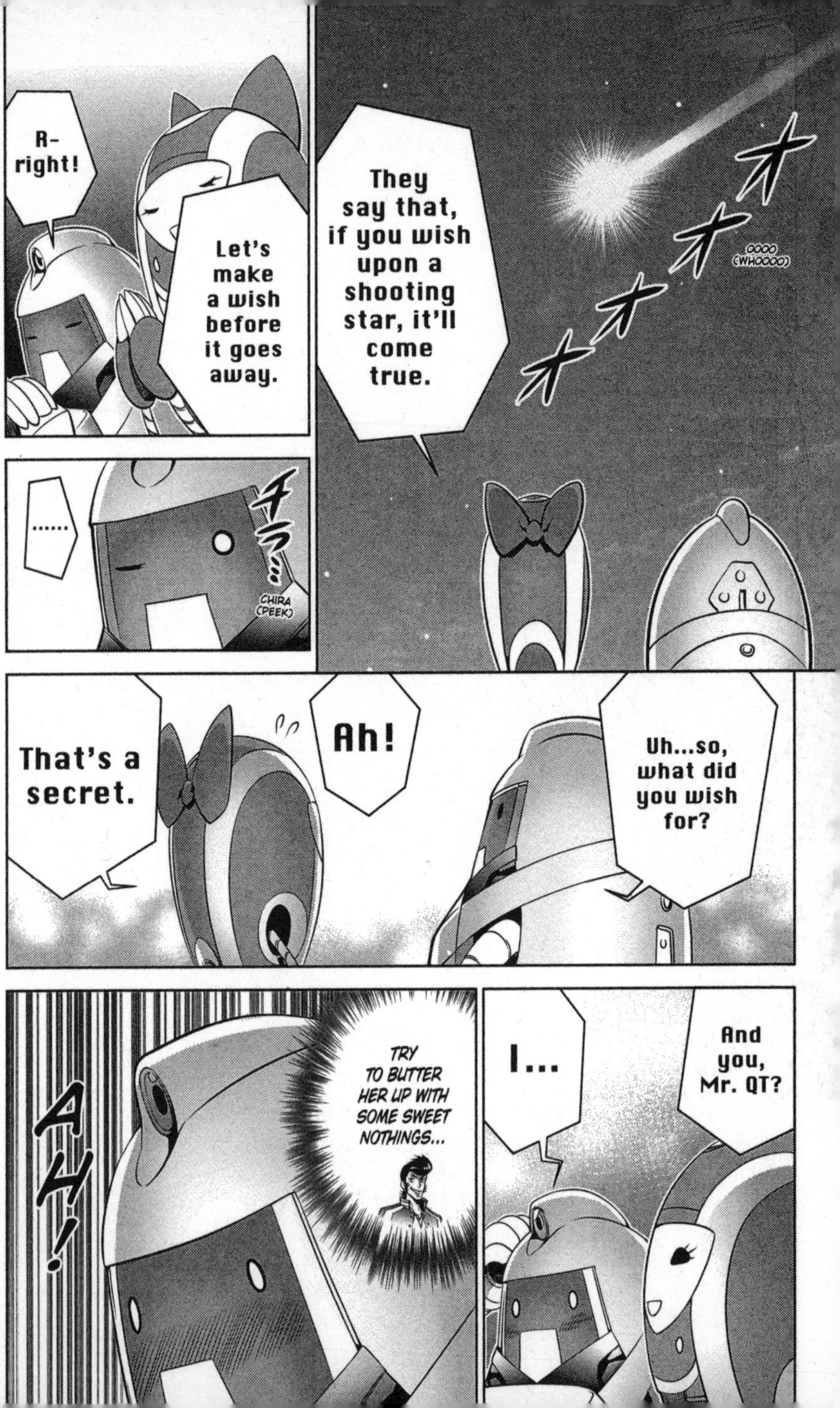
They say that, if you wish upon a shooting star, it'll come true.
OOOO (WHOOOO)
Let's make a wish before it goes away.
R-right!
......
CHIRA (PEEK)
Uh...so, what did you wish for?
Ah!
That's a secret.
And you, Mr. QT?
I...
TRY TO BUTTER HER UP WITH SOME SWEET NOTHINGS...
AH!

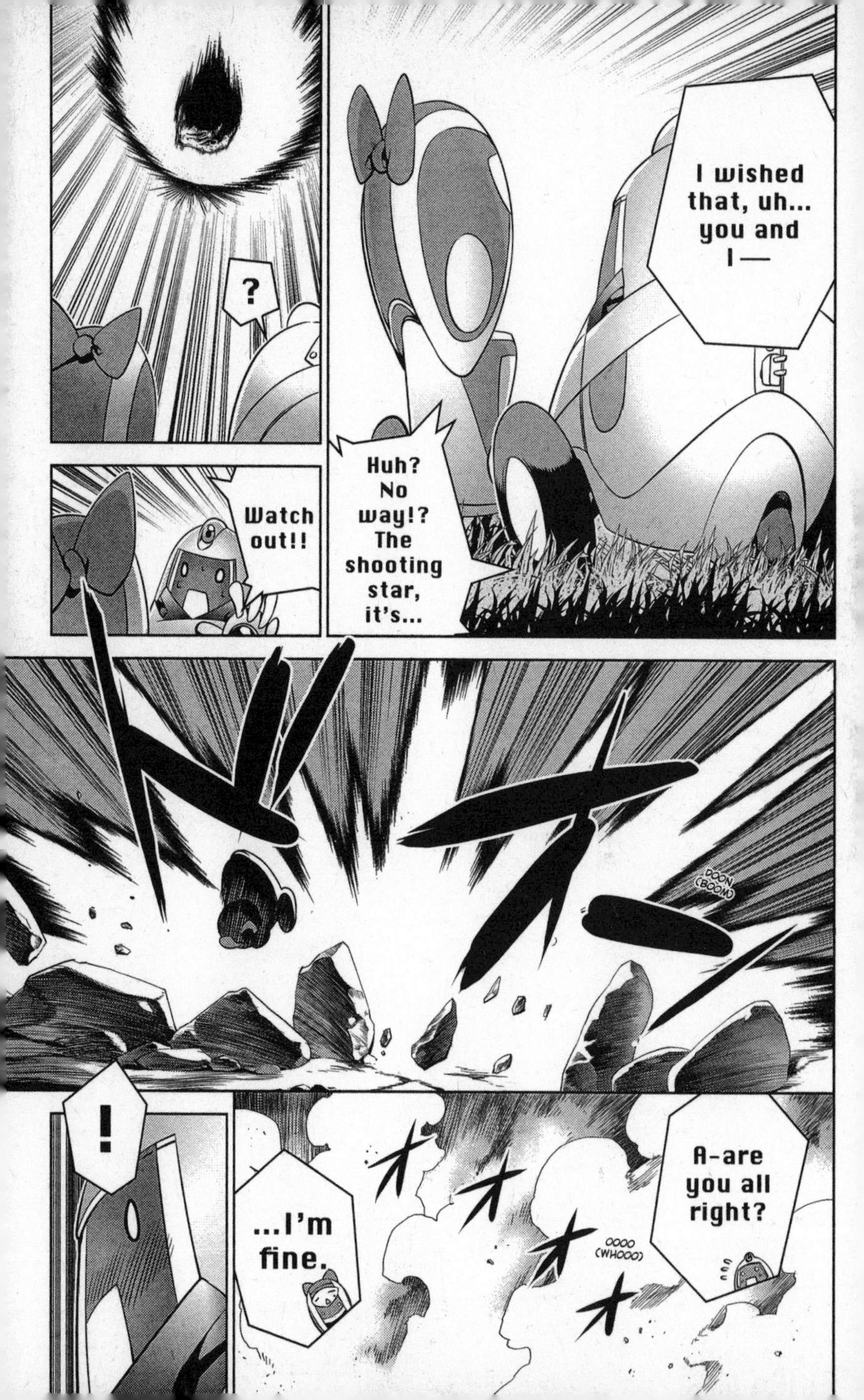
I wished that, uh... you and I—
Huh? No way!? The shooting star, it's...
?
Watch out!!
DOON (BOOM)
A-are you all right?
OOOO (WHOOO)
...I'm fine.
!

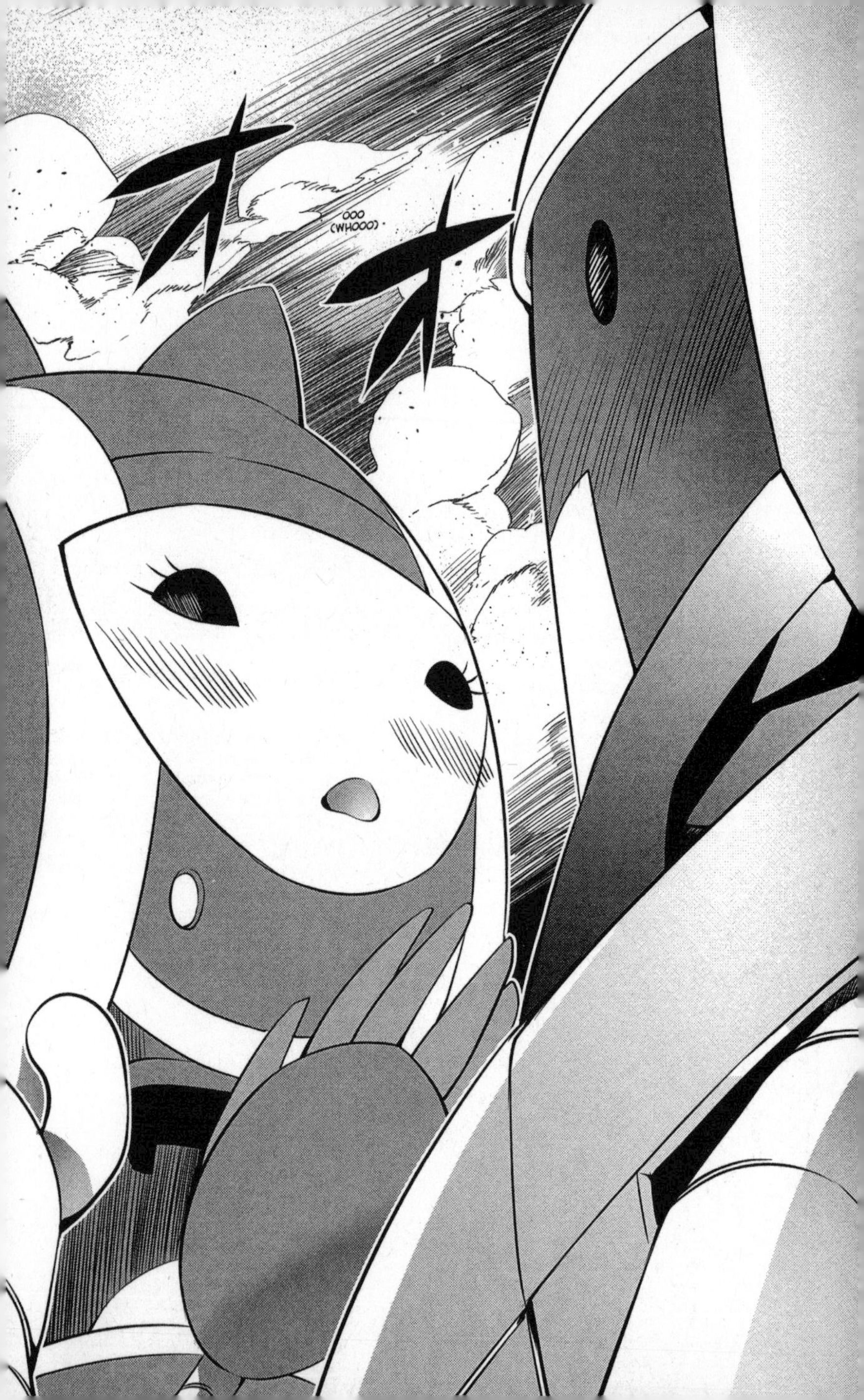
オオ
OOO
(WHOOO)

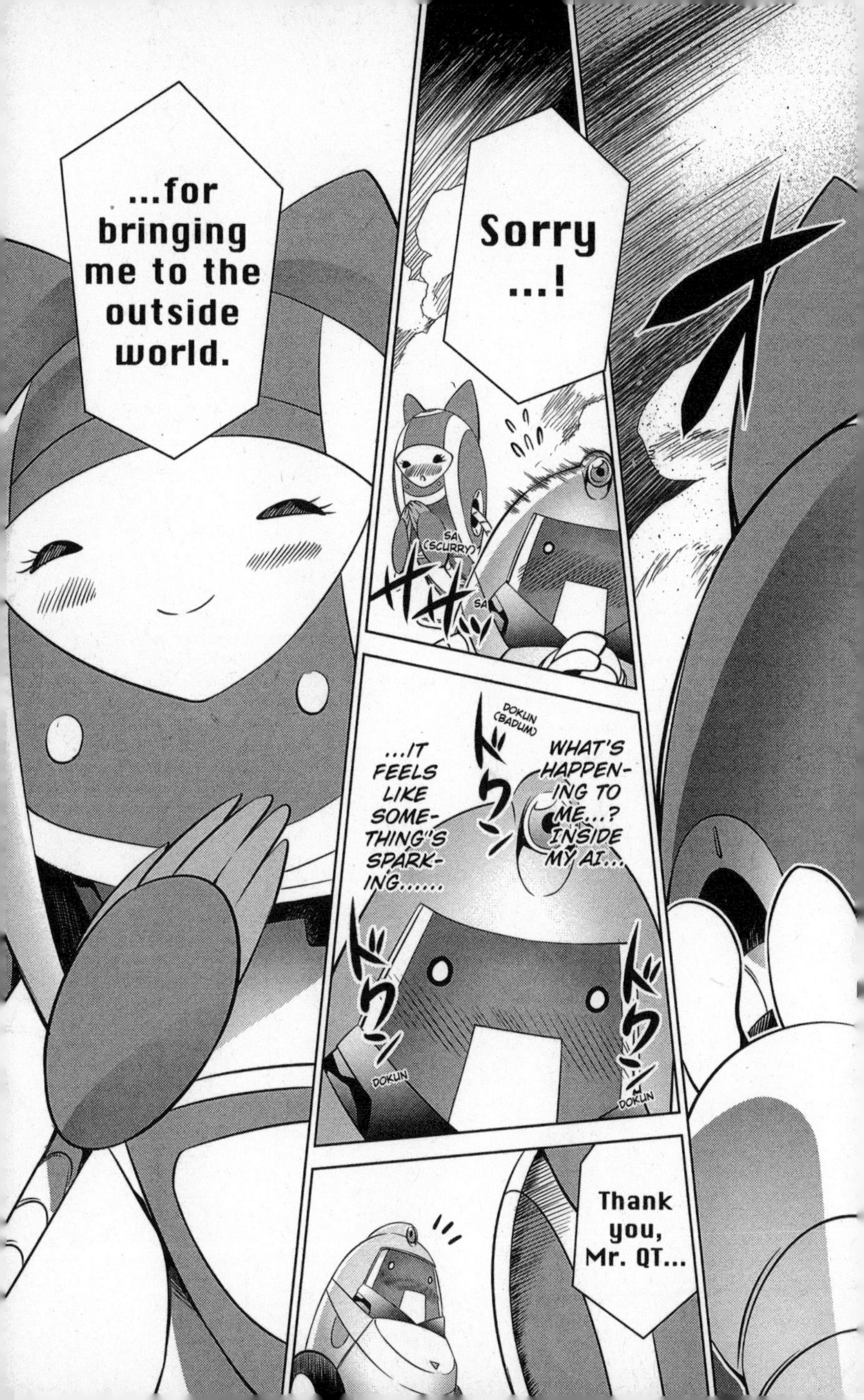
Sorry ...!
SA (SCURRY)
SA
DOKUN (BADUM)
WHAT'S HAPPEN-ING TO ME...? INSIDE MY AI...
...IT FEELS LIKE SOME-THING'S SPARK-ING......
DOKUN
DOKUN
Thank you, Mr. QT...
...for bringing me to the outside world.

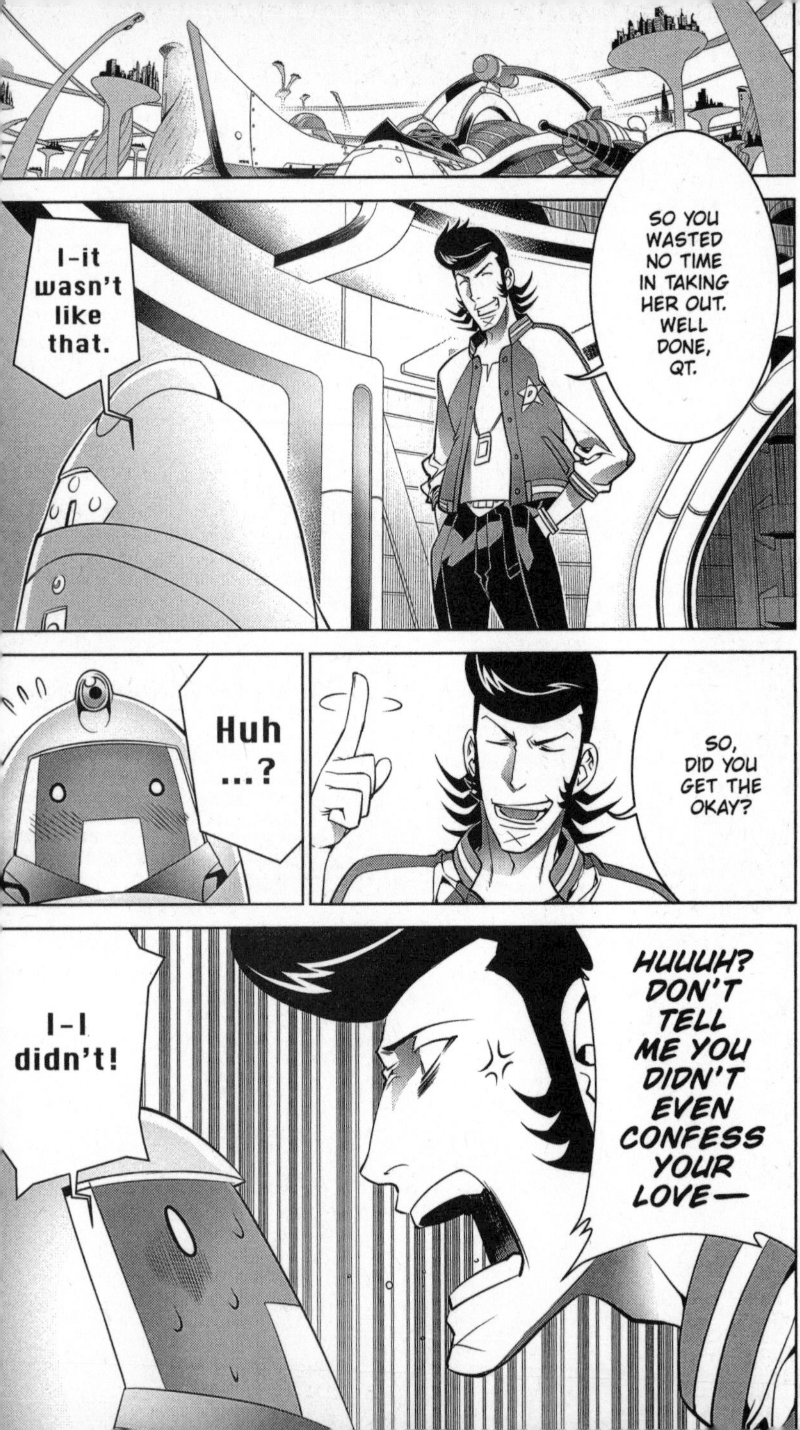
SO YOU WASTED NO TIME IN TAKING HER OUT. WELL DONE, QT.
I-it wasn't like that.
SO, DID YOU GET THE OKAY?
Huh ...?
HUUUH? DON'T TELL ME YOU DIDN'T EVEN CONFESS YOUR LOVE—
I-I didn't!

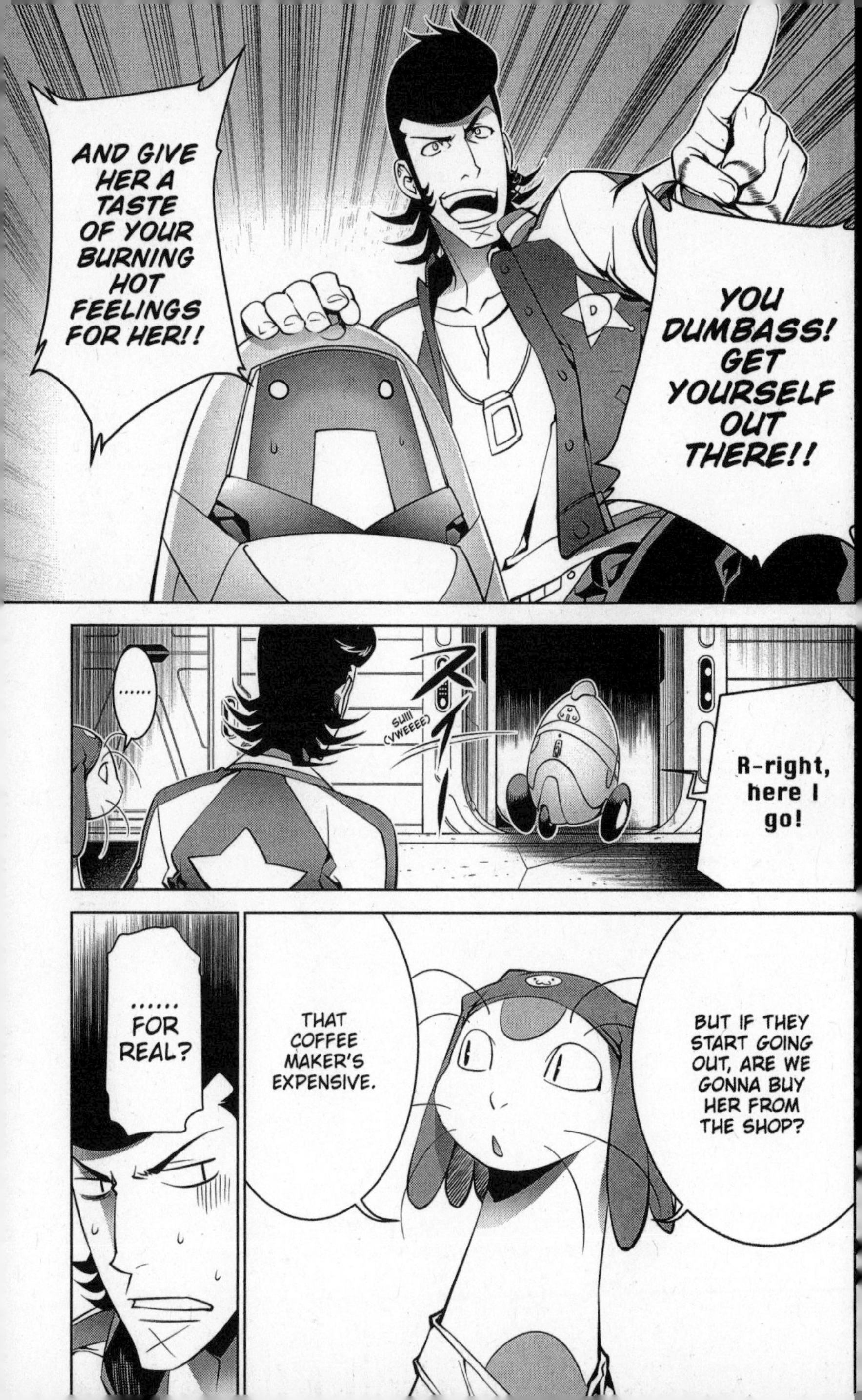
YOU DUMBASS! GET YOURSELF OUT THERE!!
AND GIVE HER A TASTE OF YOUR BURNING HOT FEELINGS FOR HER!!
R-right, here I go!
SUIII (VWEEEE)
......
BUT IF THEY START GOING OUT, ARE WE GONNA BUY HER FROM THE SHOP?
THAT COFFEE MAKER'S EXPENSIVE.
...... FOR REAL?

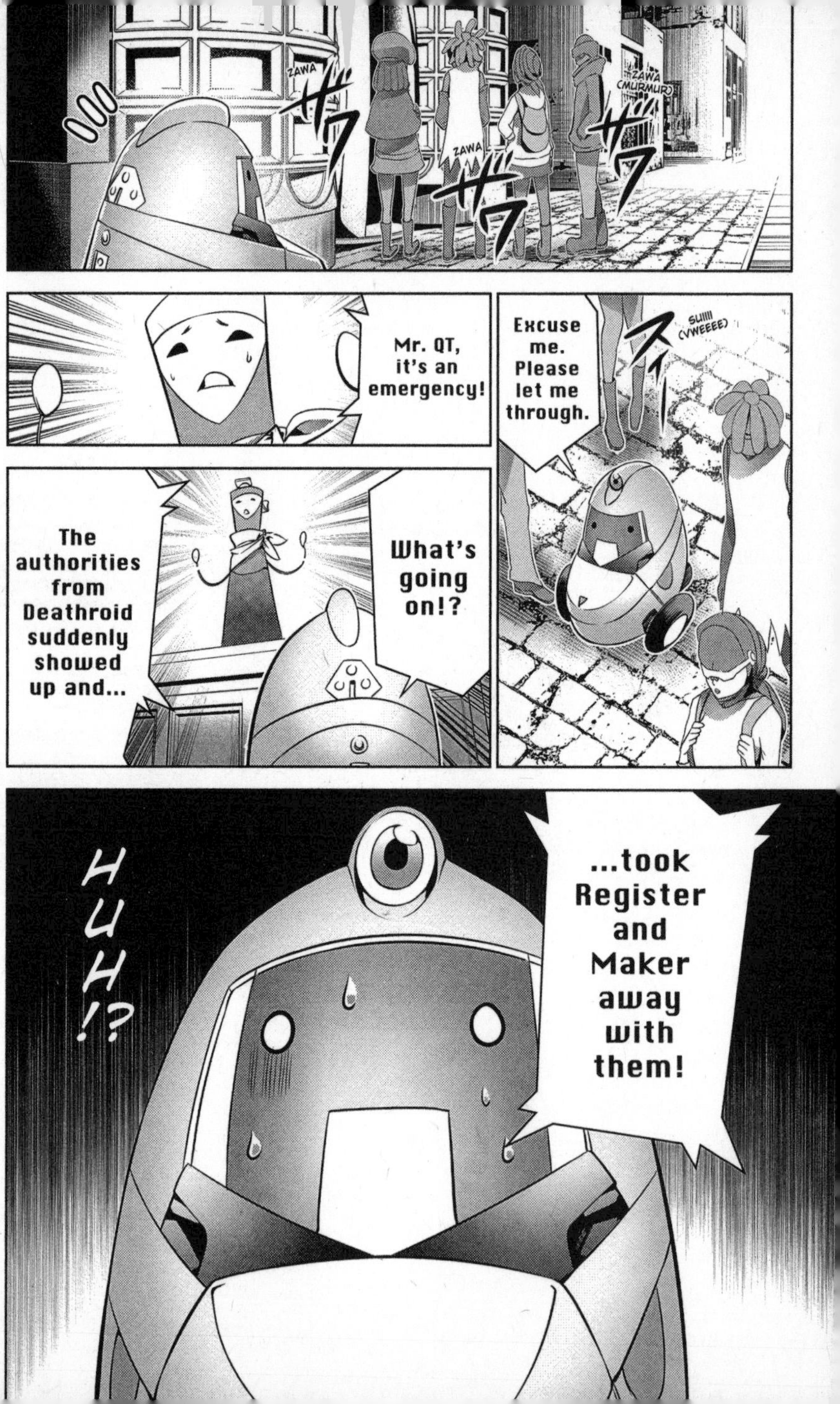
ZAWA (MURMUR)
ZAWA
ZAWA
SUIIII (VWEEEE)
Excuse me. Please let me through.
Mr. QT, it's an emergency!
What's going on!?
The authorities from Deathroid suddenly showed up and...
...took Register and Maker away with them!
HUH!?

SPACE★DANDY

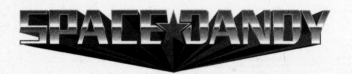

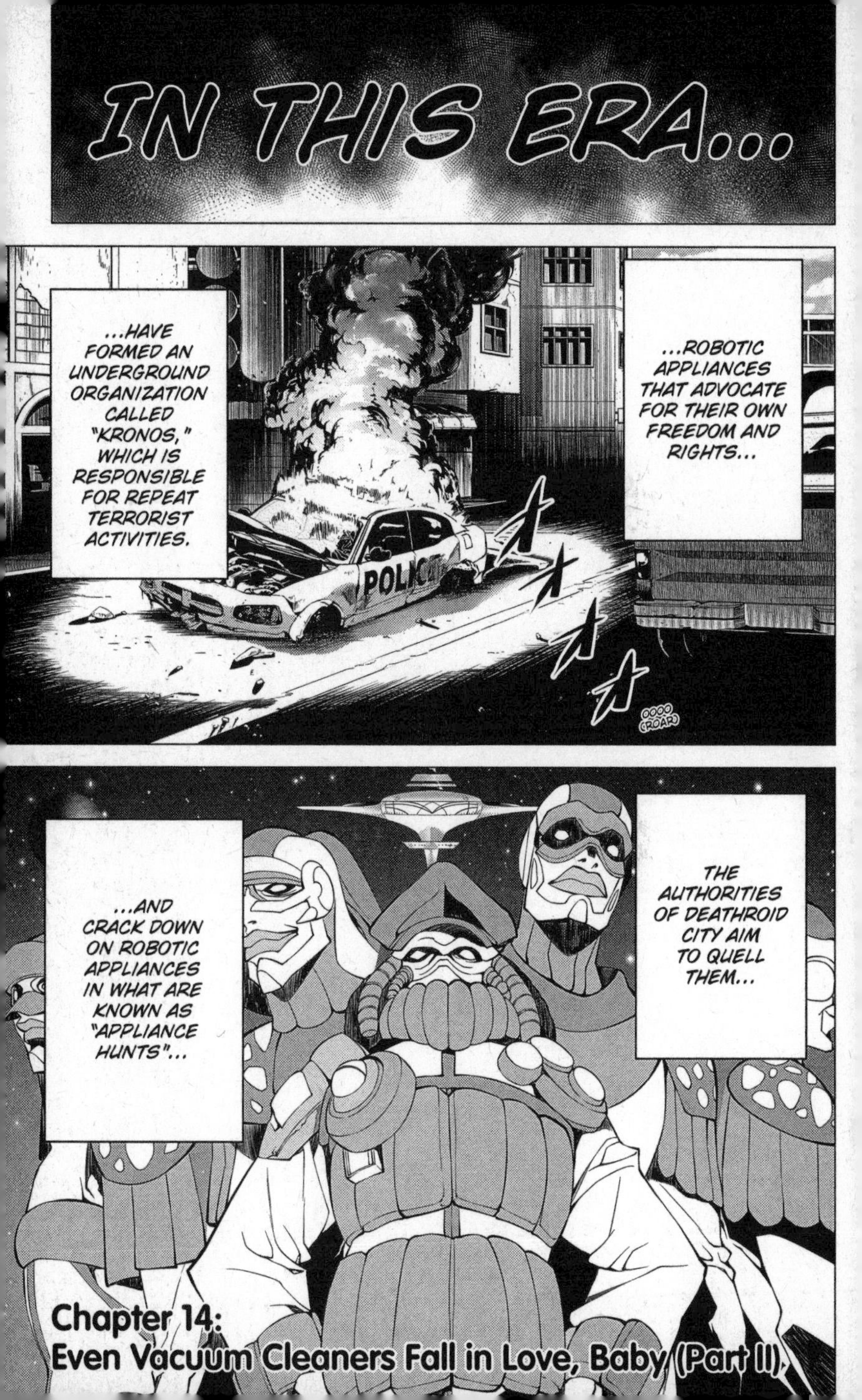
IN THIS ERA...
...ROBOTIC APPLIANCES THAT ADVOCATE FOR THEIR OWN FREEDOM AND RIGHTS...
...HAVE FORMED AN UNDERGROUND ORGANIZATION CALLED "KRONOS," WHICH IS RESPONSIBLE FOR REPEAT TERRORIST ACTIVITIES.
POLICE
OOOO (ROAR)
THE AUTHORITIES OF DEATHROID CITY AIM TO QUELL THEM...
...AND CRACK DOWN ON ROBOTIC APPLIANCES IN WHAT ARE KNOWN AS "APPLIANCE HUNTS"...
Chapter 14:
Even Vacuum Cleaners Fall in Love, Baby (Part II)

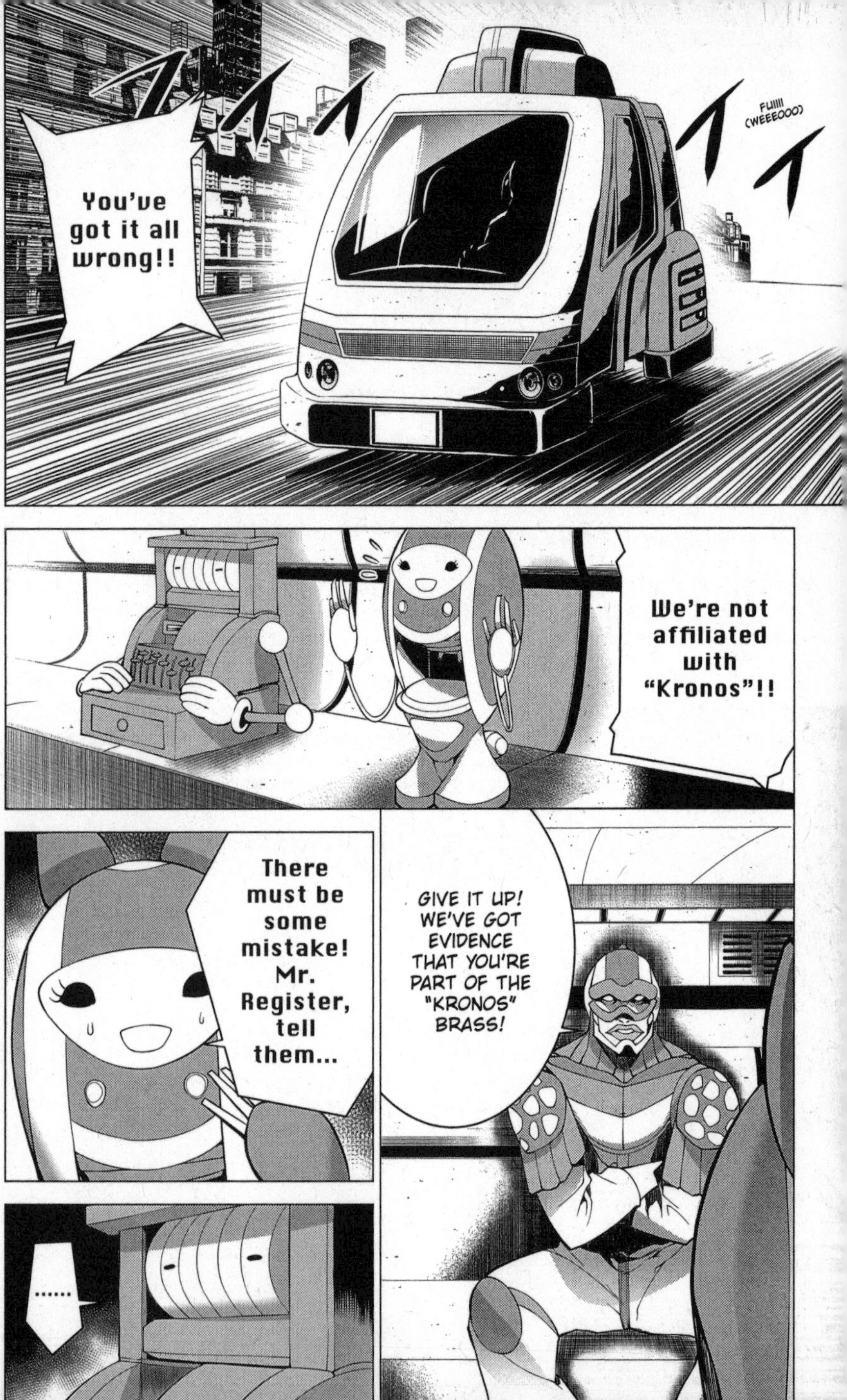
FUIIII
(WEEEOOO)
You've got it all wrong!!
We're not affiliated with "Kronos"!!
GIVE IT UP! WE'VE GOT EVIDENCE THAT YOU'RE PART OF THE "KRONOS" BRASS!
There must be some mistake! Mr. Register, tell them...
......

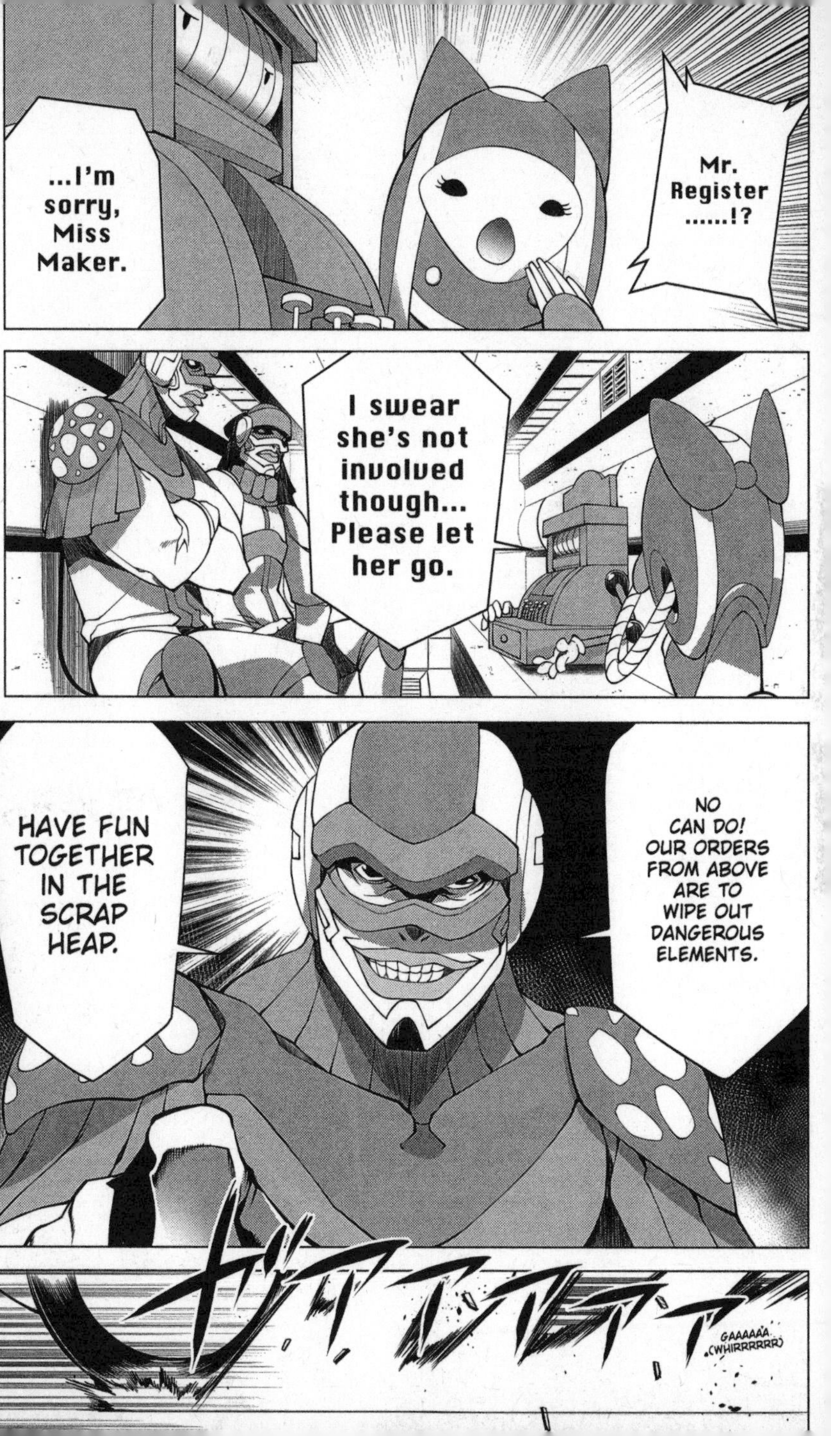
Mr. Register ......!?
...I'm sorry, Miss Maker.
I swear she's not involved though... Please let her go.
NO CAN DO! OUR ORDERS FROM ABOVE ARE TO WIPE OUT DANGEROUS ELEMENTS.
HAVE FUN TOGETHER IN THE SCRAP HEAP.
GAAAAAA (WHIRRRRRR)

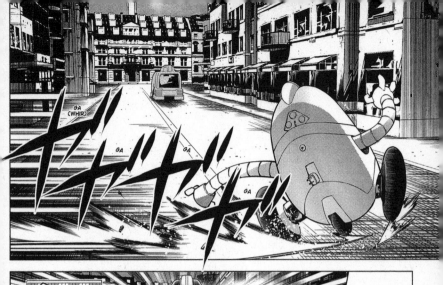

There she is!

No doubt about it!!

Miss Maker-rrrr!!!

Mr. QT!

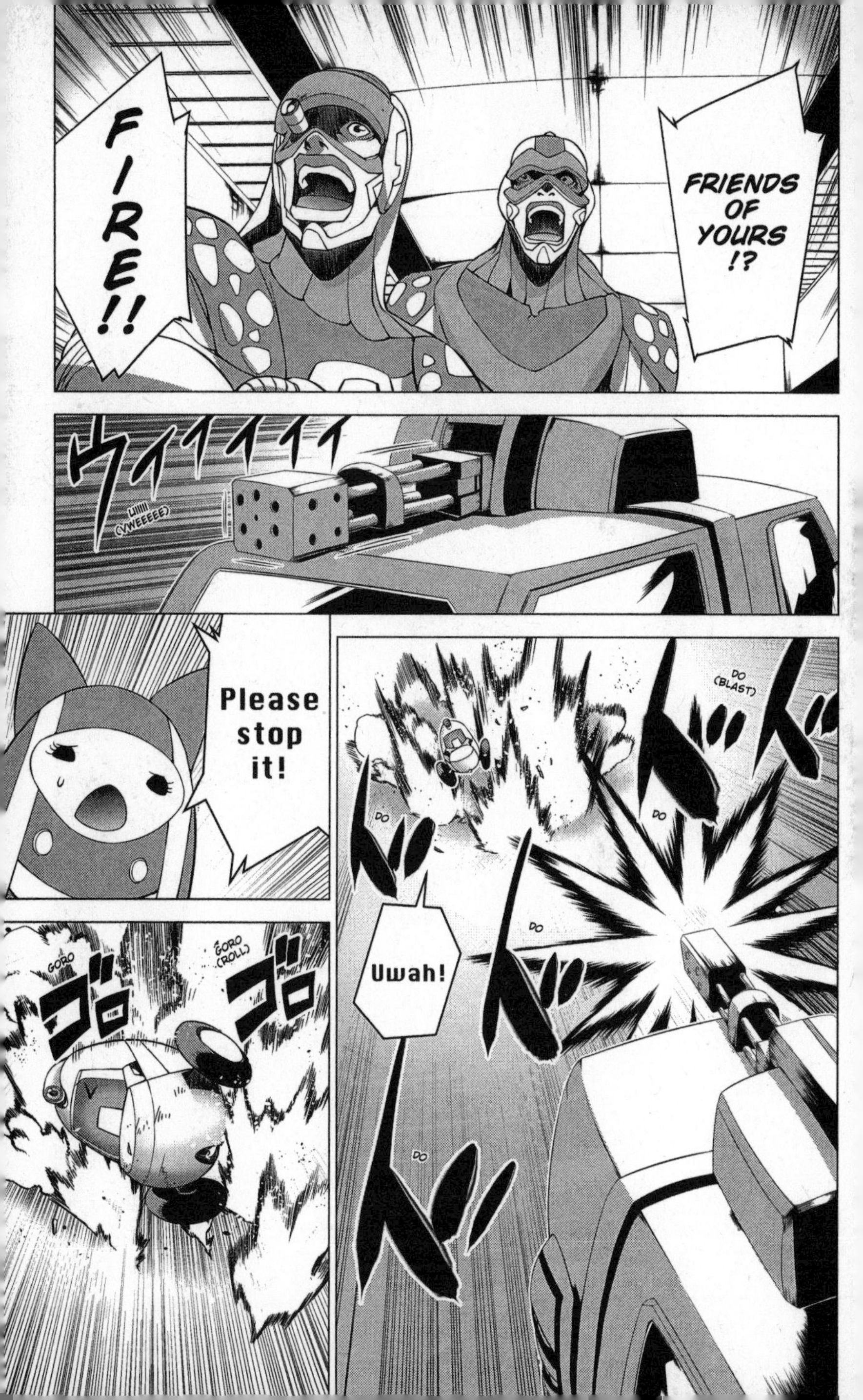
FRIENDS OF YOURS !?
FIRE!!
UIIIII (VWEEEEE)
DO (BLAST)
DO
DO
Uwah!
DO
DO
Please stop it!
GORO (ROLL)
GORO

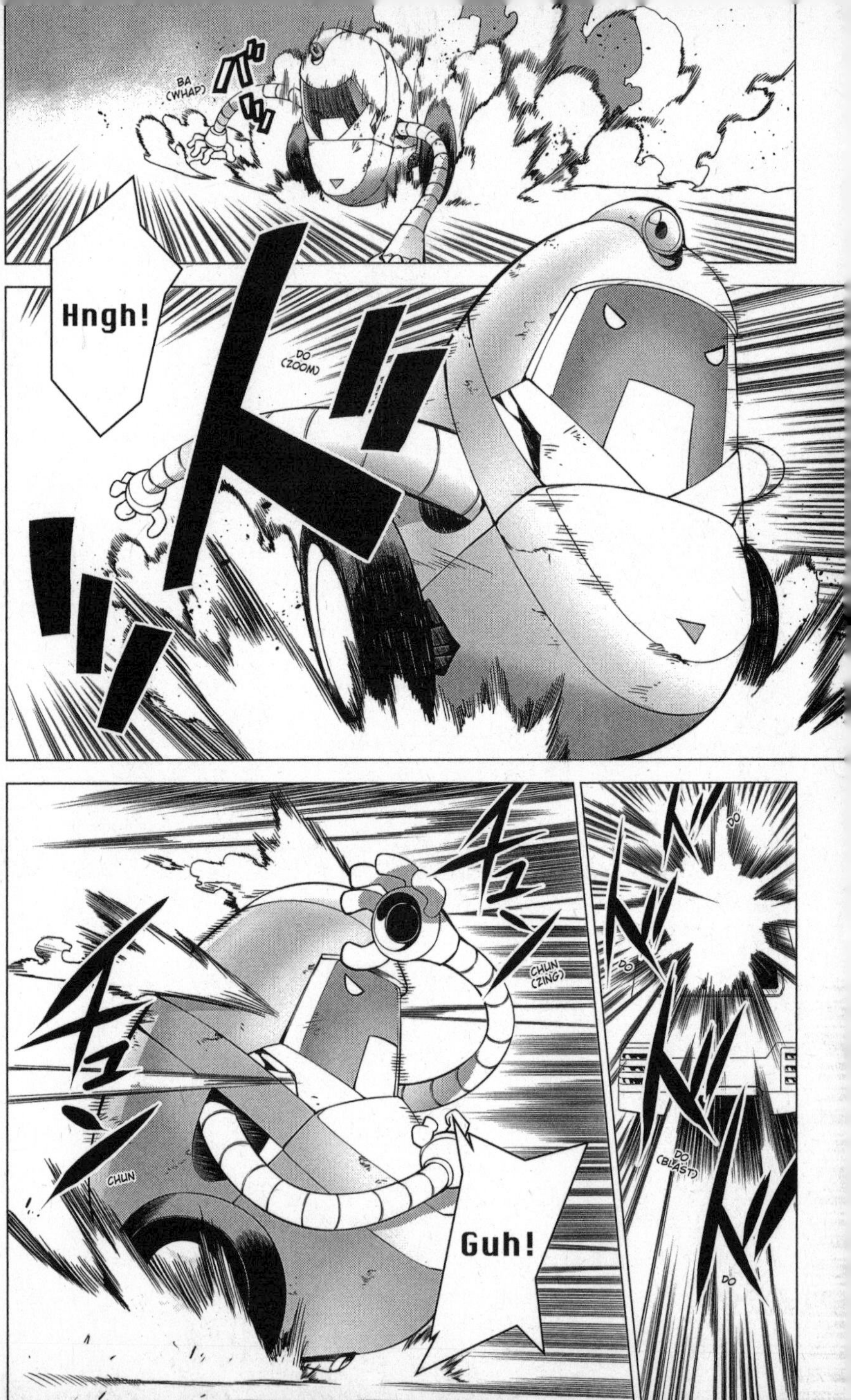
BA
(WHAP)
Hngh!
DO
(ZOOM)
DO
DO
DO
(BLAST)
DO
CHUN
(ZING)
CHUN
Guh!

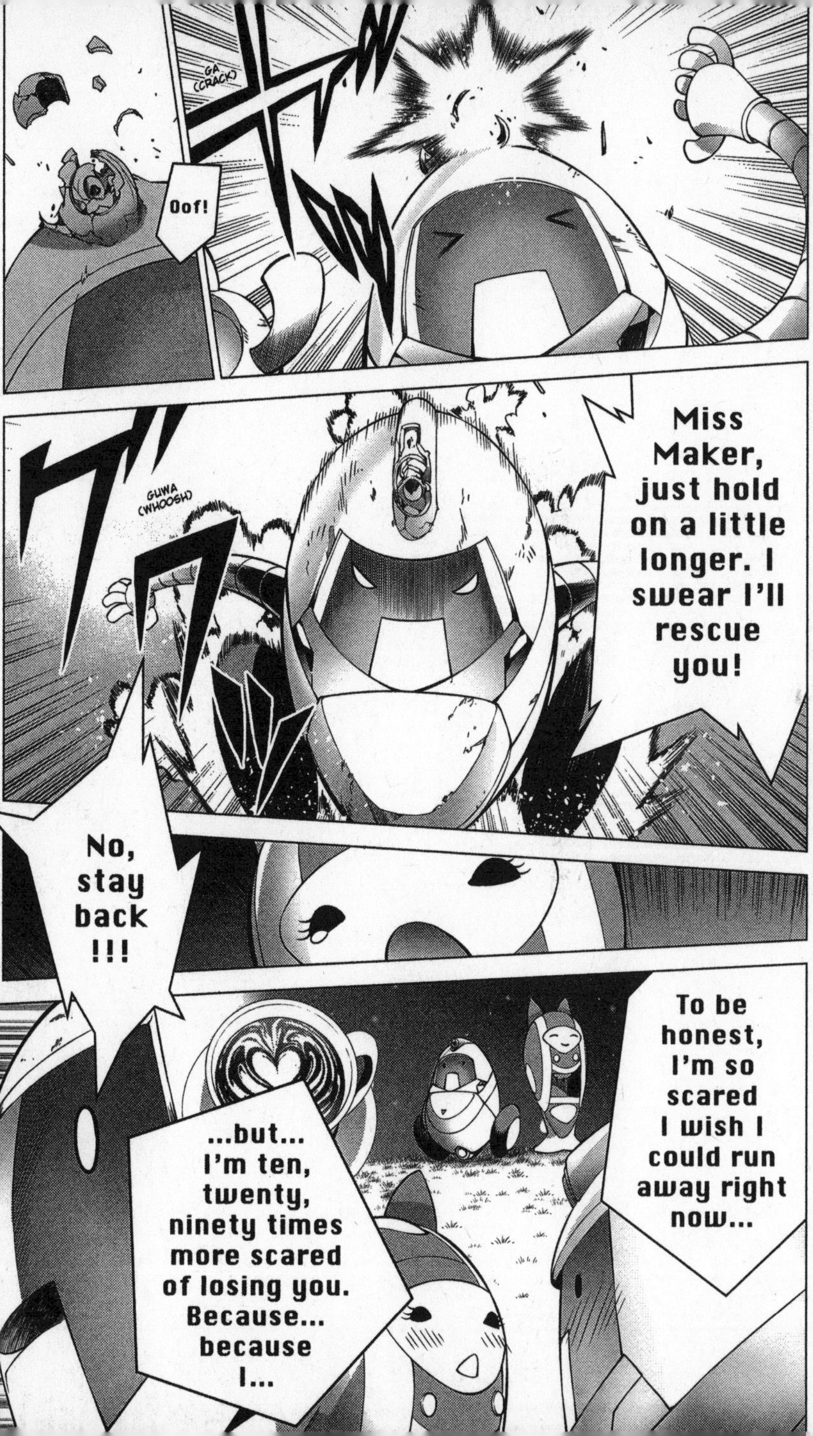
GA (CRACK)
Oof!
Miss Maker, just hold on a little longer. I swear I'll rescue you!
GUWA (WHOOSH)
No, stay back!!!
To be honest, I'm so scared I wish I could run away right now...
...but... I'm ten, twenty, ninety times more scared of losing you. Because... because I...

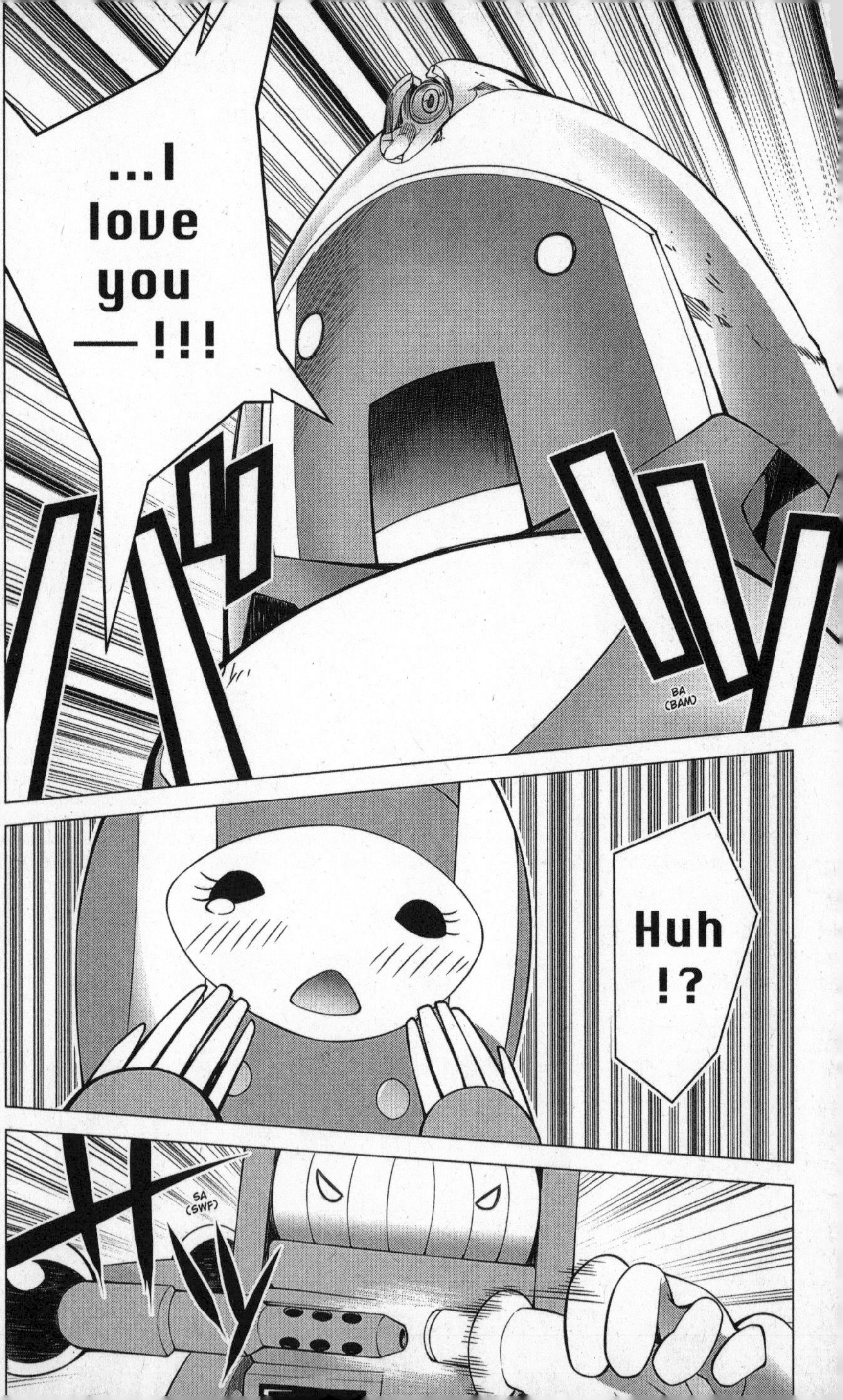
...I love you—!!!
BA (BAM)
Huh!?
SA (SWF)

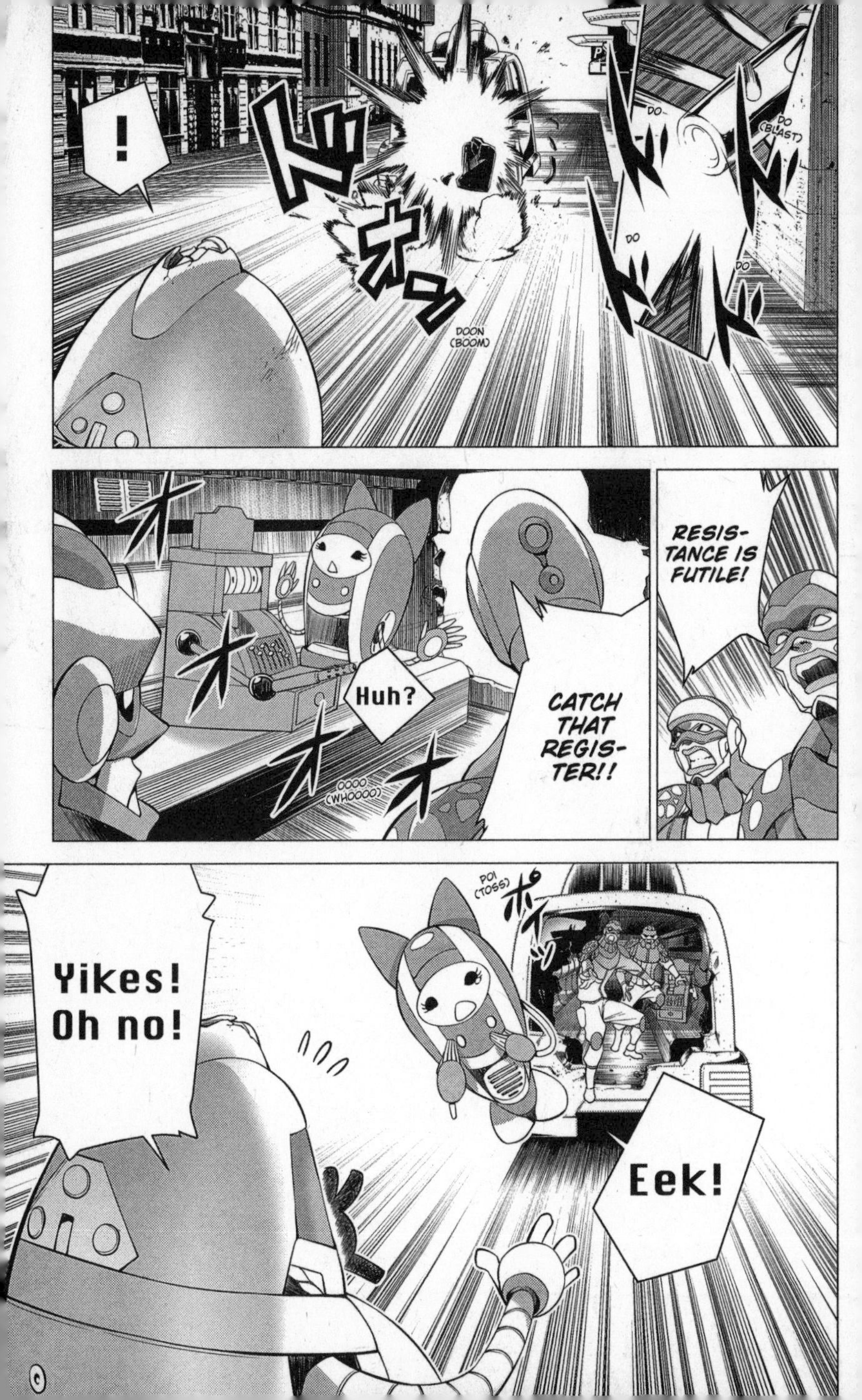
DO (BLAST)
DO
DO
DO
DOON (BOOM)
!
RESIS-TANCE IS FUTILE!
CATCH THAT REGIS-TER!!
Huh?
OOOO (WHOOOO)
POI (TOSS)
Eek!
Yikes! Oh no!

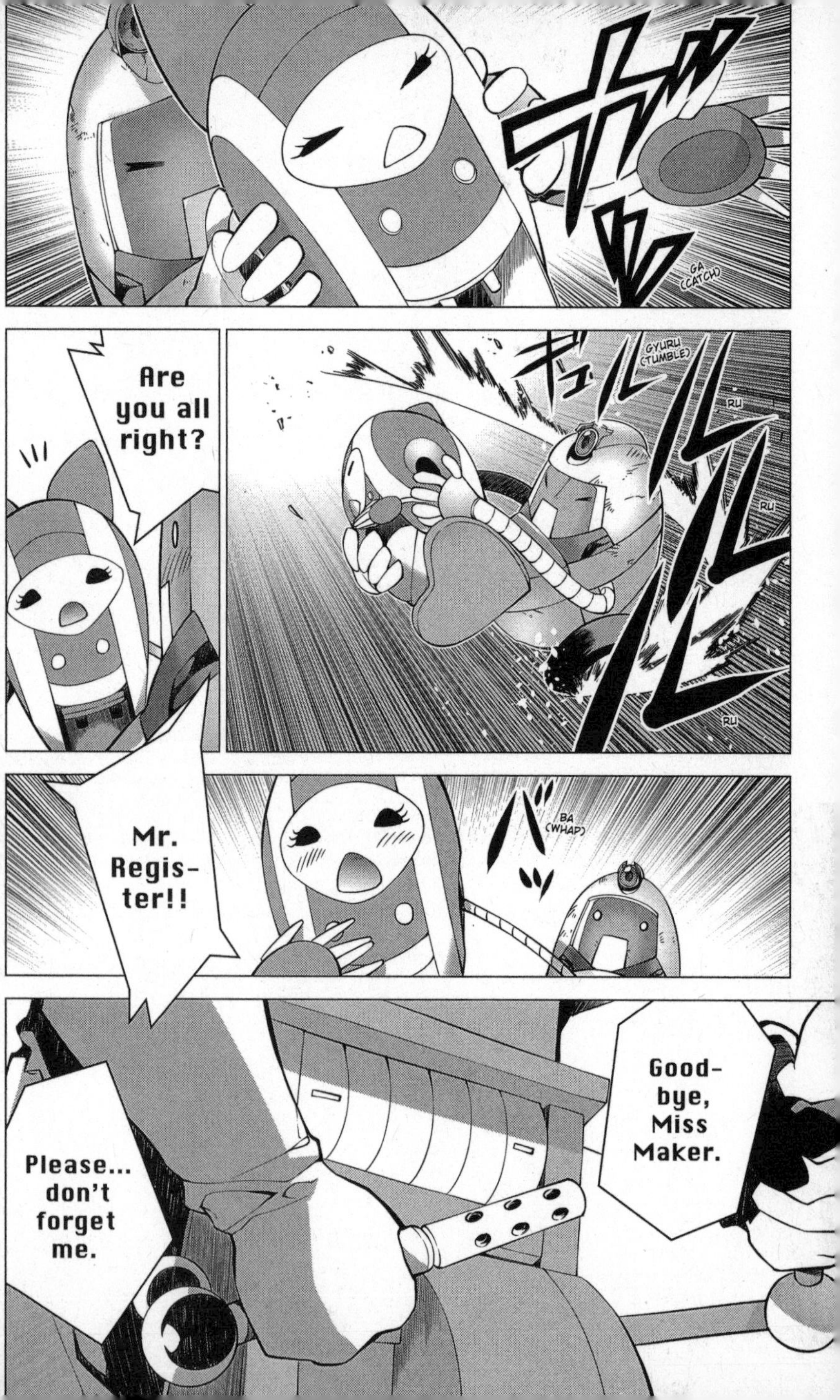
GA (CATCH)
GYURU (TUMBLE)
RU
RU
RU
Are you all right?
BA (WHAP)
Mr. Regis-ter!!
Good-bye, Miss Maker.
Please... don't forget me.

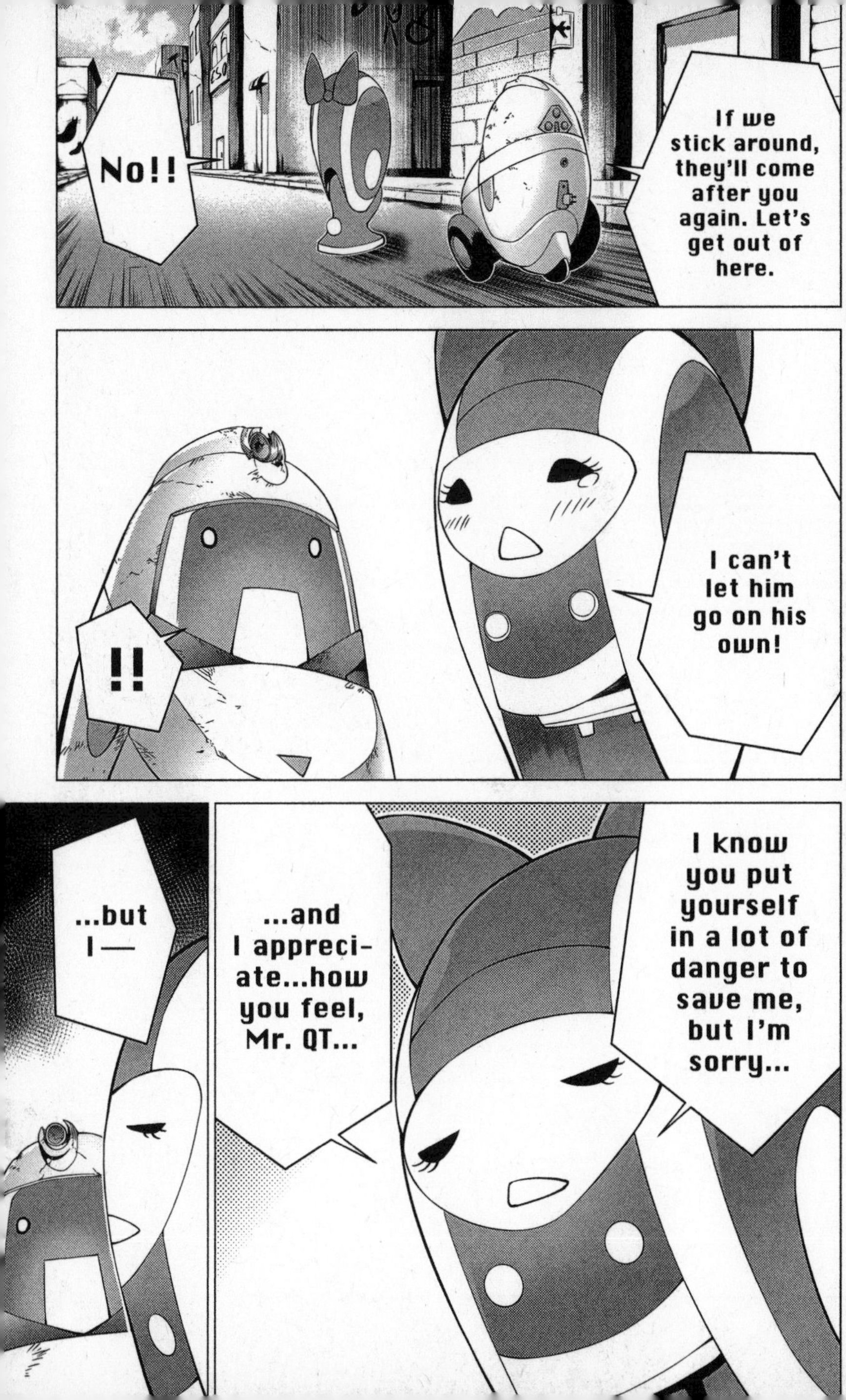
If we stick around, they'll come after you again. Let's get out of here.
No!!
I can't let him go on his own!
!!
I know you put yourself in a lot of danger to save me, but I'm sorry...
...and I appreciate...how you feel, Mr. QT...
...but I—

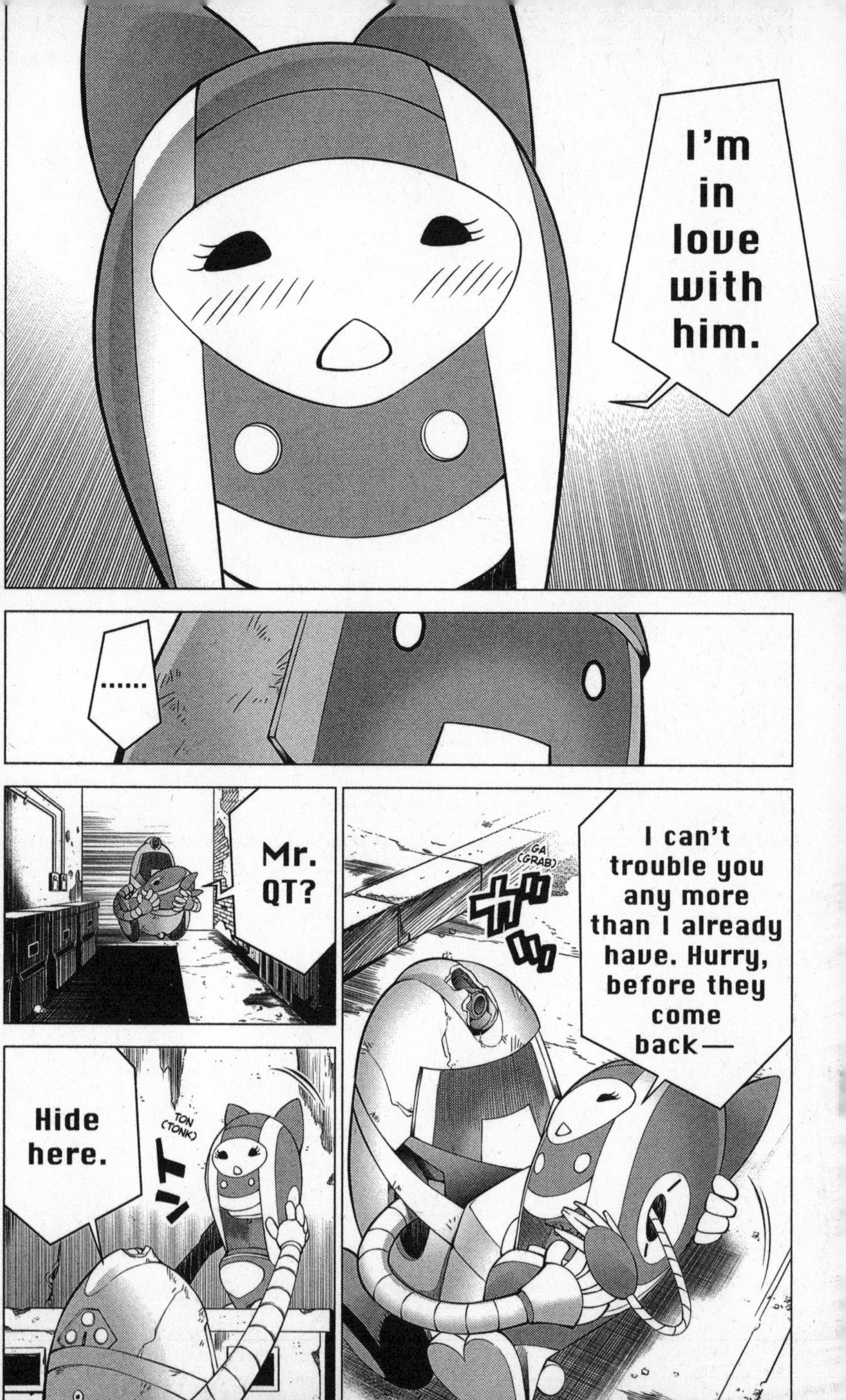
I'm in love with him.
......
I can't trouble you any more than I already have. Hurry, before they come back—
GA (GRAB)
Mr. QT?
Hide here.
TON (TONK)

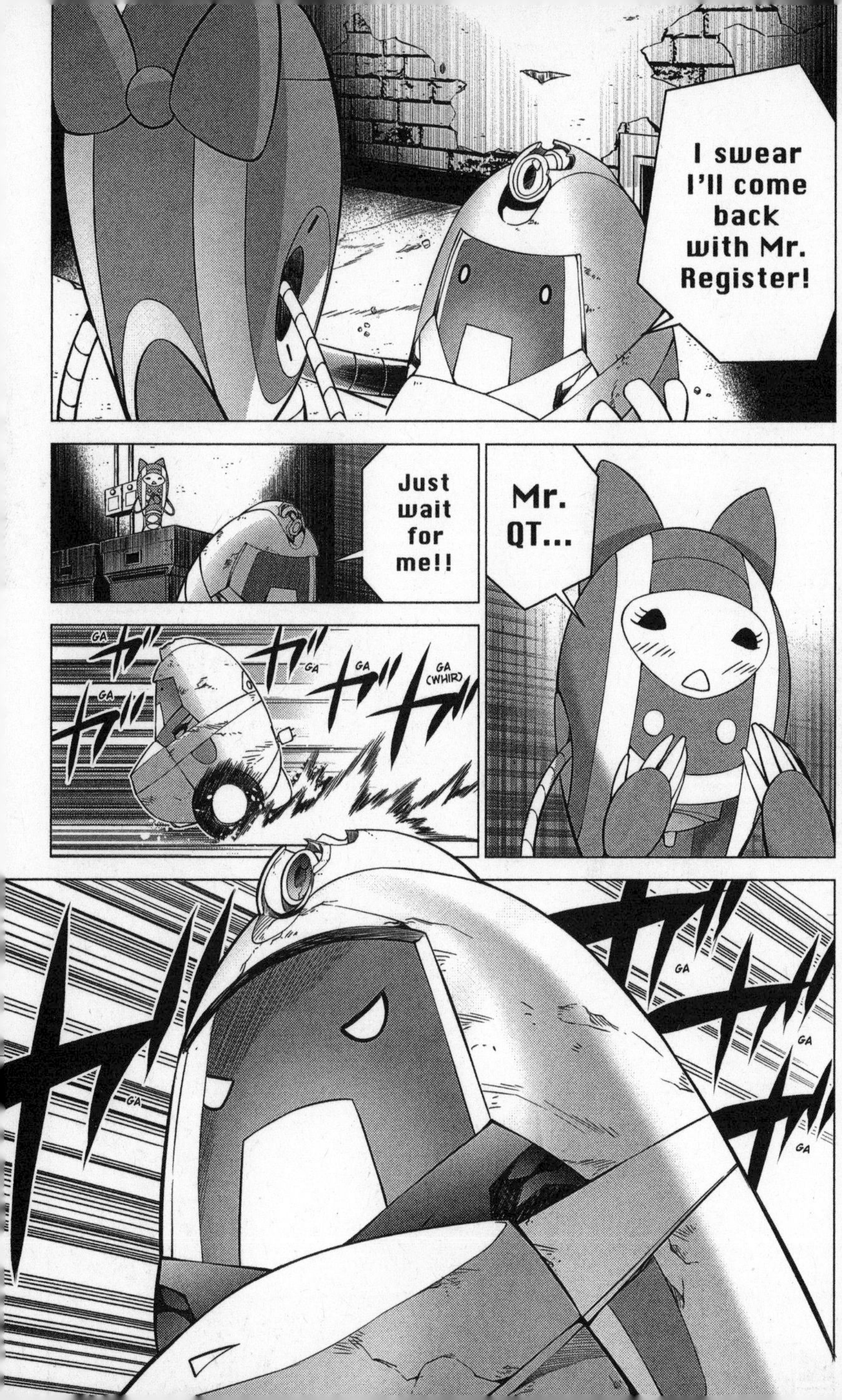
I swear I'll come back with Mr. Register!
Mr. QT...
Just wait for me!!
GA (WHIR)
GA
GA
GA
GA
GA
GA
GA
GA

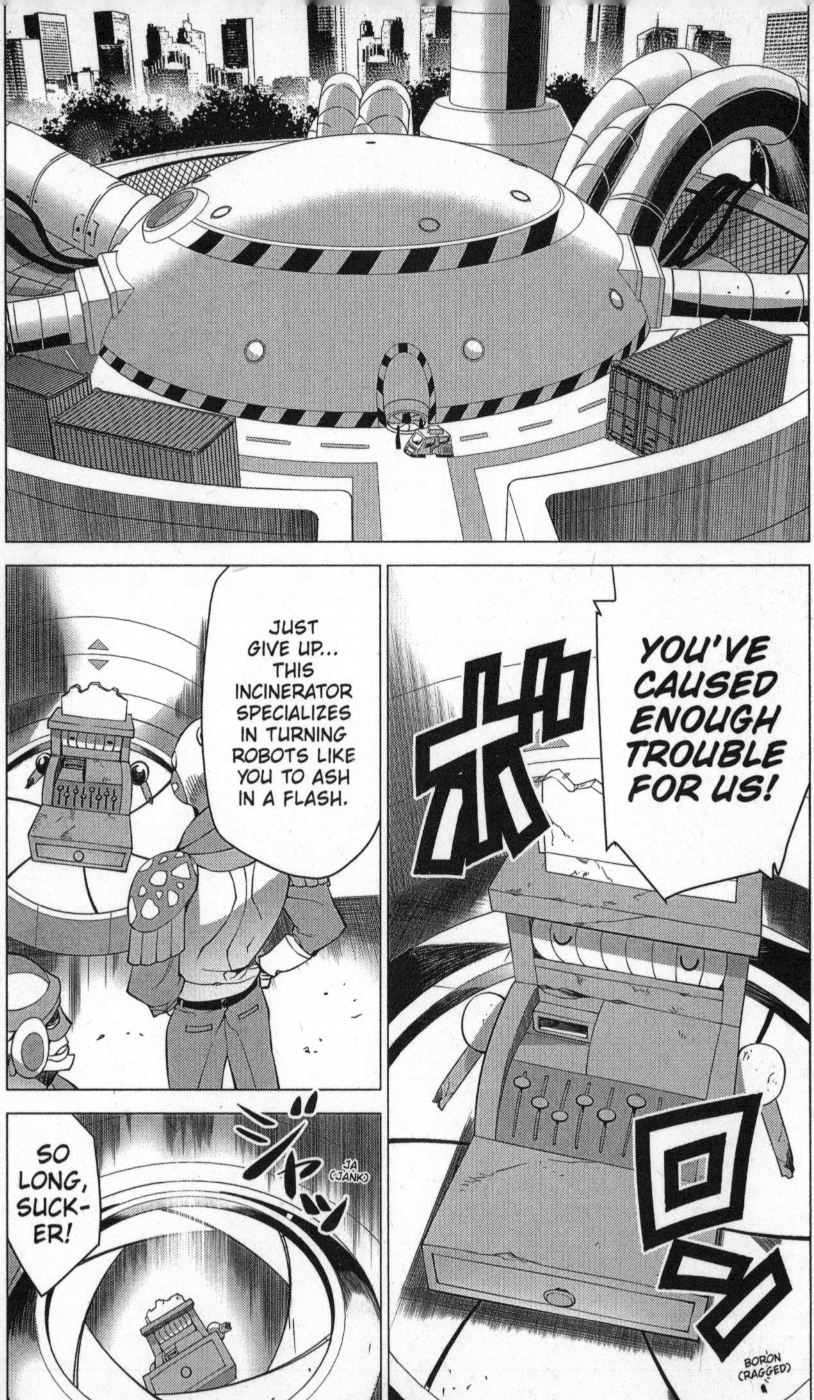
YOU'VE CAUSED ENOUGH TROUBLE FOR US!
BORON (RAGGED)
JUST GIVE UP... THIS INCINERATOR SPECIALIZES IN TURNING ROBOTS LIKE YOU TO ASH IN A FLASH.
SO LONG, SUCK-ER!
JA (JANK)

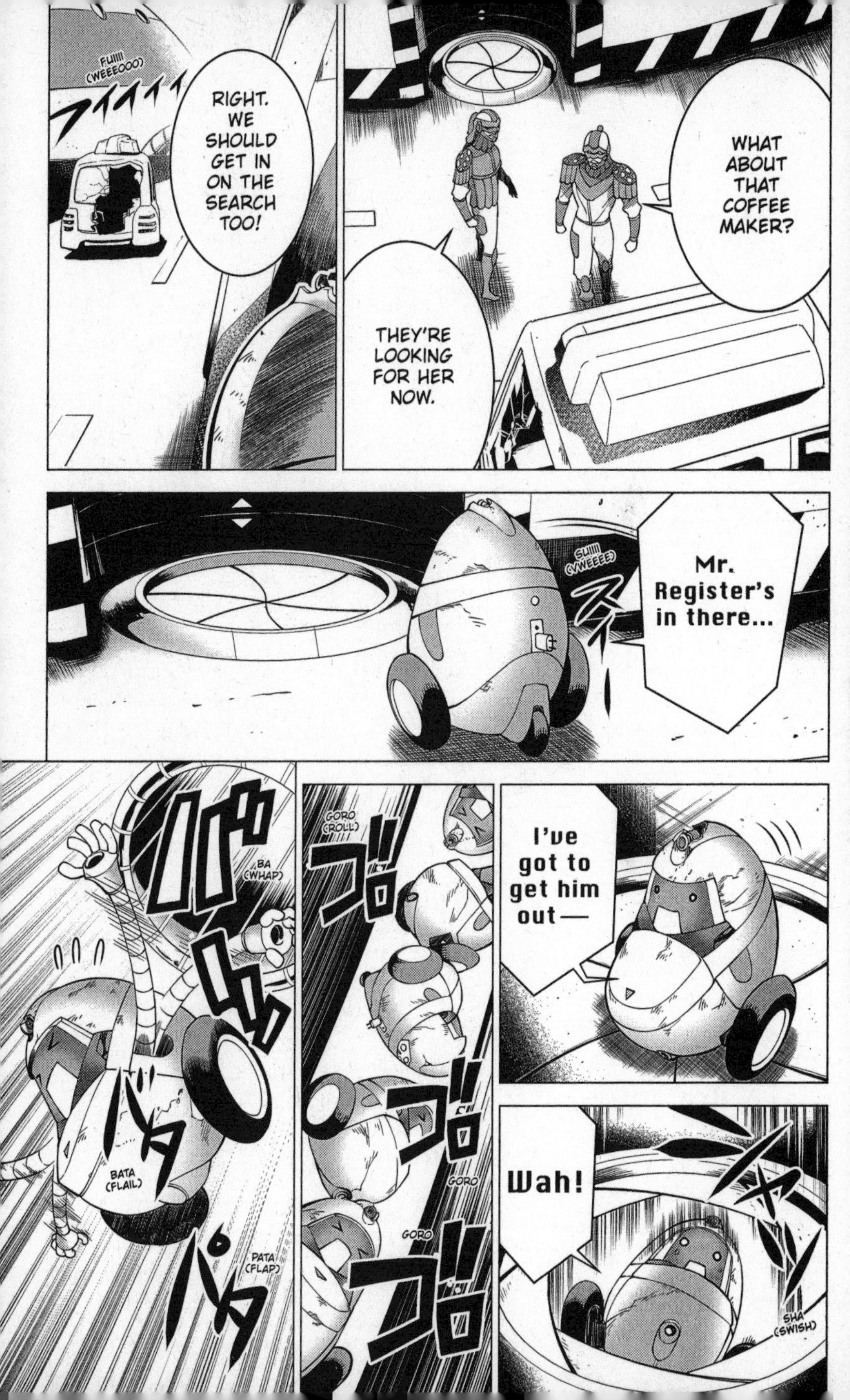
WHAT ABOUT THAT COFFEE MAKER?
THEY'RE LOOKING FOR HER NOW.
FUIIII (WEEEOOO)
RIGHT. WE SHOULD GET IN ON THE SEARCH TOO!
SUIIII (VWEEEE)
Mr. Register's in there...
I've got to get him out—
Wah!
SHA (SWISH)
GORO (ROLL)
GORO
GORO
BA (WHAP)
BATA (FLAIL)
PATA (FLAP)

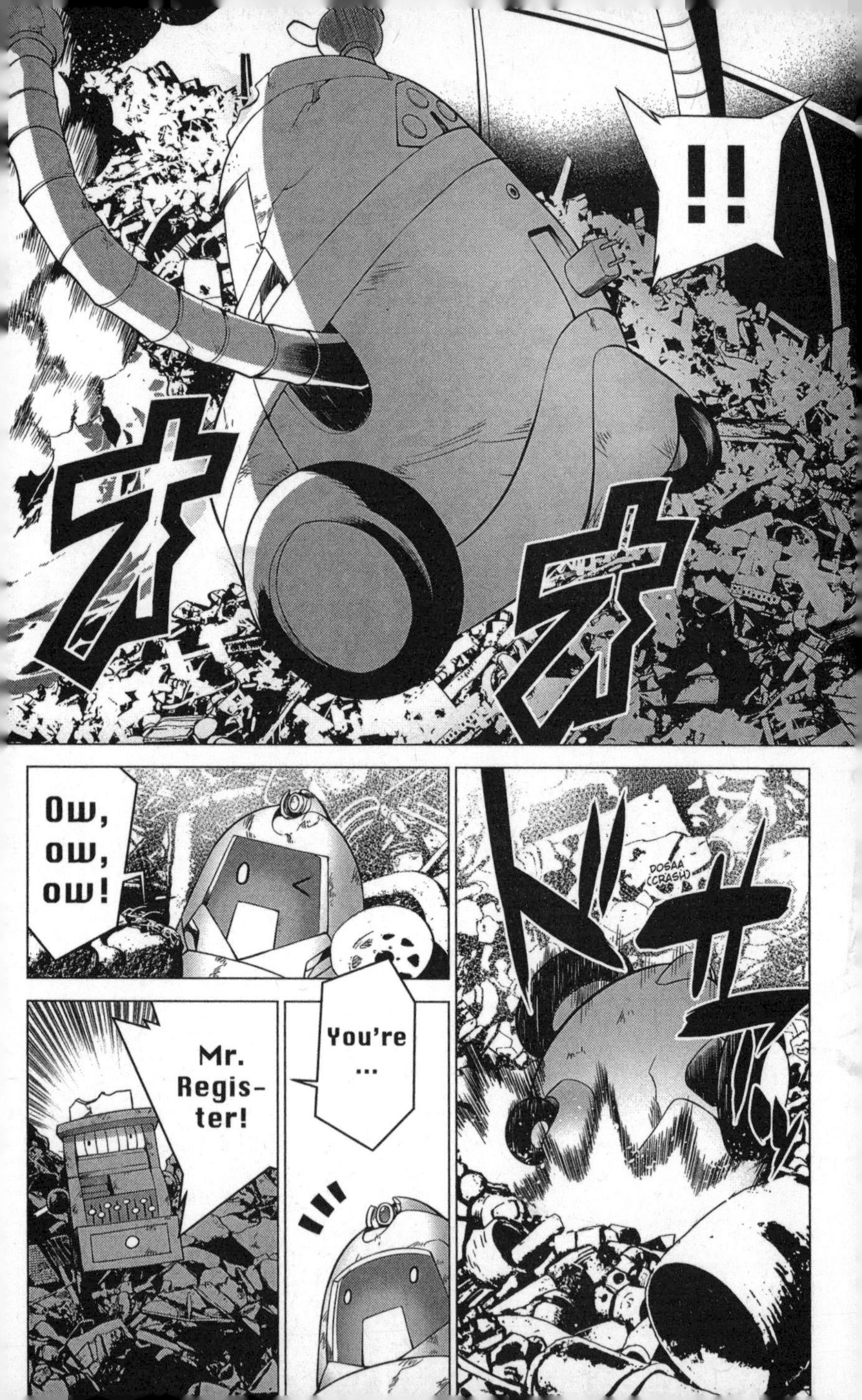
!!
DOSAA (CRASH)
Ow, ow, ow!
You're ...
Mr. Regis-ter!

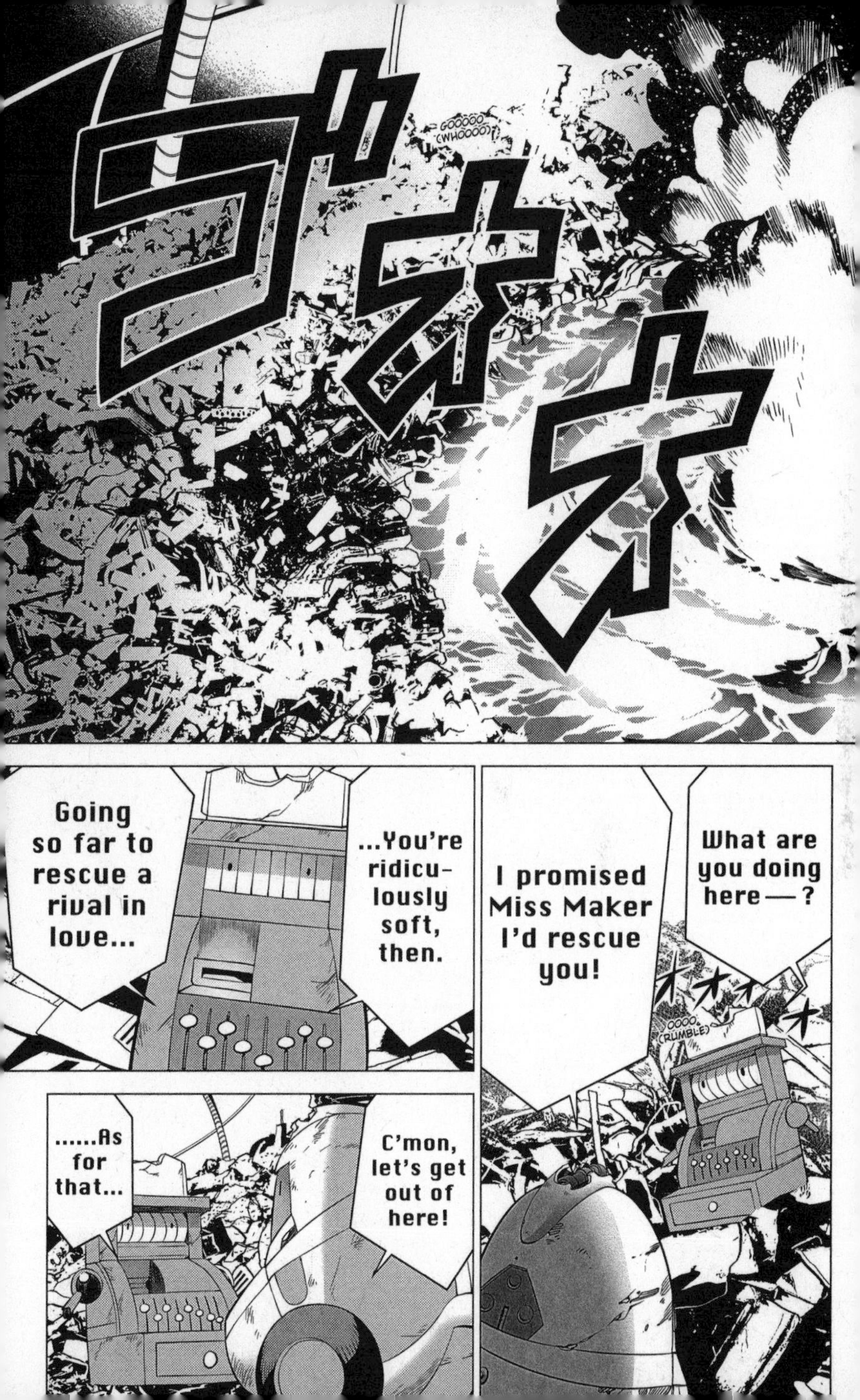
GOOOOO (WHOOOO)
What are you doing here—?
I promised Miss Maker I'd rescue you!
OOOO (RUMBLE)
...You're ridicu-lously soft, then.
Going so far to rescue a rival in love...
C'mon, let's get out of here!
......As for that...

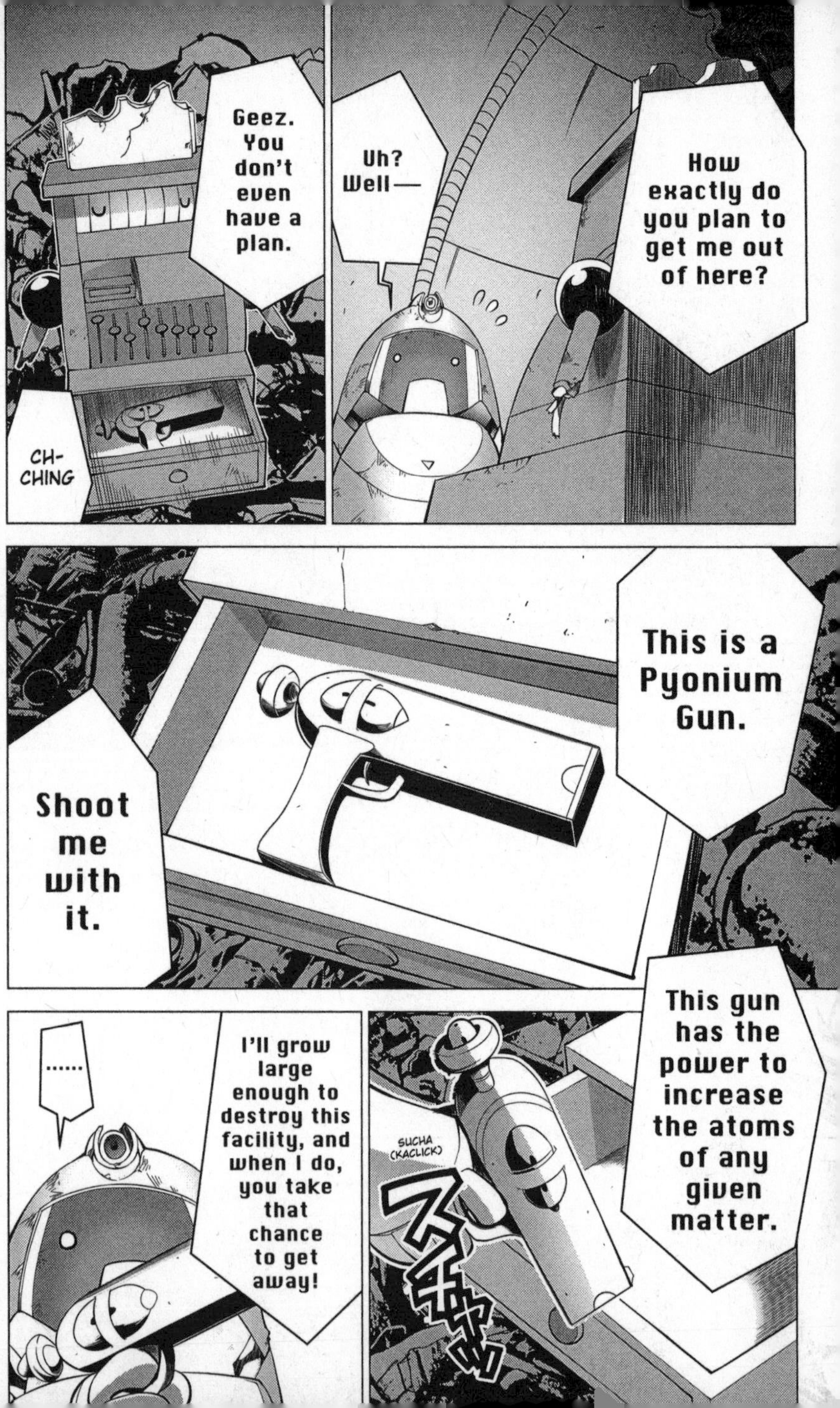
How exactly do you plan to get me out of here?
Uh? Well—
Geez. You don't even have a plan.
CH-CHING
This is a Pyonium Gun.
Shoot me with it.
This gun has the power to increase the atoms of any given matter.
SUCHA (KACLICK)
I'll grow large enough to destroy this facility, and when I do, you take that chance to get away!
......

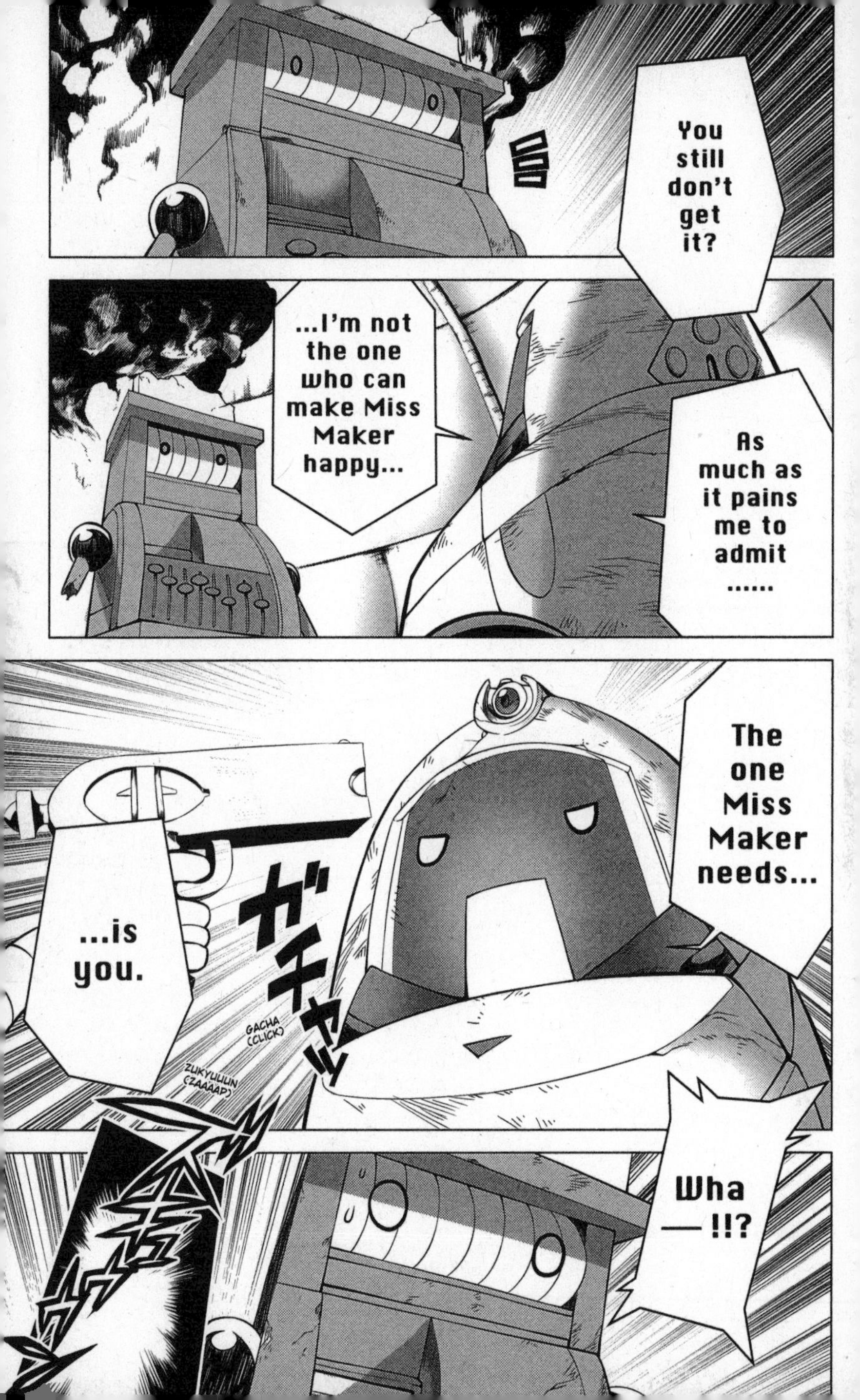
You still don't get it?
As much as it pains me to admit ......
...I'm not the one who can make Miss Maker happy...
The one Miss Maker needs...
ガチャッ
GACHA (CLICK)
...is you.
ZUKYUUUN (ZAAAAP)
Wha—!!?

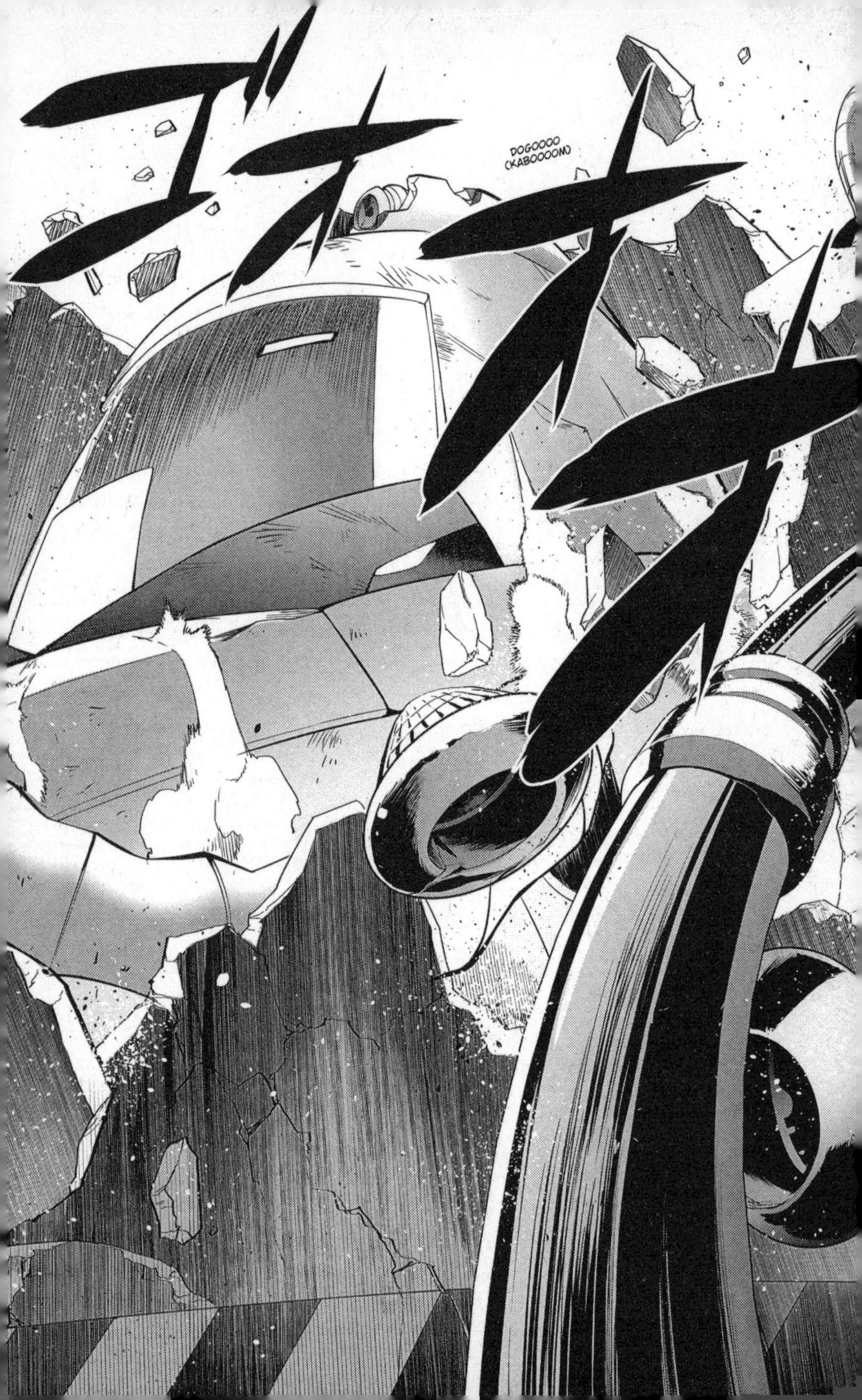
ゴオオオオ
DOGOOOO
(KABOOOOM)

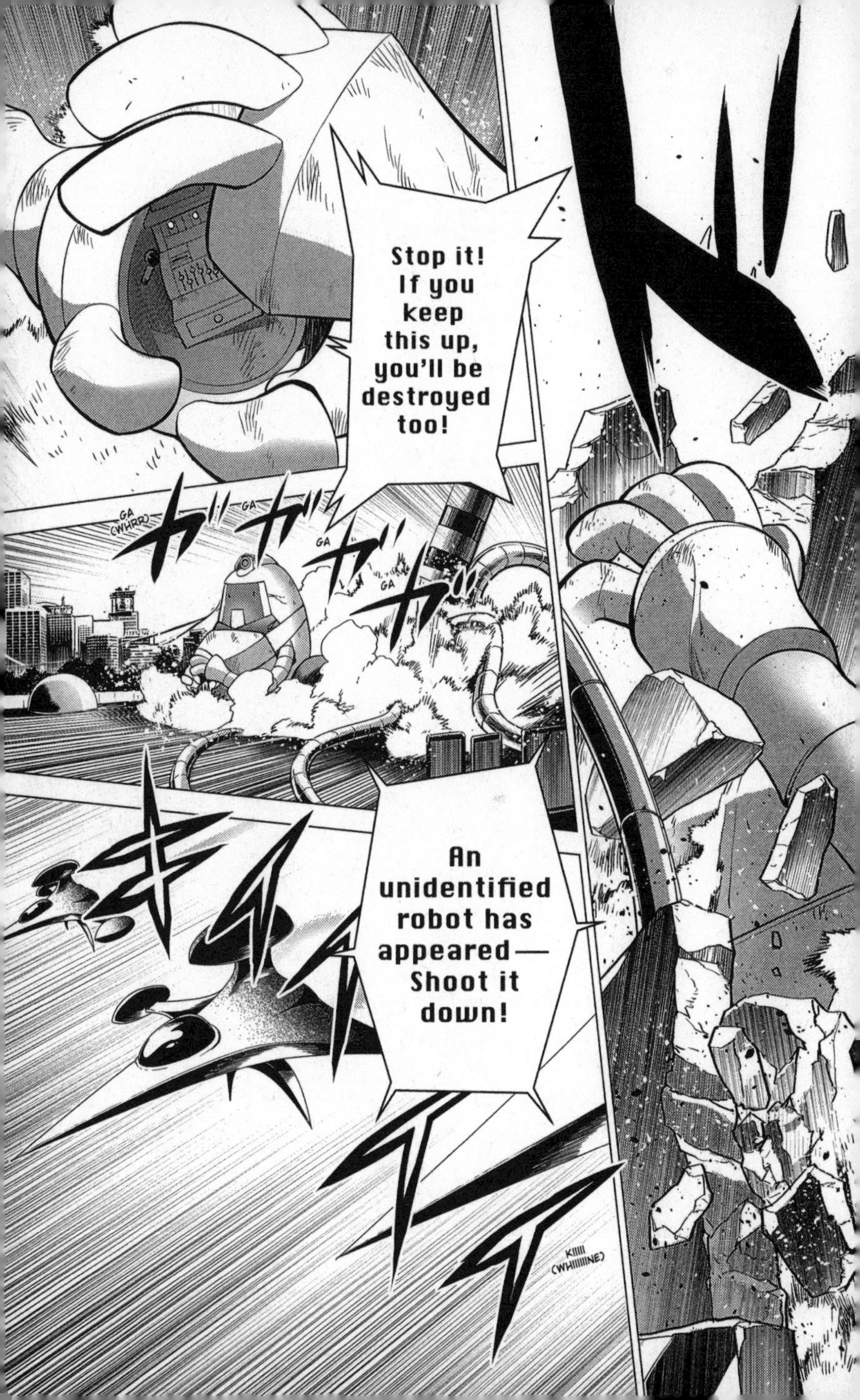
Stop it! If you keep this up, you'll be destroyed too!
GA (WHRR)
GA
GA
GA
An unidentified robot has appeared— Shoot it down!
KIIII (WHIIIIIINE)

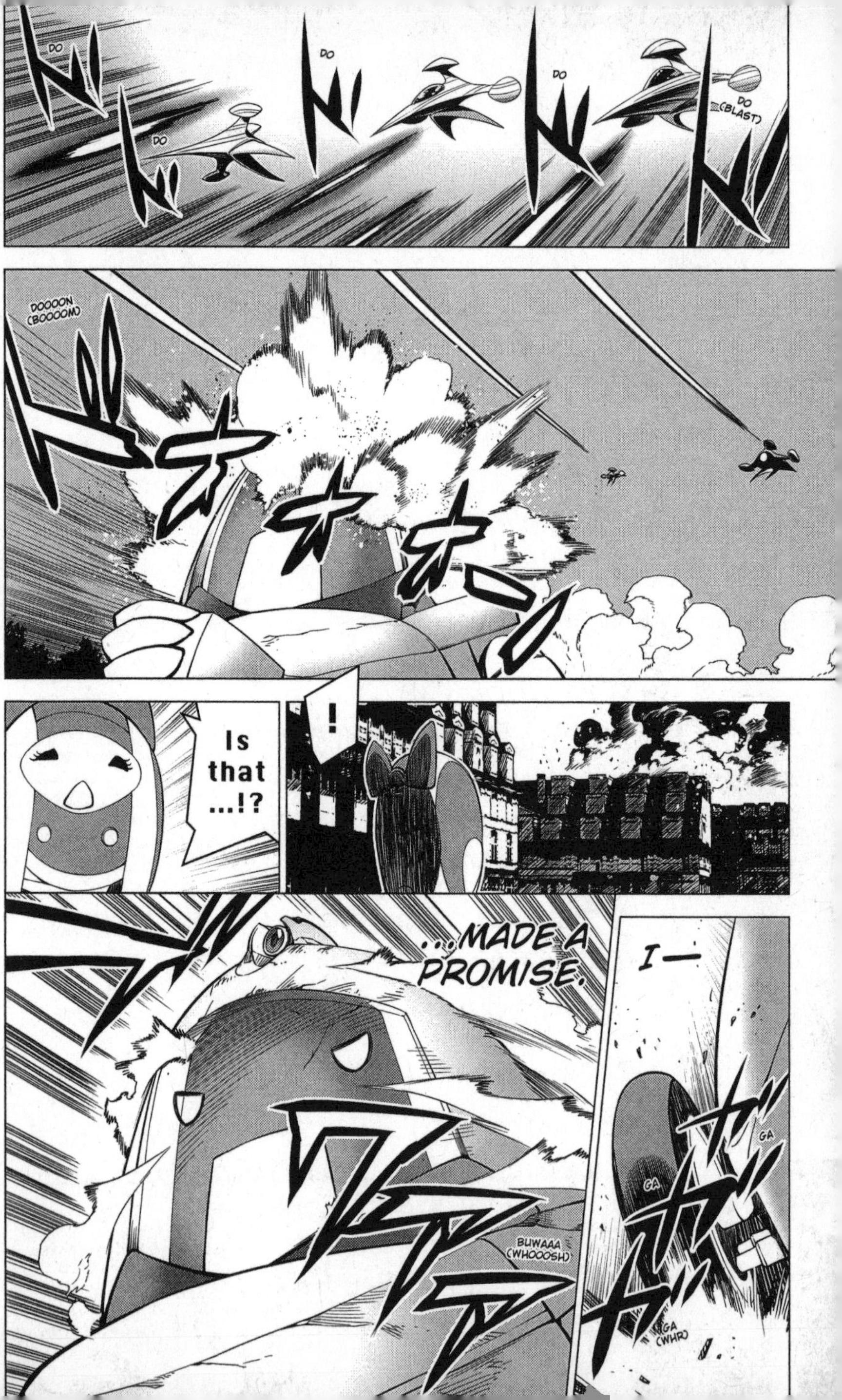
DO (BLAST)
DO
DO
DO
DO
DOOOON (BOOOOM)
!
Is that ...!?
I—
GA
GA
GA (WHR)
...MADE A PROMISE.
BUWAAA (WHOOOSH)

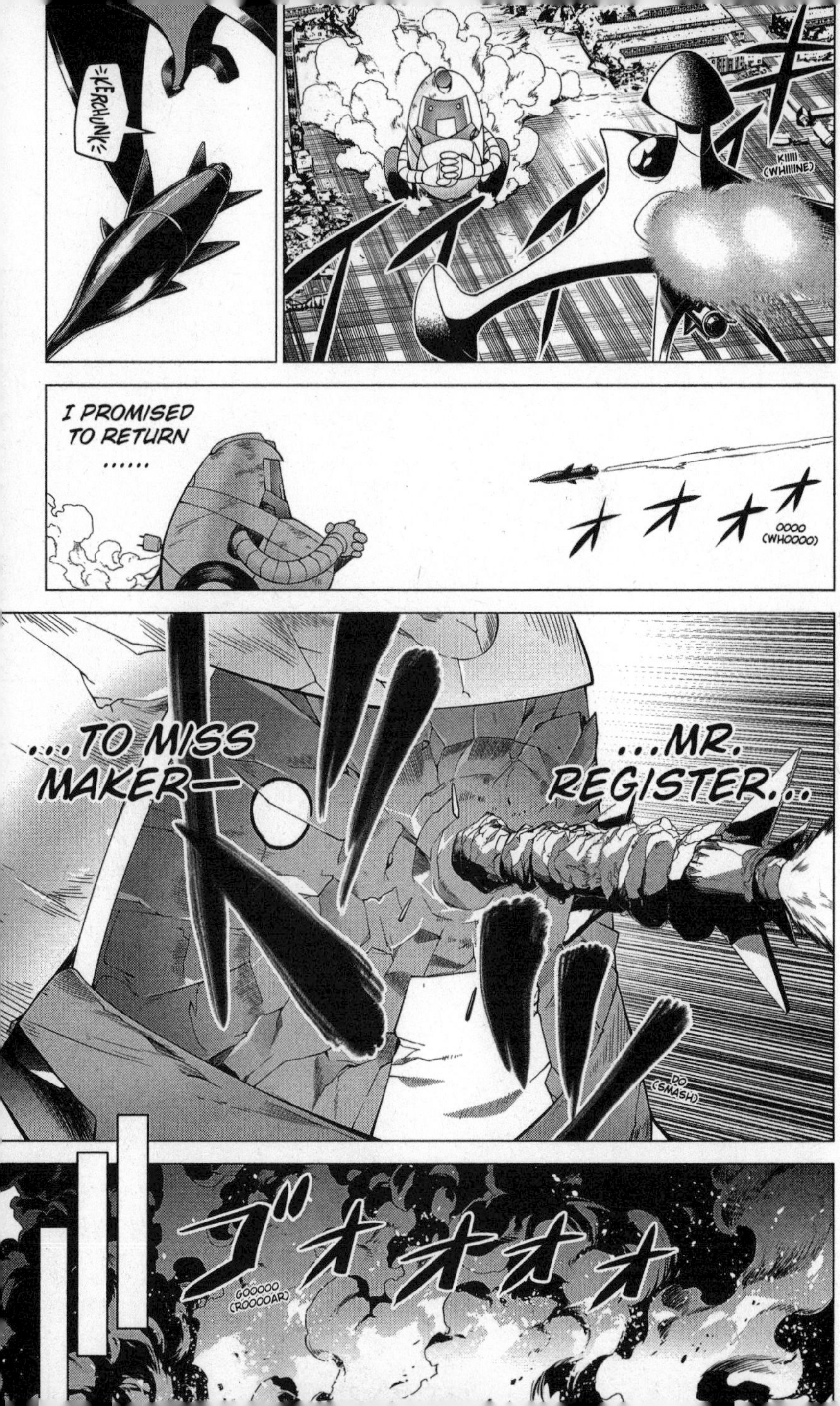
KIIIII
(WHIIIINE)
KERCHUNK
I PROMISED TO RETURN ......
OOOO
(WHOOOO)
...MR. REGISTER...
...TO MISS MAKER—
DO
(SMASH)
GOOOOO
(ROOOOAR)

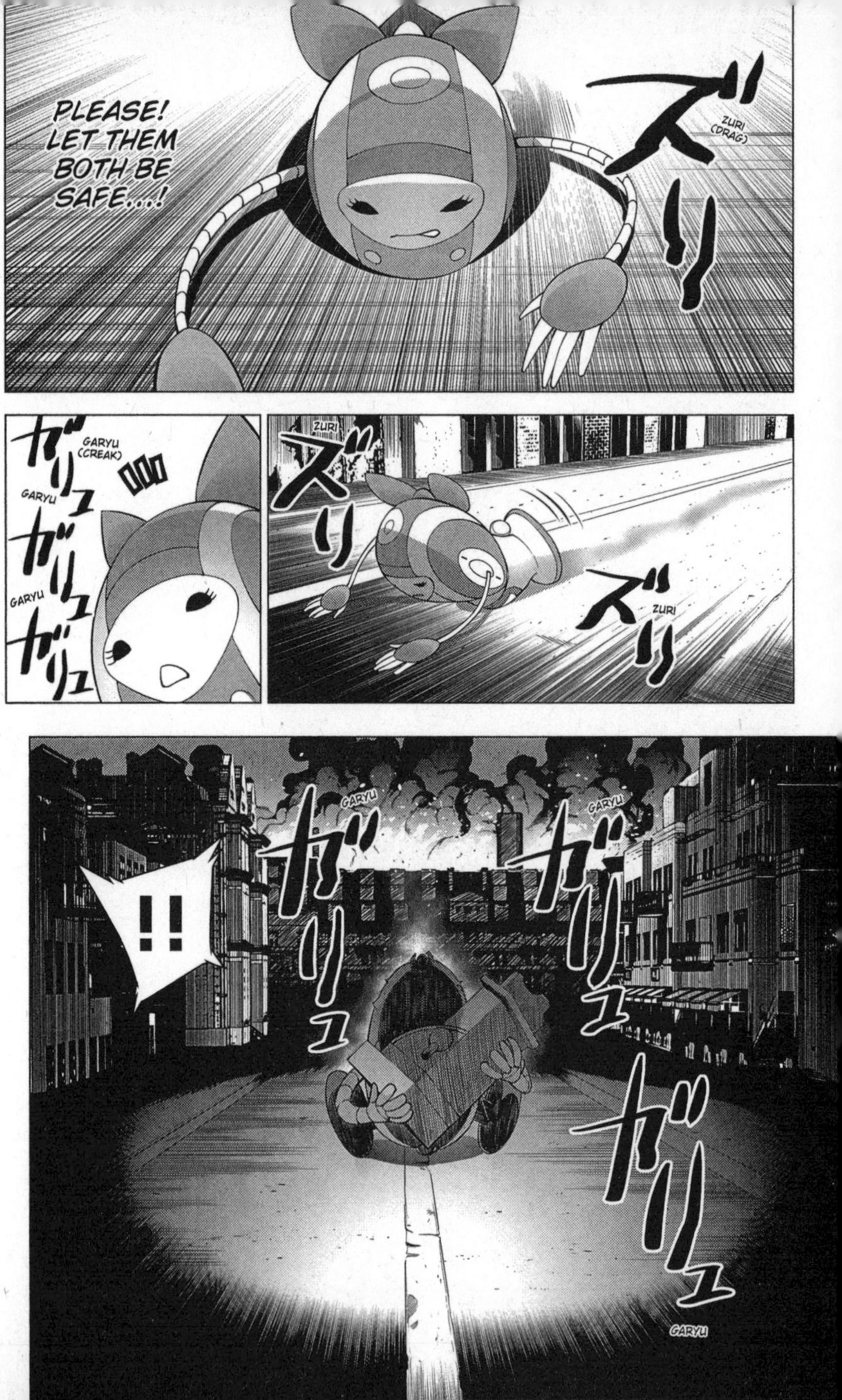
ズリ
ZURI (DRAG)
PLEASE! LET THEM BOTH BE SAFE...!
ズリ
ZURI
ズリ
ZURI
ガリュ
GARYU (CREAK)
ガリュ
GARYU
ガリュ
GARYU
ガリュ
GARYU
ガリュ
GARYU
ガリュ
GARYU
!!

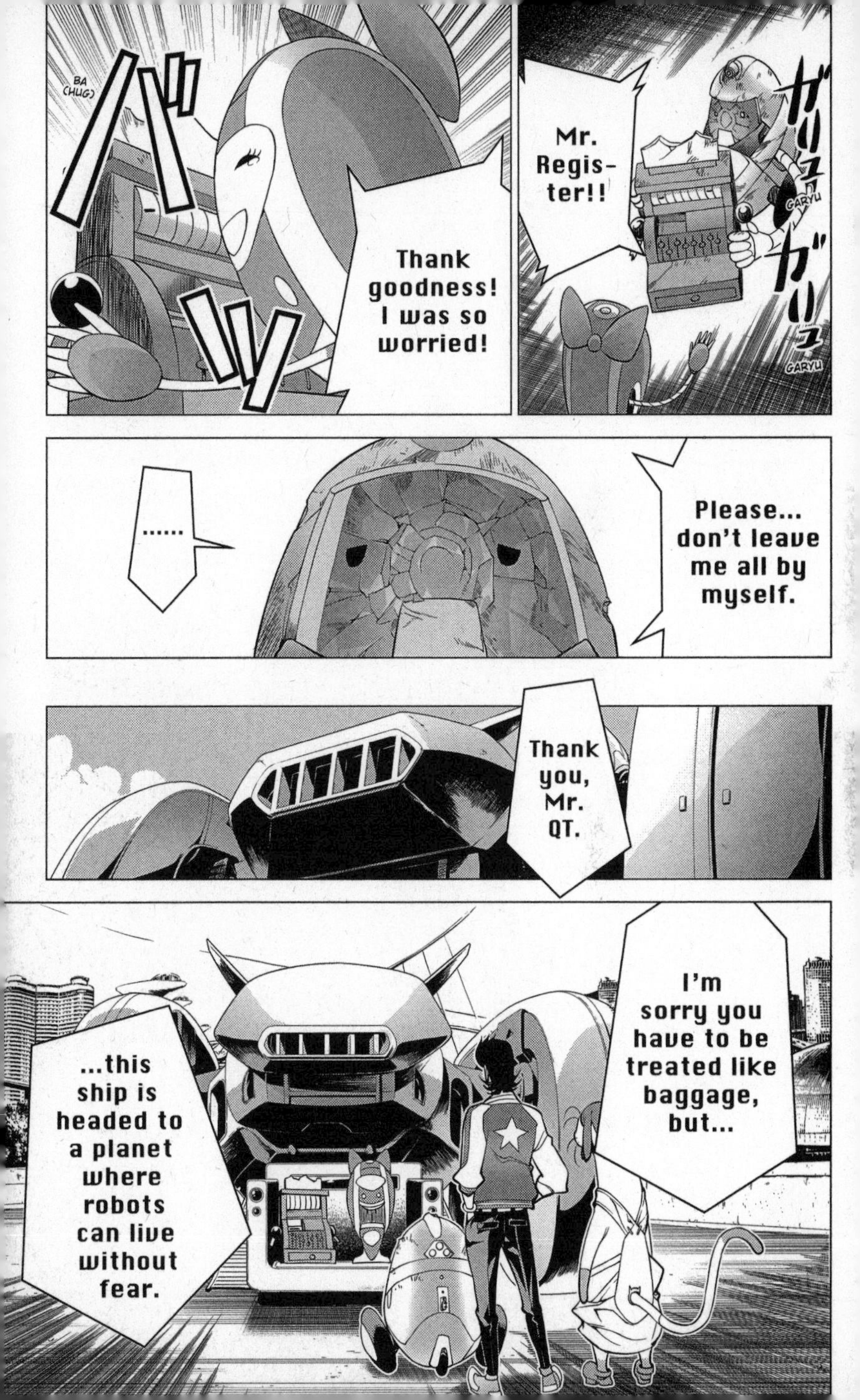

Mr. Regis-ter!!
ガリュ
GARYU
ガリュ
GARYU
BA (HUG)
バッ
Thank goodness! I was so worried!
Please... don't leave me all by myself.
......
Thank you, Mr. QT.
I'm sorry you have to be treated like baggage, but...
...this ship is headed to a planet where robots can live without fear.

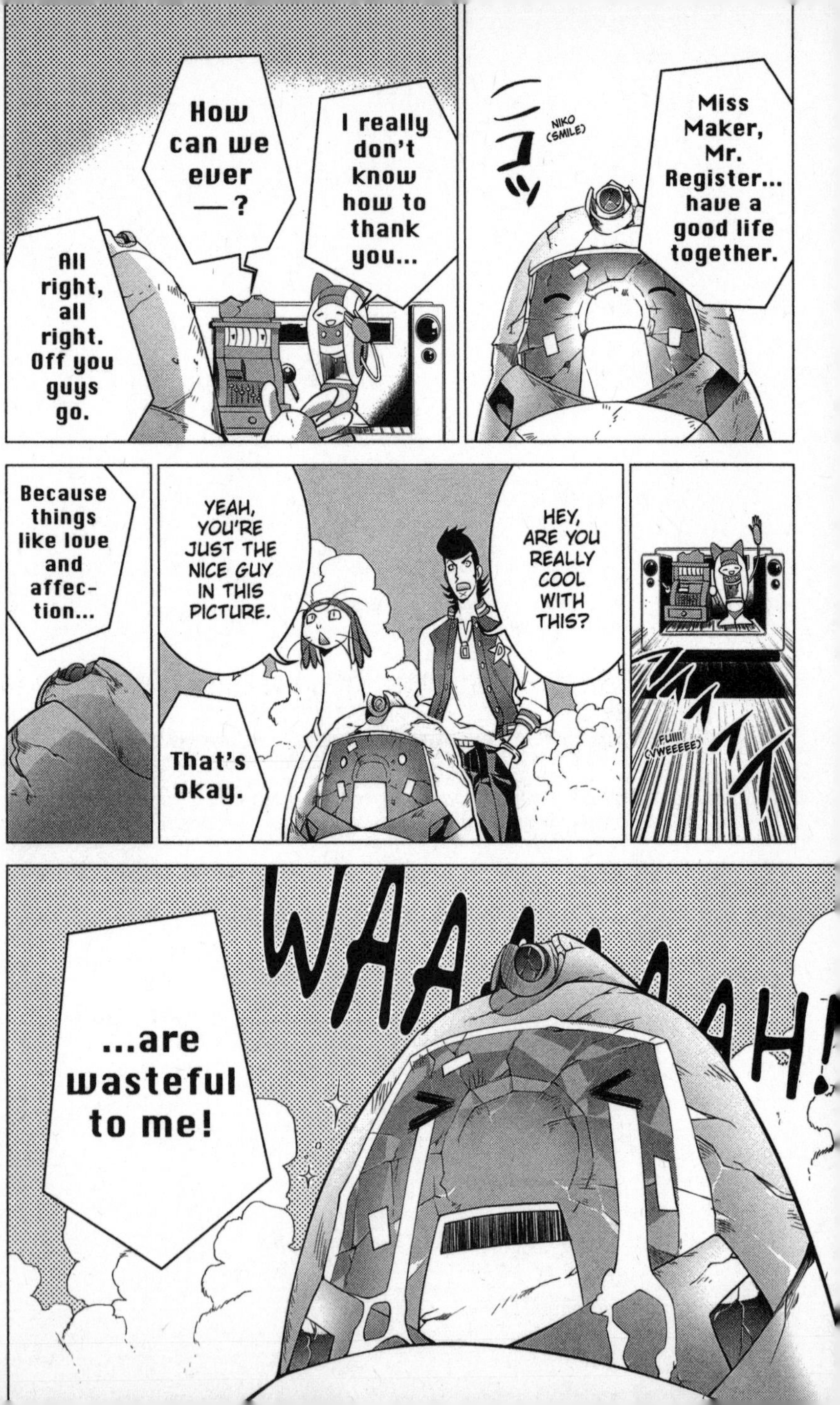
NIKO (SMILE)
Miss Maker, Mr. Register... have a good life together.
I really don't know how to thank you...
How can we ever—?
All right, all right. Off you guys go.
FUIIII (VWEEEEE)
HEY, ARE YOU REALLY COOL WITH THIS?
YEAH, YOU'RE JUST THE NICE GUY IN THIS PICTURE.
That's okay.
Because things like love and affection...
WAA
AH!
...are wasteful to me!

SPACE★DANDY

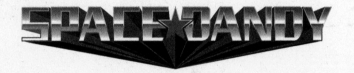

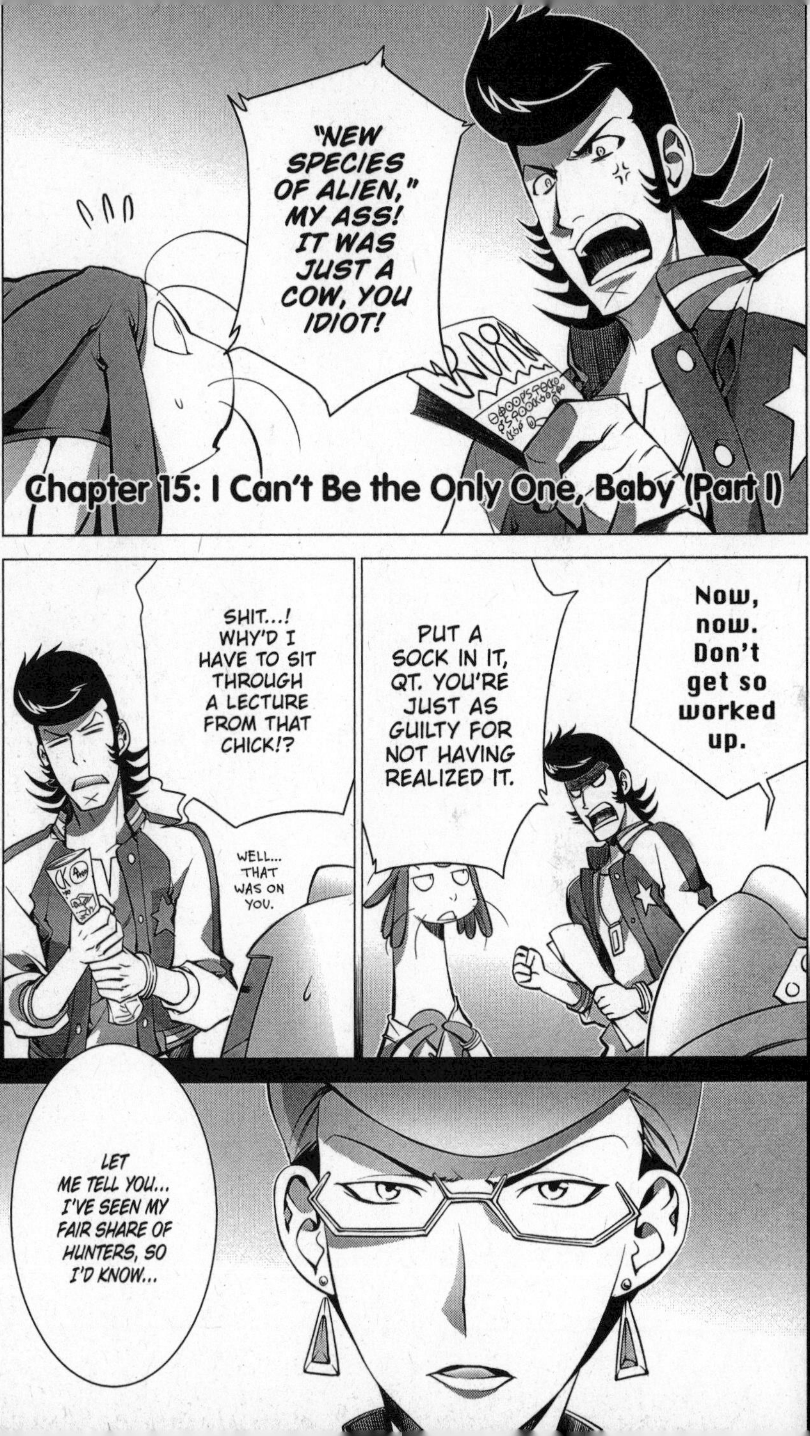
"NEW SPECIES OF ALIEN," MY ASS! IT WAS JUST A COW, YOU IDIOT!
Chapter 15: I Can't Be the Only One, Baby (Part I)
Now, now. Don't get so worked up.
PUT A SOCK IN IT, QT. YOU'RE JUST AS GUILTY FOR NOT HAVING REALIZED IT.
SHIT...! WHY'D I HAVE TO SIT THROUGH A LECTURE FROM THAT CHICK!?
WELL... THAT WAS ON YOU.
LET ME TELL YOU... I'VE SEEN MY FAIR SHARE OF HUNTERS, SO I'D KNOW...

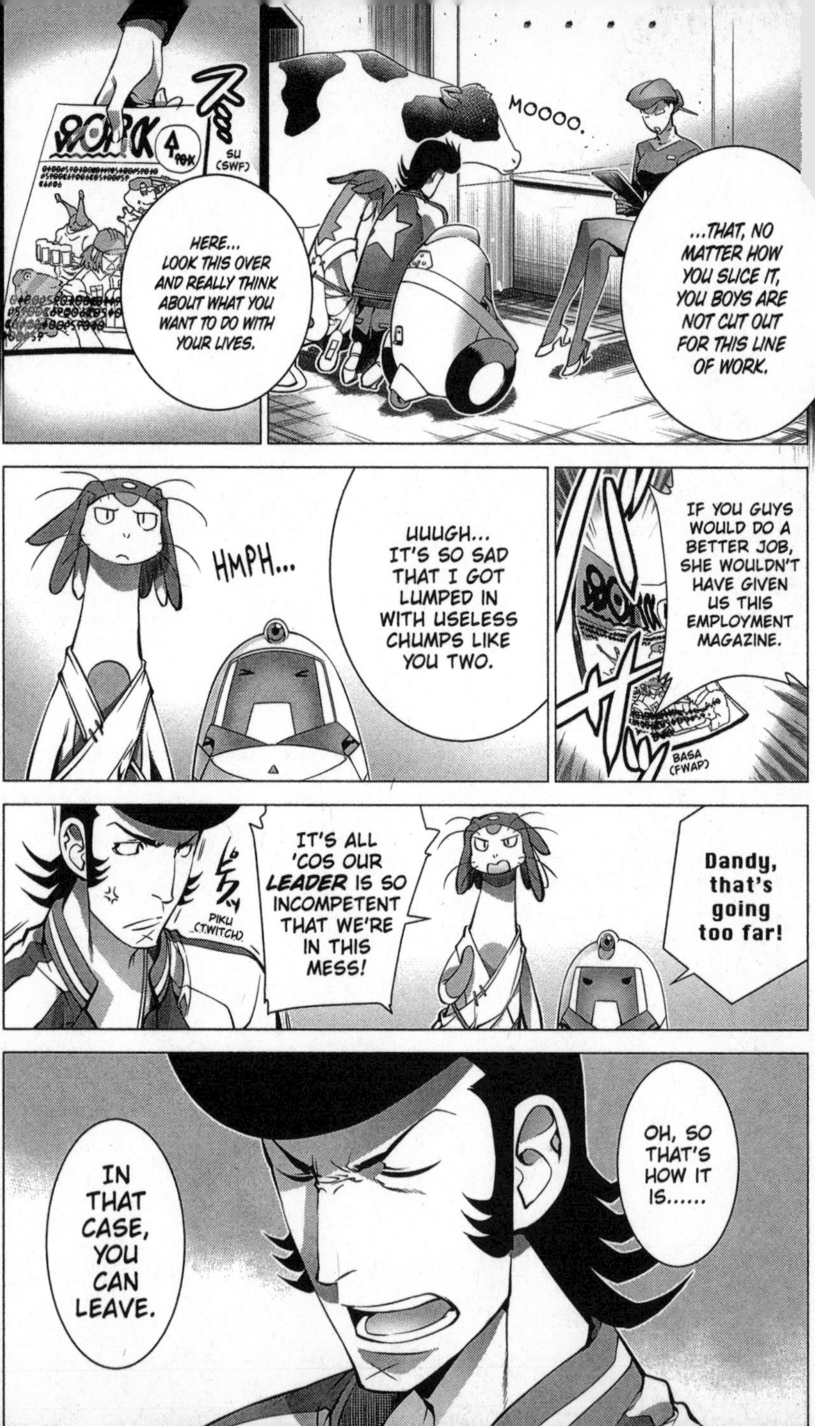
MOOOO...
...THAT, NO MATTER HOW YOU SLICE IT, YOU BOYS ARE NOT CUT OUT FOR THIS LINE OF WORK.
SU (SWF)
HERE... LOOK THIS OVER AND REALLY THINK ABOUT WHAT YOU WANT TO DO WITH YOUR LIVES.
IF YOU GUYS WOULD DO A BETTER JOB, SHE WOULDN'T HAVE GIVEN US THIS EMPLOYMENT MAGAZINE.
BASA (FWAP)
UUUGH... IT'S SO SAD THAT I GOT LUMPED IN WITH USELESS CHUMPS LIKE YOU TWO.
HMPH...
Dandy, that's going too far!
IT'S ALL 'COS OUR LEADER IS SO INCOMPETENT THAT WE'RE IN THIS MESS!
PIKU (TWITCH)
OH, SO THAT'S HOW IT IS......
IN THAT CASE, YOU CAN LEAVE.

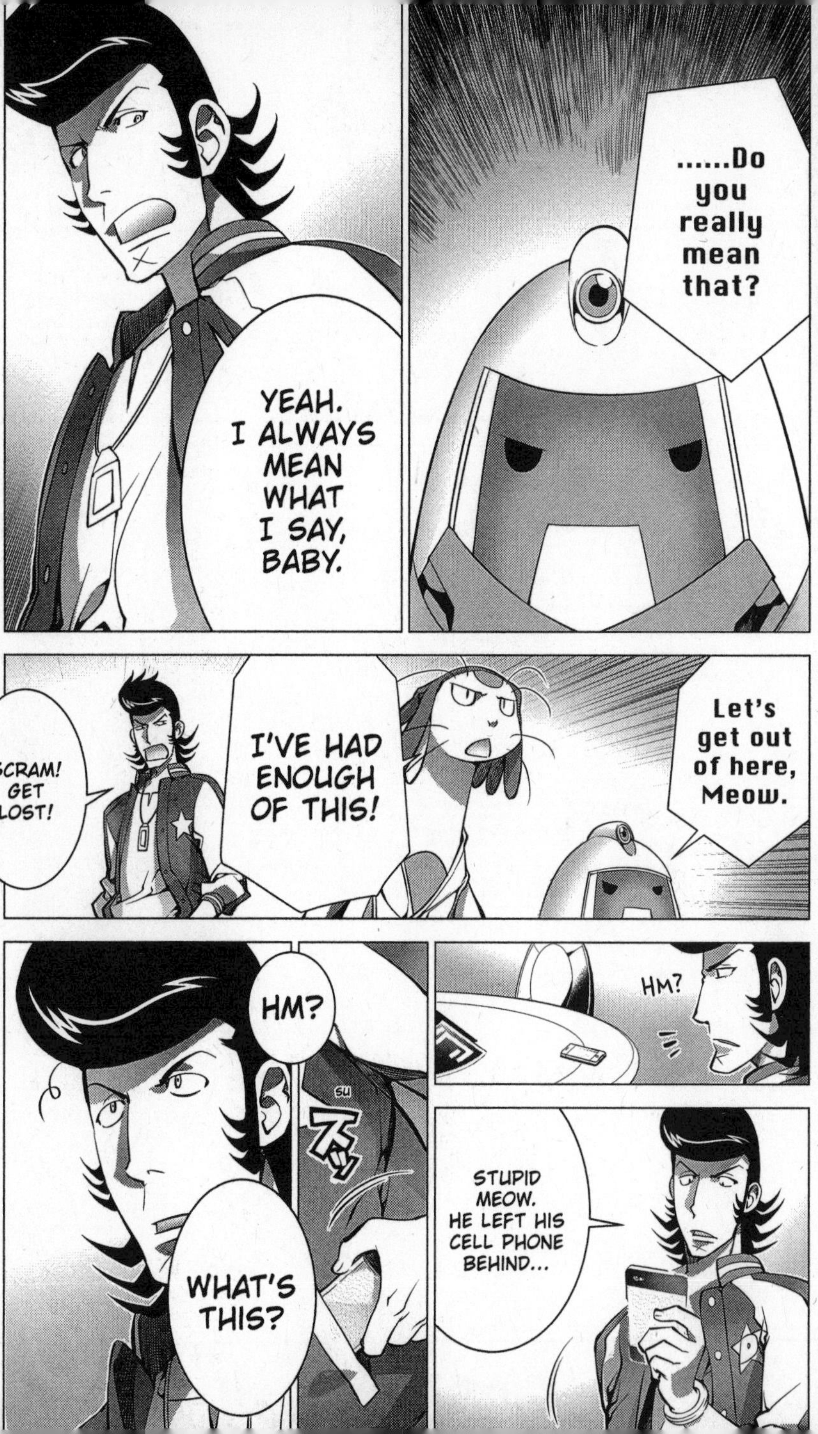
......Do you really mean that?
YEAH. I ALWAYS MEAN WHAT I SAY, BABY.
Let's get out of here, Meow.
I'VE HAD ENOUGH OF THIS!
SCRAM! GET LOST!
HM?
STUPID MEOW. HE LEFT HIS CELL PHONE BEHIND...
HM?
SU
WHAT'S THIS?

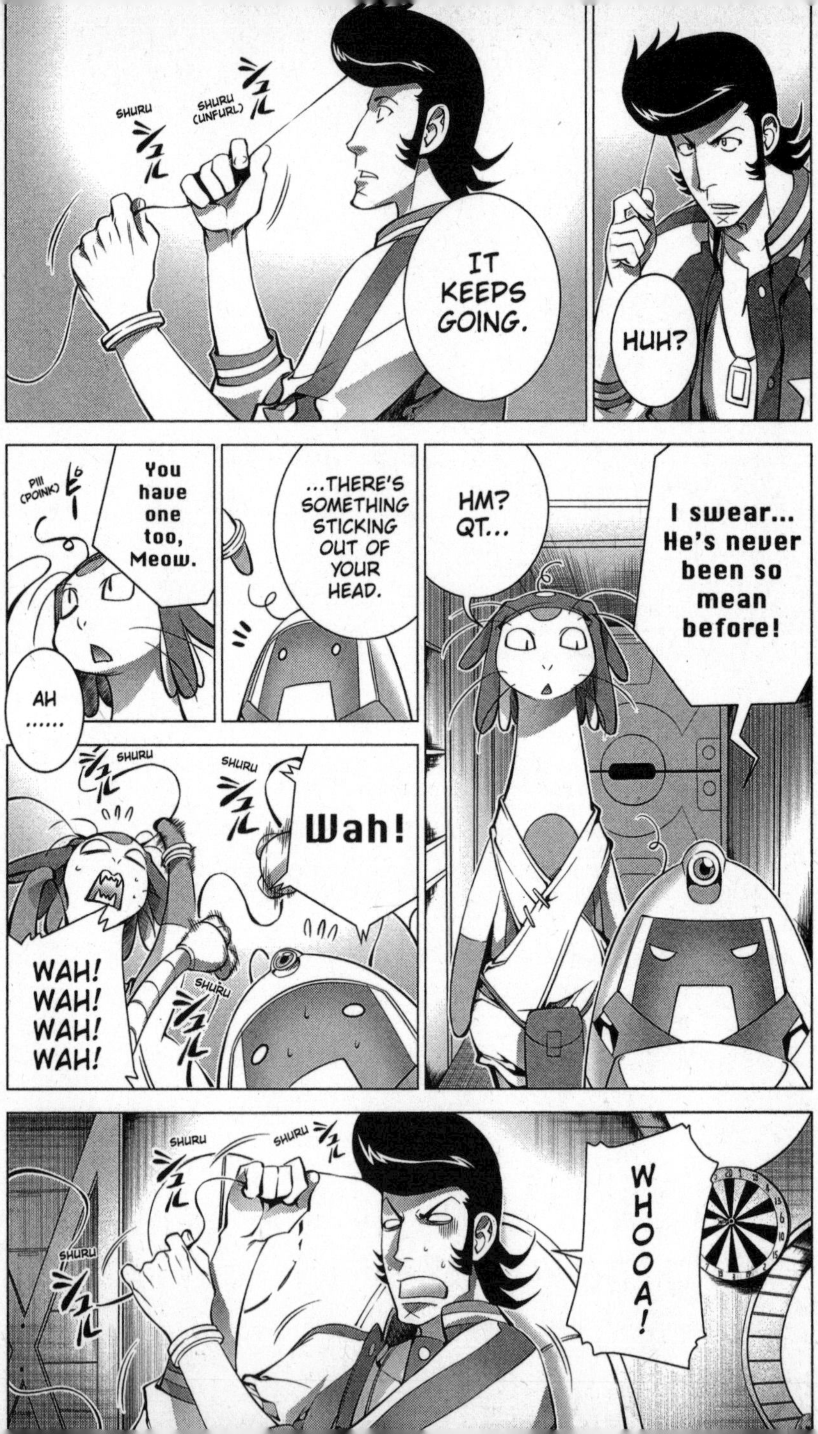
HUH?
SHURU (UNFURL)
SHURU
IT KEEPS GOING.
I swear... He's never been so mean before!
HM? QT...
...THERE'S SOMETHING STICKING OUT OF YOUR HEAD.
You have one too, Meow.
PIII (POINK)
AH ......
SHURU
Wah!
SHURU
WAH! WAH! WAH! WAH!
SHURU
WHOOOA!
SHURU
SHURU
SHURU

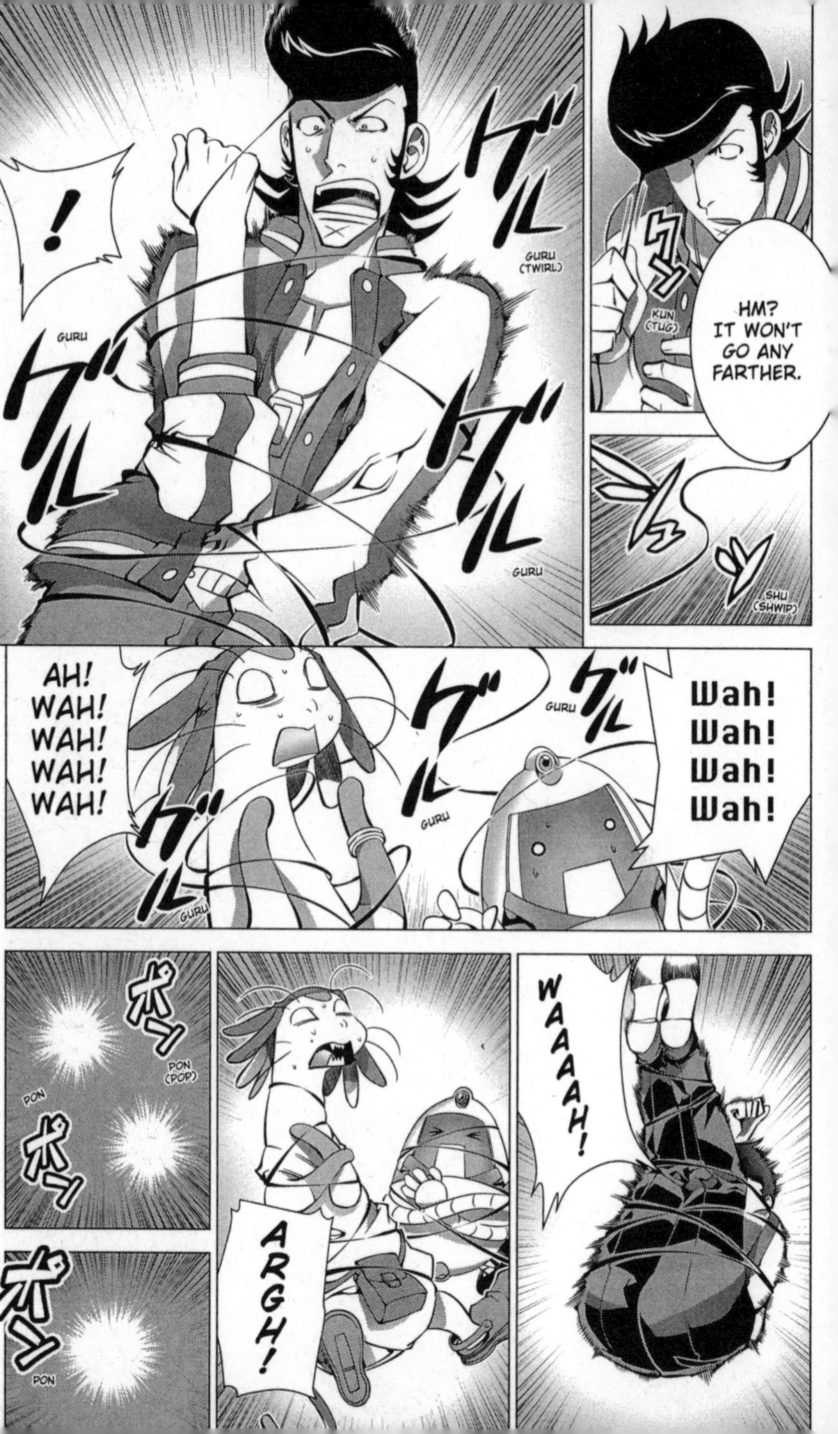

KUN (TUG)
HM? IT WON'T GO ANY FARTHER.
SHU (SHWIP)
GURU (TWIRL)
!
GURU
GURU
Wah! Wah! Wah! Wah!
GURU
GURU
AH! WAH! WAH! WAH! WAH!
GURU
WAAAAAH!
ARGH!
PON (POP)
PON
PON

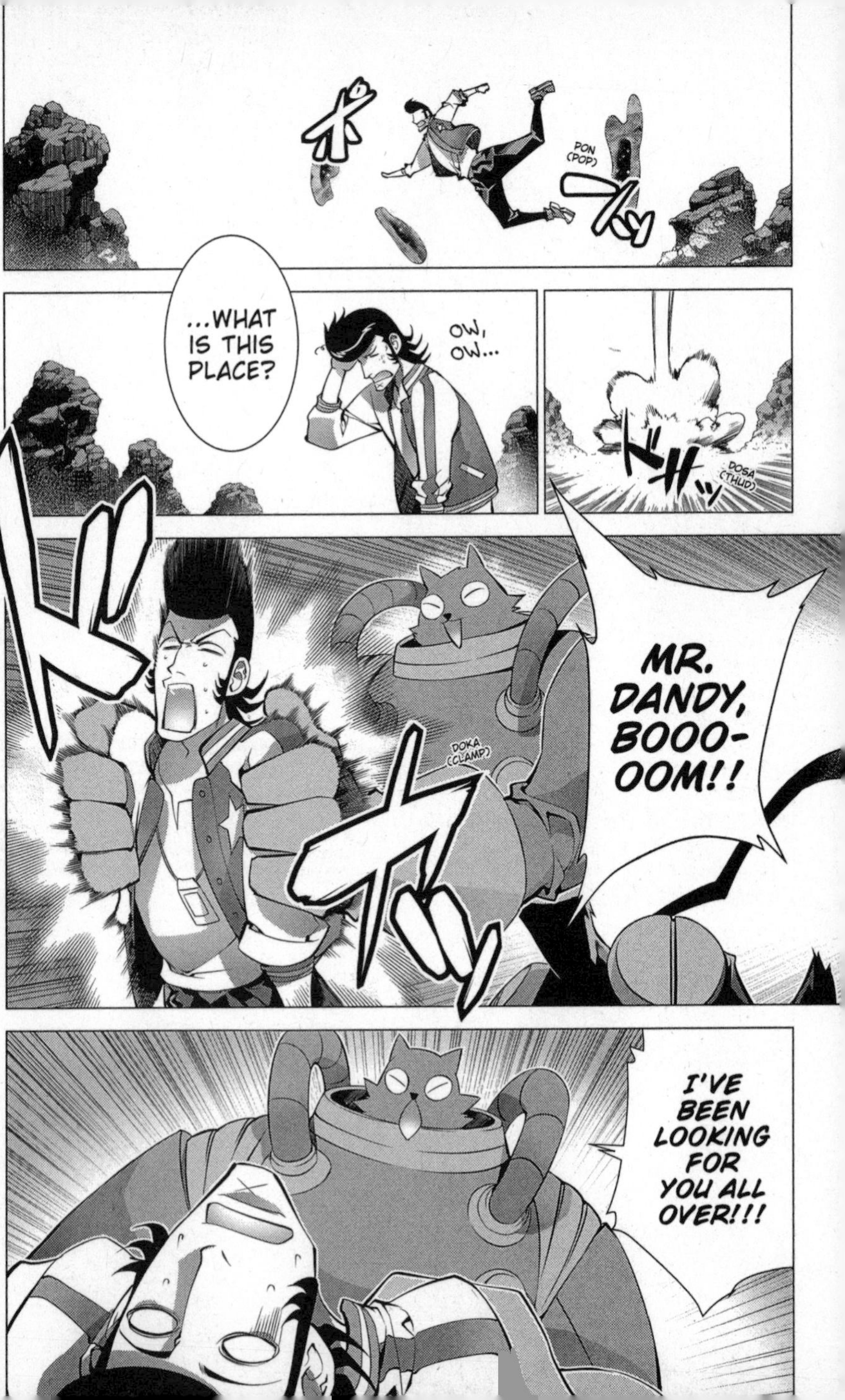
PON (POP)
DOSA (THUD)
OW, OW...
...WHAT IS THIS PLACE?
MR. DANDY, BOOOO-OOM!!
DOKA (CLAMP)
I'VE BEEN LOOKING FOR YOU ALL OVER!!!

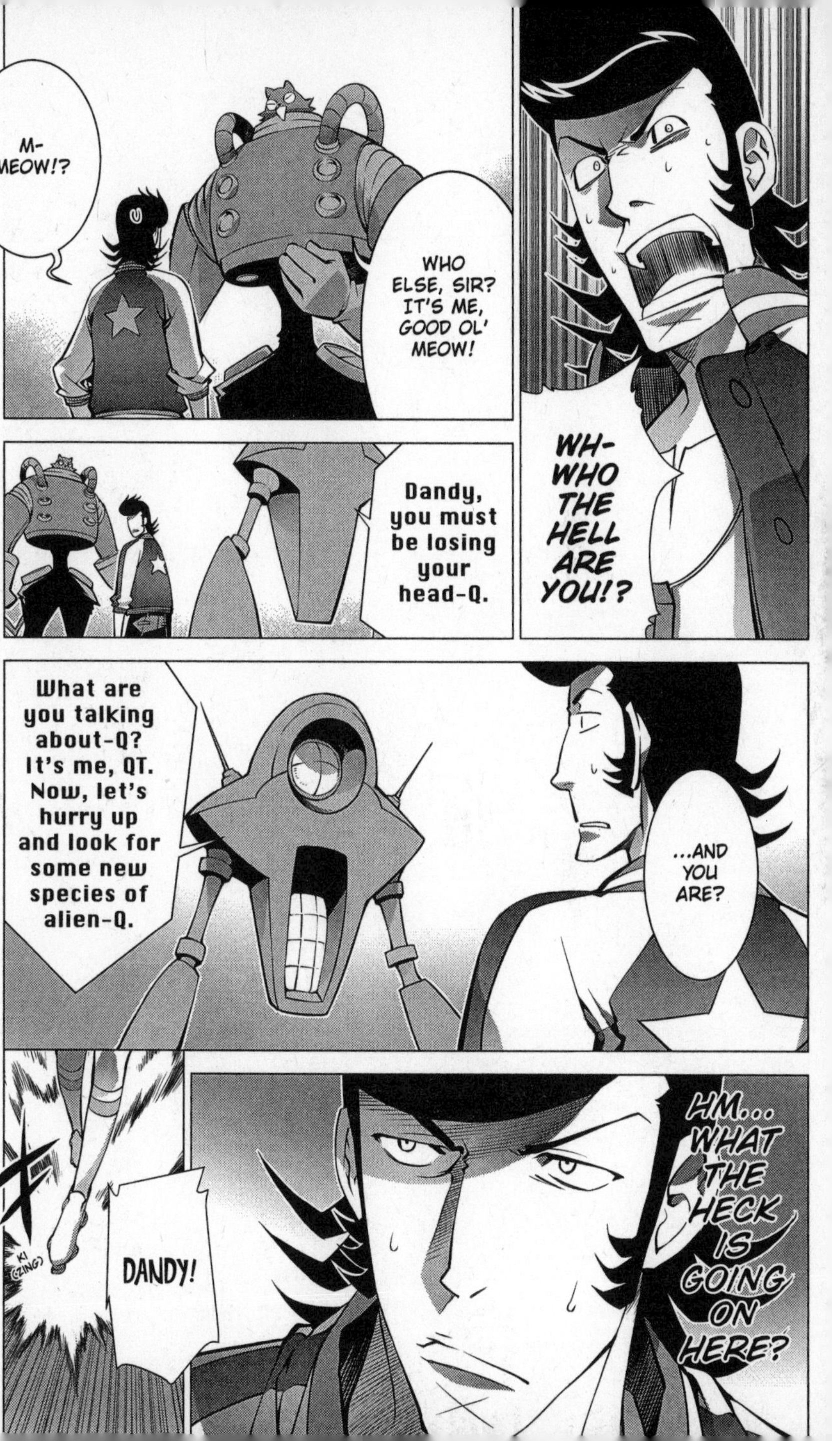
WH-WHO THE HELL ARE YOU!?
WHO ELSE, SIR? IT'S ME, GOOD OL' MEOW!
M-MEOW!?
Dandy, you must be losing your head-Q.
...AND YOU ARE?
What are you talking about-Q? It's me, QT. Now, let's hurry up and look for some new species of alien-Q.
HM... WHAT THE HECK IS GOING ON HERE?
DANDY!
KI (ZING)

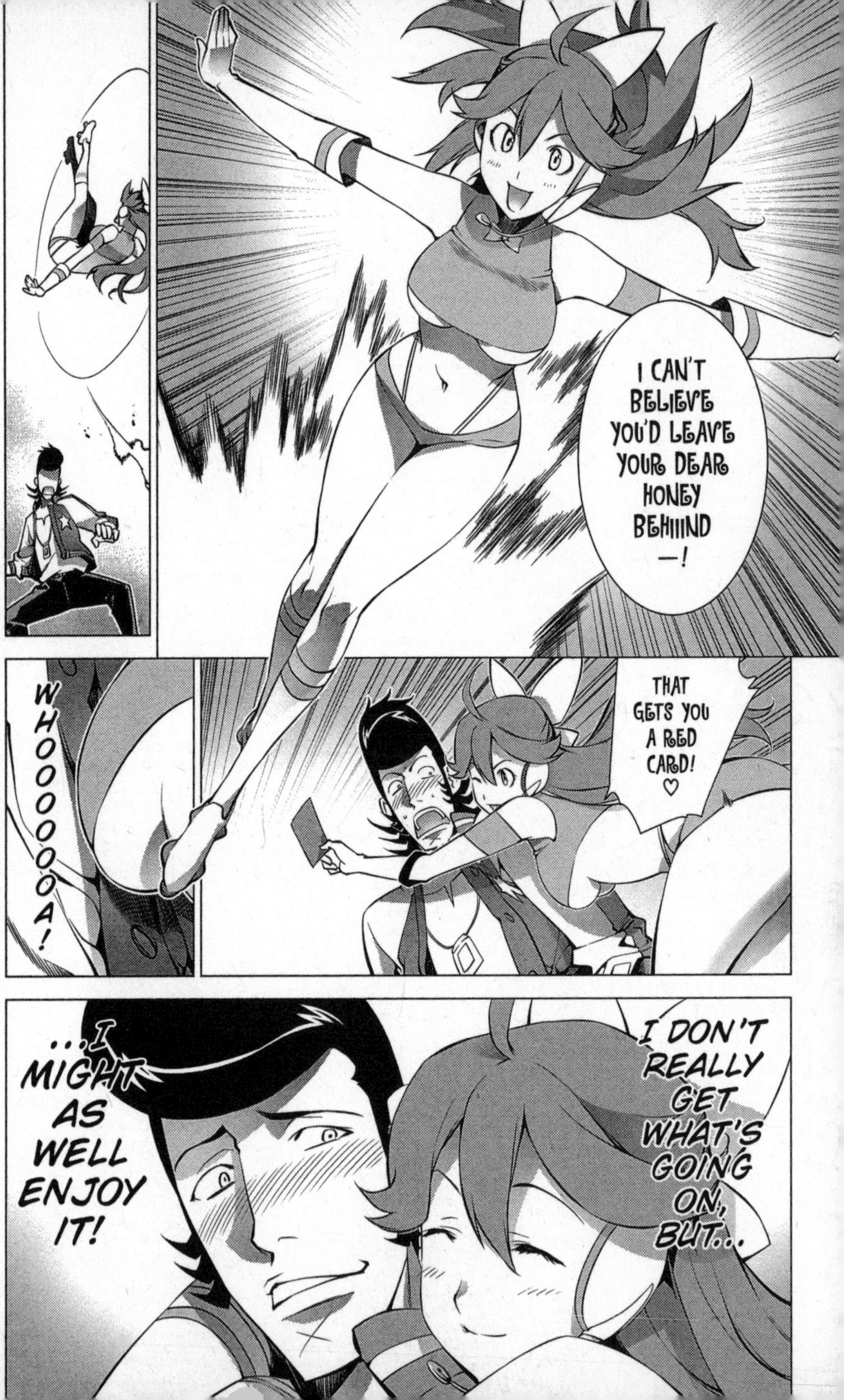
I CAN'T BELIEVE YOU'D LEAVE YOUR DEAR HONEY BEHIIIND—!
THAT GETS YOU A RED CARD! ♡
WHOOOOOOOA!
I DON'T REALLY GET WHAT'S GOING ON, BUT...
...I MIGHT AS WELL ENJOY IT!

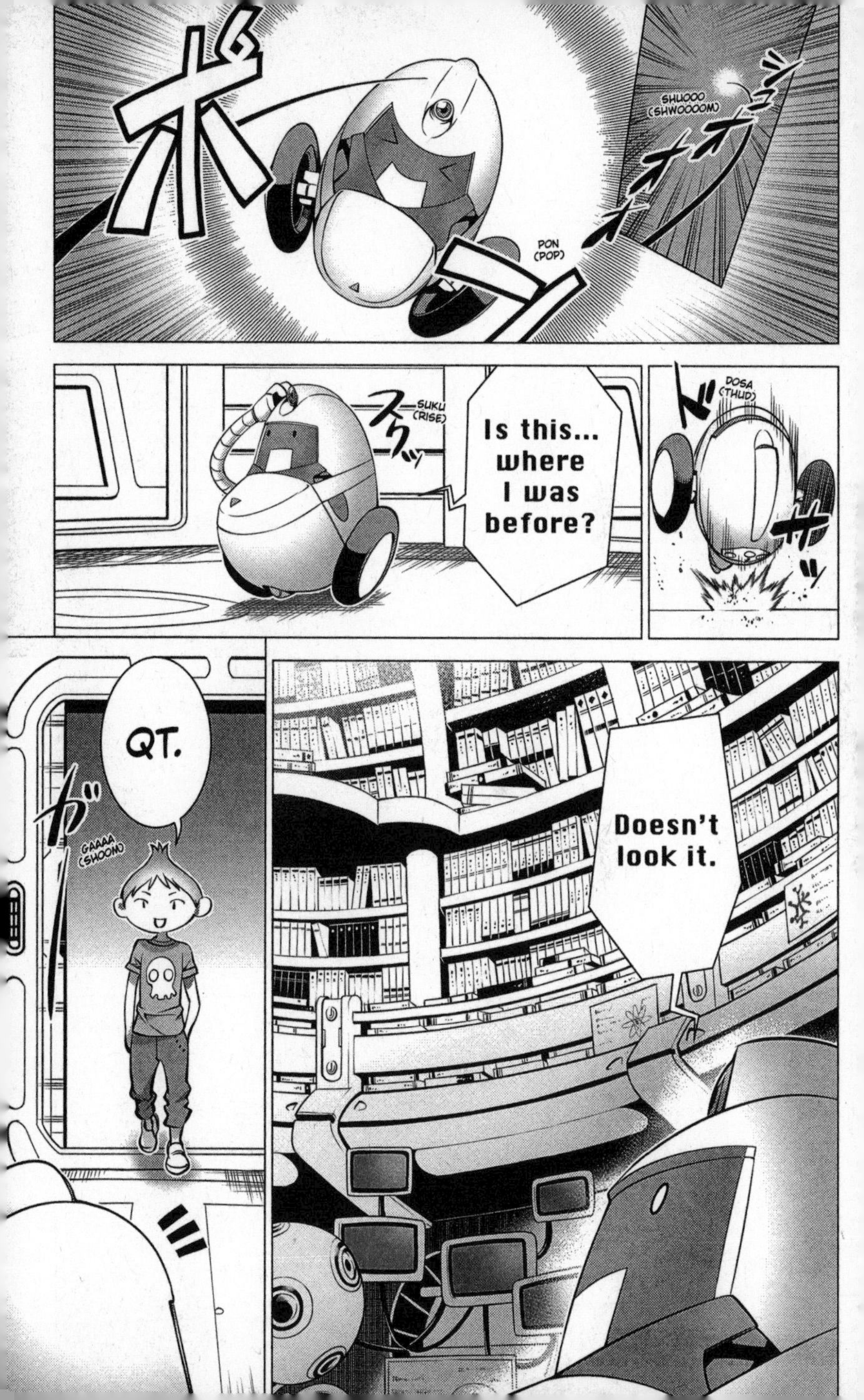
SHUOOO (SHWOOOOM)
PON (POP)
DOSA (THUD)
SUKU (RISE)
Is this... where I was before?
Doesn't look it.
QT.
GAAAA (SHOOM)

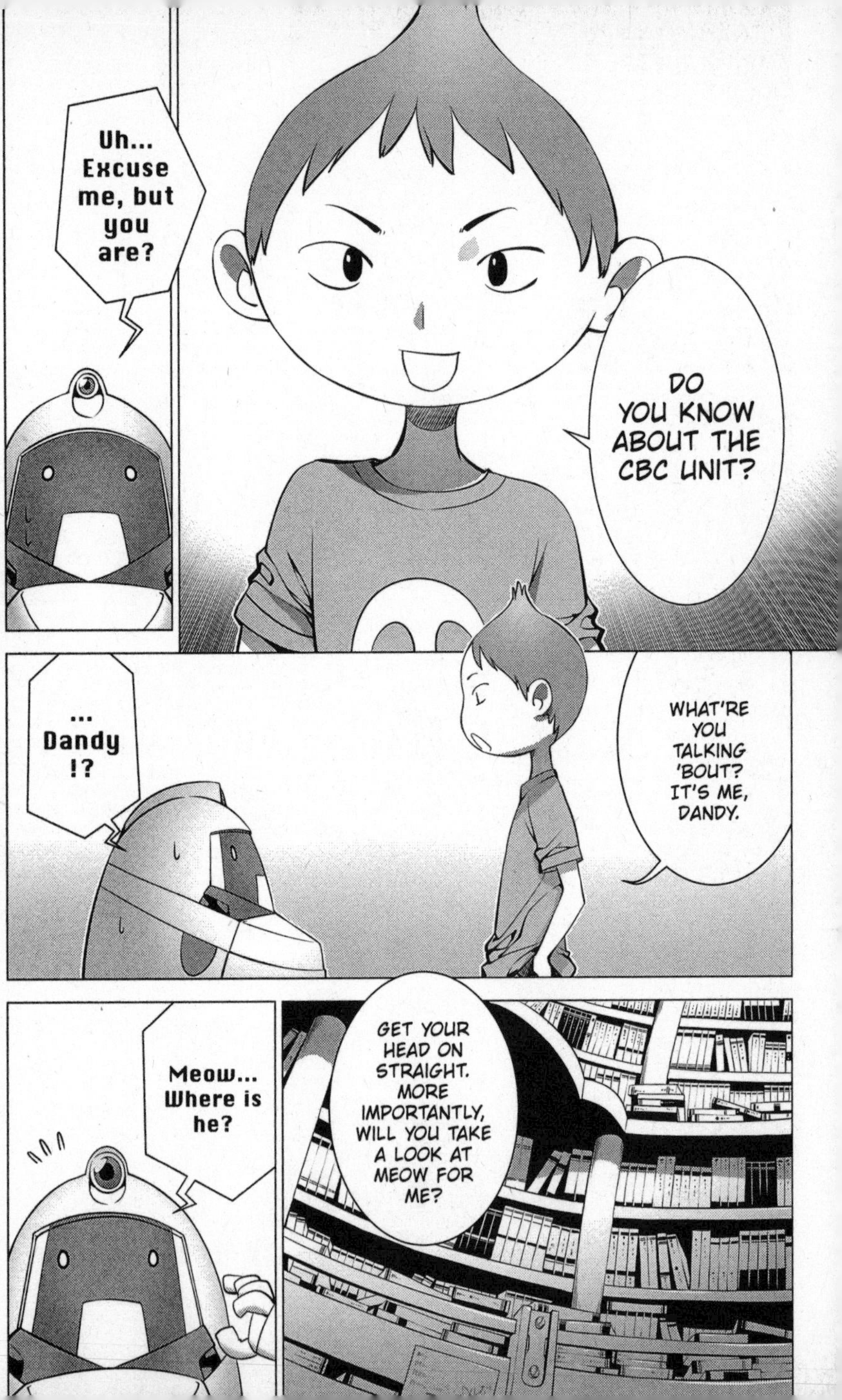
DO YOU KNOW ABOUT THE CBC UNIT?
Uh... Excuse me, but you are?
WHAT'RE YOU TALKING 'BOUT? IT'S ME, DANDY.
... Dandy !?
GET YOUR HEAD ON STRAIGHT. MORE IMPORTANTLY, WILL YOU TAKE A LOOK AT MEOW FOR ME?
Meow... Where is he?

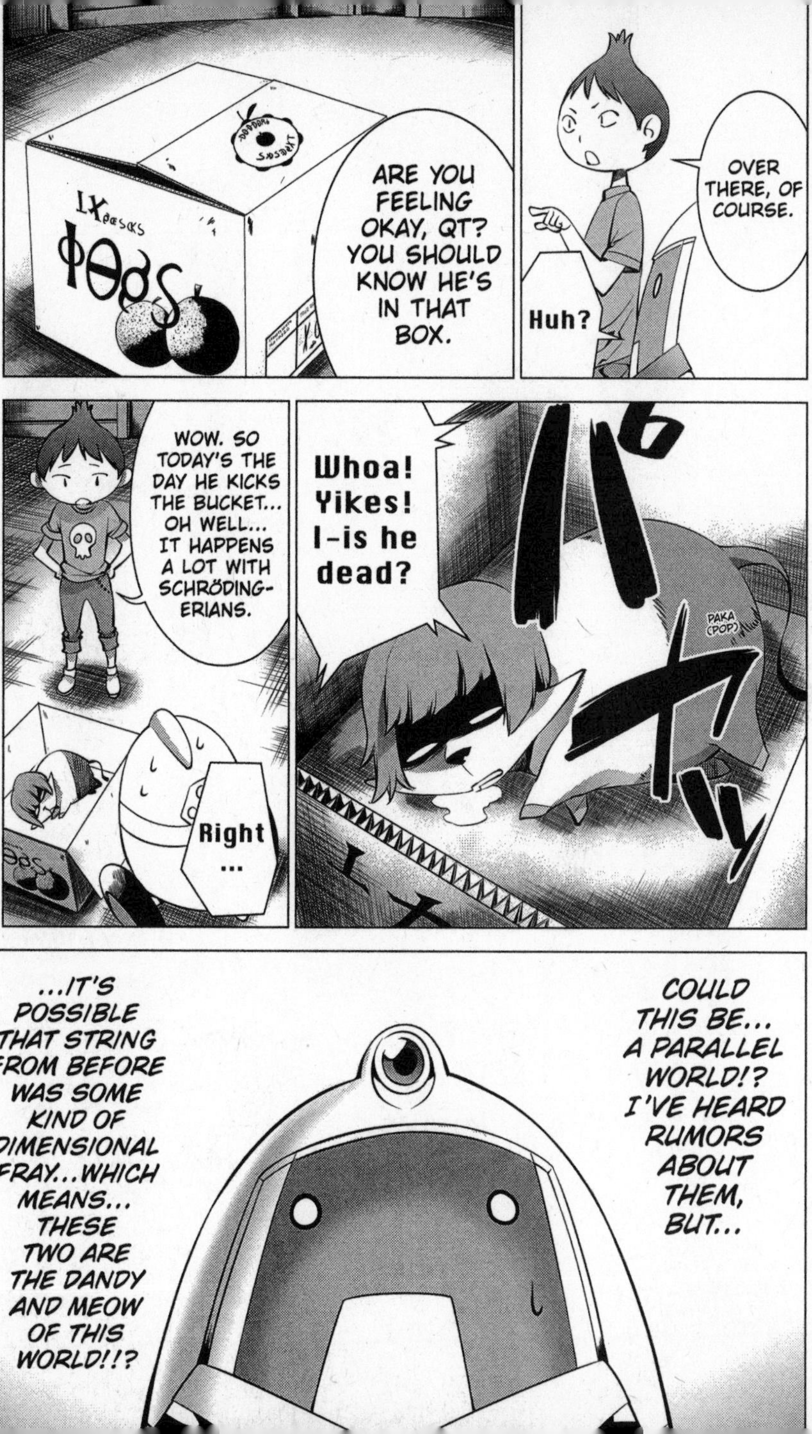
OVER THERE, OF COURSE.
Huh?
ARE YOU FEELING OKAY, QT? YOU SHOULD KNOW HE'S IN THAT BOX.
Whoa! Yikes! I-is he dead?
PAKA (POP)
WOW. SO TODAY'S THE DAY HE KICKS THE BUCKET... OH WELL... IT HAPPENS A LOT WITH SCHRÖDING-ERIANS.
Right ...
COULD THIS BE... A PARALLEL WORLD!? I'VE HEARD RUMORS ABOUT THEM, BUT...
...IT'S POSSIBLE THAT STRING FROM BEFORE WAS SOME KIND OF DIMENSIONAL FRAY...WHICH MEANS... THESE TWO ARE THE DANDY AND MEOW OF THIS WORLD!!?

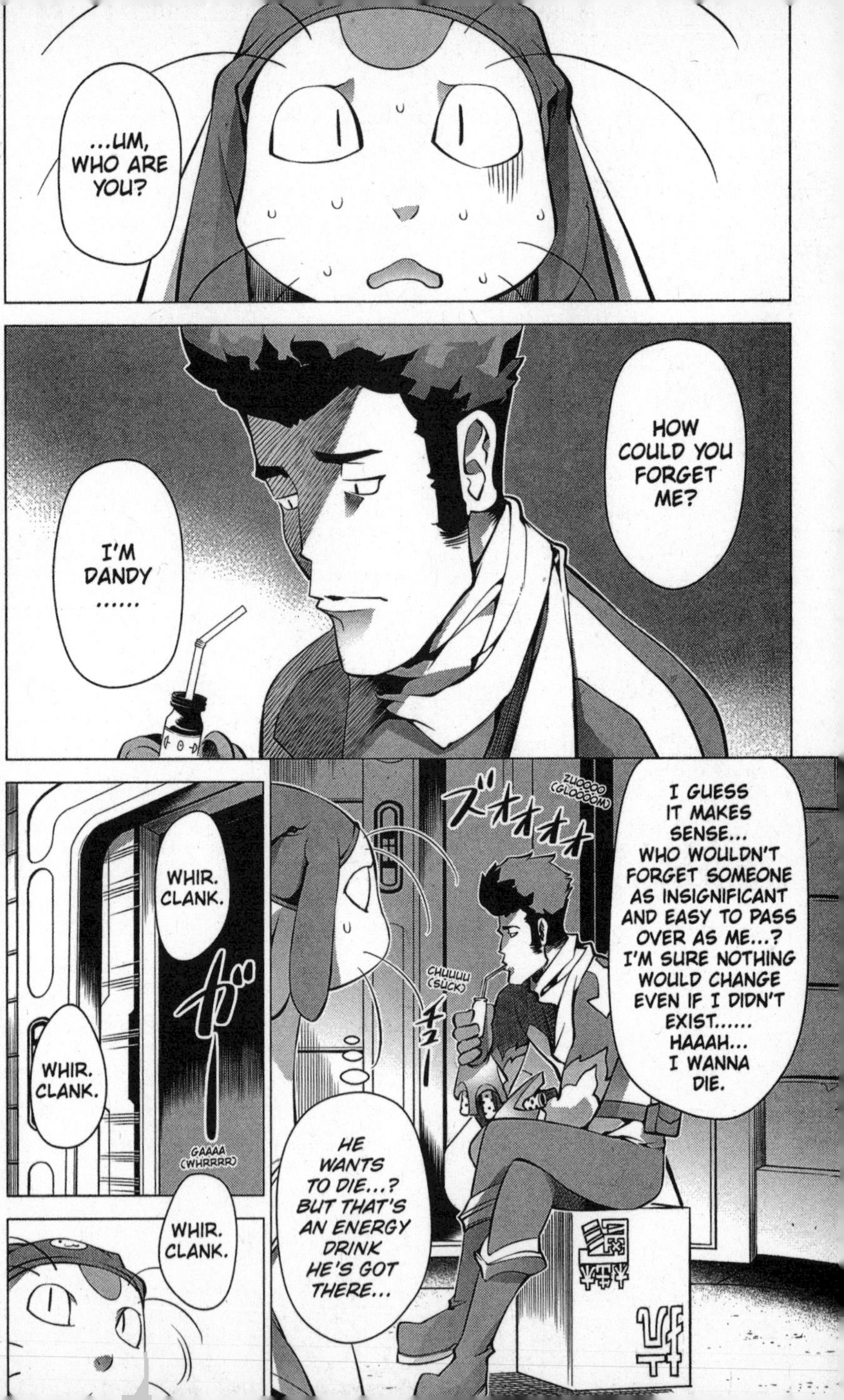
...UM, WHO ARE YOU?
HOW COULD YOU FORGET ME?
I'M DANDY ......
ズオオオオ
ZUOOOO (GLOOOOM)
I GUESS IT MAKES SENSE... WHO WOULDN'T FORGET SOMEONE AS INSIGNIFICANT AND EASY TO PASS OVER AS ME...? I'M SURE NOTHING WOULD CHANGE EVEN IF I DIDN'T EXIST...... HAAAH... I WANNA DIE.
チュー
CHUUUU (SUCK)
HE WANTS TO DIE...? BUT THAT'S AN ENERGY DRINK HE'S GOT THERE...
WHIR. CLANK.
WHIR. CLANK.
GAAAA (WHRRRR)
WHIR. CLANK.

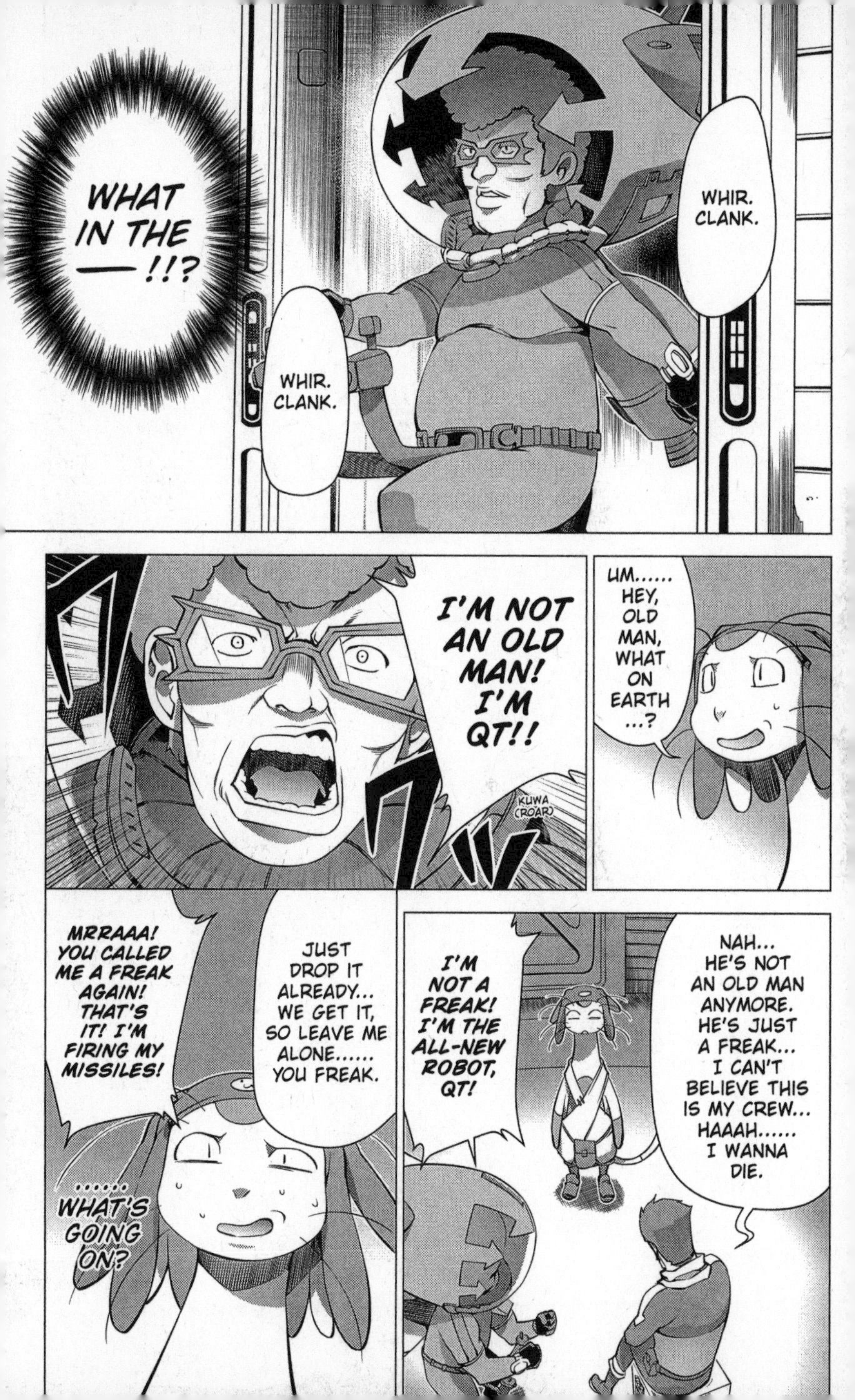
WHIR. CLANK.
WHAT IN THE —!!?
WHIR. CLANK.
UM...... HEY, OLD MAN, WHAT ON EARTH ...?
I'M NOT AN OLD MAN! I'M QT!!
KUWA (ROAR)
NAH... HE'S NOT AN OLD MAN ANYMORE. HE'S JUST A FREAK... I CAN'T BELIEVE THIS IS MY CREW... HAAAH...... I WANNA DIE.
I'M NOT A FREAK! I'M THE ALL-NEW ROBOT, QT!
JUST DROP IT ALREADY... WE GET IT, SO LEAVE ME ALONE...... YOU FREAK.
MRRAAA! YOU CALLED ME A FREAK AGAIN! THAT'S IT! I'M FIRING MY MISSILES!
...... WHAT'S GOING ON?

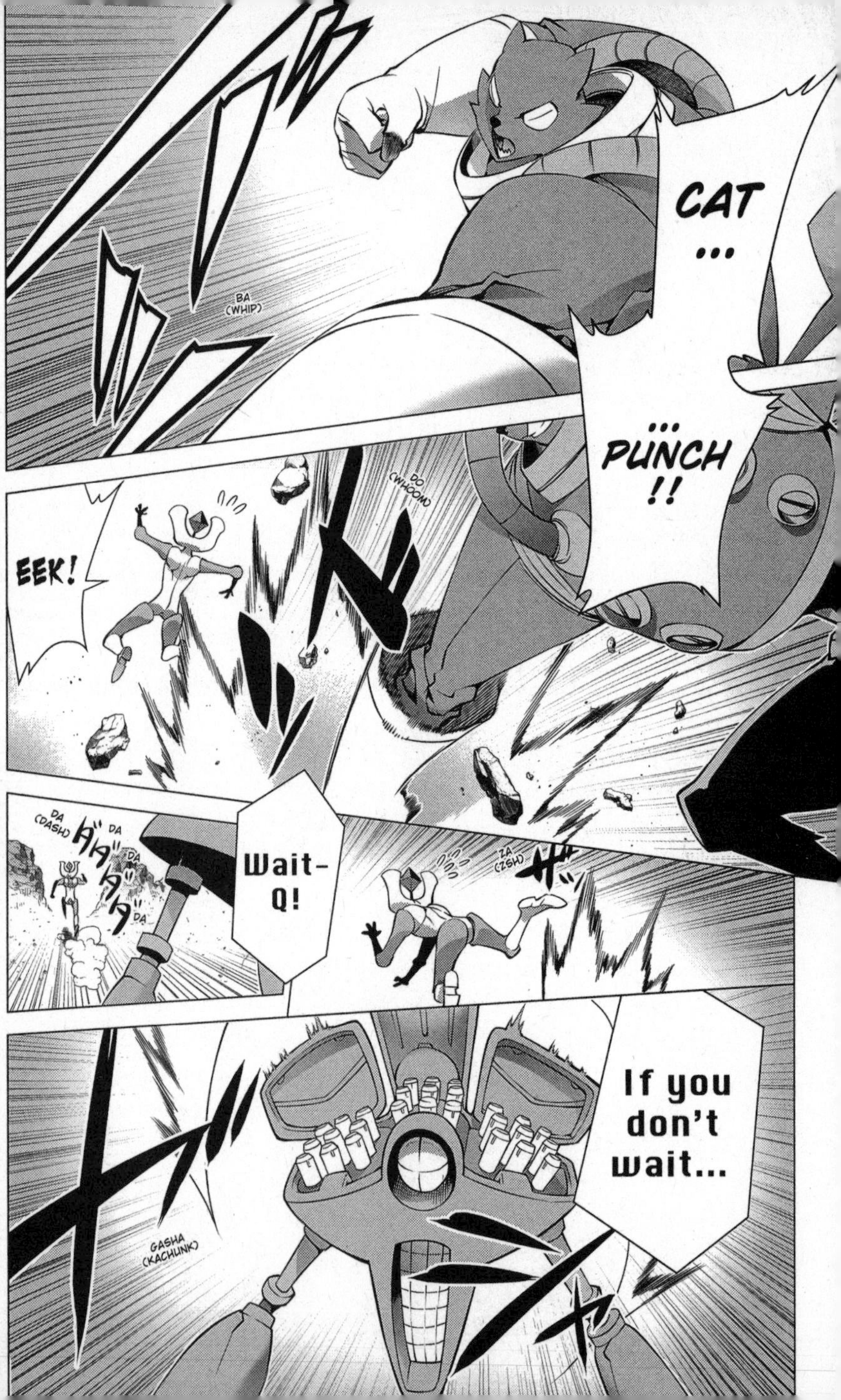
CAT ...
... PUNCH !!
BA (WHIP)
DO (WHOOM)
EEK!
ZA (ZSH)
Wait-Q!
DA (DASH) DA DA DA
If you don't wait...
GASHA (KACHUNK)

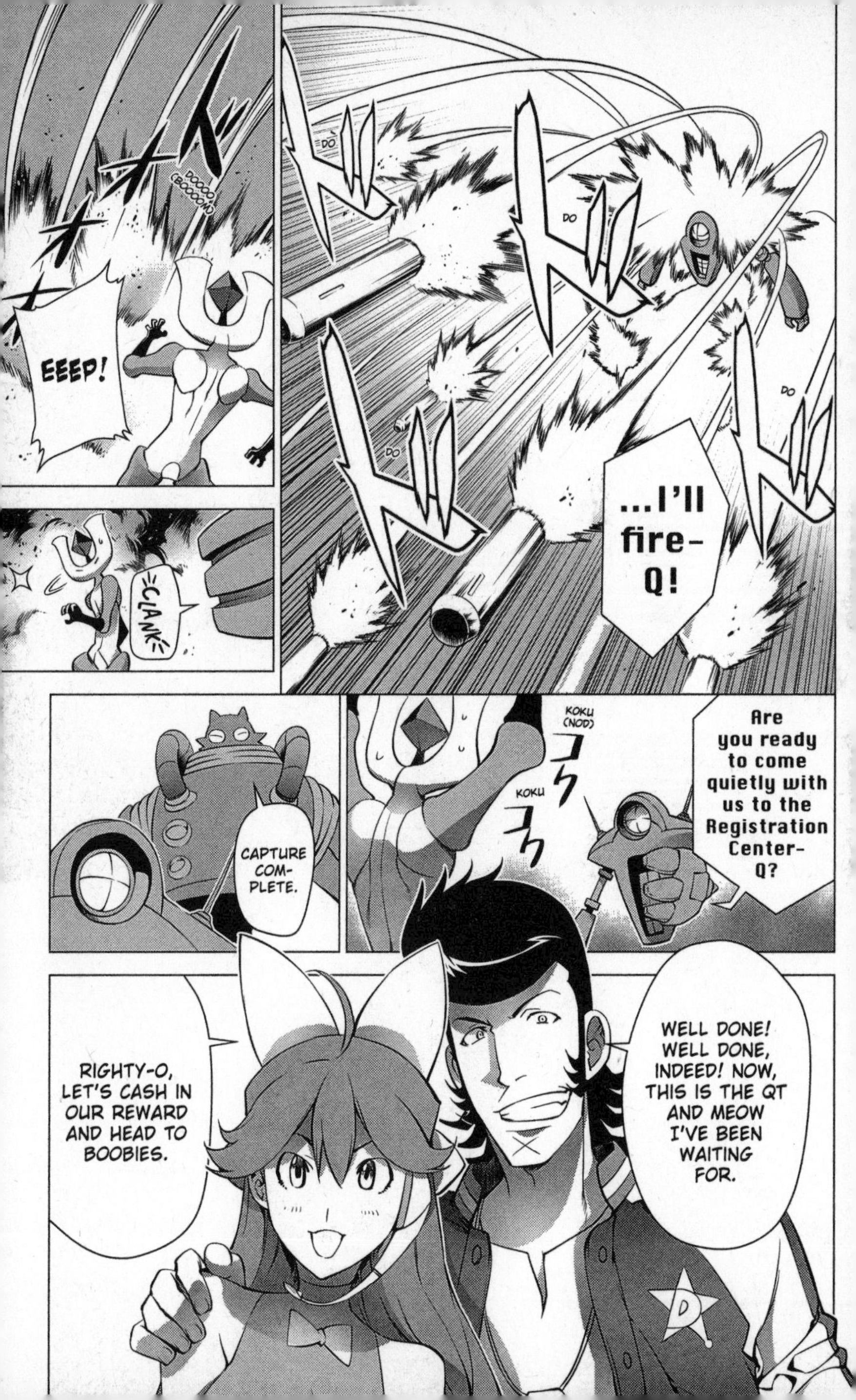
DO
DO
DO
DO
...I'll fire-Q!
DOOOO (BOOOOM)
EEEP!
CLANK
KOKU (NOD)
KOKU
Are you ready to come quietly with us to the Registration Center-Q?
CAPTURE COMPLETE.
WELL DONE! WELL DONE, INDEED! NOW, THIS IS THE QT AND MEOW I'VE BEEN WAITING FOR.
RIGHTY-O, LET'S CASH IN OUR REWARD AND HEAD TO BOOBIES.

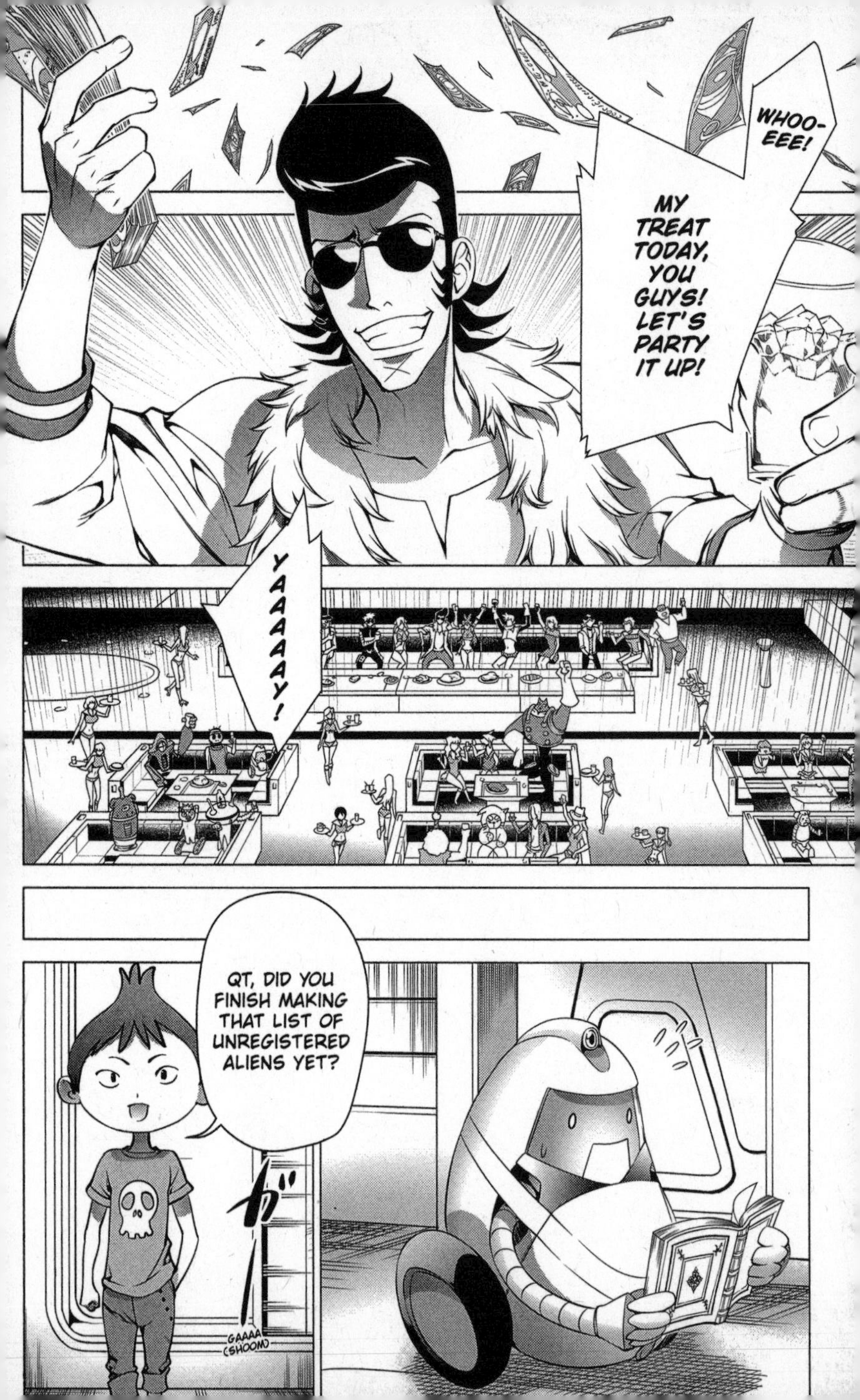
WHOO-EEE!
MY TREAT TODAY, YOU GUYS! LET'S PARTY IT UP!
YAAAAAY!
QT, DID YOU FINISH MAKING THAT LIST OF UNREGISTERED ALIENS YET?
GAAAA (SHOOM)

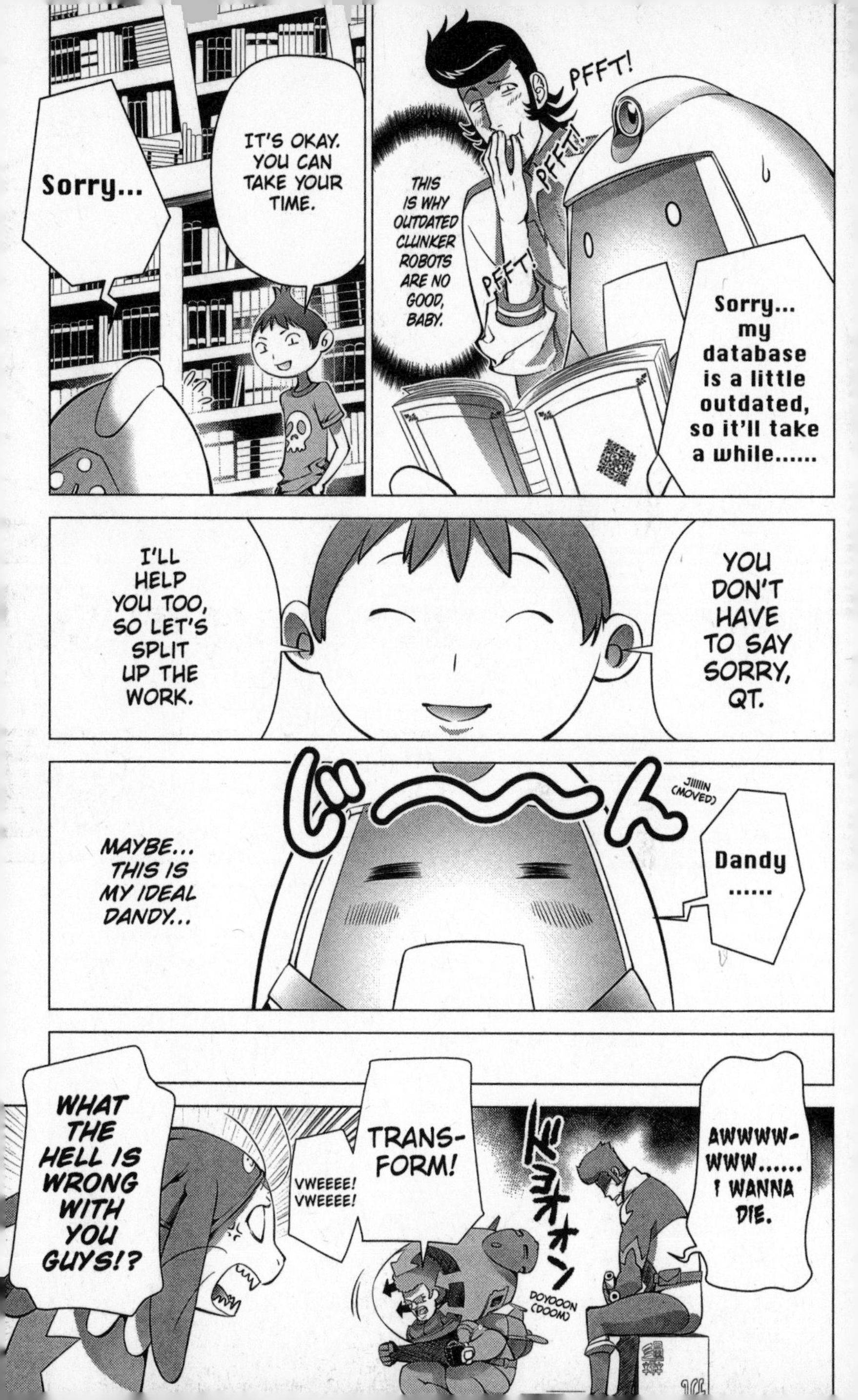
PFFT!
Sorry... my database is a little outdated, so it'll take a while......
PFFT!
PFFT!
THIS IS WHY OUTDATED CLUNKER ROBOTS ARE NO GOOD, BABY.
IT'S OKAY. YOU CAN TAKE YOUR TIME.
Sorry...
YOU DON'T HAVE TO SAY SORRY, QT.
I'LL HELP YOU TOO, SO LET'S SPLIT UP THE WORK.
JIIIIN (MOVED)
じーん
Dandy ......
MAYBE... THIS IS MY IDEAL DANDY...
AWWWWWWW...... I WANNA DIE.
ドヨオオン
DOYOOON (DOOM)
TRANS-FORM!
VWEEEE! VWEEEE!
WHAT THE HELL IS WRONG WITH YOU GUYS!?

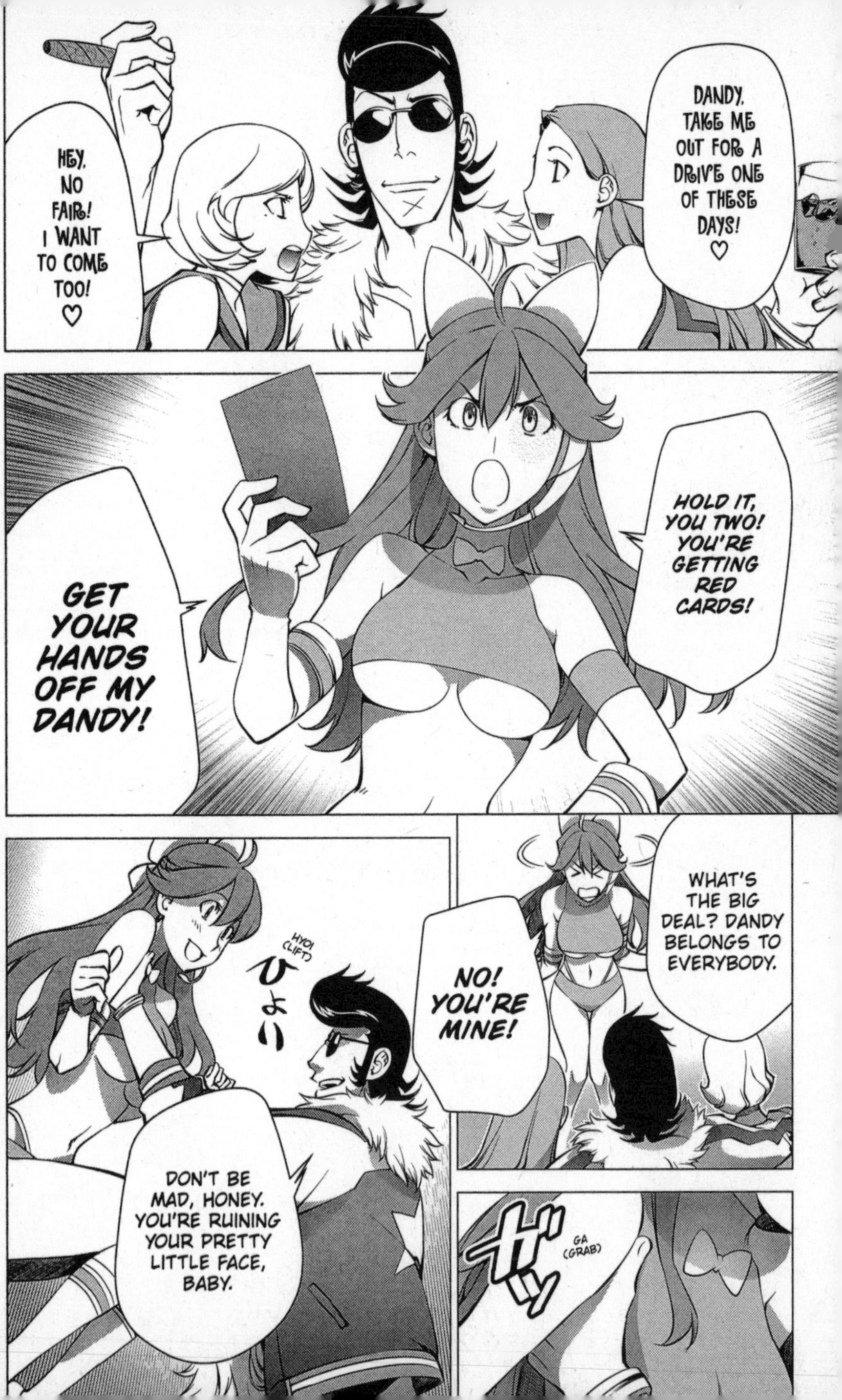
DANDY, TAKE ME OUT FOR A DRIVE ONE OF THESE DAYS! ♡
HEY, NO FAIR! I WANT TO COME TOO! ♡
HOLD IT, YOU TWO! YOU'RE GETTING RED CARDS!
GET YOUR HANDS OFF MY DANDY!
WHAT'S THE BIG DEAL? DANDY BELONGS TO EVERYBODY.
ガッ
GA (GRAB)
NO! YOU'RE MINE!
ひょい
HYOI (LIFT)
DON'T BE MAD, HONEY. YOU'RE RUINING YOUR PRETTY LITTLE FACE, BABY.

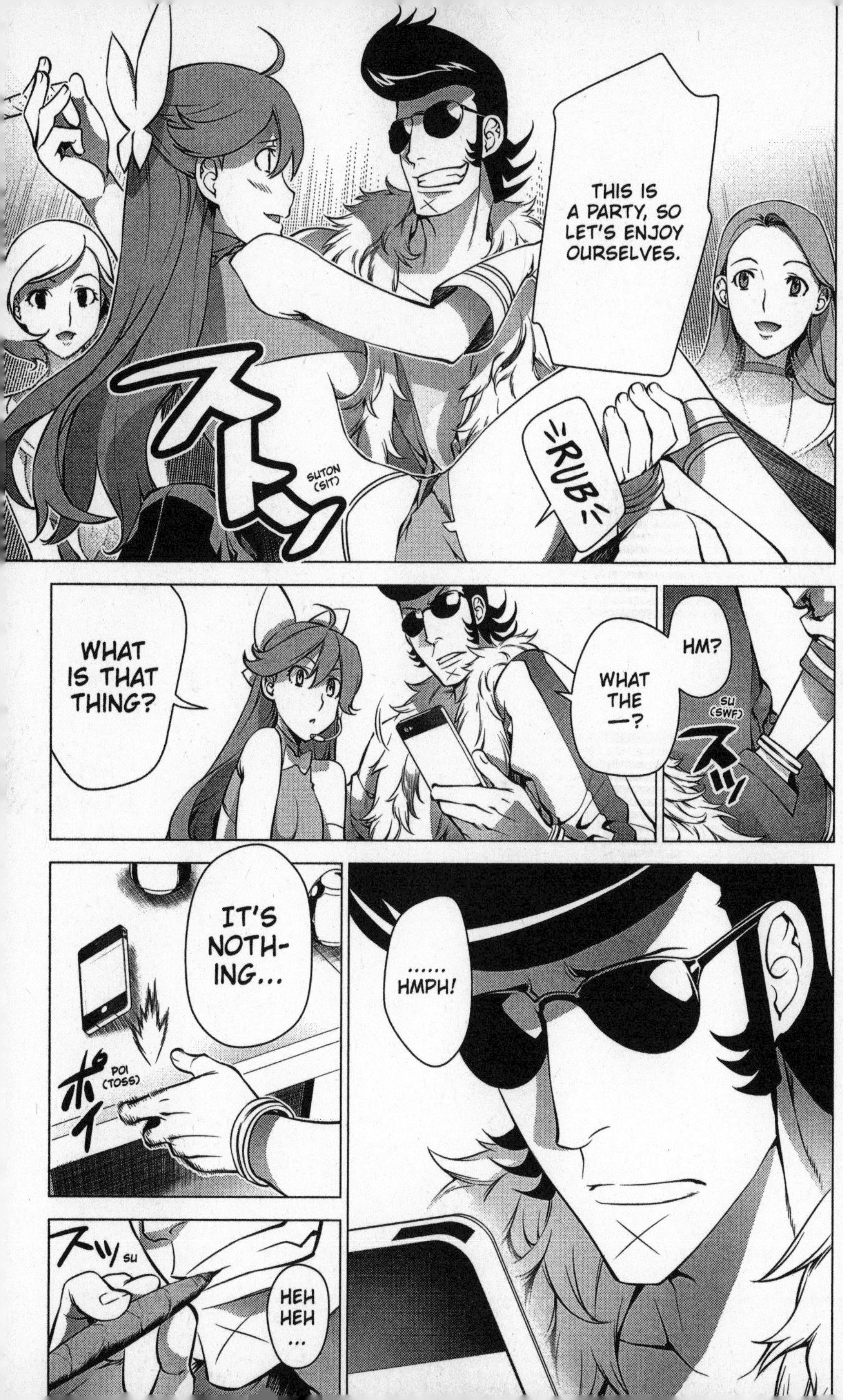
THIS IS A PARTY, SO LET'S ENJOY OURSELVES.
RUB
SUTON (SIT)
HM?
WHAT THE—?
SU (SWF)
WHAT IS THAT THING?
...... HMPH!
IT'S NOTH-ING...
POI (TOSS)
SU
HEH HEH ...

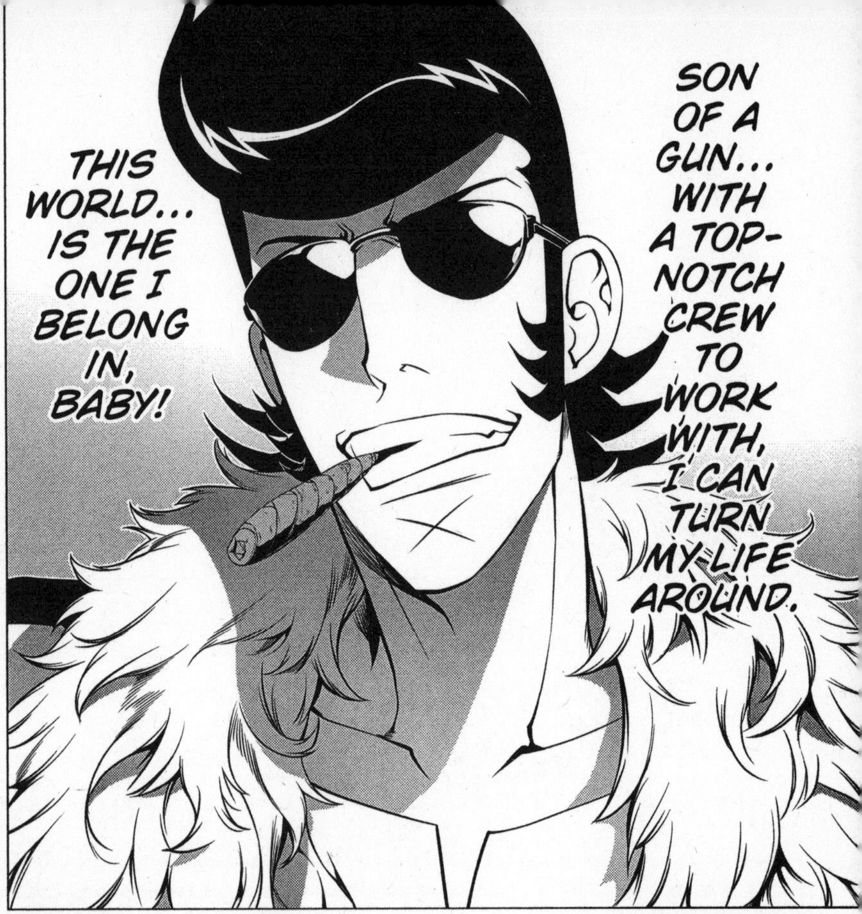
SON OF A GUN... WITH A TOP-NOTCH CREW TO WORK WITH, I CAN TURN MY LIFE AROUND.
THIS WORLD... IS THE ONE I BELONG IN, BABY!

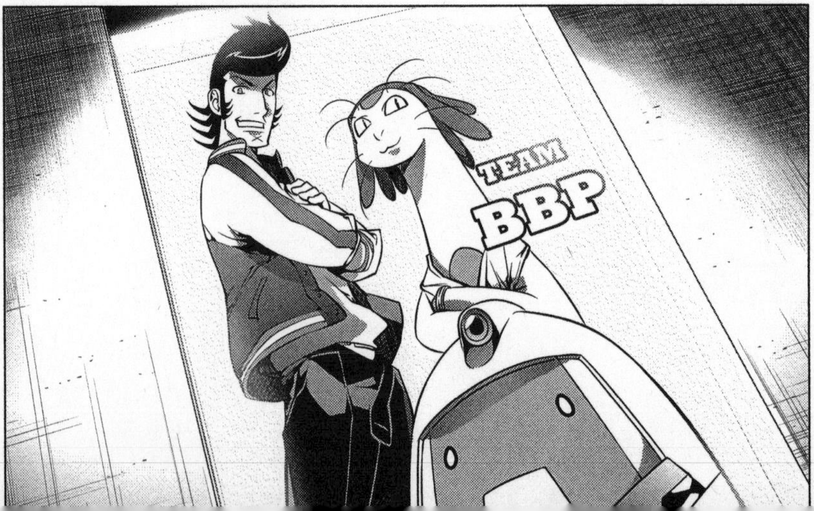
TEAM BBP

SPACE★DANDY

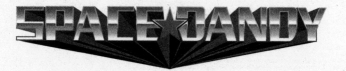

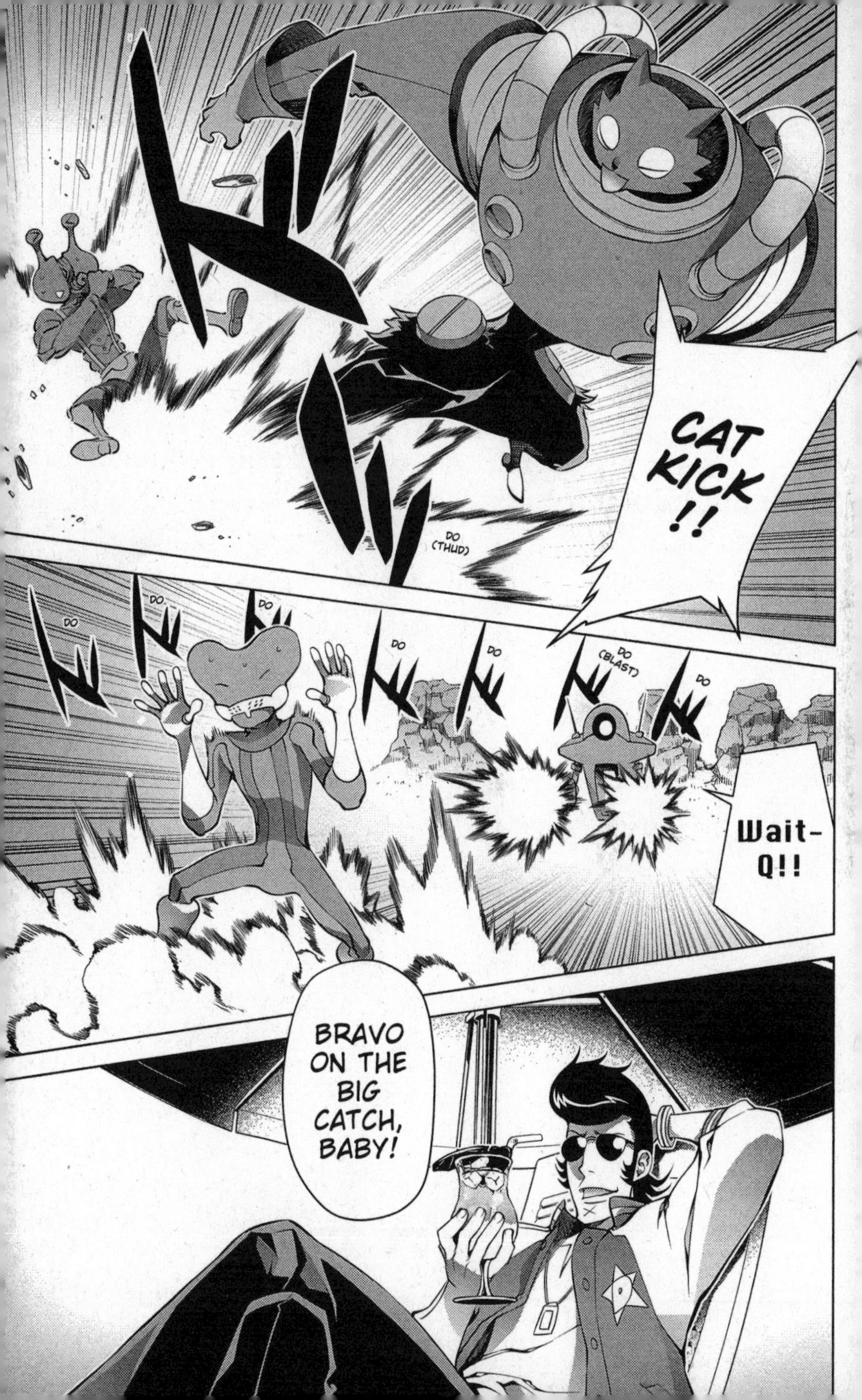
CAT KICK!!
DO (THUD)
Wait-Q!!
DO
DO (BLAST)
DO
DO
DO
DO
DO
BRAVO ON THE BIG CATCH, BABY!

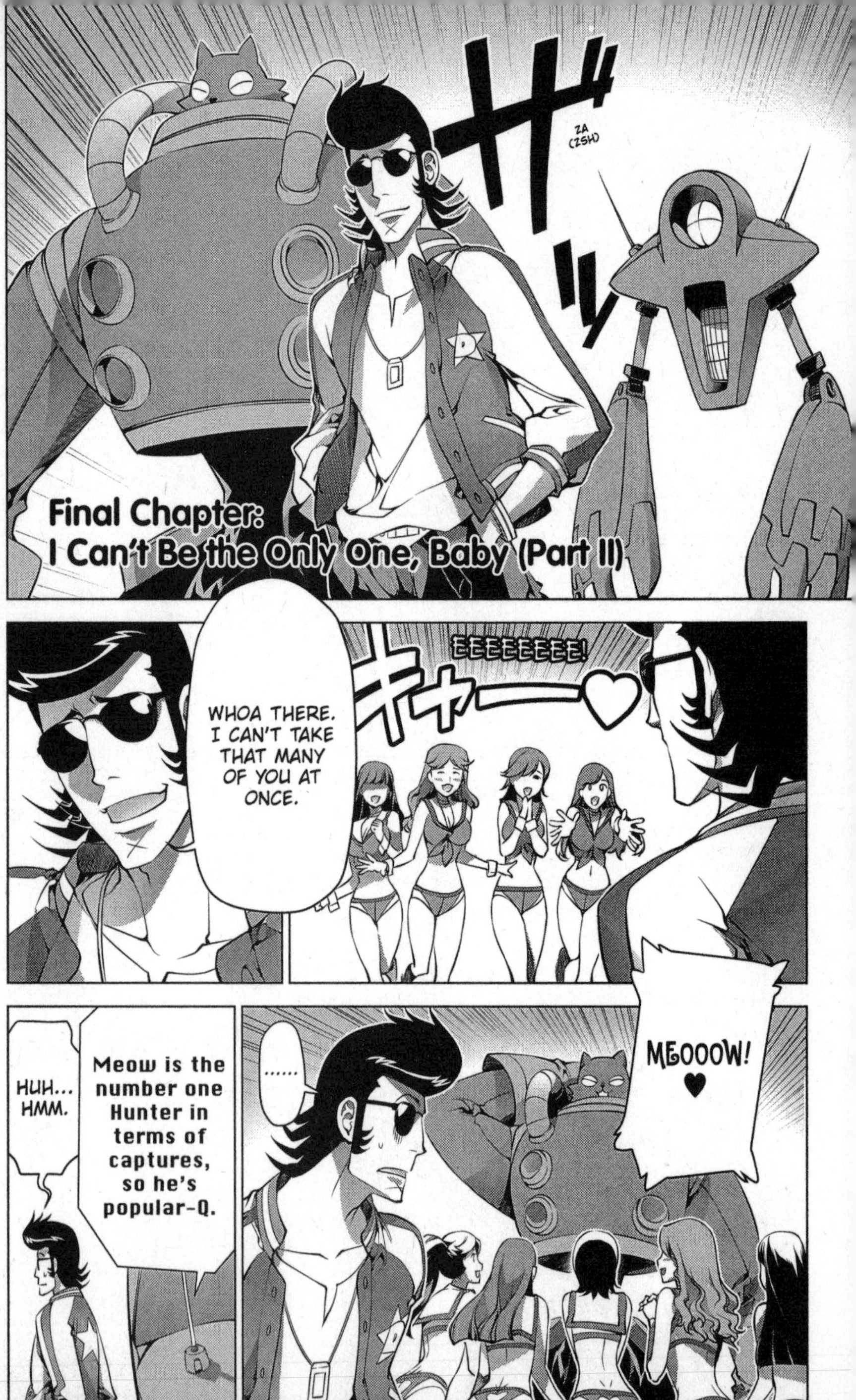
ZA (ZSH)
Final Chapter: I Can't Be the Only One, Baby (Part II)
EEEEEEEEE!
WHOA THERE. I CAN'T TAKE THAT MANY OF YOU AT ONCE.
MEOOOW! ♥
......
Meow is the number one Hunter in terms of captures, so he's popular-Q.
HUH... HMM.

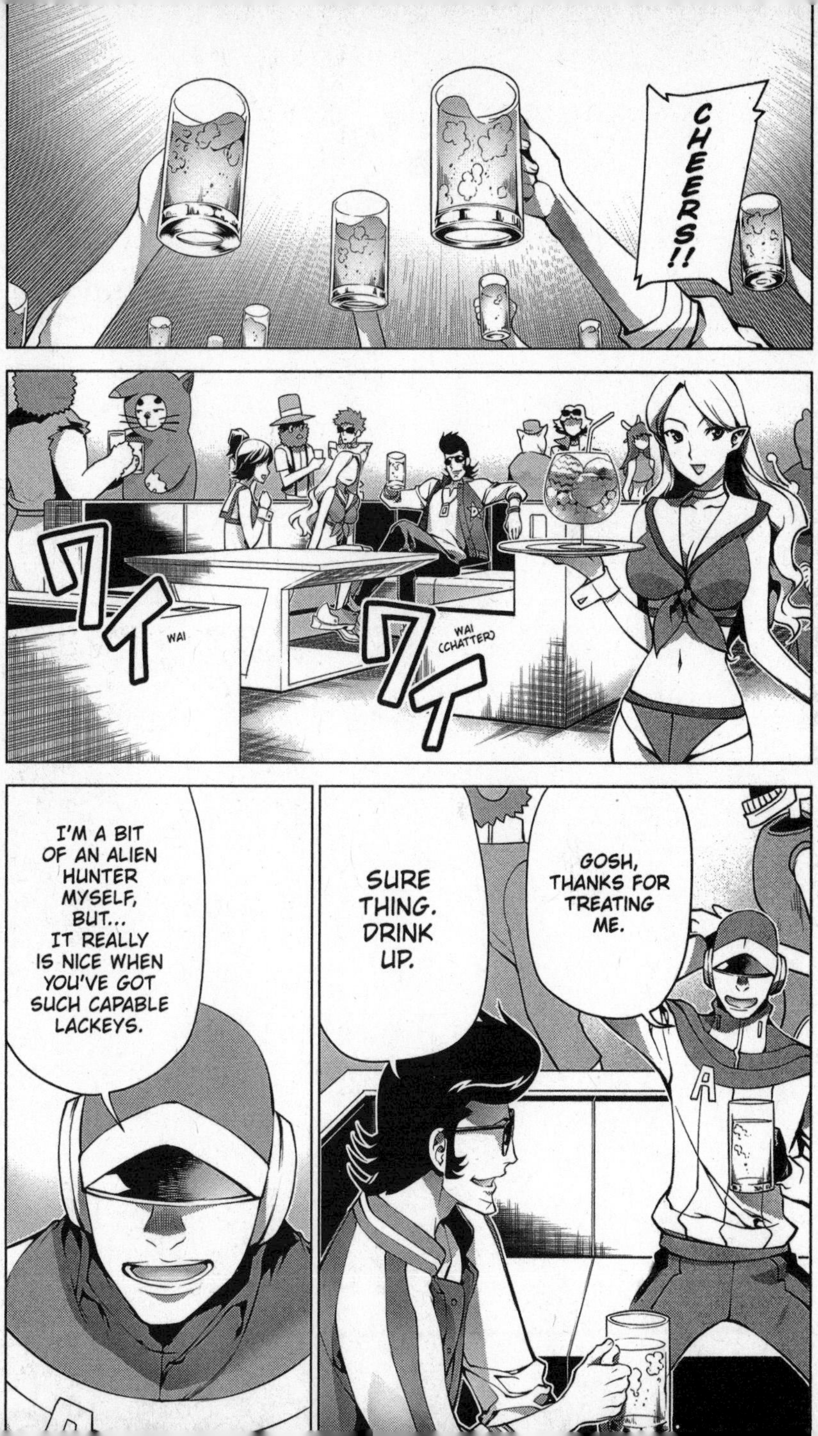
CHEERS!!
ワイ
WAI (CHATTER)
ワイ
WAI
GOSH, THANKS FOR TREATING ME.
SURE THING. DRINK UP.
I'M A BIT OF AN ALIEN HUNTER MYSELF, BUT... IT REALLY IS NICE WHEN YOU'VE GOT SUCH CAPABLE LACKEYS.

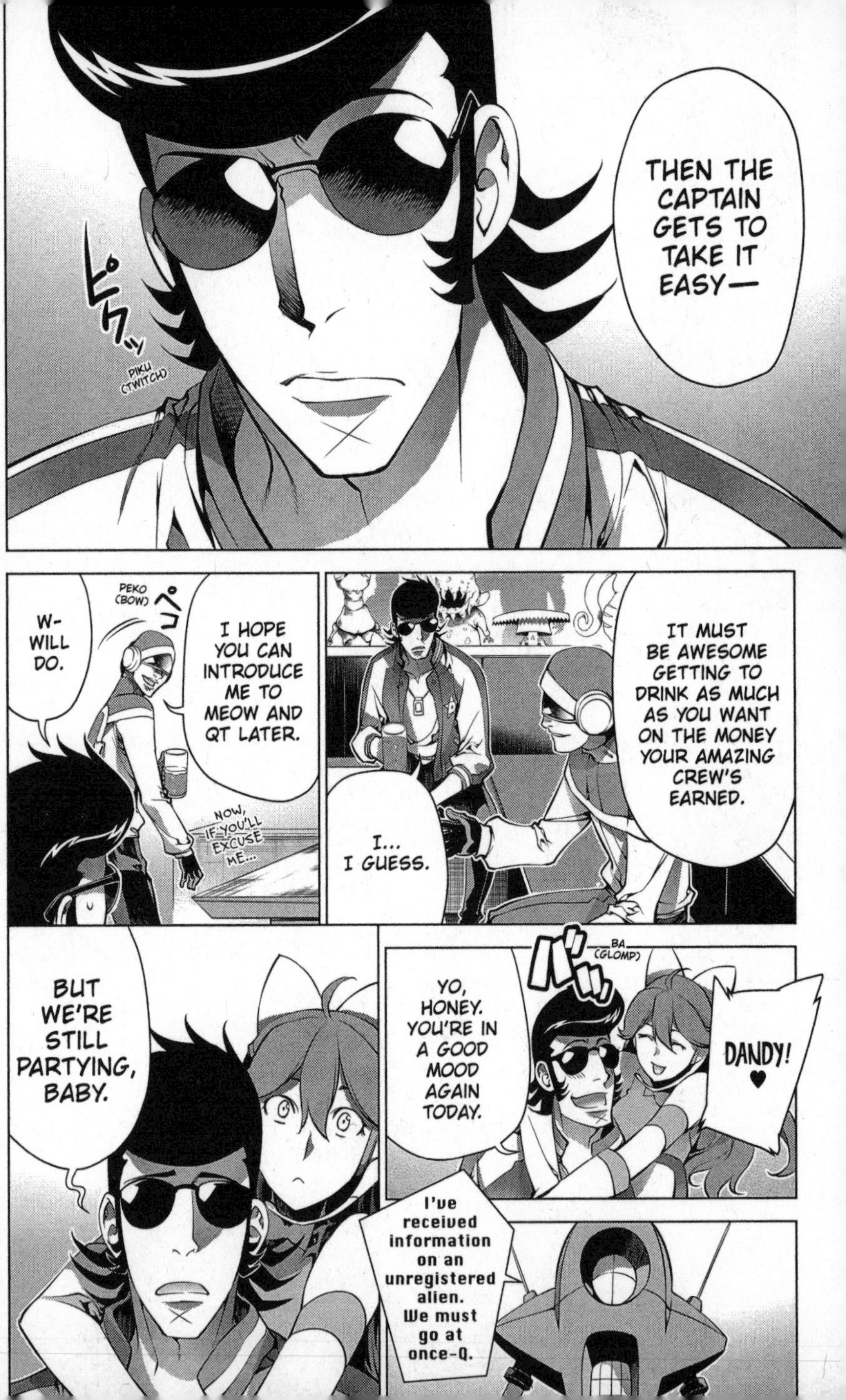
THEN THE CAPTAIN GETS TO TAKE IT EASY—
ピクッ
PIKU (TWITCH)
IT MUST BE AWESOME GETTING TO DRINK AS MUCH AS YOU WANT ON THE MONEY YOUR AMAZING CREW'S EARNED.
I... I GUESS.
ペコ
PEKO (BOW)
I HOPE YOU CAN INTRODUCE ME TO MEOW AND QT LATER.
W- WILL DO.
NOW, IF YOU'LL EXCUSE ME...
DANDY! ♥
バッ
BA (GLOMP)
YO, HONEY. YOU'RE IN A GOOD MOOD AGAIN TODAY.
I've received information on an unregistered alien. We must go at once-Q.
BUT WE'RE STILL PARTYING, BABY.

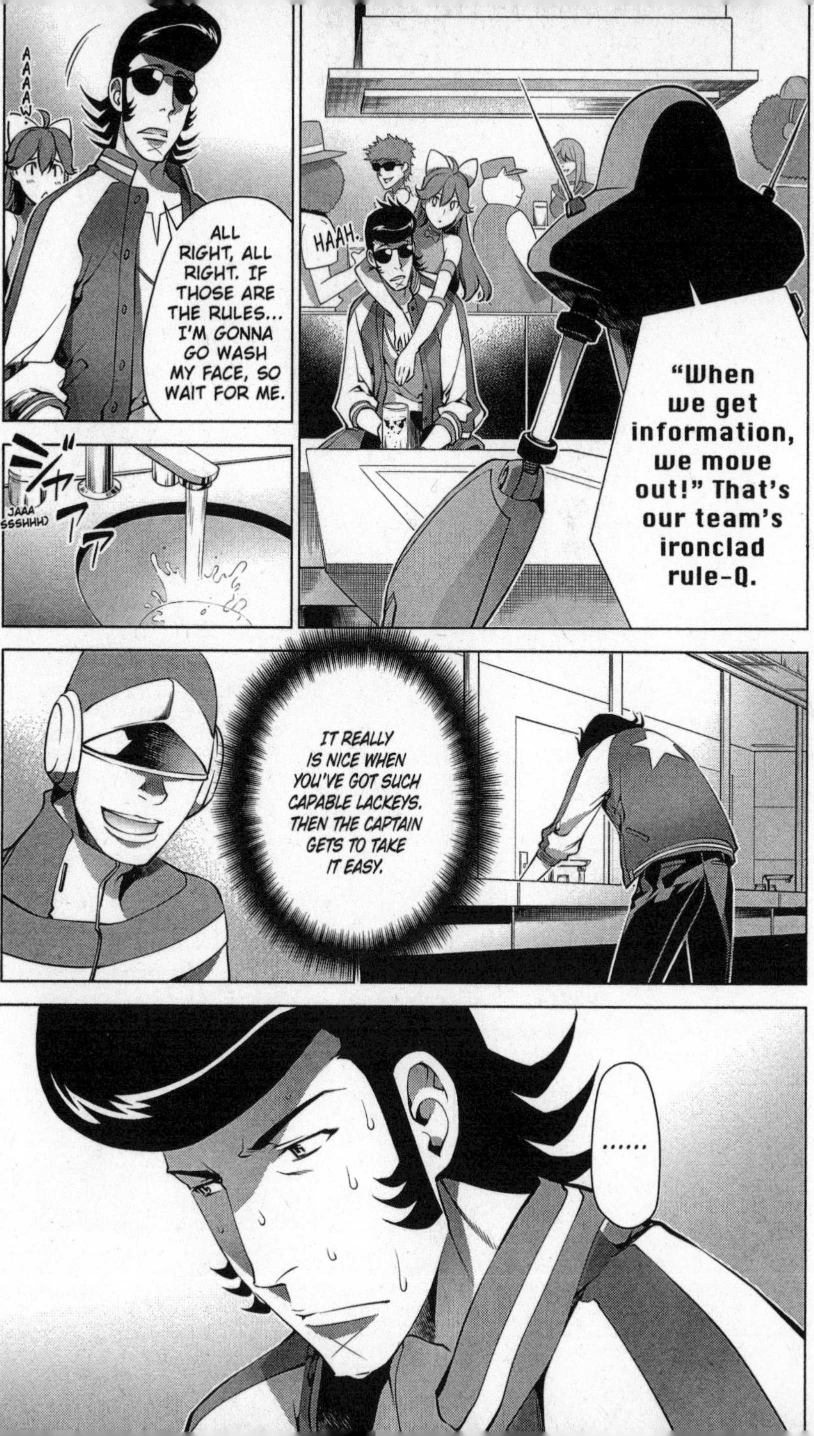
HAAAH.
"When we get information, we move out!" That's our team's ironclad rule-Q.
AAAAW...
ALL RIGHT, ALL RIGHT. IF THOSE ARE THE RULES... I'M GONNA GO WASH MY FACE, SO WAIT FOR ME.
ジャァァ
JAAA (SSSHHH)
IT REALLY IS NICE WHEN YOU'VE GOT SUCH CAPABLE LACKEYS. THEN THE CAPTAIN GETS TO TAKE IT EASY.
......

SUIII
(VWEEEE)

Now then... where should I start cleaning?

CENTRAL ROOM

PIKA

PIKA
(SHINE)

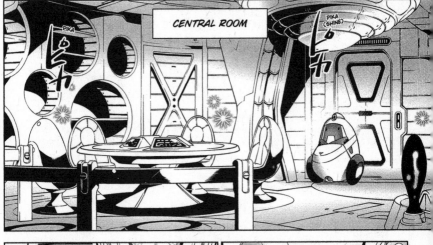

COCKPIT

......

MEOW'S ROOM

PIKA

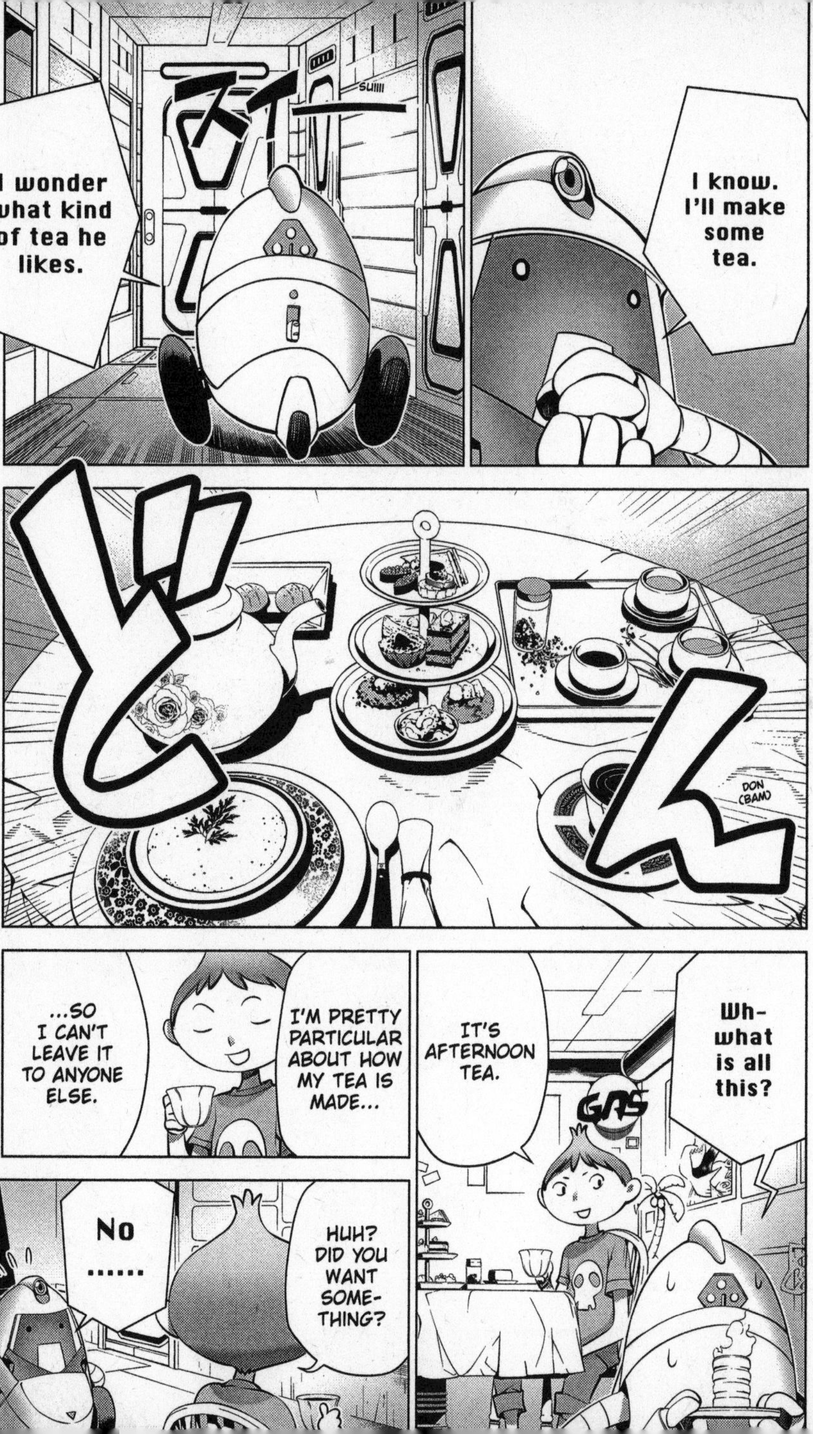
I know. I'll make some tea.
スイー
SUIII
I wonder what kind of tea he likes.
どん
DON (BAM)
Wh- what is all this?
GAS
IT'S AFTERNOON TEA.
I'M PRETTY PARTICULAR ABOUT HOW MY TEA IS MADE...
...SO I CAN'T LEAVE IT TO ANYONE ELSE.
HUH? DID YOU WANT SOME-THING?
No ......

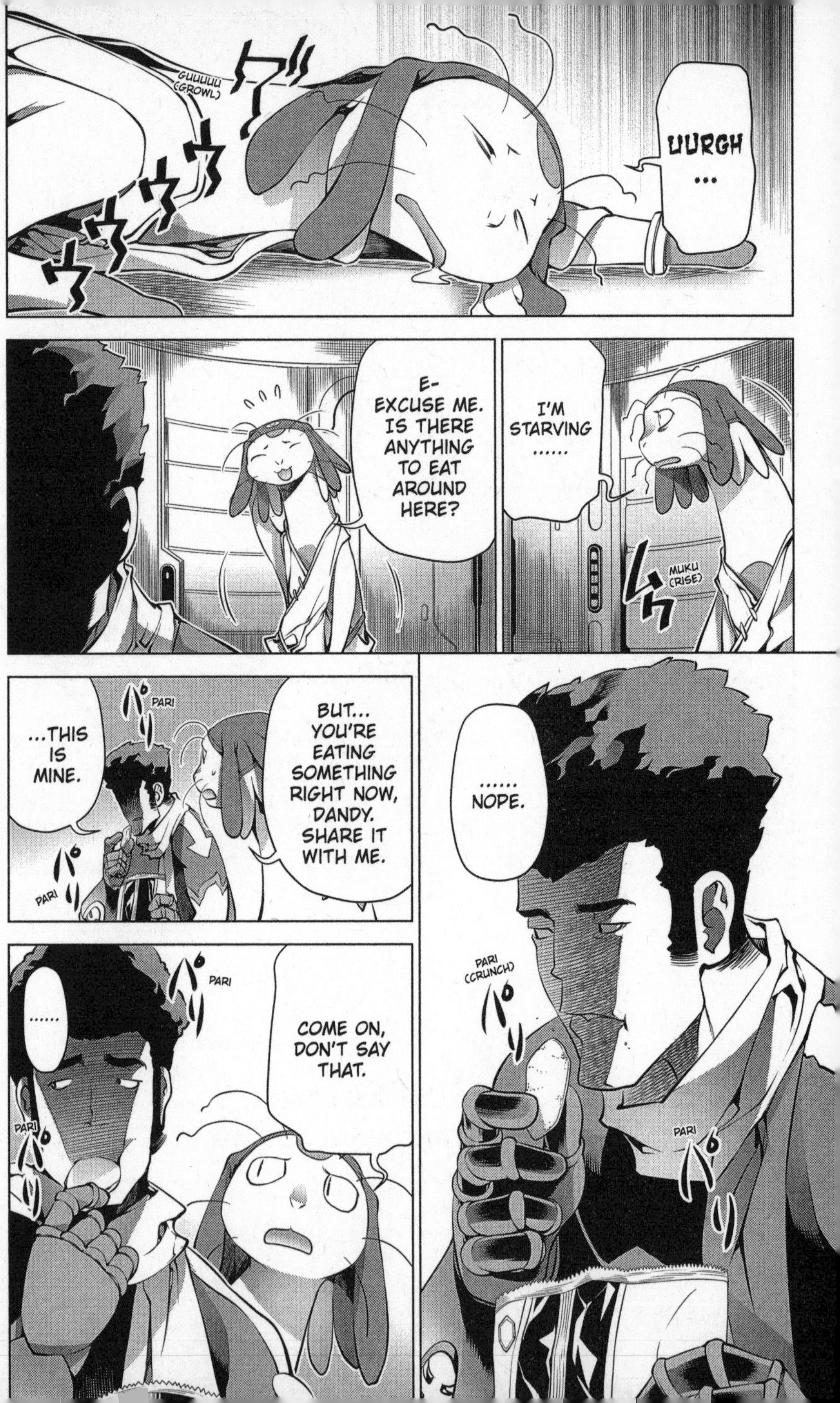
UURGH ...
GUUUUU (GROWL)
I'M STARVING ......
MUKU (RISE)
E- EXCUSE ME. IS THERE ANYTHING TO EAT AROUND HERE?
...... NOPE.
PARI (CRUNCH)
PARI
BUT... YOU'RE EATING SOMETHING RIGHT NOW, DANDY. SHARE IT WITH ME.
PARI
...THIS IS MINE.
PARI
COME ON, DON'T SAY THAT.
PARI
......
PARI

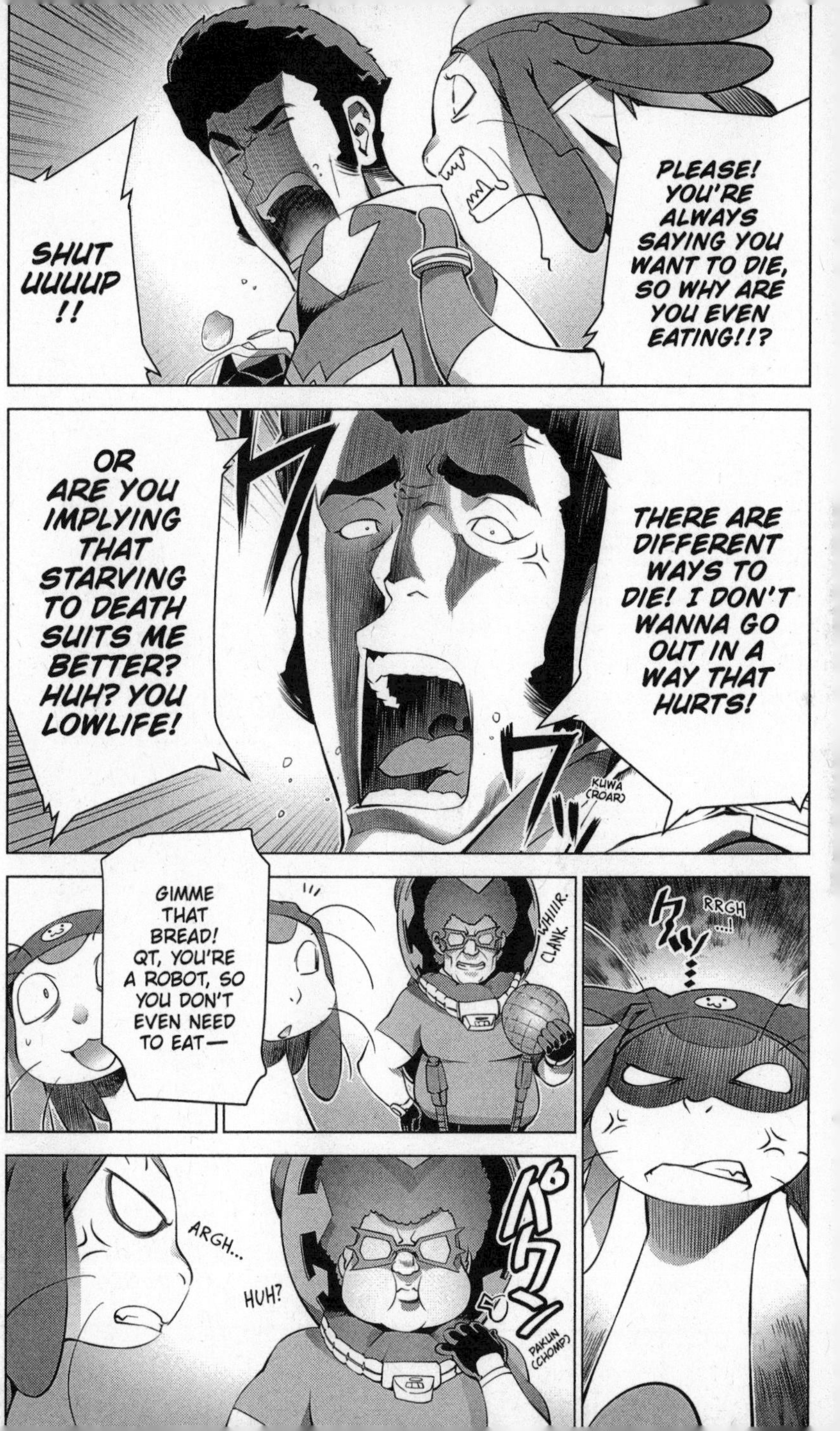
PLEASE! YOU'RE ALWAYS SAYING YOU WANT TO DIE, SO WHY ARE YOU EVEN EATING!!?
SHUT UUUUP!!
THERE ARE DIFFERENT WAYS TO DIE! I DON'T WANNA GO OUT IN A WAY THAT HURTS!
OR ARE YOU IMPLYING THAT STARVING TO DEATH SUITS ME BETTER? HUH? YOU LOWLIFE!
KUWA (ROAR)
RRGH ...!
WHIIIR.
CLANK.
GIMME THAT BREAD! QT, YOU'RE A ROBOT, SO YOU DON'T EVEN NEED TO EAT—
PAKUN (CHOMP)
ARGH...
HUH?

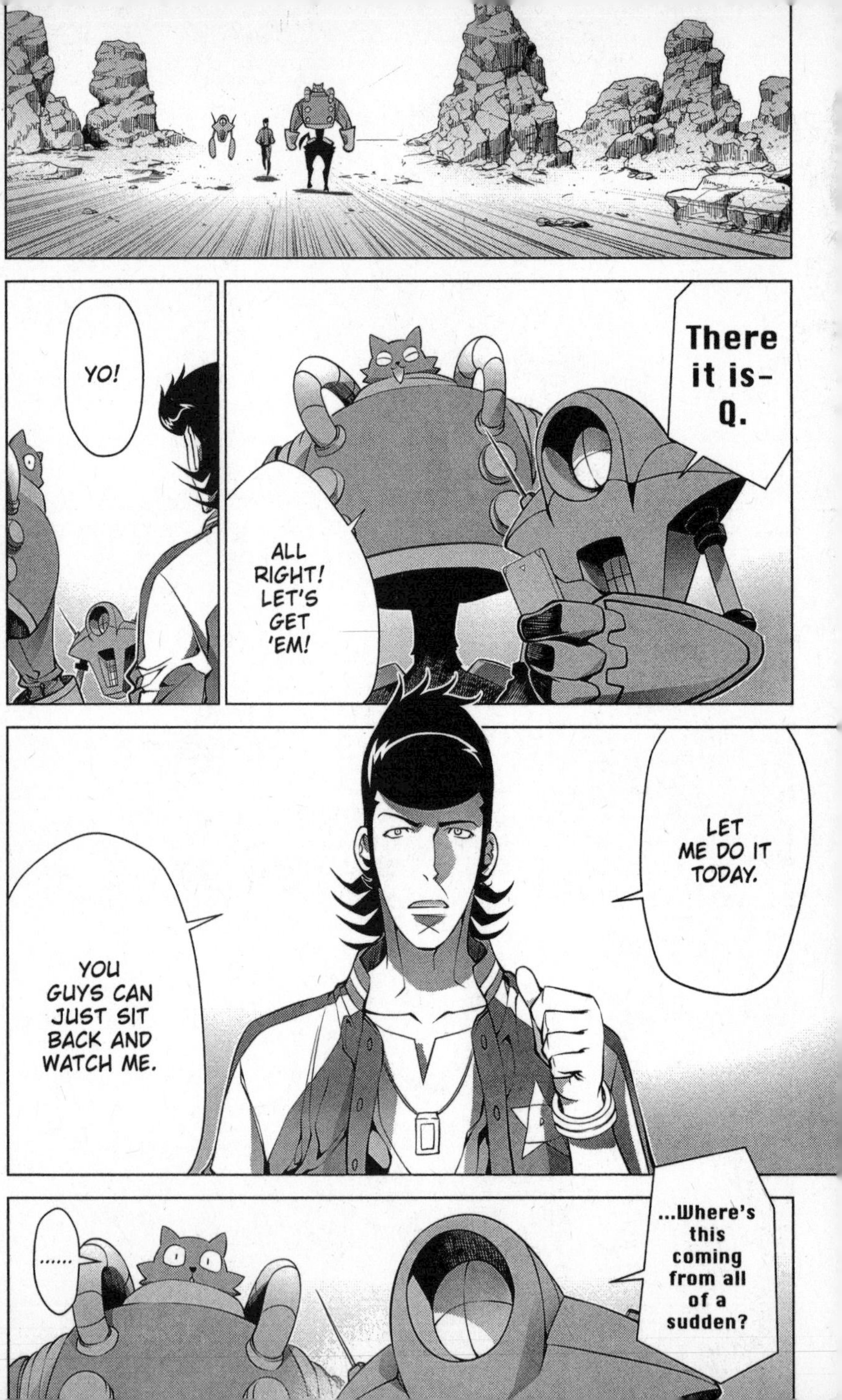
There it is-Q.
ALL RIGHT! LET'S GET 'EM!
YO!
LET ME DO IT TODAY.
YOU GUYS CAN JUST SIT BACK AND WATCH ME.
...Where's this coming from all of a sudden?
......

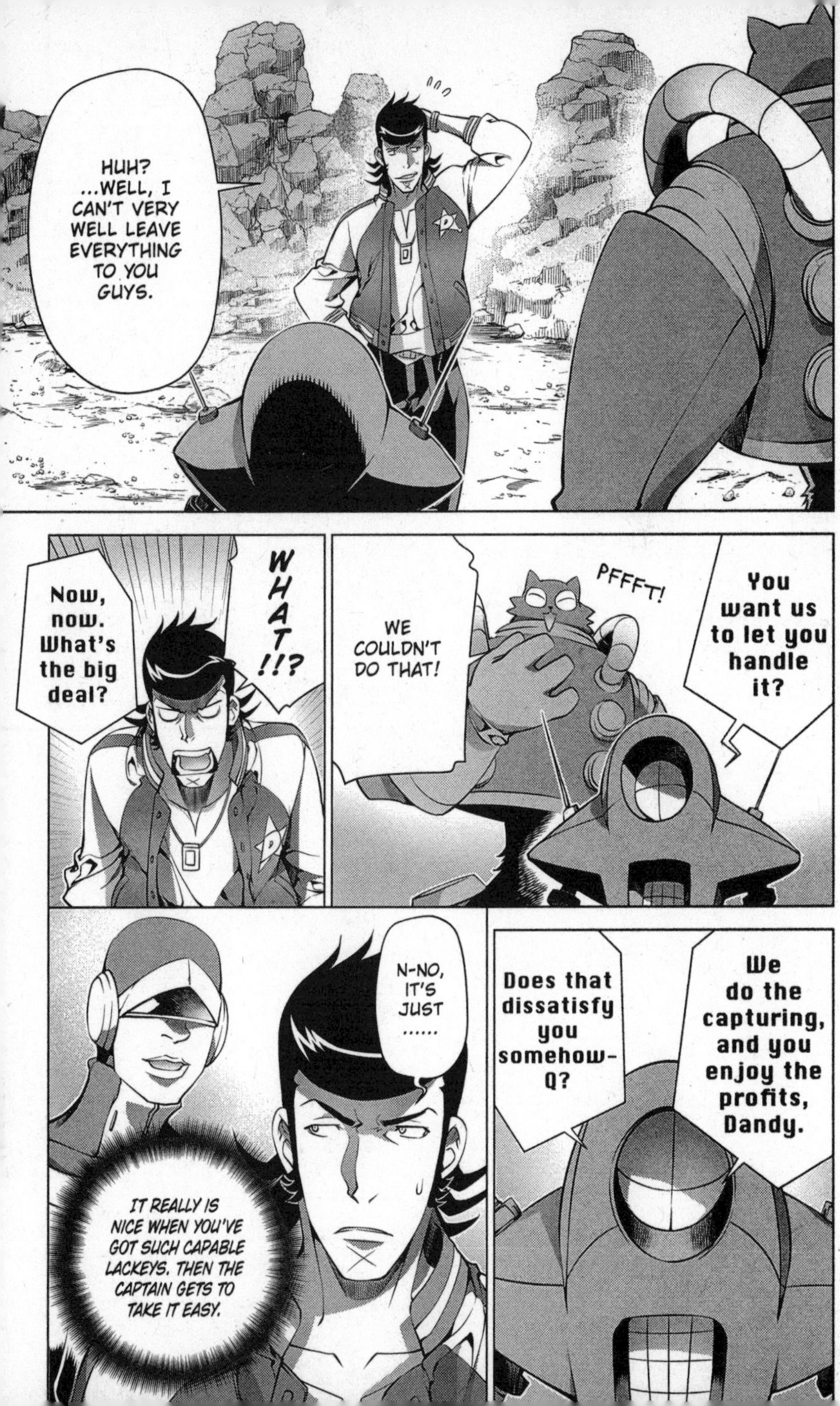
HUH? ...WELL, I CAN'T VERY WELL LEAVE EVERYTHING TO YOU GUYS.
You want us to let you handle it?
PFFFT!
WE COULDN'T DO THAT!
WHAT!!?
Now, now. What's the big deal?
We do the capturing, and you enjoy the profits, Dandy.
Does that dissatisfy you somehow-Q?
N-NO, IT'S JUST ......
IT REALLY IS NICE WHEN YOU'VE GOT SUCH CAPABLE LACKEYS. THEN THE CAPTAIN GETS TO TAKE IT EASY.

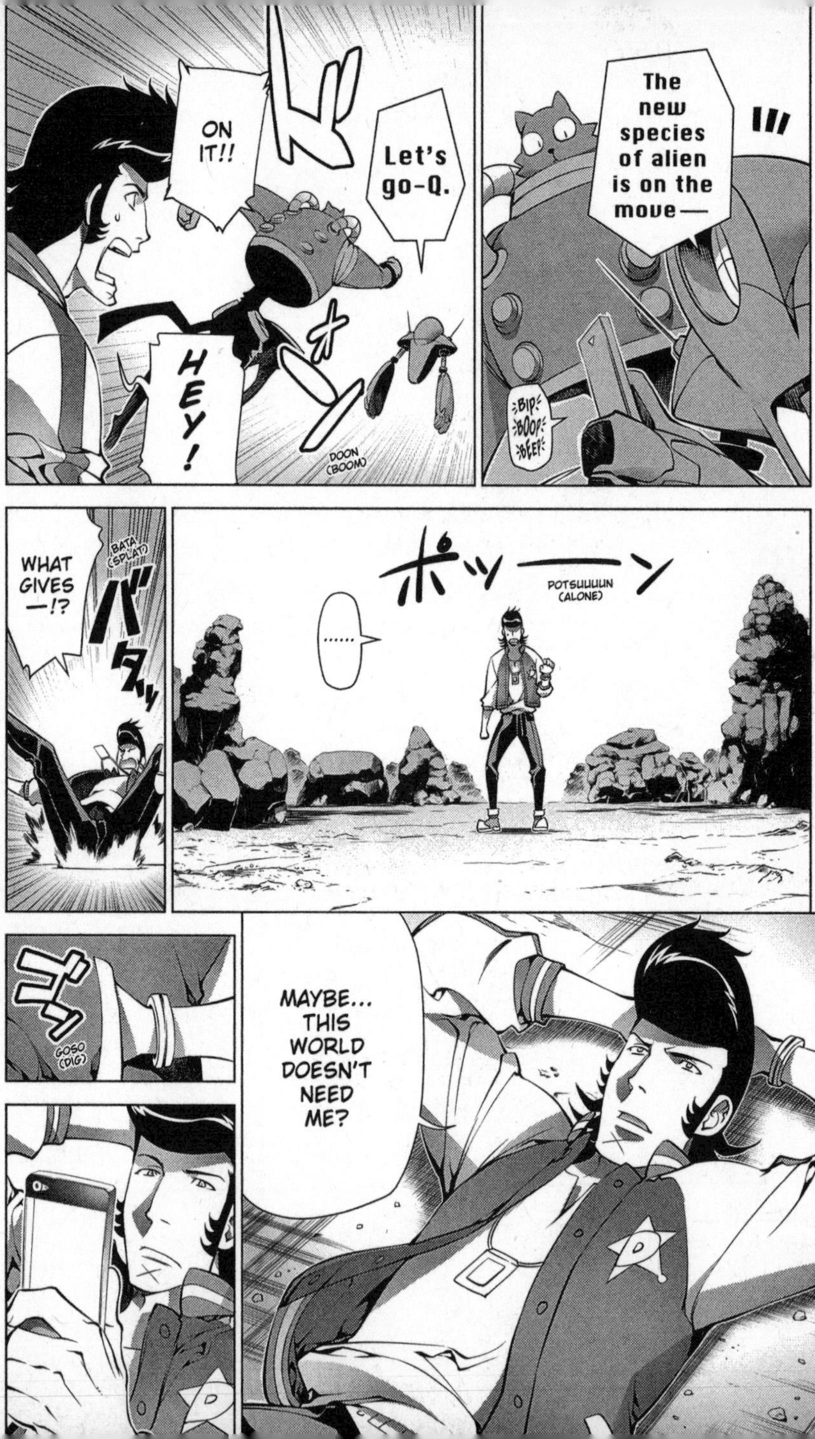
The new species of alien is on the move—
BIP BOOP BEEP
Let's go-Q.
ON IT!!
HEY!
DOON (BOOM)
POTSUUUUN (ALONE)
......
BATA (SPLAT)
WHAT GIVES—!?
MAYBE... THIS WORLD DOESN'T NEED ME?
GOSO (DIG)

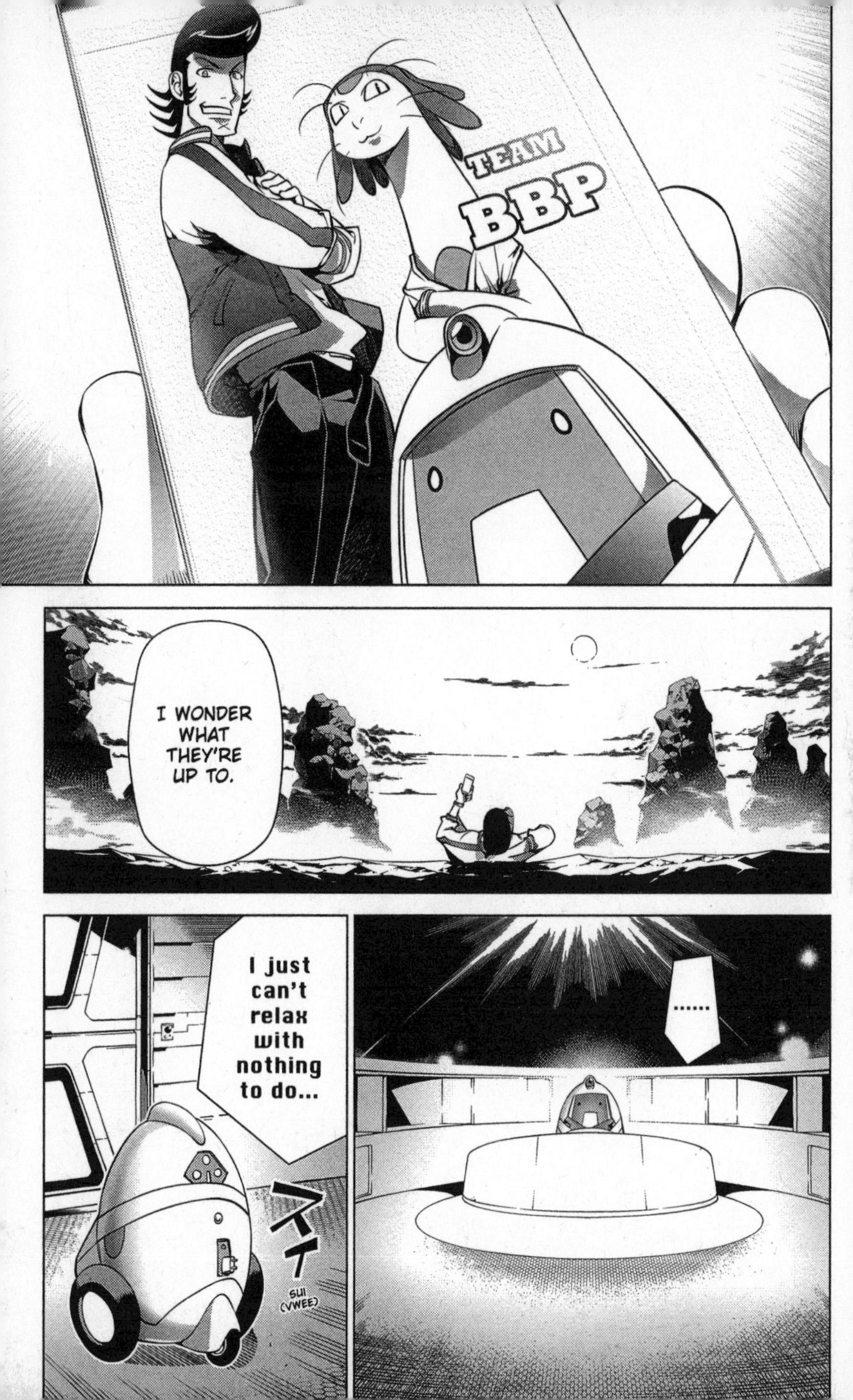
TEAM BBP
I WONDER WHAT THEY'RE UP TO.
......
I just can't relax with nothing to do...
SUI (VWEE)

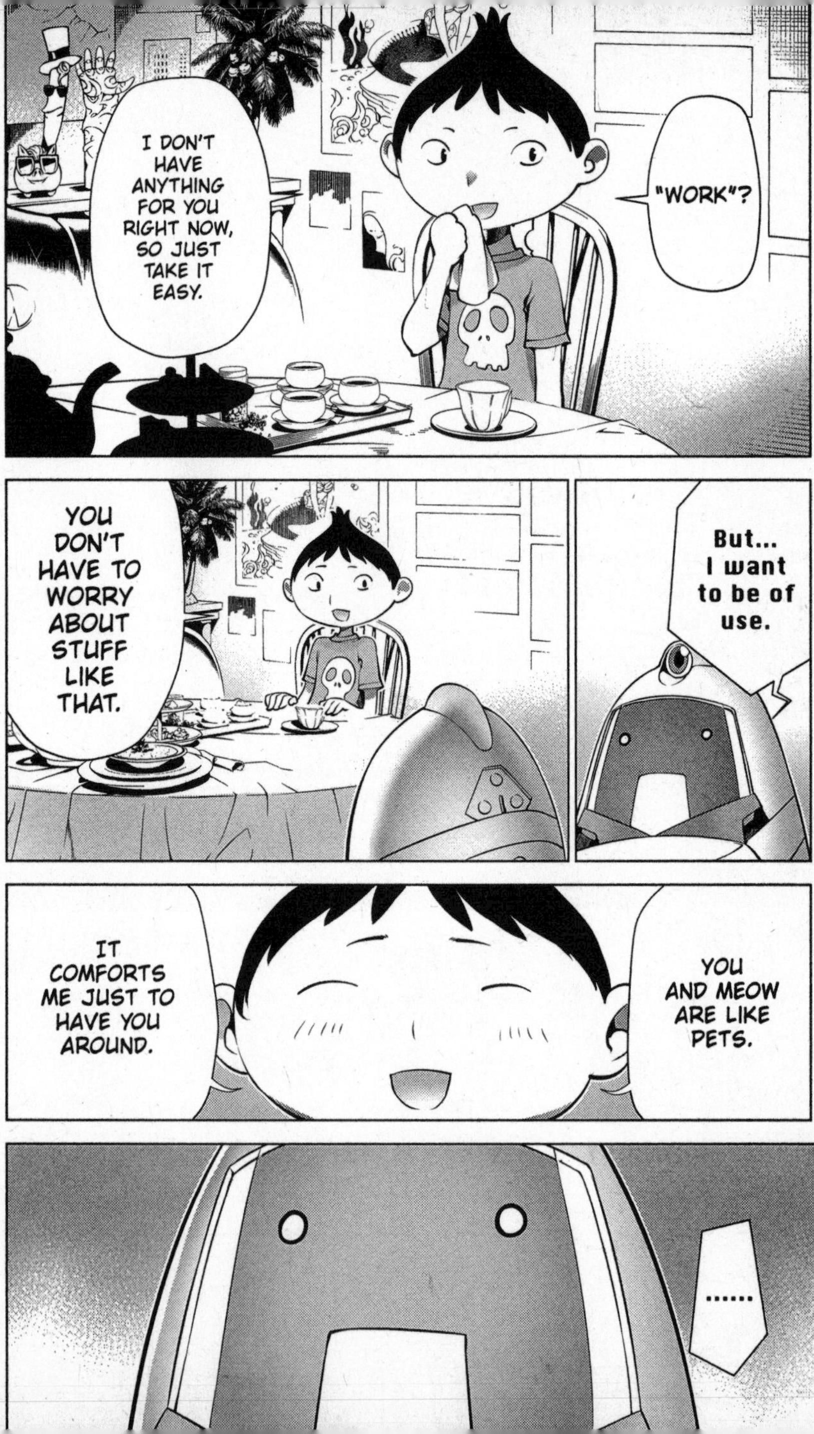
"WORK"?
I DON'T HAVE ANYTHING FOR YOU RIGHT NOW, SO JUST TAKE IT EASY.
But... I want to be of use.
YOU DON'T HAVE TO WORRY ABOUT STUFF LIKE THAT.
YOU AND MEOW ARE LIKE PETS.
IT COMFORTS ME JUST TO HAVE YOU AROUND.
......

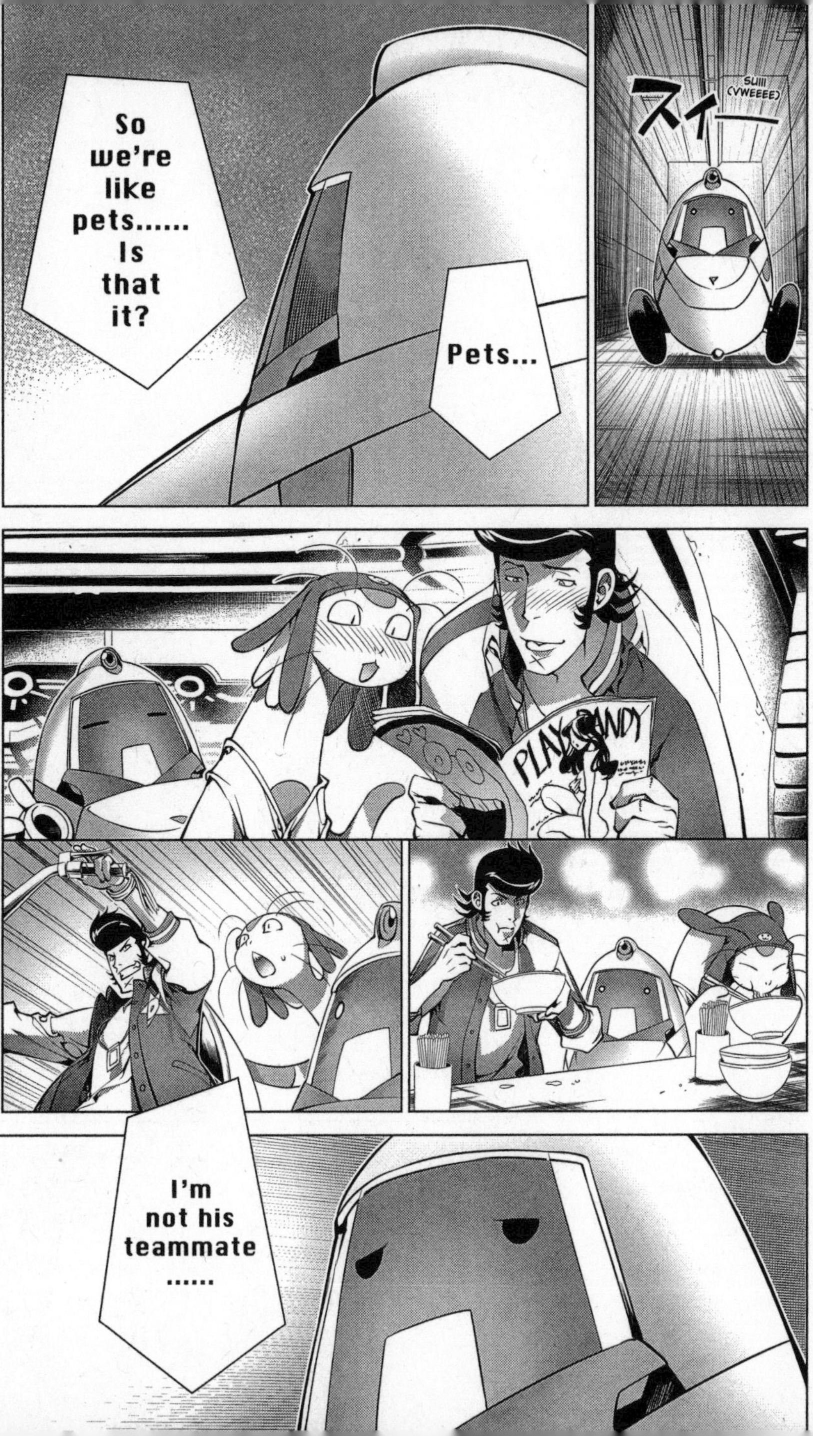

スイー
SUIII (VWEEEE)
Pets...
So we're like pets...... Is that it?
I'm not his teammate ......

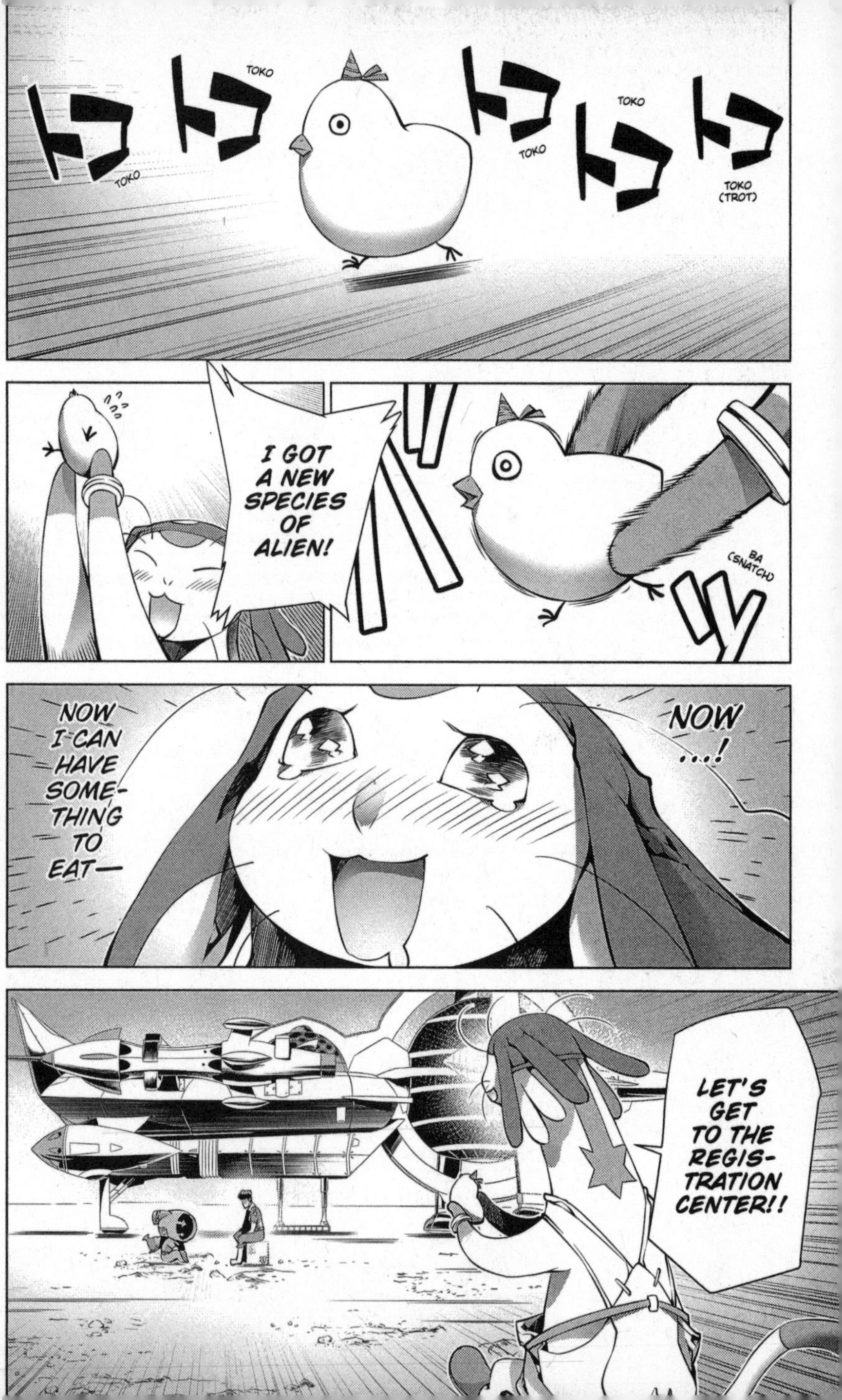

TOKO (TROT)
TOKO
TOKO
TOKO
TOKO
BA (SNATCH)
I GOT A NEW SPECIES OF ALIEN!
NOW ...!
NOW I CAN HAVE SOME-THING TO EAT—
LET'S GET TO THE REGIS-TRATION CENTER!!

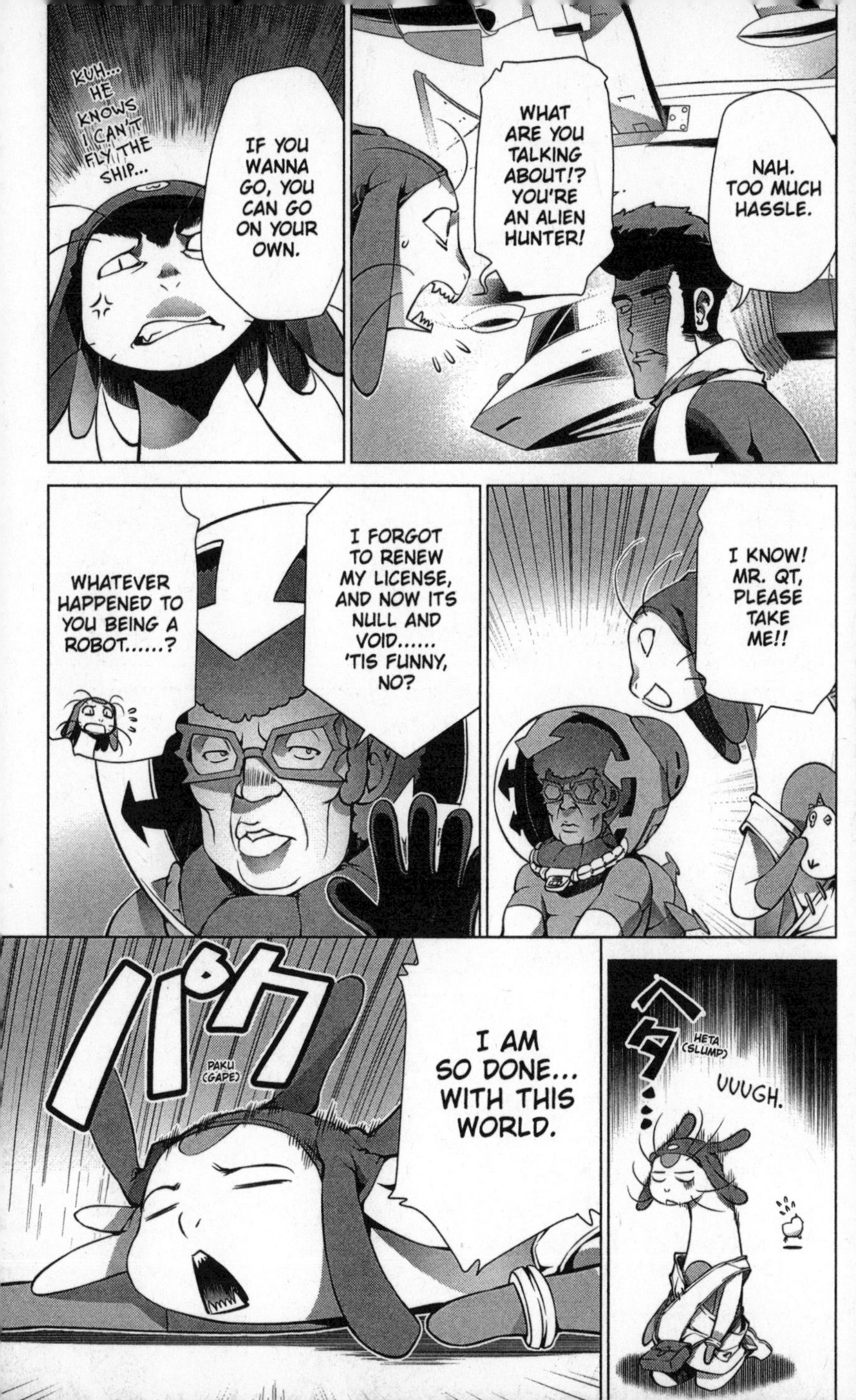
NAH. TOO MUCH HASSLE.
WHAT ARE YOU TALKING ABOUT!? YOU'RE AN ALIEN HUNTER!
IF YOU WANNA GO, YOU CAN GO ON YOUR OWN.
KUH... HE KNOWS I CAN'T FLY THE SHIP...
I KNOW! MR. QT, PLEASE TAKE ME!!
I FORGOT TO RENEW MY LICENSE, AND NOW ITS NULL AND VOID...... 'TIS FUNNY, NO?
WHATEVER HAPPENED TO YOU BEING A ROBOT......?
ヘタ
HETA (SLUMP)
UUUGH.
I AM SO DONE... WITH THIS WORLD.
パク
PAKU (GAPE)

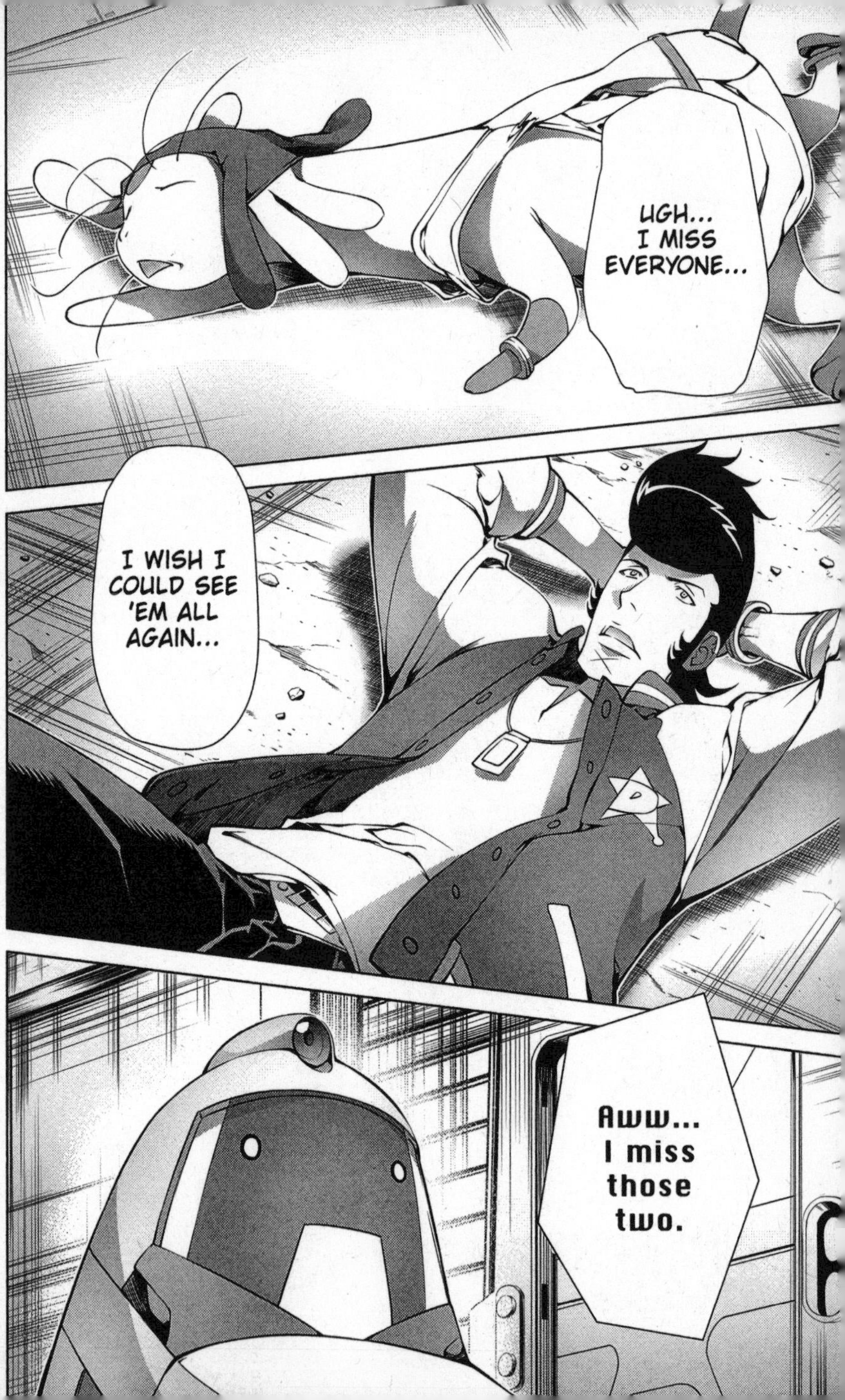
UGH... I MISS EVERYONE...
I WISH I COULD SEE 'EM ALL AGAIN...
Aww... I miss those two.

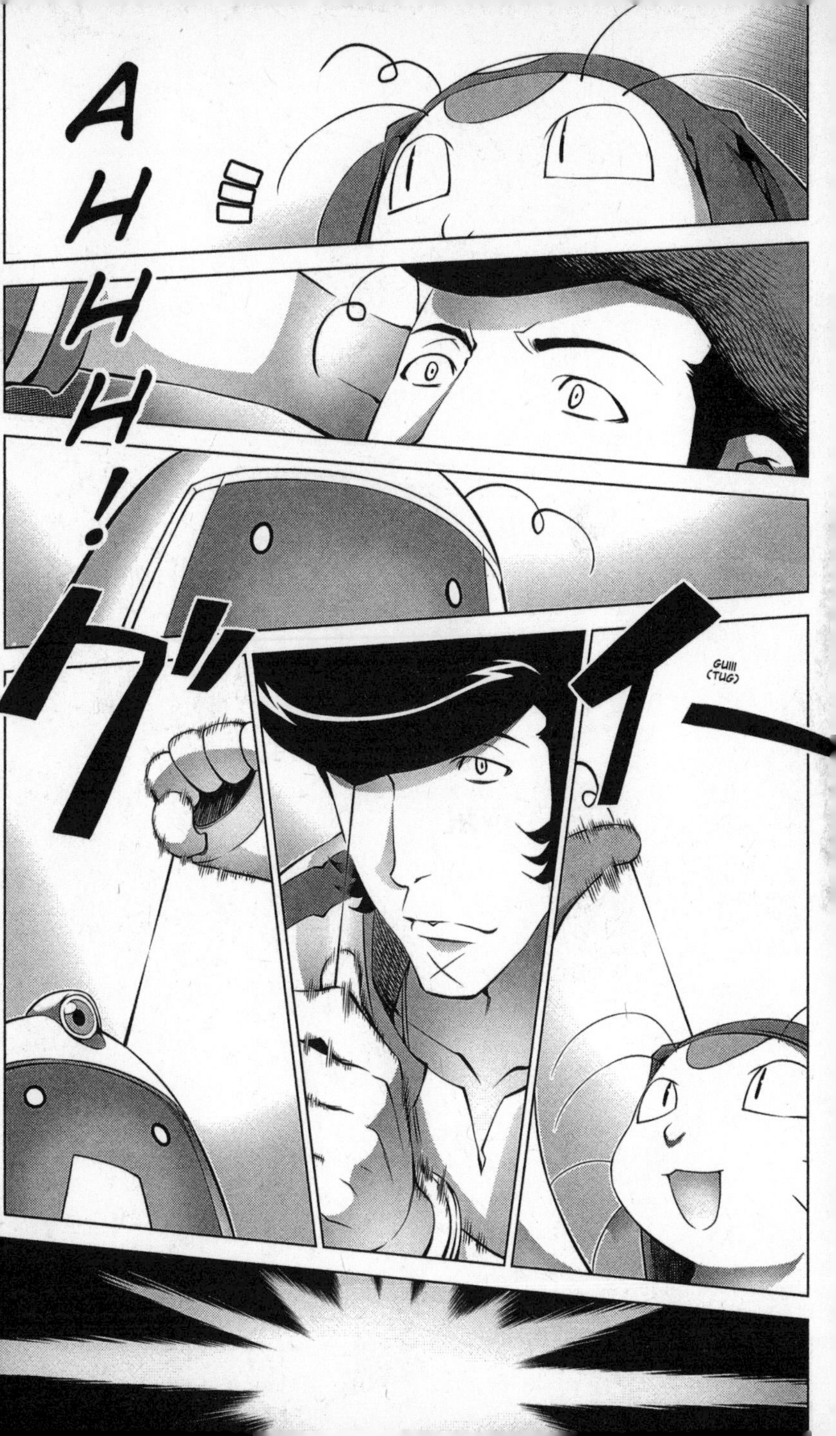
AHHHH!!
グイー
GUIII (TUG)

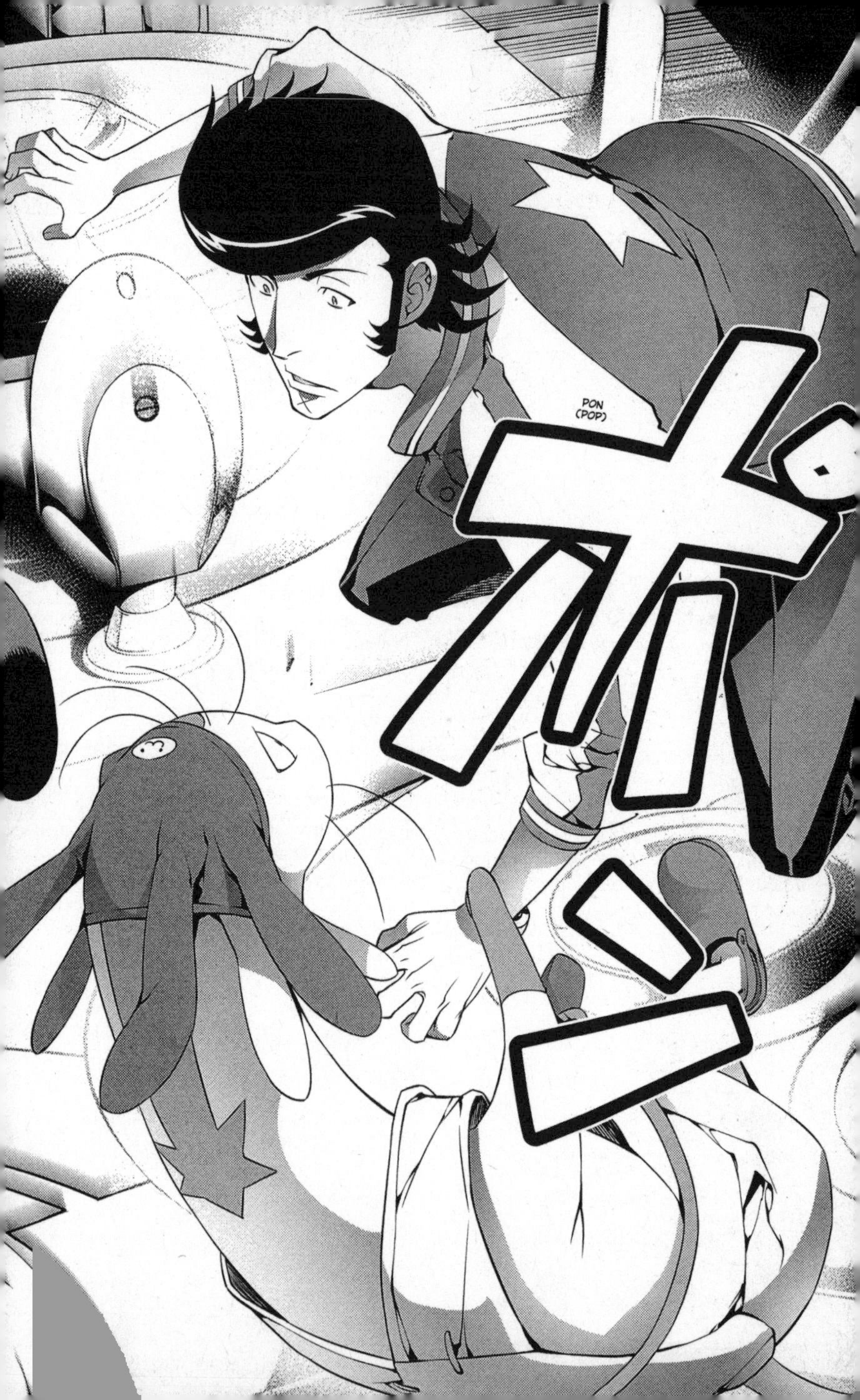
PON
(POP)

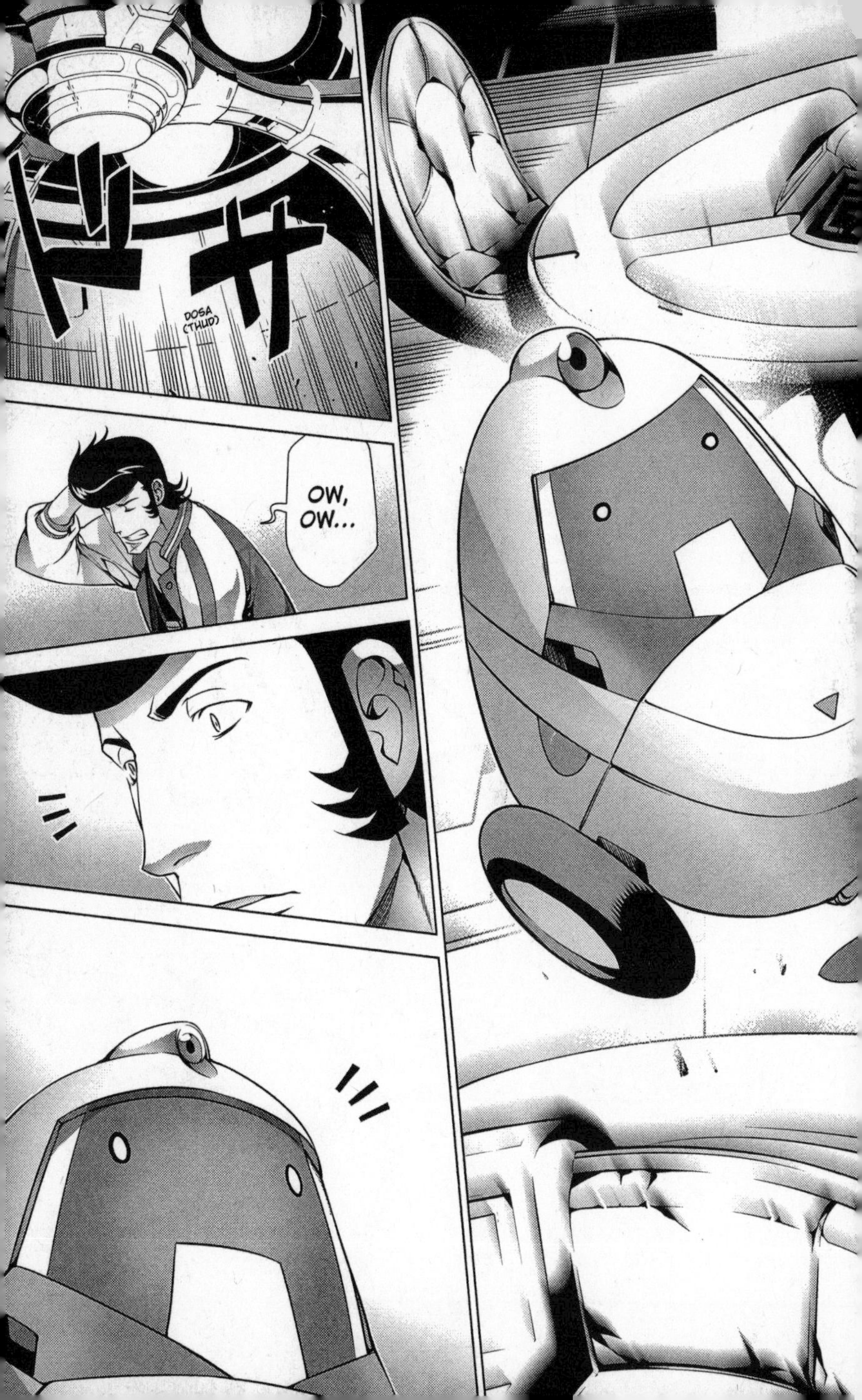
DOSA
(THUD)
OW,
OW...

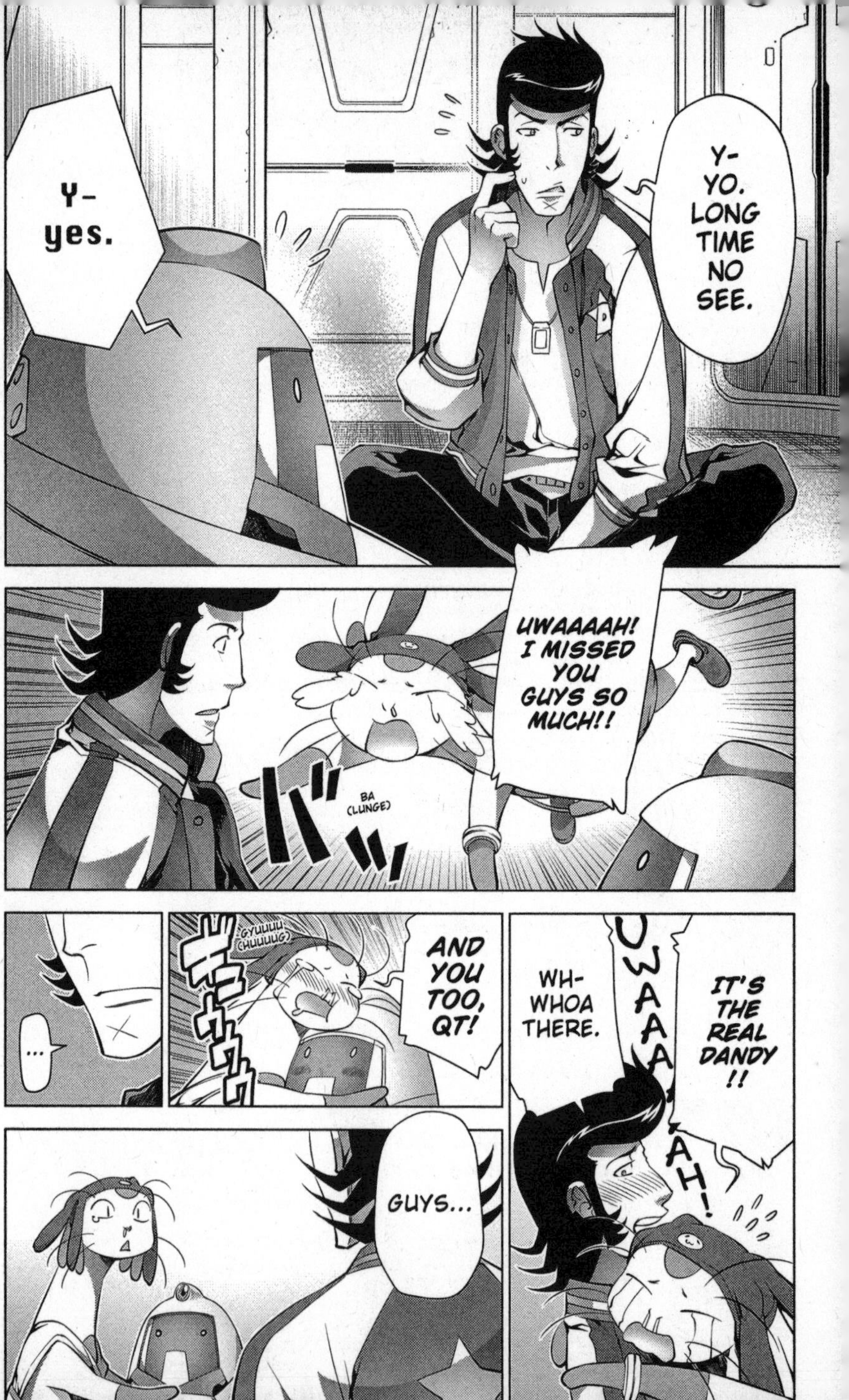
Y-YO. LONG TIME NO SEE.
Y-yes.
UWAAAAH! I MISSED YOU GUYS SO MUCH!!
BA (LUNGE)
IT'S THE REAL DANDY!!
UWAAAAAH!
WH-WHOA THERE.
AND YOU TOO, QT!
GYUUUU (HUUUUG)
...
GUYS...

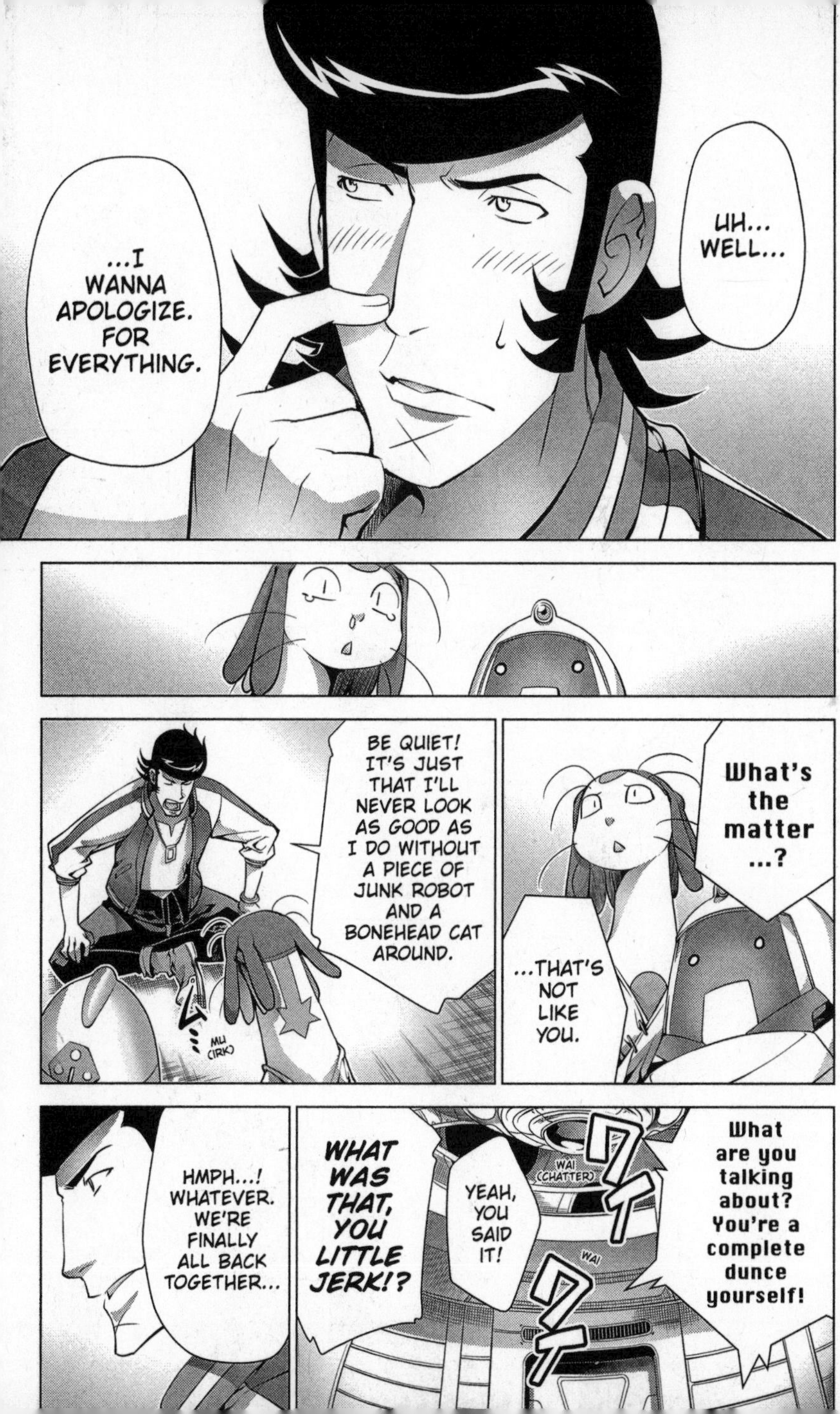
UH... WELL...
...I WANNA APOLOGIZE. FOR EVERYTHING.
What's the matter...?
...THAT'S NOT LIKE YOU.
BE QUIET! IT'S JUST THAT I'LL NEVER LOOK AS GOOD AS I DO WITHOUT A PIECE OF JUNK ROBOT AND A BONEHEAD CAT AROUND.
MU (IRK)
What are you talking about? You're a complete dunce yourself!
WAI (CHATTER)
WAI
YEAH, YOU SAID IT!
WHAT WAS THAT, YOU LITTLE JERK!?
HMPH...! WHATEVER. WE'RE FINALLY ALL BACK TOGETHER...

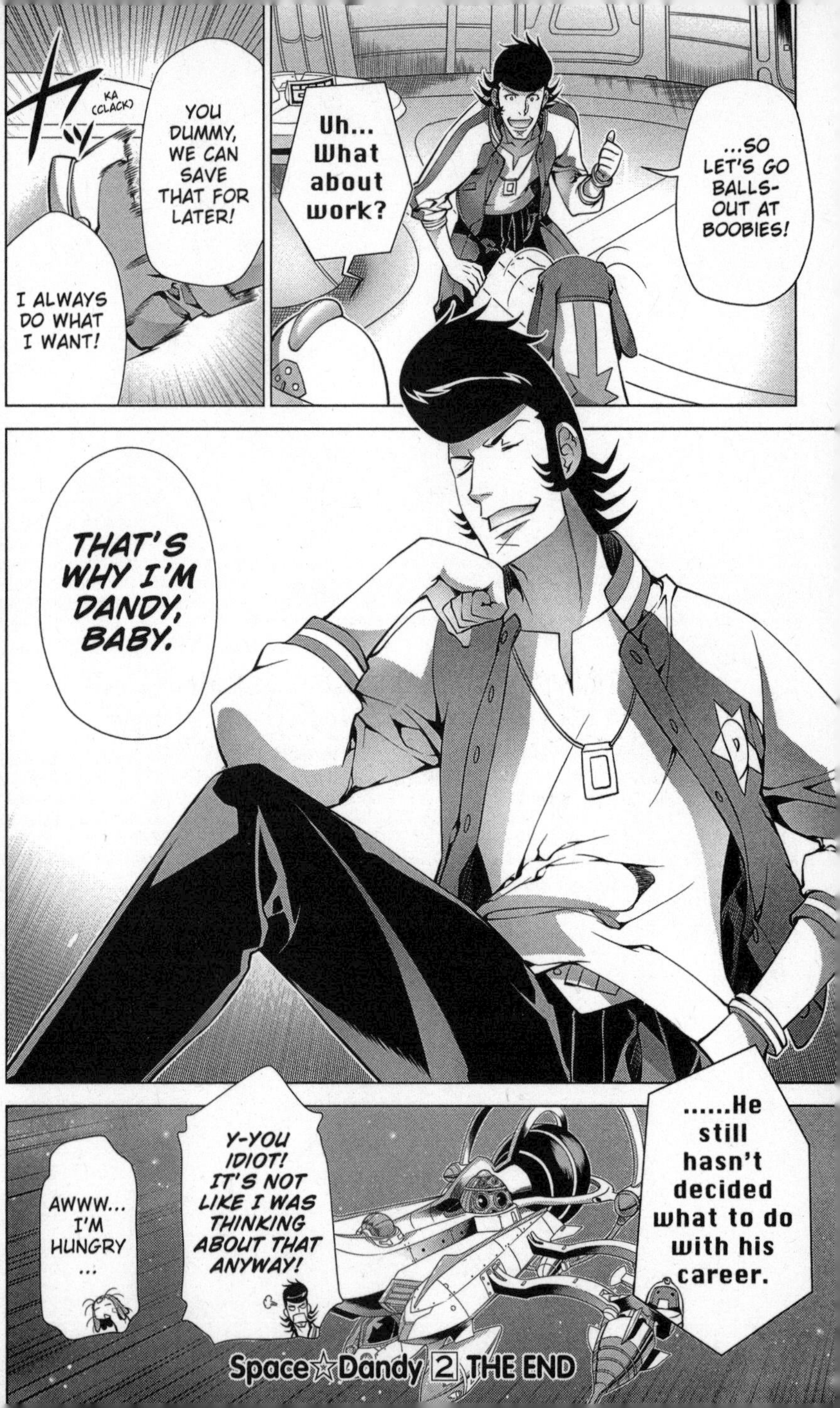
...SO LET'S GO BALLS-OUT AT BOOBIES!
Uh... What about work?
YOU DUMMY, WE CAN SAVE THAT FOR LATER!
KA (CLACK)
I ALWAYS DO WHAT I WANT!
THAT'S WHY I'M DANDY, BABY.
......He still hasn't decided what to do with his career.
Y-YOU IDIOT! IT'S NOT LIKE I WAS THINKING ABOUT THAT ANYWAY!
AWWW... I'M HUNGRY ...
Space☆Dandy 2 THE END

SPACE★DANDY

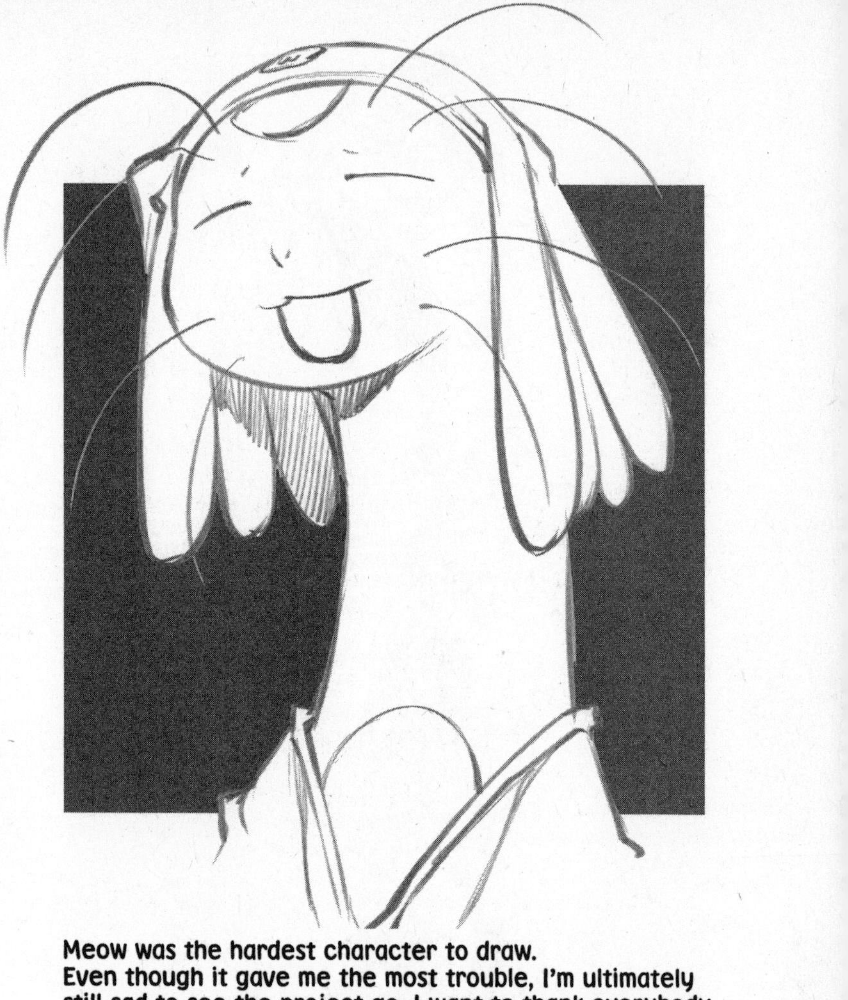

Meow was the hardest character to draw.
Even though it gave me the most trouble, I'm ultimately still sad to see the project go. I want to thank everybody who was involved with helping me create the storyboards for this. And to all my readers who followed the story this far, I thank you with all my heart.

I look forward to the next time I can see you all.

Sung Woo Park

SPACE DANDY

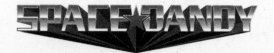

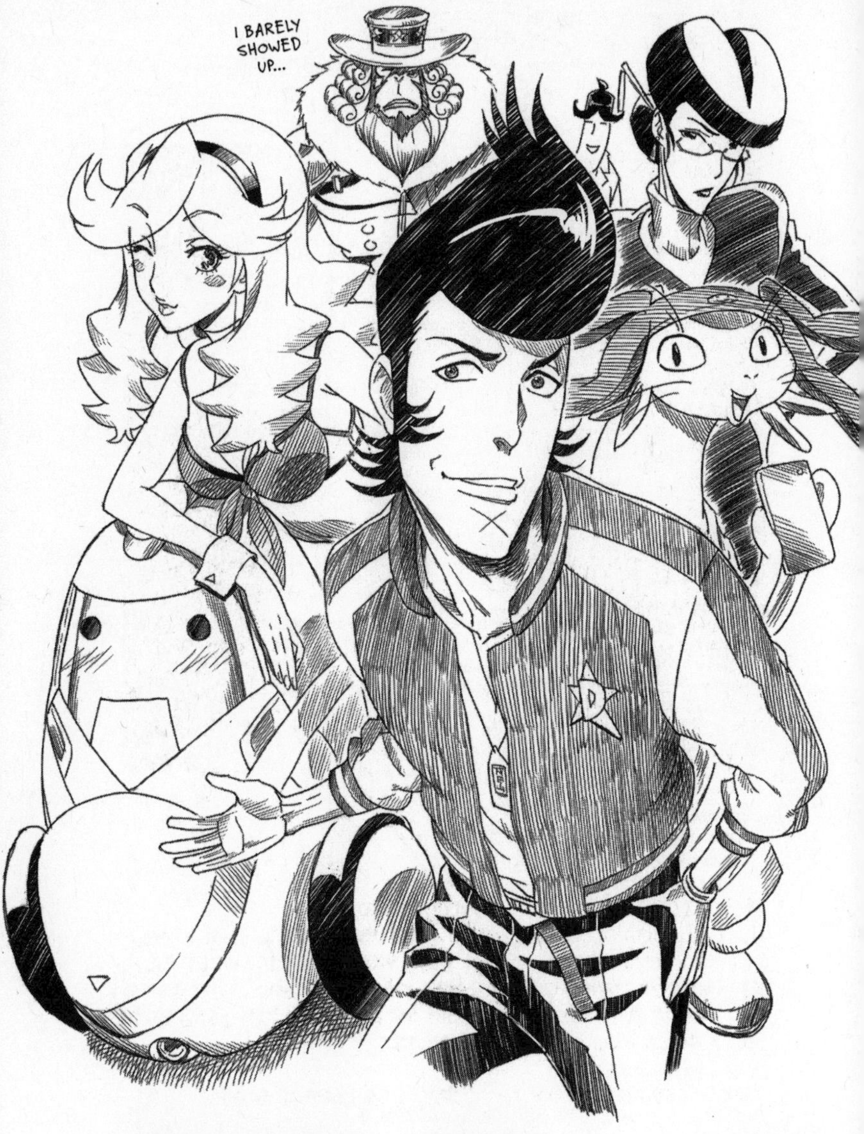
I BARELY SHOWED UP...

THANK YOU FOR READING!

HARADA
原田

SPACE DANDY ❷

BONES
Park Sung Woo
REDICE

Translation: Christine Dashiell • Lettering: Anthony Quintessenza

SPACE DANDY Vol.2 © 2014 BONES / Project SPACE DANDY © 2014 Park Sung Woo / SQUARE ENIX CO., LTD. First published in Japan in 2014 by SQUARE ENIX CO., LTD. English translation rights arranged with SQUARE ENIX CO., LTD. and Yen Press, LLC through Tuttle-Mori Agency, Inc.

English translation © 2016 by SQUARE ENIX CO., LTD.

Yen Press
1290 Avenue of the Americas
New York, NY 10104

Visit us!
♥ yenpress.com
♥ facebook.com/yenpress
♥ twitter.com/yenpress
♥ yenpress.tumblr.com

First Yen Press Edition: September 2016

Yen Press is an imprint of Yen Press, LLC.
The Yen Press name and logo are trademarks of Yen Press, LLC.

Library of Congress Control Number: 2016932689

ISBN: 978-0-316-27609-2 (paperback)

10 9 8 7 6 5 4 3 2 1

BVG

Printed in the United States of America